The Brownings' Correspondence

Volume 5
January 1841 – May 1842
Letters 784 – 966

EBB Aged 35

The Brownings' Correspondence

Edited by

PHILIP KELLEY & RONALD HUDSON

Volume 5

January 1841 – May 1842
Letters 784 – 966

Wedgestone Press

The editorial work on this volume was made possible in part by a grant from the National Endowment for the Humanities, an independent federal agency.

The plates for this volume were made possible by a subvention from the John Simon Guggenheim Memorial Foundation.

Copyright © Browning Letters, John Murray, 1987
Copyright © Editorial Matter, Wedgestone Press, 1987

All rights reserved. No part of this publication may be reproduced, stored in a retrieval system, or transmitted, in any form or by any means, electronic, mechanical, photocopying, recording or otherwise, without the copyright owners' prior permission.

Published and Distributed by
Wedgestone Press
P.O. Box 175
Winfield, KS 67156

Library of Congress Cataloging in Publication Data

Browning, Robert, 1812–1889.
  The Brownings' correspondence.
  Correspondence written by and to Robert and Elizabeth Barrett Browning.
  Includes bibliographical references and indexes.
  Contents: v. 1. September 1809–December 1826, letters 1–244 — v. 2. January 1827–December 1831, letters 245–434 — [etc.] — v. 5. January 1841–May 1842, letters 784–966.
  1. Browning, Robert, 1812–1889—Correspondence.
  2. Browning, Elizabeth Barrett, 1806–1861—Correspondence.
  3. Poets, English—19th century—Correspondence.
  I. Browning, Elizabeth Barrett, 1806–1861. II. Kelley, Philip.
  III. Hudson, Ronald. IV. Title.
  PR4231.A4 1984   821'.8 [B]   84–5287
  ISBN 0-911459-09-X (v. 1)

Manufactured in the United States of America by Inter-Collegiate Press. Shawnee Mission, Kansas.

A Request

The editors invite all users of this edition to convey any additions or corrections by writing to them through the publisher.

Contents

Illustrations	vii
Cue Titles, Abbreviations and Symbols	ix
Chronology	xii
THE CORRESPONDENCE	
1841: Letters 784–887	1
1842: Letters 888–966	195
Appendix I	
Biographical Sketches of Principal Correspondents and Persons Frequently Mentioned	365
Appendix II	
Checklist of Supporting Documents	377
Supporting Documents: Index of Correspondents	384
Appendix III	
Contemporary Reviews of the Brownings' Works	385
List of Collections	407
List of Correspondents	408
Index	411

Illustrations

EBB Aged 35 Miniature by Matilda Carter, 1841. Courtesy of the Robert Browning Settlement.	*frontispiece*

FACING PAGE

Richard Barrett Oil, artist and date unknown. Courtesy of Edward R. Moulton-Barrett.	212
Richard Hengist Horne Oil by Margaret Gillies. Courtesy of the National Portrait Gallery.	213
Willie Macready to RB Letter 953, [May 1842]. Courtesy of the Armstrong Browning Library.	330
Illustrations of "The Cardinal and the Dog" Pencil sketches by Willie Macready, 1842. Courtesy of the Armstrong Browning Library.	331
Illustrations of "The Pied Piper of Hamelin" Pencil sketches by Willie Macready, 1842. Courtesy of the Armstrong Browning Library.	350

Cue Titles, Abbreviations & Symbols

ABL	Armstrong Browning Library, Baylor University, Waco, Texas
Altham	Mary V. Altham, Babbacombe, England
B-GB	*Letters of the Brownings to George Barrett*, ed. Paul Landis (Urbana, 1958)
BN	*Browning Newsletter*, ed. Warner Barnes (Waco, Texas, 1968–1972)
Browning Collections	*The Browning Collections. Catalogue of Oil Paintings, Drawings & Prints; Autograph Letters and Manuscripts, Books ... the Property of R.W. Barrett Browning, Esq.* (London, 1913). Reprinted in Munby, *Sale Catalogues*, VI (1972), 1–192
Carlyle (1)	*New Letters of Thomas Carlyle*, ed. A. Carlyle, 2 vols. (London, 1904)
Chapman	*Harriet Martineau's Autobiography*, ed. Maria Weston Chapman, 2 vols. (Boston, 1877)
Checklist	*The Brownings' Correspondence: A Checklist*, comps. Philip Kelley and Ronald Hudson (New York and Winfield, Kansas, 1978)
Chorley	*Letters of Mary Russell Mitford*, second series, ed. Henry Chorley, 2 vols. (London, 1872)
DeVane	William C. DeVane, *A Browning Handbook*, 2nd ed. (New York, 1955)
Diary	*Diary by E.B.B.: The Unpublished Diary of Elizabeth Barrett Barrett, 1831–1832*, eds. Philip Kelley and Ronald Hudson (Athens, Ohio, 1969)
Dickens (1)	*The Letters of Charles Dickens*, ed. M. House and G. Storey (Oxford, 1965–)
DNB	*Dictionary of National Biography*
EBB	Elizabeth Barrett Barrett / Elizabeth Barrett Browning
EBB-BRH	*Invisible Friends: The Correspondence of Elizabeth Barrett Barrett and Benjamin Robert Haydon, 1842–1845*, ed. W.B. Pope (Cambridge, Mass., 1973)
EBB-HSB	*Elizabeth Barrett to Mr. Boyd. Unpublished Letters of Elizabeth Barrett Browning to Hugh Stuart Boyd*, ed. Barbara P. McCarthy (New Haven, 1955)

EBB-MRM	*The Letters of Elizabeth Barrett Browning to Mary Russell Mitford, 1836–1854*, eds. Meredith B. Raymond and Mary Rose Sullivan, 3 vols. (Winfield, Kansas, 1983)
EBB-RHH	*Letters of Elizabeth Barrett Browning, Addressed to Richard Hengist Horne, with Preface and Memoir*, ed. S.R. Townshend Mayer, 2 vols. (London, 1877)
ERM-B	Edward R. Moulton-Barrett, Platt, England
G & M	W.H. Griffin and H.C. Minchin, *The Life of Robert Browning* (New York, 1910)
Garnett	R. & E. Garnett, *Life of W.J. Fox* (London, 1910)
Kenyon Typescript	British Library Add Ms. 42229–42231, copies and typescripts gathered and prepared by F.G. Kenyon for his 1897 edition of EBB's letters
LEBB	*The Letters of Elizabeth Barrett Browning*, ed. F.G. Kenyon, 2 vols. (London, 1897)
L'Estrange (1)	*Friendships of Mary Russell Mitford*, ed. Alfred Guy Kingham L'Estrange, 2 vols. (London, 1882)
L'Estrange (2)	*Life of Mary Russell Mitford*, ed. Alfred Guy Kingham L'Estrange, 3 vols. (London, 1870)
LRB	*Letters of Robert Browning Collected by Thomas J. Wise*, ed. Thurman L. Hood (New Haven, 1933)
Macready	*The Diaries of William Charles Macready 1833–1851*, ed. William Toynbee, 2 vols. (London, 1912)
Maynard	John Maynard, *Browning's Youth* (Cambridge, Mass. and London, 1977)
MM-B	Myrtle Moulton-Barrett, Ringwood, England
Morgan	The Pierpont Morgan Library, New York
MPG	*Patrologiæ Cursus Completus . . . Series Græca*, ed. Jacques Paul Migne (Paris, 1857–80)
N&Q	*Notes and Queries*
NL	*New Letters of Robert Browning*, ed. W.C. DeVane and K.L. Knickerbocker (New Haven and London, 1950)
OED	*Oxford English Dictionary*
Orr	Mrs. Sutherland Orr, *Life and Letters of Robert Browning*, revised and in part rewritten by Frederic G. Kenyon (London, 1908)
PG-C	Philip Graham-Clarke, Abergavenny, Wales
Pope	*The Diary of Benjamin Robert Haydon*, ed. Willard Bissell Pope, 5 vols. (Cambridge, Mass., 1963)
RAM-B	Ronald A. Moulton-Barrett, Aberdeenshire, Scotland
RB	Robert Browning
RB-AD	*Robert Browning and Alfred Domett*, ed. F.G. Kenyon (London, 1906)

RB-EBB	*The Letters of Robert Browning and Elizabeth Barrett Barrett, 1845–1846*, ed. Elvan Kintner, 2 vols. (Cambridge, Mass., 1969)
RB, Sr.	Robert Browning, Sr., RB's father
Reconstruction	*The Browning Collections: A Reconstruction*, comps. Philip Kelley and Betty A. Coley (London, New York, Waco, Texas and Winfield, Kansas, 1984)
SD	Supporting Document. For checklist of contemporary supporting documents see: Volume 1, Appendix II, SD1–SD577; Volume 2, Appendix II, SD578–SD749; Volume 3, Appendix II, SD750–SD844; Volume 4, Appendix II, SD845–SD1144; Volume 5, Appendix II, SD 1145–1176
Sotheby's	Sotheby & Co., auctioneers, London
Taplin	Gardner B. Taplin, *The Life of Elizabeth Barrett Browning* (New Haven, 1957)
TTUL	*Twenty-two Unpublished Letters of Elizabeth Barrett Browning and Robert Browning Addressed to Henrietta and Arabella Moulton-Barrett* (New York, 1935)
Wellesley	Wellesley College Library, The English Poetry Collection, Wellesley, Massachusetts
Williams's Library	Dr. Williams's Library, London
Yale	The Beinecke Library, Yale University, New Haven, Connecticut
[ ]	Square brackets indicate material inserted by editors
⟨ ⟩	Angle brackets denote some irregularity in the manuscript. The absence of a note indicates that the information within the brackets is a conjectural reconstruction caused by seal tear, holes or physical deterioration of the manuscript
⟨...⟩	Angle brackets enclosing ellipsis show an actual omission caused by a defect or physical irregularity in the manuscript. Except in the case of text lost through seal tears, holes, etc., the nature of the irregularity is indicated by a note. This symbol appears on a line by itself if lost text exceeds half a line
⟨★★★⟩	Angle brackets enclosing triple stars indicate the lack of a beginning or end of a letter
| |	Vertical bars are used before and after a word which, though not physically obliterated, is a word of uncertain transcription
...	Ellipses indicate omissions from quoted material in notes and supporting documents, but in the actual texts of the Brownings' correspondence they merely reproduce the writers' style of punctuation

Chronology

1841 EBB's "Queen Annelida and False Arcite" and "The Complaint of Annelida to False Arcite" published in *The Poems of Geoffrey Chaucer, Modernized*.

January: EBB receives gift of the spaniel, Flush, from Miss Mitford.

April: RB's *Pippa Passes* (*Bells and Pomegranates*, No. I) published by Edward Moxon.

21 August: EBB's "The House of Clouds" published in *The Athenæum*.

11 September: EBB returns to 50 Wimpole St., London.

23 October: EBB's "Lessons from the Gorse" published in *The Athenæum*.

1842 8 January: EBB's "Three Hymns, Translated from the Greek of Gregory Nazianzen" published in *The Athenæum*.

February-March: EBB's essay, "Some Account of the Greek Christian Poets," published as a series of four articles in *The Athenæum*.

12 March: RB's *King Victor and King Charles* (*Bells and Pomegranates*, No. II) published by Edward Moxon.

The Brownings' Correspondence

Volume 5
January 1841 – May 1842
Letters 784 – 966

784. RB TO ELIZA FLOWER

New Cross, Hatcham, Surrey
Tuesday Morning. [ca. 1841][1]

Dear Miss Flower,

I am very sorry for what must grieve Mr Fox: for *myself*, I beg him earnestly not to see me till his entire convenience, however pleased I shall be to receive the letter you promise on his part.

And how can I thank you enough for this good news—all this music I shall be so thoroughly gratified to hear?[2]

Ever yours faithfully,
Robert Browning.

Publication: Orr, p. 125.
Manuscript: Pierpont Morgan Library.

1. Mrs. Orr states that this letter, relating to *Hymns and Anthems*, was written "In the course of 1842" (Orr, p. 125). However, we feel that RB's second paragraph anticipates publication, rather than being written afterwards; if this assumption is correct, the letter would have been written in 1841.
2. *Hymns and Anthems*, a compilation by Eliza Flower's *de facto* guardian, W.J. Fox, was published in 1841.

---

785. RB TO ANNA BROWNELL JAMESON

[London]
Wednesday Night. [ca. 1841][1]

Dear Mrs Jameson,

What *can* I say to excuse nearly a month's silence after you had told me to speak? Or, may I call one day or night and try hard to say something? Here comes in, anyhow, forlorn and halting, my explication of the Picture you described to me. Apuleius, Metamorphoseon, Lib. VI.[2] Psyche, having fallen thro' her curiosity into Venus' clutches, is dispatched on a spiteful errand to Proserpine; Venus is *out* of Beauty, having spent a deal in tending Cupid, sick a-bed with his burnt shoulder—nor can she present herself befittingly at Olympus unless replenished from Proserpine's stock: for this purpose she furnishes Psyche with a casket. Such a sample of Step-damehood causes, it should seem, the very stones to cry out—since a huge Tower, from which Psyche is about to precipitate herself in despair, takes voice, counsels her against short cuts to Hell, puts her upon another course, and after pointing out sundry snares in store for her, and proper methods of frustrating the same, especially enjoins a letting alone all

[1]

prying into casket and contents: Psyche obeys the other injunctions to the letter, gets her casket filled, and bids Proserpine farewell—but no sooner has she paid Charon[3] his back-fare ("old man in the distance") and revisited the light—than a rash curiosity takes possession of her. "Shall she fetch-and-carry Divine Beauty, and yet venture on no tiniest appropriation-clause to the Venus' Revenue Bill? Never so little a snatch would recommend her to Cupid!" No sooner said than done—the casket is opened, and forth issues only "an infernal and truly Stygian sleep"—which catching her up and casting her down—on the spot—leaves her "nothing but a sleeping corpse." At this juncture Cupid,—whose wound is well and wings want exercise,—breaks bed-room bounds, seeks out Psyche, and awakens her with the innocuous end of his arrow. "And, behold," says he, "once again had you almost perished, unfortunate that you are, thro' a like curiosity"! ("Psyche seated in a disconsolate attitude—Cupid standing with a casket in his hand.")[4]

(N.B. No attempt at *fun* in what goes before—but strict rendering, as far as I remember—having read the story this morning.)

        Pray forgive and believe me,
        Dear Mrs Jameson,
        Yours ever faithfully,
        R Browning.

Publication: None traced.
Manuscript: R.H. Taylor Collection.

 1. Although the paper is watermarked 1840, RB's general usage suggests that this letter would not have been written before 1841.
 2. Lucius Apuleius (*fl.* 2nd century A.D.) studied successively in Carthage, Athens and Rome. Many of his works are no longer extant; the eleven books of his *Metamorphoses* (better known by the alternative title, *The Golden Ass*) remain popular.
 3. Charon, son of Erebus and Nox, ferried the souls of the dead across the river Styx, for which he was paid an obolus, this coin having been placed under the deceased's tongue for that purpose.
 4. RB's description fits the painting, by William Etty (1787–1849), entitled "Psyche Having, After Great Peril, Procured the Casket of Cosmetics from Proserpine in Hades, Lays It at the Feet of Venus, While Cupid Pleads in Her Behalf." It was exhibited at the Royal Academy in 1836.

786. RB TO ANNA DOROTHEA MONTAGU[1]

[London]
Wednesday Eve^g [ca. 1841][2]

My dear Madam,
 Pray accept my best thanks for your very kind note, and believe me weather-proof after a visit to you. I shall be most happy to make one of your party next Friday, and to esteem myself,
My dear Madam,
Yours ever faithfully,
Robt Browning.

Mrs Basil Montagu.

Publication: None traced.
Manuscript: University of Texas.

1. Mrs. Montagu (*née* Benson) came, as a young widow, to take charge of the motherless children of Basil Montagu, K.C. (1770–1851), legal author and philanthropist, the illegitimate son of John Montagu, 4th Earl of Sandwich (1718–92); in time she became his third wife. Her daughter Anne, by her first husband, Thomas Skepper, was the wife of Bryan Waller Procter (Barry Cornwall).
2. Dated approximately by the handwriting and form of signature.

787. EBB TO MARY RUSSELL MITFORD

Torquay.
Jany 2. [1841][1]

"You are invincible"[2]—you, my beloved friend, & your kindness, & dear Dr Mitford & his—and I have not a word to say about Flush, except grateful ones—thanks upon thanks. Yet for obstinacy's sake, *my* obstinacy's, or rather my *perversity's* (*that's* dear Mr Kenyon's word for me!) I must go on being sure that the dog is too good, too caninely noble, for some of my base purposes. But I shall make it up to him, at least something of it, in love & care. I must love him, coming from *you*—pretty or not—ears or not! The love is a certainty whatever the beauty may be--and if I am to see in his eyes, as you say, your affectionate feelings towards me, why the beauty must be a certainty too.

 Well—dearest Miss Mitford– So I open my arms to your Flush—and shall give notice to the coachmen, that he may suffer no cruelty on his Wednesday & Thursday's journies. And pray do be sure that I did not struggle against your kindness, as if it c^d be a burden to be obliged to YOU– Oh no!– It was not *that*.

 I mean to see the London Journal since you wrote in it—far more for your writing, than the critical article.[3] As to Chaucer I w^d have sent him to you with some cream,—but I wanted Cosmo de' Medici⁴ to go besides, & M! Bezzi is keeping him by *weeks*– Chaucer is said to prosper.

My dear dear brother Charles John, from the West Indies, & my youngest brother Octavius came yesterday. They came against my will– I w^d rather, for love's sake, they had stayed at home. But since they wished to come & w^d come, dear things,—& since the *meeting* is over— (.. more full of anguish than any parting—) we shall have the comfort if not the enjoyment of those who love each other & are together—& I cannot *say* to them, looking on their dear faces 'I wish you had not come'. Indeed looking THERE, I can scarcely go on wishing it to myself.

But my headache, carried from yesterday, is very bad, & makes this note stupid to some intensity. I conjecture so—not having clear-headiness enough to be sure even of *that*.

My sense in writing, is simply to welcome *Flush*. With my most affectionate & earnest wishes for all happiness to you & yours my beloved friend—& my thanks upon thanks for all your kindness,

ever believe me
your EBB——

Publication: EBB-MRM, I, 211–212.
Manuscript: Wellesley College.

1. Dated by the impending arrival of Flush.
2. Cf. the answer given by the Oracle of Delphi to Alexander the Great: "My son, thou art invincible."
3. EBB means *The English Journal*; the issue of 2 January 1841 carried Miss Mitford's story, "Little David." The "critical article" was a review of *Chaucer, Modernized* (see pp. 385–387).
4. As letter 792 makes clear, Bezzi had borrowed several books from EBB, including Horne's drama.

---

788. EBB TO RICHARD HENGIST HORNE

Torquay
Saturday [9 January 1841]¹

Nothing of the "tragic subject" today, dear Mr. Horne: I am going to get into a scrape instead.

I tremble to do it, take a long breath before I begin, and then beg you to excuse me about the signature, and forgive me, if possible, afterwards.

Have I done it? Is it all over with me? Oh! I feel the shadow of the great Gregory hand, to match the foot, even at this distance!²

As to the petition,³ the justice of the claim lies upon the surface, and its policy not much deeper: and therefore in wishing, & predicting to you all success, I need not stir from the common sense of the question. You are sure to gain the immediate object, & you ought to do so, even though the ultimate object remain as far off as ever, & more evidently far. There is a deeper evil than licenses or the want of licenses—the base & blind public taste. Multiply your theatres & license every one.— Do it to-day. And the day after to-morrow (you may have one night) there will come Mr. Bunn,[4] & turn out you & Shakespeare with a great roar of lions. Well! .. we shall see.

You know far more than I do, & you seem to hope more: If the great mass in London were Athenians, I might hope too.

But I do *not* like giving my name to anything about the theatres. It is a name unimportant to everybody in the world except just myself for whom the giving of it would be the sign of an opinion—& I sh^d *not* like to give it in any one thing favorable to the theatres. At their best, take the ideal of them, & the soul of the Drama is far above the stage—& according to present and perhaps all past regulations in this country, dramatic poetry has been desecrated & drawn down from the sphere of her shining into the dust of our treading, yes & too often forced to desecrate & draw down morally in turn, the stage. When the poet has his gods in the gallery, what must be the end of it? Why that even Shakespeare sh^d bow his starry head oftener than Homer nodded, and write down his pure genius into the dirt of the groundlings, for the sake of the savour of their "most sweet voices",[5] & even so be outwritten in popularity for years and years by his half-brother noble geniuses Beaumont & Fletcher, because *they stooped still lower*.

Well, but, dear Mr. Horne, if you shake your head ever so much over this, & call me ever so many names .. dont let them be hard ones—dont be really angry. I can't afford to let you be angry with me. People will have their fancies and perversities. Grant me mine. If the name you asked for were not "bosh," I sh^d be still more sorry than I now am, to say 'no' to your asking. And yet even now, even as it is, I didn't like writing, either yesterday or the day before—nor do I today!—

The Monthly Chronicle has not reached me yet. I am eager for the added scene of Cosmo.

And glad, dear Mr. Horne, that you c^d like anything in the volume where there is more to forgive than like, for even the kindest.

                Ever truly yours
                EBB–

Address: R.H. Horne Esqr / 2– Gray's Inn Square / Gray's Inn / London.
Publication: EBB-RHH, I, 45–49 (in part) and *The Contemporary Review*, December 1873, pp. 154–155.
Source: Annotated copy of *EBB-RHH* text, in the hand of H. Buxton Forman, at Pierpont Morgan Library.

1. Although the manuscript of this letter is missing, an annotation by H. Buxton Forman in Horne's copy of *EBB-RHH* (now at Morgan) indicates that it was postmarked 10 January 1841.
2. Horne makes a number of references to Gregory's hands and feet in his play; see, for example, letters 756, note 6; 762, note 10; and 765, note 9.
3. Horne's petition for amended legislation regarding the monopoly of the patent theatres (see letter 767, note 3).
4. Alfred Bunn (1796?–1860), the husband of actress Margaret Agnes Bunn (1799–1883), was the manager of two of London's three patent theatres, Drury Lane and Covent Garden, and strenuously opposed any change in their legal status. A bill to abolish the patent theatres had been approved by the House of Commons in 1833, but Bunn was instrumental in securing its rejection by the House of Lords.
5. *Coriolanus*, II, 3, 172. In this and subsequent Shakespearean quotations, the line numbers correspond to those used in *The Riverside Shakespeare* (Boston, 1974).

---

789. EBB to Richard Hengist Horne

[Torquay]
[mid-January 1841][1]

My dear M![r] Horne,

So you write me down 'dozing' in courtesy for a worse word: and indeed I scarcely know another to recommend to you—yet it has not been 'dozing' either—no—nor long-drawn consideration. The truth is I have felt afraid of you, & do—and one day being the image of another to me, while the fear made me delay sending you my fancies, I lost account of the time spent in delaying, took saturday for monday still, & built up so a dozing reputation. And indeed I upon my 'rock' have less time for anything good than is supposable. Half the day, all the morning, I am just able to read lazily in that low 'spiritless lack lustre state'[2] which shows the quenched embers of opium & things of the sort, said to be necessary for me just now,—& the uncomfortable uncertain excitement before & afterwards though pleasanter as a sensation, is more congenial to dreaming ('dozing' if you please dear M![r] Horne,) than to any steady purpose of thought or fixed direction of faculty. So far to account, in part,—in some degree—for the rough sketch I send you being "very *un*like a whale".[3]

But it was thrown on paper, directly I read your reminder—'A first form' indeed I didnt wait any more—& if the *coaches do*, in the snow, it is'nt my fault– Your letter came to me most reluctantly a day too late, & mine may 'copy its paces'.[4]

Thank you for the reproof from Hazlitt—the paragraph 'to suit'—for the beauty & gentleness of the rebuke. Yet you & he c![d] both have written as finely & more congenially upon the opposite evil of compromise—of temporizing as to objects, & being indifferent as to means[5]—that 'fat weed'[6] of the day, & perhaps of the world on all days. More of us, you will admit, do harm by groping along the pavement with blind hands for the beggars brass coin, than do folly by clutching at the stars 'from the misty mountain top'[7]: And if the would be star-catchers catch nothing, they keep at least clean fingers.

This applies to nothing, you will understand, except to the passage from Hazlitt—suggestively.

And talking of beggar's coins,—will you believe me—(you MUST[8] believe me—) that I never thought until I had finished my letter to you about the petition, of my own self having something to do with the proprietorship of Drury Lane, by virtue of five shares given to me when I was a child? I really never thought of it– But I thought afterwards that if you ever came to guess at such a thing, why you might infer me into basenesses. The shares never reminded me of their being mine by one penny coming to my hands, nor are likely to do so—the national theatres being as empty of profit as of honor. But if it were otherwise, oh you could'nt suspect me of being warped by such a consideration– You will trust me that half cubit of probity, without another word.

Tuesday.

Dear M.ʳ Horne—I was not quite well & was forced to break off writing—& begin anew today. You will think me an eighth sleeper now.[9] Dont scruple to say what is in y.ʳ mind about the subject. Remember you suggested Greek instead of modern tragedy as a model for form. –My idea, the terror attending spiritual consciousness, the men's soul to the men, is something which has not I think been worked hitherto, & seems to admit of a certain grandeur & wildness in the execution. The awe of this self consciousness, breaking with occasional sudden lurid beats through the chasms of our conventionalities has struck me, in my own self observation as a mystery of nature—very grand in itself—& is quite a distinct mystery from *conscience*. Conscience has to do with action (every thought being spiritual action) & not with abstract existence. There are moments when we are startled at the footsteps of our own Being, more than at the thunders of God.

Is it impracticable?—too shadowy, too mystic, for working dramatically?

Think of Faust.

You c.ᵈ do anything!

But you are judge as to what is to be done or tried. Say yes or no—& I am prepared for 'no', most.[10]

Ever truly yours
EBB–

Did you ask Miss Mitford about the petition? You know *she* is personally interested in the theatres—has a play waiting to be acted: & I am sure she w^d sign the petition gladly.

Publication: EBB-RHH, I, 54–56 and II, 62–64 (in part).
Manuscript: Pierpont Morgan Library.

1. Dated by the further reference to Horne's petition, the subject of the previous letter.
2. We have not located the source of this quotation.
3. Cf. *Hamlet*, III, 2, 382.
4. We have not located the source of this quotation.
5. From the context, it is possible that Horne had quoted from Hazlitt's essay "On Thought and Action."
6. *Hamlet*, I, 5, 32.
7. *Romeo and Juliet*, III, 5, 10.
8. Underscored three times.
9. A reference to the "Seven Sleepers," Christian youths walled up in a cave (see letter 589, note 3).
10. Horne replied that "the subject could be worked dramatically, *i.e.*, in the spirit, everything breathing of stage-action being quite out of the question" and that he "would devise the characters, interlocutors, chorus and semi-choruses" etc. (*EBB-RHH*, II, 64).

790. MARY RUSSELL MITFORD TO EBB

Three Mile Cross,
Jan. 14, 1841.

I write, my beloved friend, by my dear father's bedside; for he is again very ill. Last Tuesday was the Quarter Sessions, and he *would* go, and he seemed so well that Mr. May thought it best to indulge him. Accordingly he went at nine A.M. to open the Court, sat all day next the chairman in Court, and afterwards at dinner, returning at two o'clock, A.M., in the highest spirits—not tired at all, and setting forth the next day for a similar eighteen hours of business and pleasure. Again he came home delighted and unwearied. He had seen many old and dear friends, and had received (to use his own words) the attentions which do an old man's heart good; and *these*, joined to his original vigour of constitution and his high animal spirits, had enabled him to do that which to those who saw him at home infirm and feeble, requiring three persons to help him from his chair, and many minutes before he could even move—would seem as impossible as a fall of snow between the tropics, or the ripening of pine-apples in Nova Zembla.¹

All this he had done, but not with impunity. He has caught a severe cold; and having on Saturday taken nearly the same liberties at Reading, and not suffering me to send for Mr. May, until rendered bold by fear I did send last night—he is now seriously ill. I am watching by his bedside in deep anxiety; but as silence is my part to-night, and I have prayed (for when those we love—*so love*—are in danger, thought is prayer), I write to you, my beloved friend, as my best solace. Mr. May is hopeful; but the season, his age, my great and still increasing love, and the habit of anxiety which has grown from long tending, fill me with a fear that I can hardly describe. He is so restless too—so very, very restless—and everything depends upon quiet, upon sleep, and upon perspiration; and yet, for the last twelve hours I am sure that he has not been two minutes in the same posture, and not twelve minutes without his getting out of bed, or up in bed, or something as bad. God grant that he may drop asleep! I read to him until I found that reading only increased the irritability. Well, I do hope and trust that he is rather quieter now; and I am quite sure that I shall myself be quieter in mind, if I can but fix my thoughts upon you. Heaven be with you all!

Ever yours,
M.R.M.

Address: Miss Barrett, Torquay.
Text: L'Estrange (2), III, 112–113.

1. Situated in the Arctic Ocean, Nova Zembla is a cold and inhospitable place.

---

791. EBB TO RICHARD HENGIST HORNE

[Torquay]
[Postmark: 21 January 1841]

Envelope only.[1]

Address: R H Horne Esq![r] / 2 Gray's Inn Square / Gray's Inn / London.
Docket, in R. H. Horne's hand: Psyche Unveiled. First outline.[2]
Publication: None traced.
Manuscript: Armstrong Browning Library.

1. It is possible, in view of Horne's docket, that this is the envelope for letter 789, as EBB speaks therein of a "rough sketch ... thrown on paper". A doubt remains, however, as the Torquay postmark of 21 January was a Thursday, whereas the conclusion of letter 789 is headed "Tuesday" and it would have been uncharacteristic for EBB to have held back the letter before posting.
2. This outline, together with other materials relating to "Psyche Apocalypté," formed part of lot 122 in *Browning Collections* (see *Reconstruction*, D754). It was included in the article on the genesis of the projected drama in *The St. James's Magazine and United Empire Review*, February 1876 (II, 478–492); the material is now at ABL.

792. EBB TO MARY RUSSELL MITFORD

[Torquay]
Thursday– [?21] [January 1841][1]

My dearest dearest Miss Mitford I am so grieved in this new grief of yours—and although I did "read the last page first" & carried from it all hopeful inferences, yet the hope is scarcely like enough to certainty to make me easy, or less earnest in my petition to hear how dear Dr Mitford is now. Send me some broken words, my beloved friend—will you? And oh may God be near your prayers, & blessing you beyond them.

I sent a little cream as soon as the lazy farm-people here would let me have it– Indeed I delayed longer than my wishes in applying for it—because I did want to send with it, besides Chaucer, Mr Horne's Cosmo which Mr Bezzi seems to hold fast with both hands[2] & much resolution. I never saw him (Mr Bezzi) you know—& he is said to be an *arch*-amiable person. But I am in the confidence of one fault .. his tendency to the 'retinence' of books. Several books he has of mine, besides Cosmo—and really my prospect of seeing them again becomes more cloudy to my own perception every day.

Tell me just what you think of Chaucer—will you, dearest Miss Mitford?

Oh and I do trust that by this time you may have a freer heart for the thought of such things. The *cause* of the attack was sufficiently salient & evident to exonerate the constitution from unprovoked failure: and a little more prudence (such as the evil itself will naturally induce) will give room (may God grant it!) for the health which returns, to remain.

Do give my love to dear Dr Mitford—my thanks (again & again) for the kindness of his thought of me at such a time, & my hope ... my humble hope, limping after all the rest .. of his being able & inclined perhaps to take a little of my cream!—& so, confer on it, a dignity above any pertaining to Mrs Trollope's dear "crème" of transcendent lords & ladies at Vienna.[3]

How I thank you for Flush!—dear little Flush[4]—growing dearer every day. He has fallen upon evil days[5] at Torquay,—for a report of 'mad dogs' has alarmed the magistrates & loaded the guns, & we dare not trust him out of the house. But he runs & leaps within it enough for exercise & keeps up his spirits & his appetite—only the latter is becoming scrupulous—demurring to any *un*buttered bread. In fact, Flush prefers muffins. However we go on delightfully together—that is, Flush & I & Crow (my maid) do. To the rest of the household he is decidedly hostile— will scarcely bestow a mark of courtesy upon either of my sisters, runs away from my brothers, & is coldly disdainful to one little page who has done everything possible to please him & is in despair at the result. But

No. 792 [?21] [January 1841] 11

Crow he is very fond of—& he prances up to the side of my bed in an ecstasy to hug the hand he can reach, between his two pretty paws. We are great friends. And when my sisters & brothers are with me, there he lies .. quite down-hearted--responding to no notice .. waiting patiently, as it seems, until he can celebrate their departure by a round of leaps!- Is'nt it strange?- We cant make it out at all. Perhaps he may associate Crow & myself with his deliverance from the basket, & love us out of gratitude—but why he sh^d be such a hater of the toga[6] (which really is the case) & so little to be won upon by my *sisters* even, is a riddle to us all.

I have not seen the 'Hour & Man' yet. This is such a place for books! But I shall soon, nevertheless.

Oh of course .. judging by extracts .. Toussaint's eloquence is Miss *Martineau's*.[7]

Do send me good news—if God give the power!-

Ever yours in truest
affection
EBB.

Who could be stern to 'Little David'[8]--but your own self?- "I w^d not hear your enemy say so"[9] nor c^d nor sh^d Think of my putting such words in a post[s]cript—Oh—the last shred of time-

Publication: EBB-MRM, I, 212-214.
Manuscript: Edward R. Moulton-Barrett and Wellesley College.

1. This is a response to letter 790.
2. Cf. Micah, 7:3.
3. In *Vienna and the Austrians* (1837), Mrs. Trollope introduces "the circle of the very highest aristocracy ... by the style and title they have chosen for themselves; they have ... taken the soubriquet of 'La Crême,'—an expressive phrase enough" (pp. 281-282).
4. The first offspring of Miss Mitford's Flush, he became a valued and pampered companion to EBB, going with her to Italy, and dying there in 1854. See *Flush: A Biography*, by Virginia Woolf (1933).
5. *Paradise Lost*, VII, 25.
6. i.e., of the male sex, the toga being worn by Roman boys and men.
7. Miss Martineau's *The Hour and the Man: A Historical Romance* had just been published. A review, with extracts, appeared in *The Athenæum* of 5 December 1840 (no. 684, pp. 958-959); it included this passage: "Toussaint L'Ouverture is The Man, and The Hour is that remarkable period when the slaves of St. Domingo first declared themselves freemen. The picture drawn by Miss Martineau is one of great moral interest; and she has treated it ... with care and ability." Pierre Dominique Toussaint L'Ouverture (ca. 1746-1803) commanded the insurgent army and was principally responsible for overthrowing the authority of France and establishing the republic of Haiti. He was, however, taken prisoner through treachery and died in captivity in France.
8. Miss Mitford's "Little David: A Country Story" appeared in *The English Journal: A Miscellany of Literature, Science, and the Fine Arts* (2 January 1841, pp. 3-6). It was reprinted in *Atherton, and Other Tales* (1854).
9. *Hamlet*, I, 2, 170.

793. EBB TO RICHARD HENGIST HORNE

[Torquay]
[late January 1841][1]

I am *so* glad, dear M!̲ Horne, that you really do like the subject—*so* glad—& something surprised—because I fancied the ink frowned through your envelope before I opened it—I never wrote down a subject before, *for anybody to see*,—& all your indulgence could'nt keep me from being afraid of YOU.

Asleep again? No—but the Sunday's no-post intervened—& even today I must write very briefly on account of my head which aches as if out of malice, & has done, from the morning "sans intermission".

Oh yes—your suggestions are excellent—& bring with them, suggestively too, new courage. I like the *genii* very much indeed.

Sh!̲ the Islanders, (the Islander chorus I mean) represent the five senses, or the conventionalities which encrust the senses, & are body beyond body .. opaker than the natural body? Will you consider? Perhaps both in a measure.

It seems to me that we sh!̲ avoid allegory in any cold strict sense,—& hold fast the individualities of the human beings– It was only for this, (to suggest the individuality of the principal personage), that I wrote down "Cymon"––not from any especial preference for the name.[2]

What will you have dear M!̲ Horne?—Philaster—Archas—Crates—Leon—Theanor—Herman? I am not sure I like either much.

For the bride .. Evadne, Luce, Berthe (no) Bianca—Violante—Viola—Elinda—Earine—a beautiful name which brings beauty of all sorts to remembrance, besides Jonson's Sad Shepherd– You remember Earine!

"Who had her very being & her name
From the first knotts & buddings of the spring–"[3]

Mariana—or shall it be German to go with Herman–[4]

The Princess Royal might be suited out of this catalogue. Decide yourself.

And as to the title generally .. why what shall be said? *That* is a graver point. 'Psyche Unveiled' w!̲ surely do—altho' it did suggest to my own associations, M!̲ Foster's 'Mahometan[i]sm unveiled'[5] & titles of the kind.

The Unveiled.
A Psychological Mystery.

W!̲ that be better?—anything better? out of M!̲ Foster's way, & the "nature displayed" people's. You speak of a Greek-English title. Such

No. 793 [late January 1841] 13

as "The apocalypse of Psyche."? or "Psyche apocalyptic"—⟨...⟩[6] Oh it wont do—will it? Shall it be more Greek than English? But then nobody, not most bodies at least, will know what we mean.

Psyche the Pursuer?—or the Persecutor? Psyche the Terrible?

Well– I know what name you will choose for *me* after all this— perhaps a Greek one .. & then it will begin with $\underline{\mu}$.[7] But it is hard upon me, to expect an answer to such a question by an early post—when everybody admits that the title of a book now a days, takes more study than all the rest of it– You must think yourself—& your first thought is better than the best of mine in the rear.

I was pleased in every way by your expression of satisfaction with the rough outline I dared to send you—I felt it to be absolute daring— pleased in every way—& not the least, with the sympathy of feeling. Only my head aches so, that I can scarcely see to write down whatever part of the pleasure w.^{d} be otherwise expressive .. Oh—I have an agreeable sense of writing nonsense—coincident with the close of every sentence. Can you make out anything?–

In regard to the question about the attack on Chaucer, I fancied it was an oratorical question, & not meant to be *answered*! You did'nt *before* say who 'the black gentleman' was, or whence protruding his blackness. *Now* I shall send for the magazines, for the present month & February.[8]

I cant write any more—but will do so in another day, or two—to tell you what Miss Mitford says of *you* in Chaucer. —— Did you see the English Journal, the first Jany number[9]—a three halfpenny publication .. but sovereignly courteous.

Ever truly yours EBB

Publication: EBB-RHH, II, 70–74 (in part).
Manuscript: Pierpont Morgan Library.

1. This is EBB's reply to Horne's response to the outline sent him with letter 791.
2. Later changed to Medon.
3. Act III, 2, 44–45, slightly misquoted. Earine, a shepherdess, was the beloved of Æglamour, the Sad Shepherd.
4. An oblique reference to Porson's epigram on Professor Hermann (see letter 508, note 8).
5. Charles Forster's edition of *Mahometanism Unveiled* was published in 1829.
6. About half a line obliterated, apparently by EBB.
7. Horne has placed an asterisk next to the Greek character and written, at the foot of the page, the word μαινάς. The Mænades, priestesses of Bacchus, became so abandoned in celebrating their festivals that they appeared mad.
8. There was a negative review of *Chaucer, Modernized* in *The Athenæum*; see letter 796.
9. *The English Journal*, 2 January 1841, included, in addition to Miss Mitford's "Little David," a review of *Chaucer, Modernized*. (For the text of the review, see pp. 385–387.)

794. EBB TO RICHARD HENGIST HORNE

[Torquay]
[late January 1841][1]

I wrote to you on Saturday dear Mr Horne, under the delusion that you might be able to read such words as I c.^d write then,—& that if you might, they c.^d be worth your reading[.]

Is *Medon* a name for our 'island monster'—& *Œnone* for the lady?[2] I doubt– I dont know! My Psyche is "perplexed in the extreme"[3] upon this important point of nomenclature– And important it is, in a measure. Blowsabella w.^{dnt} do for a heroine[4]—not for us at least.

I have just read your reply to the Monthly Critic—though not his attack, which lingers away, by an omission.[5] Yet I can discern his line of road by the dust of the chariot-wheels of your triumph, even to the sharpest turnings & fairly in to the goal– A triumph indeed! Done so excellently well too, as to candour & temperance & good humour!– The steel shines in the sunshine—& it must be a pleasure to everybody to see a little stabbing accomplished upon a "boiling bloody breast"[6] with such "great beauty" of instrument. I particularly liked the affront hurled back upon the pompous nothingness of "our tribunal" canopied & footstooled out by the critics; they mouthing their parts like any other stage Kings against the royalty of nature's making, seen & crowned in such men as Leigh Hunt!

Talking of stage kings reminds me of stages– I am perfectly aware, believe me, of the great wrong, the base wrong, trampled into dramatic genius during this present injury & injuriousness of the theatres. My doubt is as to its being removed by any 'yeas' to your "petition".[7]

In the meanwhile perhaps the dramatist has as open a door to the public imagination through the press as any other modification of poet has. I dont say an open door,—but 'as open a door'. If the trade repudiates your tragedies, it does so, less perhaps because they are tragedies, than because they are poetry. The outcry among booksellers is "Bring us prose or stay at home"– None among them will READ a poetical ms unless the 'honor' be 'thrust upon them'.[8] And as to buying one, unless its author's reputation be fixed among the stars, w.^d they do it?– Even in the starry case, wd'nt they cast down their eyes?– Murray has "up there" 'an oath in heaven'[9] never to print a line poetical! And a phrase reached me from certain bibliopolist-oracles, that "neither Shakespeare nor Milton w.^d be expected to sell at this present moment, *without pictures*"!!! Oh dead march of intellect!

Therefore you who are dramatists stand on the same ground, rather in the same ditch, with other poets—and in my mind (forgive me) you sh.^d do so.

This people is wanting in eyes to see, in ears to hear withal—in a heart to understand.[10] *Here is the evil root.*

That the state of the theatres is infamous & unjust is very clear—but dig out the evil & feel if there be not below a deeper depth of it.

Dear M! Horne, I have forgotten!— There is one paragraph of your 'reply', in which kindness says so much more than justice, that gratitude does'nt know what to say— You shall guess it for me.

Oh yes! You will settle all about the scenes. Your additional suggestions give a spring upwards to the whole scheme,—just what the encouragement of your approval & consent has given to *me*. Yet .. in spite of all .. I shall remain nervous to the last as to the temerity of working with you—

> 'And you will be the best harper
> That ever took harp in hand—
> And I SH^D. be the best singer
> That ever sang in this land—[']'[11]

But as it is, oh King Estmere, where will be the symmetry?—— The fault at least (as far as volition goes) will be your majesty's.

Yours in harp-fellowship & the minor key—
EBB—

I have read two, three times, your fine Cosmo scenes in the last M. Chronicle.[12] You did'nt quite forgive me, I *suspect*, for thinking & feeling more about Cosmo than Gregory,—the latter being allowed the highest place artistically. Well these newly published scenes have not righted my impressions— They are *very* fine—

Publication: EBB-RHH, II, 74–76 (in part).
Manuscript: Pierpont Morgan Library.

1. Dated by the reference to *The Monthly Chronicle*.
2. In response to this letter, Horne submitted to EBB a sketch of the plot for act I; he retained Medon as the name for the male protagonist, but called Medon's betrothed Evanthe.
3. *Othello*, V, 2, 346.
4. Cf. Blouzelinda, a rustic maid in Gay's *The Shepherd's Week* (1714).
5. Horne's reply must have been shown to EBB in manuscript, as it was not published. Although EBB speaks of an "attack," the review of *Chaucer, Modernized* in *The Court, Lady's Magazine, Monthly Critic, and Museum* (January 1841, pp. 58–60) was largely favourable, although it did include some disparaging remarks about previous attempts to popularize Chaucer.
6. *A Midsummer Night's Dream*, V, 1, 147.
7. See letter 767, note 3.
8. Cf. *Twelfth Night*, II, 5, 146.
9. *The Merchant of Venice*, IV, 1, 228.
10. Cf. Isaiah, 6:10.
11. Lines 159–162, slightly misquoted, of "King Estmere," one of the poems included in Thomas Percy's *Reliques of Ancient English Poetry*.
12. *The Monthly Chronicle*, January 1841, pp. 37–40, contained some "hitherto unpublished scenes" of Horne's *Cosmo de' Medici*.

795. RB TO EDWARD MOXON

Monday M^r [ca. February 1841][1]

My dear Mr Moxon,

I was not fortunate enough to find you at-home this morning when I called for the purpose of begging your advice about a work of mine I want to publish:[2] I have removed, you must know, deeper into Uninhabitableness than Camberwell even, and may call on and miss you, therefore, next week as this: do I draw too largely on your kindness if I say I shall be in Town on Wednesday—and at Dover St by 1. o-clock? Of course you would not dream of setting aside the least important engagement you may happen to have for that hour.—but if this mention of my purpose should merely postpone a ride or walk for a few minutes, it will greatly oblige

Yours very truly,
Robert Browning.

New Cross, Hatcham, Surrey. By the way, there is famous horse-way to this Chaos-and-Old-Night Quarter;[3] Hills and trees of a sort—which will be green presently: we have a garden too: why should I despair of inducing you to come over and talk of all and every thing *except* "a work of mine I want to publish"?

Publication: BN, No. 9 (Fall 1972), 36–37 (reproduced on page 32).
Manuscript: Harvard University.

1. Dated by the move to New Cross and the impending publication of *Pippa Passes*.
2. *Pippa Passes*, published in April 1841.
3. Cf. *Paradise Lost*, I, 543. This is probably intended as a further reference to New Cross, some three miles from London, being "deeper into Uninhabitableness than Camberwell even".

---

796. EBB TO RICHARD HENGIST HORNE

[Torquay]
Monday. [?8] [February 1841][1]

Anthea, Evanthe—I dont remember either—elsewhere . . prominently elsewhere. You read *Earine* right—but being *perfectly* right besides in eschewing "the names of other people's heroines,"[2] all its beauty w^d not fit it for our purpose. Besides, I sh^d'nt be brave enough (although working with you dear Mr Horne) to touch a word hallowed by the atmosphere of that exquisite 'Sad Shepherd'—which proves Ben Jonson a true poet & no mere scholar, to the critics' faces.

No. 796   [?8] [February 1841]   17

Talking of critics .. oh .. the Athenæum!– Have you seen it?—& seen in it how tender-hearted people keep themselves warm this cold weather by tomahawking their neighbours?– Everybody belonging to Chaucer is executed,—& *you* hacked at, with the degree of malice extraordinar[il]y done to you as editor! Only M.[r] Wordsworth, is slunk round in a cowardly disingenuous manner[3] (oh I *must* say it!) just because in right of his high Eminence of reputation 'among the nations',[4] weapons of their sort could not hurt him. I must call the mode of the gliding round M.[r] Wordsworth *very* cowardly .. a sword in both hands & no prick of either for him—! Why, if the work *be* an evil design, his hands are as little clean as yours—or as mine, if I dared name such things *avec*![5]–

And by the way, *I* am commended, with others for *selecting* an imaginative part of Chaucer—a commendation as little deserved you know, as the cruelty upon the collective body of your "Innocents".[6]

Now I am quite sure, or next to quite sure that Mr George Darley, is the perpetrator of 'the article'. I have no reason for it, except the *crossness*—which however is to myself unanswerable. This "Cynical poet" as some of his fellow citizens in the Rep. Lit. call him, achieves I rather believe most of the Athenæum bitternesses: & I who admire his powers when displayed lyrically & kept apart from tragedies, really wish he were a little better tempered!– Only when a poet works by profession as a critic, we sh.[d] scarcely wonder at the monstrosity of the centaur.

Aglae—w.[d] Aglae do? or Ægle? After all, my inclination is something perhaps towards *Medon* for the man's name—& to Ev*anthe* (not *adne*) for the woman's. You are perfectly right as to the poetical impertinence of a citizen chorus. Oh no!–nothing approaching to an embodiment of the conventionalities w.[d] do—but we might hint at them notwithstanding—if the opportunity comes, & the graceful possibility—might'nt we?

Though perfectly right in abjuring German names you made me smile a little by protesting against them *because* "it w.[d] be called German mysticism". Do you really suppose it will be called anything *else*, in any case? You will see what M.[r] Darley (for one) will say to us, in the Athenæum.

Yet I have an interest in the Athenæum, for all its sins. They have been as kind to me, I do believe, on different occasions, as their consciences would let them—& the editor is liberal enough to send me a number every week on account of a few very occasional contributions of mine, deserving no such gratuity.

To extract a few words from Miss Mitford's letter—"I knew something of Chaucer, & yet I rejoice to see him made quite clear & with so much taste & skill.—— Gloriously has M.[r] Horne executed his own portion. The introduction too is all that heart can wish. How thoroughly right is he in all that he says of M!" Darley, . . who is laughably in the wrong".

Oh you will build up the preface excellently well—and do you know I am watching your 'paces' altogether very curiously, besides the deeper interest! I want to see how you manage your creations—the erection of your edifices—never having stood near any poetical scaffoldings before . . except my own. And it appears that you take it very regularly—first the title page, then the preface—κ.τ.λ.[7] When you begin building, who knows but what you will send me away?

Oh no! the headache is no excuse! I have not frequent headaches—& if just now I am rather more feverish & uncomfortable than usual, the cause is in the dreadful weather—the snow & east wind— & not in our Psyche. These external causes do however affect me as little,—even *less*, my physician says,—than might have been feared—& I think steadily, hope steadily, for London at the end of May . . so to attain a removal from this place which has been so eminently fatal to my happiness.

The only gladness associated with the banishment here has been your offered sympathy & friendship. Otherwise bitterness has dropped on bitterness like the snows—more than I can tell, . . & independent of that last most overwhelming affliction of my life,[8]—from the edge of the chasm of which, I may struggle, BUT ⟨never can escape.

Ever yours,
EBB⟩[9]

I forgot the title. W!ᵈ not Psyche apocalypte (η you know) be more correct, as *well* perhaps as more pedantic? I dont mind if *you* dont. What is your thought of *Psyche Agonistes*? I lean to it a little, perhaps.

Publication: EBB-RHH, II, 92–96 (in part).
Manuscript: Pierpont Morgan Library.

1. This letter falls between nos. 793 and 799.
2. Earine, one of the names proposed by EBB in letter 793, was used by Jonson in *The Sad Shepherd*. The name eventually chosen for Medon's bride was Evanthe.
3. *The Athenæum* of 6 February 1841 (no. 693, pp. 107–108) reviewed *The Poems of Geoffrey Chaucer, Modernized*. The reviewer equates Horne's aim, expressed in the Introduction, of making Chaucer's poems "intelligible to the general reader" as being merely "to dilute them down to the level of cockney comprehensions" and says that Chaucer "is reduced to sickly weakness and effeminacy." He speaks of "gratuitous flourishes" and "wanton changes, which affect both the sense and the rhythm" and says "in every page, almost every line, Mr. Horne stumbles." There is no direct criticism of Wordsworth's contributions. (For the full text of the review, see pp. 389–391.)
4. Numbers, 23:9.
5. "Together with" [the critics].
6. The Feast of the Holy Innocents, on 28 December, commemorates Herod's slaughter of the children of Bethlehem (Matthew, 2:16).
7. "Και τα λοιπα" ("and the rest"), the Greek equivalent of "etcetera."
8. Bro's death.

9. The Morgan manuscript concludes with the word "BUT," except for the postscript, written at the top of the first page. The printed text, however, includes "never can escape" and the signature.

---

797. EBB to Mary Russell Mitford

[Torquay]
Tuesday. [9 February 1841][1]

Have you thought me the most ungrateful creature in the world, dearest dearest Miss Mitford? Or have you thought I was out of it?

Indeed the latter supposition is almost the only *responsive* one, considering the kindness & delightfulness altogether of your letter . . but although I have thought much of it & very much of you & yours, there are sometimes necessities of writing elsewhere & sometimes, especially in this trying weather, disinclinations to any kind of exertion . . & so I put off from day to day, nay, from mondays to saturdays, the expression of that grateful love to you which is always deep down in my heart.

First—I rejoice with you in the blessedness of seeing dear Dr Mitford better. Have you read to him Bulwer's "Night & Morning."?[2] Oh—I know you dont like Bulwer—& I myself consider this new romance several paces below Maltravers & Alice. Still it has a good deal of action & . . rather melodramatic . . interest . . and you could not very well,— frown as you may,—lay it down half or three quarters read. Then, if you are looking out for romances to melt away the sense of snow & long evenings from your invalid, there is the American Dr Bird's 'Nick of the Woods'[3]—which for adventure & hair breadth escapes & rapid movement from the beginning to the end, will charm you far above the freezing point, though face to face with a thermometer. I recommend to you "Nick of the Woods". I read it lately myself, & went forthwith by a metempsychosis into a pilgrim of those vast sighing forests,—& travelled so far & fast & wildly, that I c^d scarcely, on my return, believe myself an oyster.

Mr Quillinan's book I enquired for at the libraries,[4] & shall see perhaps before long. How kind of you to care for the *cause* of your mentioning it to me! "*Your* Miss Barrett"! To be sure I am! How, as you say, can I help it?– Yours in the bondage of true grateful affection!– Yours to do what you like with . . except to throw away. You would'nt do that, . . & you could'nt indeed . . you could'nt throw me *all* away . . not my love for you . . not far! It w^d creep back & cling, do what you could!——

I dreamt of you two or three nights ago. Is it strange that I sh^d dream of you? Yes—because for very very long, it is strange whenever I dream pleasantly. The sun rules the day,⁵ exclusively for me—& I have no sunshine in sleep—nothing but broken hidious [sic] shadows, & ghastly lights to mark them. But two or three nights ago I dreamt of *you* .. dreamt of seeing you at Three Mile Cross. I was there .. in your sitting room .. and what do you think I did? Sate down on your sofa, drawing up my feet beside me in my old lazy way (how impudent!–) and then said ... not, "Tell me of the Tragedy" .. not "Where are the letters" .. not even "Can you forgive me?" .. but ... "*Now let us talk about* FLUSH".!!! I dont deserve to dream of you,—do I, dearest Miss Mitford?–

It was so kind too, to copy out the long extract from Mr Chorley. You were sure it w^d amuse me—& so it did.

And in the meantime the Athenæum, by the hand as I divine of your 'cynical poet' has stabbed near the heart if not into it, our poor Chaucer .. adjusting the degrees of illtemper to the Chief chiefly, & so downwards—only gliding with most adroit cowardice, round Mr Wordsworth. Now the great poet of the Lakes was forward in spirit, in the undertaking, although the labor of the editorship fell upon Mr Horne—& if the whole design be evil, evil also was his share of it.⁶

I think about the tragedy.⁷ Historical it must be, I know—or you will have none of it—& you will 'bate no inch⁸ of the "sweeping pall".⁹ Did you ever try C Kean with *Otto*? If he is old enough for Sir Giles Overeach,¹⁰ the 'years' cant be objected to.

Dear little Flush grows dearer every day—talking of tragedies! & you may assure 'Master Ben'¹¹ that he seems quite happy & grows visibly fat. He is far more courteous to the houshold than he used to be, but keeps his love & familiarity for Crow & me, & positively refuses to stir out of the house in spite of all temptations, with anybody but herself. My sisters feed him & pat him in vain. He is very civil .. & "perverse" like his mistress .. & if carried past the threshold, runs back again at the moment of liberation. A shawl thrown upon a chair by my fireside, is his favorite place—& there he sits most of the day .. coming down occasionally to be patted or enjoy a round of leaps. Such a quiet, loving intelligent little dog—& so very very pretty! He is washed in warm water & soap twice a week, & brushed & combed everyday, & shines as if he carried sunlight about on his back! Is *your* Flush washed? Do you know,—notwithstanding all the fame & immortality of your Flush,—I am sure he cant be, essentially, more beautiful or good than mine. There's jealousy for you, instead of gratitude! I sh^d sleep in sack cloth tonight for a penance.

God bless you my beloved friend. I am tolerably well notwithstanding this intense weather, & the periodical attacks of fever & palpitation which it brings to me regularly every day at three oclock. But I am not really worse . . with a worseness which will not pass with the frost. At least I *hope* not, for poor Papa's sake—

Give my love to your dear invalid—& think of ⟨me⟩ yourself as

your own

EBB

Address: Miss Mitford / Three Mile Cross / near Reading.
Publication: EBB-MRM, I, 214–216.
Manuscript: Wellesley College.

1. Dated by the reference to *The Athenæum*.
2. *Night and Morning*, a 3-volume novel, had been published in January 1841.
3. *Nick of the Woods; a Story of Kentucky* (1837) by Robert Montgomery Bird (1806–54), novelist and physician. He had previously written *The Gladiator* (1831), which provided the actor Edwin Forrest with one of his favourite roles.
4. *The Conspirators, or The Romance of Military Life* (1841), by Edward Quillinan (1791–1851), had been labelled by *The Athenæum* of 5 December 1840 (no. 684, p. 964) as "Wearisome and devoid of artistic construction" though "not without interest, both as regards first invention and detail" despite the author's being "very prosy."
5. Cf. Genesis, 1:16.
6. See letter 796, note 3. Although Horne was the editor, it was Wordsworth who had first proposed the project, hence EBB's statement regarding his share of responsibility for the outcome. The "cynical poet" was undoubtedly George Darley, whose "able *guilty* article upon Ion" aroused EBB's ire in letter 748.
7. Miss Mitford was contemplating writing another play, and had asked EBB to propose subjects. Miss Mitford was presumably planning to respond to Charles Kean's mother's request for her to write a tragic role for him. Miss Mitford also invited suggestions from her friend Miss Jephson, saying: "The hero must be young and interesting—must have *to do*, and not merely suffer" (L'Estrange (2), III, 117).
8. Cf. Byron, *Don Juan*, XIII, 98, 4.
9. Cf. Milton, "Il Penseroso" (1673), 98.
10. Overreach was the avaricious uncle in Massinger's *A New Way to Pay Old Debts*.
11. Ben Kirby, Miss Mitford's manservant, who helped look after the Mitfords' dogs.

---

798. EBB TO GEORGE GOODIN MOULTON-BARRETT

[Torquay]

Sunday. [14–15 February 1841][1]

At last my ever dearest George, I give some sign of being sensible to your kindness upon kindness in the shape of letters. I write to you at last. You know you frightened me away from doing so before with your solemn obtestations & protestations—and even now, Stormie has just said . . "oh pray dont write to George, for he was very angry when you wrote to *me.*" But the 'lex talionis'[2] not being the law of the land, I am clear of intruding any offence between the wind & your legality,[3] in whatever other direction I may do so.

There is my beloved Papa's letter too—drawing an answer out of my thoughts, with a golden cord!——[4]

Dearest Georgie, I do think of you so much, & hope for you so much & so strongly—with a hope partaking far more of expectation than of anxiety after all. Sooner or later, if God continues life & health, you will succeed. That I never in the least doubt about—because I am, as you probably know, a great believer in the "unconquerable will"[5] as to intellectual successes. It is the beat of the drum to the soldier's march. A man with a mind may *will* himself into anything—& a woolsack[6] may be set down as a 'thing' in moderation—by no means the most glittering toy in the toyshop, or hung most out of reach. —— You cant think how many engravings my thoughts & fancies have made (working together) from the picture you sent me—of your retirement in Paper Buildings.[7] God bless you in all ways dearest, dearest George—out of Zion[8] *first*, & then from other high places of the earth[9]—& mind be careful of yourself—& dont be wet & cold—nor walk out your heart with rapidity, *tuo more*,[10] for *my* sake, Georgie!–

I was glad that you—& my dearest Papa speaks approbation too— liked my profile of the Man with a Soul.[11] Only Georgie, it isnt German, & never was. Since you thurst [*sic*] the dishonor of that suspicion on me, M[r] Horne said something which made me smile a little in relation to it. He said "Let us by no means, have German names. People will call it instantly *German mysticism*, instead of what it is, a mystery of universal nature." No beginning has yet been made. He is so hard to please about names. What do you think of, for a title .. "Psyche Apocalyptic"—or "*Psyche Apocalypte*"? Oh—Papa is quite right– We are sure not to get anybody to read it except himself & you– But it is our business, you know, to make it *worth* reading, & not to mind the rest—to work as the caterpillars do, without thinking of who is looking. Authors have low mercantile ways, sometimes, of considering things—whereas they have no business with results. If God has given them any power (though but of a fibre's strength) they sh[d] work by it, & if He has revealed any truth, according to it, without taking into account the bookseller's pay in pence, or the public's in popularity–

Stormie's cold is quite vanished, I am very glad to say. And Jocky's knees & ancles which suffered the pains & penalties of growing too fast, are quite strong again,—to give credit to his own testimony & that of his fellow-walkers. They take very long walks on every possible day—and I heard Stormie remonstrating with Arabel & maintaining that "four miles were quite long enough for a walk"—Arabel's answer being, "Yes,—four miles there & four miles back." She & Ocky are opposed on this point to Stormie Henrietta & Mary [Hunter]—the two latter being considered decidedly 'lazy', & Stormie, too practical. I never remember (or at least have not for years) to have seen Arabel so excursive & capable of exercise. And she has not had one cold this winter. It is a great mercy, & comfort to me.

For my own part I think myself better, dearest Georgie. I do *think* so. I am low & fit for nothing in the morning—but that is the consequence in great measure, I am persuaded, of being over-excited the rest of the day by the brandy & opium. The three oclock fever is less than it was. Indeed today, my face was not flushed at all—& the palpitation was slight. It was nothing but the severe weather. Now we are as hot as we were cold—no! not quite!

Flush amuses me sometimes when I am inclined to be amused by nothing else. There is no resisting his praying to be patted,—& he has some striking peculiarities.—wont eat anything unless he is pressed—& then scarcely, .. unless he sees you do the same. We must make him friends with Myrtle–[12] Write some of you—will you? do!– I did not mean to write so much after what my own dearest Papa said—but it is hard to begin & end—& still this was not written at once. Is dear Treppy with you? Affectionate love to her & the rest. God love [&] bless you George. Love to my dear Minny. I unalterably love you– No—*more than ever*–

Ba——

Tell Papa & yourself, I did not write this all at once; so it c^d do no harm.

Address: G. G. Barrett Esqr / 50. Wimpole Street / London.
Publication: B-GB, pp. 50–53.
Manuscript: Pierpont Morgan Library.

1. The letter is postmarked 16 February 1841.
2. The law of retaliation, i.e., an eye for an eye, etc. (Exodus, 21:24).
3. Cf. *I Henry IV*, I, 3, 45.
4. Marlowe, *The Tragedy of Dido, Queen of Carthage* (1594), I, 1, 14.
5. *Paradise Lost*, I, 106.
6. See letter 679, note 4.
7. George was practising law in chambers at no. 3 Paper Buildings, The Temple.
8. Psalms, 128:5.
9. Deuteronomy, 32:13.
10. "In your fashion."
11. In the projected drama with Horne, Psyche was the soul of Medon.
12. "A poor dull worthy dog, reposing / All day beside the fire" (letter 562); a "brown & yellow terrier ... whose noblest qualities lie in his mind" (letter 591).

799. EBB to Richard Hengist Horne

[Torquay]
Monday. [15 February 1841][1]

Then let it be 'Psyche Apocalyptic'. Your reasons are abundantly good–.

Now dear Mr Horne, see how we have been beguiled. The necessary name *Psyche* drew me towards the propriety of holding a certain Greekness in the other names—& this draws *you* into fixing upon Greece for a locality. Well—you are right. Only we need not be very local—need we? To tell you the truth, I had never thought about locality—or at least about our's being other than some new-new-world Island—or continent– But let it be Greece—the Spirits will murmur to our feet the more readily.

As to the time being *olden*, there are the objections you perceive, & which are insurmountable, & which we need not (happily) *try* to surmount. Indeed the endeavour w^d eeclipse [*sic*], cloud over, the high summits of our subject.

Let it be, if you please, two hundred years ago—or something less, or something more.

But now, I am unreasonable & covetous. You say 'If we have the antique time, we may have a Chorus of Satyrs.' I want the *modern time, & the Satyrs besides*. '*Want*' is too strong a word. But I am *inclined* to the Satyrs—I *lean* to them. There is something "high fantastic"[2] in them—& deeply contrastive to the Heavenly Spirits. Their 'dark earth'[3] falls with heavy suggestive noises. Your *woods* inspired you with the Satyrs.

Yet after all, there are certain objections which I glance at reluctantly .. such as the difficulty of sustaining the right satyrical tone, in the universal harmony. If we have them for a chorus, we must KEEP them for a chorus. Do *think* about it, dear Mr Horne– You know so much more of artistic effects than I do. My private instinct is after all & certainly, to venture with them.

I write on the same day on which I received your letter. That letter *ought* to have reached me yesterday—and the roads & posts being in such disorder, I am afraid by any delay on my part, to risk over passing the 'three or four days' from last saturday. And thinking longer w^d scarcely change my present thoughts.

I thought once today of sending you the Athenæum.– But no—I wont– It is not worth reading, & less, being vexed about. It is not fair criticism—or criticism indeed, at all.[4]

So you acquit Mr Darley, on the strength of Ethelstan[5]– My hand aches while it holds on to my first opinion.[6]

But I have not read Ethelstan. '*Becket*' Miss Mitford lent to me, with what appeared to me at the time, some excessive praise. I read it through, acknowledging its power *of a certain class*—but daring to think it quite deficient in *concentration & passion*, the brain & heart of the drama.[7] Was this wrong? If so, I was wrong altogether,—as unmoved by all the reading, as this paper .. if my pen & breath were turned from it.– Is it not true besides, that the blank-verse construction wants harmony & variety—from the imperfect management of the pauses? No—I could not be an enthusiast for Becket,—& Ethelstan, I never saw.

But Mr Darley is a poet—& has done very fine things in lyrical raptures.

What do you think the '*critic*' (whoever he is) says cruelly as to the 'Innocents.' Why that when we meet the great poet in the spiritual Hereafter, he may vouchsafe us the touch of his hand (through goodnature) in testimony of our excellent intentions!!—but that there can be no further communion, because *his* place is not ours!![8]—graciously intimating, you see, that *our* place is some fathoms farther down, in some low recess of Tophet—[9] Is'nt this worse than any massacre of Herod . . who was satisfied with murdering the body?———

The Tableaux with your 'Fetches' is in London with Papa . . all the books I write in, being his of right—& I cant look at Friedrich's speech.[10] I have groped in my memory for it ever since.

Oh yes—of course you must often have seen Psyche "in visions of the night[11] .. when deep thoughts fall upon men".[12] Good night now, dear Mr Horne! I must *try*, at least, to get to sleep–

Ever yours
EBB–

Address: R H Horne Esqr / 2. Gray's Inn Square / Gray's Inn / London–
Publication: EBB-RHH, II, 96–98 and 106 (in part).
Manuscript: Pierpont Morgan Library.

1. Envelope is postmarked 16 February 1841; the previous day was a Monday.
2. Cf. *Twelfth Night*, I, 1, 15.
3. Shelley, *Prometheus Unbound* (1820), II, 1, 149.
4. See letter 796, note 3.
5. *Ethelstan; or, The Battle of Brunanburh: a Dramatic Chronicle* (1841), Darley's new work.
6. i.e., that Darley was the author of the critical review of *Chaucer, Modernized* in *The Athenæum*.
7. EBB had commented on Darley's *Thomas à Becket* in letter 763.
8. The review included this passage: "When these 'mere moderns' meet Chaucer [in another world], a recognition there will be, a friendly shake of the hands, perhaps, for intentional kindness, but nothing to infer intimacy or to encourage it. Kindred spirits live together, and where Chaucer is, his modernizers cannot be." (For the full text, see pp. 389–391.)
9. A place of fire and destruction, equated with Hell (see Isaiah, 30:33)
10. Presumably EBB's reference is to his speech after Juliana, his betrothed, dies, and before he jumps to his own death (p. 62 of the 1840 *Findens' Tableaux*).
11. Genesis, 46:2.
12. Cf. Psalms, 92:5.

800. EBB TO THOMAS POWELL

Torquay.
Feby. 19.th 1841.

Dear Sir
I write three days later than I sh^d have done, to acknowledge your very kind attention in sending me your new attempt upon Chaucer[1]—

which seems to me excellently accomplish'd, with more closeness perhaps to the original (*perhaps*—is it not so .. as a whole?) than your previous performances—also 'Staffo' with its touching preface[2]—& y.^{r} 'Nature's voice'[3] a prophecy with so much beauty siding the truth. I appreciate in all your poetry its uplooking aspect. And pray do not sheathe the 'dogmatic swords'[4] or apologize for not doing it—a strong expression adapted to the strong cruelty of the thing expressed.

Thank you too, much & truly, for some kind-words conveying your own & Mrs Powell's pleasure in poems of mine. My Prometheus is rather close to the letter—but I quite disagree with you—(you wont misinterpret me into affectation—*that* w.^{d} be serving me worse than I served Æschylus—) as to its being true to the poetry. Oh no!– It is stiff & hard—a Prometheus *twice* bound, & to a colder rock than was intended .. I wish sometimes to vindicate myself by doing it again. In the meantime your goodnature is father to a too gentle thought[5] of it, by much!

But you do me bare justice again in supposing that I sh.^{d} be sorry to hear of any heaviness weighing upon that true poet Mr Leigh Hunt. "The world presses heavily on one of its finest spirits." And so it must be: or the world w.^{d} not be the world—nor w.^{d} spirits be spirits.— I do hope, he is not seriously ill—that he is better while I write. The weather is very trying—with these sudden heats upon the late bitter cold. Yet (in answer to your kind enquiry) I myself have suffered less, & am actually better than might have been thought from the circumstances.

                          Sincerely yours
                          Elizabeth B Barrett.

Publication: None traced.
Manuscript: University of Iowa.

1. *The Monthly Chronicle* for February 1841 contained Powell's modernized version of "The Nun's Priest's Tale; or, The Cock and the Fox" (pp. 119–133).

2. *Sic*, for "Staffa." This poem, on pp. 110–113 of the magazine, was by "the late Thomas Chapman." The preface explains that Chapman, "endowed with mental powers of no common order, of a lovely natural disposition ... beloved by ... all who had the happiness of his friendship," had died of cholera in 1824, in his 21st year. The manuscript was supplied "through the kindness of a friend"—presumably Powell.

3. The magazine contained three poems by Powell, but none with this title.

4. We have not located the source of this quotation; from the context, it may well be taken from one of Powell's own poems, or his letter to EBB.

5. Cf. *II Henry IV*, IV, 5, 92.

801. EBB TO MARY RUSSELL MITFORD

[Torquay]
Tuesday. [March 1841][1]

If being angry with myself, ashamed of myself, & in the metaphorical sackcloth & ashes of dry repentance can avail anything except the making me more unhappy than the sense of making you uneasy has rendered me, do my dearest kindest & ever until now forgiving friend, accept the atonement. No—nobody has the influenza & I am not worse than usual. What is to be said for me! And here have I been making you uneasy when it might have been otherwise! What is to be said for me? And after that long delightful letter of yours which brightened my spirits for a whole day—that long kind most delightful letter!!– Oh! can anything be said for me?–

Most very bad people as to reputation, are not perhaps quite as bad as they seem—& perhaps even *I*[2] am not. I loved you & thought of you through every day & night of the whole long silence, & prized your letter my beloved friend deeply as I loved you– I prized it & thought how kind you were to waste all that brightness upon *me*—besides breathing aside my clouds to let in that brightest dream of coming to see me in London when the summer comes & I am *there*. Thank you, thank you!– How *can* I thank you!– I felt myself smiling to myself over the words as I read them, & after reading them, c:d scarcely forget or willingly & consciously neglect their writer.

No– The real cause of the silence was your tragedy. I wont write (was my soliloquy) till I know of Ulfried[3]—or of somebody else who is tragic: and I who am denuded of books in this place, sent to the right hand & left, & waited for Wraxall[4] & others to be sent to me .. being disappointed on all sides & unconscious on all days of the flight of time– You cant think how when a person exists as I do, saturdays are taken for mondays, & mondays for saturdays. And then I wanted, waited for books on Spanish-Moorish times—having a fancy in my head from a word you once dropped close to me, that a subject for you was to be sought *there*. And now,—after all .. a pretty business I have made of it!– Made you uneasy!—and all my good news, .. that we have not the influenza!——

You have been ill my beloved Miss Mitford—& are not well, I fear, even now. That sickness!– I know how distressing it is, .. having suffered myself from it dreadfully—in consequence of no stomachic affection, but mere debility. All the latter part of last year, .. indeed until very lately the simplest causes .. even *speaking* a little too much, .. provoked the most violent vomiting which of course increased the weakness *in* which it originated. So I can feel for you—know fully what you suffer.

You *suffer* .. ah—may that be a wrong word now .. a wrong tense for the word. Mind you tell me exactly, when you write my dearest friend. I say, you see "WHEN you write", not daring to say "Write".

In the long letter, you mentioned friends of yours who had suffered deep affliction. Tell me how they are.

Then the little puppies, Flush's puppies, whom you & Ben were nursing. Dont forget about the puppies.

And tell Master Ben .. will you?—with my thanks for his kind message to me that I hope he may see my Flush some day & judge with his own judgment as to whether he was thrown away upon me, in the matter of being cared for & educated & *spoilt properly*. For voices north & south cry out "Flush is spoilt"! "Flush wont eat mutton—he objects to it!– Flush wont be left in the room by himself .. he cant bear it!["]– And worse than all, if somebody is'nt ready to play with Flush just when he likes, he thinks himself ill-used & begins to cry with that inward moaning cry which exacts the attention he desires. Very affectionate he is! But tell Ben that as to "going through fire & water"[5] under any possible circumstances or for any possible body, such heroic self-devotion is quite out of Flush's *line*. Flush is, in fact, the prince of cowards .. if he does not wear the crown—shudders all over at his own shadow in a looking-glass, runs away from the least of little dogs in his path, & in the case of a coal cracking in the fire, leaps upon the bed to me to be taken care of. In fact Flush is a proverb for cowardice in this household. There never was such a coward—not even his mistress!– And with that bond of sympathy added to other still faster bonds, he & I are very near and dear– The first person who comes to wake me in the morning is Flush,—to wake me & remind me of *you!* There he comes, all in the dark .. before the shutters are open .. pushes through the bedcurtains & leaps into the nearest place by me & bites each of my hands very gently after the manner of his customary salems.[6] Every morning he does this—and once when I w^{dnt} see him & kept my eyes fast shut, Flush began to moan, quite despairingly.

So you see what friends we are! But it is not only he & *I* who are friends!– Everybody likes Flush—everybody in the house. Even after he has done all the mischief possible, torn their letters, spoilt their books, bitten their shoes into holes (these favorites, these Buckinghams[7] are always full of mischief) everybody likes Flush, & nobody refuses his pretty paw when he holds it out apologetically "to shake hands & make friends".

I have written myself tired, my dearest Miss Mitford– May God bless & keep you & yours.

I sh^d like much to hear something of the tragedy—whether any suggestion w^d be quite too late now. I wring my useless hands for being so useless to you!——
Give my love to dear Dr Mitford. May he & you be both quite well—& happy .. as far as that can be here.

Your EBB.

Publication: EBB-MRM, I, 217–219.
Manuscript: Wellesley College.

1. Dated by the further reference to Miss Mitford's projected tragedy.
2. Underscored twice.
3. In a letter of 28 March 1841, Miss Mitford had written that her bad writing had misled Miss Anderdon, her correspondent "as to the name, which is Umfried" (Chorley, I, 179–180)—presumably a character in a plot she had outlined to EBB, who had been similarly misled.
4. Nathaniel William Wraxall (1751–1831); his *Posthumous Memoirs of His Own Time* (1836) is doubtless the book EBB wished to refer to.
5. Cf. *The Merry Wives of Windsor*, III, 4, 103.
6. An 18th-century version of "salaams" (*OED*).
7. George Villiers (1592–1682) was introduced to James I in 1614, and the "good-looking sprightly youth caught James's fancy" (*DNB*). He was made Cupbearer to the King, the first step in his advancement, through the king's favour, to the post of Lord High Admiral and the duchy of Buckingham.

---

802. EBB TO RICHARD HENGIST HORNE

[Torquay]
March 10th 1841

My dear Mr Horne,

I have seen Orpheus, & write just to thank you for the pleasure of the vision. 'Oh then I see that Keats had been with you'—in the manner of dealing romantically with classical subjects—painting out statues—not otherwise of course. There is plenty of your own massiveness (that best word for you)—notwithstanding which & the number of fine lines, the *whole* w^d have differed by excelling, had it been written now. You have gathered power, intensity, freedom of versification– But in my brain

——"slow the Argo ploughs her way
Like a dun dragon spreading moonlit wings",[1]

to suggest certain unsurpassable lines. That dun dragon with moonlit wings with its grand solemn movement is very fine. You are worthy of naming the Argo–[2]

I have a little spaniel called Flush the descendant of Miss Mitford's spaniel, Flush the Famous, which she sent me *for company* & besides to remind me of her. He is spoilt of course—it could'nt be helped under the circumstances— For in addition to the association, he gave me most ready affection notwithstanding all my dulness as a playmate—& it was only natural that I sh^d murmur when my maid told me she had been obliged to whip him for a misdemænor.

His sin at its first aspect, looked a heavy one. He had torn up into fragments like a critic, a volume of Lamartine's poems,—into fragments an inch square. [']'Oh—but" I said,—"how c^d he know any better?"

There's an apology for the critics! "He sh^d be *taught*" she replied— "or he'll tear up all the books in the house. He'll tear them all to pieces if he's not whipped".

Think of *that*!—'Gregory VII' Cosmo & all! Did the critics do *you* much harm formerly, dear Mr Horne, when you went for sympathy to Echo?[3]—or was it a mere pestilent silence? But you may whip *them* for ever, without making them better—I lose my moral so–

Ever truly yours
Elizabeth B Barrett.

Publication: The Pall Mall Gazette, 2 April 1890, p. 7 (in part).
Manuscript: Harvard University.

 1. We have not been able to trace a published poem called "Orpheus" by Horne, containing these lines. It was, perhaps, sent to EBB in manuscript.
 2. Jason's galley, in which he went to search for the Golden Fleece.
 3. Echo was Jupiter's confidante before being deprived of speech by Juno.

803. EBB TO GEORGE GOODIN MOULTON-BARRETT

[Torquay]
March 27.th 1841

My dearest dearest Georgie,

It is, surely in equity & law, *my* turn now to write to you .. & just as surely my wish to do the same thing. I want to write to you. I want to thank you too,—for your kindness in thinking of me more than you need have done, as proved by letters two or three. Thank you dearest George,—*dearest*!–

But still being human I am discontented—& being desirous of hearing some thing of your degree of legal success, you never say a word upon the subject– We saw your name in the paper *quoad*[1] one trial .. so that you cant be altogether briefless—which information was'nt enough to satisfy the most easily satisfied among us. You are turning your face to London by this time .. are you not? You go, I think, from Monmouth to London?- Would that I were you. And do you know, dear George, I am really going to London in *May*, or very early in the next month .. & that Dr Scully considers me "QUITE RIGHT" in meaning to do so. He has said more over that I may pass the *winters* in London: & that I may do so with perfect impunity if with care. He thinks in fact, that I must be shut up in one room during the winter *anywhere*, & that under such circumstances, I might as well be in London—to say nothing of the advantageous adjacency of medical advice, better there than in other places– So if it sh.^{d} please the Infinite Goodness to withdraw His hand from striking, we shall be at home late in May, or very early in June. Remember that. And dearest George, I beseech you, never to say a word or offer a gesture against it. All that remains to me of earthly happiness seems to me dependent upon my return to Wimpole Street. Dr Scully's *honest* opinion is in its favor. I want to be with you *all*—none away, but those whom God has taken. And as to this air, however I may eat & drink or even speak & smile in it, it is & always must be to me by day & night like the air of a thunder-storm.

There was a letter from dear Set yesterday—no—from Set the day before, & from Henry yesterday. The only news is that Papa has dined twice with Mr Kenyon, & met Joanna Baillie the poet Milnes, Mrs Coleridge, & Babbage. That sounds brilliant—does'nt it? Mr Milnes professes *Puseyism*[.][2]

I had a letter from Wolverhampton & Mr Horne this morning. He still has "millions of pots & pans for a background" but has been able at last to enclose to me the skeleton-process of the first act of our Drama. You w.^{d} like to look at it I know, but have'nt time to copy it out—more especially as Dr Scully has come while I was on the verge of post-time, to push me down the precipice. And so much as I had to say to you! Mr Horne desires me not to write a line of the drama, till the whole skeleton is completed. Did you hear of his sending me his picture "showing" how he looks when fresh-black from the pits—?[3] What a national dishonor it is, that high spirits sh.^{d} be thurst [sic] upon such work! Two thousand a year & a title for man-slaying, & for man-helping & glorifying, naught!–

My writing improves—does'nt it– And indeed *I* am improving, as a whole. I think so at least.

Stormie wont go out now I am sorry to say[4]—but take no notice. Occy & Arabel & Mary [Hunter] walk every day & Henrietta *visits*. The visiting-love is stronger than I had ever supposed.

God ever ever bless you–
My own dearest Georgie's Ba.

Address: George Goodin Barrett, Esqr / On the Circuit / Monmouth.
Publication: B-GB, pp. 53–56.
Manuscript: Pierpont Morgan Library.

1. "As far as."
2. Adherents of Edward Bouverie Pusey (1800–82), Regius Professor of Hebrew at Oxford. He worked with Newman to oppose the spread of rationalism, current in Germany, to English religious beliefs and to contribute towards the practical revival of doctrines, such as apostolic succession, which were in danger of becoming obsolete. These efforts gave rise to what became known as "the Oxford Movement."
3. Horne was currently a member of a Royal Commission investigating the employment of children in mines and factories. What Horne told EBB of conditions there prompted her poem, "The Cry of the Children," published in *Blackwood's Edinburgh Magazine* in August 1843.
4. Because of the "wall of insuperable shyness" mentioned in letter 833.

804. EBB to Julia Martin

[Torquay]
March. 29.th 1841

My dearest Mrs Martin,

Have you thought "The dream has come true"? I mean the dream of the flowers which you pulled for me & I w^{dnt} look at, even? I fear you must have thought that the dream about my ingratitude has come true.

And yet it has not. Dearest Mrs Martin, it has *not*. I have not forgotten you or remembered you less affectionately through all the silence, or longed less for the letters I did not ask for. But the truth is, my faculties seem to hang heavily now, like flappers when the spring is broken. *My spring is* broken—and a separate exertion is necessary for the lifting up of each, .. & then it falls down again. I never felt so before: There is no wonder that I sh^d feel so now. Nevertheless I dont give up much to the pernicious languor .. the tendency to lie down to sleep among the snows of a weary journey .. I dont give up much to it. Only I find it sometimes at the root of certain negligences, .. for instance of this towards *you*.

Dearest Mrs Martin, receive my sympathy, *our* sympathy, in the anxiety you have lately felt so painfully & in the rejoicing for its happy issue. Do say when you write (I take for granted you see that you will write) how Mrs Vigor[1] is now—besides the intelligence more nearly touching me, of your own & Mr Martin's health & spirits. May God bless you both!–

Ah!—but you did not come! I was disappointed!–

And Mrs Hanford!– Do you know, I tremble in my reveries sometimes, lest you sh^d think it, guess it, to be half unkind in me not to have made an exertion to see Mrs Hanford.[2] It was not from want of interest in her——least of all from want of love to *you*– But I have not stirred from my bed yet— But to be honest, that was not the reason— I did not feel as if I *could*, without a painful effort, which on the other hand, c^d not, I was conscious, result in the slightest shade of satisfaction to her, receive & talk to her. Perhaps it is hard for you to *fancy* even, how I shrink away from the very thought of seeing a human face—except those immediately belonging to me in love or relationship—(yours *does*, you know).. & a stranger's might be easier to look at than one long known.

No— I did not understand from Dr Scully that he apprehended anything serious in Mrs Hanford's indisposition. She had frequent colds, I think—& reason to complain of the humidity of the climate—but there was no cause for uneasiness. So at least I understood. His opinion too, as expressed to me, was favorable about her son. He said, nothing but care was wanted. And as to Fanny,[3] she appears to have prospered here, to have looked better & better, & become capable of a good deal of exercise. Dr Scully was delighted with them all—to *admiration* I assure you!—

For my own part, my dearest Mrs Martin, my heart has been lightened lately by kind *honest* Dr Scully (who w^d never give an opinion just to please me) saying that I am 'quite right' to mean to go to London, & shall probably be fit for the journey early in June. He says that I may pass the winter there moreover, & with impunity—that wherever I am it will probably be necessary for me to remain shut up during the cold weather, & that under such circumstances it is quite possible to warm a London room to as safe a condition as a room *here*. So my heart is lightened of the fear of opposition: & the only means of regaining whatever portion of earthly happiness is not irremediably lost to me by the Divine decree, I am free to use. In the meantime, it really does seem to me that I make some progress in health—if the word in my lips be not a mockery. Oh—I fancy I shall be strengthened to get home.

Your remarks on Chaucer pleased me very much. I am glad you liked what I did—or tried to do—and as to the criticisms, you were right—& they shant be unattended to if the opportunity of correction be given to me.

Ever your affectionate
Ba

Love to ⟨dear⟩ Mr Martin. Henrietta's love & Arabels too—
Stormie & Octavius are still here—all of them quite well thank God—

Address: Mrs James Martin / Camden House / Chiselhurst / London.
Publication: LEBB, I, 86–88 (in part).
Manuscript: Wellesley College.

1. Unidentified.
2. Mrs. Martin's friend, Mrs. Hanford, had been in Torquay for her health.

3. Fanny Hanford and her brother later visited RB and EBB in Florence, where, in May 1847, they witnessed the signing of the Brownings' marriage settlement, afterwards conveying it back to Kenyon in England (see EBB's letter to Henrietta Moulton-Barrett, 16–21 May 1847).

805. EBB TO GEORGE GOODIN MOULTON-BARRETT

[Torquay]
Thursday. [15 April 1841][1]

ever Dearest Georgie

It is a pleasure to open one's heart—and for no other reason do I write my first minutes thoughts of your kindest letter to *Paper Buildings* where the freedom may lie between you & myself—& nobody else. The truth is, I am more troubled about this Black Mountain scheme[2] than lately I have fancied it possible for me to be about any temporal circumstance of that kind—and join with you in devoutly wishing that the illusion may be dispelled by the sight. Suppose the contrary to be the case—what will happen then?– Why that the only comfort I have dared to hope for must come to an end, & WE be no longer together– You are bound to London by your profession—and unless our brothers quench the energies of their lives in hunting & fishing, they must necessarily be away too .. while I leave you to judge what possible human chance there can be for *me* to bear rough roads & the distance from medical advice— look as far as you can into the future. If our home sh^d be fixed there, it is the knell of my perpetual exile—seems so at least—& I must be anxious until the risk of the stroke be past–

I am sure my dearest Papa w^d be far happier in the end, by disposing of whatever money he has—to spend, in the purchase, for his sons, of shares or partnerships of whatever business may be suited to their inclination & capacity. Of course no one c^d suggest it to him—but he w^d, I am persuaded, be happier in witnessing their establishment, than in reigning alone at the top of a mountain where their society could neither cheer *him*, nor his hand help *them*.

Dont fancy that I am worrying myself!– Oh no!– But I have been ruffled & uneasy in a measure about this business for some time—long before your letter came—from hints in Sette's. By the way, is not Sette *advising* in this matter? I wish Papa w^d ask *me*. No—I dont–

I am not up yet George. Dr Scully does not permit it until the sun shall seem inclined to tarry; & in the mean while I am going to *lie for my picture*!: Indeed it's true. You know I always meant to do it,—to *undergo* it,—in the case of any lady painter visiting this place—& the circumstance occurring, she is to be admitted to my bedside tomorrow.³ Four interviews will suffice—& four headaches will be well endured, sh^d the result be anything which my own dear Papa can have pleasure in looking at. Of course it is for *him*—a reflection of the kindness he spent upon me last year.⁴

It is so long since I saw a stranger that I shrink at the thought of the woman's coming tomorrow—even apart from her errand. And a beautiful picture will conclude all!—at least, if she succeed in making a likeness of the white shadow of this face.

Now keep my secret, George. My plan is, to send the picture to London by the post—*as a surprise*—supposing Papa to be there then. A miniature-painting, it will be.

Oh—may we be free soon from this night-mare of Black Mountains!– *Tell me all you hear.* The removal of our home from London w^d be lamentable to me under any local advantage—but these Black mountains are black indeed!–

God bless you ever & ever, my dearest dearest George! I loved you always—but since your last visit here I have loved you *most*– You will easily gather *how* the love deepened–

Your
Ba.

Henrietta had a luncheon party here today. She goes out a good deal– I wonder she can *bear it*, much less like it—but one heart cant judge for another– Say nothing of this—nor indeed of any thing else spoken by me today. God bless you George—dearest! I am so glad you liked the chain.

Address: George Goodin Barrett Esqr / 3. Paper Buildings / Temple / London.
Publication: B-GB, pp. 56–58.
Manuscript: Pierpont Morgan Library.

1. Postmarked 16 April 1841; the previous day was a Thursday.
2. The Black Mountains are in Wales, east of Brecon. EBB's father was contemplating taking a place there, presumably in the belief that the higher altitude would be good for EBB's health.
3. The result was a painting by Matilda Carter, who had a studio at 122 Leadenhall St. in London. She had exhibited a "Portrait of a Lady" at the 1839 Royal Academy exhibition. Her portrait of EBB (reproduced as the frontispiece to this volume) formed lot 1410 of *Browning Collections* (see *Reconstruction*, F11) and is now at the Robert Browning Settlement.
4. In giving EBB his own portrait (see letter 738).

806. EBB TO MARY RUSSELL MITFORD

[Torquay]
April 16– 1841

Ever dearest Miss Mitford,

Did you write "*sweetness*" in the last line? Because I think it sh^d be 'fragrance'––for all that slip of the pen.

Thanks many & true for your 'Memorabilia' of Flush the ancient! You cannot think how they amused me & how willingly & copiously I pay my tribute of wonder before him!– The dramatic taste leaning to the high tragic, & the courtesies from the carriage to the Bench,[1] are all admirable in their way—and although I & *my* Flush bend of course to so much superiority of acquirement, I do, in certain features, & in spite of all philosophers who deny hereditary genius, trace in him downwards, some faculties of his father. But you must make allowances you know, for youth & seclusion. Your Flush is a dog of the world.

But mine is not quite happy though you think so. My Flush has a grievance—which is, that he is forced most nights to be shut up in the kitchen & consigned to a straw bed in a basket, covered indeed with green baize, & placed near the fire before it quite goes out, but still very far from being as agreeable to Flush *as my bed is*. He wants to lie on my bed—& most particularly objects to being shut up at night all by himself in the dark. It is quite a grievance both to him & me. For he begs so hard not to be taken away & cries sometimes so piteously, that I cant in every case resist—& more than once or twice, although Dr Scully said to me "Mind, Flush must not sleep on your bed" I have yielded the point & let him lie at my feet till morning in the manner of Ruth.[2] At other times he is shut up—& whenever a door down stairs has happened to be left unclosed, up he comes to this door in the middle of the night, shaking the handle with his two paws until Arabel, who sleeps on a sofa by my side, gets up to let him in. Poor Flush! That is *his* "evil of humanity".

You will never guess what I am doing—my beloved friend—or rather suffering!—oh—you will never guess.

I am sitting . . rather *lying* for my picture!!^{3}

That sounds like vanity between two worlds, indeed!—only the explanation excuses me, . . the picture being for Papa who wishes for it I know, & thinks he wishes for it [in] vain! But I mean it as a surprise to him—always meant to surprise him *so* if a *lady*- ⟨★★★⟩

Publication: EBB-MRM, I, 219–220.
Manuscript: Wellesley College.

    1. Miss Mitford's Flush liked to travel into Reading with Dr. Mitford when he attended to his duties as magistrate.

2. Cf. Ruth, 3:7-14.
3. See note 3 to the previous letter.

807. RB TO WILLIAM CHARLES MACREADY

[London]
[?late April 1841][1]

My dear Macready:—

Do forgive the delay in sending the little book I herewith beg your acceptance of—and which has only come to hand this minute.

Our friend Fox, I am given to understand, pronounces it abundantly "unintelligible"[2]—but Fox is lecturing just now on the Devil, and can hardly fail to be full of his subject—on one point, however, I should be truly sorry to be misunderstood. I have advertised three plays, or attempts at plays, one of which, I think, might succeed on the stage—now the poor but genuine compliment to yourself implied by such a course, was this—all things considered, I had rather publish, that is print—this play, sell a dozen copies, and see the rest quietly shelved—than take the chance of a stage success that would in the highest degree gratify and benefit me, at the *risk* of "mettre du gêne"[3] in a friendship which I trust I know how to appreciate, by compelling you once more to say "No", where you would willingly say "Yes."

"I hope here be proof"[4] how much I am,

Dear Macready,
Yours faithfully,
R. Browning.

Pray remember me most kindly to Mrs. and Miss Macready.

Text: Emerson College Magazine, Vol. XX, No. 3, January 1912, pp. 131-132.

1. Dating hinges on identification of the book being sent, discussed in the following note.
2. In view of Fox's comment, it appears at first glance that the book was probably *Sordello*. However, that is made unlikely by Macready's diary entry of 29 March 1840, recording that RB called to make a personal presentation of *Sordello* (*Macready*, I, 54). It therefore seems from the context that RB was sending one of the three works advertised as "nearly ready" when *Sordello* was published (see letter 747, note 6). As RB indicates that he doesn't wish to press Macready to stage this play, that excludes from consideration *The Return of the Druses*, as RB certainly did urge its performance; the choice is between *Pippa Passes* and *King Victor and King Charles*. As Macready had read "Browning's play on Victor, King of Sardinia—it turned out to be a *great mistake*" in September 1839 (*Macready*, I, 23), we reach the conclusion that the enclosure with this letter was *Pippa Passes*. Fox's comment may seem unlikely in connection with *Pippa*, as DeVane

writes (p. 95) of its "simplicity and beauty" and the expectation of success, but the shadow of *Sordello* caused it to receive a cool reception. *The Spectator* (17 April 1841) found it "without coherence or action"; *The Monthly Review* (May 1841) spoke of "obscurity that offends us" and of the "mechanical imperfection" of the language, so it is quite possible that Fox did pronounce it "unintelligible." EBB herself found it hard to understand (see letter 827). (For the full text of the reviews, see pp. 392–393.)

If the enclosure was *Pippa Passes*, the date can be conjectured from the following three letters, all sending copies of the work.
 3. "To put constraint."
 4. Cf. *Measure for Measure*, II, 1, 133.

808. RB TO JOHN ANSTER[1]

Hatcham, New Cross, Surrey.
April 28 1841.

My dear Sir,

Some years ago I received a very beautiful and melodious volume of Poetry—"Xeniola"[2]—you had been good enough to send me: it arrived by a very circuitous route and considerably after the date of the kind letter that was enclosed in it, and I very unfortunately allowed myself to imagine that a little longer delay in acknowledging your courtesy would not much matter, while it would allow me to accompany my thanks with a Poem on which I was engaged.[3] That Poem, however, took a longer time to complete than I had anticipated– I was forced to travel– I have not a single acquaintance in Dublin . . in short the thanks I should have delivered then, I only deliver now—they have kept warm all the same. The facility of the Post enables me to beg your acceptance of the trifle you receive,[4] and your leave to forward its successors in due course. If you will further signify to me any way a packet would easily reach you—(I am so unacquainted with these matters)—I will also send the work I published last year—Sordello.

Begging once more that you will accept my true thanks and forgive the tardiness of their expression,

I am, Dear Sir,
Your's obliged
R Browning.

Dr Anster.

Publication: NL, p. 24.
Manuscript: Yale University.

 1. John Anster (1793–1867), Regius Professor of Civil Law at the University of Dublin, had published an English translation of Goethe's *Faust* in 1835.
 2. *Xeniola. Poems, Including Translations from Schiller and De la Motte Fouqué* (1837).

3. *Sordello.*
4. *Pippa Passes*, published in April 1841.

---

809. RB to André Victor Amédée de Ripert-Monclar

New Cross, Hatcham, Surrey,
29 Avril 1841.

Mon cher Amédée,

Faites-moi l'amitiè d'accepter le Poème que je vous envoie:[1] c'est un effort pour contenter presque tout le monde, et vous savez comme cela réussit ordinairement. L'essentiel, c'est de vous avertir que nous avons changé d'adresse et que nous demeurons à *New Cross, Hatcham, Surrey*—vous prendrez le Kent-Road que vous savez,—vous en irez jusqu'au bout—et le premier sentier à haie verte et à droite vous conduira chez nous: c'est une vielle maisonnette avec un jardin et des petites collines tout près—que nous serons heureux de vous y voir!

En attendant, recevez les salutations les plus cordiales de toute ma famille—et n'oubliez pas de presenter mes hommages à M.ᵉ la Comtesse[2] —votre enfant[3] se porte toujours bien, j'espère.

À vous de cœur,
Robert Browning.

Publication: None traced.
Manuscript: Yale University.

Translation: My dear Amédée, / Be so kind as to accept the poem I am sending you:[1] it is an attempt to satisfy almost everyone, and you know how successful that usually is. The main point, is to inform you that we have changed address and that we now live at *New Cross, Hatcham, Surrey*—you take the Kent-Road that you know,—you follow it to the end—and the first path on the right with a green hedge will lead you to us: it's an old cottage with a garden and low hills close by—how happy we will be to see you here! / Meanwhile, accept heartiest greetings from all my family—and don't forget to offer my respects to the Countess[2]—your child is still doing well; I hope. / Yours in heart, / Robert Browning.

1. *Pippa Passes.*
2. Mary Clementina (*née* Jerningham, 1810–64), the niece of Lord Stafford. Monclar had married her in 1838.
3. Joseph Anne Amédée François (d. 1921).

810. RB TO SAMUEL LAMAN BLANCHARD[1]

New Cross, Hatcham, Surrey.
April 31. [sic] 1841.

My dear Mr Blanchard,
 I have to beg the favor of your acceptance of the accompanying little Poem[2]—and to beg that you will forgive the tardiness of its arrival on the score of my having just got up from a very sick bed indeed, where a fortnight's brain-and-liver-fever has reduced me to the shade of a shade. I shall gather strength, I hope, this fine weather. Shame—shame—shame on you that the giving of rhymes is all on my side—or—not to talk of giving—what would I do to once again run (real running, for I was a boy)—run to Bond St from Camberwell and come back with a small book[3] brimful of the sweetest and truest things in the world: it is many years ago since I gave it away to a friend nothing I could give seemed too good for—but the noble and musical lines—that fine "sun-bronzed like Triumph on a pedestal"—that bridge "dark trees were dying round"— that super-delicious "song of the wave"—live within me yet[4]—"being things immortal".[5] Will you please to notice that I have changed my address: if in a week or two you will conquer the interminable Kent-road, and on passing the turnpike at New Cross you will take the *first* lane with a quick set hedge to the right, you will "descry a house resembling a goose-pie"—only a crooked hasty and rash goose-pie. We have a garden, and trees, and little green hills of a sort to go out on– Will you come? I say in a week or two, because at present I can hardly crawl and could barely shake your hand.

Yours very truly,
Robert Browning.

Laman Blanchard Esqr.

Address, on integral page: Laman Blanchard Esq.
Publication: LRB, pp. 5–6 (as April 1841).
Manuscript: University of Iowa.

 1. Samuel Laman Blanchard (1804–45) contributed prose and verse to *The Monthly Magazine*. He published *Lyric Offerings*, a collection of verse dedicated to Charles Lamb, in 1828. He edited successively *The Monthly Magazine*, *The True Sun*, *The Constitutional*, *The Court Journal* and *The Courier*. From 1841 until his death he was closely connected with *The Examiner*.
 2. *Pippa Passes*.
 3. Noted at this point in the manuscript, in an unidentified hand: "Lyric Offerings— L.B." The publisher, William Harrison Ainsworth, was located in Old Bond Street.
 4. The first two quotations are taken from Blanchard's "A Poet's Bride" (stanzas XV and I, pp. 14 and 1, respectively); the third reference is to "The Wave" (pp. 89–91).
 5. Cf. *Hamlet*, I, 4, 67.

811. EBB TO MARY RUSSELL MITFORD

[Torquay]
May 1. 1841

My beloved friend,

Your verses are *your own* in all ways,—appropriate & graceful—& my sole regret with any cousinship to the subject is, that I stand confessed as being useless to you except in will & desire.[1] Yet—if you can disentangle my meaning—I didnt desire to be of this precise kind of utility to you—feeling your sufficiency to yourself, & my own personal awkwardness in strutting about with a reputation on, not made for me. The last decision is quite right—and the verses prove it so, without other logic. May I ask how they prosper? Be sure of the *secresy*.

Dearest Miss Mitford! The lithograph is out of the question.[2] I have not friends enough who care enough for me! Ah—you dont know what a life I have led—what a solitude it has been—to count beyond my immediate family. A few country neighbours, seen at long intervals for an hour, talked to with one half one's mind, or a quarter of it—*that* has been the degree & sort of society by which the solitude was chequered. I make guesses at the world—sometimes wrong, sometimes a little right—and if at all the last,—'ah Signorina', as my Italian master once said to me .. "indovina benessimo [*sic*]"[3]—it is the bare faculty of guessing.

So that I have not you see,—could'nt have by a possibility,—a crowd of friends to catch at lithographs of my picture.

To *you*—certainly—to *you* it shall be lent at any time & for any time—but you must come to Wimpole Street & see whether it is like. My sisters & my two brothers here, say "yes, very"—and I myself am so far satisfied as to think it a quiet unpretending picture, with the right degree of simplicity in the dress & gesture, to accord with the pale worn cheek. But Papa—what will Papa say?– He will see it on wednesday morning. How disappointed I shall be, if he shakes his head & wonders who it can be.[4]

Dearest friend, wont all this sunshine which I see on the walls & the floor, revive & exhilarate the dear object of your anxious watching? I fancy & hope it will & must. Give him my love & the wishes which belong to its sincerity. There shall be some more cream soon—but I am half fearful of its passing under so much sunshine. The unseasonable heat cant last long, & *then*—

I meant to have told you long ago, rather to have whispered to you as a secret, something of a poetical lyrical-dramatic plan of M.[r] Horne's & mine—but the paper when I write to you seems to shrivel up under my fingers & leave no room for such things to be written about. Well— another day, I must mean *with a result*–

Not that I have heard from M？ Horne for weeks & weeks—so that he may be exhaled, plan & all—& my *front* plan, is about your tragedy. —— [5]

Perhaps tomorrow, certainly the first day without an east wind, I am to try a removal to the sofa!—the first footstep to London.

God bless you—dear & kind! Tell me how Ben is—[6] Think of Flush being lost & cried [over] yesterday, & found in a wood at eleven oclock at night! They did not tell me of it—until concealment was impossible— and his return happened just afterwards. I could not help a few tears for his sake—& yours. Naughty Flush. But nobody c^d scold him—& his ecstasy on finding us again was an indescribable thing.

Y？ EBB

Address: Miss Mitford / Three Mile Cross / Near Reading.
Publication: EBB-MRM, I, 220–222.
Manuscript: Fitzwilliam Museum.

1. Miss Mitford had apparently asked EBB for suggestions for reworking a poem, perhaps "On the Portrait of the Countess of Burlington," printed in *The Athenæum* of 24 July 1841 (no. 717, p. 556).
2. The inference is that Miss Mitford had suggested that lithograph copies be made of Matilda Carter's portrait of EBB.
3. "Excellent prophet."
4. Despite the approval of the family members present in Torquay (Henrietta, Arabel, Charles John and Octavius), those in Wimpole Street were dissatisfied with the likeness (see letters 816 and 819).
5. See letter 797, note 7.
6. Miss Mitford had told a correspondent that Ben Kirby, her manservant, had been "very ill indeed" (L'Estrange (2), III, 116).

812. EBB to Richard Hengist Horne

Torquay.
May 6.th 1841

I do *not* write to teaze you, dear M？ Horne, *indeed*. But it is so very long since I heard from you, & appears so strangely long, that I *do* write to enquire.

As to the 'Drama,' my questions wont turn their faces that way—although—*by* the way .. if it ever is completed by these degrees, you will have to take into partnership some successive generations of such as I am. But I dont ask about that, nor—pour le coup[1]—*think* I am wondering why you make no sign—& exercising my architectural genius for building Bastilles in the air,[2]—& running the risk of standing confessed an intruder, a teazer, an impertinent, in one- Did I say anything wrong, anything it was possible to be wrathful at, when I wrote last? If I did, it was my blind fate writing in me—but I dont remember–

Truly yours
Elizabeth B Barrett.

Publication: EBB-RHH, II, 66–70 (in part).
Manuscript: Pierpont Morgan Library.

1. "This time; for once."
2. A reversal of "castles in the air," to give the meaning of a dark fantasy rather than a bright one.

---

813. EBB TO HUGH STUART BOYD

1 Beacon Terrace.
May 10.th 1841

My very dear friend,

Throughout this long silence, embracing the most afflictive time of my whole life, I hope you have known me better than to believe ANY grief could force me to forget you. I have thought of you on the contrary often, and wished that you might be very happy,—and regarded you as truly as if I could smile and say so to you in the light of days gone for ever. But you will understand the shrinking from writing,—when one's heart is full—and *that* has been my case often and often—after the *power* of writing had returned to me. Lately I have been impatient with myself about you, lest you sh^d murmur to *your*self "Ah she forgets me"—and thus I would'nt let Arabel write although she proposed it. So you must forgive her for my sake, and me ... for my own sake– There is no help for me otherwise.

Arabel heard from Annie a day ago—and thus I became aware that you had lately been grieved by the loss of your old valued friend Mr Spowers.[1] Receive my sympathy, dear Mr Boyd. I fear this event will sadden Hampstead to you as a residence—or perhaps you have other friends there. Will you write to me and tell me a little about yourself—and not as to one who could ever forget you. Bright hours of my life have been spent at your side, and you know the metaphysicians say that contrast is a principle of suggestion– So that I could'nt forget *them* now and here.

Do you remember when you told me that I clung too much to human affections?– And therefore perhaps it was, that the Divine Hand cast me down in the place of graves[2] and struck me terribly in the very life of my heart. But I cannot write of this, even now.[3] Only I know & recognize

God's chastening in it, and my own transgression—my God & my sin .. eminent in the sweeping agony as causes & interpretations. Presently, & perhaps very soon, all will be calm & smooth in Christ Jesus. Oh dear friend! What an "anarithmon gelasma"[4] *that* will be, in the eternal world!

I have been much better this spring—really better, I think—and am waiting only for some fine days, to remove from my bed to the sofa, as an almost immediately previous step to a removal to London. You *cannot* know how the only strong earthly wish I have left, relative to myself, is set towards being once more *at home*—and my physician hopes that I shall be able to travel quietly & slowly in June. It may please God for you & me to meet again, after all.

Storm & Octavius besides my sisters are with me.

Will you write to me when you can conveniently,—and will you speak, (*not* of *me*, but of yourself)—& let me hear whether you listen still with charmed ears to the charming clocks?—above all, whether you are as well as usual & with good spirits? May God bless you in Christ!– I have a counterpart to your clock amusement, in a little spaniel dog which was sent to me by Miss Mitford, for company. Now you wonder at my pastime as I at yours—although Flush does'nt bark I assure you.

I have written very little poetry lately—but I love it as I always did—and shall write on if I live on.

Do try to forgive this letter for not going to you before—believing with how much earnest truth its writer remains

       Your affectionate
       Elizabeth B. Barrett–

Henrietta & Arabel are quite well, thank God.

Their kindest regards to you.

Address: H S Boyd Esq! / 21 Downshire Hill / Hampstead / London.
Publication: EBB-HSB, pp. 239–240.
Manuscript: Harvard University.

1. He had died in Hampstead on 11 April, aged 77. Spowers' influence on Boyd was acknowledged in Boyd's translation of *Agamemnon* (see letter 377, note 9).
2. Cf. Ezekiel, 39:11.
3. i.e., Bro's death.
4. Æschylus, *Prometheus*, 90. EBB's own translation (*Prometheus Bound*, 100) was "laughter innumerous."

814. EBB TO RICHARD HENGIST HORNE

[Torquay]
May 13.th 1841

My dear Mr Horne,

I had your note yesterday & have today the second act . . and shall be sorry & remorseful on all tomorrows until sure that you will give up the thought of Psyche till you give up the cough. As to serving me ill . . dear Mr Horne, you did no such thing! I am not a desperate hunter—I like waiting in the dew—and provided we have the *antlers*, it may as well be in the afternoon as forenoon. Shall the clock make us quarrel?– No—no! I leave unbeaten that "deep dell of silence",[1] just as long as you please to lie there, and are not well.

What made me write was indeed impatience—there is no denying it—only not about the Drama. Do you know what it is to be shut up in a room by one's self, to multiply one's thoughts by one's thoughts—how hard it is to know what "one's thought is like"—how it grows & grows, & spreads & spreads, & ends in taking some supernatural colour, . . just like mustard and cress sown on flannel in a dark closet?– First I begin with the simple impertinence of wondering why you did'nt write to me—simple enough—altho' I dont call it altogether my own fault when I miss your letters– Then came the complex—*per*plexing in the extreme–

I am very sorry about the cough. Do not neglect it lest it end as mine did—for a common cough striking on an *insubstantial* frame began my bodily troubles—and I know well what that suffering is, though nearly quite free from it now. So let it be understood, consented & agreed to, & well approved on each side, that *until your return to London, Psyche is suspended.*

The new act shall go to you in a day or two. Your spiriting is most excellently done—and the Drama half alive already. I am not impatient, but contrariwise *satisfied*. Yet one thing I must ask . . no—not today— another day.

Ever & truly yours
EBB–

Publication: EBB-RHH, II, 82–84 (in part, as 10 July 1841).
Manuscript: Pierpont Morgan Library.

1. We have not located the source of this quotation.

815. EBB TO GEORGE GOODIN MOULTON-BARRETT

[Torquay]
May 26.th 1841.

Although I have written to Papa and sent you almost message enough in reply to your letter, I must attempt I find, before I can be satisfied, some reply to its philosophy. Thank you first for its kindness. Ah—but you know I did in my heart, however lightly I might speak of anything besides. Yet *not* lightly,—gravely & seriously, my beloved Georgie, I do assure you that there is no "fever," no "excitement" in the thoughts you refer to—on the contrary common sense and a rational deference to a "MEDICAL OPINION". I know myself that I sh.^d be better anywhere than here—and Dr Scully says—not to *me* (to please me) but to others—"she will be as well in London as anywhere." Now do, George, consider these things—and refrain from starting again, when I speak of setting out in a few weeks– Why sh.^d I not move when it is possible? Why sh.^d I not be better when I can? Instead of starting, suggest to Papa the advisableness of sending a carriage for me when the time arrives for its use,—and enquire as to the *easiest springs*. Not that I am afraid. Not the least fear is in me. I am in a different state altogether from what you saw me in, and cannot be liable to the danger apprehended then. If there *were* danger, I w.^d go—I dont deny *that*. But there is none—and I shall act this time by what you call with dignity "the advice of my medical attendant". And mind George—mind this truth—*if God has an earthly blessing for me He will take me home*. I do not limit his power or His mercy—but I have no hope or capacity of joy, except for being once more, not indeed as we were, but as we can be, together in Wimpole Street.

In regard to that detestable Michael Church,[1] what you say in this note, disquiets me again *rather*. Papa's answer was obviously "a pertinent one to an impertinent question", the *evasion of an intrusion*—and even implies the possibility of his family being settled there as a residence—which idea from what you told me before about the "mere investment" and the decision against parting with his London house, appears a new evil. My wonder is great that under any circumstances he sh.^d think of Herefordshire—thickly sown as it is with pain for all of us.[2] I w.^d rather live in a wilderness, than there—how far rather!– Matters of feeling are not however subjects of argument–

Henrietta, it appears, very improperly (but you need not mention it in writing or otherwise) told the Holders[3] that Papa was "thinking of purchasing an estate"—mentioning the name of this– Well!– They knew all about it. A cousin of their own was a resident in it– And their report went on to describe it as "a miserable place & quite unimprovable!—

wretched house impossible roads—fine mountainous scenery, but not a tree."

Not that I care a feather, if it be thus *or Eden*. My objections are of another sort,—quite unremoved by your philosophy, George—& unremoveable by any other. We are however here to suffer—and I have little heart or strength left to struggle out towards the light. It will be as God wills.

I was wrong in my last letter, (long ago) to dwell at all upon SELFISH objections.[4] I[5] ought not to be thought of, and certainly w^d not *consciously* say that I wish to be thought of unduly.—— *You* were wrong too in interpreting words of mine into an opinion that I sh^d w^d or might have constant medical attendance after leaving this place. *I do not think of that*. Indeed I determine just the contrary. When I go to London, I will see nobody unless it sh^d be necessary. Only you see, Georgie, when certain attacks come on—these hemorrhages for instance—it is necessary to see somebody instantly or to take the bad consequence. Well—but this is nonsense! I am not thinking of it, however I may talk.

Dearest Stormie, I grieve to say, never *goes out at all*. He is just as he used to be—only he talks *quite enough*, . . if I may judge through the walls. Henrietta does just the contrary—I dont mean about the talking, or the walking, but the going out in another sense. Only the place is thin just now of visitors. But there is Lady Bolingbroke still.–[6] Arabel paints resolutely– Dont let Papa fancy that Ocky wishes to be idle—because indeed he does'nt, dear boy!——

You have my condolence about Mrs Trant—and poor Papa seems to groan as deeply as any of you.[7] He never hints to me of Michael Church— merely of his prospect of having us back in Wimpole Street. God bless you all there, and us in our return.

I am much much better—and sh^d not have been ill at all, but for the mistake.[8] Certainly this last hemorrhage which was very bad for some days, proves the weak state of the pulmonary vessels—but still, there is the sunshine which I can feel, *though not look at while I remain here*, and a whole summer, for gaining strength and being reunited to *you*. So no word more against the moving, dearest Georgie!– I do love you. I have written till I am tired.

Your most affectionate
Ba—

Address: George Goodin Barrett, Esq. / 3 Paper Buildings / Temple– / London.
Publication: B-GB, pp. 58–61.
Manuscript: Pierpont Morgan Library.

1. Michaelchurch, some 12 miles S.W. of Hereford, was on the slopes of the Black Mountains. From the context, it was one of the locations being considered by EBB's father to benefit her health.

2. i.e., memories of Mary Moulton-Barrett.
3. Local acquaintances; Henrietta mentions going riding with Miss Mary Holder (SD1006), and SD1059 speaks of Bro's presenting a sketch to Mrs. Holder.
4. No. 805, dated 15 April.
5. Underscored twice.
6. Isabella Charlotte Antoinette Sophia, formerly Baroness Hompesch, was the second wife and widow of George Richard St. John, 3rd Viscount Bolingbroke (1761–1824). Henrietta writes of a group singing glees "under old Lady Bolingbroke's windows" on New Year's Eve (SD977). Another letter, from Arabella (SD1023), speaks of Lady Bolingbroke's consulting George Moulton-Barrett on legal matters. She died in Torquay in 1848.
7. Mary Trant, a first cousin of EBB's paternal grandmother, had been a neighbour of the Barretts in their Hope End days. The reason for condolence is not known.
8. In the following letter, EBB explains that she had taken the wrong medicine, resulting in a hæmorrhage.

816. EBB TO MARY RUSSELL MITFORD

[Torquay]
May 30.th [1841][1]

My beloved friend,

Indeed you sh^{d} have heard before—long ago—for I have felt both you and your Tragedy pulling long and strong at my thoughts every day of many. But I have not been well—*my* old tragedy, so trite and dull, which keeps all the unities except *time*.[2] I *was* very well—considering the "I"—much better, much stronger; and 'tomorrow' they said 'you shall get to the sofa as the first step to London.' Well—and what do you think I managed to do to make myself worse again?– Took a *wrong medecine*—a medecine which w^{d} have hurt nobody in the house except me, had anybody else mistaken and taken it. But *I* took it,—and it was too much for a system weakened to an extraordinary degree of sensitiveness. I was made unwell—thrown into a state of excitement—& the whole resulted in an attack of hemorrhage from the chest far worse than any I have had through the winter. Well—I wrote to you when I was better again—but the exhaustion & above all the disappointment about the London journey were *in the letter*. It was a moaning letter—you might have heard it moan in your hand. And so I did justice to you and to my own philosophy, and w^{dnt} send it—waited till I had the heart to write something more serenely. It was not the illness itself– The sword which pierces only the body and nothing beyond,[3] pains little. But I fancied an invisible Hand 'pushing me from my stool'[4]—quenching the only earthly light left to burn for me, .. the hope of being at home. One disappointment seemed the seed of another—for a perpetual generation.

It was wrong to write so, and w^d have been more wrong to have sent the letter. I sh^d have learnt in my darkness to count the stars of God's mercies better. Would that we acted as rightly as we suffer.—— And the end is, that I am well again—that is, for *me*—and have my physician's permission to try the sofa tomorrow, with his opinion that at the end of June, sh^d no further evil occur, the journey will be feasible. My heart is lighter again,—and leaps up directly to speak to you.[5]

I enclose a *subject* which has struck me,[6] and clung to me of many which struck me, almost alone. I have taken up many & thrown them down as objectionable from some point of view or other. In this there appears to me great tragic capability—a strong *struggle of heart*. I wished much to consult Bentivoglio who is the authority[7]—but here I cant—and sh^d you think it worth while to think more of it, some other friend may do for you in this respect what I w^d gladly do if my situation in the bookless wilderness w^d let me. If however you fail with others, I will try again. I shall be in London in June– But you may not require much more—even in the case of y^r adoption of the subject.

And after all the other subject you once mentioned to me may be preferable—or yet another subject. I beseech you to try mine by your own judgment, *without a reference to me*: and if I did not believe you w^d do so freely my tongue sh^d have been tied.[8] It is not used to suggest subjects for the stage,—it has as little experience as intuitive wisdom about such things,—and "no one has taught this parrot its '*How d'ye do*'["].

As to all the dreams you dream, with an angel of perfect kindness lighting the vision, about my power of combining with Mr Horne in the production of a real actable tragedy, .. well, my only comment is "you dream". Dearest dearest Miss Mitford! You praise me with your love!——

No—neither my power nor my wish touch that point. What Mr Horne and I are engaging ourselves in, is a mere *Lyrical Drama*; & the title of it, is to be "*Psyche Apocalyptic*"!—the subject, as is obvious, balancing itself between the high fantastical[9] & the high philosophical—the hero neither a Manfred nor a Faust[10] (we shall keep clear of either) but pretty nearly as mad to vulgar eyes, and suffering persecution from the hauntings of his own soul,—the Psyche—seen in vision, and heard in solitude or crowds. Ah—you shake your head!– *I* feel it,—as the Olympians did a Jove-shaking—I feel it all this distance off. But we are to have real situations, I mean tangible—men and women talking loud out to one another—.& only Psyche is purely psychical. There will be joy and grief—a child and a bridal—we are not quite in the clouds—we keep one foot on the ground.

The mystery is, how *I* sh^d have the vanity to consent to a combination with Mr Horne,—whose genius I take high measure of. And besides—there does seem to me an objection to such combinations in general, even with more balanced powers—and to this moment I am not sure how I shall succeed in working by allotment, after the necessary fashion.

The truth is, that Mr Horne long & long ago, more than a year ago said in one of his kind letters that 'he sh^d like to write a Lyrical Drama with me.' I answered more laughingly than I c^d now .. joke to joke, as it seemed to me—it was very ingenious in him to want to set up a show, with a dwarf and giant together—some nonsense of that sort—not all nonsense either. Then he was serious and pressed his wish upon it. And I was made serious—and we talked or rather wrote it over—& it was agreed to be done some time—sometime when he & I became acquainted face to face.

A pause came—when this spring Mr Horne (half out of kindness, and the wish to amuse my mind, and perhaps *whole*) proposed that we sh^d begin at once—desiring me to consider for a subject. My thoughts grew fantastical, and hummed down upon Psyche—and I was surprised at his accepting the suggestion eagerly,—as a difficult subject but still feasible, and a very fine one. We were agreed in a minute. And now he is arranging the sketch I sent him, into *acts* (oh we call them 'acts' I assure you) and dividing the labour between us. You see the weak sides of Mr Horne and myself bend the same way—to the *mystic*. That is why we agreed,—and the only excuse for such a partnership.

Have I told you enough? or too much? You are tired of me surely. And now *keep the secret*—will you?- There was none to you from the first—only I had not breath for a long story: and the simple fact "I am going to write a drama with Mr Horne" might, I thought, sweep you away in a whirlwind with the overwhelming sense of my vanity.

How is dear Dr Mitford? How are *you*? You were not well, when you wrote. You sit up too late—you do everything too much, even to loving .. no, not loving, .. thinking well of .. *me*!-

God bless and keep you.

The picture—ah the poor picture!- I will tell you of *that* another day. Papa said it was'nt like!!-[11] I and the grand Sultan are not people to have our likeness taken.[12]

Your faithful & affectionate
EBB.

Not a line of the dramatic poem is written. Nothing but the plan. We daudle and dream. Mr Horne declared I was asleep & dreaming—and

now he has gone down to Wolverhampton on government business[13] about pots & pans & pits, NOT poetry but pottery–
Flush sends his love–
Do you know M.rs Sigourney—the American poetess?[14] I had a very flattering letter from her just before she sailed, saying that she had tried long & vainly for my direction–
Is the M.r Edward Quillinan who married M.r Wordsworth's daughter, the 'Love & War' Quillinan.[15]
Do write when you have time to throw away– Nobody picks it up so gladly as I—because--no room for reasons.[16]

Publication: EBB-MRM, I, 222–225.
Manuscript: Wellesley College.

1. Dated by the references to Miss Mitford's tragedy and EBB's portrait.
2. The three unities—of time, place and action—were held, particularly by Corneille and other French writers, to be essential to the construction of tragic drama. This theory was an expansion of Aristotle's dictum, in his *Poetics*, that unity of action was an absolute dramatic law.
3. Cf. Luke, 2:35.
4. Cf. *Macbeth*, III, 2, 48 and III, 4, 81.
5. Cf. Wordsworth's poem beginning "My heart leaps up when I behold" (1807).
6. For Miss Mitford's proposed tragedy (see letter 797, note 7).
7. Guido Cardinal Bentivoglio (1579–1644) was the author of *Della Guerre di Fiandra*, translated into English in 1654 as *The Compleat History of the Warrs of Flanders*, by Henry Carey, 2nd Earl of Monmouth (1596–1661).
8. Whatever EBB's suggestion may have been, letter 819 indicates that Miss Mitford did not accept it.
9. *Twelfth Night*, I, 1, 15.
10. The protagonists in Byron's *Manfred* (1817) and Goethe's *Faust* (1808) both make pacts with the Devil in return for temporal power.
11. Matilda Carter's oil painting (see letter 805).
12. Describing a ball given by the Turkish Ambassador in *Vienna and the Austrians* (1838), Mrs. Trollope wrote: "The next object that attracted notice was a full-length portrait of the Sultan Mahmoud; as the taking such a portrait at all, has been considered till very lately to be a sort of trifling with such august features too familiar to be permitted" (II, 230).
13. As a member of a Royal Commission (see letter 803, note 3).
14. Lydia Howard Sigourney (*née* Huntley, 1791–1865) was the author of *Moral Pieces, in Prose and Verse* (1815) and *Letters to Mothers* (1838). She contributed to *The Ladies' Companion* and was editor (1839–40) of *The Religious Souvenir*.
15. EBB had mentioned Quillinan's earlier work, *The Conspirators*, in letter 797. *Love and War* had just been announced. He had married Dorothy ("Dora") Wordsworth on 11 May 1841, despite her father's objections.
16. The concluding three sentences are squeezed in the top margin of the first page.

817. EBB TO SEPTIMUS MOULTON-BARRETT

[Torquay]
Friday. June 11.th 1841

My dearest Set,

To show that I am not ripe with ingratitude,—which w^d be like a medlar, ripe & rotten at once,—here I am writing to you at last!– Thank you my dear dear Set for all your kind letters, inclusive of the one received yesterday. If I never loved you in my life before I should be forced to do it now.

There you see is my "compliment" in exchange for yours!—and both compliments, unlike their race, are worth something. And if I do not say besides that *I*[1] too will be "pretty considerable jolly" to see *you*, yet the thankfulness & contentment will be deeper perhaps on my side—ought to be & must be.

As to 'deciding' my own dear Set, that does not belong to me, nor will I try that it should. Our dear Papa is in possession of all my thoughts wrong or right, & I am waiting now for his 'finality-measure'. In the case of his still leaning to Clifton on account of a personal preference,[2] I wont say a rebellious word more—only reserving my own right of solitude next winter under certain circumstances: and in the case of its seeming good to him to meet me somewhere twenty miles from London, more or less, why I shall be *equally pleased* with any place—not only equally *contented*, but equally *pleased*. Dr Scully says "Why there are a hundred places near London, from Twickenham to Windsor, & one as good as another". And do understand that the only object I have in the world is to be *with you all, & not in danger of being separated again*. That is all I care for in the world. So settle it, you who have wider carings & a more extended 'point of sight'.

⟨...⟩[3]

Arabel tells me that she told you of Miss Mitford's proposition;[4] but dont take it into your heads that I have taken *that* into mine. I have taken nothing into my head. I wish for nothing except what you read in my confession– And indeed to confess a little more, I have scarcely strength of heart & spirits to consider with any fixed & unwavering pleasure the vicinity of even Miss Mitford, though I dearly love her. I want *you*—*just you*.

So do *you*, just *you*, settle how it is to be.

Only remember my carriage. Has anybody enquired about the carriage, so as to be sure of the easiest? Dr Scully's favorite balloon wont do, you see—and it w^d be foolish to run an unnecessary risk. I was up yesterday for an hour, & might have stayed much longer, had there been anything to gain by it. The day before he w^d not let me move: and indeed the change of weather here from intense heat to wintry cold was trying, without stirring to meet it— Yesterday was warmer again, & today seems warm— Perhaps I shall be up again today. Quite ready to go, & more than willing—that is my account of *me*.

Dear Joc is well—but Arabel, through manifold imprudences, I must say & scold, has had some return of the swelled face,—which however is better, & has not caused her, at the worst, a great deal of pain. Stormie, on the other hand, I am sorry to say, was very far from being well yesterday, & is not, however better, very near, today. It was sickness & headache—nothing to be uneasy about except in sympathy: and he has had recourse to sufficient remedies. Therefore by the time you read what I write, you may count upon his perfect convalescence,—& on Arabel's also. Indeed if it were not for me, she w^d be out walking now. *But I wont let her.*

She took Flush to Upton on tuesday, upon the Bible business—& he soon understood it so well, that he ran on before, & stopped & waited for her at every cottage,—and only troubled her upon three occasions when he met three cats & was thrown into paroxysms of fright. Flush does not seem to understand the glory of fighting— Whether through philosophy or good temper, "the pomp & circumstance of glorious war"[5] never move his ambition. Every other sort of understanding he possesses to a perfection wonderful considering his canineity. It amazes me to hear Crow talk to him with a full consciousness & expectation of the exercise of this faculty of comprehension—"Naughty Flush!— How dare you carry the shoes out of their place! How often have I spoken to you about it, Sir! No—you need'nt hold out your paw—I wont shake hands with you, I can assure you". But if she threatens extreme punishment, he rushes to me & lays his head down on my shoulder.

Even Dr Scully said the other day "Really that dog seems to understand every word you say—. I met him on the stairs" (Flush has a great fancy for Dr Scully & always comes with him to my room, if not happening to be there before) "I met him on the stairs & just said "You must'nt come into Miss Barrett's room Mr Flush,—your feet are dirty",—& round he turned directly & walked away."!— And Crow's "Go away & lie down quietly", or "go to the chair" or "go down stairs" or "go to Miss Barrett" are obeyed to the letter. He fixes *his* eyes on yours while you speak—obviously understanding. It is not gesture which is understood—it is verbal expression. Well, Set,—you shall see—you shall admire—you shall confess that nothing in dog-nature & your experience ever equalled this. Certainly there is Flush the elder, Miss Mitford's Flush, who discerns as she assures me French from English. But then mine is young & too playful to be so deep a linguist,—hating indeed the discipline of the schools, & running away to me from everybody who wrongs him enough to attempt to teach him anything. Wait a little,—& he may understand Greek as well as Cerberus.[6] Why should'nt he?——

June 12.

Dearest Set, I wrote so far yesterday, forgetting the no-post—& now I may tell you that Arabel is well again, & even poor Stormie nearly so—only he has a headache tonight. They have all (except Stormie) been to Mudge's farm with Miss Baldwin & little Fanny & the governess,[7] to have tea in an orchard—& I do hope Arabel's part in the expedition will not be proved an imprudence. She is quite well *now*.

The weather is cold again—at least cold to *me*—cold out of the sun—with an east wind in supremacy. I am well however, *but not out of bed*.

Are you wrapt or rapt in politics, dear Set? Joc calls you a republican—"Set is a republican". I hope the ministry will be strengthened to the strength of the Queen's heart by the new elections,[8] & I think well enough of the popular intelligence to expect it.

May God bless you my dearest Set—my dearest Papa—my dearest all of you!– I will write to George. Decide about the house, arrange about the carriage—dont let me wait here—love me, & believe me ever your

own affec.^{te}
Ba.

Our love to your visitors——

Address: Mr Sept Barrett / 50, Wimpole Street / London.
Publication: None traced.
Manuscript: Myrtle Moulton-Barrett and Ronald A. Moulton-Barrett.

1. Underscored twice.
2. Clifton, close to Bristol, was yet another location being considered by EBB's father for the family home, perhaps with the idea that EBB's cousin, John Altham Graham-Clarke, and his wife, who lived there, would provide her with company.
3. A little over one line obliterated, apparently by EBB.
4. As letter 819 makes clear, Miss Mitford had told EBB of a house in her neighbourhood, suggesting that EBB ask her father to consider taking it.
5. *Othello*, III, 3, 354.
6. Pluto's many-headed dog, the guardian of the gates of the underworld.
7. "Little Fanny" was EBB's cousin, Fanny Hedley, so called to distinguish her from "Big Fanny," their aunt Frances Butler. Miss Baldwin has not been identified.
8. A general election was pending, to vote for members of the new Parliament to meet on 19 August. However, rather than strengthening Melbourne's administration, as EBB hoped, the election returned Peel to power with a majority of 76 seats.

818. EBB TO RICHARD HENGIST HORNE

[Torquay]
June 13.th 1841.

My dear Mr Horne,

I am so sorry about the hooping cough. As a means of "rejuvenescence", why one might as pleasantly pass into & through Medea's kettle.[1] Do try to remember when you write again, & tell me how you are; & if the change of air perfects the good it has begun. For my own part I never had the hooping cough at all. I stood alone in my family & would'nt have it when everybody else was hooping.

Mind, if you please!– I wrote two notes to you instead of one, & had it not been for the fear of teazing you beyond bounds, should certainly have written a third to ask about the cough. The first was put into a dangerous envelope—out of perverseness, & faith in the right measure, & perhaps glided away. But I have sent a hundred of these little letters & received still more, & never missed or was missed till now––*if* now. So why should'nt I be perverse?

I am revived just now .. pleased, anxious, excited altogether in the hope of touching at last upon my last days at this place. I have been up, & bore it excellently—up, an hour at a time, without fainting—& on several days, without injury: and now am looking forwards to the journey. My physician has been open with me & is of opinion that there is a good deal of risk to be run in attempting it—but my mind is made up to go, & if the power remains to me, *I will go*. To be at home & relieved from the sense of doing evil where I w^d soonest bring blessing, of breaking up poor Papa's domestic peace into fragments by keeping my sisters here (& he wont let them leave me) w^d urge me into any possible "risk"—to say nothing of the continual repulsion, night & day, of the sights & sounds of this dreary place. There will be no opposition—for Papa promised me at the beginning of last winter that I sh^d go when it became 'possible'. Then, Dr Scully did not talk of 'risk', but of certain consequences. He said I sh^d die on the road. I know how to understand the change of phrase. There is only a 'risk' now—& the journey is 'possible'. So I go–

We are to have one of the patent carriages with a thousand springs from London—& I am afraid of nothing—& shall set out, *I hope*, in a fortnight. Ah but, not directly to London. There is to be some intermediate place where we all must meet, Papa says, & stay for a month or two before the final settlement[2] in Wimpole Street,—and he names "Clifton," and I pray for the neighbourhood of London, because I look far (too far, perhaps, for me) and fear being left an exile again at those Hot Wells during the winter. I don't know what the "finality measure" may be. The only thing fixed is a journey from hence:—and "if I fall," as the heroes say, why you and "Psyche" must walk by yourselves. *She*, at least, won't be the worse for it.

Who taught this parrot its "How d'ye do?" and so much irrelevancy? You would be tired of me, even if you hadn't the hooping-cough.

Is it true that Mr. Heraud's magazine is downfallen?[3] And why?

But don't answer my questions—don't indeed write at all until you are better, and able and inclined to write. Writing is so bad—leaning to write is so bad, and I don't suppose that you could write in the way that I do, leaning backwards instead of forwards—lying down, in fact. I write *so* "to the Horse Guards."

How you would smile sarcasms and epigrams out of the "hood" if you could see from it what I have been doing, or rather suffering, lately! Having my picture taken by a lady miniature-painter who wandered here to put an old vow of mine to proof. For it wasn't the ruling passion "strong in death,"[4] "though by your smiling you may seem to say so,"[5] but a sacrifice to papa.

Are you tossed about much by the agitation of political matters, or indifferently calm? I hear nothing from London, except what Lord Melbourne has done, or the Queen said.

Dear Mr. Horne, don't let me mar anything in your conception with regard to the drama. Push any foolishness aside which seems to do it.

I did *not* understand your particular view. I thought that our philosopher (Medon), having laboriously worked himself blind with the vain, earthward, cramped strivings of his intellect, was suddenly thrown upon the verge of awaking in, and to, the spiritual world, by a casualty relating to his body itself. It was something of that sort which I seemed to discern in what you wrote. Don't mar anything for *me*, dear Mr. Horne.

Truly yours,
Elizabeth B. Barrett.

Perhaps we may not be gone from hence so soon as a—a fortnight, after all. If you are inclined to write, do not hesitate about directing *here*, as usual, until I say more. I remember something of Broadstairs, deep in a cloud of childish thoughts.

Address: R H Horne Esq! / Post Office / Broadstairs / Kent.
Sources: Manuscript (in part) Harvard University. Text (in part) *EBB-RHH*, I, 25–27 (as 12 June 1841) and *The Contemporary Review*, XXIII, December 1873, pp. 151–153.

1. Medea, to demonstrate her powers to the daughters of Pelias, cut up an old ram, boiled the pieces in a cauldron, and then produced from them a young lamb.

2. The manuscript ends at this point; the remainder of the text is taken from the printed sources.

3. John Abraham Heraud (1799–1887), poet and dramatist, was the author of *The Descent into Hell* (1830) and *The Judgment of the Flood* (1834). He had become editor

of *The Monthly Magazine* in 1839, a post he held until 1842, when he became editor of *The Christian's Monthly Magazine*. *The Monthly Magazine* ceased publication in 1843. He later became dramatic critic for *The Athenæum*.
4. Pope, *An Epistle to ... Viscount Cobham* (1734), line 263.
5. *Hamlet*, II, 2, 309–310.

---

819. EBB TO MARY RUSSELL MITFORD

[Torquay]
June 14. 1841

Thank you my beloved friend for your kindness in writing & wishing to have me within teazing distance– Ah!—I hope you would'nt have reason to repent it if I were to go!– I should be on my guard, and never say "Do come," and *look* it as seldom as possible.

I have told Papa about the house, but have urged nothing,—because under the circumstances & in the state of feeling natural to me at this time, my only full contentment can be in his doing his own full pleasure. I want to be with him & in a situation which w^d least threaten a future separation—a want which involved the objection to Clifton, I c^d not keep concealed. But if his wish remain fixed upon Clifton, even to Clifton I must go. And in any other case, the reason is strengthened for my suspending every form of interference.

I came here, you see, not indeed against his desire, but against the bias of his desire. I was persuaded—he was entreated. On his side, it was at last a mere yielding to a majority.

Well!—& what has been the end?– The place .. no! I will not say that it was accursed to me—but the bitterness suffered in it has been bitter, (in regard to present endurance) as any curse. All the sorrow of my life besides, & that life not free from sorrow, showed without sting or agony in comparison with the deep deep woe of last year. It was the sharpest laceration of the tenderest affection—an affection never agitated till then except with its own delight. Oh my beloved friend—There was no harsh word, no unkind look—never from my babyhood till I stood alone– A leaf never shook till the tree fell. The shade was over me softly till it fell. And although what I cannot help feeling as an unnatural tenacity to life, prevented my following my beloved, quickly quickly as I thought I sh^d,—and although I have learnt even to be calm & to talk lightly sometimes, yet the heavy sense of loss weighs at my heart day & night, and *will*, till my last night or day.[1]

There is much much to love, left to me, close to me always– But there is no one close to me always, to whom I can say 'Is this which I have written, good? Is it worth anything?' and, be sure of the just answer.

The nearest sympathy, the natural love which was friendship too, is not close to me now.

I have thrown down my paper & taken it up again. It was wrong, very wrong, to write so— It has pained your kindness, & done no good to me—except indeed for the pleasure's sake of speaking out a pain. Take no notice of it dearest friend!—ever kindest & dearest you are!—— I know that the stroke fell in blessing & not in cursing, & that when we see each other's smiles again in the light of God's throne, not one will be fainter for the tears shed here. Blessed be God in Christ Jesus, who consummates grief in glory.

But you will understand from all, that my poor most beloved Papa's *biases* are sacred to me, & that I w^d not stir them with a breath.[2] Yet he says to me "Decide". He is so kind, .. so tender. No love of mine can echo back his, as far as the demonstration goes— I love him inwardly, I was going to say better than my life .. but that is worthless, was so always, & is now so most of all.

I shall like you to know Papa—ah, you smile at my saying *Papa*—I am too old for such a baby-word I know—but he likes to be called so, & therefore I dont like to call him otherwise even in thought— I heard him say once "If they leave off calling me 'Papa', I shall think they have left off loving me". I shall like you to know him. You will certainly like & estimate him. Mr Kenyon does thoroughly— Mr Horne, who has seen him once,[3] has begun to do it already. He is not poetical, or literary even in the strict sense—but he has strong & clear natural faculties & is full of all sorts of general information. I have consoled myself sometimes when you were abusing the professional literati with the thought that you w^d be sure to like 'Papa'. You like, you know, sensible men who dont make a trade of their sense,—reading country-gentlemen who dont write books. I have hopes of you.

Well—and thus then it remains. I have put him in possession of your report about the pretty house—but have received no notice of his decision, or of any sort of decision about any place. Thank you, thank you, for thinking of me in reference to the Chiswick show.[4] How kind! how *welcomely* kind! and how probable it is, as far as any pleasure can be probable, that I may see you somewhere this summer!–

Ever dearest Miss Mitford, I dont like what you say of yourself—I fear you are very far from being well, to say nothing of the 'strong'. Do you ask Mr May's advice—and take it?– Do you ever try *gruel* instead of warm water?– It is considered more soothing & effective. Reading so much aloud must be wearing & bad for you—& if I were near, I could'nt help being mischief-maker enough, just to hint to dear Dr Mitford the injury it must do to you, & to him *because to you*. Can there be nobody in the village or a little without it, whose reading he w^d listen to & spare your's? Not that anybody c^d do it as well—oh I understand the whole!—but that anything were better than your suffering. Tell me how you are, & how he is.

No— The picture, they said in Wimpole Street, was not like. The head was too large, & the features too large, & the expression a void. So said the critics there. Those here, consisting of my sisters & two brothers & one or two persons who had looked at me (some time ago) for an hour or two, vowed deeply on the other hand that no picture ever was will or could be a more complete facsimile of the thing pictured.— Well—but it was for Papa, & Papa was dissatisfied. So I begged him to return it & let the artist muse upon the means of amendment. She mused,— drew out her brushes, perhaps in some little fluttering of annoyance,—& straightway made all the critics of one mind—straightway everybody said "Oh, it is'nt like at all now!" Was'nt it provoking?–

And then my sisters went to her & prayed her to come again & do something—& she came & did it, took away something of the wooden look, & left the whole under improvement. So "the critics here" say now "It is very like—*only not quite so like as it was at first*",—and what they will say "there", remains yet unknown. A satisfactory business altogether!⁵

Is your picture like?– I mean the one you yourself had painted—happier in its destination than mine. I liked to hear of my thought being your thought once on a time. Love *will* do the same things.

You dont very much like the tragedy-subject, I discern without wonder⁶—but there may be time for looking further. Of what "prose thing" do you speak? Of the novel I do trust? Will there be *Tableaux* for 1842—or will you embark, as I wish earnestly, in some work of a new character, illustrated, if you please, annual-wise and as fit for the drawing room as any that ever walked in purple & gold,—but not an annual nor of its grade nevertheless?–⁷

My dearest friend, in what you say of me you speak wisely & truly as far as your kindness lets you. A cold mystical poetry strikes & falls from us like the hail—it does not penetrate or abide. And in this work, if Mr Horne & I ever compass it, as well as in others, I will try to clasp & keep in mind what you tell me, & make my access to human feelings *through* human feelings– The plan of the work in question admits of the natural workings of humanity: there are real persons & events—there is not a naked allegory, or a mere embodiment of abstractions. Even the Psyche herself, with her persecutions & her terrors, is intended to present an absolute & universal truth, not barely incident to our humanity but common to every thinking human being. However I sometimes fancy that the work, whether for good or evil, will never pass much beyond the threshold of its conception. Mr Horne lingers— He seems quite earnest about it—but he has been oppressed with business (England never cares you know, to give leisure to her poets) & is just now suffering from the *hooping cough*. I had a letter from him to say so two days since, from Broadstairs where he fled for change of air. He says "There's a re-juvenility for you."!—but I really fear that he has been & is still exceedingly unwell.

But although I admit your verities, I will not deny my mysticism. The known & *the unknown* both enter into our nature & our world. Our guesses at the invisible belong as much, & more nobly, to the part played here by the spirit within us, as do our familiar thoughts upon the flowers of June— Our terror before 'Psyche', (as in my view of her revelation) is not surely more alien to our humanity, than a child's or a poet's pleasure in a daisy.

At the same time I quite submit to the truth of your remarks—only entreating that your view (& it need not) may not *exclude* mine. I confess to a love & reverence for Goëthe above any to which Schiller c^d move me. Goëthe was surely the greater genius—and he did not, as you admit, neglect the humanities, in their strict human sense. It was Shelley that high, & yet too low, elemental poet, who froze in cold glory between Heaven & earth, neither dealing with man's heart, beneath, nor aspiring to communion with supernal Humanity, the heart of the God-Man. Therefore his poetry glitters & is cold—and it is only by momentary stirrings that we can discern the power of sweet human love & deep pathos which was in *him* & sh^d have been in *it*.

Do you call me ungrateful, or stupid? Have I not the sense of kindness or its memory, never to thank you until now for the geraniums? Ah Papa did better. He told me that the gift, together with the recollection of all your goodnesses to me, touched him so, that he could'nt help intruding a note upon you. It was well done of him—and *you* did not call it an intrusion, I know as well as if you told me.

They will take great care of the geraniums—they must: and if Wimpole St is left to itself this summer, the pots must transmigrate to *me* with the gardeners.

I have been up day after day, & an hour at a time, & bore it gallantly. *I am going away*. Pray for us, my beloved friend, that we may meet really, & not in hope alone.

Your ever attached
E B Barrett–

Give my love to dear Dr Mitford—& some cream is going to him. Have you seen Blanchard's life of LEL?[8]—& what *is your mind*?–
I am ashamed of this quire of little sheets[9] & wonder if you ever will get through it. God bless you– I truly & gratefully love you *indeed!*–

Publication: *EBB-MRM*, I, 225–230.
Manuscript: Wellesley College.

1. EBB is referring, of course, to Bro's death.
2. Cf. Milton, *Paradise Lost*, II, 214.
3. Letter 829 describes their meeting.
4. An annual flower show.
5. Matilda Carter's miniature of EBB (see letter 805).
6. i.e., that suggested by EBB in letter 816.
7. Miss Mitford was not involved in the 1842 edition of *Findens' Tableaux*. She turned her attention instead to the editing of *Schloss's English Bijou Almanac for 1843*, to which EBB contributed.
8. Samuel Laman Blanchard, as literary executor of Letitia Elizabeth Landon (Mrs. Maclean), had just published his *Life and Literary Remains of L.E.L.* EBB's copy formed part of lot 813 of *Browning Collections* (see *Reconstruction*, A257).
9. EBB's letter was written on 32mo stationery, and covered 20 sides (10 sheets).

820. MARY RUSSELL MITFORD TO EBB

Three Mile Cross
. June 20, 1841.

I have not written to you, my beloved friend, because until to-day I could have given you no pleasure. I have been very ill, but I am now getting well. Did I tell you that just before I took to my bed I drove out with K⎯⎯[1] for a few miles?—very ill *then*. About four miles from home one of the traces came undone. The horse (an old Irish thoroughbred) feeling the trace beat against his side, began kicking; and the splashing-board of our little chaise being very high, so that he could do no harm, galloped off at a speed such as few horses could have exceeded. He trod upon the trace and broke it—a fresh jerk and an additional fright. We met men, ten or twelve; we passed a turnpike-gate, but the men flew from us as we passed; the gate was flung open (wisely, or the horse, an excellent leaper, would have taken it), and for a mile and a half we had as close a view of death as has happened to many people. K⎯⎯ behaved bravely. She gave me the whip, or rather I took it from her, and wound the reins round her arms to increase her power. At last, the remaining trace brought the collar into such a position as to half choke the horse; and a boy driving a donkey across the road, we stopped—I so frightened that I could not stand. We were forced to be tied up with string and led home. If I had not been ill I should have stood it better; as it was, I kept it from my father till next day, when it became necessary to tell him for fear he should hear it from another. And since then I have been very ill, or rather, I was very ill, and now I am getting better. But I have not sent for Mr. May. I very seldom do; it frightens my father.

After all, a wretched life is mine. Health is gone; but if I can but last while my dear father requires me; if the little money we have can but last; then it would matter little how soon I, too, were released. We live alone in the world, and I feel that neither will long outlast the other. My life is only valuable as being useful to *him*. I have lived for him and him only; and it seems to me, God, in His infinite mercy, does release those who have so lived, nearly at the same time. The spring is broken and the watch goes down. Have you not seen it so?

I have been reading Mr. Blanchard's life of poor L. E. L.[2] When looking into the chronology you will be struck with the closeness of the two events—the acceptance of Mr. McLean and the other affair of the rejection.[3] There was another, too, about the same time, Mr. C____[4] tells me. Then Mr. Blanchard alludes to the scandals of different persons (I don't remember the words, but they implied scandals regarding more than one), and the very manner in which our very slight intercourse is mentioned proves that there was a dearth of female friends. She had written to ask me to write something for somebody, and apologised for addressing me as "My dear Miss Mitford." I, of course, replied, as you will see.[5]

Poor thing! The book is to me deeply affecting. She was a fine creature thrown away; and just when that mysterious event occurred there seemed to me more hope and chance of happiness, and more development of power, and (which is more important than either) a greater chance for goodness and usefulness than there had ever been before. Poor thing! Nothing seems to me so melancholy as the lives of authors—Sir Walter Scott, Mrs. Hemans, this of Miss Landon. I hardly know an exception. And these are the successful! Heaven bless you!

Ever yours,
M. R. Mitford.

Address: Miss Barrett, Torquay.
Text: L'Estrange (2), III, 117–119.

1. Miss Mitford's maid, replacing Martha. Always referred to in the correspondence as "K," she was named Kerenhappuch, after the third of Job's daughters (Job, 42:14). In 1844, she had an illegitimate child, and was dismissed, but Miss Mitford took her back the following year, and she stayed in service until Miss Mitford's death in 1855.
2. See letter 819, note 8.
3. A reference to Miss Landon's having broken off her engagement to John Forster.
4. Doubtless Chorley. He may have told Miss Mitford about the rumours of an affair between Miss Landon and the Irish poet and journalist William Maginn (1793–1842),

the prime reason for the breaking of the engagement to Forster (see *DNB*), or of the linking of her name with that of William Jerdan (see letter 727, note 22).
5. In Blanchard's *Life of L.E.L.*, Miss Mitford is quoted as replying: "My dear Miss Landon, I do not address you as a stranger because I cannot think of you as one" (I, 265).

821. EBB TO GEORGE GOODIN MOULTON-BARRETT

[Torquay]
[*Postmark:* 21 June 1841]

Ever dearest Georgie, I write on the only fragment of paper within reach,—my strength being another fragment: for I have been up today & tired by my letter to Papa besides. "Conspiracy!" Yes!- Conspiracy!- That is the word. I beseech you, George, not to acquiesce in it quietly, but to speak for me if you have not spoken & help to avert the evil I have no courage to face, of remaining another year in this miserable place—another year—involving perhaps the rest of my life.

The sending for Occy c^d mean only one thing—that *some weeks* (AT LEAST) delay in the removal was contemplated. I must judge of things as I see them—& this is obvious! You say "Dont come to London because we want country air"—& immediately you send for Joc to London!- What am I to infer?- Are you *not* conspirators?-

Now, Georgie, my dearest kindest Georgie, do try to produce a decision, and let some sort of carriage be sent to me at once. Why not Harman's?[1] Twenty guineas—what is it, as a consideration?

Dr Scully is nervous about the journey, & will say so. But it is *about the journey*, about *any* journey & *at any time*—and his opinion is that if I have resolved to do it (AND I HAVE) it had better be done without loitering. He said himself—"Well—Harman's carriage is the best means I can recommend," and he hoped some decision might reach us by tuesday. And now it seems as far off as ever.

As to Clifton .. if I dislike it!- IF, George!- There is no *if*. Why you everyone must know perfectly that there is no hypothesis in the matter. Clifton w^d be better than Torquay because any place w^d be better—but almost any *other* place, Salisbury Plain for instance, w^d be better than Clifton. My object is to be within reach of London—choose the place & I will thank you all. But then Papa!- He must not be displeased—he must be pleased. He must, Georgie, to please me. But why sh^d he care for that horrible Clifton? As to the rail-road Dr Scully bids me beware of it. He wont hear of my trying it. And ask Joc what he said about "three days". I cant help being anxious—& the sort of twilight I am kept in is not likely to do me or anybody good.

Ah Georgie!—if I were well it w^d be different!— But as it is, if the thing be not done now, I may be forced into quiescence in this place. And I say solemnly that in such a case *not one of my family shall remain with me!*— God bless you dear kind George. I dearly love you a⟨ll—⟩ every on⟨e.⟩ This f⟨or⟩ y.^{r} private hand.

Ba.

Address: George Goodin Barret Esqr / 3. Paper Buildings / Temple / London.
Publication: B-GB, pp. 62–63.
Manuscript: Pierpont Morgan Library.

  1. It is not clear whether this was James C. Harman, coach maker, of 27 Charles St., Tottenham Court Rd., or Samuel Harman, coach builder, of 100 Gt. Russell St.; both are listed in *Pigot's Street Directory of London for 1840*.

---

822. THOMAS CARLYLE TO RB [1]

5. Cheyne Row, Chelsea
21 june, 1841–

My dear Sir,

Many months ago you were kind enough to send me your *Sordello*; and now this day I have been looking into your *Pippa passes*, for which also I am your debtor. If I have made no answer hitherto, it was surely not for want of interest in you, for want of estimation of you: both Pieces have given rise to many reflexions in me, not without friendly hopes and anxieties in due measure. Alas, it is so seldom that any word one can speak is not worse than a word still unspoken;—seldom that one man, by his speaking or his silence, can, in great vital interests, help another at all!–

Unless I very greatly mistake, judging from these two works, you seem to possess a rare spiritual gift, poetical, pictorial, intellectual, by whatever name we may prefer calling it; to unfold which into articulate clearness is naturally the problem of all problems for you. This noble endowment, it seems to me farther, you are *not* at present on the best way for unfolding;—and if the world had loudly called itself content with these two Poems, my surmise is, the world could have rendered you no fataller disservice than that same! Believe me I speak with sincerity; and if I had not loved you well, I would not have spoken at all.

A long battle, I could guess, lies before you, full of toil and pain, and all sorts of real *fighting*: a man attains to nothing here below without that. Is it not verily the highest prize you fight for? Fight on; that is to say, follow truly, with steadfast singleness of purpose, with valiant humbleness and openness of heart, what best light *you* can attain to; following truly so, better and ever better light will rise on you. The light we ourselves gain, by our very errors if not otherwise, is the only precious light. Victory, what I call victory, if well fought for, is sure to you.

If your own choice happened to point that way, I for one should hail it as a good omen that your next work were written in prose! Not that I deny your poetic faculty; far, very far from that. But unless poetic faculty mean a higher-power of common understanding, I know not what it means. One must first make a *true* intellectual representation of a thing, before any poetic interest that is true will supervene. All *cartoons* are geometrical withal; and cannot be made till we have fully learnt to make mere *diagrams* well. It is this that I mean by prose;—which hint of mine, most probably inapplicable at present, may perhaps at some future day come usefully to mind.

But enough of this: why have I written all this? Because I esteem yours no common case; and think such a man is not to be treated in the common way.

And so persist in God's name, as you best see and can; and understand always that my true prayer for you is, Good Speed in the name of God!

I would have called for you last year when I had a horse, and some twice rode thro' your suburb; but stupidly I had forgotten your address;— and you, you never came again hither!

Believe me,

Yours most truly,
T. Carlyle

Address: Robert Browning Esq / E. Moxon Esq, Publisher / Dover Street / Piccadilly.
Docket, in RB's hand: June 21. '41.
Publication: Carlyle (1), I, 233–235.
Manuscript: Berg Collection.

1. For details of RB's friendship with Carlyle, see pp. 365–368.

---

823. EBB TO MARY RUSSELL MITFORD

[Torquay]
June 23– 1841

I cannot delay my beloved friend expressing to yourself the thrilling thankful sense of escape with which I read your letter.[1] May God bless you & keep you among those who love you & look to *you* for love, as long as they live to do so!–

But do *do* tell me––how are you now? How is the spine, the jarring of which I liked least of all to hear of? Do you lie down rightly & prudently, & remain quiet in every way until the system recovers itself? Because, *indeed* you should—indeed dearest Miss Mitford, you MUST. Leave the garden to the wind & the dew, and trust the strawberry-gathering to .. K! That is the only letter you ever told me of your maid's name, & I guess it stands for her name! Tell me if you do everything right, & nothing wrong .. & whether the swelling upon the spine has passed away. I dont like hearing of that, indeed!–

For the rest of your dear delightful letter whence are the words to come which sh^d thank you!—for what you say of Papa—for what you say of me—for your wish that I were near you .. without one word or fear about the teazing! How kind you are! How grateful I am to you!– How I love you out of a heart which *can* love though it has not loved many!– How I count your love for me among the blessings left to me, to be remembered among the tears left too. May God bless you & return it to you, my beloved friend!–

I have heard from Papa & he has heard (so he tells me) from you. You who speak pearls & diamonds without any fairy but yourself, must be used to hear of the pleasure conferred by your words. *He* seems to [be] pleased & over-pleased—for he is inspired into an impertinence wonderful in a country gentleman & scarcely tolerable in a poet. Shall I tell you what it is? Will you be angry? He is'nt a poet I do assure you—so dont think very ill of him. Nevertheless he had the impertinence to say (to *me*, mind) that the writer of such kind words as some which somebody wrote, "*sh^d be kissed by all of us*" in answer.

Ah!– I wish I were near enough to do my part in the kissing!– But dearest friend there is no settlement yet of the grand question,—& in what direction I am to remove remains less certain than the removal. To be patient during the long process of deciding, or rather of being decided for, is hard: and I who thought, not many months ago, that I never c^d. care more about anything earthly relating to myself, am detected in the very act of caring a good deal, .. more than I ought, more than you w^d think or do think I ought!—about this simple turning to the left or right. I dread so another separation—or isolation—such as it w^d be at Clifton. No!—my physician does not recommend the place. He w^d rather, I believe, that I went straight to London, & shut myself up in a large airy room, & took counsel & quietness with Dr Chambers. But he fears the *journey*—a journey anywhere—& has tried hard & vainly to frighten me out of the thoughts of it. I on the other hand, hold fast—& *wont* be

frightened—simply because the moral terrors which rise up with the prospect of remaining here, are more terrible to me—
Your old houses delight me as they do you.[2] If I had a house at all, it sh^d be an old one—that is, if ⟨★★★⟩

Publication: EBB-MRM, I, 230–231.
Manuscript: Wellesley College.

1. Although letter 820 gives details of Miss Mitford's narrow escape from injury, it is apparent from EBB's comments about her father that there was an additional letter from Miss Mitford, now missing.
2. See letter 825.

824. EBB TO GEORGE GOODIN MOULTON-BARRETT

[Torquay]
[*Postmark:* 24 June 1841]

My ever dearest Georgie,

Not to be over maniacal I propose myself to you as a person ready to believe for the best, that all anxieties & tribulations in relation to the journeying subject will end in a bonâ fide removal & not merely in one bona spe.[1] You will admit however that apart from your interpretation, Joc's recall wore a strange aspect. You will admit, that without any "maniacal" tendency, it was enough, when taken in conjunction with the delays & the discussions & the contradictions & the universal tendency towards treating me as a baby, . . to excite the most unexcitable!– Forgive me (then) this mania!——

Dr Scully himself has been vibrating in a manner provoking to me. I dare say you put down as sure that all his sayings in relation to "the beginning of the argument," such as, "she is quite right", "it is very natural", "it is very reasonable", "it is very possible," were misrepresented or at least warmly coloured by me. Nothing of the kind!– It was all clear approbation at first!– But when he saw that I was actually *in earnest*, he fell straightway into a tremblement– Then came, a list of the risks & the dangers & of all the things which would could or might peradventure befall me. He sate by this bedside & tried hard to frighten me—not as to *the time*, mind, my dear George, but as to the movement essentially. He sate at this bedside, & endeavoured to persuade me to go into another house & to another part of Torquay!! You may suppose how I answered— admitting that he had done right in telling me all, but resolute as to the act. Indeed he c^d not deny, when I put the question to him, that *if he were I, he w^d go.*

Well—we must allow for the unpleasant feeling of responsibility. I do not blame him—although all this prudent counsel, not being confined to my ear as I begged it might be, makes everybody cry out in different voices & keys, so as to consummate the discord of indecision. Now *I*[2] AM GOING—THAT IS SETTLED. And I leave it (no! I dont *leave* it) I *put* it to the wisest amongst you, whether, granting there is a risk, it be not increased by delaying & discussing one week after another.

Dr Scully calls me "excited". Now the two last conversations on the subject, began with himself—& all the impatience about getting me away, was expressed BY himself. Two days ago, he came with earnest anxious looks!—"Had I heard?" "Was the house taken?" "What! not yet?" "Oh! it w^d be far far better for you to go at once. You are excited, naturally, & must remain so until the journey is over—and there is no use in doctoring the body while the mind is restless. In your case, this is eminently true. IT IS THE LEAST OF TWO EVILS THAT YOU GO AT ONCE".

Then he went on to tell me how he got up at four in the morning to make notes about me, & to examine a map of London & the situation of Wimpole Street. He approved of the latter, and after enquiring about the aspect of my bedroom, expressed his opinion for the twentieth time that I sh^d be *as well there as here in the winter*. The thing necessary for me, he said, was an airy room which c^d be warmed,—with a south or western aspect,—and the neighbourhood of good advice. His own leaning evidently is to send me *direct to London*. He thinks it w^d be better for me, and that the journey being begun had better be ended at once. That was his opinion as he rendered it to me, two days ago—Crow being witness– But of course I explained to him that Papa's plans for my brothers, did not allow of this direct passage to Wimpole Street. Oh no!– I w^d not break upon *them*. At the same time it does appear to me hard, rather hard, that the Clifton question sh^d be carried against me, when I am the only person affected either for good or evil by that particular locality, & when the evil threatened to me by it, is all unmingled evil. Dearest George, do say a word, when the opportunity occurs. You must see how it is, as plainly as I do. I shall have no rest of spirit at Clifton– I shall have encountered this "risk" which is talked of, without an equivalent object. Certainly I shall have left Torquay—but a removal to the first stage from Torquay to Chudleigh[3] w^d accomplish *that*, without a step beyond. All the effort, all the expense, will be made & paid for next to in vain. It will be a sovereign in change for sixpence. Not that I forget the blessing of being free from this place—but all besides,—and I have lived upon the blessed hope of being settled at home with you all—will be *lost*!– Do you not see?– Do you not feel how it is?– Dr Scully himself says "I understand. *You object reasonably.*" As to Reading, I do not say Reading more than Twickenham or any other place of the vicinity. I dont want to have my own way about it—indeed I have no "own way" to carry— I want you all to choose— I want Papa to choose. Only, if he persists in this Clifton plan, I shall scarcely, I feel, have spirits to travel away from all my hopes, to another place of exile & scene of separation!— yes, & of more than separation, George, *of* ISOLATION .. such as Clifton SHOULD be to me if I went to it— Why I might quite as well remain at Chudleigh—quite as well. There w^d be an escape from the pressure of actual associations[4]——and nothing more. But nothing more can be said of Clifton.

I leave these things with your 'professional' judgment to turn over & discern. Remember!—I am forbidden, in any case, to attempt the rail road. That is that. And I ask you to task your fancy, as happily you cannot your experience, & try to image what peace & rest & *safety of heart* there w^d be for me in the feeling of being at home or close to home, after this present sense of banishment & seperation.

Ah dearest dearest George! It is all very selfish!— How selfishly I have written!— Only INDEED I w^d not that one of you sh^d sacrifice a good or a pleasure for *me*!— I have no good or pleasure but your's—except *you*!— It is the living apart from any of you which drives me to say so much,—or to say anything—& I cant bring myself to think that living apart from you can be the cause to you of good or pleasure. Hemel Hampstead [*sic*], or Twickenham, or Reading, or Tunbridge or Walthamstow .. all places where we can be together & whence we can remove together, are equal to me. Would it not be hard—no!—not hard perhaps,—but unhappy, if the only place where I cannot rest, sh^d be fixed upon for me to travel to.

My mind turns round & round in wondering about Papa's fancy for Clifton—that hot, white, dusty, vapory place, & scarcely an inland place too!— And then sometimes I grow dizzy & fearful that he looks to Michael Church!— Oh but I WONT[5] fear it. I wont fear anything. I will hope a little, while there is room. So you are going next week my dear dear George.[6] I will write to you on your way. *I* will be the "kind heart,"[7] George, & write—that is, if they dont wear me out with these "rubs" backwards & forwards. The "conspiracy" is discredited upon your assurance. One word more. Dr Scully did not like the idea of a carriage from Bristol, & seemed to think too much depended upon *the best*, not to have it from Harman himself, or Willoughby,[8] without considering the expe⟨nse &⟩ the safe⟨ty &⟩ besides that *twenty guineas* is no extortion— that on the contrary a patient of his who removed from hence to Brighton in a conveyance of the kind, paid more. But I think I shall say this to Papa, or have it said. God bless you. When I reach you, I will not talk so of myself. I shall subside in contrast.

Your ever attached
Ba

I dont want Papa to come! Is there any use? He will be over anxious & nervous, & uncomfortable. Tell him not to come[.] Do you know Dr Scully *wants* YOU?⁹ He distrusts dear Storm's firmness, it appears—*but say nothing*- Oh of course you would not! Storm w^d do everything very well—& I am fearless.

Address: George Goodin Barrett Esqr / 3. Paper Buildings / Temple / London.
Publication: B-GB, pp. 67–71 (as [24 July 1841]).
Manuscript: Pierpont Morgan Library.

1. i.e., an actual removal rather than an anticipated one.
2. Underscored twice.
3. Chudleigh, on the Exeter road, was some 13 miles north of Torquay.
4. i.e., continual reminders of Bro.
5. Underscored four times.
6. George was going on circuit again; EBB's next letter to him (no. 830) was addressed to Stafford.
7. *Parœmiologia Anglo-Latina* (1639), p. 45, by John Clarke.
8. Solomon Willoughby was a coach builder with premises at 1 John Street. Harman may have been James C. Harman or Samuel (see letter 821, note 1).
9. Underscored three times.

---

825. MARY RUSSELL MITFORD TO EBB

Three Mile Cross,
June 28, 1841.

First, my beloved friend, let me answer your most kind inquiries. I am greatly better. It has been a most remarkable escape; but a real escape. I can not yet turn in my bed; but when up I get about astonishingly well. To say truth, I am, and always have been, a very active person—country-born and country-bred—with great fearlessness and safety of foot and limb. Even *since* this misfortune, Ben having said that half the parish had mounted on a hay-rick close by to look at the garden, which lies beneath it (an acre of flowers rich in color as a painter's palette), I could not resist the sight of the ladder, and one evening when all the men were away, climbed up to take myself a view of my flowery domain. I wish you could see it! Masses of the Siberian larkspur, and sweet-Williams, mostly double, the still brighter new larkspur (*Delphinium Chinensis*), rich as an oriental butterfly—such a size and such a blue! amongst roses in millions, with the blue and white Canterbury bells (also double), and the white foxglove, and the variegated monkshood, the carmine pea, in its stalwart beauty, the nemophila, like the sky above its head, the new erysimum, with its gay orange tufts, hundreds of lesser annuals, and fuchsias, zinnias, salvias, geraniums past compt; so bright are the flowers that the green really does not predominate amongst them!

Yes! I knew you would like those old houses! Ockwells surpasses in beauty and in preservation anything I ever saw.[1] Our ancestors were rare architects. Their painted glass and their carved oak are unequalled.

Heaven be with you, my dearest!

Ever yours,
M. R. Mitford.

Address: Miss Barrett, Torquay.
Text: L'Estrange (2), III, 119-120.

1. Ockwells Manor, a timbered house near Maidenhead, was described by Miss Mitford as having "a hall, with the dais and music gallery, and two tiers of windows covered with the arms of the Romeyns (by whom it was built in 1437), in the most perfect preservation ... the front of the house, with its gables, is ornamented by the most splendid oak-carving, as delicate as an Indian fan" (Chorley, I, 186).

826. EBB TO MARY RUSSELL MITFORD

[Torquay]
July 2. [1841][1]

I am so glad—so glad & thankful that you are really better, & that the effect of the accident is not likely to be lasting.[2] When knights hand ladies over 'fair floors', they sh^d do it more cautiously, lest too 'trippingly', if the boards be wanting. I have trodden castle floors (in the air) where there were neither boards nor beams—and to fall *there*, is peradventure a sadder thing.

The ascent of the "ladder" was very much in my way too .. my old way .. in my days of tree climbing & wall-climbing, which are hard to look back at now. I remember wondering why in the world Jacob did not set about climbing up *his* ladder[3]—and my sympathy grew intense in the matter of Jack's beanstalk, just in proportion as it reached the sky– Well—I cannot climb now, nor ever shall again. Yet it is something compensative to have climbed high enough to touch your love. Is'nt it my beloved friend? I think so– It is little to think so now: but indeed I *should* have thought so years & years ago at the top of an appletree!——

What a history!—which was meant only to be a sympathy in regard to the ladder—to *your* ladder. How bright & beautiful the garden must have looked from it—& as if all the flowers of the country kept tryst just there—as they might well do, if only to live with *you*!–

And speaking of flowers, I must have walked in a poppy field with my thoughts, never to have thanked you for preparing or promising a geranium to crown 'Psyche' with. It was not gross ingratitude, however you may have thought of the silence. I forgot my gratitude while I was writing to you—(when so many kinds of gratitude are apt to rise up & try to thurst [*sic*] themselves in)—but not a minute after I had sealed my letter. May Psyche be worthy! In the meantime it seems to me questionable whether she will *be* at all.

Before I forget again . . have you looked into the 'History of a flirt'?[4] The name may daunt you—but the writer 'leans to Miss Austen's side',— as I remember dear D.[r] Mitford & yourself do—& there is some power & much truth to nature– If you have not seen it & can see it, will you?– There is nothing high toned or passionate—& supposing you safely over the monotony of the subject & the odiousness of the heroine, it may not prove heavy light reading for your evenings– Cold praise, after all! You wont catch at it from my praises. But I under-praise it purposely—for an obvious reason. It did indeed strike me as one of the very best domestic novels which have fallen upon these evil days.[5]

Have you read the new Memoir by Blanchard, of poor LEL. Do tell me (if you have) what your thought is—only extracts by the reviewers having reached me.[6] The '*calumny*' refers to M.[r] Jerdan—does it not?–[7] But I grope in the mournful darkness for the signification of her own allusion to "the *vanity of a man* and the tongue of a vulgar woman".[8] Poor, poor LEL!

Strange in M.[r] Blanchard & Miss Roberts[9] or any friend of hers, to dwell so emphatically upon the contrariety of her own nature to the thing *called* her nature & expressed in her poems. Why *there*, just *there*, was the plague spot—*there*, her poetic mortality. She was the actress, & not Juliet. Her genius was not strong enough to assert itself in truth. It *suffered* her to belie herself—& *stood by*, while she put on the mask. Where is the true deep poetry which was not felt deeply & truly by the poet? What is the poet, without the use of his own heart? And thus, the general character of Miss Landon[']s most popular poems is . . melancholy without pathos. A conventional tone pierces through the sweetness.

Poor LEL! Just as she had outstretched her hand to touch nature, & to feel thrillingly there that poetry is more than fantasy . . to die so! I have dropped tears on tears over some of her later poems, which par-

⟨. . .⟩[10]

Oh M.[r] S Talfourd! How c.[d] he desert you & why?!![11] I saw no letter. We are slaying ourselves in the elections, we free Britons!

M.[r] Chorley's book—have you seen *that*? The extracts promise for a good book. They are very living.[12]

Publication: EBB-MRM, I, 231–234.
Manuscript: Wellesley College.

1. This is a reply to letter 825, which provides the year.
2. Miss Mitford had suffered "a terrible jar upon the spine" as a result of a fall (see L'Estrange (2), III, 123).
3. See Genesis, 28:12.
4. *The History of a Flirt: Related by Herself* (1840) by Lady Charlotte Susan Maria Bury (*née* Campbell, 1775–1861), daughter of the 5th Duke of Argyll. She had previously published *Flirtation* (1828).
5. *Paradise Lost*, VII, 25.
6. *The Life and Literary Remains of L.E.L.*, by Laman Blanchard, was reviewed, with extracts, in *The Athenæum* of 29 May 1841 (no. 709, pp. 421–423) and *The Examiner* of 13 June (no. 1741, p. 371). EBB has apparently forgotten that Miss Mitford mentioned reading the book in letter 820.
7. The writer in *The Athenæum* felt that either certain references should have been passed over or else have been fully explained, to prevent "the most assiduous of evil-speakers from ever again writing his epitaph of open calumny . . . upon her grave." EBB questions whether this "calumny" refers to the rumours that had linked Miss Landon romantically with William Jerdan, her literary mentor and first editor. EBB had previously mentioned "the Jerdan murmurs" in letter 727.
8. Probably a reference to another speculation, tying Miss Landon to the Irish journalist William Maginn, whose wife claimed to have found compromising letters to her husband from Miss Landon. The gossip about her alleged affairs was the reason for her breaking off her engagement to John Forster. For a more detailed account, including comment from Miss Landon herself, see *Bulwer: A Panorama* (1931) by Michael Sadleir (I, 387–390).
9. Miss Landon's friend had also written a memoir of her (see letter 687, note 25).
10. The conclusion of the letter is missing, except for the following sentences, written at the top of the first page.
11. Apparently a reference to another disagreement between Miss Mitford and Sergeant Talfourd; an earlier quarrel was mentioned in letter 716.
12. Chorley's latest work, *Music and Manners in France and Germany*, was reviewed, with extracts, in *The Athenæum* of 26 June 1841 (no. 713, pp. 485–487) and 10 July (no. 715, pp. 518–520).

---

827. EBB TO MARY RUSSELL MITFORD

[Torquay]
[*Postmark:* 15 July 1841]

⟨★★★⟩ be repeated no where. But is it not abominable cant to cry out as people do in behalf of domestic delicacy, whenever a great man is spoken of abstractedly from his works, as a man? Is'nt it folly besides cant?—or rather, w^{dnt} it be, if all cant were not folly. For my own part, I do feel strongly that when a man has either by great deeds or noble writings, passed into the heart of the world, he gives that world the *right of love* to sit at his fireside & hear him speak face to face & with a friend's voice. The man being ours to love, is ours to look at as our familiar—and if he be a man who can love as he is loved, his countenance will gather more brightness from our 'curious eyes'[1] than from the sense of his own dignified privacy. Dont you think so? Dont you laugh to scorn Monsieur Neckar's complaint of the wrong done to men of genius by calling them out of their titles?[2] As if Shakespeare, our Shakespeare, were not better than Master Shakespeare, or for the matter of that, than Monsieur Neckar? As if love were not the best dignity!– And after all, to return to my position which of us w^{dnt} like to know how Shakespeare came down stairs one Wednesday morning with his hose ungartered? W^{dnt} you climb your ladder ten times,[3] to catch the colour of the garters? I know how you agree with me!—and how, admitting my principle, you give your gracious forgiveness to Miss Sedgewick for that graceful characteristic sketch of your own self in the midst of the geraniums. The words too—the very words full of you & true to you—"I love my geraniums next to my father"—why sh^{dnt} we every one hear those words? Well done, Miss Sedgewick!– And you my beloved friend, will guess that I have been reading all this in the Athenæum[4] .. feeling a smile upon my own lips almost as if I saw *you*!——

But what a wandering from my beginning in which I began to thank you for your letter with its details. They did indeed amuse me—& I have been explaining the length & breadth of one of my 'Whys', to you!– Nevertheless it w^d be plain to others both from your letter & my answer to it, that we are not quite of a mind as to certain things & that I am deeper in hero- & heroine-worship than you are. Yes! and you shant make me blaspheme my poets, or cease to love people "for blotting paper"—provided the blot be such as I like!– Dearest dearest Miss Mitford, why YOU love them too! To be sure you do!– What w^d your Fletcher say if he heard with his subtle spiritual ear, that you loved nobody for blotting paper? .! Poor wretched LEL!– I grieve for her. But I hold stedfastly— perversely perhaps you think .. (yet dont!) that her faults were not *of* her poetry but *against* it.

To speak generally, there are errors which make a blaze & a noise, more than some of a worse kind, & which are peculiar to quick irritable excitable temperaments—such as go commonly with vivid imaginations. Sin is sin—but it often happens, and did happen in the case of poor Ld Byron, that we do not deal tenderly & pitifully enough with the sinner. We are apt to judge the man of genius by his own ideal—& to apportion our severity by his eminence. This w^d be cruel if it were not ungrateful. By the pleasure he has brought us, we measure back our stripes.

The end of it all is, that *I do not believe there is or was or ever will be a "good for nothing" poet in the world.*

There is a doxy for you!——

But poor poor LEL!– I feel all you say of the material unworked!– She might indeed have achieved a greatness which her fondest admirers can scarcely consider achieved now. And do you know (ah!—*I* know that you wont agree with me!) I have sometimes thought to myself that if I had those two powers to choose from .. Mrs Hemans's & Miss Landon's .. I mean the *raw* bare powers .. I w.^{d} choose Miss Landon's. I surmise that it was more elastic, more various, of a stronger web. I fancy it w.^{d} have worked out better—had it *been* worked out—with the right moral & intellectual influences in application. As it is, Mrs Hemans has left the finer poems. Of that there can be no question. But perhaps .. & indeed I do say it very diffidently .. there is a sense of sameness which goes with the sense of excellence,—while we read her poems—a satiety with the satisfaction together with a feeling "this writer has written her best",—or "It is very well—but it never can be better". It is the flat smooth ground at the top of a hill—table-ground they call it—& many hills in Devonshire are shaped so:—a little to their loss in picturesqueness– If she had lived longer w.^{d} she have been greater? "*I trow not*".[5]

I have read the Bells & Pomegranates!– "Pippa passes" .. comprehension, I was going to say!–[6] Think of me, living in my glass house & throwing pebbles out of the windows!! But really "Pippa passes", I must say, Mr Browning[']s ordinary measure of mystery. Now laugh at me!– Laugh, as you please!– I like, I do like, the 'heart of a mystery'[7] when it beats moderate time! I like a twilight of mysticism—when the sun & moon both shine together! Yes—and I like 'Pippa' too. There are fine things in it—& the presence of genius, never to be denied!– At the same time it is hard .. *to understand*—is'nt it?– Too hard?– I think so!– And the fault of Paracelsus,—the defect in harmony, is here too. After all, Browning is a true poet—& there are not many such poets—and if any critics *have*, as your critical friend wrote to you, "flattered him into a wilderness & left him"[8] they left him alone with his *genius*,—& where those two are, despair cannot be. The wilderness will blossom soon, with a brighter rose than "*Pippa*'. In the meanwhile what do you think of *her*? Was there any need for so much coarseness? Surely not. But the genius—the genius—it is undeniable—is'nt it?–

I have sent some more cream, which you must tell me about, in the case of its *not* arriving safe. *Only in that case.* I have found it to be a possible case lately, in regard to other parcels.

No decision has yet been made.[9] I hold fast to my patience—and everything will be well at last—but I do fear with all my fine words, that if my heart were bare it w.^{d} be found a very very impatient heart. This is why I say so little of what is close to it!–

This is a long long letter, & I must put off Flush to another. He is well & happy—as playful as a kitten,—& *with* a kitten for a playmate! Think of his condescending to a kitten! What w^d his great ancestor say? Think of his carrying this little white, snowball of a kitten, no larger than his head, *carrying* it about the room in his mouth—& playing with it for hours together!– Dear goodnatured Flush!– We are very fond of him—I & the kitten are!– And if he is ever in a scrape, up he leaps to me, & lays his head on my shoulder for sanctuary!– I protect him! He knows *that*—& so we love each other.

Do you look up under the shame of these elections? I feel abashed!–[10]

God bless you my beloved friend! Tell me of yourself & dear Dr Mitford—of both in detail!– Did Mr Chorley pay you the visit you hoped for? *I* hope he did. And is his health better than it used to be—and have you read his 'Manners & Music'?–[11]

God bless you my dearest friend. Love me as long and as much as you can! I love you as long as I cant .. help it!

Ever your EBB–

Address: Miss Mitford / Three Mile Cross / near Reading.
Publication: EBB-MRM, I, 234–237.
Manuscript: Wellesley College.

1. Cf. *Romeo and Juliet*, I, 4, 31.
2. Jacques Necker (1732–1804), the father of Mme. de Staël, was a French banker, statesman, and sometime Minister of Finance.
3. EBB's reference is to the incident recounted by Miss Mitford in letter 825.
4. The passage cited by EBB occurred in the review of Miss Sedgwick's *Letters from Abroad to Kindred at Home* in The Athenæum of 10 July (no. 715, pp. 516–518). Catharine Maria Sedgwick (1789–1867), an American, was the author of *A New England Tale* (1822) and other works. The book under review was an account of 15 months spent in Europe in 1839–40, with very candid descriptions of some of the people she had met. As later letters show, Kenyon had arbitrarily edited her manuscript when he chanced upon it at the printer's shop, and Miss Mitford was incensed by some of the comments about her.
5. Luke, 17:9.
6. *Pippa Passes* had been published in April.
7. Cf. *Hamlet*, III, 2, 366.
8. The "critical friend" is assumed to be Chorley, who is said, in the following letter, to have read the poem four times.
9. i.e., regarding EBB's return to London.
10. Allegations of manipulation in the general election were rife. *The Examiner* of 17 July, reporting the result, wrote: "The country is sold to the highest bidders. By bribery on the largest scale, and intimidation strained to the uttermost, the Tories have obtained a majority of seventy. The sums given for votes have been of unprecedented magnitude."
11. Apparently Chorley did pay Miss Mitford a visit at this time, as the following letters contain references to his comments to her about Horne. He had suffered a heart condition since childhood (see *Henry Fothergill Chorley: Autobiography, Memoir, and Letters*, ed. H.G. Hewlett, 1873, I, 158). For EBB's comments on his new book, see letter 826.

828. EBB TO MARY RUSSELL MITFORD

[Torquay]
July 17. 1841.

My impulse was to begin answering your letter before I reached its end!– Am I in a scrape? Am I *not* in a fright? To be sure I am!– And was it not a cross destiny which led to such a "hands across"[1] as our crossing letters? To be sure it was! But then there's another "to be sure" surer than all the rest & *that* is your indulgence to me. You will have mercy, as Flush has for the kitten—carrying it about softly with its head in his mouth, tho' *without* biting it off. I mew a little, & you let me fall softly. *To be sure* it is so, or will be so, or at least may be so. I will thank you as if it were so—& I will love you my ever beloved friend, if it be so or not.

I have been beating my brains to remember exactly what the nonsense of my last letter was. I beat them—and the chaff flies up in my eyes & blinding me leaves me my obscurity. But you will do me the justice (this is my hope) of inferring from the very nonsense, that I could have seen only the corrected Athenæum & was altogether unaware of the want of delicacy & respect towards you, demonstrated in the work itself.[2] The little vision of you made me feel glad .. something as if I really had seen you. There seemed to me nothing in it which was not true to your nature, & therefore pleasant & good for other natures to contemplate. And I was pleased—as I always am when you are brought closer to me by thought or word—& in the crisis of my good humour, achieved every sort of benediction for all sorts of literary gossippers. Well!—I do like them after all. And if I did'nt, the generations after me, would!—now, would'nt they?– Oh yes!– I do like,—with the strong eager earnest liking of an enthusiast in books, shut up a life-long among books *only*, .. to look at the book's motive-power & externity! *You* do not feel this so strongly— just because you have "seen, touched, & handled"!–[3] *You* cant imagine how happy I felt once, to know,—nay, to have beheld with my eyes, that the poet Campbell had red stuff curtains in his dining room.[4] But push back the clock—& think! Push it back to Shakespeare's day! The colour of his hose—or was'nt it of his garters—did'nt I say his garters?— *their* colour is a case in a point—. Think of 'The Shakespeare *garters*'!

But you must do me justice, & believe in the breadth & blackness of the line I draw between innocent & objectionable gossippings. That line sh.^{d} be very broad & very black. For without any absolute falseness, or positive breach of confidence, details may be given & tittle-tattle re-tittle-tattled, in a way most vexing & improper. Dont, therefore, call up an image of me, clapping my hands over Miss Sedgewick's sins of indelicacy—oh *dont*!– Think how the thorns ran into me all the time I read the first part of your letter, & dont give me up—dont love me less—dont even set me down among the "good for nothing poetesses".

After all, was it so very bad of me to like that vision of you, given in the Athenæum? Read it over again, & think! Now was it?– My only word against it at the moment, was to my sister who happened to stand at my bedside! And what do you guess it was? .. "Why there is one peculiarity in her face without a notice! The eyes!—and *not* the forehead! Oh something sh^d have been said of her forehead".

Is it very very wrong of me?– But you have, you know, a peculiar, massive forehead. Coleridge was

"The creature of the godlike forehead"— [5]

& Mr Kenyon once said to me (There!—now *I* [6] am the gossipper!) Mr Kenyon once said to me, "I never saw any forehead like Coleridge's, except Miss Mitford's."

Try to forgive me. I *may* be forgiven—because it was my love of you which did wrong .. by being pleased. But it did not know—it c^d not see!– It was love in a *poke!*– [7]

Thank you, thank you for Browning's poem. My thought of it crossed your question about my thought, Mr Kenyon having kindly sent me *his* copy ten days since. But I must tell you besides that I read it three times—in correspondence with Mr Chorley's four—& in testimony both to the genius & the obscurity. Nobody sh^d complain of being forced to read it three or four or ten times. Only they w^d do it more gratefully if they were not forced. I who am used to mysteries, caught the light at my second reading—but the full glory, not until the third. The conception of the whole is fine, very fine—& there are noble, beautiful things everywhere to be broken up & looked at. That great tragic scene, which you call "exquisite" [8]—& which pants again with its own power! Did it strike you that there was an occasional *manner*, in the portions most strictly dramatic, like Landor's, in Landor's dramas, when Landor writes best. Now read—

—"How these tall
Naked geraniums straggle! Push the lattice—
Behind that frame.—Nay, do I bid you?—Sebald,
It shakes the dust down on me! Why of course
The slide-bolt catches—Well—are you content
Or must I find you something else to spoil?–
Kiss & be friends, my Sebald!" [9]

Is'nt that Landor? Is'nt it his very trick of phrase? Yet Mr Browning is no imitator. He asserts *himself* in his writings, with a strong & deep individuality: and if he does it in Chaldee, why he makes it worth our while to get out our dictionaries![10] Oh most excellent critic 'in the glass house[']!–[11]

After all, what I miss most in M.[r] Browning, is *music*. There is a want of harmony, particularly when he is lyrical—& *that* struck me with a hard hand, while I was in my admiration over his Paracelsus.

This is for *you*—I *do not know him*.

Ten oclock—& not a word of the last subject—the last dread subject!–[12] I will write tomorrow. But I must say before my eyes shut tonight, that I thank you most gratefully & fondly, beloved kindest friend, for the frankness of your words. Oh advise me always—tell me always what I ought to do—or ought'nt!– It is so, that I feel sure of your loving me.

I will write tomorrow—but do not wait until then to be in true grateful attachment

Your EBB–

Can you read? My hand shakes, .. goes east & west .. today—& it is *tonight* now.

I have sent for the *Literary Gazette*.[13]

Publication: EBB-MRM, I, 237–240.
Manuscript: Wellesley College.

1. "The Belle of the Ball," verse 2, by Winthrop Mackworth Praed (1802–39).
2. See letter 827, note 4. The extracts in *The Athenæum* did not disclose the remarks to which Miss Mitford took exception; EBB later saw these in *The Literary Gazette* (see letter 834, notes 1 and 3).
3. Cf. Colossians, 2:21.
4. See letter 706.
5. Cf. Wordsworth, "Extempore Effusion Upon the Death of James Hogg" (1835), lines 17–18.
6. Underscored twice.
7. i.e., blind love; cf. the expression "a pig in a poke."
8. The work under discussion is *Pippa Passes*, published in April. The scene praised by Miss Mitford may be that between Ottima and Sebald in part I.
9. The lines quoted appear in part I, "Morning," (lines 7–13).
10. A reference to criticism of RB for obscurity, particularly in his previous work, *Sordello*.
11. "People in glass houses shouldn't throw stones"—a wry reference to criticisms of EBB's own style (see, for example, letter 538, note 20).
12. The "last dread subject" was her developing relationship with Horne, discussed in the following letter.
13. As noted above, *The Literary Gazette* (10 July 1841) contained more extensive and more offensive extracts from Miss Sedgwick's book than those EBB had read in *The Athenæum*.

829. EBB to Mary Russell Mitford

[Torquay]
July 18. 1841

And now to finish yesterday's letter. With a deep true sense of the value of every word from *you* & of the *love-value* of these particular words, & thanking you over & over again for a frankness so dear to me, I shall yet be .. I shall *therefore* be correspondingly open with you & confess that I have not for a moment since the ringing of Mr Chorley's alarm-bell,[1] felt frightened or embarrassed or distrustful of my invisible friend with his visible kindnesses .. Mr Horne. Certainly the dreadful black book, "The false medium between men of genius & the public"[2] is his own perpetration. It is his acknowledged work. There is no mystery about it. I never read it: & I remember hearing of it, long before the Medeist[3] & the poet became identified in my knowledge & still longer before I knew Mr Horne under either character,—as a clever & eccentric work—eccentric—no more– Mr Chorley's "silent gravity" being 'the full sum'[4] of evil imputation in relation to it that ever reached *me*. Again & again I meant to get it—but never did. I never did read it, or look at its outside— never, up to this moment.

"And now'['] (you are murmuring) "what is she going to do?["] "*What* (as Mr Kenyon says) *will come next*?" ["]What will she do? Defend thro' thick & thin the infallibility of a book she never read, for the sake of a person she never saw? Walk into "good-for-nothing-ness" deliberately, leisurely, & without holding up her petticoats."!!

You see how I want you to smile a little, & draw from Mr Chorley's "gravity," something scarcely as grave as the first deduction. Let us consider. Perhaps the book may be 'black' from its politics!– W.^d Mr Chorley look grave over a levelling principle? He might, you know!– But I will get the book & read it & put off my apology for it until then. I shall be worth just as much as a defender, after I have read it—dont you think so?–

But dearest kindest friend, why w.^d I talk lightly when you spoke to me with such serious kindness. Perhaps I ought not. I am serious enough *within*– And the seriousness is within & without too, indeed, .. it spreads itself all over .. while I look back & consider the whole long story of this unseen friend's kindness to me. Surely he must have in him an abundant goodness to have done by me as he has. What claim had I in my solitude & sadness & helpless hopeless sickness, such as he believed it to be, upon a literary man overwhelmed with occupation & surrounded by friends & fitnesses of all sorts in London? Nevertheless from the first kind little note which he sent to me on learning the straightness of my prison (he learnt that from a mutual friend)⁵ to ask me to allow him to help in amusing me, he has never forgotten or seemed to forget me. There has ever been coming some slight detail, some witty word, some notice of book or writer—the whole made acceptable & even touching to me by a delicacy & unostentatious sympathy which are rarer even than the attention. But the attention itself is rare. How few w^d have thought of the thing!— How fewer still w^d not have wearied of it?— There is your own beloved self who are never tired of me!— And there are my own dearest ones at home who are never tired of me!— But although I have nothing to complain of, & have received from my slight intercourse with the world a more than proportionate good will, there is scarcely another .. yes, scarcely another, who continues writing, writing to me as if I were well & c^d amuse them back again. So that it w^d be impossible for me not to feel this strange kindness from a stranger, or not to dismiss, so, the thought of strangership. Why even our dear Mr Kenyon, with all his overflowing benevolence towards all, & that regard for myself which I sh^d be both unjust & sorry to doubt, .. why even he cant find time to spend in such a way. He scarcely ever writes a word to me—scarcely ever!— Never above twice indeed, since I was exiled.

Well— You will grant then the reason I have for gratitude. But *that*, you will say, is not a reason against the intimation conveyed in the "silence"!

But then I recur to this sa⟨me⟩ correspondence. It has been very frequent—short letters but many of them—and perfectly open & unceremonious on each side. We became quick friends—& by passing through a multitude of subjects, cannot be ignorant of our mutual modes of thinking & feeling upon many. And I have liked very much my knowledge, so derived, of Mr Horne. I have liked & estimated it all. And if he is not a true gentleman, of "fancies chaste & noble"⁶ I sh^d not recognize one anywhere.

True, that Leigh Hunt is his friend! Poor Leigh Hunt!— I never c^d help to cry down that hapless, industrious, imprudent man of genius— loved much by the few—scorned much by the many,—& to be extolled & respected by more future generations than he can reckon now, individual well-wishers. Will the Roggers's, or even the Moores measure genius with him hereafter? "I trow not".⁷ You w^d not wish me to speak or think lightly of the true poet Leigh Hunt—& for the universal reason which as far as I can understand it is no reason at all. You w^d not yourself. When Mr Horne told me once that Leigh Hunt spoke affectionately of me, I felt proud all the day after.

Of Fox I never heard—except—is'nt he a unitarian preacher?— There is another friend—a Mr Powell, who is a very dear friend also of

Wordsworth's. M! Powell has written to me two or three times, & sent me his poems, which are marked by poetical sentiment & pure devotional feeling, but by no remarkable power. You know we had him with us in the Chaucer. Then there's D! Southwood Smith[8]—& M! Bell,[9] editor of the Monthly Chronicle, & the Monthly Chronicle people perhaps, generally, M! Carlyle that profound thinker, is a friend of M! Horne's: & the Landors & Milnes's & Talfourds visit him at least—to say nought of Ld Northampton's soireès.[10] Oh!—it almost seems to me *a wrong*, to set up all these paltry wooden props for a circumstantial respectability—yet let them stand! And so it stands "proven" I think that he does move in a society which the world accounts "respectable"—M! Chorley's expression, *when he was not silent*, rather intimating the contrary.

Does this sound as if I were angry! No no!—indeed, indeed my beloved & kindest friend, whom I shall love dearly when hereafter you have found me out to be far less worth loving than you first supposed .. indeed I am not angry. I love you & thank you from my heart for the interest which led you to write the words you wrote. I am *grateful*—& you will be understanding. For *you*, who are of a generous trusting nature, *will* understand how one cant help springing up warmly when persons we esteem & have learnt to be obliged to, are deprecated by others. Not by you! You are not the deprecator! You have only performed a *necessity of love* in telling me what you thought I sh^d know– And I on the other side, have told you everything I remember & as far as I remember it, about the individual in question—and all my thoughts besides.

Papa who hates visiting to the point of desease—so painfully that I c^d not ask him to call upon anybody—was yet moved to leave his card upon M! Horne. And they seemed to meet with mutual satisfaction—one saying—"I seem to have known him a hundred years" (M! Horne said *that* of Papa—) and the other—"A gentleman—plain & quiet manners— not ætherial enough (so said Papa!) for a poet."– Papa had been touched too .. soothed back into gratification after his furious anger with the Quarterly (because M! Lockhart did'nt seem to love me as himself did)[11] by those beautiful stanzas of M! Horne's in the Monthly Chronicle.[12] And those pleased *me*! Not that I cared after the manner of my own dear Papa, for the Quarterly's stripes. Perhaps they were as 'gently done'[13] as I might hope for. And then few things moved me at that time. The review was one of the first readings I got through with—& even in accomplishing *that*, it was by a painful mental effort that I c^d compass the meaning of it, sentence by sentence. If they had set me up on the top of a pyramid with a foolscap on, what w^d it have been to me?–

Oh my dearest friend! That was a very near escape from madness, absolute hopeless madness– For more than three months I c^d not read—c^d

understand little that was said to me. The mind seemed to myself broken up into fragments. And even after the long dark spectral trains, the staring infantine faces, had gone back from my bed,—to *understand*, to hold on to one thought for more than a moment, remained impossible. That was, in part, because I never c^d cry. Never! The tears ran scalding hot into my brain instead of down my cheeks— That was how it happened.[14]

But I might well spare you this— The Athenæum has not done the most limited justice to Mr Horne as a poet. I like the Athenæum!— I am interested in it, & Mr Dilke is kind enough, do you know, to send it to me regularly. But I wish sometimes that it's poetical were like its *musical* criticisms, justified & beautified by the love of art.[15] When however the critic passes to the poets, he grows blue with cold, & his finger-ends insensate! Not that bad versifiers do not depreciate poetry more than cold critics. Not that we have poets to spare!— But surely there *are poets!* ⟨★★★⟩

Publication: EBB-MRM, I, 240–244.
Manuscript: Folger Shakespeare Library and Wellesley College.

1. As indicated later in this paragraph, Chorley had expressed to Miss Mitford some reservations about EBB's relationship with Horne, due in part to his reputation for eccentricity.
2. Horne's book, *Exposition of the False Medium and Barriers Excluding Men of Genius from the Public* (1833), had earned him a certain opprobrium for his dismissive comments about various literary figures of the day (see, for example, the reference to Fanny Kemble's *Francis the First* in letter 839).
3. Medism described the attitude of Greeks in the 6th and 5th centuries B.C. who unpatriotically sympathized with the Persians; hence, by extension, it connotes the holding of unpopular opinions.
4. *The Merchant of Venice*, III, 2, 157.
5. Mrs. Orme, the former governess at Hope End.
6. We have not located the source of this quotation.
7. Luke, 17:9.
8. Thomas Southwood Smith (1788–1861), preacher and physician, advocated major improvements in sanitation to reduce disease and mortality, especially among the poor. He was one of the personalities treated in Horne's *A New Spirit of the Age*. Coincidentally, he died in Florence a few months after EBB.
9. Robert Bell (1800–67), journalist, author and playwright, collaborated with Bulwer-Lytton in establishing *The Monthly Chronicle* in 1838, subsequently becoming its editor. He was one of the contributors to *Chaucer, Modernized* (see letter 780), and later produced a 24-volume annotated edition of English poets (1854–57).
10. Spencer Joshua Alwyne Compton (1790–1851), 2nd Marquis of Northampton, was President of the Geological Society and (1838–48) President of the Royal Society. A minor poet, he assembled a miscellany of verse, *The Tribute* (1837), which included, as well as some of his own poetry, contributions by many of the foremost poets of the day, such as Wordsworth. RB attended at least one of Lord Northampton's soirées (see letter to EBB, 20 February 1846).
11. In an article entitled "Modern English Poetesses" in *The Quarterly Review* (no. 66, September 1840, pp. 382–389), John Gibson Lockhart (1794–1854), the editor, spoke of EBB's being "too dogmatic in her criticism ... too positive in her philosophy" and lacking "that clearness, truth, and proportion, which are essential to beauty" (for the full text of his comments, see vol. 4, pp. 413–416).

12. In *The Monthly Chronicle* for November 1840 (p. 480), Horne contributed a 19-line poem "To the Greek Valerian; or, Ladder to Heaven. Addressed to Elizabeth B. Barrett, on the inadequate notice of her Poems in the last Number of the Quarterly Review." A footnote qualifies his comment: "Inadequate, except in conferring upon her the above most appropriate title."
 13. Cf. *The Tempest*, I, 2, 298.
 14. EBB refers, of course, to the trauma of Bro's death.
 15. Chorley contributed both literary and musical reviews to *The Athenæum*, but EBB felt that his primary interest was in music and that his remarks were kinder to musicians than to writers.

830. EBB to George Goodin Moulton-Barrett

[Torquay]
July 20, 1841

Dearest dearest Georgie,

I dont promise faithfully to fill you this goblet up to the brim[1]—but my own little half pint sheets have all, I find, been put into the post at different times & nothing is left to me but to "speak small"[2] on a large surface. Dearest George, I meant & meant again, to write to you before. Two or three letters of yours have witnessed to your thoughts of me, while mine of you said nothing. Mine of you, *were* nevertheless. I have been whetting my patience upon silence—or rather muffling my *im*patience in my silence—for that is the right metaphor after all. And then I felt smitten in conscience about having vexed Papa,—& made a deep vow at the moment, not to say a word more directly or indirectly .. not even if it became clear, as I half feared it might do, that I was'nt to go at all. I w^d rather stay, than really vex him—and particularly if, as depended more on my own resolve, I got everybody away, except myself & Crow.

But however, Papa said something yesterday about the present fine weather being open to the experiment—& that sounds as if he had not given me up. George, you are a very violent tempestuous person!– First, you look fierce at me for my impatience,—& then at others for their dilatariness [sic]!– No– No!– Georgie!– There is no unkindness *ever*, & least, now– It w^d have been better for me (that is my immoveable impression) to have performed this journey some weeks ago—better in several ways—but others did not account it so, or I sh^d have gone. And then—delay—delay—delay!– The sum about the snail is the "full sum of us".[3] We cant go on at all without stopping short– Our lagging is a part of our progression. And nobody knows *quite* (not even you, George!) the degree & detail of the repulsion with which this place acts upon me, whenever my mind is left, as all minds, however their will-organs may sternly turn them into abstracting occupations, must be sometimes, to the full influence of the locality.

Well—but never mind!— It will end, I dare say now, in our going. Papa's expression in last Sunday's letter certainly seems, as if even he thought the time for action had arrived—or was near—although, by the way, he says not a syllable of decision on the point of our destination. May God bless you all,—& grant the blessing to me of seeing you well, when I do see you,—well, and open to the pleasantnesses of life. Now I sh^d like to know (but without hoping that you will tell me!) if you meet gracious attorneys & take from their smiles any business at all. My fear is, that you look out over the hills, up to the present moment, for prosperity. But I dont fear what is behind the hills— No—not in any measure. A strong will, such as yours, will carry a city. You know my doxy— And Miss Mitford, by a letter I had from her some days ago, extends it into a paradox—holding that *strong wishes fulfil themselves*. Ah! *that* is not true! or the earth w^d be one or two shades lighter. But if it sH^D be true Georgie, why you have only to "put to" my strong wishes for you to your strong will for yourself, and the two teams will take you up a mountain as steep as the Jungfrau.[4] I do love you, my dear dear George!—

I dont deny my "hankering for Wimpole Street." If I did .. [']'Thou liest, thou liest, thou little foot-page",[5] might be said to this page. But honestly, sincerely, I am ready with a full heart of content, for any place *very near London*. I sh^d be quite content with Reading—Reading being only half an hour off Marylebone. Or I sh^d like Twickenham or Windsor. The choice however, is very properly & very *pleasantly* (for I dont want to choose) out of my own hands.

Dear Miss Mitford is very anxious for Reading—and then I c^d write an "and", and then a "but". The truth is, I shrink from the thought of looking upon anybody except yourselves—even upon such as I love. Well—no more of the going away.

Arabel gave a rural entertainment yesterday to the school—in a meadow at Upton—Henrietta very wonderfully wrath about it, I cannot make out why. Tea & cake & a run in the grass—were the head & front of the offending. She w^d.nt go—or—. I was vexed a little I confess—but say nothing of this. A person may be as High Church as one steeple upon another, & yet care for the innocent enjoyment of poor children. Which is my 'end of controversy'—

Do you hear of the business in London at Moxon's?—how Miss Sedgewick who was here you remember, two years ago, & received with open arms & kisses on each cheek by all the literati, (they never once suspecting "The deil, amang them taking notes",[6]) put everything down about their eyes & noses & other humanities & sent it to the printer's—and how M.[r] Kenyon surprised these interesting proof sheets at Moxon's half an hour previous to the publication, & after reading therein what a delightful person he was in particular, presumed upon the fair author's good opinion of himself to become her corrector of the press, & positively & then & there *cancelled* the things which appeared to him objectionable! He said he had "a moral right" to do it, and wrote this distinct opinion to America, to Miss Sedgewick. What is your thought? Is the moral right the legal? Was he justified *either* way? I doubt stedfastly. I am very sorry for the "altogether" about it. Miss Mitford wrote me a letter full of just indignation, at the wrongs perpetrated against her by the authoress— whom she had received as her friend, & who took advantage of opportunities so derived, to ask questions & take answers from the maid-servant where with to illuminate the new world. With all my love for literary gossipping, this is too much. It is a littleness—if not a baseness—a treachery, *in small*.

But, on the other hand, I am astonished at M.[r] Kenyon's dagger scene at Moxon's! Think of the consequence, if everyone who pleased, walked into a publisher's shop, and cut down every writer's proof sheets to the measure of his own opinions! It w^{dnt} do—w^d it?

Tell me–

Oh such a hurry. No time to read over– God bless you ever–

Your ever & ever attached

Ba

Address: G. G. Barrett Esq.[r] / On the Circuit / Stafford.
Publication: B-GB, pp. 63–67.
Manuscript: Pierpont Morgan Library.

1. A reference to the size of the pages (8vo) on which she was writing.
2. Cf. *The Merry Wives of Windsor*, I, 1, 48.
3. Cf. *The Merchant of Venice*, III, 2, 157.
4. The mountain, 13,667 ft. high, 10 miles S.E. of Interlaken in Switzerland.
5. Taken to be a reference to the "lying page" in stanza XLII of "The Romaunt of the Page."
6. A play on Burns's "A chield's amang you takin' notes, / And faith he'll prent it" ("On the Late Captain Grose's Peregrinations Thro' Scotland," 1793). EBB refers, of course, to the furor occasioned by Miss Sedgwick's *Letters from Abroad*.

831. EBB TO RICHARD HENGIST HORNE

[Torquay]
July 24. 1841

There was a blank, dear M.[r] Horne, in your last note, when you ought to have said something about the cough. I hope the silence meant that you had quite forgotten all the cutting up & boiling—the whole process of

No. 831 24 July 1841

your "rejuvenescence"—& that your present suffering is concentrated in the Parliamentary reports. They are enough at a time, certainly. Why Napoleon was better!–

It is an atrocious system altogether, the system established in this England of ours—wherein no river finds its own level but is forced into leaden pipes, up or down—her fools lifted into chairs of state, her wise-men waiting behind them—& her poets made Cinderellas off [*sic*] & promoted into accurate counters of pots & pans. We need not wonder at the elections.[1] *Everything* is rotten in the state of Denmark–[2]

Have you seen Miss Sedgewick's book, & heard the great tempest it has stirred up around you in London,[3] without a Franklin to direct the lightening?[4] She was received from America two or three years since by certain societies with open arms—none ever suspecting her to be "the deil amang them takin' notes".[5] The revelation was dreadful– My friend & cousin Mr Kenyon,—admitted to be one of the most brilliant conversers in London,—fell upon the proof sheets accidentally, just half an hour previous to their publication, and finding them sown thick with personalities side by side with praises of his own agreeable wit, took courage & a pen & "cleansed the premises".[6] Afterwards he wrote across the Atlantic to explain "the moral right" he had to his deed. For my own part, strongly as I feel the *saliency* of Miss Sedgewick[']s fault (it struck repeatedly & ungratefully against dear Miss Mitford who had bestowed some cordial attentions upon her sister authoress, & less as an authoress— so she tells me—than as a friend) I am not quite clear about Mr Kenyon's "right." The act was .. *un peu fort*[7] .. in its heroism,—& probably his American admirer may not thank him as warmly as her victims do.

Not that I ever do or could join in the outcry against Boswell & his generation,[8] I like them too well. But there is a line—a limit .. to their communicativeness—& such as pass it, dirty their feet.

Thank you very very thankfully for wishing me away from this place. No—you "do not counsel madness" but the sanest wisdom. Nevertheless nothing is yet fixed. Perhaps I may hear more tomorrow when I shall hear from Papa. I always do on *Sundays*. I hope the cream passed the Bishop of London yesterday, on its way to Guido–[9]

Truly yours
E B Barrett.

Address: R H Horne Esqr / 36. New Broad Street. / City / London.
Publication: Lyle H. Kendall, Jr., *A Descriptive Catalogue of The W. L. Lewis Collection* (Fort Worth, 1970); pp. 6–7 (in part).
Manuscript: Pierpont Morgan Library and Texas Christian University.

1. A further reference to the implications of corruption in the electoral process (see letter 827, note 10).
2. Cf. *Hamlet*, I, 4, 90.

3. See letters 827, 828 and 830.
4. A reference to Benjamin Franklin's invention in 1752 of the lightning rod.
5. An adaptation of Burns's line (see letter 830, note 6).
6. Probably an allusion to the cleaning of the Augean stables, one of the labours of Hercules.
7. "A little too much."
8. A reference to James Boswell (1740–95) and his ilk, who committed their subjects to print "warts and all."
9. The significance of this remark eludes us.

832. EBB TO MARY RUSSELL MITFORD

[Torquay]
July 25. 1841

My kindest, ever beloved friend,

I understand, I acknowledge, I love all your love. It was only *you*. And yet I thank you as if it were more than you! The frankness & truthfulness of it are so dear to me, that I say once more, .. Ever be so with me, my beloved friend, and do not suffer a reserve to deprive me of an advantage.

I have sent for the book[1]—that is, I have asked Papa to send it to me directly—*without* telling him the 'because'. Of all particularly particular people he is chief; and I sh^d not like for obvious reasons, to startle him in his particularity by what may prove, as I hope & believe it will, the shadow of a silence, the negative of a negative & to be treated negatively. If it sh^{dnt} .. why what shall I do? How difficult, yet how necessary, to retreat from this poetic alliance—which has been so long pending—& the papers preparatory to which, are actually prepared!–How shall I get up a 'caprice' dramatically, & not ungratefully?– Well—it is my own fault as my vexation!

I see too that you think the John Bull-Fraser-people may say all sorts of disagreeable things, even if the black book turn out a Biblical commentary. But then, sh^d we mind it? Mr Horne means to say in the preface[2] (so he wrote to me once) that the work is the joint production of two persons *who had never seen each other*. Now if he said so, nobody w^d have the power to dissert upon our degree of forgone intimacy—w^d they?–

After all, as I told you before, the whole thing if left to itself, may & probably will, break like a bubble. I said to him some time ago, that if his delays were so abundant, it w^d take several generations of people like me, to work with him to the end of Psyche. He is overwhelmed with business of various kinds– That work of Tyas's, the history of Napoleon, is his you know—besides the preliminary Essay to Schlegel—besides some Mexican directorship³—besides, oh I cant tell you what!–

Yes—the disadvantage is to *me*. I shall say afterwards—'Tout est perdu hormis l'honneur.'⁴ There is honor to my own *consciousness* in working with him, but when we have both done, everybody will ascribe the weak parts of the performance to *my* responsibility, & all the good to my coadjutor's. When a man & a woman write together, it's almost always so—to say nothing of poetic degrees– But this I sh.ᵈ not mind. The critics could never mortify me out of heart—because I love poetry for its own sake,—and, tho' with no stoicism & some ambition, care more for my poems than for my poetic reputation.

Does it sound vain?—or will you understand the plain verity of it? Indifference to golden opinions, even when not *yours*, even when not associated with love, is not philosophy for me—or rather I am not a philosopher for it! Not even now, .. when the green leaves have fallen from my tree. But I mean that revelations of the beautiful are reward enough for the desiring. Let those sit, who please, among the laurels—as long as I catch sight of the Egeria!–⁵

And this, bringing me to Leigh Hunt, reminds me that I do not wholly agree with you in regard to him. I think he has been wronged by many,—& that even you, your own just truthful & appreciating self, do not choose soft words enough to suit his case. For instance—it never was proved either to my reason or my feelings that *Rimini* had an immoral tendency.⁶ Indeed my belief is exactly the reverse. The final impression of that poem, most beautiful surely as a poem, appears to me morally unexceptionable. The 'poetical justice'⁷ is worked out too from the *sin itself*,—& not from a cause independent of it,—after the fashion of those pseudo moralists who place the serpent's sting anywhere but in the serpent. We are made to feel & see that apart from the discovery, apart from the husband's vengeance on the lover, both sinners are miserable & one must die. *She* was dying, without that blow– The sin involved the death-agony!– Who can read these things tearless, & without a deep enforced sense of [']'the sinfulness of sin"?⁸

. I admit that there are here & elsewhere, descriptions too glowing: sometimes perhaps but very seldom (—I believe *very* seldom ..) expressions less delicate than might be chosen– But comparing Parisina⁹ & Rimini, what is the conclusion? Or comparing Moore's early, yes, & later performances with Hunt's collected poems, what is the conclusion? Why to my mind Hunt sings like a seraph beside Moore!– Yet *he*, born beneath a bright star is looked upon brightly– It is "respectable" & something better to be the friend of Moore!

The Examiner under the Hunts,[10] came a step before me—but I have here, in the house, a volume of his collected poems—the effect of which, to judge from my own pulses, is for beauty & for good. Now I sh^d like to lecture you out of that book! My text book sh^d make amends for my impudence!– I w^d begin with the verses to his sick child

> "Sleep breathes at last from out thee
> My little patient boy—"[11]

I w^d dare you to read *that* without a tear! & then again as a prose gossipping essayist—his delightful Indicator!–[12] Oh I plead for Leigh Hunt. He has been very unfortunate, & very imprudent as to money affairs—but it is the way of poets, as a race,—and we c^{dnt} be very hard upon him for wasting too much money (one story went so!) upon a stair-carpet,—could we—should we, dearest Miss Mitford?– Now how I *am* teazing you.

Thank God for the escape, my beloved friend—the *second* escape within so short a time!– The thought of that flame mounting & burning, made me tremble almost like your Flush![13] Do tell me that you are really none the worse for the fright. Such frights do not do good—although *your* mind is comparatively safe, in the sevenfold wrapping of care for others.

How sorry I am for poor Miss Martineau! Dying with her intellect in her hand—wielding it to the last, bravely!– The very fortitude makes us shrink a little. I have not seen her last work.[14]

But if an operation be possible, will she not endure it?– May there not be a hope?–

Thank you for your delightful letters! Thank you for the "royal gossip"– *They* do not need a royal gossip or a gossip royal of any sort to be delightful—to be three times welcome—to be my fairy gifts of sunshine for the hour on which they fall! A word about the garden—about Flush,—how it beams & makes me glad! Still the long Windsor letter had its charm. I sate down with you & Miss Skennet in the Monkey heat, & saw the queen & the queen's baby, & the prime minister musing in a scene to himself!–[15] I enjoyed it all—& wont deny my entertainment,— for all your "fishing" questions with large hooks!–

Seriously—gravely, gratefully, I feel deeply my dearest kindest friend how many golden guineas of time I cost your dear kindness. I give them back to you in more golden affection—but my hand strikes against your gift in *that* kind also, & I find myself still your debtor.

And so let it be!– There is a tender pleasure, you shall not grudge me, in remaining

Your indebted as attached
E B Barrett–

Oh I hope I may know Ben some time. Will you tell him, that I hope to know him & to ask him whether Flush is better or worse for my company!– Everybody admires Flush—& in my private opinion, he grows prettier & prettier every day,—although as Ben says, the beauty is quite secondary. I sometimes comb his glossy golden ears myself—but I always think *that*. His intelligence is a wonderful thing– But there is such a noise again. They are letting off fireworks!– I cant write any more—my tales of Flush must be for another day & letter.

There has been the dreadful regatta today—& through shut windows & close-drawn curtains I could'nt help hearing the cannons firing & the people shouting! It has been so painful—so hard to bear![16] And I hoping all was over, took up this letter to turn aside my thoughts from the morning's sadness. This house is the lowest down on the beach, of all! W^d we were gone!——

God bless you! I knew your sympathy before you uttered it.

Ever yours.

Address: Miss Mitford / Three Mile Cross / Near Reading.
Publication: EBB-MRM, I, 244–248.
Manuscript: Folger Shakespeare Library, Edward R. Moulton-Barrett, and Wellesley College.

1. Horne's *Exposition of the False Medium*, mentioned in letter 829. EBB's copy formed lot 766 of *Browning Collections* (see *Reconstruction*, A1248).
2. To "Psyche Apocalypté."
3. Robert Tyas, of 50 Cheapside, was publishing *Tyas's Illustrated History of Napoleon* in parts, the first two having been announced in May 1839, with text by Horne. *The Spectator* (no. 557, 2 March 1839, p. 211) said it was "clearly and concisely written, in a vigorous and racy style, combining anecdotical liveliness of narration with compression of facts." Horne had also contributed the introduction to *A Course of Lectures on Dramatic Art and Literature* (1840), by August Wilhelm von Schlegel, translated by John Black (1783–1855), author and editor of *The Morning Chronicle*. Details of Horne's Mexican directorship are not known, but it was presumably a result of his visit to Mexico in 1825.
4. "All is lost but honour"; said by François I (1508–65) after the French forces were defeated at the Battle of Pavia in 1525. Dryden used the phrase in connection with King Charles's defeat at the Battle of Worcester in *Astræa Redux* (1660), line 74.
5. The nymph Egeria gave advice to Numa Pompilius, King of Rome; hence her name has come to signify a woman counsellor.
6. Hunt's *The Story of Rimini* (1816) was based on Dante's tale of Francesca's adulterous love for Paolo. *Blackwood's Edinburgh Magazine* (October 1817) said that "The story of Rimini is not wholly undeserving of praise ... But such is the wretched taste in which the greater part of the work is executed, that most certainly no man who reads it once will ever be able to prevail upon himself to read it again.... [Mr. Hunt's] works exhibit no reverence either for God or man." After speaking of "those glittering and rancid obscenities which float on the surface of Mr Hunt's Hippocrene" the writer observed that "The author has voluntarily chosen a subject ... in which his mind seems absolutely to gloat over all the details of adultery and incest" (pp. 38–40).
7. Cf. Pope, *The Dunciad*, I, 1, 52.
8. "Jesus, If Still Thou Art Today" (line 32), by John Wesley (1703–91).
9. Byron's *Parisina* (1816) tells of Parisina's incestuous love for her husband's illegitimate son and of his consequent execution.

10. Leigh Hunt, with his brother John (1775-1848), established *The Examiner* in 1808 and both remained associated with it until 1821. They espoused liberal causes and were frequently in trouble with the authorities for their outspokenness; both were imprisoned for two years after being found guilty of libelling the Prince Regent.
    11. EBB had previously quoted these lines (to Thornton Leigh Hunt at age six) in letter 737.
    12. *The Indicator*, a non-political magazine, was founded and edited by Leigh Hunt in 1819; it ceased publication in 1821.
    13. Writing to William Harness on 22 July 1841, Miss Mitford told him how "two nights ago I was writing with a low candle by the side of the desk when the frill of my nightcap . . . took fire. . . . I flung myself upon the ground and extinguished it with the hearth-rug; frightening nobody except poor dear little Flush, who was asleep on my father's chair . . . My head was a good deal scorched" (L'Estrange (2), III, 123-124).
    14. Miss Martineau had just finished "Feats on the Fiords," the third volume of *The Playfellow*, and was engaged with "The Crofton Boys," the last volume, which, she later said, "was written under the belief that it was my last word through the press" (Chapman, II, 169).
    15. EBB has again misread Miss Mitford's writing, taking "Skennet" for "Skerret," the name of the Queen's Dresser. Victoria Adelaide, the Princess Royal, had been born on 21 November 1840. The current Prime Minister was Victoria's favourite, Lord Melbourne. The reference to "Monkey heat" is not clear; it may have to do with a summer outing to Monkey Island on the Thames, not far from Windsor.
    16. These activities would have brought painful memories of Bro's death, just over a year before.

833. EBB TO GEORGE GOODIN MOULTON-BARRETT

[Torquay]
July 25. 1841

Ever dearest George,
    I squeeze myself in, you see, out of my turn, & intent to write to you again. The usual letter came yesterday (my first thought must be my first word) but with no decision in it!– Indeed Papa says justly that the weather was miserable all last week—only taking no note of the brightness of the saturday on which he wrote—that is, if the saturdays here & there wear the same aspect. Here, we have had one two & three days full of sunshine & warmth– Something must surely be decided soon– The weather refuses to hold up the train of a delay, an hour longer!–
    Dearest Georgie, why dont we hear from you. It seems almost strange that we dont. I begin sometimes to think about the rail roads. Write, dearest George,—if but a line with a pencil under the bower of your wig!–
    They are well in Wimpole Street—and here we are well too– For myself I gather strength,—get daily to the sofa, & *sit up on it*. Dr Scully has not seen me these three days. But what's the use of it, if I stay on, wait on, in this dreary way? Well—there is not a remedy!– I cant vex Papa again, or have him vexed!– He will decide presently . . I hope still!–

From what he says, there has just arrived a bad, or worse than bad, account of the West Indian crops,—very bad indeed it seems to be. He hopes to pay the expenses of cultivation—but fears for his Statira[1] who cannot be properly laden– Altogether he felt too annoyed, he said, to go on writing.

Did anybody tell you (while we are on commercial matters) that the Newton bank had broken,[2] & that poor Dr Scully among others yet poorer, was a sufferer by six hundred & fifty pounds?–

Stormie, kind fellow, gave me Blanchard's Life of LEL, the other day,[3] which though a wrong thing to do, was a thing I c^d not choose but suffer gratefully. It is a dreary melancholy book—by no means satisfactory, in touching either upon her life or death. I sh^d like to hear you talk legally upon the evidence & the witnesses connected with the latter's dark mystery, and leap at some conclusion for me. And then the biographer is parsimonious of her letters,—which always tell a story of life better, than the best abstract of it, elaborated by the cold hands of another.

I shall like to introduce Flush to you, Georgie, when we see each other—Mr Flush as they sometimes call him. He is such a companion to me all day long—lying close beside me—& when I move to the sofa, leaping there, beside me still, and always marking his sense of the change of place, by kissing me in a dog-way, most expressively. If Crow tells him to "go to Miss Barrett" in any part of the house—indeed she tried it this morning from the outside of the house—up he comes leaping & dancing & shaking the handle of my door. A sort of dog, George, to whom you could'nt reasonably refuse the franchise, in the case of any liberal extension of it. He understands almost every word you say! I like him to be beside me! It does'nt do anybody any harm.

Arabel's rural entertainment to the school children answered very well—so everybody said—and they made delightful tea in kettles, upon a foundation of sugar & cream—or milk I think it was. Crow went—and I had my tea at four oclock instead of six on purpose not to cross their purposes.

Henrietta goes out indefatigably—quite wonderfully to me!—day after day, week after week—the consequence of course being, that when she falls back upon *only us*, we are found hard & dry. Stormie stands on the remote pole—refusing to leave the house, even for the purpose of worship. He is just as he was, dearest George,—just, altho' I had hoped differently!—*just*,—except in a greater freedom & tendency towards conversation. With us, he talks continually & very cheerfully—I hear him talking for hours together through the wall. But I do wish the other wall of insuperable shyness c^d be thrown down or blown down—or at the very least w^d admit a window.

God bless you—ever & ever

Your most attached
Ba

Address: George Goodin Barrett Esqr / On the circuit / Hereford.
Publication: B-GB, pp. 71–74.
Manuscript: Pierpont Morgan Library.

1. Named after the wife of Alexander the Great, this was described by EBB as "Papa's own ship" in a letter of 1 September 1844 to Miss Mitford; we believe, however, that Edward Moulton-Barrett was a major share-holder in, rather than the sole owner of, the ship.
2. Newton Abbot, 6 m. N.W. of Taunton.
3. This volume formed part of lot 813 of *Browning Collections* (see *Reconstruction*, A257).

---

834. EBB TO MARY RUSSELL MITFORD

[Torquay]
July 26. 1841

My beloved friend,

I have seen the Literary Gazette,[1] and cannot help telling you the whole truth of my thought in regard to Miss Sedgewick's memoires pour servir–![2]

Well then!– I really do think that some BAD TASTE constitutes the head & front of the offending—that she meant all reverence to you, even while she counted upon her fingers your men-servants & maid servants,— & that the *general* impression of what she has said must be felt to be pleasing, among those who admire & love you most.[3] She is evidently not a person abounding in refinement & delicacy—and as evidently, of warm feeling turned warmly towards you. Forgive her my dearest friend! And just smile at what you shrank from at first. Dr Mitford takes my side, I see, for "he laughed" long ago!--She sent you the book– To be sure she did!– It never entered into her dreams that you c.^d be vexed by one word in it,—that you c.^d take these details any other way than as proofs of the high estimation & deep interest in which you are held, not simply by herself & her family, but by that great new world whose large listening ears stand erect to hear all about you, through Niagara!–

I am at once surprised & relieved by this Literary Gazette revelation— feeling absolutely certain that no human being c.^d look with uncharmed eyes or irreverent thought at this little picture of you & yours—whatever coarse Dutch lines be in it.[4] The sin of them (if *sin* be not too stern a word—& indeed my dearest friend, it is!–) & the shame of the sin, both together rest with the artist & not the subject. It is natural that you sh.^d

be sensitive. It is natural that I^5 sh^d be so, if the least shadow of a shadow fell upon you the wrong way—even to the injury of your *picturesqueness*. But I have read this paragraph scrutinizingly & jealously—& I dont feel sensitive any more— Do not *you*, dearest Miss Mitford—do not *you*! And as to the Duke of Bedford——why I will just tell you what my physician Dr Scully, an intelligent sensible man though no man of letters, said the other day, when I was talking over the Athenæum article with him. He began the subject,—& of course I did not enter into detail with him upon it. But I said that you, with other of Miss Sedgewick's victims had been vexed, by her giving you to the public piece meal,—& leaving the same public to suppose that she had everything from authority—that you (for instance) had said to her .. "Here am I, a near relation of the Duke of Bedford besides being so & so, doing such & such things for my father"! He smiled & answered instantly—"No, Miss Barrett. Nobody c^d say such a thing!— It is obvious to everybody that the Duke of Bedford is more likely to boast of being related to Miss Mitford, than Miss Mitford of being related to *him*".[6]

And that is the obvious truth! It quite amused me while I read your fear upon that especial point. And although I am (they say) a republican, & take republican measure of such things, people who live under a monarchy w^d agree with me to an inch. The honor, as Dr Scully said, is all the Duke of Bedford's.

I fear there are worse sins in this book than the one against you. It is apprehended that she may have endangered the safety of the Italian patriots, by her unreserved communications—!!—[7]

After all, was dear Mr Kenyon justified in the active thrust of his heroic dagger? Because do you know, I cannot at all think so.[8]

Proof sheets are private papers—are they not?—

The bride-cake simile is admirable[9]—too good!— I wish it were not so good!— For I have a true regard for *him*—

Ever your most affectionate
EBB—

Do give my love to Dr Mitford—& say particularly how you both are—& .. that you are not angry with me for not being angry enough with poor Miss Sedgewick!—

Publication: EBB-MRM, I, 249–251.
Manuscript: Wellesley College.

1. *The Literary Gazette* of 10 July 1841 (no. 1277, pp. 433–436) contained a review, with extensive extracts, of *Letters from Abroad to Kindred at Home* by Catharine Maria Sedgwick.

2. Literally "recollections to be of service"; in view of EBB's indignation at Miss Sedgwick's remarks about Miss Mitford, it is obvious that some derogatory slant is intended, suggesting "ingratiating" or "self-serving."

3. Miss Mitford had probably taken exception to Miss Sedgwick's having discussed her in regard to the coachman, who "professed an acquaintance of some twenty years' standing with Miss M., and assured us that she was one of the 'cleverest women in England,' and 'the Doctor,' (her father) 'an 'earty old boy.' And when he reined his horses up to her door, and she appeared to receive us, he said, 'Now you would not take that little body there for the great author, would you?'" After describing Miss Mitford as "dressed a little quaintly" with "hair as white as snow," Miss Sedgwick spoke of a voice with "a sweet low tone" and a manner of "naturalness, frankness, and affectionateness." Later, Miss Sedgwick recounted that Miss Mitford "keeps two men-servants (one a gardener), two or three maid-servants, and two horses. In this very humble home ... she receives on equal terms the best in the land."

4. Taken to be a reference to the exactness of detail and truthfulness that characterized the Dutch School of painters.

5. Underscored twice.

6. The book was also reviewed in *The Athenæum* of 10 July (no. 715, pp. 516–518), again with copious extracts, although those referring to Miss Mitford were considerably shorter than those in *The Literary Gazette*, making no reference to the number of her servants or to the remarks of the coachman.

The Athenæum made no reference to the Duke of Bedford, but the *Gazette* had said (p. 435): "Her literary reputation might have gained for her this elevation, but she started on vantage-ground, being allied by blood to the Duke of Bedford's family" (i.e., the Russells). The connection was through Miss Mitford's maternal grandfather, Dr. Richard Russell, Vicar of Overton and Ash, a descendant of one of the collateral branches, but we have been unable to establish the exact degree of kinship with the Duke.

7. In the second volume, Miss Sedgwick refers (p. 65) to a visit paid to "Madame T." and mentions this lady speaking freely of forbidden topics and of "the petty and irritating annoyances" suffered under Austrian rule.

8. Despite Kenyon's desire to protect friends from Miss Sedgwick's revealing scrutiny, EBB obviously disapproves of his self-imposed task of censorship (see letter 830).

9. Miss Mitford's simile is lost to us; in the Roman wedding ceremony for the patrician class the bride cake, a mixture of flour, salt and water, was partaken of by the contracting parties in the presence of ten witnesses.

---

835. EBB TO MARY RUSSELL MITFORD

[Torquay]
[late July 1841][1]

Here is a train to my last letter. In writing to you my dearest friend, I always seem to have an *arriere pensèe*,[2] if not two or three,—and this time it's of the Life of poor LEL. I *have* read it & fancied I had told you so,[3]—& certainly agree with you in all you say of it. Yes! those dates do clash in discordant accordancy, & *not* to the tune of

'Tis good to be off with the old love' &c[.][4]

On the contrary old & new loves are shuffled together. And what struck me especially is, that, rejecting one man whom she seemed to love, lest the shadow of her cloud sh^d fall upon him, she sh^d marry another directly under precisely the same circumstances & without the slightest misgiving.[5] How comes that inconsistency to be? Either the compliment to M^r

Maclean wears a strange aspect—as if he were not *Cæsar*![6]—or the generosity of the first rejection sh[d] be called by another name– There are in fact contradictions all over the book– Too much is said—or not enough: and *I* think, not enough. I sh[d] have liked to see more letters, her own letters, both to men & women. M[r] Blanchard presses in his words where we want hers, & his commentaries & explanations where we want none at all. It is an interesting painful book. The fatal point was, .. she believed that great lie, *that poetry is fiction*—and it was fatal to her not merely as a poet but as a woman. It is a creed desecrative of the soul, & of nature, & of 'supernal spirits['].[7] The ruin of it, extends beyond literature.

I observed the manner———

So far I wrote yesterday, was interrupted, & now cant the least in the world remember what manner I observed! Never mind. Probably you have'nt lost much philosophy after all.

She had, poor thing, many sensible critics who exhorted her loudly. Not so much love, they said! Not so much melancholy!– Not so much partridge!—or rather, not so constantly, toujours *tourterelle*![8] Now that sounded sensible enough of the critics, but it was superficial advice without roots to it, & scarcely deserved being taken. They sh[d] have said (with reverence be it spoken) "*Twice* as much love & melancholy, if you please,—only feel them—or wait till you do". There is no human passion & sentiment capable of being worn out in the writing of it. Nature is very deep. The misfortune was, it was'nt nature at all, .. & the passion was pasteboard from the first. Every word which this M[r] Blanchard has devised in order to sunder the identity of poet & woman, is a stroke at her fame.

Only one letter to her mother, & that of the coldest! There is a mystery somewhere. Indeed everywhere over the book, we are perplexed in the extreme.[9] Poor thing!—I wish you *had* been her friend!– I wish you had!– How the association w[d] have rescued her! Did you read the tragedy?[10] One might have guessed that her silken sentiments & dialect w[d] never fold into tragedy,—but I did not expect anything quite so weak. It's all blank—except *the verse!*–

No—she never w[d] have been tragic. But otherwise, she was rising into light & power & knowledge, when the death-stroke came. Some of those lyrics in M[r] Blanchard's second volume, are very beautiful—full of beauty– What "a lovely song" is that "A long while ago"!– The last cadence is in my ears now—

—"and I have felt them all
A long while ago!"[11]

Poor, poor, LEL!–

What you say, of the "calamities of authors" is sad with truth!–[12] But surely you sh[d] except Walter Scott from that mourning multitude.

As an author, he triumphed gloriously—from the first, to the last. The Seward coterie clapped their hands at his rising,—the Byronian school doffed their caps to him—the Lakers passed him reverently—the Cockneys (mind—I protest against the use of that word in using it!) did him honor.[13] Personally, no man mocked him. The martyrdom of genius was a *name* to him. He had a crown on his head, and a check in his pocket. He was the *shirra*[14] as well as the poet. Most happy he was in his family—most beloved & most blessed—blessed in their lives & loves. What was wanting in the destiny of this man!–

Surely, only that it sh^d last!–

Surely there was no darkness but in the closing scene,—and out of his faults arose that cloud. It was his ambition of landed proprietorship (a false pitiful thing!) which wrecked him[15]—his love of money & land!– Ld Byron with all his wrongs & his *sins*—& he had many of both—seems to me worth ten Walter Scotts, as a *man to be loved*. But you will quarrel with me for saying so!– *Dont*–

Mr Kenyon is expected every day, I hear. He will not, however, have his "hut," which is bought—to my pleasure.[16] What is there here, for *his*?– Mr Bezzi certainly–

You never wash your Flush. Well– Mine w^d be clean too, without washing, I dare say—only I sh^d scarcely fancy so, (when he creeps up in his usual irresistible way, & lays his head down on my pillow) if it were not for the precessory soap & water.

Do tell me how you are—do! I am so anxious– Did you ever try simple water-*gruel*, without sugar or salt? If you have not, will you? Dearly, dearly I love you. ⟨★★★⟩

Publication: EBB-MRM, I, 251–253.
Manuscript: Wellesley College.

1. Dated by EBB's comments on Blanchard's *Life of L.E.L.*
2. "Afterthought."
3. EBB's previous comments to Miss Mitford about Blanchard's book derived from extracts read in magazines; as letter 833 makes clear, EBB had only recently had access to the book itself.
4. *Songs of England and Scotland* (1835), II, 73, line 3 of "Song."
5. See letter 820.
6. Presumably a reference to the explanation given by Suetonius of Cæsar's divorcing Pompeia: "Cæsar's wife must be above suspicion."
7. *Paradise Lost*, VII, 573.
8. "Always the turtle-dove."
9. *Othello*, V, 2, 346.
10. Miss Landon's drama *Castruccio Castracani*, published in 1837 but never staged.
11. Blanchard's *Life of L.E.L.* (II, 256), slightly misquoted.
12. See letter 820.
13. i.e., the Lake poets and those of the Cockney School (see letter 737, notes 18 and 19).

14. Sheriff (of Selkirk).
15. EBB refers to the expense incurred by Scott in maintaining his Abbotsford estate; in fact, his "ambition" was to pay off, from the proceeds of his writings, the debts incurred when his publishing venture with John Ballantyne went bankrupt in 1826.
16. Kenyon had been contemplating buying a house in the Torquay area.

---

836. THOMAS CARLYLE TO RB

Newby, Annan, N.B.
29 july, 1841–

My dear Sir,

Lest you chance to have the trouble of a fruitless journey to Chelsea, and so be discouraged from coming back, I had as well apprise you straightway that your loyal-minded, welcome little Note finds me not there but here,—on the Scotch shore of the Solway Firth; I might say on the very beach, amid rough sea-grass and gravel; remote from all haunts of articulate-speaking men; conversing with a few sea-mews alone, with the ocean-tides and gray moaning winds! I have fled hither for a few weeks of utter solitude, donothingism and sea-bathing; such as promised to prove salutary for me in the mood I was getting into. London in the long-run would surely drive one mad, if it did not kill one first. Yearly it becomes more apparent to me that, as man "was not made to be alone,"[1] so he *was* made to be occasionally altogether alone,—or else a foolish sounding-board of a man, no *voice* in him, but only distracted and distracting multiplicities of echoes and hearsays; a very miserable and very foolish kind of object!

My Wife[2] is here too, with her maid; a wondrous little cabin of a "furnished cottage," built as if expressly for us, has been discovered here; a savage of the neighbourhood even takes charge of a horse; Annan a sufficient little Burgh stands but two miles off, and yet our place is lonely (owing to its ugliness), lonely as if it were on the coast of Madagascar;—a place altogether as if made for us! Thank God, there are still some places *ugly*, if that is the price of their loneliness!– We are to continue here for some four weeks yet; and do not count certainly on Cheyne Row again till the last hope of sunshine, perhaps in the end of September, have abandoned us for this year. Pray observe the date; and let us hope we may actually see you then.

The spirit you profess is of the best and truest: perhaps one man only, yourself only, could do much more for you than I who can do nothing, but only say with all my heart, Good speed! Doubt it not at all, you will prosper exactly according to your *true* quantity of effort,—and

I take it you already understand that among the "*true* quantities of effort" there are many, very many which the "public," reading or other, can simply know nothing of whatever, and must consider as falsities and idlenesses, if it did. But the everlasting Heart of Nature does know them, as I say; and will truly respond to them, if not today or tomorrow, then some day after tomorrow and for many and all coming days. Courage!

With much goodwill,

Yours very truly always
T. Carlyle

R. Browning Esqr

Address: R. Browning Esqr / New Cross, Hatcham, / Surrey.
Docket, in RB's hand: 29. July. '41.
Publication: Carlyle (1), I, 239–240.
Manuscript: Yale University.

1. Cf. Genesis, 2:18.
2. Jane Baillie Carlyle (*née* Welsh, 1801–66), whom Carlyle had married in 1826.

837. EBB TO MARY RUSSELL MITFORD

[Torquay]
[*Postmark:* 30 July 1841]

⟨★★★⟩ I had a kind note & some stanzas of much beauty from Mr Townsend yesterday, & a *visit from him today*. That is, he called at the door in passing through Torquay to Devonport. Very kind!– But of course I could'nt see him.[1]

Address: Miss Mitford / Three Mile Cross / near Reading.
Publication: EBB-MRM, I, 254 (as 31 July 1841).
Manuscript: Wellesley College.

1. These sentences are written on an envelope. It is possible that they form the missing conclusion of letter 835.

838. EBB TO RICHARD HENGIST HORNE

[Torquay]
August 4. 1841.

My dear Mr Horne,

I am so sorry to hear of the obstinacy of this cough of yours. Why do you not get away from London and keep moving about? Continual change of air, says Dr Scully,—my physician who says everything of that sort wisely,—is the *specific* for hooping cough at its advanced stage—that is, when it lingers as yours does. Surely you should not allow the winter months to surprise you coughing!– And surely (pardon my impertinence) it w^{dnt} be much harder to go round London in a circle, if it were only from village to village, previous to the settling down in chambers, than to settle immediately.

For my own part I am gasping still for a permission to move too—but Papa has gone suddenly into Herefordshire, and I am almost sure not to hear for a week. Some thing however must soon be determined,—& in the meantime, being tied hand & foot & gagged, I am wonderfully patient.

Did you hear of Mrs Orme's kind proposal about coming here? It was very kind—& I felt it so—even as an impossibility.

If you have no "vow in Heaven",[1] *never* to answer a question,—will you tell me whether the Monthly Chronicle is extinct, & why?[2]

Truly y^{rs}
EBB–

Address: R H Horne Esqr / 36. New Broad Street / City / London.
Publication: EBB-RHH, I, 31–33.
Manuscript: Pierpont Morgan Library.

1. Cf. *The Merchant of Venice*, IV, 1, 228.
2. *The Monthly Chronicle*, edited by Bulwer-Lytton and Robert Bell, ceased publication with the June 1841 issue. EBB comments in letter 842 on Horne's explanation of its demise.

---

839. EBB TO MARY RUSSELL MITFORD

[Torquay]
August 4. 1841

My beloved friend,

I have seen & read *the book*,[1]—and although perfectly understanding why any critic by profession w^d naturally look 'grave' upon it,[2] and even admitting myself that all the words of it are not scrupulously & wisely said, yet my conclusion remains .. that no plague-touch need be feared from its author. It is written by an enthusiast in the cause of genius upon the spectacle of its misery, lighted up to ghastliness by the torchlight of D'Israeli[3] & other memorialists. Its thunderbolts are hurled against all false media—such as interpose between men of genius & the public, in the form of *readers* for publishers & Theatrical managers, &c &c—which aforesaid thunderbolts do occasionally smell a little over much of sulphur. There is in fact, with much talent & power, a sufficiency of acrimony & indiscretion. Nothing & nobody escape. Universities, Royal academies,

Literary societies .. there is a sweep of scorn over all!– For my own part, after all .. notwithstanding my private reasons for weighing faithfully .. notwithstanding the sense forced upon me of the overweight of certain words—I did feel myself taken off my feet & carried along in the brave strong generous current of the spirit of the book– It is a fearless book, with fine thoughts on a stirring subject– I myself once, long ago, fancied & began to fashion a poem drawing near to the same subject—at least, recording the sorrows of poets—("The poets' record" was to be my name for it)[4] and D'Israeli's mournful tales were my incitement to it. The wrongs done & the sorrows suffered by men of genius (for whom genius itself seems to cut down & curtail of fair proportion the common sympathies of man to man, .. not always but very often) turn the whole heart into sickness. I forgive the book its indiscretion, with tears in my eyes. And that you may forgive it too, I must try to get it to you soon .. I must be satisfied with your opinion. Surely nobody but poor Southey's snow Lady,[5] need be afraid of approximation to the author of the book—I mean that no woman need, on the point of womanly delicacy, .. of moral delicacy .. be afraid. There is nothing in it touching womanly offices & conduct. Even women of genius (except Fanny Kemble, whose Francis the first & its fourteen editions are dismissed coldy & briefly .. ("a weak subject" he says "& weakly treated")[6] even women of genius pass silently,

⟨...⟩[7]

as I cannot write here. Dearest, "warmest of friends" ("that warmest of friends Miss Mitford" said M! Townsend to me!) may God bless you. If I c^d do anything for you in any way, so as to soften one of your cares, I sh^d feel it to be well worth the cost of many cares of mine. I wish I c^d have *such* cares!– Mine are selfish things. Yet I love you through them all.

M! Kenyon is not yet heard of—but if he comes while I am here, I will see him—but (an honest 'but') I hope he will not come while I am here. It is not prudery. It is faint-heartedness. I seem to shrink from people's faces & voices—& most of all *here*. Still it w^d not be altogether kind, to refuse seeing M! Kenyon—particularly when I can get to the sofa—& most particularly when you wish it. So I shall see him if he comes. And I shall hope to get away in time to be too late.

But our uncertainties continue: and to clench their character, I heard suddenly yesterday of Papa's having gone into Herefordshire for a few days!! What will become of me? My patience has dreadful chilblains from standing so long on a monument![8] To go away, without coming to a definite resolution, or sending a carriage for me!– Well—I *am* a little bit vexed—which proves how human *I* am, & *not* how human *he* is .. except in his love for me. I have not climbed so high in ingratitude, as to *complain* of the delay, the least bit! And everybody says that a few more days will see the solution of the problem. Indeed they *must*—Dr Scully beginning to talk of the unfitness of my setting out on a journey, *after* the tenth of September—, this being August!

In regard to places, I am blind too—as blind as Fortune[9]—or Misfortune. And I have been so afraid of annoying that dearest Papa of mine, that I have not asked him for very long to take off the bandage. Still, voices come to me from London—younger voices, which try to say what I may like to hear best—flattering apocryphal voices, which are not to be trusted. And *they* say "You are sure either to go to Reading or to London". But *I* say .. "I dare not believe them"—and I dare not.

I can walk very closely by your side (always a dear position) in the matter of these poets—but scarcely all the way. We think just alike of Moore, for instance—who w^d be a truer poet, if poetry were a bundle of fancies—as Hume thought the soul a bundle of ideas.[10] As it ⟨★★★⟩

Publication: EBB-MRM, I, 254–256.
Manuscript: Wellesley College.

1. *Exposition of the False Medium and Barriers Excluding Men of Genius from the Public* (1833). See letter 829.
2. A review of Horne's book by Christopher North (John Wilson) in *Blackwood's Edinburgh Magazine* (October 1833, pp. 440–468) castigated Horne: "He must, without delay, be drenched with drastics—purged within an inch of his life ... but all this will be of no avail, unless he be denied access to pen and ink."
3. Isaac D'Israeli (1766–1848), the father of Benjamin Disraeli, published *Curiosities of Literature* (1791–1834), *An Essay on the Literary Character* (1795), *Calamities of Authors* (1812–13) and *Quarrels of Authors* (1814).
4. EBB mentioned this project in 1831 (see *Diary*, p. 93). Three manuscripts exist at Wellesley (see *Reconstruction*, D733–735); one was published in *Anthony Munday and Other Essays*, ed. Eustace Conway (1927), pp. 105–111.
5. Laila, the daughter of Okba the sorcerer, had been sequestered in a snowy region as a protection, her only companions figures made of ice; see Southey's *Thalaba the Destroyer* (1801), bk. X.
6. Horne wrote (p. 48): "As to style, it is not poor or negative ... but inexcusably bad throughout. 'Francis the First' is an abortive attempt, because its chief character commences with the greatest pretensions of inherent power, and ends with the weakest compromise ... It was a weak subject, weakly treated, and passed through fourteen editions in a short time."
7. Pages of the manuscript missing.
8. Cf. *Twelfth Night*, II, 4, 114.
9. Cf. *Henry V*, III, 6, 32.
10. See "On the Immortality of the Soul" (1779).

840. EBB TO MARY RUSSELL MITFORD

[Torquay]
August 5. 1841

Now for Flush's turn .. after the poets!— And he may "side the gods"[1] as well as another.

I think I told you, I am sure I meant to do so, that pretty as he was when he came here first, he is prettier now and does indeed grow prettier & prettier every day. He is not merely fatter comparatively, but fat positively—& *how* we cant quite make out, for his appetite matches in delicacy a May Fair lady's at the close of the season. It is the milk, I suppose, that does it. He is fond of milk—& when any is brought to me in a cup he wont let me drink a whole half without a hint that the rest belongs to him. He waits till his turn comes, till he thinks it *is* come—and then if I loiter, as I do sometimes pretend to do, Mr Flush tries to take possession of the cup by main force. His ears which you were inclined to criticise are improved—grown thicker & longer, and fall beautifully in golden light over the darker brown of his head & body. He is much admired for beauty—particularly for that white breastplate which marks him even among dogs of his colour—Flush the silvershielded!—

But the beauty sh^d come last. I assure you that he does not in intellect & sensibility disgrace his high lineage!— I c^d tell you two or three volumes of wonderful stories upon either count. If I were another Scheherazade[2] I c^d save my head by talking of Flush.

What really astounds me sometimes is his intelligence of words—not of gesture, not of countenance but articulate words .. Whisper them in his ear & its the same. Crow says (*she* taught him, which accounts for the ceremony) "Go to Miss Barrett"—and up he rushes to my side in a moment. Nay—if she says so in another room or down stairs or even out of doors, straightway he is galloping to my door, & I hear him turning the handle after his fashion, not scratching dogwise, but turning & shaking the handle, in a way which suggested itself to his observation as the ordinary means of opening a door. Nobody taught him *that*—but he always does it—& the effect is curious. Then if you say to him "Kiss me Flush", he does it directly. "Lie down"—"Be quiet"—the action follows the phrase.

His greatest pleasure of all is to be taken out to walk—and when some of the walkers pass through my bedroom into one adjoining to put on their bonnets, you sh^d see Flush's eyes brighten as he leaps off my bed to investigate the subject & discover if really they are going. The sight of a head in a bonnet stirs him into an ecstasy. He dances and dances, & throws back his ears almost to his tail in Bacchic rapture. More than once he has lost his balance & fallen over. And then if after all, the cruel person in the bonnet sh^d say .. "No Flush! I cant take you today". Ah then is the change! Now dont think me romancing,—but at the utterance of those words, he stands still, suddenly still, looking up to the cruel eyes in visible consternation! He stands so, just a moment,—and then leaps up to me, & kisses my hands & face after his fashion, that I may intercede for him. Now I do assure you it is'nt romancing! He always does this. It is not once or twice—but always. I am his friend & take his part and spoil him—and in every disappointment & fright he always comes to me, that I may do my best for him. And if in the going out business, I can do nothing,—and the sentence is repeated "No Flush—you cant go out today" .. why then, Flush is a philosopher & lies down again by me & never tries even to follow the bonnet out of the room. Now is'nt it clever of Flush?

He is washed twice a week notwithstanding your threat of premature grey hairs. But what c^d I do? He insists upon lying close by me on the bed,—& we must as a consequence see to the ablutions. He hates them though,—& is only comforted afterwards, by being wrapt up in my shawl for the rest of the evening. I forgot to do it properly the other day. The shawl was there, & he was lying on it, but the wrapping up was not perfected—and Mr Flush did make such a fuss—licked my hand, & then bit & scratched at the shawl with tooth & paw, until my memory came back to me, & I covered him up all but the nose like a Turkish lady!

Crow says "he is as particular about his dinner as her Majesty." That is Crow's opinion. She often tells me—"Flush has scarcely touched his dinner today, because it was only *boiled mutton.*" He & she have been from the first most tender friends—and I am jealous sometimes. Yes, I do think that he is both most afraid of her & loves her most of any— You see, she has had a good deal to do with necessary parts of his education— has whipped him a little,——and played with him a good deal. I cant play with him as Crow can & does—and a game at ball or at romps generally, touches Flush's heart, next the cockles. How his eyes glisten whenever she comes into the room!– But he wont stay away from me even for her. He wont rest anywhere but by me. He considers this room to be between us, part mine & part his—& if the door is not opened to him directly, I hear him cry on the other side. In regard to the matter of courage I sh^d be sorry to shock Ben or to disgrace you, but certain it is that Flush was never born for a hero. Certainly he is not so bad as he was. For instance, he does not shiver much when he sees himself in the glass,—and, out of doors, he does not expect, upon meeting a dog or passing near a flock of geese, to be taken up & carried. We are braver than we were. But still—if a cat stands & stares at us, we retreat prudently—if it runs our way by accident however free of hostile intention, we cry out piteously—if a stranger tries to pat our pretty head, we shrink away, backwards or sidewards—we have not, in fact, reached the point of heroism.

But when everybody cries out "I never saw such a coward as that dog is," my apology for him is just this. It is the predominant sweetness & softness of his disposition which keeps him aloof from the "shadow before"[3] of 'wars alarms'.[4] He says to himself—"Now this may be the first step to a fight—and it being quite contrary to my principles & temper to fight, I shall beware of taking it". Flush has never, since he has been here, hurt any living thing or tried to hurt it—& he wont do so. Even the other day when that naughty boy Edwin[5] tied a live mouse by the tail to a chair's leg, & Flush's friend the kitten, yet too young to slay, was trying to beat it down with its paw, Flush stood by superior, close by, with eyes as large as four, looking Crow says "very much amused" but "never attempting to touch" the poor little victim himself. She cut the string & let it escape.

The friendship with the kitten continues fast as ever. It runs after him like a puppy—and he thinks nothing of carrying it up stairs in his mouth. Then he lies down, & suffers the little snowy thing to roll over him & play with his ears & thurst [sic] its paw into his mouth. There is love on both sides. But Flush has a passion besides, for young children & babies. So have I—and if ever one is carried in for me to look at, as happens now & then, he is in ecstasies—dancing round & round the room after the person carrying it,—& carressing it after his fashion most tenderly. When Arabel goes into a cottage & Flush is with her, he is by the cradleside in a moment, with his nose pushed under the bed-cloaths— till the poor mother comes to the rescue, in the natural belief that her baby is about to be eaten. It's just the same in the street. If he meets a nurse & baby, he forgets all strangership & dances round it, & pulls peradventure at its frock. A child sixteen months old came here the other day. He was delighted—w^{dnt} lie down—could'nt keep still a moment,— & made the poor child scream more than once with his fearful familiarities,—& won its heart at last by suffering it to feed him with breadbutter which he w^{dnt} take from any hand but just that little infantine hand. So there they settled down at last, his two paws upon her knee & his eyes on her face! No notice from Flush to anybody else as long as she stayed!- Even the kitten was neglected,—& took comfort by playing with his tail while he wagged it unconsciously-

The degree of his timidity may be measured by the fact, that although he delights beyond delight in going out to walk, he never attempts to do it by himself. He never attempts to go beyond a few yards from the door. Once indeed he was missed for an hour, & came home just at dinner time quite out of breath. I dont know how he was incited to this—but it happened some time ago, & he never has repeated it.

I fancy sometimes that he was used to be in your stables a good deal. Was it so? They tell me of his running up to all the horses he meets! He was not at first quite a Brahmin as to cleanliness[6]—a young dog & perhaps not kept strictly in the house .. was he?—but now (wh.^{ch} indeed was the case after the first week or two) he is faultless in this respect.

A letter sacred to Flush! Well—you asked me for his history, so must pardon the length of it. It's a post[s]cript to the letter yesterday.

Do let me hear how you are beloved friend! If many of my thoughts end in you, this of Flush *must*. How he makes me think of you! How every pleasure he gives me, is one drawn from you! How I love him *for your sake!*—which is the sure way of loving him dearly.

God bless you my beloved friend. There are faults of construction in Cosmo—but in Gregory[7] the constructive faculty seems to me strong. At the same time it might not do upon what we call the stage.

Again the post hour surprises me. Love to dear Dr Mitford. Now do say how you both are—particularly you. I am not easy yet about the effect of the fire.[8] You are shaken by it. Ah do take care of yourself my dearest friend!–

Ever your attached
EBB–

Is there any annual this year? Or are (which w.^{d} be so much better) the letters coming out?[9] Perhaps you are too occupied for either. *No Mr Kenyon.*

Address: Miss Mitford / Three Mile Cross / Near Reading.
Publication: EBB-MRM, I, 256–260.
Manuscript: Edward R. Moulton-Barrett and Wellesley College.

1. EBB may have had in mind Θεοι παρεδρος, "those sitting near the gods"; she had alluded to the phrase in *Diary*, p. 48.
2. The daughter of the Grand Vizier, who staved off death by recounting the 1,001 stories of *The Arabian Nights*.
3. Thomas Campbell, "Lochiel's Warning" (1802), line 56.
4. Thomas Hood, "Faithless Nelly Gray" (1826), line 2.
5. Edwin Hingson, at this time just a boy, remained in the Moulton-Barretts' service for a number of years; references to him in secondary material point to his being the senior male servant in the household at the time of EBB's father's death in 1857.
6. The Brahmins, a priestly order, formed the highest Hindu caste.
7. Horne's *Cosmo de' Medici* and *Gregory VII.*
8. Miss Mitford's accident the previous month (see letter 832, note 13).
9. Miss Mitford was not involved in the 1842 *Findens' Tableaux.* Her projected edition of correspondence with Sir William Elford (see letter 737, note 1) never materialized.

841. EBB TO MARY RUSSELL MITFORD

[Torquay]
August 9!ʰ [1841]¹

My beloved friend,

The pleasure with which I always put out my hand to clasp a letter of yours turned, today, soon indeed into pain. My dearest friend, you have been, you are still, very very unwell—& you are suffering in another besides! Do you exert yourself too much? Is the right care taken of a health so precious to more than yourself? Does Mʳ May come to see you?— Surely that remedy which costs so much as to appear a desease of itself, shᵈ not be recurred to without absolute necessity. Without much experience in the sort of thing, I wonder at & fear it. Did you ever try castor oil administered the same way? Its properties are healing you know,—free from the acrimony of salts,—however taken: & I do venture to conjecture that if a small quantity were administered after your own custom, you wᵈ suffer less & be freer from exhaustion than can be the case now. If you have not tried it in vain, will you?— Gruel is recommended sometimes, I know,—as being more active than water. But even that might not do. The oil surely wᵈ—

Do ask Mʳ May about it, my dearest friend. Of course you shᵈⁿᵗ trust such an ignoramus as I am—for with all my experimental philosophy on the subject of sickness, the kind of suffering which distresses you is not & never was mine. Indeed it sounds like a very peculiar case. But upon the face of it, lies the propriety of changing or modifying this terrible remedy. You ought to do it, indeed— And you go on, I do fear, week after week, suffering & suffering, & thinking, with all the suffering,— nothing at all in proportion to the real value of the thing lost, of the constitutional habit of good health you are losing. Let me hear how you are, by one word .. when it is not a strain upon your time to write it. God grant it may be a happy word for one who loves you as I do, to listen to!—

Here is your post[s]cript to Mʳ Kenyon back again!— No indeed,—I will not deliver it. He shall have the letter, & shall see me if he shᵈ wish it & I am able— No indeed!— I shᵈ seem even to myself, half unkind in refusing to see him. I almost fell under my own reproval for it last year, when I had better reasons on the side of my cowardice. If he comes before we go, I will unlock my iron mask² & put the iron on my heart & see him. As for your vexing me .. my dearest dearest friend, when did you do it—& how cᵈ you do it?— You never did such a thing in yʳ life as vexing *me*! In all that I have received from you, *that* one thing is wanting .. vexation!— Dearest Miss Mitford, what *did* I say to make you fancy it? Vex *me*! I must be a vexable person indeed to be vexed by your tenderness to me, & your sacrifice of time & kindness to please me—me—who by retaining few pleasures am not likely to fall into the fault of undervaluing those left! Do not *you* undervalue the grateful thoughts you cannot see. I love you far more than you know of!— But if I did'nt, how c^d I be vexed! There I come back to the key note of wonder.

Mr Kenyon is not here yet, & perhaps will not come until we go. I heard too from George & the circuit[3] this morning,—& he tells me of Papa's having returned to London & of his pondering my "*immediate*" removal from Torquay. George is diplomatic & does not say a word about localities. Those are left as usual to my imagination.

But hope may spring up again you see—Papa is in London—and I MAY be about to remove immediately.

In the meantime he has had a pleasant excursion in Wales, George says, & looks the better for it, & I am the better pleased.

Think of Mr Flush yesterday, refusing to drink his milk out of a soup plate— He w^{dnt} have it at all, except from a glass!— He'll want silver soon!— I hear Crow talking to him sometimes after this fashion— "Ah Flush!—sh^{dnt} you like to see *Aberleigh*[4] again!" She is an excellent young woman—intelligent bright-tempered & feeling-hearted,—more to me than a mere servant; since her heart works more than her hand in all she does for me! And her delight in your Village which I gave her to read, was as true a thing as ever was that of readers of higher degree. She says to me that if we go to Reading, she means to visit the Village, and will know every house in it just as if it were an old place to her!— Flush's love! I often make him kiss your letters—which he does readily, only fighting afterwards for a full possession!

Dont forget *the word* about yourself. I am anxious—& shall be, till I hear.

Yours in truest affection
EBB—

How glad I was to see the graceful stanzas in the Athenæum!—Lady Burlington's I mean!—[5]

Publication: EBB-MRM, I, 260–262.
Manuscript: Wellesley College.

1. Year provided by the reference to *The Athenæum*.
2. A reference to the man, imprisoned for more than 40 years by Louis XIV, immortalized by Dumas. He is now thought to have been Count Girolamo Mattioli.
3. Letter 833 was addressed to him on the Hereford Assize circuit.
4. A "little hamlet" in Miss Mitford's *Our Village*.
5. *The Athenæum* of 24 July 1841 (no. 717, p. 556) contained Miss Mitford's verses "On the Portrait of the Countess of Burlington, Painted after her Death by Mr. Lucas."

She was Blanche Georgiana (*née* Howard), daughter of the 6th Earl of Carlisle. Born on 11 January 1812, she married William Cavendish, 2nd Earl of Burlington, on 6 August 1829; she had died on 27 April 1840.

842. EBB TO RICHARD HENGIST HORNE

[Torquay]
August. 14. 1841

"I would not hear your enemy say so"[1] .. dear Mr Horne, .. that you were a bad correspondent, much less say so myself. You are a bad *catechumen*—& that's the worst of you—& I am sure it does'nt deserve a bad cough. Therefore if you receive a jar of tamarinds from the West Indies viâ Wimpole Street—and you *will*, in the case of Papa's having received any himself as he usually does—pray use them both as they are, & with hot water poured over them, & try if they relieve you at all. But the pilgrimage thro' the villages is the remedy. And dear Mr Horne, never mind Psyche. There is plenty of time for Psyche—in the future, if not now. She is persecuting you, *I fear*. *Remember*—when one is tied with cords, to struggle only strengthens the knots. Put Psyche away, out of thought for the present, and dont fancy that I (for one) am even inclined to be impatient about it. I shall not expect any more news of her for six months, from this fourteenth of August, eighteen hundred and forty one.

And so your angelic sin is so rampant that 'you'd be an Abbot,' (not a butterfly, despite of Psyche!) if you went into a monastery—an abbot of misrule[2]—unless St Cecilia who "drew the angel down"[3] did the like by your reverend desires!– Ah, when I was ten years old, I beat you all you & Napoleon & all, in ambition—but now I only want to get home.

Nevertheless I fear I do fear, the light words may be bubbles at the top—that it may be darker underneath. I know the secret of *that* you see!– And I fear that the hooping cough & pressure of business dont do blythely together, & that you are walking your imaginary cloisters with a graver, perhaps sadder step than should be– Can it be so? Is it so? The louder the call then to the villages. Neither cloisters nor graves are ready for you yet, nor you for them. So I do hope that "generally you dont think about" either. Whom sh^d we have for Dramatic professor in the great new Genius-establishment, where the moth will be sworn never to corrupt, & the thief never to steal?–[4] Whom, if you were away? If you were only an Abbot, or an organist, it w^d be different. Do remember that if you are not so tranquil as they, you are greater & to be valued more—*and valued more–*

So the Chronicle is gone—self slain because it w^{dnt} condescend to be lively.[5] There was power enough in it for three or four magazine-popularities—but the taste of caviare preponderated, & people turned away their heads. They said of it, as my own ears witness, "dull & heavy"– Then it was such a fatal mistake to keep back the *names*! I saw it to the last.

God bless you! I am going I think in the face of the weather, if it wont turn round.–

Truly yours
EBB

Address: R H Horne Esqr / 36, New Broad Street / City / London.
Publication: EBB-RHH, I, 33–36 (in part).
Manuscript: Pierpont Morgan Library.

1. Cf. Ezekiel, 36:2.
2. The Abbot (also Lord or King) of Misrule was the ancient director of Yuletide festivities.
3. St. Cecilia, who was blind, was the patroness of music and the supposed inventor of the organ. Legend recounts that an angel fell in love with her musical skill and descended from heaven to give her a crown of martyrdom.
4. Cf. Matthew, 6:19.
5. Its last number was published in June 1841.

---

843. EBB TO MARY RUSSELL MITFORD

[Torquay]
August 19– 1841

My ever & beloved friend,

Your letter distresses me. You seem to live under a star of accidents, as Mr Varley w^d put it[1]—and what is worse, since God's dear mercy has cut off the evil ends of these frightful chances, you are, I am sure you are, both unwell & out of spirits in a measure which it grieves me to think of & which is beyond my reach to help. How painful yet how obvious the last thought is. To love much & to be capable of little—that is my fate!– But in regard to yours my dearest, dearly valued friend, do suffer me to say how wrong it is to suffer in this way without seeing Mr May, & only lest you sh^d give some momentary alarm to Dr Mitford. Yes—I wrote that "only" advisedly. You do injustice to his love for you in weighing a transient anxiety against your ultimate injury. He w^d start away in grief from the thought of such a sacrifice of blood. Now do you not think, that the fever you have lately suffered from was the effect of the constant inward irritation which has been going on? And may not the evil return & increase? Why not see Mr May *secretly*? There may be a compromise between your fear & mine. I beseech you to remember the value of your life as before God & men—and also before those who love you. Many love you– Ah, DO not many? I beseech you not to talk of springs breaking & watches going down.[2] I do not enter into it. It's a wrong metaphor. You yet owe much to literature, much to life, much to love. There is a life precious to you, most precious—and my prayer is that it may be prolonged very very long to bless & to be blessed by your devotion. But oh my beloved friend the ties of love are not those of life—they do not break together—or *I*[3] should not be *here*. And while I am, a heart remains to love you, as even *you* cannot be loved by very many, and to be rent by the thought of losing you,—*you too*– May God bless you & make you happy, my beloved friend. I said that of myself, I scarcely know why, except that I felt it strongly. There are stronger holds for you on life, through love, (—I mean there w.^{d} be, under the grief of a possible deprivation,—) than can be found in *me*—in me who live on from week to week, more precariously far than the very aged do! *There are strong holds for you on life*. And since you have administered the sweetest offices of nature with an almost unexampled devotion & tenderness, it remains for you not to wrong her at the last by sinking beneath the pains they involve. "God is above all",[4] in mercy as in decree. And it is something to know how the Chief Love is higher than death—how the Chief Love is the Central Love, where all loves may meet at last! The same in eternity or even time—"Jesus Christ, the same yesterday, today, & for ever".[5] What other name c.^{d} go with those following words, & not be mocked at?——

Is it your habit to drive out, without Ben—only you & K⸺ together? Dearest friend, what chances do befall you!– Write to me—*do*.

Your Flush "IS a .." dog! Nature may stand up & say so!–[6] He is king of the isle of dogs[7]—& his son, Prince Royal. He eats too right royally. As to my Flush, he is very fat with very little *de quoi*[8]—often touches nothing, *will* touch nothing until one o'clock in the day, and then if he does not like his dinner, *only touches* it. Mutton & veal he eschews in general—& even his favorite roast beef, must be cut free from fat or outside, & into very little pieces on a plate, or Mr Flush turns away. He will take a bone sometimes—but I think that it's more for the sake of playing with it & hiding it in a corner, than anything beside. Crow has occasionally cut up mutton & beef together—& then he has picked out all the beef. He does not dislike roast rabbit or chicken. As to those large biscuits, not all the praying in the world c.^{d} recommend them to his attention. The little crisp desert biscuits he does not refuse—& gingerbread he likes when in the humour: but altogether I never saw a dog so indifferent about eating at all, unless in "Epecurus's stye".[9] Tell me if y.^r Flush is silver-shielded like mine—marked white on the breast!–Yes—I must see him– Oh we must meet. Do you know I *believe* we shall go direct to London after all. But it's so near you still!–

Your own attached
EBB.

I have had it in my head long & long, to make a petition to you. W.^d you send me the least shred of your hair,¹⁰ my beloved friend? W.^d you?– It w.^d be such a gift. Yet say *no*, freely, if you *think no*. Mr Kenyon is expected every day—but he wont buy his "hut" since it met with (I am glad to say) a purchaser long since.¹¹

Address: Miss Mitford / Three Mile Cross / near Reading.
Publication: EBB-MRM, I, 262-264.
Manuscript: Wellesley College.

1. Miss Mitford's latest mishap was a spill from her carriage when accompanied only by her maid. John Varley (1778-1842), a landscape-painter who exhibited at the Royal Academy and the Water-colour Society, was also a devoted student of astrology, casting his own horoscope daily, and standing ready to "read the stars" for friends or pupils. Several of his predictions were said to have come true.
2. Miss Mitford had used this phrase in letter 820.
3. Underscored twice.
4. Cf. John, 3:31.
5. Hebrews, 13:8.
6. Cf. *Julius Caesar*, V, 5, 74-75.
7. The Isle of Dogs, a peninsula on the bank of the Thames opposite Greenwich, derived its name from the hounds kept there by Edward III for hunting in Waltham Forest.
8. "Wherewithal"; i.e., Flush grows fat though eating little.
9. James Beattie, *The Minstrel* (1771), I, 40, 6.
10. For incorporation in a locket or bracelet, a popular Victorian custom witnessed by the inclusion of no less than 37 locks of hair in *Reconstruction* (H473-508).
11. See letter 835, note 16.

---

844. EBB TO MARY RUSSELL MITFORD

[Torquay]
[Postmark: 22 August 1841]

⟨★★★⟩ Do take care of y.^rself, & avoid trusting that terrible horse any more–¹ What w.^d dear Dr Mitford do without you? Think of *that*! And when you have done, think what *I*² sh.^d do! God bless & keep you–

Ever your gratefully affectionate
EBB–

Address: Miss Mitford / Three Mile Cross / near Reading.
Publication: EBB-MRM, I, 264.
Manuscript: Wellesley College.

1. A reference to Miss Mitford's latest mishap (see letter 843, note 1).
2. Underscored twice.

845. EBB TO MARY RUSSELL MITFORD

[Torquay]
August 25. 1841

My beloved friend,
Thank you again & again for gilding a little the cloud which was up in the sky when you wrote before. No—do not forsee miseries. It is not good for us to do it. It w^d be the bitter part of prudence—if it were prudence at all. Only in the case of any sadness, dont let me go for nothing, while a true & tender love can go for anything. True that I have still a broad circle of family affection,—even now—even with these gaps in it—the dearest of the dearest away!—but how wrong you w^d be, how you w^d wrong me, should you suppose for such a reason that I c^d love you less. There are two ways of loving, you know— The "after the flesh" way, & the "after the spirit"[1] way. Both may go together—but they do not always: and a bare relationship-love, (beyond the very nearest *cordon*), is a cold skeleton-love. What heaps of cousins & uncles & aunts I have, whom, for love's sake, I sh^d be ashamed to mention in the same page with you— Two aunts out of them, I do love–[2] Hearts wont branch out after the pattern of genealogical trees—at least not mine! And it does not wrong my very nearest, (for whose lives or for whose delights, this frail life of mine sh^d be laid down quickly as a thought, & without a thought of withdrawing it)—that you hold a place all to yourself in my affection & power of appreciation, dear in a manner peculiar. Let me love you, although I love them. If I did NOT love them,

"I could not love thee, Sweet, so much".[3]

Look at them as my sureties for loving you!—& dont look at *me*, as if I had a heart of '*bride-cake*'![4] I have'nt, I do assure you. I can count my friends (beyond *my own beloved's*) on the fingers of one hand—& indeed sh^d be at a loss to get from the thumb quite to the little finger. I never tried the homœopathic infinitesimal system of love! I give it to you, dearest friend, by handfulls! But you dont *say* whether you mean to give me (in exchange) the precious shred of hair. Refuse it if you like—say 'no' freely in a moment!—only *not* because you dont think I love you enough!

Thank you for speaking to Mr May. Or rather I sh^d thank Mr May for making you. Ah! do—do take care of yourself. You are in the prime of life & faculty—and England looks to you for the infusion of still more freshness & sweetness into her literature. Take care of your health—and do, do beware of that horse. I cannot approve of your daring—you & K— alone. It's independence certainly—but it[']s not safety. If I were with you—I driving too—I might perhaps like it—there's no saying—although Flush & I are much on a par as to cowardice: but since I am away, I very decidedly protest against the whole system.

Your letter found me considering whether I sh^d send you the playbill, or trust to the probability of Mr Horne's having enclosed one to you when he did so to me.[5] He merely did so—without note or comment—therefore I cant answer from authority one of your questions. But of course Cosmo & Gregory will take their turns, if the thing survive the first step across the threshold. I apprehend it will not—although the first step wont be less costly for *that*: & I am sorry Mr Horne sh^d involve himself in such a gulf. The getting out, as the poet said of his Avernus, will be harder than the getting in.–[6] Should they succeed, or show like it, what do you say to trusting your *Otto*.? I thought of you directly—that is, I thought silently—for not a word has passed my lips to Mr Horne, I do assure you. By the way—in sending the cream yesterday, I doubted for a minute whether I w^d or would not send you the *Medium* together with your *Pippa*, by the same opportunity. And then I considered how we were on the verge of setting out to London, where communications might be thick & rapid–

We are going, I believe. The carriage, the patent carriage, was to have set out yesterday—& if it arrive in time, we may leave this place on Monday. Dr Scully, a most kind intelligent man—as in his department there cannot be more—is yet very nervous, & as the hour approaches, seems frightened out of his wits. I can only say again & again—"If I suffer, it's my own fault"—which it is altogether. And whatever be the consequence, my beloved friend, I never shall regret the step I am about to take. It is necessary to my happiness—and what is of far more importance,—to Papa's. If I stay here, I *stay alone*—I must & will. And even *that* w^d be painful to my family—while a continuation of the present state of things, w^d be still more destructive to their domestic union & peace. For myself I ought not to care. And dreadful as this place must ever be to me, & oppressive & miserable, I yet might be talked into staying—if I stayed alone– But even that w^d give pain. I cannot. I have considered the subject in all ways, & I must go– And after all I may go quite safely, perhaps. There is a bed in the carriage—and its springs are numberless—and I am so much better—and Papa's permission frees me to my bravery. You shall hear everything– So dont fancy a single evil out of a silence!–

Your romance of your Flush is delightful! and dont think, because I say romance, that I disbelieve the least detail of it. But he must stand high amid his species, in regard to intelligence. The "Nodding" is his prerogative—shared between him & Olympian Jove. My Flush has not attained to it. He is however, I think, trying to speak, & may burst out some day in a "Romans, countrymen & lovers",[7] when we least expect it.– Indeed already he deals in all sorts of inarticulate sounds—low & not inharmonious for the most part. Whenever he is scolded long together, he answers (first throwing himself into my arms) with a plaintive apologetic cry—as much as to say "I did'nt mean any harm—pray have mercy on me." Or sometimes, if he appears to be very ill used, he grumbles to himself,—"This really is past bearing". There is never the least sign of ill humour. His temper w^d show well in a monastery—among the most saintly. I say sometimes that we may all take a lesson in minor morals from Flush!

Mr Kenyon, I understand, is expected here today, with Miss Baillie & another lady. What Miss Baillie? Any other than the poetess?[8] They have taken a house for a week, & Mr Bezzi only *hopes* to detain them longer. You shall hear the details. I will write again before I go– My love to dear Dr Mitford with my wishes that he may like the cream– I must try to find some other way of pleasing myself by pleasing him, when I get to London & lose this one.

Your ever affectionate
EBB.

Address: Miss Mitford / Three Mile Cross / near Reading.
Publication: EBB-MRM, I, 265–267.
Manuscript: Wellesley College.

1. Romans, 8:1.
2. Arabella Graham-Clarke ("Bummy") and her sister, Jane Hedley.
3. Richard Lovelace (1618–58), "To Lucasta, Going to the Warres" (1649), line 11.
4. See letter 834, note 9.
5. The playbill was of *Martinuzzi, or The Hungarian Daughter*, a tragedy by George Stephens (1800–51), produced at the English Opera House on 26 August 1841. In an effort to circumvent the monopoly of the patent theatres (see letter 767, note 3), songs had been arbitrarily introduced to convert it to a musical drama. Horne's interest, of course, was in the test of the monopoly, the subject of his petition to Parliament.
6. Cf. *Æneid*, VI, 126: "Facilis descensus Averno."
7. *Julius Caesar*, III, 2, 13.
8. The lady was not Joanna Baillie the poetess; she was Sarah Bayley (?–1868), Kenyon's close friend and companion, to whom he bequeathed £5,000 and his house in Wimbledon. She had an adopted son, Watkin William Lloyd, and there seems to have been speculation that he was really her illegitimate son—perhaps by Kenyon; RB, in a letter to Isa Blagden on 19 October 1869, after Miss Bayley's death, spoke of "a mild little doubt" about Lloyd's being her "adopted son."

846. EBB to Hugh Stuart Boyd

[Torquay]
August 26.th 1841

My very dear friend,

I have fluctuated from one shadow of uncertainty & anxiety to another, all the summer, on the subject to which my last earthly wishes cling—and I delayed writing to you, to be able to say, I am going to London. I may say so now—as far as the human may say "yes" or "no" of their futurity. The carriage, a patent carriage with a bed in it, & set upon some hundreds of springs, is, I believe on its road down to me—and immediately upon its arrival, we begin our journey. Whether we shall ever complete it, remains uncertain—*more* so than other uncertainties. My physician appears a good deal alarmed, calls it an undertaking full of hazard, & myself the "Empress Catherine",[1] for insisting upon attempting it. But I must. I go, as "the doves to their windows,"[2] to the only earthly daylight I see here. I go to rescue myself from the associations of this dreadful place. I go to restore to my poor Papa, the companionship of his family. Enough has been done & suffered for *me*. I thank God I am going home at last.

How kind it was in you, my very kind & ever very dear friend, to ask me to visit you at Hampstead! I felt myself smiling, while I read that part of your letter,—& laid it down, and suffered the vision to arise of your little room & your great Gregory[3] & your dear self scolding me softly as in the happy olden times, for not reading slow enough. Well—we do not know what MAY happen! I MAY (even that is possible) read to you again. But now—ah my dear friend—if you c.d imagine me such as I am!—! You w.d not think I c.d visit you!—— Yet I am wonderfully better this summer—& if I can but reach home & bear the first painful excitement, it will do me more good than anything—I know it will! And if it does not,—it will be *well* even so!-

I shall tell them to send you the Athenæum of last week, where I have a "House of Clouds",[4]—which Papa likes so much that he w.d wish to live in it if it were not for the damp. There is not a clock in one room—that's another objection! How are your clocks? Do they go? and do you like their voices as well as you used to do?

I think Annie is not with you—but in case of her still being so, do give her (& yourself too) Arabel's love & mine. I wish I heard of you oftener. Is there nobody to write? May God bless you.

Your ever affectionate friend
EBB

Address: H S Boyd Esq.ʳ / Devonshire [*sic*] Hill / Hampstead / London.
Publication: LEBB, I, 88–89.
Manuscript: Wellesley College.

1. Assumed to be a reference to Catherine I (1683–1727), who had insisted on campaigning with her husband, Peter the Great.
2. Blake, *Jerusalem; The Emanation of the Great Albion* (1804), XXX, 13.
3. A 1690 edition of Gregory Nazianzen's works; it was given to EBB by Boyd, and formed lot 718 of *Browning Collections* (see *Reconstruction*, A1093). It is now at Wellesley.
4. The issue of 21 August (no. 721, p. 643).

---

847. EBB to Mary Russell Mitford

[Torquay]
Saturday. [28] August [1841][1]

My dearest friend,

I read your letter just after sending my own to you, with a sympathy as true & full as the love it came from. That "*it*" seems to mean your letter, but does mean mine—and might, I know well, mean either. God bless & keep all who are dear to you, & bless & surprise your heart with still more riches in the consciousness of many being dear. Life is dreary indeed without love—the sand were not worth the footsteps.[2] And love is nearer to us than even the more sanguine of us reckon upon—over us, in the Heavens—& *with* us perpetually, whatever we may lose, in what is called lost. "He will not come to me—I shall go to him".[3] The connection, the meeting, the embrace, remain as sure in the case of death as life—the change being simply in the action .. in the going instead of the coming, .. & in the person acting .. '*I* shall go', instead of 'he shall come'. It is well for us perhaps—not—to live without love—& not—to die, because we have not love—but to have love on each side the grave.

Do not omit telling me, my beloved friend, how Mʳˢ Edward May[4] continues to be!– Your little picture is vivid to my eyes .. better, as all your pictures are, than Mʳ Lucas's. A lovely picture—fragrant as well as beautiful. Oh may she indeed be spared to her husband, & the dear unconscious children, & to you!– I feel so, all you must have felt!–

Mʳ Kenyon arrived the day before yesterday,—& as that day went down, he had your letter. Yesterday morning before my sofa-hour, he kindly came to see my sisters, & promised to be here again today—which promise he is perjured in. So I have'nt seen him! But I may still! He looks, my sisters say, most excellently well & is in his usual spirits—those you know, being holiday ones. Was there ever anyone who made such a holiday of life as this dear friend of ours? Is there anyone under twelve years old?—or ten perhaps?—or six?—to antedate the Latin grammar! I know of nobody.

He is here, he says, for a week,—"with two ladies",—and as they feared the noises of an hotel, has taken a house for their common use. "Two ladies", he said—naming no name.[5] One house, one carriage, "two ladies" (introduced namelessly) & M^r. Kenyon! Can you pluck the heart out of the mystery?[6] Is'nt it a mystery? *Is'nt* THERE A HEART? I assure you I am pondering it gravely. And then the broken vow about coming here today! And another vow, which he mentioned besides, not broken yet & strange upon *his* lips—to abstain from the society of the place during his stay!!- They were a week too at Sidmouth,—& from hence cross to the north of Devonshire! Dear, dear, M^r. Kenyon, what can you be about?

He *is* very fond of Miss Garrow—and so is M^r. Bezzi, and so is M^r. Landor. But how am I to answer your question in regard to my sisters? I open my heart to you always,—& I have wondered sometimes whether you ever wondered at my saying so very little about her, when everybody else of better judgment, said so much .. Well—my sisters do *not* very much admire Miss Garrow—and now the IN*ness* is *out*. I may trust you. I DO trust you—for I sh^d. be very averse to any word of mine on this subject being repeated to anybody in the world. *I* DO *trust you solely.* My sisters—I sh^d say, my sister Henrietta—since Arabel has seen so little of her—my sister Henrietta then, does not admire her, for manner or simplicity, or any other quality than her superior musical accomplishments. A musical talent goes a great way with Henrietta, & she can appreciate it more fully than literary attainment—but with all this appreciation of & admiration for Miss Garrow's remarkable proficiency in her own favorite art, she does not .. to speak plainly .. she does *not* admire the musician. And it is not merely Henrietta. There is a great lack of popularity here I understand—and (which I think of more gravely) there have been those, whose general charity & particular sensitiveness to certain graces of character failed to include them among her admirers. The charges are—affectation—at least want of naturalness—& a leaning to light flirty manners.

For my own part, I have seen her twice, & from that limited experience, I did not infer the 'affectation', & had of course no opportunity of inferring the rest. She came with her sister Miss Fisher, her half sister,— who has been far the most cordial to me of the two,—altho' the whole family has been kind in sending me now & then a present of vegetables & flowers. Miss Fisher spoke however & wrote—& seemed the more inclined to *like* me—and as a kind person entirely without pretension, & not very particularly polished, I liked her.

In regard to Miss Garrow's poetry, I cannot to please any person in the world take the Landor & Kenyon estimate of it. M.ʳ Landor, you know, says "Sappho"⁷—and M.ʳ Kenyon says,—said *in my ears*—"wonderful genius!" while M.ʳ Bezzi does, I believe, strike the full chord. The best poem I have seen of hers, is the Ballad in Lady Blessington's Keepsake for next year⁸—but we must all think & feel for ourselves, if we think & feel at all—and I think & feel of that ballad as of the rest, that it is flowingly & softly written, with no trace of the thing called genius, from the first stanza to the last. She has a good ear, & has caught the tune of the poetry of the day. I told her, when she kindly sent me a previous annual—a Book of beauty⁹—(oh such trash as those beautiful books rejoice in!) that I thought her verses graceful & flowing. But power—originality, which is *individuality*—the sign of the separate mind—you seek in vain for them. At least *I* do. And the philosophy I have drawn from the mystery of the admiration of such very good judges, is an additional reserve & guardiness in my own case against trusting the applausive opinions of friends. I myself always thought, & perhaps think still, that I c.ᵈ love a person to the top of my heart, & yet judge their writings fairly. But it is presumption in me—or it is otherwise with *them*. Think of M.ʳ Landor saying "Wordsworth never wrote anything like this"!! I heard he said so! Why even friendship which covers so many sins, lies scant upon the blasphemy!–¹⁰

It is right to admit that I have seen only four or five poems—but those were selected ones .. for Lady Blessington¹¹—(two selected by M.ʳ Landor) and the master-hand is seen in a stroke. In German & Italian literature she is I believe highly accomplished—speaking both languages. But from all I can hear the *forte* is music. She composes & performs—& there is genius in each. Quite enough various attainment, you see, to render her remarkable & admirable—without touching Wordsworth's laurel. Push just praise into extravagance, and you undo it! If the world recognize her as a poet, I shall be surprised—but certainly not so much so as I have been already.

Oh my dearest Miss Mitford, the carriage is come!– We are going!– We shall probably go on tuesday or wednesday.

There is much to bear—much to dread– The physical danger almost passes from my mind. How I shall thank God, if He *do* reserve to me the comfort of being at home again. Poor Papa is too frightened to come, & will meet us, he says, somewhere on the road—while D.ʳ Scully, repeating "If a lady *must*, she *must*" is obviously drawing philosophical inferences upon the indomitable obstinacy of womanhood generally. How can I help it? *I* CAN'T *stay*.

God bless you—dearest & kindest!– I am leaving a place where in the midst of unspeakable anguish, I have known when I c.ᵈ know anything

the truest kindness—the soothingest ceaseless touch of yours. I thank you, thank you for it all.
While I live, I am
your attached
EBB–

You shall hear.
God bless you & dear D.[r] Mitford!
You shall hear—but dont be uneasy if you sh.[d] not immediately. We may be days & days on the road, if not longer– Write to 50 Wimpole Street–
You are aware perhaps that M.[rs] Garrow was a public singer. The whole family is musical.[12]

Publication: EBB-MRM, I, 268–271.
Manuscript: Wellesley College.

1. Dated by Kenyon's arrival, anticipated in letter 845.
2. Cf. Longfellow, "A Psalm of Life" (1838), line 28.
3. Cf. II Samuel, 12:23.
4. Assumed to be the sister-in-law of Miss Mitford's physician, George May.
5. One of the ladies was Sarah Bayley; see letter 845, note 8.
6. Cf. *Hamlet*, III, 2, 365–366.
7. The poetess of Lesbos, ca. 600 B.C.
8. *The Keepsake for 1842*, edited by Lady Blessington, contained Miss Garrow's poem "The Doom of Cheynholme" (pp. 87–107). EBB must have seen the poem in manuscript, as the book was not published until November 1841.
9. See letters 670 and 671.
10. Although Landor's friendship with Miss Garrow's father, Joseph Garrow, might have contributed to the extravagance of his praise, EBB later ascribed his comments to "the personal feeling which speaks in him" (letter of 20 November 1845 to RB).
11. Two of her poems were included in the 1839 *Book of Beauty* and two in the 1840 edition.
12. Theodosia Garrow (*née* Abrams, 1766–1849) sang at public concerts in London for several years with her sisters Harriet and Eliza. Joseph Garrow was an accomplished amateur violinist.

---

848. EBB TO MARY RUSSELL MITFORD

[Torquay]
Monday night– August 30.th 1841

My beloved friend,
I have seen our dear Mr Kenyon. I saw him today. It was like waking out of a sleep—and *my* reality must always have its pain. But I am glad I have seen him, very glad! You were right, as you always are, my dearest Miss Mitford! He was so kind, so very very kind & feeling—and, do you know, I have thrown the "bride cake" simile[1] out of the window. It

is'nt true of him at all. It wont do for a simile at all! If he likes to use it literally & bodily—very well—provided we have the consent of one of the two fair mysteries domiceled on the Upper Terrace!– But for a simile, its a villainous bridecake—and the maker of it sh^d be put to death as a murderous maker. It's worse than a peppery cheesecake—far! I protest against it!

We could not talk very much, but some of the little was of you, my beloved friend, of course. I told him how I did'nt think Miss Sedgewick meant any harm, or achieved much more than is comprised in the excess of bad taste. But he is strong in disapprobation—& quoted severely the imputed irreverences of the Reading coachman.[2] Oh—but they were not uttered irreverently, nor can be so understood by the majority of readers. Everybody who knows the idiom of a certain class will read that "hearty old boy" into a warm cordial expression of regard. I who lived nearly my whole life long in Herefordshire, have heard it applied a hundred times by the poor to such of the class above them, as they dared to love, heart to heart, without formality. It's an idiom!-- Well—but we who talked of Miss Sedgewick without quite, altogether, agreeing, could do it heartily & utterly in regard to *you*!– Dearest friend! It w^d be a merit in me to love you as I do, if there were any possibility of doing otherwise!

I enclose under this envelope a collar—a little specimen of the Honiton lace for which Devonshire is famous– You will wear it—will you not?—for my sake. You never, you know, w^d eat my cream.

Good night—I am so tired!

Mr Kenyon encourages me in my undertaking,[3] telling me of his "*faith in impulses*"!– He pretends too to think me looking much better than he expected to see me. But all *that* may be flattery.

Ever your affectionate &
grateful E B Barrett.

I w^d not have written what I did lately,[4] but for your question, & considering the value of your good opinion almost regret having done so now. There are differences of opinion—& certain judges & familiar friends are both in regard to judgement & friendship, more trustworthy on a certain subject than I. *Suspend your opinion*. The very blindness of affection may feel its way to the right place—& if not—*I*[5] sh^d be the last to say that it is not to be prized—I, who have been so overpraised & overloved. Codrington's panegyric upon Garth is worth all the critics' scales in the world——

"I read thee over with a lover's eye—
Thou hast no errors, or I none can spy—
Thou art all beauty, or all blindness I"–[6]

God bless you! Forgive me everything wrong–

Publication: EBB-MRM, I, 271–273.
Manuscript: Wellesley College.

1. See letter 834, note 9.
2. For the coachman's "irreverences," see letter 834, note 3.
3. i.e., her determination to undertake the risky journey to London.
4. i.e., about Miss Garrow's poetry, in the previous letter.
5. Underscored twice.
6. Christopher Codrington (1668–1710), sometime Governor of the Leeward Islands, addressed these lines (here slightly misquoted) to Samuel Garth (1661–1719) on the occasion of the publication of *The Dispensary* (1699).

849. EBB TO HUGH STUART BOYD

[Torquay]
August 31. 1831 [*sic*, for 1841]

Thank you my ever dear friend, with almost my last breath at Torquay, for your kindness about the Gregory,[1] besides the kind note itself. It is however too late. We go or mean at present to go, tomorrow—and the carriage which is to waft us through the air upon a thousand springs, has actually arrived. You are not to think severely upon Dr Scully's candour with me, as to the danger of the journey. He *does* think it "likely to do me harm" & therefore, you know, he was justified by his medical responsibility, in laying before me all possible consequences. I have considered them all, & dare them gladly & gratefully. Papa's domestic comfort is broken up by the separation in his family—and the associations of this place, lie upon me, struggle as I may, like the oppression of a perpetual night-mare. It is an instinct of self-preservation which impels me to escape—or to try to escape. And in God's mercy,—though God forbid that I sh^d deny either His mercy or His justice, if *He* sh^d deny *me*,—we may be together in Wimpole Street, in a few days. Nelly Bordman has kindly written to me Mr Jago's[2] very favorable opinion of the patent carriages, & his conviction of my accomplishing the journey without inconvenience.

May God bless you, my dear dear friend! Give our love to dearest Annie! Perhaps if I am ever really in Wimpole Street, *safe enough for Greek*, you will trust the poems to me, which you mention. I care as much for poetry as ever, and could not more.

Your affectionate & grateful
Elizabeth B Barrett.

Address: H S Boyd / Downshire Hill / Hampstead / London.
Publication: LEBB, I, 89–90.
Manuscript: Wellesley College.

1. EBB had mentioned Boyd's "great Gregory" in letter 846 and he had apparently offered to lend the book to her; he later gave it to her (see *Reconstruction*, A1093).
2. Dr. Francis Robert Jago (d. 1862) later attended EBB professionally. Miss Bordman, whom he married in 1848, was now an orphan, living in his house as his *de facto* ward.

850. RB TO WILLIAM CHARLES MACREADY

New Cross, Hatcham, Surrey
Monday Sept 6. [1841][1]

Dear Macready,

Have you found time to look over the Play I left with you?[2] This Autumn weather produces the old rubbing of eyes and unfolding of arms in me—a wake-up bodily and spiritual. I shall be glad to hear from you—and, *par parenthèse*, that your family is as I hope—au mieux[3]–

Ever yours,
R Browning.

Publication: None traced.
Manuscript: Scripps College.

1. During RB's residence at New Cross, 1841 was the only year in which 6 September fell on a Monday.
2. This must have been the manuscript of *A Blot in the 'Scutcheon*. After Macready and Forster had read the play, they were doubtful of its suitability for the stage and the manuscript was sent to Dickens for a third opinion. He did not return it with his comments ("full of genius . . . simple and beautiful in its vigour") until November 1842. Macready then promised RB that he would mount the play, but his handling of it gave offense to RB and caused a breach of their friendship. For a more detailed account of these events, see DeVane, pp. 137–141 and Orr, pp. 109–118.
3. "At best."

851. EBB TO MARY RUSSELL MITFORD

50 Wimpole Street
Monday Sept 13.th [1841][1]

My ever beloved friend,

The first line written by my hand in this dear home is, as it sh.d be, written to you. I arrived on saturday just after post time—& yesterday being sunday there were no means, you know, of passing a letter upon it. I c.d only read over & over *your* letters, & thank & bless you for them!

I write only a line. I am tired of course, with a sense of being thoroughly *beaten*,—but bad symptoms have not occurred—at least the spitting of blood increased *very* little in proportion to what might have been expected—and the whole amount of God's mercy to me is told in the fact of my being *here*. "How great is the sum of it"![2] Here—with Papa—in the midst of all left! No more partings—nor meetings which were worse!—almost *much* worse, sometimes! I thank God for the undeserved mercy!–

For the rest, there was of course much to remember & suffer both in leaving Torquay & coming *here*. But my weakness helped to spare me—and now, I try to be alive only, or most, to the sense of blessing.

Thank you thank you for your too much kindness!– The precious ringlet![3] It might serve, as far as the preciousness goes, to hold a city by—only being cut off, it is precious still. The fable ends there—and the truth begins. And is'nt it truth that I love the least part of you?–

You say too much—far too much! It's all too much kindness. Give my love to dear Dr Mitford. How close we are now!—and how I w^d say a hundred other things which I cant!–

Goodbye– God bless you!

Dont you know that Martinuzzi has perished.[4] I fear so–

Ever your
EBB–

Publication: EBB-MRM, I, 273–274.
Manuscript: Wellesley College.

1. Dated by EBB's return to London.
2. Cf. Psalms, 139:17.
3. The lock of hair requested by EBB in letter 843.
4. EBB is a little premature in her comment; despite a disastrous first night (see letter 854), the play was kept in the repertory for a month after its 26 August première.

852. EBB to Mary Russell Mitford

[London]
[*Postmark:* 20 September 1841]

Envelope only.

Address: Miss Mitford / Three Mile Cross / near Reading.
Publication: None traced.
Manuscript: Edward R. Moulton-Barrett.

853. EBB TO MARY RUSSELL MITFORD

[London]
Sep.! 21. 1841

Dearest dearest Miss Mitford, the note I wrote yesterday had scarcely passed from my hands when the flowers came!– I have looked at them & seen you in them, & borne for your sake that some of them sh.^d be put into a vase in my room. It is the first time since the time I cannot speak of, that I have borne to look at flowers so nearly as to have them in my room. They *used* to find free entrance there, & the people at Torquay were kind in sending me bouquets—but *after that time*[1] I grew changed you know altogether & shrunk from the things I liked best—& the colour & the smell of these beautiful creations became terrible to me, as if they were noisome instead of beautiful. Since that time, there have been no more flowers in my room until now—& here are yours!– Yes!—here are yours. I denied nature, but could not deny *you*! And do not think that it has been an effort to me, a bare duty of love! I used to think at Torquay—"I cannot while I stay in this place—but if I live ever to be free from it, one dearest person may send me some of *her* flowers, & *then I will have those*!" That was my promise to myself built upon the presumption of your liberality. For you did'nt want notes or commentaries to explain who the "dearest person" was? Oh no!—you guessed *that*! —because you know *me*! My beloved & kindest friend, how I thank you for your splendid flowers! Instead of their encomium I have written what is as grave as an epitaph! Yet I do praise & admire them—do today & did yesterday—& can look at them without crying, for your sake!– Dont take any notice of all this weakness. But I felt impelled to explain how I owe a new spring to you—among the rest of the debts!—among *all* the rest, my beloved & kindest friend!–

All the rest indeed! For how could I thank you first for flowers, when you promise me the gift of yourself. Is it possible?– Come to see *me*, such a long long way! Oh—how can I thank you enough for even the thought of it? And will you do it? Ought I to let you? I, who am so spent & worn of the little good-for-companionship that ever was in me? Ought I to *let* you?

There is a question for a debating society of starch consciences!—but mine, I fear, wont make a very long speech about it. It will "*let* you", I see from the beginning.

But not just yet—do not come just yet, my beloved friend! I must *quite* take breath before that joy, & have time for a dream of it. In the meantime—when you come, must you go back the same day?—must you? We are full here, I am sorry to say—but still, I do think with a little more thought, we might conjure up a bedroom for you. I feel myself smiling at the very thought of it. *Will* you come—or is it too much pleasure for me? I was confessing the other day that I felt myself (now that I had come *home*) growing credulous of joy, again! The credulity seems to roll on like a bowl. What if I sh.^{d} set up again for a castle builder!–

When you come, you wont see any "little brothers"—& when *I* came, I looked for them in vain! Not a brother to be seen out of a long-tailed coat—& even Set (Septimus—you must learn our names!) sidling away from Papa's morning kiss, because he's too old!²–

But nobody's too old to like geraniums—not even I!– Yet hold your generous hand, & let us consider a little. Is it the very best time? And if it is, will you promise to send only one or two? We have been luckless in attempts of the kind hitherto. And will you instruct us how we are to prepare the two plants you sent some time ago, for the winter? They appear drooping & inclined to eschew London & winter together. Should we cut them down—quite down—? or should we take them up, out of their pots, & garner them in the cellar. Do give us some advice. And do believe how we thank you! You are Flora herself to us³, carrying Plenty's horn, because there's nothing else in mythology large enough to hold your gifts of nosegays!

Mr Haydon's letters shut up in the best letter of all,⁴ I received this morning & will return to you in a day or two. I must let Papa just look at them. They interested me much. How I do like the "self glorying" (in the sense of Longinus) of genius⁵—the devotion of heart to noble ends, overlooking life—the joy in self-sacrifice—the consciousness of power! How fine this life of genius is!—& its religion too! If any smile as perhaps they might, & [*sic*, for at] the artist's supplication before the great creator, I at least am not one. I like these letters. They spring up like a fountain among the world's conventionalities—they & such as they.

He is said, you know, to be a vain man, & it may be true for aught the letters say.

"Poor little Flush." You may well say so. He did'nt like London at all at first—not through rural preferences so much, as through fear of the crowds of strangers which presented terrors to him on all sides. The journey, Mr Flush enjoyed no less than any other classical traveller inclusive of Eustace.⁶ He w.^{dnt} sleep in the carriage, but sate at the window upon Arabel's knee or Crow's, with his two paws on the sill, & his glittering ears dancing up & down over his nose—the eyes dilating with the prospect. Through all my exhaustion, I could'nt help now & then smiling at Flush. No student of the picturesque ever gazed more intently upon hill & valley—only he had a decided preference for animated nature. A flight of crows—for instance—drew him half out of the window—a flock of sheep produced a wag of the tail—a man on horseback, of the whole body––and, best of all, from this "high sphere"⁷ he had the honor of barking at many a large dog who, if both had been on equal ground, w?. have gobbled him up– At the inns too, M! Flush took his pleasure. My bed used to be drawn out of the carriage like a drawer from a table & was carried, by men, with a shawl over the face of the occupant, up stairs to a bedroom. Well!—Flush thought himself bound in duty to pay every attention to this process. He walked & stood & paused & gazed, just as others did—& when I was laid down safely, the first living thing I used to see was Flush standing on his hind legs to reach up & kiss me. Then he established himself on my bed until he was taken down to dinner, always returning, finding out my bedroom door in the strange houses, with as little delay as possible, & most absolute in his resolve of passing the night with me. And every morning, he watched all the preparations for setting out again, evidently rejoicing in all & the first to spring into the carriage & take his usual seat. I am by no means sure that Flush wont bring out as good a two volumes of "Travels" some day—of notes & documents—as anybody from the new world.

Well, but—when he came here—it was different. He liked my room very much indeed,—but my brothers he altogether disapproved of—and, what was rather worse, he thought it necessary (being a moralist & a traveller) to express his disapprobation most loudly & tumultuously—starting up, whether by night or day, everytime he heard a footstep, throwing himself upon my shoulder & barking like a pack of hounds in one. My quiet Flush!—whom I always praised for quietness! Was there ever such a beginning! I was in despair—not so much for myself as for Papa who is not perhaps very particularly fond of dogs & most particularly, of silence. Papa said Flush made him nervous, & that he must not sleep in my bedroom until he was reformed altogether. So Crow took him for a night—& everybody paid court to him—&, in a little time, his terrors passed away & he permitted himself to be walked near & talked to & even patted. Oh—he is quite contented now—quite friends with the whole world. Poor dear little Flush! And he likes London "pretty well, thank you". He has had two long runs the Hampstead way, & runs out in the Parks, & thinks it pleasant enough.

Oh the post, the post—I shall be too late—& must'nt & wont.

I heard from M! Horne last night– Tomorrow you shall hear. Yet there is not much—only that he thinks they have made a "pretty good floundering beginning" in the English Opera speculation.[8] I must write again—perhaps tomorrow—certainly next day.

Thank you for thinking of Arabel in regard to the studios.[9] Over-kind you are!– All their love to you—& mine to dear D! Mitford. Tell me if the tamarinds relieve the thirst.[10] God bless you. *I do love you indeed*[.]

Your own EBB.

No. 854 23 September 1841 129

Address: Miss Mitford / Three Mile Cross / near Reading.
Publication: EBB-MRM, I, 274-277.
Manuscript: Wellesley College.

1. i.e., the death of Bro.
2. At this time the two youngest members of the family, Septimus and Octavius, were 19 and 17 respectively. Sette had always been his father's particular favourite (see, for example, letter 462).
3. The Roman equivalent of Chloris, the Greek goddess of flowers and gardens.
4. Benjamin Robert Haydon (1786-1846), the painter, had known Miss Mitford since 1817 and had painted her portrait, ca. 1825 (reproduced in *EBB-MRM*, facing I, 158). He later became one of EBB's major correspondents, and left his personal papers to her care when he committed suicide on 22 June 1846. (For details of his friendship with EBB, see pp. 370-373.)
5. Cf. *On the Sublime*, cap. xxxiii.
6. John Chetwode Eustace (1762?-1815), a close friend of Edmund Burke, had published *A Tour Through Italy* in 1813 (entitled *A Classical Tour Through Italy* in later editions).
7. Cf. Milton, "On the Death of a Fair Infant Dying of a Cough" (1673), 39.
8. A reference to the production of *Martinuzzi* in an attempt to circumvent the legal monopoly of the patent theatres (see letters 845, note 5, and 854).
9. i.e., those of Haydon and Lucas; Miss Mitford provided letters of introduction to them (see letter 857) and letter 861 tells of a visit to their studios by Arabel and Sette.
10. Letter 857 affirms that they gave "great relief."

---

854. EBB TO MARY RUSSELL MITFORD

[London]
Thursday. Sept 23[d] 1841

My beloved friend,

Here are the letters returned to you,[1] for which I thanked you yesterday .. & I think Arabel will be tempted into the impudence you encourage, (you being the tempting angel) of using your charmed name to gaze upon the new manifestation of Uriel.[2] When *you* come you will visit the artist, wont you?,—& help him on from rapture to rapture?[3] And this consideration helps *me* to a juster one of times & seasons. We must'nt put off your avatar until the winter—must we?- When is the best hour for my gladness? Think yourself. But oh—how remorseless, to "*let* you come"!-

I remember M[r] Lucas perfectly. A pale body-thinking looking person—diffident in his manners. I remember perfectly.

With the other things, which accident delayed until they c[d] be sent in your flowerbasket, you will find M[r] Browning's *Pippa* & M[r] Horne's "False Medium". Tell me your thoughts of the last. They will not pass over it, of course, in entire approbation—they will find some rashness & violence—much magnanimous madness. What I regret most is a note upon Shelley's expulsion from the university, together with a page or two *round about* it!⁴ The generous indignation will occasionally like ambition 'overleap itself'.⁵ I *know*, I think I may say, I *know*, that Shelley's sins against the God of his own poetry are more lamented by Mᵣ Horne than by the fiercest lifter up of the collegiate brand. As to the brand, Milton was struck first.⁶

Mᵣ Horne sent me *Martinuzzi* to read, a day or two ago,—together with these sentences upon the great speculation, .. "Of course in such an undertaking we never expected to *make money*. Owing to the disasters of the first night, the press with its usual intelligence & high principle, has made a crusade against us⁷—but there are certain parties in this matter who are not to *be* put down. On the whole we have made a good floundering beginning."

Such being the opinion of the persons concerned, 'the mourners' need not "go about the streets".⁸ The fact is—that *Martinuzzi* is in a course of performance still—if it has'nt a run, it has a walk.⁹ After the fatal first night, sundry corrections & reformations were made in the tragedy—& then, it walked! I have however, in my secret self, & so far out of the way that nobody can say "get out of it,["] I have an opinion of my own which walks too. *I cannot think highly of* MARTINUZZI. There it is, alive & upright, though most innocent.

The tragedy has fine things in it, but not very frequently & always broken into chips. Both story & character seem to be (that is, seem to *me*) defective, & the building up of the lofty verse, is tumbling down instead. Mᵣ Horne lent me the play—& now I have only to stutter out the truth to him in all courtesy. I never could admire *in a train*—& least of all, poetry. And I do wonder that those members of the new Theatrical committee who are *not* Mᵣ Stephens, shᵈ have dared to take their first step upon *Martinuzzi*.

In regard to certain other poets (so called) you may be right, my beloved friend, although I do not know enough of the parties to be sure that you are. For my own part, I dare to believe of myself that I am not hypercritical, & that I love poetry too deeply, not to recognize & kiss the faintest mark of her foot. At the same time, I have no business in the judgment seat.

Mᵣ Bezzi I never saw, & never read a word from his pen—only recollecting of him gratefully that he ran down once through the rain, with a book which he heard I wanted, & had borrowed for me. He is, you know, very musical—& by some occult enchantment independent of his music he draws everybody after him like Orpheus.¹⁰ Never was anything like his popularity—but popularity is *naught*—& I can quite understand something of what you intimate. Does it refer to *the talent*—or the what? As to the former, a man who *produces nothing* is after all second rate. Henrietta likes him very much—but then she saw him in society & in reference to it.

Well—perhaps we may have a little gossipping before long—if I shall be able to do anything but look at you dearest dearest friend, when I have you to look at. You must be prepared for the change that has come over the spirit of my dream in many ways—notwithstanding the surprising revival of this summer & notwithstanding that everyone here says "Oh, you look so much better than I expected to see you"!- But then my voice—my poor voice has shrunk away into the mythological destiny of the nymph Echo-[11] I cant speak out of a whisper- I cant recover my old tones! I lost my voice again & again & recovered it—but it is gone now so long & far that it cant get back!

They gossip dreadfully at Torquay—past the ridge of scandal- Perhaps this voice may tell you a little, if you can hear it! Oh how pleasant to think, to dream, of hearing *you*? Do you repent leading me into this extravagance of hope? Do you? Say yes—if you do.

The post is going.

My love to dear Dr Mitford. Flush is in high spirits. He likes London, he says, very much indeed.

Ever your own
EBB–

Address: Miss Mitford / Three Mile Cross / near Reading.
Publication: EBB-MRM, I, 278–280 (as 22 September 1841).
Manuscript: Wellesley College.

   1. EBB means Haydon's letters to Miss Mitford, mentioned in the previous letter, but, as the following letter indicates, EBB forgot to enclose them. Miss Mitford has interpolated "Haydon's," on the manuscript.

   2. The archangel Uriel, described by Milton as the "regent of the sun" (*Paradise Lost*, III, 690). In a letter to Miss Mitford of 26 August 1841 (presumably one of those EBB speaks of returning), Haydon had described how he decided to experiment with fresco: "getting leave of my worthy landlord to knock my walls to pieces, if necessary, I proceeded ... to chip off the outer coat ... and, following Cennini, spread the requisite quantity of wet mortar ... In four hours I produced a colossal sketch of 'Uriel disturbed by Satan in disguise of an Angel'." (*Benjamin Robert Haydon: Correspondence and Table-Talk*, 1876, II, 137.) Haydon's son, Frederick Wordsworth Haydon (1827–86), described it as being of "ideal and unearthly beauty" and said that he was the model for it (Pope, V, 83). For a report on the fresco by Arabel and Sette, see letter 861.

   3. Miss Mitford did see the fresco when she came to London at the end of October. She described it as "a very interesting specimen of a restored art, the first ever executed by an English painter" but thought "the want of shadow will tell against it in a large picture—no depth" (Chorley, I, 191, 283).

   4. On p. 241 of his book, speaking of men of genius, Horne referred to "their probable inability to shine, or even make a moderate progress in the usual collegiate studies" and

of their behaviour being "deficient in proper respect to professors, and their general conduct, wild, refractory, and not to be endured." A footnote stated "One of the highest honours that can attend a youth's outset in life, is to be expelled from college, for manifesting a resistance to servile ignorance and brutal tyranny. Such was the case with Shelley, and many others."

5. *Macbeth*, I, 7, 27.

6. Milton had had some quarrel with his tutor, which resulted in a temporary departure from Cambridge (see *DNB*).

7. *The Examiner* of 28 August 1841 (no. 1752, pp. 548–549) dealt with the presentation of Stephens's drama under the auspices of "the Council of the Dramatic Authors' Theatre. Established for the full Encouragement of English Living Dramatists." Although wishing "heartily well to every attempt to throw open the stage," the writer had serious reservations about the selection of *Martinuzzi* for that purpose: "the construction of the whole must be characterized as eminently unfortunate. The stage at the last was strewn with dead bodies: each having fallen to the untragical accompaniment of a roar. So mirthful an audience never before presided over a matter of so much gravity." *The Times* of 27 August reviewed the play in similar terms, commenting that "From an unfortunate anti-climax that was uttered about the middle of the piece ... the audience caught an unlucky humour, and a constant disposition to seize on the ridiculous side of everything was manifest to the end" and concluding that the injustice of the managers of the patent theatres in refusing to produce it had not been proved.

8. Ecclesiastes, 12:5.

9. The play only survived for a month; its last performance was on 25 September.

10. Orpheus, son of the Muse Calliope, was such a master of the lyre that even inanimate objects were moved by his music.

11. Echo was deprived of freedom of speech by Juno, being permitted only to answer questions put to her.

---

855. EBB TO MARY RUSSELL MITFORD

[London]
Sept. 24. 1841

Oh my stupidity, to have left out M.ʳ Haydon's letters! Here they are.

Do you know the poor Laureate's full desolation? Do you know that his wife, CAROLINE BOWLES, & his beloved children have quarrelled—are at variance—& that the latter have left his roof? They visit him occasionally—claiming their filial rights! Oh what a picture! What a picture! And he unconscious either of love or hate, in the midst of them!—All gone but life—and life springing up like a wallflower from a ruin—strong & green as a weed—and *to last*! Poor poor Southey!—— M.ʳ Kenyon told me of it—& that he was more likely to live than ever.¹ Say how you both are.

Flush has made friends with all my brothers, & enjoys his new gaiety very much—only preferring my society to everybody's & keeping near me as a prudent precaution.

Your most affectionate
EBB–

Publication: EBB-MRM, I, 280-281.
Manuscript: Wellesley College.

1. Southey's first wife had died insane in 1837. Despite his own failing faculties, Southey re-married in 1839, his second wife being Caroline Anne Bowles (1786-1854); her stepchildren apparently detested her (*DNB*). Within three months of the marriage, Southey's health had seriously declined, and he gradually became insensible to externals. The last year of his life was "a mere trance" (*DNB*); he died on 21 March 1843.

---

856. EBB TO MARY RUSSELL MITFORD

London.
Sept. 25. 1841.

The pause of a day brings me another dear letter for which to be glad & grateful. Thank you my beloved friend—and thank you above all for what you say of the coming. I am sure I am in fairyland all at once—I must be! Only think of how I was a few weeks ago—shut up in a dark room with its associations tugging at my heartstrings—everything I could see, everything I c^d hear, to the very footsteps on the stairs, giving me pain—& just beneath the window (for our house was the lowest down of all upon the shore) that dreadful perpetual sound!– When I think of it, it makes me shudder & wonder how I c^d live on there so long!– But we dont know what we can bear—and only a few weeks since it was so! And now—to be at home again—to see the dear faces—no more thought of goodbyes—everybody smiling as if grief were not in the world—& this dream of seeing *you*, set as a crown upon the general gladness. No wonder that I sh^d wonder! Thank you & dear Dr Mitford for being glad for me! It is a renewing of life to me. Not that the deep grief is not here still—like the clay beneath the grass. That must be: but I could not without sullenness, be insensible to the full pleasantness of the sweet dewy verdure, which has sprung up so suddenly after a long desolation. 'Shall we receive *evil* from the Lord's hand, & not *good*?'[1] May His goodness forbid that evil!–

Forgive my wanderings, beloved friend! Fairy-bewitched people dont always know what they say & are very apt to "wander in their talk[.]" I was thinking last night that when you come & drop the silver penny into my shoe,[2] our dear Mr Kenyon might just as well be here to take his chance for a penny too! What do you think? His time for returning to town will soon strike! And would'nt it be selfish of me not to give him a chance? 'I pause for a reply'.[3] You see how conscientious I am grown. But not to be overvirtuous so as to lose my cakes & ale,[4] could'nt we prevail upon dear Dr Mitford to part from you without sighing oftener than once, for longer than the day? Could'nt we! I w?. not grieve him for the world, & I know too so well how the very fancy of his sighing twice w?. make you restless & unhappy away from him. But then my fancy is, that he w?. be better satisfied *in securing you from fatigue*. He knows, & so do I, that you w?. certainly be tired in that sudden going & coming. You w?. be out of breath with it!–

Thank you for the delightful chronicle of Flush. *He* must come too, you know! I long I long to see him. And pray dont forget to thank K. & Ben for their kindness about putting up the basket so beautifully!– How fully & truly & utterly I agree with you in all you say about the luxury or rather necessary of having people round you who love you, yes, & whom you love again. The Edgeworth doctrine (not peculiar to that rational cold school) in regard to domestics, was always abhorrent to me. To teach children "not to talk to servants"!! And a bible in your room—and God above you—& the quick sense of universal brotherhood at your heart!– It is an atrocity both in morals & instincts!–[5]

I must not let you fancy that Papa does not like Flush, because Flush for a day or two made Papa nervous. No indeed—I prophecy that M?. Flush will, in time, climb into favoritism. He is admired already.

My brothers Charles John (Stormie we call him) & Henry have two splendid dogs chained up in the yard—one of them a bloodhound & the other an Alpine mastiff, Catiline & Resolute—and Flush who violently objected to them at first, admits them now occasionally into his society— that is, he has condescended to walk out with them once or twice.

God bless you my ever beloved friend! *Thank* you for all y?. kindness—but to the geranium extravaganza I say "Oh no, no indeed!" That is too much–

But ever & ever yours
E B Barrett–

I am very glad of your judgment upon the *medecine*—very glad— altho' I anticipated it.

Address: Miss Mitford / Three Mile Cross / near Reading.
Publication: EBB-MRM, I, 281–283.
Manuscript: Wellesley College.

1. Cf. Job, 2:10.
2. We cannot identify EBB's allusion. The editors of *EBB-MRM* refer to a suggestion that a silver penny purchased entry to Fairyland (see *EBB-MRM*, I, 282, note 2).
3. *Julius Caesar*, III, 2, 34.
4. Cf. *Twelfth Night*, II, 3, 115–116. The expression "cakes and ale" was synonymous with pleasure and revelry.
5. Chapter IV of *Practical Education* (1798) by Maria and Richard Lovell Edgeworth offered advice on teaching privileged children how to comport themselves with servants. "Familiarity between servants and children cannot permanently increase the happiness of either party.... A boy who has been used to treat a footman as his playfellow, cannot

suddenly command from him that species of deference, which is compounded of habitual respect for the person, and conventional submission to his station ... Children should never be suffered to speak imperiously to their attendants ... There is, however, a great deal of difference between treating servants with kindness and with familiarity."

857. MARY RUSSELL MITFORD TO EBB

Three Mile Cross,
[early October 1841][1]

I prefer the man of action to the man of letters—the *mere* man of letters. But, certainly, the cultivation and faculty enhances and embellishes the sterner stuff. But I am made for mere country pleasures, rather than for those of literature. I was this afternoon for an hour on Heckfield Heath:[2] a common dotted with cottages and a large piece of water backed by woody hills; the nearer portion of ground a forest of oak and birch, and hawthorn and holly, and fern, intersected by grassy glades; a road winding through; and behind us the tall trees of Strathfieldsaye Park.[3] On an open space, just large enough for the purpose, a cricket match was going on—the older people sitting by on benches; the younger ones lying about under the trees; and a party of boys just seen glancing backward and forward in a sunny glade, where they were engaged in an equally merry and far more noisy game. Well, there we stood, Ben and I and Flush, watching and enjoying the enjoyment we witnessed. And I thought if I had no pecuniary anxiety, if my dear father were stronger and our dear friend well, I should be the happiest creature in the world, so strong was the influence of that happy scene.

Let me say, my sweetest, that the "Romaunt of the Page" (which is a tragedy of the very deepest and highest order) always seems to me by far the finest thing that you have ever written; and I do entreat and conjure you to write more ballads or tragedies—call them what you will—like that; that is to say, poems of human feelings and human actions. They will be finer, because truer, than any "Psyche" can be.

I enclose a note to Mr. Haydon. Miss Arabel will like his vivacity and good spirits. Those high animal spirits are a gift from heaven, and frequently pass for genius; or rather make talent pass for genius—silver-gilded. Mr. Lucas is of a far higher and purer stamp. There is no gilding there, it is the true metal and without alloy, as far, I think, as can be said of any mortal.[4]

Did I tell you his story? His father was a clerk in the War Office, an inferior clerk; and he, showing very strongly a genius for design when a boy, was apprenticed to Reynolds the mezzotint engraver.[5] At Mr.

Reynolds's he worked six days in every week from eight o'clock in the morning till eight o'clock at night, and he did work so honestly towards his master and himself that he could *now* earn from £1200 to £2000 a year as an engraver; but his aim was higher. His master being of so much eminence as to have such pictures as the "Chapeau de Paille,"[6] &c., to engrave, he rose at four in the morning, abstracted from his breakfast and dinner hours every moment not absolutely required for the support of life, and devoted every stolen minute to the study of oil-painting in those great pictures, and that with such success that the moment he was out of his time he was ready and able to earn his bread as a portrait painter—not only to earn his own bread, but to support (as he has done ever since) a widowed mother.[7] One of his early patrons was Mr. Milton,[8] Mrs. Trollope's brother, and at his request, he thinking that any one whose name was at all known would be of service to the young artist, I sat to him for my portrait.[9] Of course it was a failure. A plain, middle-aged woman could hardly be otherwise. We paid for it the too modest sum that he required, and never demanded it after it returned from the exhibition, where, in spite of its ugliness, it had a good place. He did not like the picture and did not send it back. We had, however, been charmed with *him*; had heard with delight of his rapidly increasing reputation; and had perhaps been of some little use to him in the early part of his career, by recommending him to different friends. This, however, was nothing; his own great talent, astonishing industry, and exemplary character were his best patrons. However, when we met in town, I said to him, "You used to like our poor cottage. Come and see us again; will you not?" and he answered, "I have been hoping that you would say this, because that head of you is upon my conscience, and I want to paint it over again." I replied, of course, "No; I asked you to come and see us for recreation, not for work. I shan't sit to you, I assure you." "Well," said he, "if you won't let me paint you, you'll let me paint your father?" And I could not resist; and he did come; and the portrait of my father is one of the very finest ever painted, and only less precious to me than the original.[10] Think of the difference of his prices now and then; think of his coming to my father as he would to Prince Albert, and you will feel the full value of his unostentatious and generous piece of kindness.

I love John Lucas. He is less talked of than many who have not half his real reputation; but next to Sir Thomas Lawrence, no man has painted half so many of the highest nobility.[11] The Duke of Wellington (an excellent judge) will sit to nobody else.[12] The Duchesse de Dino,[13] Princess Lieven,[14] and all the great foreigners preferred him to any portrait painter at home or abroad. I must enclose you a letter about him, from a dear friend, received to-day, and a note to him for Miss Arabel. He has now more pictures bespoken than he can paint for two years. Oh! if I had but a head of you by him! What a head of you he would make! I should like Mr. Barrett to see his portraits, and to know him. He is modest almost to shyness; but it is such a mind, so well worth a little trouble to get at. I love John Lucas. His wife[15] have never seen.

The tamarind water has been my father's best friend; it has given great relief. Love to all.

Yours most faithfully,
M. R. Mitford.

Address: Miss Barrett, Wimpole Street.
Text: L'Estrange (2), III, 63–66 (as 17 October 1836).

1. Dated by the reference to letters of introduction to Haydon and Lucas; EBB acknowledged these in letter 860.
2. Heckfield Heath was about 5 miles S. of Three Mile Cross.
3. The Duke of Wellington's estate.
4. For a report of Arabella Moulton-Barrett's visit to the studios of Haydon and Lucas, see letter 861.
5. Samuel William Reynolds (1773–1835), painter and engraver, studied under William Hodges and John Raphael Smith and was employed by Turner.
6. The portrait of Susanna Fourment, now in the National Gallery, London, painted ca. 1620 by Peter Paul Rubens (1577–1641).
7. Mrs. William Lucas (*née* Calcott).
8. The 1829 Royal Academy exhibition included Lucas's portrait of the twin sons of Henry Milton (1784?–1850). The 1830 exhibition included Lucas's painting of Milton himself. Lucas also painted Milton's wife. All three are reproduced in *John Lucas, Portrait Painter, 1828–1874*, by Arthur Lucas (1910), facing p. 6.
9. This was also shown in the 1829 R.A. exhibition. It is reproduced in *Mary Russell Mitford: The Tragedy of a Blue Stocking*, by W.J. Roberts (1913), facing p. 290.
10. This portrait, painted in 1836, was exhibited at the Royal Academy in 1838, where Arabella and Henrietta Moulton-Barrett saw it (see letter 636). It is reproduced in vol. 4, facing p. 41.
11. Sir Thomas Lawrence (1769–1830), Portrait-Painter in Ordinary to George III and George IV and President of the Royal Academy, had painted many of the members of the royal family and nobility, several European sovereigns and notables, as well as Pope Pius VII.
12. One of Lucas's portraits of Wellington was shown at the Royal Academy in 1840. Sixteen portraits of Wellington are catalogued in *John Lucas, Portrait Painter, 1828–1874*, six of them being reproduced.
13. Dorothea, Duchess de Dino (*née* de Courland, 1793–1862), later Duchess de Talleyrand (1838) and Duchess de Sagan (1843), was in London while Talleyrand was Ambassador, where she exerted considerable social and diplomatic influence.
14. Dorothea Christopherovna, Princess de Lieven (*née* Benckendorff, 1785–1857), spent many years in London, where her husband was Russian Ambassador; her influence was greater than his and her correspondents included Prime Ministers Earl Grey and the Earl of Aberdeen. Lucas's portrait of her, painted in 1833, is reproduced in *Princess Lieven*, by H. Montgomery White (1938), facing p. 236.
15. The former Miss Milborough Morgan.

858. EBB TO HUGH STUART BOYD

50. Wimpole Street
Oc.! 2ᵈ 1841

My very dear friend,

I thank you for the letter & books which crossed the threshold of this house before me, & looked like your welcome to me home. I have read the passages you wished me to read—I have read them *again*: for I remember reading them under your star (or the greater part of them) a long while ago. You on the other hand, may remember of *me*, that I never could concede to you much admiration for your Gregory as a poet[1]—not even to his grand work *De virginitate*. He is one of those writers of whom there are instances in our own times, who are only poetical in prose.

The passage imitative of Chryses, I cannot think much of. Try to be forgiving. It is toasted dry between the two fires of the Scriptures & Homer[2]—& is as stiff as any dry toast out of the simile. To be sincere, .. I like dry toast better.

The Hymns & Prayers I very much prefer; & although I remembered a good deal of them, it has given me a pleasure you will approve of, to go through them in this edition. The one which I like best, which I like far best, which I think worth all the rest (*De virginitate* & all put together) is the *second* upon page 292, beginning *Soi charis*.[3] It is very fine I think—written out of the heart & for the heart,—warm with a natural heat, & not toasted dry & brown & stiff at a fire, by any means.

Dear M.ʳ Boyd, I coveted Arabel's walk to you the other day. I shall often covet my neighbour's walks,[4] I believe, although (& may God be praised for it) I am more happy, that is, nearer to the feeling of happiness now, than a month since I could believe possible to a heart so bruised & crushed as mine has mine.[5] To be at home is a blessing & a relief beyond what these words can say.

But—dear M.ʳ Boyd,—you said something in a note to Arabel some little time ago, which I will ask of your kindness to avoid saying again. I have been through the whole summer very much better,—& even if it were not so, I should dread being annoyed by more medical speculations & consultations. Pray do not suggest any. I am not in a state to admit of experiments—and my case is a very clear & simple one. I have not *one symptom* like those of my old illness—& after more than fifteen years absolute suspension of them, their recurrence is scarcely probable. My case is very clear—not tubercular consumption—not what is called a "decline",—but an affection of the lungs which leans towards it. You know a blood vessel broke three years ago—& I never quite got over it. M.ʳ Jago not having seen me, could scarcely be justified in a conjecture

No. 858   2 October 1841

of the sort; when the opinions of four able physicians, two of them particularly experienced in diseases of the chest, & the other two the most eminent of the faculty in the east & west of England, were decided and contrary, while coincident with each other. Besides you see I am becoming better—and I could not desire more than that. Dear Mr Boyd, do not write a word about it any more, either to me or others. I am sure you would not willingly disturb me. Nelly Bordman is good & dear, but I cant let her prescribe for me anything except her own affection.

    I hope Arabel expressed for me my thankful sense of Mrs Smith's kind intention. But indeed—although I would see *you* dear Mr Boyd, gladly, or an angel or a fairy or any very particular friend, I am not fit either in body or spirit for general society. I *cant* see people—and if I could, it would be very bad for me. Is Mrs Smith writing?[6] Are you writing? Part of me is worn out; but the poetical part,—that is, the *love* of poetry,—is growing in me as freshly & strongly as if it were watered every day. Did anybody ever love it & stop in the middle? I wonder if anybody ever did.

    My dear friend, I remember your once telling me that you were at a loss sometimes for objects of charity—that you would sometimes gladly give if you knew to whom. I do therefore take the liberty of apprizing you of the melancholy circumstances under which Mrs Hopkins (*Cousins*)[7] is at present. She is very industrious—& unexceptionable as a wife & mother—but her husband is so involved in debt, that all her struggles cannot rescue herself & her poor little children from a state of deep poverty. She knows nothing of my resolve to mention it to you—and I do so, simply as friend to friend, & out of compassion & sympathy, . . because I am sure that if you can give her anything it will be a gift to the much-afflicted. Nevertheless you will of course do as you think best—& not through courtesy to me. When do you expect Annie?

                                  Believe me
                                  Your affectionate
                                  EBB–

Address: H S Boyd Esqr / 21 Downshire Hill / Hampstead.
Publication: EBB-HSB, pp. 241–243.
Manuscript: Wellesley College.

    1. In 1831, EBB had written: "Gregory is not a great poet, scarcely a real poet" (*Diary*, p. 105).
    2. When Lyrnessus was taken by Achilles, Chryseis, wife of the King of Lyrnessus and daughter of the priest Chryses, was taken captive, becoming part of the spoils of war claimed by Agamemnon. *The Iliad* opens with Chryses begging Agamemnon to free Chryseis and being scornfully refused.
    3. We have not been able to identify the specific edition to which EBB refers. The poem in question is Gregory Nazianzen's *Poemata Dogmatica*, 34 (*MPG*, 37, 515).

4. Cf. Deuteronomy, 5:21.

5. *Sic*, for "mine has been." The mistake is indicative of EBB's lifelong distress whenever she thinks or speaks of Bro's death.

6. Mary Ann (Mrs. Richard) Smith had edited volumes II and III of the biography of her father, Boyd's friend, Dr. Adam Clarke. At this time, she might have been engaged in preparatory work on *The Life of the Rev. H. Moore, Including ... the Continuation Written by ... Mrs. R. Smith* (1844).

7. Not identified.

859. RB to Charles Dickens[1]

New Cross, Hatcham, Surrey.
Thursday M^g [7 October 1841][2]

Dear Dickens,

I am far luckier than the rest of your friends in having heard of your illness no sooner than of its partial abatement.[3] Pray get well, and keep so, for all our sakes.

Forster tells me you don't absolutely reject an apple, roasted or otherwise! May I offer you two or three?—no more, because the Scripture blessing of the good man in "his basket and his store"[4]—has only been half-accomplished with us here—the only remains of the best article we can muster for the moment being spectrally true to one's notion of "Osier's Ghost"![5]

Ever yours faithfully,
R Browning.

Chas. Dickens Esqr.

Publication: Dickens (1), II, 401.
Manuscript: Huntington Library.

1. For details of RB's friendship with Dickens, see pp. 368–370.

2. Dated by reference to Dickens's illness.

3. On Friday, 8 October 1841, Dickens underwent an operation for the removal of a fistula; Macready visited him that evening and "suffered *agonies*" as the details were recounted to him, and saw Dickens again on 11 October, this time in the company of RB (*Macready*, II, 145).

4. Cf. Deuteronomy, 28:5.

5. Francis Hosier (1673–1727) was in command of a naval squadron blockading Porto Bello, in the West Indies, to prevent the sailing of Spanish treasure ships. While he was thus engaged, a virulent fever broke out among the crews, claiming some 4,000 lives, including that of Hosier himself. A poem dealing with these melancholy events, "Admiral Hosier's Ghost," was included in Thomas Percy's *Reliques of Ancient English Poetry*.

860. EBB TO MARY RUSSELL MITFORD

50 Wimpole Street
Oct. 9.th 1841

My beloved friend,
It is my remorse & your pardon which I must think of first, in writing to you at last! What is to be said for me? That the flowers sh^d be withered before I thank you for them, withered, & the last stalks thrown away—what is to be said?— And the worst is, I have no very good very iron reason for silence. I have not been ill, no, nor gagged!— And I did receive the beautiful beautiful flowers, and the books, & your letter dearest of all!—, with gladness & thankfulness, besides the dumbness. I stand in my sackcloth & ashes,[1] without a spark of excuse left in them—if this sh^d be none—that I put off from one lazy day to another my duty & pleasure of writing to you, having some letters of paramount propriety to write, & some disinclination through a little more languor than usual (which has passed now) to writing at all—so that it was convenient to me to think to myself "Now I am not *up* to writing today—& to prove it, I wont even write to Three Mile Cross". Besides—I wanted to fix a day for my holiday or holidays——& in order to that, wanted to hear something of dear Mr Kenyon. Not a word comes!— But surely surely he must come back soon. Yes!—it w.^{d} be hardhearted & ungrateful of me, not to give him a slice of my cake, a part of my pleasure, when under similar circumstances *he* has remembered *me*. Dear Mr Kenyon! Scandal about Mr Kenyon! Why who c^d dream of such a thing? Nobody, that I ever heard. Whatever I gossipped about the fair double mystery he carried with him,[2] was for joke's sake! There might as well be scandal about your double dahlias!— Very elderly intelligent women I understand they were—one of them, the Miss Baillie, but no relation to "Queen Joanna",[3] said to be, said by Mr Kenyon to Papa to be, the deepest thinker for a woman, he ever met with!— There is no marrying or giving in marriage[4] in question any more than in heaven—neither marrying nor gossiping my dearest friend!—

The scandal referred to other parties altogether—& I am sorry almost I referred to *it*.[5] Some of it is *so bad* that I reject the belief of it on the ground of the badness. I sh^d not like to write down the least odious of it—but when we meet, I will give you a shadow by which to measure the pyramid!—

I understand that Lady Blessington is ill with dropsical symptoms. Not that *she* is a party!—

Dearest, dearest Miss Mitford, I am punished for my not writing to you by not hearing! When shall I hear you best,—face to face?— When?

You are to listen to all the voices in Wimpole Street, Papa's loudest, through the voice of this letter,—& all saying "Come"—but all saying besides, my dearest friend, that we cant & wont have you (except by an effort & with a lessening of pleasure) unless you will condescend & consent to one night's rest at least, under this roof. Oh will you? Will dear Dr Mitford spare you to us? Is there no friend, if society is necessary to him, who w^d take your place in some imperfect way, for a day or *two*?– I tremble to count on. I fear to presume on your affection even with mine. Speak what your real wish is, & I will try to keep my wishes silently within the bound. I have no right I feel, to pray for even half an hour beyond the time you first spoke of—& perhaps I sh^d scarcely have courage if it were not my persuasion that to come & return as quick as thought & steam would be too great a fatigue for you, as well as a disturbed delight to me!– I told you once, we had a full house. Nevertheless I deny myself now. There is full room for you—there is indeed!– *Full room!*– Papa's only fear is, our quietness—[']'How will she be amused?" You know, you celebrated authors pass over our heads in such an awful roll of thunder, that we are afraid sometimes to look up! How afraid I was to see you the first time!– And I observe that gentlemen are not the less afraid when the celebrities are feminine, but the more!—— Nevertheless the associations connected with your name are so many & various—so dear, as well as so distinguished—the writer is so, not sunk, but, softened in the friend, & in the thought of that beloved friend's kindness to one undeserving of such except by love—that every heart here will spring out to welcome you whether you please to care for the welcoming or not.

And now, dearest dearest Miss Mitford, tell me what my destiny is! Is the *being spared* possible? I mean your being spared by dear Dr Mitford?——

I have not heard from Mr Horne since he wrote to me of Martinuzzi .. A friend of mine, Mrs Orme (who lived once with us as my governess & my sisters',) promised to procure for me from Dr Stone⁶ a copy of *Martinuzzi* which he had marked the margin of, with "great laughter", "peals of laughter", as the spectators laughed where they ought to have cried.⁷ This copy I sh^d like to show you as well as myself. It was a transcript of the impressions of the first night. Now the English Opera House is, I hear, no longer the authors' theatre—the "good floundering beginning" having floundered to a bad end!–

I was quite sure that you w^d like the canadian workman in his tarpaulin hat,⁸ .. & liking him as much as *you* do, I doubt as little that Mr Horne himself *heros* his tale. He has resolute energies in all things—and what is rare, can suffer bravely as well as act. On the first night of the "floundering", when the audience was in fits (of laughter) & a friend of his, a lady, sent a message to him praying his presence to conversation then & supper afterwards, his reply was that he c^d not stir or speak the whole night long,—& there he sate side by side with the poor author, they two together in a conspicuous box, the only two in the theatre, with grave faces!

Mr Stephens[9] is a man of some fortune I believe, & can afford his losses.

There is no time to speak of the books for which I thank you. There is much that is interesting in them!

Dearest friend, may God bless you.

Say how you both are. Give my love to Dr Mitford & beg him not to begin to hate me because I want to steal you away.

Ever your EBB–

Everybody's kind regards– Believe it of them!–

How Arabel thanks you for the introductions.[10] Will you believe it of her that she has not yet delivered them. But she has had some swelling in the face—the cold which is making the circuit!——

Address: Miss Mitford / Three Mile Cross / near Reading.
Publication: EBB-MRM, I, 283–285.
Manuscript: Wellesley College.

1. Esther, 4:3.
2. i.e., Kenyon's two female companions, mentioned in letters 845 and 847.
3. See letter 845, note 8.
4. Matthew, 24:38.
5. The reference to the scandal is not clear; it may have related to an amplification of EBB's remarks about Miss Garrow's lack of popularity, mentioned in letter 847.
6. Tom Stone (d. 1854), a physician, was a friend of Horne.
7. For comments on the audience's inappropriate laughter, see letter 854, note 7.
8. Horne's hat, "preserved as a trophy," is referred to in more detail in the following letter.
9. Stephens was the author of the ill-fated *Martinuzzi*.
10. To Haydon and Lucas, furnished by Miss Mitford with letter 857.

861. EBB TO MARY RUSSELL MITFORD

50 Wimpole Street
Wednesday [13] Oct. 1841.[1]

My beloved friend,

I upbraid myself bitterly ("Should I upbraid"[2]—surely—yes!) for having been the cause to you of such unnecessary uneasiness. It was very wrong in me: and the anxious thoughts you speak of are the only fruit which I would entreat your precious love for me *not* to bear. I must try not to be so guilty again.

Dearest friend, what you tell me of the reasons you have for forbidding us to think of detaining you even one night long, are too sacred to be reasoned against. I will not say a word .. but *this*—that as we have agreed to put off the avatar until a missing high priest of the divinity be here,[3] the little pause may admit of a great improvement in your dear invalid, & your courage may come back, & Dr Mitford himself may say "Do not return until tomorrow or next day". Is'nt it possible, my dearest friend? I used to be a sanguine person, an Inigo Jones in the air[4]—& now I'm at my dirty work again you see!– I must hold on to a hope still. But I dont reason against your reasons—do not suspect me of wishing to do it—and if dear Mr Kenyon comes while things remain otherwise unimproved, I will either embrace gladly & gratefully the amount of joy you promise now, just as it is, or, in the case of everybody's fearing the fatigue & excitement for you too much,—as I do myself,—beg you to put it all off until you can without anxiety join two days together. However it may be, I am angry with myself for talking of 'a full house.' It was wrong of me—& a mistake besides. The house is large for London—and although our family is large too, there is a room for you, a large room,— large enough for K. besides yourself, if you liked her to be there with you & if she could be accommodated on a sofa—& this without *any degree of inconvenience to any of us*– Think of it—keep it in your mind—dearest Miss Mitford. There is the room ready for you at any time. I only wish we could offer one to Dr Mitford—I only wish we could. But we are so many—and the long coats I find, take up more room than the jackets I left behind me![5] Many as we are, we have one heart between us in relation to the affection & admiration due to you. No! I cant put it quite as you tell me! I cant keep it all as affectionate thankfulness for your goodness to *me*! I cant keep away the admiration from working besides—and I would'nt if I could. You remember, I dont share your opinion upon the "good for nothingness" *par excellence* (a construction scarcely odder than the opinion) of authors & authoresses. And oh— dearest Miss Mitford—if I did not fear to shock you, I *could* say something dreadful of *you*——! nothing less than that you never cease, waking or sleeping, grave or playful, in letters or conversation, to appear & be that very terrible thing whatever it is, that you are in your published works. Therefore how can I say to Papa what you tell me—that you are nothing like an authoress?– How can I? Where is my conscience? Indeed I can say no such word. Never was there a more perfect unity than that between the individual & the writer in your case. Do forgive me for thinking so—because *that* was one of the *whys* that I loved you at first sight—& *that* too *was* one of the *whys* that the whole world of us loved your writings long before any first or second sight of mine. They are earnest writings,—sealed to universal truth by an individual humanity.

But I must tell you of Arabel's visit to Mr Haydon & Mr Lucas, by the grace of your goodness to her. Mr Haydon was not at home—"out of town" the servant reported him to be, admitting her however without hesitation into the fresco room– Set (Septimus) went with her, & they both turned their eyes round & round in search of the angel Uriel & could scarcely believe they had found him in the form of what they both talked of as "a sketch in the corner". This however was of course the *fresco*.[6] Do you call to mind the artist's enthusiasm about his new creature standing in the gap of the wall? Now—although Arabel is unlearned upon frescos & did not probably expect rightly, yet we may gather from her report & Set's behind it, that nothing generally striking & obviously great has been effected in the new fresco apocalypse. I should like much to know how others of your friends under the same circumstances, have been impressed or unimpressed. Do tell me. Arabel was utterly disappointed—"*That* all!!" *That* was her feeling.

Well—afterwards they passed to Mr Lucas's—& there, were delighted. One picture, Arabel says particularly captivated her—one of Mr Serg.^{t} Talfourd's children.[7] Did you ever see it? Do you remember it? Then there was the lovely portrait of Lady Burlington[8]—most lovely—& which so little impressed her with the sense of sadness, that she quite started when I told her of the circumstances relating to it—"Taken after death!– Why it looks so youthful & smiling & full of life!–" How differently the light falls on different minds!– Your friend, whose letter you sent me, c.^{d} even see the parting pitying look!—and I hope she is right.[9]

Mr Lucas was very kind & pleased them in everyway—talked of Prince Albert & his talents—"If he had studied five years under Raffael,[10] his remarks could not have been acuter"—thought him very handsome, & the Queen charmless if you except the pleasant countenance & youthful freshness. There were too earnest enquiries about you & Dr Mitford & the probability of your coming to town–

Arabel said "Did you ever paint a portrait of Miss Mitford, Mr Lucas!" "Oh yes!—but it was a failure—he had destroyed it—" (prophane man!) "he had made a great mistake,—& instead of preserving her characteristic of simplicity, dressed her up in a hat & feathers. All was wrong together."

Dearest friend, are you aware that you, as you appeared in this picture & that hat & feathers, are engraved & given to the public to pass judgment on?– Before I went to Torquay, in my yearnings to look upon you I enquired about this matter of engraving. They—Ackermann's people I think—sent me an engraving from Mr Lucas's picture,[11]—and I, in utter discontent, sent it back again & preferred waiting until I could get the profile likeness which at the National Gallery exhibition, appeared to me so like & characteristic.[12] This I *will* have. I am glad Mr Lucas repented of the hat & feathers. It was a sin, verily!——

I forgot, quite forgot, to answer a question, in my last letter. That is, I forgot to send you my last contribution to the hardhearted Athenæum—but it will come in today as an illustration of my Inigo Jones-ship, if Crow can find it.[13] Mr Dilke is kind in sending me the paper—& I respond sometimes, just to show myself alive & grateful–

I had a note from Mr Horne today, to express his remorse at having wandered to "things less worthy" than Psyche,—& "to return". I did not "whistle him back"[14] I assure you—nor even "sign him back"—but as he sends me the modelling of the third & last, department of our drama, little remains I suppose but to set to work. I had been 'revolving in my altered soul'[15] all your gracious & good advice about a subject, & having been haunted for a long while before it came—oh long long ago,—by one of the interdicted ("*A day from Eden*"—half dramatic[16]) was beginning to clear my mind by writing it off previously to doing something better. But this Psyche has the first claim of all you see—has'nt she? There is no room or excuse for a departure on my side—is there?– I think not!– And indeed Psyche, if we only write up to her feet, will make a noble subject—will *show* as a noble subject. Oh I think so– I do indeed!–

I said to Mr Horne that you as well as another less worthy person, had admired the energy under a certain tarpaulin hat– Was I wrong to say "*you*"? I hope I was not. It would give pleasure I knew. And thus he replies, confessing the identity. "The tarpaulin hat, having weathered every storm & vicissitude, is preserved as a trophy of a traveller who visited every place he intended, and after six or seven thousand miles, arrived at his mother's house with one halfpenny.[17] I had a great mind to send it off straight to you (the hat—not the halfpenny, for that alas!— was obliged to go long since) but when I routed it out, the thing was too real & w.^d have much soiled the idea"– I have made them laugh here by saying that if he *had* sent it to me, I w.^d have hung it up by my bust of Plato!——

You are spared my "House of Clouds" today. Crow cant find the Athenæum. I will send it to you—but for today it's too late.[18]

Give my love to dear Dr Mitford!– God bless you both.

Your ever attached
Elizabeth B Barrett–

Address: Miss Mitford / Three Mile Cross / near Reading.
Publication: EBB-MRM, I, 286–289.
Manuscript: Wellesley College.

1. The continuing discussion of arrangements for Miss Mitford's impending visit clearly places this letter between nos. 860 and 862.

2. A reference to the popular air, "Should He Upbraid," from *Two Gentlemen of Verona* (1821) by Henry Rowley Bishop (1786–1855).

3. i.e., until Kenyon returns. In Hindu mythology, an avatar was the appearance of a deity in visible form.

4. Inigo Jones (1573–1652) designed the scenes, costumes and machinery for Jonson's *Masque of Blackness* (1605) and for other stage presentations, pioneering the use in England of movable scenic devices. He was also responsible for the design of a new Banqueting Hall for Whitehall Palace, to replace the structure burned down in 1619. A further mention of Inigo Jones later in this letter indicates that EBB is referring obliquely to her poem, "The House of Clouds."

5. A reference to the physical change in Septimus and Octavius during EBB's absence in Torquay; they were now 19 and 17 respectively.

6. See letter 854, note 2. Miss Mitford had enclosed notes of introduction to Haydon and Lucas in letter 857.

7. This portrait, exhibited at the Royal Academy in 1835, is reproduced in *John Lucas, Portrait Painter, 1828–1874*, by Arthur Lucas (1910), facing p. 14.

8. This was the painting that inspired Miss Mitford's verses (see letter 841, note 5). It is reproduced in *John Lucas*, facing p. 33.

9. Miss Mitford had sent this letter with no. 857.

10. Prince Albert was sitting for the first of four portraits made by Lucas; finished in 1842, it is reproduced in *John Lucas*, facing p. 41. Raphael (Raffaello Sanzio, 1483–1520) was one of the most famous of the High Renaissance painters, specializing in religious subjects.

11. Rudolph Ackermann (1764–1834) was born in Saxony, but settled in England after studying in Germany and France; he established a print shop and drawing school, and was instrumental in refining lithography into a fine art.

Chorley recounts how Miss Mitford "instead of wearing the simple cap, and the soft lace cape folded over the dark dress she usually wore" was persuaded by Lady Madalina Palmer "to accept the loan of a large black velvet hat, surmounted by a plume of white ostrich feathers, and a gorgeous cloak of gentianella blue, lined with white satin" and sat thus to "the secretly demurring artist ... [who] fretted over the bad taste of these sumptuous and unnatural accessories, [and] at last cancelled the picture in a fit of desperation" (Chorley, I, 17–18).

12. EBB saw this portrait, made for Chorley's *The Authors of England*, in 1837 (see letter 570 for her comments on it).

13. "The House of Clouds" appeared in *The Athenæum* of 21 August 1841 (no. 721, p. 643).

14. Cf. Goldsmith, "Retaliation" (1774), line 108.

15. Cf. Dryden, "Alexander's Feast" (1697), line 85.

16. Published as "A Drama of Exile" in *Poems* (1844).

17. These references are to Horne's travels in Canada in 1826.

18. The poem was finally sent with letter 863.

862. EBB TO MARY RUSSELL MITFORD

[London]
18.ᵗʰ Dec.ʳ [*sic*, for October] 1841[1]

Thank you my dearest friend beyond what the expression can convey, for catching my hopes just as they fell, and leaving to our prospect a green "perhaps" on which our eyes may rest. Thank you, thank you!– It is almost too much good to happen really—but the very possibility lets in sunlight. Thank you, dear D.ʳ Mitford,—for coming over to the "faction"–[2] Oh I hope you may be better & better. I hoped so before *indeed*, and now I have another reason for hoping it. I do hope you may be better. And for yourself my dearest friend, I hope you may resolve on doing as much & going to see as many delightful people as possible, so as to save me the remorse of drawing you into dulness. Otherwise I shant be able to help being ashamed. The room is of no awful size, but will admit of another bed on a sofa, if *you* will. Shall you mind having K. to sleep in the same room?– Of course she must come. No inconvenience indeed!–

Oh what a "vision of delight"[3] this visit will be to me!– And, do you know, I am recovering my voice so as to be able to talk to you!– It has threatened to come back again & again through the summer—audible sounds breaking hazily through the whisper—but now, they are repeated thickly & the tone is clearer—is recognized in fact as my own voice—although when I say so, Papa laughs & tells me I am proud of it & meditate a performance at the Opera whereas I am actually farther than ever from being a daughter of harmony. And that's true—I mean the lack of harmony is true!– My poor voice *is*, in this state of transition hoarser than the whisper was. Only it is something to be sensible of a transition.

So that story of the Duke of Devonshire is a verity after all. Of course I had heard the gossip of it,—but never believed a word. And he then is vowed to celibacy.[4] Well—the motives were strong—and yet I do not *think* I could act out my life player-like, even as a Duke of Devonshire,—& especially not, in the face of the world. If my motive *compelled* me, I w.ᵈ have thrown down all I could throw down silently, & have "recoiled into a wilderness".[5]

I had heard of Lucretia Davidson, but in a passing way, & I never read her memoir.[6] Therefore notwithstanding the obviousness of the influence of her memory, the book you sent me suggested something better & brighter than an "imitation".[7] Yes!—& there is, I think (in the midst of the muck which is mere *warbling*) indication of something capable of growth & survival beyond the hour of excitement & desease—deeper tones than those caused by the pricking of the thorn. It is a natural question to ask—"Was it genius—or a show?"—and in the multitude of rhymings

I stopped to ask it. There *are* verses—those for instance in answer to her mother's foolish almost cruel question as to her desire of posthumous renown[8]—which seemed to answer the question in the right way. Still, I scarcely know—!- Was Lucretia older than her sister at the time of death—& was her poetry more promising? Any way, it is an interesting memoir—interesting to pain.[9] I thought it very painful. I would willingly hope that she was something more than a precocious prodigy- Surely she was something more than an *imitation*. But any way, her story is painful,—and her music the very singing within her of the angel of death.

Your's is the poetical view of the Lady Burlington portrait, & is, I surmise, the right one. A painting so associated, which the most loving sigh to look at, should not *smile wholly*.[10] For my own part, I should eschew a little even "white satin" & "the ornaments". They are an anachronism .. and the sentiment must look ghastly by them.

Indeed I have a preference—or I have an aversion rather, to full dresses, hats & feathers & ball costumes, in the portraits of those who have any to love them. The everyday look, not the preparation for a crowd, is what we want to keep by us—the everyday look with not even a smile in it—or if a smile, a gentle musing one expressive rather of love than gaiety. Otherwise, there may be moments as I sometimes think, yes, hours & days & weeks, when the too bright countenance & array may cut us like a knife- It is foolish to think of such things—but I do!-

Your hat & feathers struck me as objectionable for other reasons. It was out of costume altogether. It gave you a '*dowager*-aspect'.[11]

Will you really get the cast for me? Oh if you *will*, if you can conveniently, I must say "yes yes" in my impudent part of acceptance. To have the cast from your own self w.^d increase the value of course—and—I do indeed my beloved friend, think it like you, I really do. There is a harshness which you have not—I am aware of *that*: but the intellectual character is fully caught & conveyed—the thinking mouth—the Coleridgean brows.[12] It is worth fifty "dowagers"—only dont tell Mr Lucas-

And now I must finish. Tell me always how you both are. I fear from one expression that you yourself continue far from quite well. Oh may God bless you- All our love!——

Nay—but I must not forget. A friend of mine, Miss Bordman the daughter, now the orphan daughter of a clergyman in Kent, orphaned of father & mother & thrown upon the kindness & protection of one ready to extend both to her, the excellent Mr Jago of Hammersmith with whom she lives entirely, is as well as her friend a true & understanding admirer of yours my dearest Miss Mitford. Well- That is not wonderful at all—much less so wonderful as to justify a long story & sentence- But I am to go on & tell you how she has supplicated me to supplicate you to

vouchsafe to her some little cutting or plant out of *the* garden—Miss Mitford's garden! She is helping Mr Jago to construct one at Hammersmith as an appendage to his new cottage & upon the model of a garden described in your books. And now if she could but attain to one plant from Miss Mitford's very own garden, by way of link between the ideal & the real!– You see how it is! I promised to be ambassador—to "stretch my sacred hands",[13] fillets & all!– Will you be so gracious? Say 'no' freely. She is a gentle meek creature besides her intelligence, and will take the 'no' as the most natural thing. For "yes" I w^d thank you as well as herself–
God bless you—

Ever your own
EBB.

Disappointed about the Athenæum—*tomorrow*.

Address: Miss Mitford / Three Mile Cross / near Reading.
Publication: EBB-MRM, I, 290–292.
Manuscript: Fitzwilliam Museum and Wellesley College.

1. Confirmation of EBB's erroneous dating is provided by the continuing discussion of topics contained in the previous letter, and by the envelope with a Reading Receiving Office stamp of 19 October 1841.
2. In letters 860 and 861, EBB had urged Miss Mitford to stay at least one night in London; EBB is now thanking Dr. Mitford for agreeing to this.
3. Wordsworth, "The Sparrow's Nest" (1815), line 4.
4. The 5th Duke of Devonshire, during the life of his wife, Georgiana, daughter of Earl Spencer, had had children by Lady Elizabeth Foster, daughter of the 4th Earl of Bristol. Because of this liaison, speculation arose regarding the legitimacy of his heir, William George Spencer Cavendish (1790–1858), fuelled in part because the birth took place in Paris rather than at Chatsworth or Devonshire House. The Duchess died in 1806, and the Duke married Lady Elizabeth in 1809. He died in 1811 and his son became the 6th Duke; he never married. (See *Dearest Bess: The Life and Times of Lady Elizabeth Foster*, by Dorothy M. Stuart, [1955], pp. 51–52.)
5. Wordsworth, "Effusion in the Pleasure-Ground on the Banks of the Bran, near Dunkeld" (1814), line 128.
6. Lucretia Maria Davidson (b. 1808) started writing poetry at the age of four; she died a month before her 17th birthday. A reference in letter 874 suggests that the memoir was *Poetical Remains of the late Lucretia Maria Davidson . . . With a Biography by Miss Sedgwick* (1841).
7. References later in this paragraph indicate that Miss Mitford had sent EBB the *Biography and Poetical Remains of the late Margaret Miller Davidson*, by Washington Irving (1841). Lucretia's sister (b. 1823) also wrote poetry, from the age of six. She died of consumption in 1838, eight months after her 15th birthday.
8. "On one occasion . . . her mother ventured to sound her feelings upon the subject of literary fame, and asked her whether she had no ambition to have her name go down to posterity. . . . retiring to the other room, in less than an hour [she] returned with the following lines ['To Die and Be Forgotten']" (p. 93 of Irving's *Biography*).
9. EBB would have been particularly affected because the details of Margaret's illness mirrored EBB's own experience.
10. In the previous letter Arabel had expressed surprise that a portrait "taken after death" should look "so youthful & smiling & full of life".
11. i.e., in Lucas's portrait (see letter 861, note 11).

12. See letter 828.
13. We have not located the source of this quotation.

863. EBB TO MARY RUSSELL MITFORD

[London]
Tuesday. [*Postmark:* 19 October 1841]

My beloved friend,

After all we cant get a stamped number of the Athenæum. Papa has tried in vain. It appears that through the popularity of the Scientific association reports which helped to fill it, not a single one remains unsold.[1] But I do as well in sending you a page or two—as far as my castle in the air is concerned, & your kind care to see it. As to the castle, you will perceive at once that it is no fit lodging for the critics.

Thank you from my heart, for your kind propitiousness towards my dearest dearest Papa. Yes! I think you *will* be sure to like him! I thank you for the leaning forwards to tell me that you will! What a precious kindness your's is!–

Dearest friend, I have been wondering to myself since I wrote last, as to whether it was greedy & grasping of me to say 'yes' so suddenly upon your offer of the cast. If so, or (without quite such a terrible if) if you cannot very easily & conveniently get the cast for me, do not think that I said 'yes' at all. Otherwise I stand upon it—and how rich I shall be with that memorial of you, besides the soft silken lock, all the prettier for its silver glittering! I never said half enough of *that*!—& dont blame me, for I could'nt!–

So they wont let your Flush travel per railroad!– How uncivilized the world is still!– And *I* am so disappointed—I w^d give anything to see Flush—w^d rather see him than all their machinery! Could'nt he be put into a basket, & smuggled, at the price of somebody's reputation?

As to my Flush he is in great spirits & very well—has taken up a new taste .. for spunge cakes & ratefies,[2]—and thinks it good to be a citizen. But after all he is as true to me as in his days of rural virtue, and wont be led astray far from the door of my room by anybody—except when the body has a hat on its head, & then the temptation carries it. Poor Flush!– Think of his sleeping every night on my bed! I resisted a long while! I would'nt do such a thing on any account. It was wrong & foolish—scarcely cleanly indeed!– Some women might do such things— but no—I never could!– After all Flush persevered, was pathetic, &

gained his object. Flush is 'invincible' like Alexander!—and I had to admit it from the tripod.³ He was in *such* despair when he was sent away!

My brothers,—I forgot to say of them how proud they are of your approbation of their great monsters in the yard.⁴ One is *called* a St Bernardian; but I doubt. The other, the Cuba bloodhound, roars like a lion. You must see & try to approve of them. My doves too, you must see again⟨.⟩

Ever y⟨our⟩ EBB–

No account yet of M⁺ Kenyon. What *is* he doing?–

Address: Miss Mitford / Three Mile Cross / near Reading.
Publication: EBB-MRM, I, 293–294.
Manuscript: Wellesley College.

1. The issue of *The Athenæum* containing EBB's "House of Clouds" (no. 721, 21 August) devoted ten pages to a report of the Eleventh Meeting of the British Association for the Advancement of Science.
2. A ratafia or ratafie was an almond-flavoured biscuit, similar to a macaroon.
3. See letter 787, note 2.
4. The dogs Catiline and Resolute, mentioned in letter 856.

---

864. EBB TO GEORGE GOODIN MOULTON-BARRETT

[London]
Thursday. [*Postmark:* 21 October 1841]

Thank you my dearest George for your obolus–¹ I dont reproach you for not being generous, over-generous I mean, when all I begged you to attain to was the first element of charity. Thank you for the note & the line. I jumped as high as I could for it.

Arabel wrote to you yesterday. I meant to write to you first, although not yesterday—if it were only to prove what 'a lion' or a 'mouse' I could be in gratitude. That I write to you for pleasure's sake besides, ceases to be fabulous.

Dearest George! I am trying to be as glad as possible at your being away—particularly since people say that the result of the absence must be your increase round the waist by an inch. I try to be glad by the ell. And if it were not for the wild horses & the guns, I shᵈ wish you to go to Kinnersley & Frocester, & stretch your stay (not stays) & waist together. Oh, you are sure I think, to go to Frocester. I make myself sure of *that*. Give my love with everybody's to dear Bummy & Arlette & Cissy [Butler]—& dont forget to say how remorseful I was about remembering them all too late.

Now let me see what there can be to tell you– That Trippy is in your place, Arabel has told you of course. Mʳˢ Orme dined here yesterday &

thought me or flattered me "looking better". Henrietta dined with Lady Bolingbroke on saturday, on monday, & went with her on wednesday (with her & Daisy) to Exeter Hall to hear Spohr's Judgment.² On monday she dined in company with Mrs Whitbread—& yesterday I heard such things of the latter, of her reputation or the lack of it, that I mean you to use your authority in putting an absolute end to the acquaintance—³ Under Henrietta's circumstances—unmarried & without a chaperon—it is incumbent that she sh^d be particular in regard to her associates. I am more annoyed about this business that [*sic*] I can tell you here, but not more than I will tell you. I am above (or below—which you please—[)] the suspicion of prudery or particularity or I-would-not-do-such-a-thing-ness, but some *thing* must be done under certain circumstances, the present being those. Well— The scandal will do for some day after tea.

I sent back the third skeleton act of the Psyche, revised & emended, yesterday—& perhaps we may begin to build in the course of another ten days. My hand shakes before it takes up the trowel. The poem looks so well in my head that I am afraid of disappointing myself. But I'll try—that is sure!— And do you know, George,—my plan is, to bind the book (when it's done) in a bright, perhaps a rare fashion—so that it may outwit the annuals—and to have the back overspread with mystical figures—perhaps a great rampant lambent silver serpent lifting its solemn crest & uplifting from the earth in the dreadful pressure of its folds, a man—to typify how, according to our subject,—the humanity agonizes within the sense of Psyche's eternal. Well, then—we need only have some black-&-white spiritual-pictures, by Martin,⁴ to put in between the leaves—and the book will "have a run". That's my plan, Georgie!

I have Capt Maryatt's America from the library—& Pepys.⁵

The gossip down stairs is, that Papa is going to have a stove put into the back drawing-room instead of the fire-place. The bookbinder was here this morning & waited for orders about binding the work-table (yes—binding the top of it) but Papa w^d give no orders because "Sette was'nt at home". How could he, they said, when the master of the house was'nt at home?— Sette is studying at the London university, Logic, Metaphysics, ancient & modern history, the English language & literature, to say nothing of debating & gymnastics. I think it must be a little overwhelming. But he is resolved on being a special pleader & wants to be historical & logical & oratorical all at once. Sundry "dreadful notes of preparation"⁶ appear to him necessary.

God bless you, dearest dearest George. I am very tolerably well—my voice continuing to make inharmonious progress towards audibility—the sense of fitness & comfort in being *here*, increasing day by day. God be thanked. He is tenderer to me than I deserve—oh how far! He might well have denied to me this *remaining blessing*!—— May you have business!—— But dont be discouraged if you have'nt!–

Ever your Ba–

Flush's love! His present taste is for ratafies, but his affections he says are unchangeable.

Address: George Goodin Barrett Esq!. / M!. Palmer's / Westgate Street / Gloucester.
Publication: B-GB, pp. 74–77.
Manuscript: Pierpont Morgan Library.

1. EBB is obliquely reproaching George for the brevity of his note; the obolus was a small Greek coin.

2. *The Last Judgement*, by Ludwig Spohr (1784–1859), was one of the works performed on 20 October 1841 as part of the opening concert under the auspices of the Sacred Harmonic Society. Composed in 1826, it was first performed in England in 1830.

3. We have not been able to identify this lady, or explain "her reputation or the lack of it."

4. John Martin (1789–1854) was known for his historical and landscape paintings, "Belshazzar's Feast" (1821) being probably the most noteworthy. Bulwer-Lytton thought him "more original, more self-dependent, than Raphael or Michel Angelo" (*DNB*).

5. Frederick Marryat (1792–1848), a naval officer and novelist, spent 1837 and 1838 in Canada and the U.S.A., subsequently writing *A Diary in America, With Remarks on its Institutions* (1839).

The diary of Samuel Pepys (1633–1703), Secretary of the Navy, was first published posthumously in 1825.

6. *Henry V*, IV, Chorus, 14.

865. EBB TO MARY RUSSELL MITFORD

[London]
Monday Oct. 25 1841

My beloved friend,

I am in a straight—& know not what to do or say. You are coming on thursday, and I must be glad—overjoyed—that is certain! But you will know what it is that I dont know what to say about!– There's an "about & about"[1] for you!

I suffer under one terror—*that* being lest I may have expressed myself coldly or awkwardly or mysteriously in relation to the room in this house which awaits your acceptance, or, worse than all, to the will of this house's inhabitants to make it available. Dearest dearest Miss Mitford—my ever beloved friend—if I have been so guilty, or say rather so unfortunate, I do entreat you by that dear loving heart of yours to forgive my misfortune. There *is* a room—without disturbing any separate bandbox belonging to any individual petticoat or long coat. There IS a desire on everybody's part (petticoated or longcoated) to have you here. We all feel the honor of it & desire the gladness of it! If I spoke obscurely at first, it was through my ignorance, & because the subject had not been talked over with Papa. Will you believe this; however you determine?– And will you be sure that in the case of your coming, it sh.^{d} be our ambition to give you an 'at home' feeling—that you sh^d dine at luncheon-time, and go in & out to your friends or receive them here just as you pleased?– We have not a carriage at present—altho' Papa talks of getting horses—but if you dont mind the lack of "purple pall & array"[2] there is the carriage which our people use when they want one, & which looks 'respectable', they say although falling short of 'an equipage'. If you condescend to it, my sisters will be too glad to take you anywhere & everywhere, & leave you with your friends, calling again for you—and this they w.^{d} too gladly do, in the case of your sleeping here or elsewhere, should it be the slightest convenience. As to your walking about London— oh no no—indeed my dearest friend, you must'nt think of it. There is excitement & fatigue enough, without walking even from one street to another. And now I have told you all!

What remains?– Just that you sh^d decide according to your own preferences. I say preferences, you see—& not in a passion or a jealousy! I promise not to forget (how c.^{d} I?) that you my dearest dearest friend are coming all this way to see *me*—and so I could'nt be jealous of anybody in the world. My heart is bare to you my beloved friend. I want you first to believe that a room here is open & prepared for you—& next .. *to do as you please*. Decide exactly as you think best. I quite see some reasons leaning to the Chapel Street plan. Your friend may claim a promise[3]—and she may help to lighten your evenings—while I (luckless wretch!) am shut up myself between eight & nine .. soon after sunset!– Altogether I leave it to you—promising to be contented with your finality-measure. I do promise. And now I shall turn my face to the full light, & think of nothing but the great great joy which I am sure to have on thursday. Thank you a thousand times, my beloved friend! 'Ready to see you?' Yes, to be sure. Ready & eager. And as to your tiring me—oh never think of it. I wish there were time to be tired in!– I shall throw away all pruderies of costume & place,—& not mind intruding myself upon you before I get up. I wish there were time for etiquettes—but being on the sofa only for two hours, I cant afford to waste all the rest—can I?

Talking of pruderies,—I agree with you my beloved friend altogether upon that particular matter. Your expression "such are exactly they who w.^{d} not go to *balls*" is pregnant—and we may look to it for the precise restriction between mercy & licentiousness. For my own part I do think somewhat differently from many on this very subject. The censure *'with a difference'*[4] extended by our gracious world to male & female offenders—the crushing into dust for the woman—and the 'oh you naughty man'ism for the betrayer—appears to me an injustice which cries upwards from the earth. Fair wives of honorable husbands who shrink from breathing the same air with a betrayed woman, yet bend their graceful heads & sit in quiet association with such arch-traitors as Lord Fitzharding,—him of Berkeley Castle.[5] The offence is rank, & smells not merely to heaven but in our own nostrils.[6] For my own part & apart from this 'difference', I should not dare to refuse either my forgiveness or my society to a repentant sinner—even altho' *that sinner be a woman*. I sh^d not *dare*. And the world's reasoning against the moral policy of it, weighs lightly as all such expedient arguments do, against the whole grand system of Christian truth. Still the penitence must be as overt as the crime—and as you say, the *so* penitent "w^d not go to balls"– You are not "prudish" my beloved friend, but wise & generous. I never read Leigh Hunt's book—but I will. I never read it—because (now comes a foolish reason) I had understood that he said cruel things & ungrateful of poor Byron & I hated to read them.[7] Lately, wishing to think Leigh Hunt above that shame, I have been wishing to myself to get the book & make it out 'not so bad'.[8] Strange, that you sh^d read it only now!—just now!– I tell you everything, you see.

The post—I shall be too late—& really I cant & must'nt today.
My dearest friend, may God bless you! May God bless both of you–
Your ever & ever attached
Elizabeth B Barrett–

Kind Mr Haydon!——[9]

Address: Miss Mitford / Three Mile Cross / near Reading.
Publication: EBB-MRM, I, 294–296.
Manuscript: Folger Shakespeare Library and Wellesley College.

 1. Cf. Donne, "Satyre III" (1633), line 81.
 2. Cf. "The Cherry Tree Carol," verse 13, line 2 (*The Oxford Book of Carols*).
 3. It is apparent that Miss Mitford was considering staying with a friend in Chapel Street during her visit to London, rather than with the Moulton-Barretts. Unfortunately, an examination of a contemporary street directory does not reveal any immediately recognizable name as her potential hostess.
 4. *Hamlet*, IV, 5, 183.
 5. William FitzHardinge Berkeley (1786–1857) was the eldest son of the 5th Earl of Berkeley by Mary Cole, whom the Earl married in May 1796. After the Earl's death, when William claimed the title, his mother swore before a committee of the House of Lords that there had been an earlier marriage ceremony in March 1785, but the Lords declared the issue of legitimacy "*not* to be proved" and the title devolved upon the fifth son, born in October 1796.
 EBB's reference to FitzHardinge as an "arch-traitor" probably reflects the widely-held belief that his being created Earl FitzHardinge in August 1841 was contingent upon his securing Parliamentary seats for his four brothers in the 1841 elections. They were returned, for Gloucester, Bristol, West Gloucestershire and Cheltenham (see Vicary Gibbs, *The Complete Peerage*, 1926, V, 411, note c).
 6. Cf. *Hamlet*, III, 3, 36.
 7. *Lord Byron and Some of His Contemporaries* (1828). The picture Hunt delineated of his relationship with Byron certainly showed the latter "warts and all." *The Athenæum*

of 23 January 1828 (no. 4, p. 55) said "Mr. Hunt has done a bold deed by publishing this work.... Mr. Hunt says, and we firmly believe him, that he has withheld much which we might have been told; but he has also told much which many will think, or say, that he ought to have withheld. He has presented us with a totally different view of Lord Byron's character from any that has previously appeared in print ... There are hosts of persons who ... will be eager ... to pour upon him, in every imaginable variety of outrage, the accusations of treachery and ingratitude ... [but we] give the most implicit credit to all his assertions."

8. EBB did obtain the book; it formed lot 538 in *Browning Collections* (see *Reconstruction*, A1269).

9. Perhaps an allusion to his undertaking to encourage and advise Arabella Moulton-Barrett on her painting (see letter 874).

866. EBB TO MARY RUSSELL MITFORD

[London]
Tuesday [*Postmark:* 26 October 1841]

I broke off so abruptly yesterday, my dearest friend, the post constraining me, that I forgot one word which must be said today. If you decide upon coming directly to us—*which I dont expect*—so do not vex yourself by prefiguring my disappointment—but if you do decide upon this unlikely step,—ought we not to meet you at the station? *Say the hour.* One word to say it by, & in reply to this!—

Miss M A Browne's poems I never saw collected—but a few snatches of her lyrics, which reached my knowledge, appeared to me, not original, not powerful, rather perhaps the contrary,—however touched with a cordial natural sweetness. I am sorry to hear so sad a story of her.[1] That she was ever one of M.[r] Jerdan's fair poetic saints I never heard before—& assuredly it is a pity he left her for Eliza Cook. Her hand is fitter for the palm– He *may* have desecrated Eliza by this time—I never see the Literary Gazette—and if so the [']Brutus' in the frontispiece looked very likely to rise up in every particular hair with very particular indignation.[2]

To think of how much you have written & edited which has floated away from me, out of my reach, down the current!– Your American stories of children, I bought for Mary Hunter, much to her delight–[3] Your memorials of Lucretia Davidson I do not remember to have heard of even!–[4]

Much of the verse of the day, rather poetic than poetry, rather tuneful than music, stands in the same relation to poems of endurant construction, as the soft sweet moanings of the Æolian harp[5] do to the works of Handel or Beethoven.

Keats—yes—Keats—*he* WAS a poet. But Jove is recognized by his thunder. A true true poet, from his first words to his last, when he said he "felt the daisies growing over him."⁶ Poor Keats! Do you know, did I ever tell you, that Mʳ Horne was at school with him & that they were intimate friends? "The divine Keats"—he says of him—and will not hear the common tale, which I for one thought deteriorative to the dead poet's memory, that he suffered himself to be slain outright & ingloriously by the Quarterly reviewer's tomahawk.⁷ No, said Mʳ Horne to me once—"He was already bending over his grave in sweet & solemn contemplation, when the satyrs *hoofed* him into it."⁸

I am going to confess to you my dearest friend, & when you come you must advise me—for I have a weary conscience about a person whom I heartily admire—Lady Dacre. Three years ago, after the passing between us of a few notes which left me her debtor for much graceful & gracious kindness, she called upon me. It was a strange sort of visit. Oh I do believe she thought me in a strange sort of situation, if not strange myself. She was announced one Sunday, when we were all together in the drawing room, & I, very unwell & helpless, had'nt time to crawl into another room & receive her as I should have done. There was a crowd in the drawing room. Two of my cousins, the Mʳ Clarkes of Kinnersley castle were there—& in addition to our ordinary household helped to produce the effect of a crowd of young men—besides two lady-neighb[o]urs of ours when we lived in the country, country neighbours of Irish extraction who had come to town 'to see the lions'—the sort of people who look quite out of place in town,—very kind, very warm-hearted, very broad Irish, anything but very refined,—what is worse than all, very præternaturally smart,—looking as if they had just emerged from a bog into a rainbow! Well—Lady Dacre found us just so!⁹ And I, proud & pleased to see her, yet a little vexed at the combination, & very vexed with myself at my own half consciousness of being ashamed of my friends,—(& really I could'nt help being the very least in the world ashamed of the blues & pinks & lilacs) had not half the pleasure from her visit which under ordinary circumstances I shᵈ have had.– Well—but, here proceeds the confession. You know how unwell I was—& how distressed to be forced away from home. I was not able to return Lady Dacre's visit, but I might have sent a card, & *I*¹⁰ DID'NT. Never from that day to this hour has her visit been returned or acknowledged. What should I do? Nothing, I suppose. I cant go now—that is sure—and as to sending a card, it wᵈ be out of time & tune now. She wᵈ finish thinking me out of my wits. Have'nt I disgraced you?

God bless you, my beloved friend– My love to dear kind Dʳ Mitford. How I DO thank him!– But it seems like the dream of a dream, this thought of seeing you on thursday. I return your suggestion of High

Priestess-ship & thank M.ʳ Haydon for his kindness to a friend of *yours*!—
That is a prouder name th⟨an "*High*⟩ priestess" for your attached
EBB

Thank you (how gratefully!) for your smile on my verses.¹¹ That is always a crown to them. I have directed the few still worse rhymes in the last Athenæum to be sent to you—not for a smile but a pardon[.]¹²

Address: Miss Mitford / Three Mile Cross / near Reading.
Publication: EBB-MRM, I, 297–299.
Manuscript: Wellesley College.

1. Mary Ann Browne (afterwards Gray, 1812–44) had published several volumes of verse, including *Mont Blanc* (1827), *The Birth-Day Gift* (1834) and *Sacred Poetry* (1840). We cannot shed light on the sad story to which EBB refers.
2. See letter 720.
3. *American Stories for Children* had been published in 1832.
4. We have not found any record of a work by Miss Mitford about Lucretia Davidson.
5. Æolus was the god of the winds. An Æolian harp, usually placed in an open window, produced sounds by the passage of the wind over its strings.
6. Joseph Severn, in a letter to John Taylor, 6 March [1821], told how Keats, four days before his death, had said "I shall soon be laid in the quiet grave—thank God for the quiet grave— O! I can feel the cold earth upon me—the daisies growing over me— O for this quiet—it will be my first."
7. *The Quarterly Review* (April 1818) said of *Endymion* "we have made efforts almost as superhuman as the story itself appears to be, to get through it; but ... we are forced to confess that we have not been able to struggle beyond the first of the four books of which this Poetic Romance consists.... we are no better acquainted with the meaning of the book through which we have so painfully toiled, than we are with that of the three which we have not looked into." The article later said that Keats "is unhappily a disciple of the new school of what has been somewhere called Cockney poetry; which may be defined to consist of the most incongruous ideas in the most uncouth language."
8. Although Keats did not die until February 1821, it was generally believed that the harsh reviews of his work had hastened his death.
9. For EBB's comments on Lady Dacre's visit, see letter 651.
10. Underscored twice.
11. "The House of Clouds" in *The Athenæum* of 21 August (no. 721, p. 643).
12. "Lessons from the Gorse" in *The Athenæum* of 23 October (no. 730, p. 810).

---

867. EBB TO MARY RUSSELL MITFORD

50 Wimpole Street
Nov. 2.ᵈ 1841

Thank you my dearest dearest friend for doing what it was at once so kind & so wrong to do—writing that long note to me when you were tired & when it was too late to write at all. The two words "Quite safe" were the only ones I asked for—and if I had known (as I might,—knowing *you*) the excess that asking for them w.ᵈ induce, I w.ᵈ have tried to be reasonable instead & to suppress my fear of the railway. Well—but you are no longer tired I hope—and here is the dear letter surviving its own evil.¹ I will think of that, and love you my beloved friend for everything.

Ah—you are too kind to me!—both of you—dear Dr Mitford & you!– And how at the end you deceive yourselves in a way which makes even my grave gratitude smile—pretending yourselves to be obliged,—& thanking others for your own goodness! What a curious delusion it is, dearest friend! You for instance, coming this long way by that noisy railway, just to see *me*—as in your naïvetè you admit—and immediately turning round to thank me for my infinite kindness in being not actually a flint, & pleased to see you!– You for instance, with your touching kindness & varied powers of charming, falling down in the midst of us all like a goddess—& then thanking everybody who by imperfect gesture of hand or knee acknowledged the avatar!– As to Papa he is quite overwhelmed. He stopped me in the midst of the delivery of your message to him. "What had HE done"—he said—"What had been in his power."? What have *I* done, is to be said still more emphatically. What have I ever done,—ever since I first looked at you—but honored you as all the world does, and loved you as I could'nt help?

I am only just awaking from the dream which began last thursday. Since saturday, I have been rubbing my eyes. It was so strange, so supernatural to me—so happy besides! How hard to thank you. We *talk Miss Mitford* now, constantly. I am still nearer to you my beloved friend!– And altho' the more you know of me, something must ever more be taken from the superfluity of your estimation of me, yet as you never can find out that *I do not love you*, I am not afraid of falling down the worst depth—while your improved knowledge of what is *mine*, of those who are the dearest to me, and their own experience of the charm which is in you, must draw us more closely together. May God bless you always!– I am not worse as to health, indeed.

The night before last I went to sleep & had a dream of you & the Haymarket. I think the omen was good. Otto was certainly accepted²—but a glorious confusion of personality between Celeste³ & my Flush, prevents my giving a very distinct account of the process. I am so glad you found the scene. That was something to go back for.⁴ And now do tell me, oh do tell me the whole result. The uncertainty keeps me swinging backwards & forwards between a cypress & an olive tree!—every now & then, pricking my feet against a holly.⁵ If I tumble, it will be among the nettles!– Judge how uncomfortable I must be!–

Half an hour ago I received a letter a *psychi*cal letter,⁶ from Mr Horne, which made me smile almost to laughing, it struck with such an unconscious rebound against your *love-opinion* upon my dramatic faculty. Now hear what he says: & "My enemy does not say so"⁷—but my friend—one who is most generous in his general praises, & most, not merely inclined but resolute,—to think well of my poetry. Now hear—& hear besides that I in my inmost conscience recognize his judgment on this point, as being very nearly if not altogether just & righteous as Daniel's!–[8] "—Inasmuch as I have perceived .. or fancied I saw .. that all the different characters in your various writings, are not very different, nor very much of characters in themselves, but rather the medium or vehicle of certain abstract thoughts & images & principles; and forasmuch as they are not of any age, nor of any period of time, nor of any sex character nor physiognomy—but *pure abstractions*, & as such perfect, though not dramatic——"

That is, perfectly undramatic. I need'nt quote any more—need I? And oh how convicted I feel!–

My beloved indulgent friend's own EBB—

What am I to say from everybody? 'All the love they dare[']. [9] Mine to dear D.r Mitford. Thank God he is so well. Do say to K. how sorry both Crow & I are that she w.dnt come in. Of course I had not repeated your excess of kindness to M.r Horne. It was a coincident contradiction.

Publication: EBB-MRM, I, 299–301.
Manuscript: Wellesley College.

1. EBB refers to the letter announcing Miss Mitford's safe return home after her London visit of 28–30 October.
2. As previously indicated (letters 729, note 4, 733, note 15), there had been a revival of interest in Miss Mitford's *Otto of Wittelsbach*.
3. Madame Céleste (1815–82) was a celebrated French dancer and actress. After appearing before enthusiastic audiences in America, she returned to England in 1837 and acted at the Drury Lane and Haymarket theatres. She later (1844) shared with Benjamin Webster the management of the Adelphi.
4. The implication is that, after discussions with the management of the Haymarket, Miss Mitford left behind part of the manuscript of her play and had to return to retrieve it.
5. The cypress was associated with funerals, its wood having at one time been used in making coffins (cf. Shakespeare's "in sad cypress let me be laid," *Twelfth Night*, II, 4, 52). The olive symbolized peace and prosperity (as in Genesis, 8:11) and the holly, used as decoration in the Roman festival of Saturnalia and our Christmas, signified rejoicing.
6. i.e., relating to "Psyche Apocalypté"; presumably the letter to which 868 is a reply.
7. Cf. *Hamlet*, I, 2, 170.
8. Cf. *The Merchant of Venice*, IV, 1, 223ff.
9. Cf. Donne, "The Undertaking" (1633), line 19.

868. EBB TO RICHARD HENGIST HORNE

50 Wimpole Street
Nov. 4.th 1841.

My head has ached so for two days (not my temper I assure you) that I thought it was beheading itself—and now, that 'distracted globe'[1] having come to a calm, I hasten to answer your letter. A bomb of a letter it is, to be sure!– Enough to give a dozen poets, a headache apiece! "No sex—no character—no physiognomy—no age—no Anno Domini"– A very volca*no* of a letter!–

After all, dear Mr Horne, your idea of *revenge* is not tragic enough for a great dramatist, & I may criticise back upon you, on such grounds!– Your vengeance is not tragic enough. But then again I spare you on others. You need'nt "try to recant". I am not angry—dont even feel myself ill used—(that feeling of melancholy complacency!)—and beg you to extend your dramatic sceptre within reach of my subject hands, & with the "diagram" at the top of it!–[2]

When Socrates said that it was worse to suffer, being guilty than being innocent,[3] was'nt he right,—and am I not like Socrates?—in the sentiment . . which I am right in—not position . . which I am wrong in.

At the same time, it does seem hard,—hard even for Socrates,—to drink all this hemlock without making a speech—to die & make no sign. The general criticism is too true a one—absolutely true—but not equally, altogether true, perhaps, in everything. I think for instance that my Page—the Page-lady in the Page-romaunt—has some sex & physi[o]gnomy, however the anno domini may be mislaid, even in her case. Well—but it's a true general criticism—& true particularly besides—& do send the diagram, dear Mr Horne—& be sure that however lightly I have spoken, I must always be gravely grateful to you for telling me all such truths. Miss Mitford came to town last thursday in her abundant affectionateness, just to see me, & returned home on saturday. I saw her for a good part of each of the days—& she asked far more about you than I was able to answer. She measures your dramatic stature by cubits!– She prefers *your Cosmo to Gregory*. So do I you know—altho' the artistic power is greater in the Gregory– And—oh—she told me that the late struggle of the unacted authors has done good already in the theatres. "How" I asked. "Because it disproves the late idea of there being an immense deposit somewhere of excellent unacted dramatic works. People say to one another, '*you see they c.^{d} find nothing more excellent than Martinuzzi*'[4]—& thus the theatres open their doors a little wider to the *rare* virtue![""]

But you c.^{D}[5] *have found something more excellent than Martinuzzi–* There, was the––

Well—but do send the diagram. I wish I c^d "transfuse" into George, who talks of meeting you face to face this evening at Mrs Orme's.

Truly yours
Elizabeth B Barrett–

Of course I could'nt object to listen to your arguments upon the title page, as long as they do not touch my "foregone conclusions".[6] But those—pray, dear Mr Horne remember,—are fixed as Danton's hat.[7]

Address: R H Horne Esqr
Publication: EBB-RHH, I, 39–42.
Manuscript: Pierpont Morgan Library.

1. *Hamlet,* I, 5, 97.
2. In explanation of this diagram, Horne noted: "Referring, probably, to certain geometric figures I had suggested as private 'working' illustrations for the 'Psyche'." *(EBB-RHH,* I, 40.)
3. Cf. Plato, *Georgias,* cap. 469, sections a–c.
4. This comment echoes the doubts of *The Examiner* as to the choice of *Martinuzzi* (see letter 854, note 7).
5. Underscored three times.
6. Cf. *Othello,* III, 3, 428.
7. Danton's hat would, of course, no longer be fixed when the head that wore it was removed by the guillotine in 1794. EBB apparently suggests that her "foregone conclusions" are subject to modification in the light of changing circumstances.

869. EBB TO MARY RUSSELL MITFORD

[London]
Nov. 8. 1841

I hasten to return Mr Haydon's letter,—altho' I shall be driven to write hurried lines in the process. Of course it can only be felt as an honor that he sh^d take any care about coming here—and he may like to see two or three of the pictures whatever else he may not.[1]

As for the fresco, the ideal fresco,—wiser than you all, I mean to postpone my opinion until I see it.[2] Mr Haydon's mystical way of talking of the "poetry of dark" is winning to certain of my weaknesses—and I could'nt help smiling at my own inward sense of approval, clashing as it did just exactly with dear Arabel's "Now what *can* he mean by *that*? I cant understand it"– Well—but—one thing is clear .. these frescos cant be after visible nature .. they cannot—and therefore I hesitate to believe their suitableness to historical pictures, exclusive of queen Elizabeth. On the other hand I dare to perceive or imagine the grandeur of spiritual subjects—spirits & angels—spreading their faint shadowless glories over a vast surface,—with an effect more lustral & supernatural than even the seraphic Guido c^d drag up into his skies together with those dark blue many-shaded draperies.[3] Tell me if this may not be. And do tell me besides why M[r] Haydon seems sure of the immutability of his frescos in our atmosphere of fog-smoke—why he does'nt fear for the water colour the fate of the oil. I like his letters. That intense love of Art & self-renunciation before it & selfglorying within it, I love— Even when the object is not poetry, "I love love".[4] Do not *you*?—

How I loiter on my way,—never till this moment thanking you for your kindest letter. Every drop of your affection being precious to me my beloved friend, am I to say nothing to such an overflowing? Yes— nothing—or the next thing! or I will answer it better,—indeed in the only possible availing way,—by loving you back again.

But now you want to hear something of dear M[r] Kenyon, who must have reached London as you say about the beginning of last week, absolutely in time to be too late! He came, we never hearing a word of it!—he living at I wont count the precise number of paces from where we live. He might have sent us a word—an "all hail"—might'nt he? But he did'nt—he did'nt. Henrietta & Septimus came into collision with him in the street on *saturday*—and though no lives & tempers were lost, he looked a little remorseful, & I, if I had been there, sh[d] have looked a little ruffled. He had had a cold, however, since his arrival, & he was coming to us, & w[d] come the next day at two oclock & see me. I wish he had, for the sake of what I might tell you of him, & also for the sake of seeing him—dear M[r] Kenyon—my own self. But he did'nt come, because Papa, in ignorance of the arrangement, went to his house instead, & I have not seen him or had a line from him up to this moment. Papa says he is to remain in town a very short time—perhaps a very few days—that he has been journeying through Herefordshire, to Malvern . . "tramp tramp across the land"[5] with his fairer demon[6]—& is now about to return . . to Torquay!! He goes to spend a fortnight with M[r] Bezzi!—

Dearest dearest Miss Mitford, may God bless you. I feel unreasonably disappointed (perhaps) at the drama's making no more rapid progress towards representation.[7] I want you back again you see. There was the only evil in coming! I shall be always restless, & catching at the possibility of looking at you! Give my love to dear D[r] Mitford, if I really may say so. Flush is quite well—and siezing upon M[r] Haydon's letter, left his autograph. The letter was barely rescued. Naughty Flush! As mischievous as a magpie, Crow says he grows—more & more mischievous.

Ever your own
EBB—

Publication: EBB-MRM, I, 301–303.
Manuscript: Wellesley College.

1. Haydon did visit Wimpole Street on 21 November (see letter 874).
2. For previous references to Haydon's fresco, see letter 854, notes 2 and 3, and letter 861.
3. Guido da Reni (1575–1642), a painter admired by both EBB and Miss Mitford, favoured bright, lighter colours. He had created numerous fresco decorations, including an "Aurora" (1613) on the ceiling of the Casino Ludovisi.
4. Shelley, "Song" ("Rarely, rarely, comest thou," 1821), line 43.
5. A slight misquotation of Scott's "William and Helen" (1796), line 185.
6. i.e., Sarah Bayley (see letter 845, note 8).
7. A reference to renewed hopes for the staging of Miss Mitford's *Otto of Wittelsbach*.

---

870. EBB TO MARY RUSSELL MITFORD

50 Wimpole Street.
Novr 9. 1841

Dearest friend,

Nelly Bordman came here yesterday too late to be a post[s]cript to the letter I had just sent & yet eager & anxious to be written about. She was delighted up to the full height I expected, with the seeds.[1] I am to tell you how much she feels your kindness—& having felt & loved other qualities, common to you, it must be pleasant to her (—judging from my own experience, it must be—& looking at her animated grateful face, it *is*—) to recognize kindness to oneself as crowning all–

And now, my kind beloved friend, will you send by the railway to me, the two pilgrim-pots—the very two? I see plainly that she w^d. rather not wait—& that there is even a *prestige* in regard to those very two pots, on account of their adventures & their fellow-travellership with you. Nobody likes waiting—& I hate it myself—so I quite take her part in prefering the immediate transference of the very same pots—that is .. if you have not repented!——

Mr Kenyon has not come yet. No—I am not angry, for all the knitting of my brows yesterday. I write all my *humeur*[2] to you, as it comes & goes. It is gone now. Poor dear Mr Kenyon was not well—had a cold—& who knows but it may have returned to him—& that he may fly away in haste & fear without seeing me at all. To obviate whatever part of this disastrous chance might effect [*sic*] your American parcel, I will send it to him at once, I think. Yes—I will!

Did I tell you that he is meditating, & more & more seriously, the purchase of a house at Torquay? *I* am quite sorry!–

I turn away to brood upon all the kindest words you say upon all of us. I thank God day by day, for His unspeakable mercy in bringing me home again—whether to live or die, be it according to His will. You can understand what the deep gladness must be .. although YOU never experienced the bitter anguish of bestowing evil, unmitigated evil, where you w^d only cause good.[3] The scars of that anguish I shall take down with me to the grave. Things past remain present—*some* things. And however I look around me & love them all, dear things,—for *my best beloved*—I may as well say it for it always was so—for *my best beloved* I look up to that Heaven whence only comes any measure of true comfort & adequate endurance. The crown fallen from our heads as a family, can be restored only there.

But it is wrong to write so to you. Do not notice it. It is wrong. May God bless you ever & ever.

Your attached
EBB–

Publication: EBB-MRM, I, 303–304.
Manuscript: Wellesley College.

1. For the garden Miss Bordman was helping to construct at Hammersmith (see letter 862).
2. "Ill-humour."
3. As Bro had been allowed to remain in Torquay only because of EBB's pleading, she always felt herself to be in some way responsible for his death there.

871. EBB TO JOHN KENYON

50 Wimpole Street
Nov 10. 1841

My dear cousin,

What I hear of your having alighted in the midst of us only on one foot & on your way back to the west, makes me fear the possibility of your not finding time (for all your kind intentions) to come here, & so of your going away without this parcel which Miss Mitford directed me to commit to your hands– I therefore resolve upon sending it to you at once.

I was so glad to hear you had come—so sorry that it is but a flash in the pan—that I had better say nothing of being either–

You have heard of our late vision of Our Miss Mitford[1]—but did Papa tell you how she delayed coming on purpose to see you .. I being generous enough to wish that she might ..? and how at last, despairing of you, she came just in time to miss you? Perhaps on your way to the west you may look in upon her? In that case, do let me advise you to bestow the pleasure in the pleasantest manner .. by letting her know *when* beforehand, & by consenting to have luncheon or dinner at her house. I do not speak unadvisedly myself. She complains of your one fault—or two faults .. the not *saying*, & the not *staying*—and I resolved to be impertinent enough to try & work out your perfection.

Your kindness will induce you to be not sorry to hear from me that every day I am more & more thankful to the mercy which permitted my removal. It was the loosening of chains whose iron entered into the soul–² I continue better in all ways—& in my spirits & sense of repose, to a degree surprising to myself–

Dear M! Kenyon, may God bless you!– I have not quite given up the hope of seeing you—but I do not expect what might prove an inconvenience to you—what probably indeed would.

I have been wandering in Lower Austria—very much pleased—by the help of your music-tongued & smiling philosophy.³

Ever affectionately yours
Elizabeth B Barrett–

Publication: None traced.
Manuscript: Armstrong Browning Library.

1. A reference to Miss Mitford's 28–30 October visit (see letter 868).
2. "The Captive. Paris" in *A Sentimental Journey Through France and Italy* (1768) by Laurence Sterne (1713–68).
3. EBB means "Upper Austria," Kenyon's contribution to *The Keepsake for 1842*, just published. EBB repeated the incorrect title in the following letter.

---

872. EBB TO MARY RUSSELL MITFORD

[London]
Nov! 12. 1841

Thank you my ever beloved friend for what did not after all go nearest to my heart, but which I must thank you for first if I mean to do so at all today—your kindness to Nelly Bordman, & the milk for Flushie & me, & the cream, & the lovely flowers!– Oh but it was too good of you to make such a struggle with the Fates for those two bottles, after they had spun them away into Kent out of my reach! I never once thought to have them again,—indeed—& you sh^{dnt} have sent them. Such milk & cream, with the "flower & the lefe"¹ in them!– Worth all the Devonshire cream .. which—between you & me .. does look & taste most insipidly *nasty*—I never c^d bear that liquidity of butter! never did try to bear it, after the first trial! But your cream is real cream—the natural crown of the milk—& clear of the artifice of fingers. While for the milk .. I sh^d leave the praise of it to Flush if he c^d but talk. Flush estimates it infinitely—& watches me with large suspicious stedfast eyes lest I overstep the modesty of justice & take more than my half. And oh the flowers! How lovely—how kind! I sh^d sing instead of *say* about them—& that reminds me of a verse in a little flower lyric I wrote once, some time ago, allusive to your flowers. Probably it will be printed hereafter—but thus runs the verse belonging to you. I had been praising the Devonshire gardens—when mindful of the rival garden in the east, without th.^{r} climate, I diverge in a natural apostrophe—

> "Yet, gifted friend!— The flowers are fair
> By Loddon's stream, that meet thy care
>   With prodigal rewarding—
>
> For Beauty is too used to run
> To Mitford's bower, to want the sun
>   To light her thro' the garden.["][2]

Nelly Bordman is 'ware by this time of your munificence. How she *will* clap her hands & look pleased! Thank you my dearest friend.

No—I have not seen dear Mr Kenyon. I *ebb & flow* about him. I think if I were encouraged, I c.^{d} work myself up into a wrath. Scarcely had I written a note to escort the parcel left in my care, when he came—called—stayed one minute in the drawing room. Arabel said—"I will run up stairs & see if Ba is ready." Oh no—he w^{dnt} hear of it. He had come just for a moment, & c^{dnt} wait to see me—but w.^{d} come another day on purpose. There it remains! To be sure he *may* come!— I sent your book & letters to him that night.

During the moment he was here, he told them he had changed his mind about going to Torquay immediately. He found his home so pleasant that he c^{dnt} part with it immediately. But, that he actually offered a sum of money (in vain) for a certain house there, we have heard from himself—& that he is likely to be persuaded or tempted into the purchase of an uncertain one, we may derive from the circumstances. He admires the scenery passionately—& then that is not all.[3]

As to seclusion—it is not *that*, believe me. There is not such a dancing, fiddling cardplaying gossipping place in all the rest of England as Torquay is—there is not such a dissipated place, in the strongest sense. And it's a ghastly merriment. Almost every family has a member either threatened with illness or ill. Whoever is merry, is so in a hospital. They carry away the dead, to take in benches for the company.

I do not say this from a soreness of individual feeling, which perhaps you may suspect—because long before my own miserable associations with that miserable place, I had a strong apprehension of the ghastliness of the collision there between life & death, merriment & wailing. It has made my flesh creep sometimes.

"Wretches hang that jurymen may dine"[4] being a fainter antithesis than is suggested on everyside. Think of a grand ball being given, where Moses stood . . between the dead & the living?[5]—no!—between the dead

& the dying– A woman in the last agony in one house—a corpse laid out in another—& the whole of surviving Torquay dancing intermediately!– And this not a case to observe, but an instance of a general custom. There is not at any rate a question of seclusion—while the sort of society, with the exception of Mr Bezzi & the Garrows, I cannot imagine to be suitable to a taste formed among the intellectual. I shall be sorry if he goes there—that is, if he settles there.

In the last Keepsake, which I must try to let you see, there is besides Mr Kenyon's graphic philosophy upon "Lower Austria," a long poem of Miss Garrow's, superior in force & picturesqueness (the Athenæum commends it for "picturesque power") to anything I had seen of hers.[6] It is a story in Scott's manner—at least the opening is—& I have been thinking that you may like it better than I do,—even while I admit the accession of force. I w^d. not cheat anybody of that precious thing, your praise—far less a woman—& a student in the great Art I love so devoutly. What I miss myself is individuality & inspiration—the *poet's power over the pulses*. Individuality & inspiration I do *not* find in her. Enclosed is a paper I laid my hand on this morning—some stanzas of hers on poor LEL's death, & in her own autograph.[7] Read it & tell me what you think—& I will try & borrow the Keepsake for another day.

To think of dear Dr Mitford remembering me in the midst of the pain! How kind! Do say how earnestly I hope he may be better—& tell me whether he is so.

And now, in reply to your question, my beloved kindest sympathizing friend–– YES. Yes—YOU DID—& you were estimated aright & fully.

There, went a high soul to *God!*—high talents—only not distinguished among men, because the heart was too tender for energy– Only God who is love, knew how tender to *me*.[8]

I cannot write of these things—you see I cannot—I cannot write or speak– I never have spoken—not one word—not to Papa—never named that name anymore. He was & IS the dearest in the world to me—the first dear & dearest—& because he loved me too well to leave me I am thus—& he is thus—earth's sorrows & God's angels between us. The great Will be done. I am weak & ignorant, & cannot speak of the doing of it–

Thank you for saying it *was not I*—& for your tender tears. It was not I in a sense. I w^d. have laid down this worthless life ten times, & thanked God—but the sacrifice was unacceptable. On the contrary, I was used, I & my love were used as the wretched ever miserable instruments of crushing ourselves in another.

I beseech you to say no more. I love you more dearly for what you have said—but do not say any more. My head turns to write. I never knew DESPAIR before those days—never. And the grief I had felt before so lately,[9]—nay, all my former griefs & I have had many, were bruised out of my heart by one.

'Let us praise God in Christ'[10] for the hereafter—*His* hereafter—the place of meeting & everlasting union–

Your own attached
EBB–

Publication: EBB-MRM, I, 304–307.
Manuscript: Wellesley College.

1. *The Flower and the Leaf* is a 15th-century anonymous allegorical poem, long attributed erroneously to Chaucer.
2. EBB's reference is to "A Madrigal of Flowers," submitted to *The Monthly Chronicle* (but not published) in 1839 (see letter 710). These lines appeared in a modified form as stanza XI of "A Flower in a Letter" in *Poems* (1844).
3. EBB's comment, "& then that is not all", probably refers to the rumours of Kenyon's romantic involvement with some lady in Torquay, quite possibly the subject of the "scandal" about him, mentioned in letter 860.
4. Pope, *The Rape of the Lock* (1712), III, 22.
5. Numbers, 16:48.
6. *The Athenæum* of 6 November 1841 (no. 732, p. 852), in reviewing *The Keepsake for 1842*, said Miss Garrow's contribution, "The Doom of Cheynholme," had a "picturesque power, far beyond the common range of young poets." EBB's reference to Kenyon's poem is incorrect; its title was "Upper Austria." For other comments on Miss Garrow's poem, see letter 847.
7. The manuscript was presumably returned by Miss Mitford, as it is not at Wellesley with this letter. We have not traced any publication of this poem.
8. EBB's writing becomes very erratic at this point, as was always the case when referring to Bro's death. The introduction of this painful subject suggests that Miss Mitford's question related to her having met Bro (see letter 662).
9. EBB was still grieving over the death of her brother Sam, in February 1840, when she was prostrated by Bro's loss in July.
10. Cf. II Corinthians, 12:19.

873. EBB to Mary Russell Mitford

[London]
Novr 18.th 1841.

I felt yesterday & the day before as if I ought to write to you, as if I wished it—& my heart had a pen in its right hand: but the cold dreary weather came between me & the light of your countenance[1] & left me with scarcely energy enough to lay upon paper the thoughts belonging to you.

Oh—I am so glad that you have the habit of returning upon your steps to give me the golden kisses—to put end upon end to your letters— because, as you must observe, that is just my fashion towards you, & I know so well the meaning of it! You must observe how I sometimes, nay, often, write one, two, three, letters running after one another with "last words". They laugh at me for it here. "What! another letter to Miss Mitford, today!" The fountain once unsealed, will flow on.

But I cannot write much today. I began with being tired—and oh, this frost! I have enough to do, lying still here & bearing it.

Do tell me if the title of the book be simply *Joan of Arc*²—for if I call it so, Saunders & Otley may send me Southey's epic or Schiller's play.³ I shall like very much to read it— Your story of the author is a stirring one, to say nothing of your praise of the book. And how w^d you look at me, sh^d I after all take Joan & leave Napoleon?⁴ Sh^d I be right or wrong? Think of it, as you walk once round your garden. I have been turning Napoleon round & round—& after all, I turn myself wistfully towards Joan. Perhaps my original sin of mysticism is struggling towards her visions—and then I have an inverted enthusiasm about military glories, such as Napoleon's were for the most part. Walk once round the garden when the sun comes out, & think. The objection of the ground being pre-occupied by Schiller & Southey, I care the less for, that I w^d treat the subject differently (—yes—very differently, quoth a critic—) & that Southey sang of that inspired maiden in his youth & not with his best music. By the way—I see that a great epic in six books has just appeared, under the very name of *Napoleon*—probably greater lengthwise than otherwise.⁵

Here is a little note from Nelly Bordman. Nelly *is* a pretty name—and the bearer of it, quite a Nelly in herself—with simple, gentle manners, & a sweet voice, & a sense & cultivation & a true womanly loveable nature which do not go necessarily with either. Her delight & pride in your kindness w^d please you—and as for me, she is so grateful to me for saying what I did to you, that I really feel as if *I* had done something great too!! So thank you again, for my share of the pleasure & honor!– She tells me to inclose this note to you, & to take the blame of the blots outside.

You do "encourage" me indeed!– The most modest ill-humour, might, by favour of such fostering, arise & assert itself. Nevertheless I have not frowned myself blind up to the present moment.

No no no—my beloved friend! I do not measure what ought to be, by what *is* in *you*—it w^d be unfair to everybody. YOU are too kind—too tender—*I*⁶ love you too much!– And to prove how it is between you & me— –if *you* were to be in London a fortnight without coming to see me, I sh^d cry myself blind instead of frowning.⁷ There w^d be the difference.

I will send the Keepsake in a day or two, & you shall complete your judgment– God bless you!—& keep you better. Do say particularly how you are & how dear D.ʳ Mitford is. I did hate so, to hear of the indisposition. But the weather—the weather. I feel it too. I c.ᵈ scarcely speak thro' it yesterday—& today I seem writing in a fog, so gropingly & heavily & wearily.

The end must be another day.

Your ever attached

EBB–

Oh but Joan. My belief is that she was *true*. Did you ever hear of Stilling, the German's, book upon Pneumatology?[8] If you have not read it, I mean to make you, when I send the keepsake. There are more things in Heaven & earth than are in other people's philosophy[9] just now– *We*, you know,—you & I—believe everything—and Heinrich Stilling wants us to believe more than everything—for all of which, his book interests *me*.

Publication: EBB-MRM, I, 307–309.
Manuscript: Wellesley College.

1. Cf. Psalms, 4:6.
2. The play (1841) by Thomas J. Serle (1798–1889) did have this title.
3. Southey's poem, also entitled *Joan of Arc*, was published in 1796. The first English translations (1835 and 1836) of Schiller's *Die Jungfrau von Orleans* bore the title *The Maid of Orleans*.
4. Miss Mitford had suggested Napoleon as the subject of a projected epic poem by EBB (see SD1165).
5. *Napoleonis Reliquiæ: a Poem, in Six Cantos* had been published anonymously by Hatchard in October.
6. Underscored twice.
7. In letter 869, EBB reported Kenyon's return to London and his promise to visit her on 7 November, but he had failed to do so, hence her "frowning."
8. *Theory of Pneumatology* by Johann Heinrich Jung-Stilling (1740–1817), translated by Samuel Jackson (1834).
9. Cf. *Hamlet*, I, 5, 166–167.

874. EBB TO MARY RUSSELL MITFORD

[London]
Thursday. [25 November 1841][1]

My beloved friend,

I was half uneasy about your silence & half remorseful at the idea of causing it myself–-remembering how I sent you only the first canto of a letter in my last, & how you might besides, have expected the books I promised some seven days ago. Well—here are the books!– And if you find no 'inspiration' in Lady Blessington's Annual, why there is plenty in Jung Stilling's Pneumatology, to make up for it. Now pray do, I beseech you, read Stilling. His auto-biography (I wish it were here) struck sparks from me, each time I read it[2]—& the impulsion thence taken, of

No. 874 [25 November 1841] 173

interest in the individual Stilling, w^d have carried me clear through these reveries, without another. Faustic touches of the familiar & the sublime cross each other abundantly in the biography—& then the true, the credulous, the elevated, the extravagant .. all meet in the biographer. His first volume is quite a poem—a Hermann & Dorothea melted out into real life,³ by the common sun & air—and to read it with dry eyes is as impossible, as to do the same with a grave mouth. So much for the autobiography which I cant send you. The pneumatology is at least as curious. Tell me your thoughts of it. I hesitate which to wonder at most, the 'facts' or the 'philosophy'—and be sure, that altho' I have smiled sometimes—just when I c^d not help it—I have recognized again & again the charm of the mystical which is in fact the voice of our own souls calling to us thro' the dark of our ignorance, yes, & stood still & awed in MY dark, listening to those rustling sounds of what may be verities, beyond the shell of the body. And then the very commonplace everyday intonation of the writing adds something to the effect. There is no poetry, you see! Not so much odour of poetry in it all, as in five pages of the autobiography!- "I know of a spirit having appeared, on whom the little brass buckles were distinctly recognizable—and this is quite natural &c".⁴ Is not this simplicity quite .. *new* .. at least!—& this within hearing of steam-engines!- They have not utterly ruined us, after all.

Read in the Keepsake, Mr Milnes's sonnet on the death of the Princess Borghese. I do think it exquisite. What a true poet he is!⁵

So you turn the light of your countenance⁶ away from Joan of Arc⁷—& perhaps wisely—considering my infirmities. Nevertheless I do not think with you that an objection to a military-glory-subject reverberates necessarily against Joan. If I wrote of her, it w^d not be of "a great general" but of a great enthusiast—admitting perhaps some actual impulses, according to Stilling, from the spiritual world—nay, admitting them certainly—& preserving faithfully & tenderly her womanly nature unrusted in the iron which sheathes it. Yet, however capable of love, in the sense of the passion, I w^d not make her actually *in love*—because where the imagination is much pre-occupied, the heart is all the less liable to impressions of that particular character. I take Mr Serle's part, you see, against you!- Not that I have seen his book! I have not, up to this moment.

After all, I shall disappoint, my beloved friend, every feeling of yours, except your love- *That* I meet—love to love—heart to heart .. nay, loving you better, in some wise, because more gratefully, than you can ever have reason to love me. For the rest, the dramatic action & real-life-interest, which you expect from me demand peculiar faculties, & such as have not always been possessed by writers more highly gifted than I. Well!- When you are disappointed, you wont love me less—will you?- When you praise me "over head & ears" as the phrase is, I always say to myself .. "She loves me"--& it is pleasanter to think *that*, than the consciousness of the praise being deserved, c.ᵈ ever be!- You will never love me less,—my beloved friend!-

M.ʳ Haydon came on Sunday. It was kind to come at all—it was kind to encourage & counsel Arabel upon her painting—he must be a kind person altogether.

Oh—and M.ʳ Kenyon came, the day before yesterday, & spoke of having been too much occupied (qr.ʸ distributing bridecake!) to do so before. I, despite my wrath, w.ᵈ have gladly seen him,—but I was unwell that day & c.ᵈⁿᵗ get up under any temptation. He was good enough to remind me of y.ʳ goodness, by bringing Marg.ᵗ Davidson's memoir, & also Lucretia's (written by Miss Sedgewick) & also an American version of LaFontaine which I have not looked at yet.[8] He said he was still wavering on the matter of the purchase at Torquay. It is'nt done yet-- Ah yes!—you are right. M.ʳˢ Niven is right!-[9] The ghastly gaiety of such places *is* revolting!—and altho' Hastings takes rank among them, not one conjoins to the desecrating degree of Torquay, the hospital & the assembly—at not one, are the funeral baked meats[10] so hot for the ballroom supper tables! I w.ᵈ not live there—apart from the perpetual pain of certain recollections—for any scenery in the world. And certainly nature is very lovely there!-

Does M.ʳˢ Niven live entirely at Reading[?]- She must be a remarkable woman indeed. And does *Agnes* (I know her as Agnes!) write verses still?

Tell me exactly your mind upon the Keepsake. You will find dear M.ʳ Kenyon[11]— .. oh I can forgive him!

He said—he told them .. that all your friends were jealous of *me* because you were a spendthrift of your time upon me!! See what harm you did by that visit- Not exactly the 'mille mecontents et un ingrat',[12] but a great many jealous ones besides the vain one!!- But that one is very very grateful too!-

No—my dearest friend—dont send any more of the milk & cream just now .. I beg you not to do it. Let it be for the time when you come yourself .. I will consent to have it then!- But not before—not before, my dearest friend!-

God bless you! How I wish I c.ᵈ see you by a glance, as in a dream!- Say how you are & how D.ʳ Mitford is & make my affectionate wishes & remembrance acceptable to him!

It is warmer, but I am not comfortably well even today- It is an effort to drive on my words—& they run uniformly with my metaphor, like a flock of geese. I need not tell you. May it be as clear that I am

ever your attached
EBB-

The Roman Brother—& thank you!—— There are fine things in it—very—but it wants continuity, interest altogether—& leaves you cold as a stone.[13]

I am interested, not par connoissance but *recon*noissance,[14] in the author, who was, as I have lately heard, the editor of that 'Sunbeam' Gazette which shone so benignantly upon my Seraphim.[15] You remember?

Publication: EBB-MRM, I, 309–313.
Manuscript: Wellesley College.

1. Dated by the books promised "some seven days ago" (in letter 873).
2. See letter 516 for EBB's earlier comments on the book.
3. *Hermann und Dorothea* (1797) was a romantic epic by Goethe, set during the post-Revolution invasions of Germany by France. Goethe intended it to show "as in a mirror, the great movements and changes of the world's stage."
4. Chapter IV of Jackson's English translation (1834) of Jung-Stilling's *Theory of Pneumatology* discusses apparitions, stating that the spirits of the departed appear in the form most vividly remembered, and recalls one "spirit having appeared, on whom the little brass shoe-buckles were perfectly cognizable."
5. "On the Death of the Princess Borghese, at Rome; November, 1840."
6. Cf. Psalms, 4:6.
7. In the previous letter, EBB had mentioned Joan of Arc as a possible subject, in preference to Miss Mitford's suggestion.
8. Probably the 1841 edition published by F. Sales of Boston. For details of the memoirs of the Davidson sisters, see letter 862, notes 6 and 7.
9. Mrs. Niven was Miss Mitford's friend and frequent visitor. She had recently emerged the victor in a protracted lawsuit over her inheritance (see letter 900).
10. *Hamlet*, I, 2, 180–181.
11. i.e., his poem, "Upper Austria."
12. "A thousand discontented and one ungrateful" (Voltaire, *Siècle de Louis XIV*, ch. XXVI; he says "a hundred," not "a thousand").
13. *The Roman Brother; a Tragedy*, by John A. Heraud, was published in 1840, but was not performed.
14. "Not for the sake of knowing, but from gratitude."
15. Heraud edited *The Sunbeam* in 1838–39; however, the author of *The Seraphim* review (see vol. 4, pp. 387–400) was identified by Mrs. Orme as a Mr. Frank (see SD945).

---

875. EBB TO MARY RUSSELL MITFORD

[London]
Dec.r 1. 1841.

Dearest dearest Miss Mitford,

No indeed, I am not unwell—and I do not want your D.r Chambers—and when I do, I *will* see him just as you please & Papa pleases & I ought to please. But I am not unwell now. How crossly I must have written to make you think so. How cross I am with myself for making you think so! Forgive me that I may be self-forgiven.

The cold weather had its effect certainly for a day or two—& the result was a languor & dulness & idleness which *pressed* instead of dissipating. You understand!– But my beloved & kindest friend, if I *had* sent to Dr Chambers—, the dialogue w^d have turned in some such way as this—"What is the matter?" "It's very cold."– "What do you want of *me*?" "Why, Dr Chambers, if you w^d only, just .. it's too much to ask, I know! ... but if you w^d only, just, develop the sun for me, & expel the frost, & bring on a chronic stage of summer"!– I do assure you my dearest friend—*that* is all I c^d say to Dr Chambers! And perhaps he might laugh at me! There's no knowing!–

On the other hand, on the nearest hand, I am afraid you have been very unwell yourself, and I cant be quite satisfied with the account of the betterness. Tell me—oh do!—exactly & in detail how you both are. May God bless you!–

You have written *me* a letter full of your own delightfulness, & I cant return you one today, even full of my dulness. Crow says "Indeed you must write very fast", because I stand consciously upon the edge of the last post-hour. Tomorrow or next day shall carry you more—& what is written today must serve & be received as a title page to the letter to come.

To be sure!– Mrs Niven may keep the Pneumatology as long, just as long, as she pleases. I am glad she cares to look into it. I am pleased that the first glance into it has interested *you*. I have a love for pneumatology & for Stilling besides, & love them to be loved. Is not part of the charm of the book owing to the nearness in it of what we are pleased to call *the real* & what we affect to call *the ideal*? That spirit with the little brass shoebuckles represents the whole Stilling-system—does'nt it?[1] The Germans *are* a strange people—a strange, noble people!

We agree then entirely upon the estimate of Miss Garrow's poetry— and I agree with you as to the *idiotic love*[2]—which *is* idiotic & rests there—not kindling & exalting into intellect, as in the beautiful old tale of Cymon–[3] The poetry is however more radically defective, as poetry. It is not a poet's poetry—& leaves the reader's pulses at leisure. How different, Mr Milnes! Oh how different! That sonnet lived by me for nights & days. I am so glad you like it. It is exquisite in all its different movements, each conveying a new mood of tenderness & pathos—

"Now that thou canst not blush at thine own praise—"[4]

What a line it is!—so full of life & death! Beautiful! I quite agree with you. He stands next the throne.

And Mr Kenyon's *are* Mr Kenyon's—not *inspired*, but delightful in their way, & fresh with Nature as he saw it, & philosophy as he feels it, & owing nothing to book-nature & book-philosophy.[5]

I MUST end. This tiresome post!

Your own attached EBB

Publication: EBB-MRM, I, 313–314.
Manuscript: Fitzwilliam Museum and Wellesley College.

1. See letter 874.
2. This doubtless refers to exaggerated praise of Miss Garrow's poetry by Landor, Kenyon and others (see letter 847 and SD1164).
3. "Cymon and Iphigenia" was included in Dryden's *Fables, Ancient and Modern* (1700); it was based on the story told on the fifth day of Boccaccio's *Decameron.*
4. Line 4 of "On the Death of the Princess Borghese, at Rome; November, 1840." This was Milnes's contribution to *The Keepsake for 1842,* just published.
5. Kenyon's "Upper Austria" appeared on pp. 18–23 of *The Keepsake.*

876. Thomas Carlyle to RB

5. Cheyne Row, Chelsea
1 Dec.' 1841—

My dear Sir,

The sight of your Card instead of yourself, the other day when I came down stairs, was a real vexation to me. The orders here are rigorous: "Hermetically sealed till 2 o'clock!" But had you chanced to ask for my Wife, she would have guessed that you formed an exception, and would have brought me down. We must try it another way. For example:

The evenings at present, when not rainy, are bright with moonlight. We are to be at home on friday night, and alone: could you not be induced to come and join us? Tea is at six or half past six.— If you say nothing, let us take silence for yes, and expect you!

Or if another night than friday will suit you better, propose another; and from me in like manner, let no answer mean yes and welcome.

At any rate contrive to see me.

Yours very truly,
T. Carlyle

Address, in Carlyle's hand: Rob' Browning Esq.; *in unidentified hand:* 3 Peckham / Guildford. *Redirected:* New Hatcham / Surrey.¹
Docket, in RB's hand: Dec. 1. '41.
Publication: Carlyle (1), I, 241–242.
Manuscript: R.H. Taylor Collection.

1. Due to the incorrect address, Browning would not have received this invitation in time to attend. Latest postmark is a London stamp for 4 December, 10 a.m.

877. MARY RUSSELL MITFORD TO EBB

Three Mile Cross,
Dec. 3, 1841.[1]

—Mr. Hughes, too, told me the other day of a dream of a friend of his father's, a country gentleman of fortune and character. He thought that his gardener was digging a pit in a certain part of his garden; he watched him, wondering what it could be, until it assumed the form of a grave. Then the gardener went away and fetched the body of a young woman, in whom he recognized his own dairymaid, and deposited the corpse in the ground, and shovelled the earth over it. Then he awoke. He awakened his wife and told her his dream. "Nonsense," said she; "go to sleep again; it is the nightmare." Again he went to sleep, and the dream returned. He again awakened his wife, and she, although a little startled, persuaded him that it had arisen from some talk which they had had respecting the dairymaid's appearance; and at last he composed himself to sleep once more. For the third time the dream returned, and then, arming himself with his pistols, he walked down into the garden. At the very spot indicated he saw the gardener just finishing the operation of digging the grave, and rushing upon him suddenly, the man in his panic confessed that the dairymaid was pregnant by him; that she had threatened to appeal to her mistress; that he had appointed to meet her in a retired part of the grounds at that very hour; and that, in short, if not prevented by his master, before the sun rose the poor young woman would have lain murdered in the pit before them. *This* is a certain fact.

K——, a young woman of remarkable intelligence and presence of mind, has told me frequently of an appearance that she saw, about five years back, when living with a respectable grocer in Buckinghamshire—not as servant but as shopwoman. Her bedroom opened into an anteroom common to two or three chambers belonging to the family. In this room a rushlight was burnt, and she had the habit of leaving her door open, and, after laying her head down upon the pillow, of half rising to look if the rushlight were safe. Two of her brothers and a favourite cousin were at sea in different merchant vessels, and she had that evening expressed to the grocer's daughter her strong impression that she should never see her cousin again. On raising herself up, as usual, to look at the light, she saw just before her, standing in the doorway, the figure of a young sailor. She felt that *it* was no living man: the head drooped on the bosom, and the straw hat fell over the face, which she could not discern. The dress was the usual jacket and trousers, the open shirt, and loosely-tied neckerchief of a seaman. It might have been, from height and appearance, either her elder brother or her cousin. She believed it to be the latter, and spoke to it by his name. It made no answer—but remained during two or three minutes, and then slowly and gradually melted into air. She was as strongly convinced of the reality of the appearance as of her own existence, and is so still.

Both her cousin and her brother returned to London, but the former had had a fall from some part of the rigging of the vessel on that very day (the day of his apparition), and died on shore without her seeing him. Nor has she again seen her elder brother, who, shortly after his return, sailed on another voyage and must have been lost at sea, since, although four years have elapsed since he was expected, neither he nor the vessel has ever been heard of; indeed the underwriters have paid the insurance-money. K⎯⎯ was not alarmed, she said; the only painful sensation was the immediate fear that something had occurred to one or other of these dear relatives, and she shall always, she says, be sure that *it* was her cousin who appeared to her. I believe that these are her very words, and I have no doubt whatever that she did see what she describes; nor would you if you could hear the truthful simplicity, the graphic minuteness, and the invariable consistency with which she relates both the apparition and her own feelings on the occasion. The story, as she tells it, is exceedingly impressive, from the absence of exaggeration and of those circumstances which are usually thrown in for the sake of effect. The door opening upon the staircase was fastened, bolted within; no man slept in the house except the master of the shop, a grave elderly man who officiated as a Wesleyan minister, and whom no money would have bribed into attempting a trick upon such a subject; and the females, besides a general coincidence of character with their husband and father, were all considerably shorter, and in every respect different from the figure in question. K⎯⎯ has never used the word ghost or spirit or apparition, in speaking to me; she generally says "*it*," and certainly thinks of the appearance with great awe.

I agree partly with you that there are glimpses of another world. It seems impossible to refer all these well-attested stories to imposition or credulity.

Another story I remember well. Old Mr. Knyvett, the king's organist[2] (George the Third's—one of whose favourite pleasures it was to hear this splendid musician play and sing the "Hallelujah Chorus" upon a grand pianoforte thrown open—I have heard it often; a wonderful feat it was, accomplished by a perfect knowledge of the score, wonderful dexterity of hand, and a matchless power and compass of voice)—this old man, a wit and a jester, one whose sin was levity—lightness not of conduct but of speech—the very reverse of superstition—this wag lived at a pretty village near Reading, called Sonning, a river-side village reached by a deep winding lane, now shaded by tall close hedgerows, now by the high irregular paling of Holme Park. Over the latter at one particular point, regularly as the clock struck twelve (and it was within hearing both of the church clock and of that belonging to the park) a woman was seen to emerge from the shady lane and disappear *over* the paling—rising gradually and sinking slowly—always the same figure, dressed in the costume of the middle of the last century, and with the self-same disposition and fluctuation of drapery—not a hair's breadth more or less. There was no background to form a phantasmagoria deception, since the part plainest to be seen was the figure as it rose and sank above the paling. When the moonlight was strong the apparition appeared semi-transparent. I have heard Mr. Knyvett speak in answer to a skeptical friend of his and mine, upon this subject—in answer only, for voluntarily he never approached the topic; and the manner in which this thorough man of the world trembled and quivered—cheek and lip blanching as the topic was approached—the doubtful half-glance around and behind him, and the low tremulous voice I shall never forget. It would have been a study for a tragedian in "Hamlet," for it was real. I do not disbelieve in the possibility of such appearances, though I heartily agree with Stilling in the sinfulness and danger of seeking them. By danger, I mean the peril lest such presumption should be punished by madness, or such tremor as is one form of that awful infliction; or by fits or other physical infirmities brought on by mortal fear.

I wonder, my sweetest, how you will get through this sadly tedious scrawl. My father has a grievous cough: it is while in and out of his room that I have written, partly on a low stool at the foot of the bed, using a chair as my table.

Once, again, Heaven be with you!

Ever yours,
M. R. Mitford.

Address: Miss Barrett, Wimpole Street.
Text: L'Estrange (2), III, 127–131 (as 30 December 1841).

1. L'Estrange dates this letter 30 December; this must be in error, as EBB comments on K.'s story in her letter of 6 December.
2. Charles Knyvett (1752–1822) was organist of the Chapel Royal from 1796 until his death.

878. EBB TO HUGH STUART BOYD

[London]
[*Postmark:* 4 December 1841]

Envelope only.

Address: H S Boyd Esq.ʳ / 21. Downshire Hill / Hampstead.
Publication: None traced.
Manuscript: Armstrong Browning Library.

---

879. EBB TO MARY RUSSELL MITFORD

[London]
Dec.ʳ 6. 1841

A bunch of thanks in change for such a nosegay of flowers is shabby merchandize. Yet thank you, thank you. Beautiful flowers they are, & just in time to help the unseasonably warm weather to confront this December of ours which does'nt "behave as sitch". Was there ever such a winter? For three successive days I & my thermometer looked at each other confessing that we c^{dnt} bear a fire. No fire in December for three successive days! Think of *that*! It is wonderful. And I only wanted the flowers you sent to complete the scenery & confirm the illusion. Thank you my dearest friend. Now it is August.

But in regard to Stilling—and in regard to you—and in regard to me who have something to do with it too since I love you so . . oh no—my beloved friend! dont be a Roman Catholic—dont ever. My heart is white of bitterness towards that sect, as my conscience knows. Their great men—& their poor men—have achieved love upon earth. Their saints shine brightly in Heaven. But I cant call their faith "the old faith"—& what is more uncommon, my imagination is never pricked to lean on their side. The old faith was,—by the witness of the Scriptures & the early Fathers,—an older & holier & higher thing. And for the imagination—there seems to me more room for it with the Covenanters[1] under the broad slope of heaven, or with the puritans[2] before they grew narrow & decrepid thro' the force of external pressure, or with the German Lutherans[3] who see celestial visions between the tops of the pines, or with the best of our own dissenters, as they worship God in their simplicity, in words fresh-shed from the heart, & with no other ceremonial that [*sic*] the lifted eye & bent knee—there seems to me more room, more fit & noble room for the imagination with *all these*, than in any forms & festivals peculiar to Roman Catholic observance. That is not, to my mind, what it is often called "the religion of the imagination", but the religion of the senses—nay it is—is it not?—religion sensualized. The opera in the place of the tragedy! The dancers in the place of the poet. Theatrical effects in the place of God's grand scenery! My imagination pricks me away from it all, instead of into the midst of it.

What a singular movement is this Puseyite one[4]—this new *emeute*[5] in the Church of England! If I got as far as Puseyism I w^d go the whole way to Rome. Mr Milnes is a Puseyite & wrote the "One tract more,"[6] which I read at Torquay by grace of Mr Kenyon's kindness, but thought little of. It is an aspect unworthy as it seemed to me, of so true a poet. I kiss his feet as a poet!– I am so glad you estimate the sonnet.[7]

No—again, no!—my dearest friend. I am obliged to say another 'no' to you!—— My feeling is that when our beloved go from us, *The beloved*, he who is so to God & man by right of title, stands there in the chasm—there, to be cried to—there, to be wept before,—there, to lift up the bruised affections—there, to be all-sufficient. Our dead are our absent ones!—and if as Stilling thinks their spiritual abode be in the midst of us, it is not less a state of separation,[8]—& our cry, (happily for that new blessed peace they have won) cannot more reach & wound them. How can they hear any cry of ours?– Does Death invest them with ubiquity—with omnisciense—with God's own attributes?—or are they forced to walk step by step with us—they in their divine sympathy, and we in our earthly sorrowfulness—the one rent by the other?– No—it is not reasonable, I think, that we sh^d wish it—nor is it scriptural that we sh^d believe it. They suffered enough here for some of us—and now He the blessed divinest Saviour who suffered ALL, both for them & us, offers on . . His unwearied sympathy, His pitiful consolation, His witness to what man is & what God is. He is enough for us my beloved friend. Let us not wish to trouble the new peace of our dead.

I am very glad you like Stilling—very—and—oh I quite agree!—there is in his interesting book, a good deal of very perceptible *credulity*. La Harpe's story, besides others, is self-confutable—[9]

Thank you for your delightful letter. I fell down flat under the spell of K's story[10]—and felt my wings grow in the ghostly atmosphere of the whole. But it is'nt possible to write much more just now. I have written myself into such deep gravities that it is'nt possible to emerge all in a moment. Oh letter of mine!—you must be a grave dull letter to the end!——

It was wrong of me, not to have followed close the title page which went before[11]—but just as I took up my staff,—sundry persons insisted upon being written to—sundry persons, not one of whom was half as dear as you!– Yet I obeyed then by a solemn necessity.

Not to forget the question—M.[r] Garrow was not Sir William Garrow's son in any sense—but he was his natural brother—M.[r] Garrow's father not having married the "dark ladie"–[12] To the darkness, his own complexion is said to testify—but he is a sensible intelligent man & an active magistrate & useful citizen, sufficiently so to put his pedigree out of people's heads!

God bless you my dearest dearest friend! I have'nt seen M.[r] Kenyon. He has not tried again. But as to my anger, it is so old that it's quite worn out. Miss Clarke comes to us today– Say how you both are, & if there is a breath of news, or uncertain gossip even, about the tragedy.[13]

Your own attached EBB.

Address: Miss Mitford / Three Mile Cross / Near Reading.
Publication: EBB-MRM, I, 314–317.
Manuscript: Edward R. Moulton-Barrett and Wellesley College.

1. The Covenanters were Scottish Presbyterians subscribing to a covenant for the advancement of their cause; their aims included the extension of Presbyterianism to England and Ireland, and suppression of the prayer-book mandated by Charles I.
2. The Puritans, one of whose principal adherents was Oliver Cromwell, sought the simplification and purification of the forms and rites of the Church of England and looked increasingly to the Bible as the sole authority in religious matters. After the restoration of the monarchy, they became known as Dissenters or Non-Conformists.
3. The Lutherans opposed many of the practices of the Roman Catholic Church, challenged the supreme authority of the pope, and advocated a more personal approach to faith.
4. Edward Bouverie Pusey (1800–82), Regius Professor of Hebrew at Oxford and Canon of Christ Church, Oxford, became fearful that the advance of rationalism would undermine the concept that the church was divinely instituted. With Newman and Keble, he commenced a series of *Tracts for the Times* with the object of reviving and strengthening obsolescent doctrines—efforts that became known as the Oxford Movement. His particular contributions to the movement's publications related to baptism and the eucharist.
5. "Disturbance."
6. *One Tract More, or, The System Illustrated by "The Tracts for the Times," Externally Regarded: by a Layman* [R.M. Milnes], 1841.
7. Milnes's lines on the death of the Princess Borghese, in *The Keepsake*, called "exquisite" by EBB in letters 874 and 875.
8. Jung-Stilling postulated the notion that spirits are not removed to some far-off heaven, but remain close to their loved ones, to act as intermediaries between man and God.
9. Jean François de La Harpe (1739–1803) was a member of the French Academy of Sciences. In his private papers, he left an account of a dinner in 1788, during which he and the others present were amused when Jacques Cazotte (1719–92), a man of great piety, prophesied the specific manner in which each of them, de La Harpe and the host excepted, would die, all within six years. When de La Harpe, a freethinker, queried his omission, Cazotte told him he would die a Christian. Cazotte also prophesied the Revolution and the execution of Louis XVI. All happened as he had predicted. Jung-Stilling, who included this account in chapter 3 of his *Theory of Pneumatology*, accepted de La Harpe's words as true, advancing reasons for dismissing suggestions that they had been written after the event.
10. See letter 877.

11. EBB had said that letter 875 "must serve & be received as a title page to the letter to come."

12. A reference to the "Dark Lady" of Shakespeare's sonnets and to the fact that Joseph Garrow's mother was a high-caste Brahmin. EBB's remarks are contradicted by T.A. Trollope, Garrow's son-in-law, who states that a marriage did take place, and, further, that Sir William Garrow (1760–1840) was Joseph's great-uncle (*What I Remember*, 1887, II, 150).

13. A further reference to revived hopes for the staging of Miss Mitford's *Otto of Wittelsbach* (see letter 729, note 4).

880. EBB TO MARY RUSSELL MITFORD

[London]
Decr 8.th 1841

Oh my dearest friend, how you prove to me day by day (if I wanted other proof than my own self conviction) that you measure out a broad bright ideality with a rood of your own,¹ & call it ME!² But supposing one fault you speak of, to be yours, .. why, not so much in truth & honesty, as in pride & selfgloriousness, do I claim it for mine also!– An Italian said to me once—"There's an expressive word in your language which just expresses *you*. I cant pronounce it, & I cant give an Italian synonym to it, .. but I can Italianize it into *testa lunga*". He meant of course 'headlong'.³ Well then—one of the dearest I have loved & lost—one who loved me most dearly & indulgently—Papa's only brother .. *he* told me years & years since, that I ought to thank God everyday for being born a woman—for that otherwise I sh^d achieve mortal scrapes for myself by my rashness & impetuousity. How proud I am to liken myself to you in that last sentence!– It *is* like—is'nt it?—what was said of you. So take back your praise, and leave me the dear likeness.

I have not read *Self formation*,—& *have* read 'Gaston de Blondeville'.⁴ Perhaps you dont know it, but I am, have been .. in all sorts of tenses—a profound reader of romances. I have read Gaston—and now I am going to disagree with you about him a very little. The fault of Mrs Radcliffe's preceding works was her want of courage in not following back the instincts of our nature to their possible causes. She made the instinct toward the supernatural too prominent, to deny & belie the thing. It was want of courage & power in her imaginative faculty, and want of skill in her artistic, which reduced her books from the high poetic standard to which they aspired, down to the low vulgar level of a satire upon cowardice!– Can anything be much more irritating than the Key to her mysteries,—& the undressing rooms of her ghosts?–⁵

Just in proportion to the degree of this disagreeableness, is Gaston better & nobler in *design*. Inasmuch as the ghost is real, it is excellent—but inasmuch as the book hath three volumes (or two)—it is naught. It did hang upon me[6] (with all its advantages as a ghost story) with a weight from which her preceding works are sacred. It quite disappointed me!– There are fine things—fine glimpses of the spiritual world! But the whole appeared to me heavy & not impressive—&, what is strange, not so terrible with its actual marvels, as were the waxen mimicries of the Castle of Otranto–[7] You are right, I dare say, my dearest friend—& I am wrong. Still it w^d be more wrong to hold back my thoughts unfrankly—& thus spoil the pleasure, when it occurs as it does so frequently, of agreement & sympathy. And I have been reading your Mr Serle's Joan of Arc—confessing with you the talent of the book, while I groaned a little under the heaviness. That art of interesting, does not lie upon the surface. I have read books with scarcely the hundredth part of the talent of this book, which yet were a thousand times more interesting: the proportions being scarcely exaggerated!– Even Joan is not very interesting—true & beautiful as is the aspect she wears. She is seen as in a picture—attitude, countenance—but we dont feel her heart beat—we know nothing of her inward life. Our faith in her is drawn from circumstantial evidence, & not direct knowledge—and the author himself evidently doubts whether it is'nt rather genius than Heavenly illumination after all.

How is dear Dr Mitford's cough? How are *you* my beloved friend? Miss Clarke is surprised to see me looking & seeming so well—remembering how I was at Torquay. Did I tell you of my having achieved a walk .. a yard long?– Crow held me up of course—I cant say, "alone I did it"[8]—but it was a great thing to do with any help–

God bless you, dearest dearest friend! Ah how I wish you *were* as near as Mr Kenyon! How I wish it! But it w^d be too much gladness for such as I am. I have not seen him yet—he has not been here.

Mrs Niven must indeed be a delightful companion. Does she write? Has she written? Or are her hands clean before you?[9] And sh^d I be afraid of her? Is she a person to be afraid of? Those brilliant conversational people are frightful sometimes.

Mr Haydon did not see Papa, but Mr James Clarke, my uncle. His golden opinions[10] are of price.

With the kindest regards of this house to yours, & my love to dear Dr Mitford—I must be the most intimate, out of impudence you see, . . .

ever & ever your EBB—

Address: Miss Mitford / Three Mile Cross / Near Reading.
Publication: EBB-MRM, I, 317–319.
Manuscript: Fitzwilliam Museum and Wellesley College.

1. The rood was a linear measure, varying from locality to locality between six and eight yards.
2. Underscored three times.

3. This was said of her by her Italian teacher (see letter 705).
4. *Self-formation or the History of an Individual Mind* (1839) was written by "A Fellow of a College." Mrs. Radcliffe's *Gaston de Blondeville* was published posthumously in 1826.
5. Mrs. Radcliffe's Gothic novels dealt with frightening and solitary adventures, building up suspense and terror by apparently supernatural incidents, but ending with a rational explanation of these events.
6. Cf. *Much Ado About Nothing*, I, 1, 86.
7. Horace Walpole (1717–97), in his *Castle of Otranto* (1764), also used the popular Gothic form, but without attempting any rational explanation of supernatural events.
8. *Coriolanus*, V, 6, 116.
9. Cf. Job, 18:9.
10. *Macbeth*, I, 7, 33.

881. EBB TO JOHN KENYON

[London]
Dec.r 11. 1841.

My dear M.r Kenyon;

I shall be very glad to see you any day—unless I am more unwell than usual—any day between three and five. I am on the sofa at three & ready & glad to see you. Only dont come,—dont think of coming .. when you do not stand quite free from every pleasanter engagement. Let me feel sure of that.

Thank you for the books. The ballads make a vision of a book, certainly! A book with a glory round it! The difficulty is to read out of it! One may turn the leaves of a rose with less remorse than these—& fear less to leave a stain behind. A south wind in full garden practice, sh^d be retained for the purpose. It's too beautiful for a book.[1]

Channing has delighted me—not only in the 'Self Culture'—but with the divine fervent world-wide Christ-wide spirit of the Congregational discourse.[2] How he puts the Puseyites[3] to shame!– I except a few phrases, a few words & lines here & there, and then admire & embrace the whole! *Virtue* sh^d be considered to include *right ideas of God*—and then he does not admit original sin, nor the tendency to sinning.[4] Everything besides I admire & receive & embrace. He *must* be, I sh^d think, an Arian rather than a Socinian[5]—and whichever he may be, he honors Christ more in this true grand view of Church fellowship, than many Trinitarians do,—for instance than those at Oxford or Rome!

Believe me
Your affectionate cousin
Elizabeth B Barrett.

Publication: None traced.
Manuscript: Wellesley College.

1. EBB may be referring to *Translations of the Ancient Spanish Ballads*, by John Gibson Lockhart, included in the listing of new books in the November 1841 issue of *The Gentleman's Magazine*.
2. William Ellery Channing (1780–1842) was an American Unitarian preacher and author, whom EBB had described as "obviously & prominently an extraordinary man" after reading *The Importance and Means of a National Literature*, published in 1830 (*Diary*, p. 155). The works EBB now discusses are *Self Culture* (1839) and *A Discourse, Preached at the Dedication of the Second Congregational Unitarian Church, New York. December 7. 1826* (1826). The Congregationalists held that each congregation should be entirely autonomous; the Unitarians did not accept the doctrine of the Trinity.
3. See letter 803, note 2.
4. In his *Discourse*, Channing held that the belief in original sin was one of the errors of the Trinitarians.
5. For an explanation of the beliefs of the Arians and Socinians, see letters 511, note 14 and 483, note 3, respectively.

882. EBB TO MARY RUSSELL MITFORD

[London]
Dec.r 16th 1841

My beloved friend I sh.d have written to you today,[1] even if I had not heard from you. The void of your letters .. the aching void .. was becoming oppressive to me—and like a child in the dark I was fancying all sorts of fearful sights just because I c.d see nothing– Ah—and after all, it *is* true that you have been unwell & harrassed by worse than personal painfulness! My beloved friend, how I feel for you! How I understand yet wonder at and admire the strength of your endurance!– How I pray that the burden borne by that tender & strong affection may be lightened, through the Heavenly mercy. Yes—it must be hard—very hard!– In such pain yourself, joined to mental anxiety—& still forced to talk on as the lighthearted & healthy might talk—and 'no response'! No response!– That is hardest of all. But the recognition of your devotedness must be made inwardly & silently, for all the 'no response'. You are blessed a hundred times when you do not know it! And you *will* be blessed hereafter, my beloved friend, were it only in the recollection of this consoling ministry—in the thought that you have been an angel of comfort to the dearest in the world to you! Your incomparable discharge of these hard & high duties *will* have a crown.[2] You are paying a high price for priceless thoughts. Think so, my dearest dearest friend. Do not let your heart sink. Above all do not permit yourself, *for the very work's sake*, to do more than the actual necessity demands. I am so afraid for you! The nobler the energy, the more precious *you*! And I do fear so, lest your health quite fail under the labour you are vowed to! Oh that he w^d admit some one else as a reader & talker . . so as to give you a little rest. May God bless & strengthen you, my beloved friend!– The truest sympathy that ever went from heart to heart, goes from mine to yours!–

Think of dear Mr Kenyon sitting an hour & a half with me yesterday— looking so well, talking so well . . holding up a mirror so full of all the notabilities!

⟨. . .⟩³

it was! "That goes without talking of" as the French idiom says clumsily in my English.⁴ And his plan is to write to you some day that you may take lodgings for him & make no more complaints of his obstinacy for ever & ever.⁵

Oh Flushie! How you *have* tumbled my letter!——

Address: Miss Mitford / Three Mile Cross / near Reading.
Publication: EBB-MRM, I, 319–320.
Manuscript: Edward R. Moulton-Barrett and Wellesley College.

   1. Miss Mitford's 54th birthday.
   2. In letter 877, Miss Mitford had told EBB that Dr. Mitford had "a grievous cough"; writing to William Harness, February 1842, she said "My poor father has passed this winter in a miserable state of health and spirits. His eyesight fails him now so completely that he cannot even read . . . the newspaper. Accordingly, I have not only every day gone through the daily paper, debates and all . . . but, after that, I have read to him from dark till bedtime, and then have often (generally) sat at his bedside almost till morning . . . I have been left no time for composition . . . so that we have spent money without earning any" (L'Estrange (2), III, 136–137).
   3. The remainder of the letter is missing, except for the following sentences, written on the flap of the envelope.
   4. i.e., "cela va sans dire."
   5. Kenyon was contemplating a visit to Miss Mitford (see letter 886).

883. RB to Euphrasia Fanny Haworth

Thursday M^g [16 December 1841]¹

Dear Miss Haworth,

You are kindest of the kind, now and always. —I just remember having said something about wanting to know Etty²—but some owl-faced people perched opposite my desk and looked at me– I don't know what I said—"that I worshipped Etty"? —Well, and why not—as well as Polidoro da Caravaggio?³ But then "my worship is not like other men's"— to quote Mr Poole's friend's play– Who is Mr P's friend? —One who, quoth P., made somebody thus soliloquize—

> I love her so—
> That when I see that beauteous cheek of hers
> I long to bite it as ye would a peach–
> Nay, there's no part in all my mistress['] frame
> But I could cut it off, devour it up ..
> —To show my love is not like other men's.[4]

(Very possibly I quote ill—I remember thro' a mist of claret—) However, thank you, dear friend of mine—if I can I'll call at this week's end—(do I understand you that the note should precede me by post?) I am getting to love painting as I did once—do you know I was a young wonder (as are eleven out of the dozen of us) at drawing? My father had faith in me—and over yonder in a drawer of mine lies, I well know, a certain cottage and rocks in lead pencil and black currant jam-juice (paint being rank poison, as they said when I sucked my brushes)—with his (my father's) note in one corner "RB ætat. 2 years 3 months—"How fast, alas, our days we spend– How vain they be, how soon they end!"–[5]

I am going to print "Victor," however, by Feb.[y][6]—and there is one thing not so badly painted there– —Oh, let me tell you—I chanced to call on Forster the other day—and he pressed me into committing verse on the instant, not the minute, in Maclise's behalf—who has wrought a divine Venetian work, it seems, for the British Institution– Forster described it well—but I could do nothing better than this wooden ware (All the "properties," as we say, were given—and the problem was how to cataloguize them in rhyme and unreason)——

> I send my heart up to thee—all my heart
>   In this my singing!
> For the stars help me, and the sea bears part,
>   —The very night is clinging
> Closer to Venice'-streets to leave one space
>   Above me whence thy face
> May light my joyous heart to thee—its dwelling place.[7]

Singing and stars and night and Venice streets in depths of shade and space and face and joyous heart are "properties," do you please to see. And now tell me, is this below the average of Catalogue original poetry? Tell me—for to that end, of being told, I write it. (It is, I suppose in print now and past help)

I dined with dear Carlyle and his wife (catch me calling people "dear", in a hurry, except in letter-beginnings!) yesterday—I dont know any people like them—there was a son of Burns' there, Major Burns[8] whom Macready knows—he sung "Of all the airts"—"John Anderson"— and another song of his fathers.

I am forced to go and dress— I shall be very glad to see you when you return to Town—tho' sure to do something or other snub-worthy— witness what you say about my absent thoughts—but I will do my endeavours.

Truly yours,
R Browning.

Publication: LRB, pp. 6–7 (as [ca. 30 December 1841]).
Manuscript: British Library.

1. Dated by the reference to RB's dining with Carlyle, also mentioned in letter 884.
2. William Etty (1787–1849) studied with Sir Thomas Lawrence and then in Italy. He is now remembered mainly for the texture and coloration of his nudes.
3. Polidoro da Caravaggio (ca. 1500–43) executed a number of façade paintings in Rome, imitating classical reliefs; only drawings of these survive. His fresco in Rome's S. Silvestro al Quirinale foreshadowed later landscapes in heroic style by such as Claude and Poussin.
4. John Poole (1786?–1872) was a prolific playwright, whose works, such as *Paul Pry* (1825) and *'Twixt the Cup and the Lip* (1826), advanced the reputation of Charles Kemble, among others. We have not been able to identify his friend, or the quotation.
5. We have not located the source of this quotation.
6. DeVane (p. 97) gives the official publication date of *King Victor and King Charles* as 12 March 1842, but some copies must have been circulated prior to this, as the play was reviewed in *The Spectator* of 5 March (see pp. 400–401).
7. These are the first seven lines of "In a Gondola." In a letter of 15 September 1881 to Furnivall, RB recounted how, without having seen Maclise's painting, he composed these lines impromptu from Forster's description of it. *The Serenade* was exhibited at the British Institution in 1842, and RB told Furnivall that, having seen it, he thought his lines "too jolly somewhat for the notion I got from Forster—and I took up the subject in my own way." This he did by adding a further 226 lines and presenting a situation of his own devising; the revised version appeared in *Dramatic Lyrics* in November 1842.
8. It is not clear whether this reference is to William Nicol Burns (1791–1872) or to James Glencairn Burns (1794–1865); both reached the rank of colonel in the employment of the East India Company.

---

884. RB TO ALFRED DOMETT

New Cross, Hatcham,
Dec 19. 1841–

My dear Domett,

It surely is a long time since we foregathered. What say you to coming here next Wednesday?– Our little hills are stiff & springy underfoot with the frozen grass—and you crunch the thin-white ice on the holes the cattle have made—hedge & tree are glazed bright with rime—(to speak Bucolically)– *Do* disappoint all other lovers of good-company and promise me to run over not later than 2. o'Clock. Last week I spent an evening with Carlyle and the next morning with Landor– "What are all these seeings worth, if thou &c &c"

Yours ever,
RB.

Publication: BN, No. 1 (October 1968), 14–15.
Manuscript: Armstrong Browning Library.

885. RB TO CATHERINE FRANCES MACREADY

New Cross, Hatcham, Surrey.
Dec. 23. 1841.

My dear Mrs Macready,

Do me the favor to return my best thanks to Mr Macready for the honor he has done me.[1] I shall avail myself of the Ticket on every possible opportunity. A brilliant Season to Old Drury––a merry Christmas and happiest of New-Years to you and yours!—so wishes (in humble imitation of the Bellman),[2]

Yours much obliged and
ever faithfully,
Robert Browning.

Publication: None traced.
Manuscript: Armstrong Browning Library.

1. There is nothing in Macready's diary to illuminate this remark. The context suggests a complimentary pass to the Drury Lane Theatre.
2. i.e., the Town Crier, who rang his bell to attract attention when announcing momentous news.

886. EBB TO MARY RUSSELL MITFORD

[London]
[23–25 December 1841][1]

My dearest dearest Miss Mitford,

You spoil me for even the kindness of the common world by the subtlety & sweetness of yours. But dont—dont—(hear my prayer against myself!) dont let *me* be one of the multitudinous things congregated together for the work of your weariness. Dont write such long letters to me, my beloved friend! You have too much to do & think of without me—& indeed I cant give up being thought of now & then for all of it; & so I only ask you not to write long letters to me when you have other charities heavy upon your dear hands! How is Ben's mother! How kind you are! & how precious *your* kindness must be to her! When you write, mind you dont forget to tell me how she is.

I will let M.ʳ Kenyon understand your preference about the period of his visit: but you know, my dearest friend, he mentioned his intention as an unfixed thing & in a cursory manner,—and it seems to me as likely as possible that he may not work it out for months. Talking of you made him think as it w.ᵈ anybody that he w.ᵈ like to see you!– "I sh.ᵈ like," he said, "to go & see her. I must write some day & beg her to take a lodging for me." So dont vex your thoughts over the hypothesis of the hope of it. Even hopes are vexing sometimes, when the spirits are worn & the heart, occupied!—and dont *you* be vexed with the hope of it. He seems & professes to be, deep in engagements, besides law-business .. and I am sure it is by an effort of good nature, that he throws it aside for a moment & walks to this door– He has a more 'gentle river'² than "Styx nine times round him"³—& there is'nt a ferry to it!——

M.ʳˢ Jameson's early writings—the Ennuyée for instance—have an adroit leaning to sentiment, which is *sentimentality*, & provokes one the more for the excellent artistic taste observable & admirable even there. In her later books, I do, I confess, see much to admire. The conversations, for instance, on the state of art & literature in Germany .. oh surely, we cannot all but admire their acuteness & eloquence & high intonation.⁴ Of herself individually I know nothing & have not heard much—& what I have heard has the advantage of being self contradictory at every sentence. Now I will tell you *my* story of M.ʳˢ Jameson, which M.ʳ Kenyon said something to confirm the other morning. M.ʳ Jameson proposed to her & was rejected—upon which, goaded by vanity into hatred, he vowed to win her & be avenged. By the apparent devotion of years the first object became attainable. They were married—when, at two steps from the altar, he broke upon the echo of his own oath to love, by words of this kind .. "I have overcome—I am avenged– Farewell for ever."!–⁵

This is *my* story—close, you see, upon L.ᵈ Lyttelton's,⁶ but not, perhaps, less true for the resemblance—it may be true *twice*: and it goes on to describe how the lady, cast out so abruptly & cruelly from the sphere of her conjugal duties, devoted herself with a brave & high tho' sad heart to the discharge of all filial & sisterly ones, .. & in possession of an independent income sufficing for social enjoyment among her chosen friends in Germany, sacrificed taste & comparative luxury in order to inhabit & brighten a poor lodging at Notting Hill which is the home of her family. There, her father lies bedridden,⁷ & her sister keeps a little school,—& she supplies a necessary in one place & a comfort in another by her literary industry—reserving one morning (thursday) in every week for the reception of those friends who crowd in to her society with emulous respect & admiration. This is *my* story—& if like Troy, it[']s to fall to the ground & leave .. M.ʳˢ Sherborne!!!⁸ ... why I must remain very sorry! Who is the romancer? Do tell me! But M.ʳˢ Sherbourne! my dearest friend, M.ʳˢ Sherbourne, M.ʳˢ Sherbourne! She is everything of a devil but it's sublime! I can scarcely catch & carry the idea of such a thing!– As to Marchmont, I suspected before, the identity you speak of. Between M.ʳˢ Trollope & her "grateful *though* obliged friend" Lady Bulwer, poor M.ʳ Foster is done to no gentle death!⁹ But he consoles himself I suppose by dining *en trois*¹⁰ with Charles Dickens & M.ʳ Kenyon!– It was an arrangement of not many days ago, I assure you!–

Have you read the "Blue Belles"? Do– It is very clever—and besides I want you to send me the little key which belongs to the personalities. Who is Lady Dort?—& M.ʳˢ Stewart Gardiner? Who is the painter? It is very clever—good for its bad class! Nevertheless the poet's character, Mortimer's .. I must believe to be altogether unnatural & impossible, indeed self contradictory from first to last.¹¹ She goes upon that falsest of all fallacies .. that poetry is fiction,—but which, being the commonest as well as the falsest, can scarcely surprise us from a quarter the most *antipodic* to poetry, of any on 'mortal ground'.¹²

My beloved friend—I have kept back my letter that I might send you Stilling's Autobiography! But I cant—I cant get it anywhere. Dear George went for me .. with an under-hope of pleasing you .. to sixteen shops the day before yesterday, & to fifteen shops yesterday—& the only bookseller of all who knew the book, told him that probably it was not to [be] met with in London. I *am* so disappointed. Cant M.ʳˢ Cox¹³ get it for you from the place where she read it herself?– I *am* so sorry. I sh.ᵈ like to make you read that first volume—but like the bodiless monumental cherubim, I have not, you see, *de quoi*.¹⁴

This goes to you on Christmas day! May God bless & love you my beloved friend & *your* beloved!– Would that I c.ᵈ look at you for one moment!

Your attached EBB.

Dear little Flush is not well .. out of spirits & appetite. It is however only since yesterday, & we hope he is better already. Dear little Flush! The queen seems happier I think, than she sh.ᵈ be, with her new friends!¹⁵ What do *you* think? Oh—for me—I *did* feel those cold days, but am safely over them my dearest friend.

Address: Miss Mitford / Three Mile Cross / near Reading.
Publication: EBB-MRM, I, 320–323.
Manuscript: Wellesley College.

1. EBB has dated the envelope "Dec.ʳ 25.ᵗʰ 1841."

2. Byron, *Don Juan*, canto III, verse LVI, line 6.
3. Cf. Pope, *Ode for Musick. On St. Cecilia's Day* (1713), line 91.
4. *The Diary of an Ennuyée* was published in 1826 (after prior publication anonymously as *A Lady's Diary*); her later works included *Loves of the Poets* (1829); *Characteristics of Women* (1832); *Visits and Sketches* (1834); *Conversations on the State of Art and Literature in Germany* (1837) and *Social Life in Germany* (1840).
5. Whether or not Kenyon's anecdote be true, Mrs. Jameson's marriage was certainly uncongenial. She was engaged to Robert Jameson in 1821, but the engagement was broken off and she went to Italy. She was later reconciled to him, and they married in 1825, but a few days after the wedding, Jameson went off to visit friends without her (see *Memoirs of the Life of Anna Jameson*, by her niece, Gerardine Macpherson, 1878, chapters II and III).
6. George William Lyttleton (1817–76), 4th Baron Lyttleton of Frankley, Lord Lieutenant of Worcestershire; his version of Mrs. Jameson's misfortunes is not known.
7. Denis Brownell Murphy, Painter-in-Ordinary to Princess Charlotte, died in March 1842.
8. Unidentified.
9. Marchmont is a character in Frances Trollope's *The Blue Belles of England* (1841). We cannot guess at the identity which EBB "suspected," or at Mrs. Trollope's participation in John Forster's "gentle death." He had been unkindly portrayed as Fuzboz in Lady Bulwer-Lytton's *Cheveley, or the Man of Honour*.
10. "As a threesome."
11. See letter 896 for Miss Mitford's key to the personalities in *The Blue Belles of England*.
12. Cf. Donne, "Holy Sonnet" (1633), VII, 12.
13. Mrs. Cox is mentioned several times in the correspondence as a friend of Miss Mitford, but has not been further identified.
14. "The wherewithal."
15. A reference to the new Prime Minister, Sir Robert Peel, whom EBB disliked, and his administration, formed as a result of the general election criticized by EBB in letters 826 and 827.

887. EBB to Hugh Stuart Boyd

50 Wimpole Street
Decr 29.th 1841

My dear friend,

I sh.^{d} not have been half as idle about transcribing these translations[1] if I had fancied you could care so much to have them as Arabel tells me you do. They are recommended to your mercy, O Greek Daniel!–[2] The *last* sounds in my ears most like English poetry—but I assure you I took the least pains with it. The second is obscure as its original, if it do not (as it does not) equal it otherwise. The first is yet more unequal to the Greek. I praised that Greek poem above all of Gregory's, for the reason that it has *unity & completeness*—for which, to speak generally, you may search the streets & squares & alleys of Nazianzum[3] in vain!– Tell me what you think of my part!——

Ever affectionately yours
Elizabeth B Barrett.

Have you a *Plotinus*?[4] & w[d] you trust him to me, in that case?– Oh no—you do not tempt me with your musical clocks. My time goes to the best music when I read or write—& whatever money I can spend upon my own pleasures, flows away naturally in books.

Publication: LEBB, I, 93–94.
Manuscript: Wellesley College.

   1. EBB's translations of three hymns of Gregory Nazianzen appeared in *The Athenæum* of 8 January 1842 (no. 741, pp. 39–40).
   2. i.e., for judgement (cf. *The Merchant of Venice*, IV, 1, 223ff).
   3. The town in Cappadocia where Gregory Nazianzen was born, ca. 329 A.D.
   4. Plotinus (d. 270 A.D.), a Platonic philosopher, wrote on metaphysical subjects; 54 of his treatises are extant.

888. EBB TO JOHN KENYON

[London]
Wednesday night– [ca. 1842][1]

My dear M[r] Kenyon At last I come upon your kindness, empowered to ask a "specific question"—and this is, whether there is at Dresden any academy or institute of the military character where a young Englishman who is waiting for a commission, may wait advantageously—? My uncle[2] would be very glad & obliged if you were to procure this information for him—and yet, knowing how much occupied you are, I almost reproach my own words for saying so.

                                    Ever yours EBB

Publication: None traced.
Manuscript: Wellesley College.

   1. Dated by the handwriting, which could be of this period or any of the next several years.
   2. Probably Thomas Butler, who had four sons.

889. EBB TO UNIDENTIFIED CORRESPONDENT

[London]
[ca. 1842][1]

Henrietta has just had a note from M[r] Kenyon who is "coming to see Ba", he says, today if he can, expressing himself doubtfully– Now this being the case & its being past the hour for him[2]

Publication: None traced.
Source: Draft copy in the hand of EBB, Brown University.

1. This item was found with some manuscript items by EBB known to have been written about 1842.
2. EBB apparently never completed this draft.

890. RB TO JANE WELSH CARLYLE

New Cross,
Wednesday [ca. 1842].[1]

Dear Mrs Carlyle,
　I will breakfast with you gladly indeed, and sit on the proper side of the Countess.[2] She is very much as you say; and Mr Carlyle knows a great deal more about true beauty than anybody else, "comme de droit"[3] – How good you were to me that day![4]

Ever yours and his faithfully,
RB^g.

Publication: LRB, p. 8.
Manuscript: Armstrong Browning Library.

1. Dating inferred from RB's last sentence (see note 4).
2. Countess Pepoli (*née* Elizabeth Fergus, d. 1862), a particular friend of Mrs. Carlyle, had married Count Pepoli in 1840. He was known to Miss Haworth (see letter 656, note 12).
3. "As of right."
4. RB may be referring to the evening he spent with the Carlyles in December 1841 (see letter 884).

891. RB TO RACHEL TALFOURD

[London]
[ca. 1842][1]

Offered for sale in Sotheby's Catalogue, 23 July 1903, lot 196. 2½ pp., 8vo. RB writes: "Out of great mountains come little mice, and out of certain projects of calling personally and saying my thankful say—comes this poor paper and ink acknowledgment of the Sergeant's great kindness ... to see Paris, and the Rhine, and the Alps, and be silent: *I* am, I know grateful that he has spoken out. I have read the 'Recollections'[2] with the greatest delight, seeing in my mind the whole party at every turn. Will you have the goodness to tell him this, mending my imperfect phrase."

1. Dated by the reference to Talfourd's book.
2. *Recollections of a First Visit to the Alps, in August and September 1841*. The volume was privately printed and is undated; the British Library catalogue gives [1842?].

This copy formed lot 1134 of *Browning Collections*, and is now at ABL (see *Reconstruction*, A2245).

892. THOMAS CARLYLE TO RB

Chelsea,
1 Jany., 1842.

My dear Sir–

If you happen to possess, among your Commonwealth Books, a copy of Heath's *Chronicle of the Civil Wars*,[1] I could like to look at it for a while. It is a dim, close-printed scraggy old folio, not of the thickest; the author (who wrote the *Flagellum* too)[2] is a noisy blockhead; but his old farrago serves one as a kind of dictionary now and then. If you have it not, pray never mind, never regret;—who knows if that will not even be a kind of benefit to me! The stupidity of those old dead Books excels all that it has entered into the imagination to conceive.

With many true regards, and hoping to see you again in person before long,

Yours always,
T. Carlyle.

You do not happen to have Dugdale *on the Imbankment of Fens*,[3]—or any Book that will give one an idea of Oliver's locality two hundred years back?[4]

Text: Carlyle (1), I, 246–247.

1. James Heath (1629–64), historian and Royalist, was the author of *A Brief Chronicle of the late Intestine War in the three Kingdoms of England, Scotland, and Ireland* (1661).
2. Heath had also published *Flagellum; or the Life and Death, Birth and Burial of Oliver Cromwell, the late Usurper* (1663).
3. William Dugdale (1605–86), archæologist, topographer and Garter King-of-Arms from 1677 until his death, was the author of *History of Imbanking and Drayning of divers Fenns and Marshes* (1662).
4. Carlyle sought these books in connection with *Oliver Cromwell's Letters and Speeches*, which he published in 1845. An admirer of Cromwell, he stigmatized Heath as "Carrion Heath." If RB did possess any of these titles, they did not survive as part of the library existing at the time of his death.

893. EBB TO MARY RUSSELL MITFORD

[London]
Saturday [1–6 January 1842][1]

My beloved friend,
I had hoped to lay by this morning to my pleasure & a letter to you .. when my aunt changed her mind or had her mind changed & left us today instead of *mon*day. Therefore I have been thinking & saying goodbye goodbye .. the spring of my pen is broken!– George is going too—dear Georgie! Only to be away a week though—but still a parting is a parting—and these things have grown graver to me lately.

Dearest dearest Miss Mitford, I have pondered a week past, whether Dr Mitford or even yourself w^d care to have a little of the West Indian Chocolate which we have sometimes. It is scarcely possible to get it in London unless one's face be set in toward Jamaica—and a week since Papa had some directly from thence. I w^d have sent it as soon as the thought struck me—but he said "Stop—wait! wait till we ascertain the goodness of it"—because there's a doubt—a difference of form & colour from the orthodoxy of Jamaica chocolate. If they adjudicate it *good*, you shall have it on monday my dearest friend. I do think it might suit Dr Mitford. It is even recommended by the Homœopathists .. & Dr Jephson of Leamington smiles over it.[2] At least three weeks ago, my cousin Isabel Butler[3] a patient of his just now, sent for some to Papa .. in vain at the moment. Oh I shall be so pleased if you, either of you, like it better than I do!

Mr Kenyon has been here again, & I told him without your name in the tale, that I wanted to know "the rights" of Mrs Jameson. I had heard, I said, two stories of her, perfectly different, & didn't know which to prefer.[4] 'Well'—he answered—'tell me your stories, & then you shall hear mine.' So I told him, and his witnessing third story confirmed the one I told *you*. She has suffered much, by his account, very much & undeservedly, even from the altar steps down to these poor laborious days at Notting Hill—and as to this Mr Jameson, he is a master-man only in cruelty & takes no eminence from talent or accomplishment. He is only superiorly *bad*!– Therefore my dearest just & merciful friend, you will think better of one authoress at least in the world, & no longer withhold from her your dear esteem. The rights of her do, you see, turn out to be the *wrongs* of her. Did you not *really* like the introductory dialogue to those translations from the Princess Amelia?–[5] Well, but *personally*, you will be glad, (for I know you), to do her justice .. justice as a wife & daughter & sister. Mr Kenyon says that she wins her way with you, the more you know her. She is very plain—has red hair—but all that vanishes when she talks & you come to know her– The object of her voyage to Canada was conciliation. She hung by a hope to it—which hope broke off like a Canadian icicle. She returned home without having even looked in his face!——[6]

Dearest Miss Mitford I began these little sheets on saturday morning & have been drawn out of sight of the post ever since. Have you wondered about my silence? Ah I do hope it did'nt look unkindly. I think of you, my beloved friend, long foolscap sheets-full & crossed! Never think I do not think of you.

Tell me how the chocolate seems.[7] They call it good—but it does'nt look quite as I w^d have it. The next excellent, which comes within my reach shall go straight to you.

Did you see Mr Hunter's treatise upon the Tempest?[8] Mr Kenyon 'caused it to pass before my face'[9] & I did not complain of the briefness of the vision. I hate (be it uttered in Christian charity!) I do hate all those geographical statistical historical yea, & natural-historical illustrators of a great poet. I hate them & excommunicate them! I dont care a grain of sand on the shore whether Prospero's island was Bermuda or Lampedusa! Certainly says Mr Hunter, it's Lampedusa—and he embraces with his title-page a map .. an absolute map of Lampedusa! And we are to put it, my dearest friend, into all our editions of Shakespeare!! The proof is complete! Lampedusa has a troglodytal coast, & Prospero lived in a cave! And there are lime-trees in both places! As if Shakespeare c^{dnt} make lime trees grow any where—out of granite stone if he pleased—and find caves in a wood! As if Shakespeare's Island was'nt Shakespeare's island—and as if *that* was'nt enough for us!–

But listen—here is another discovery! Ariel, the dainty Ariel, that creation of beauty .. who do you suppose Ariel is? Of all the birds in the air & beasts on dry land, which is Ariel? Answer!– "A BEE!" A BEE!! Do you understand?– "Where the bee sucks, there suck I"[10]—& therefore, says the Shakespearian *Ergoteur*,[11]—Ariel must be, I think, more like a bee than anything else. Well—now you are surprised, but I have'nt done yet with my natural history. Who do you think Caliban is! *I* sh^d guess "*a fly*"—if I did'nt know—thinking, not merely of an antithesis for Ariel, but of the derivation of Beelzebub or bul, that king of the flies,[12] & of Mr Hunter's evident tendency to consider Calibanism a species of devilry. But no—it is'nt a fly .. & you will never guess. Who is Caliban? Answer—"a kind of tortoise!" Poor Shakespeare! If he had'nt been twice immortal, how he w^d have died miserably in the hands of his commentators! He w^d not have lived up to these last lashes.

Mr Hunter is a Unitarian minister, & an execrably ingenious man.

I have been reading too by the same grace .. of dear Mr Kenyon .. Mr Alford's Chapters on the Greek poets.¹³ I dont like them at all. Such criticism, on the surface & of long familiarity with the common eye, the sense of the world has outgrown. It w^d have done for those days when poetry was considered a pretty play like skittles, but is not suitable to this *now*, when its popularity as a toy is passed, & its depth & holiness as a science more surely tho' partially regarded.

Dear little Flush is quite well, thank you! His illness did not extend over the evening of Christmas day & he recovered just in time to take a little turkey! He is quite well now, & in most abounding spirits,—& goes out most days,—although, when in the house it is as hard as ever to tempt him from the duskiness & solitude of this room. He wont stir out of it with anybody except Crow! They all 'pay him every attention' and he recognizes & returns it courteously ..., in everything except the presentation of Papa's snuffbox. But he wont leave the room, *unless they have their hats on*, for one of them! If Crow happen to be away, I am forced to send for his dinner,—or Mr Flush falls into low spirits for the lack of it. He wont leave me even for *that*, .. & a few days since, three o clock found him dinnerless yet resolute not to go. He cried a little now & then .. & at last I sent for it!—& he thanked me for my courtesy as emphatically & eloque⟨ntly⟩ as tail could wag!– How are you, both of you? How is Ben's mother?

Dearest friend, I do not speak of Mr Kenyon's movements because I know he was going to write to you. You wont see him this winter! God bless you always.

Your most affectionate
EBB

Address: Miss Mitford / Three Mile Cross / Reading.
Publication: EBB-MRM, I, 323–326.
Manuscript: Folger Shakespeare Library, Edward R. Moulton-Barrett, and Wellesley College.

1. Inclusive dating provided by London postmark of 6 January 1842.
2. Henry Jephson (1798–1878) was a well-known physician, practising at Leamington Spa.
3. Isabella Horatia Butler (1822–46) was the 3rd daughter and 7th child of Sir Thomas and Lady Frances Butler.
4. For EBB's prior reference to Mrs. Jameson's unhappy marriage, see letter 886.
5. *Social Life in Germany, Illustrated in the Acted Dramas of ... the Princess Amelia of Saxony*. Translated from the German, with Introduction and Notes by Mrs. Jameson (2 vols., 1840).
6. EBB is misinformed; Mr. Jameson had been pressing his wife, who had gone to Germany in 1834, to join him in Canada and this she did, with some reluctance, in September 1836. However, the hoped-for reconciliation did not transpire, although Jameson did agree to give his wife an annuity of £300 when she left him in 1838 to return to Europe.

7. Miss Mitford told Miss Anderdon that Dr. Mitford disliked the flavour, but that she herself "found astonishing relief from the use of it" (see SD1165).

8. Joseph Hunter (1783–1861) was a Presbyterian minister, antiquarian and author, who devoted much of his adult life to the interpretation of Shakespeare's texts. In 1839, he published *A Disquisition on the Scene, Origin, Date, etc. of Shakespeare's Tempest*, in which he suggested that the play was one of the earliest in the Shakespeare canon, rather than one of the latest, as is generally believed. He also hypothesized that Prospero's island was Lampedusa, off the coast of Tunisia.

9. Cf. Job, 4:15.

10. *The Tempest*, V, 1, 88.

11. "Wrangler; disputant."

12. Beelzebub, the god of Ekron, was described as "the chief of the devils" (Luke, 12:15); to the Jews, he personified the false gods. The name was popularly held to signify "Lord of Flies."

13. Henry Alford (1810–71), Dean of Canterbury (1857–71), a prolific author, is now best known for his edition of the Greek Testament (1849–61). EBB refers to his *Chapters on the Poets of Ancient Greece* (1841).

---

894. EBB TO HUGH STUART BOYD

50 Wimpole Street
Jany. 6.th 1842.

My dear friend,

I have done your bidding & sent the translations to the Athenæum, attaching to them an infamous prefatory note which says all sorts of harm of Gregory's poetry.[1] You will be very angry with it & me.

And you *may* be angry for another reason—that in the midst of my true thankfulness for the emendations you sent me, I ventured to reject one or two of them. You are right probably, & I wrong—but still, I thought within myself, with a womanly obstinacy not altogether peculiar to me, .. "If he & I were to talk together about them, he w^d kindly give up the point to me .. so that, now we cannot talk together,––*I might as well take it*." Well—you will see what I have done. Try not to be angry with me. You shall have the Athenæum as soon as possible.

My dear Mr. Boyd .. you know how I disbelieved the probability of these papers' being accepted. You will comprehend my surprise on receiving last night a very courteous note from the editor,[2] which I w^d send to you if it were legible to anybody except people used to learn reading from the pyramids. He wishes me to contribute to the Athenæum some prose papers in the form of reviews—"the review being a mere form, & the book a mere text." He is not very clear .. but I fancy that a few translations of *excerpta*, with a prose analysis & synthesis of the original author's genius, might suit his purpose. Now suppose I took up some of the early Christian Greek poets, & wrote a few continuous papers so?[3] Give me your advice, my dear friend! I think of Synesius for one. Suppose you send me a list of the names which occur to you! *Will* you advise me? Will you write directly? Will you make allowance for my teazing you? Will you lend me your *little* Synesius[4]—and Clarke's book?[5] I mean the one commenced by D[r] Clarke & continued by his son. Above all things, however, I want the *advice*.

Ever affec[tely] yours.
EBB

Address: H S Boyd Esqr / 21. Downshire Hill / Hampstead.
Publication: LEBB, I, 95–96.
Manuscript: Wellesley College.

    1. EBB's translation of three of Gregory Nazianzen's hymns appeared in *The Athenæum* of 8 January 1842 (no. 741, pp. 39–40). Her "prefatory note" included the statement that "There are poetical writers who are not poets ... Of such is Gregory. He is an ORATOR;—less wordy and monotonous than Chrysostom, but more laborious and antithetical ... He can build anything lofty, except a 'rhyme'."
    2. i.e., Charles Wentworth Dilke.
    3. The outcome was "Some Account of the Greek Christian Poets," published in four issues of *The Athenæum*, commencing with that of 26 February 1842.
    4. EBB probably refers to the edition by Franciscus Portus that she had borrowed earlier (see letter 446).
    5. *A Concise View of the Succession of Sacred Literature* (1830–32). Commenced by Boyd's friend, Adam Clarke, who died in 1832, the work was completed by his son, Joseph Butterworth Bulmer Clarke.

895. EBB to Thomas Westwood[1]

50 Wimpole Street
Jany. 7th 1842.

Miss Barrett—inferring M[r] Westwood from the handwriting,—begs his acceptance of the unworthy little book he does her the honour of desiring to see.[2]

    It is more unworthy than he could have expected when he expressed that desire—having been written in very early youth when the mind was scarcely free in any measure from trammels and *Popes*, &, what is worse, when flippancy of language was too apt to accompany immaturity of opinion. The miscellaneous verses are, still more than the chief poem, 'childish things'[3] in a strict literal sense—& the whole volume is of little interest even to its writer except for personal reasons—except for the traces of dear affections, since rudely wounded .. & of that *love* of poetry, which began with her sooner than so soon, & must last as long as life does without being subject to the changes of life. Little more therefore can remain for such a volume than to be humble & shrink from circulation.

Yet M.ʳ Westwood's kind words win it to his hands. Will he receive at the same moment, the expression of touched & gratified feelings with which Miss Barrett read what he wrote on the subject of her later volumes, still very imperfect altho' more mature & true to the *truth within.*—? Indeed she is thankful for what he said so kindly in his note to her—

Publication: LEBB, I, 94–95 (as 2 January 1842).
Manuscript: Wellesley College.

1. For details of EBB's friendship with Westwood, see pp. 375–376.
2. *An Essay on Mind.* This copy is now at Wellesley (see *Reconstruction*, C34).
3. I Corinthians, 13:11.

896. MARY RUSSELL MITFORD TO EBB

Three Mile Cross
January 9th 1842

My dear love—I have just looked through the Blue Belles—and so far as I can guess at Mrs Trollope's people[1]—not of course myself thinking of all of them as she does—I should say that Lady Dort was Mrs Skinner of Portland Place[2]—who is really quite as absurd if not more so- Lady Stephens Lady Hessey[3]—Lockhart Miller of course Lockhart Milman[4] and I suppose Lady Robinson Lady Morgan- Jane Beresford Joanna Baillie[—]Lenient and Contrarius, Sidney Smith and Rogers (very like)— Bradley Edwin Landseer,[5] like but a caricature- Lord Willoughby Lord Normanby-[6] The position and description of Henry Mortimer, especially the conceit and affectation resemble Henry Taylor, author of Philip van Artevelde- The extract from an American book is really an extract from Cooper's Eve Effingham[7]—a book worth reading since it shows exactly what the-highest-in-pretention-society of New York is—very much what that of Birmingham or Manchester or Liverpool people may be I suppose at this time- Do read it. That the picture is true can be in no way better proved than by the fact that the book gave such disgust to our Transatlantic friends that Cooper was well nigh as unpopular in America in consequence of it as his American impertinences had long ago made him in Europe. Mrs. Trollope had conceived herself to have an especial cause of offence— on being asked to meet her in Paris he declined adding "No woman on earth is worth talking to—nor is any one worth looking at after fifteen"- He added another saying that he had also been invited to meet Sismondi[8] but had refused as having no opinion of European Republicanism or European liberty- In fact our friend Mr. Cooper is a Cooperite in the sense in which Douce Davie Deans[9] was a Deansite—he believes in no one's talent or virtue except his own. Do read Eve Effingham—the book as a fiction is worthless but very curious as a true and unconscious picture of society amongst these pretenders. Lady Georgina is Lady Emmeline Stuart Wortley–[10] Mr. Rolfe doubtless Mr. Matthias now dead[,] Marianne Skerrett's uncle—author of the Pursuits of Literature and of many fine translations into Italian–[11] Till forty he did not know a word of the language and had never been in Italy and although living there during the latter years of his life and finally dying at Naples could not either talk or understand Italian. —My friend Mrs Fitzgerald told me that she one day invited him to dinner by some idiomatic phrase (which I have forgotten) tantamount to our potluck and was obliged after twice repeating to translate it into English for the benefit of the great Italian Poet. By the way the stuff about Petrarch and the disgusting flattery of Lady Dacre whose translations are just ladylike is perhaps the most offensive and the most degrading thing that I have known Mrs Trollope do.[12] —Let me see– These seem to me the principal people– *One* puzzles me—the official man whom she represents somewhere (I can't find the passage) as giving glimpses through some glass of character etc. —It's somewhere in the early part of the volume– The American reading Cooper's book[13] is meant for Willis[14]—but a flagrant caricature because in accent and conversation you would not have distinguished him from an Englishman. —Where Lady Dort is making her memoranda about her coachman[15] she of course means a hit at Dickens—and I think this is pretty nearly all the mystery that the book contains. As a story it seems to me a very bad copy of Miss Edgeworth's excellent Manoeuvring[16]— and the "dear friend" and "Do you understand me?" of Mrs Hartley are chiefly curious as being what especially the first Mrs Trollope uses the affectation herself[—]"Sons are expensive, dear friend" and so forth I have heard from her lips and read in letters over and over– As to Mrs Skinner (I don't know if she be extant still) her absurdity cannot be overcharged– I must tell you one calamity that befel her in her love of lionizing– General Pepe[17] and she met at some I expect watering place she having seen him in London—forthwith she hooked her arm under his and finding that he had not yet been to the Library insisted on his accompanying her there that their names might be inscribed close to each other on the book—the lady's was of course first written and after some slight hesitation the unfortunate exile wrote a short inscription immediately after– "My name" said the General "is unhappily so notorious just now that I have borrowed that of another exile one of my aide-de-camps"– Mrs Skinner much disappointed (for the notoriety was what she wanted) looked—and imagine her horror when she saw that all unconscious of its Sadler's Wells celebrity the General had written down the name of

"Grimaldi"[18] and so they stood poised upon the Library book Mrs Skinner—Mr. Grimaldi!!!

Yours ever
M.R.M.

What does Mr. Kenyon say to Moxon's having produced a cheap edition of Miss Sedgwick?[19]

Publication: None traced.
Source: Transcript supplied by Mrs. E.E. Duncan-Jones.

1. In letter 886, EBB had asked Miss Mitford for "the little key" to the personalities in Mrs. Trollope's book, *The Blue Belles of England* (1841). In the following notes, we only deal with those people not identified previously.
2. We have not been able to trace Mrs. Skinner; contemporary directories do not list anybody of that name in Portland Place.
3. Unidentified.
4. We have not traced anybody of this name. Perhaps Miss Mitford meant that the character was a compound of John Gibson Lockhart (1794–1854) and Henry Hart Milman (1791–1868), the poet, Canon of Westminster and (1849) Dean of St. Paul's.
5. Edwin Henry Landseer (1802–73), the painter, discussed in more detail in the following letter.
6. Constantine Henry Phipps, 1st Marquis of Normanby (1797–1863), had been successively Lord Privy Seal (1834), Lord Lieutenant of Ireland (1835), Secretary of War (1839) and Home Secretary (1839). After Melbourne's administration fell in 1841, he held no further ministerial office.
7. *Eve Effingham; or, Home* (1838), first published as *Home as Found*, by James Fenimore Cooper (1789–1851), who is now best remembered for *The Last of the Mohicans* (1826).
8. Jean Charles Léonard Simonde de Sismondi (1773–1842), Swiss historian and economist, was the author of *Histoire des Républiques Italiennes du Moyen Age* (16 vols., 1807–18) and *Histoire des Français* (31 vols., 1821–24).
9. In Scott's novel, *The Heart of Midlothian* (1818), Douce Davie Deans was the father of the accused child-murderer, Effie Deans.
10. Lady Emmeline Charlotte Elizabeth Stuart-Wortley (1806–55), poetess and playwright.
11. Thomas James Mathias (1754?–1835), satirist and Italian scholar, had published *The Pursuits of Literature, or What You Will* in 1794–97. He composed and published verses in Italian, edited the works of a number of Italian writers, and translated English works into Italian, including Spenser's *Faerie Queene* and Milton's "Lycidas."
12. In chapter XIX of *Blue Belles*, Mr. Rolfe expatiates on Petrarch, his idol, observing "How strangely impossible, too, has it ever seemed (excepting in one miraculous instance) for any language in the world to produce a translation of Petrarch! ... impossible, save ... in one single case, wherein a Maga ... has produced an echo which startles one into the belief that the disembodied spirit of Petrarch has revisited the earth." His listener responds "you can only mean the translations of Lady Dacre" (pp. 201–202).
13. "Mister Wilmot of New York" (ch. XXV).
14. Nathaniel Parker Willis (1806–67), American author and journalist, wrote *Pencillings by the Way* (1835) and *Melanie, and Other Poems* (1837). He is discussed in more detail in the following letter.
15. In chapter XIII.
16. Published in *Tales of a Fashionable Life* (1809) by Maria Edgeworth (1767–1849).

17. Baron Guglielmo Pepe (1783–1855), a Neapolitan general who served under Napoleon, fled to London in 1821 to escape the sentence of death passed on him after the Bourbon restoration.

18. We have not been able to identify the Grimaldi who was Pepe's aide-de-camp. The Sadler's Wells Grimaldi was the actor and pantomimist Joseph Grimaldi (1779–1837). When ill-health prevented his continued appearance on the stage, he was appointed assistant manager at Sadler's Wells (1825).

19. Moxon was advertising a four-shilling edition of *Letters from Abroad* in *The Athenæum*.

897. EBB TO MARY RUSSELL MITFORD

[London]
Jany. 11. 1842

My beloved friend,

I should not have paused two days before I told you how very very glad & half-proud I felt about the chocolate. I never hoped for so much as that *you* sh^d be able to take it. I overpower myself with congratulations. "Benedetto sia il giorno"[1] when I thought of it! As to dear Dr Mitford, it is easier to meet his taste & capability,—but my ambition stopped short in its thoughts before it touched *you*—& now just in proportion to the surprise, is my gratitude, .. to your digestion! Oh I wish there were more shaddocks! And it is'nt the time of ships![2] nor will it be (for the coming in of them I mean) until June!

Thank you my dearest friend, for the *Key*.[3] I used it with the eagerness of Blue Beard's wife[4]––& am satisfied, thank you, to the uttermost of the curiosity of my malice––or of the malice of my curiosity .. whichever it sh^d be philosophically. I had guessed a good many of the names—but, from the want of personal knowledge, was quite at a loss for many—for instance I stared myself blind at Lady Dort, Lady Stephens, Bradley! I did not guess *Contrarius* either the least—& mistook Rolfe for Roscoe[5] instead of Mathias! Willis appeared "in naturalibus" from the hearts & darts attributed to his poetry—to say nothing of the juxtaposition with Cooper in the quotation from Eve Effingham which I had read & recognized. Still the coarse American accents puzzled me—not that I ever heard or saw him—but that his writings produce an idea ... scarcely so much of Shakespeare .. praying Miss Porter's permission,—as of a literary petit maitre[6] .. very fine & finical .. lisping adroitly [']'To make his English swete upon his tongue"[7]—peradventure with a diamond ring on his little finger & a rose in his button hole, & a "Thy pardon, fair London brides"[8] among his compliments!—in fact anything except a coarse man or a great genius! & one nearly as little as the other!– I remember! He went with Miss Porter on the pilgrimage to Stratford.[9] There he must have bewitched her! *He* a great writer!! How you astonish me! Pretty & fanciful he often is, graceful sometimes, vivacious generally! And there, is said the outside of all .. & perhaps you may think beyond it! How *wonderful* of Miss Porter!–

You cannot think how your letter has amused me. ONE[10] of the portraits of Miss Pardoe, engraved & attached to her work upon Hungary, suggests certainly *twice eighteen*.[11] And so she w.d take M.r Henry Chorley in lieu of the Sultan! You know how *he* turned a longing lingering look upon her in the streets of Constantinople .. with a view probably to the seraglio![12] And she w.d catch M.r Chorley's handkerchief after *that* .. & settle down into the armchair of an English matron![13]—as if she had never touched a Turkish cushion—or seen a dervish spin!! Allah Kerim![14] It is astonishing indeed!–

She has talent—she can even be eloquent occasionally—& word-painting is an art with her. And her last book (it *is* the last—is'nt it?—the *Hungary*?) has far less wordiness & affectation—a less smell of the theatre! As she *grows older*, my dearest friend, she may be worthier & truer, & more secure of your esteem. I hope she may. Not that I wish her ever to marry y.r friend unless you desire it!–

M.rs Trollope's book *is* clever, do you not admit?

And Bradley is Edwin Landseer! Well! I have heard only now, only today a dreadful story relating to him! Do you know that he is insane—has a keeper now, while I write?– The story is terrible! That he had been subject to cruel agitation through an attachment to the Duchess of Bedford—that they were secretly married—that after the murder of L.d William Russel, he was employed to paint a portrait of the dead .. to which effect he, & *the Duchess only*, were shut up with the murdered man—that the picture was never finished .. that the artist overcome by a dreadful complexity of feeling & emotion went mad at his task & has never recovered his mind from that dreary day to this.[15] Tell me, if you can, that there is'nt a word of truth in it. It makes me shudder while I write it. The *fact* is that no picture of his has been exhibited since,—& the rest, I do hope, rose up armed out of somebody's tragic head.[16]

My dearest friend, what kind things you tell me of Miss Anderdon's kindness of thought about my poetry. You knew it w.d please me—& be sure that it *did*! Papa has sent you my 'last appearance' in some translations from Gregory, of which I sh.d like to hear y.r full mind. You know they are not mine—except as far as the 'doing into English' goes—so your love for me need not pull at your sleeve when you w.d give me a free opinion of the poetry. I have translated them almost literally.[17]

Since then, M.[r] Dilke has written to me very courteously, to ask me to send him some prose papers in the form of reviews .. to which I said a kind of 'yea' .. altho' nothing is settled as to subjects. I ventured to propose a series of sketches of the Greek poets of the early Christian centuries with translations[18]—& have heard nothing. Of course whatever I write shall be sent to *you* my beloved friend!–

That cramp!—and that watching by night & day! I grieve to think of it– I pray that God's dearest comforts may be with you, whether of earth or Heaven! How I love you! How I look up to you! Look down on me & love *me* my dearest friend!

Ever your attached EBB–

O my forgetfulness! I saw M.[r] Kenyon on Saturday—when he was on the verge of a departure for Hastings—an unwilling one, he said, but for friendship's sake. We talke⟨d of⟩ you stedfastly—& agreed *so* well in measuring YOU[19] some cubits higher than your books .. high as they are! He means to write to you soon.

I am tolerably well for the *weather* but not very comfortable. I have sent twice to Saunders & Ottley for *Aurelian*[20] & must have it soon.

Address: Miss Mitford / Three Mile Cross / near Reading.
Publication: EBB-MRM, I, 327-330.
Manuscript: Wellesley College.

1. "Blessed be the day."
2. i.e., from Jamaica.
3. Miss Mitford's interpretation of Mrs. Trollope's *The Blue Belles of England*, contained in the previous letter.
4. Blue Beard's wife, entrusted with all the keys of the castle during his absence, but ordered not to enter one particular room, cannot master her curiosity. On opening the forbidden door, she finds the bodies of his former wives.
5. Thomas Roscoe (1791–1871) had, like Mathias with whom EBB confused him, published several translations from the Italian, including *Memoirs of Benvenuto Cellini* (1822) and Sismondi's *Literature of the South of Europe* (1823).
6. "Fop."
7. *The Canterbury Tales*, Prologue, 265.
8. We have not located the source of this quotation.
9. In a letter to Miss Mitford, 22 September 1835, Willis told of visiting Kenilworth, Warwick and Stratford-upon-Avon with Miss Porter while both were guests of Sir Charles Throckmorton (L'Estrange (1), I, 295–296).
10. Underscored three times.
11. The frontispiece of *The City of the Magyar, or Hungary and Her Institutions in 1839–40* (1840) shows Miss Pardoe as a somewhat mature woman. EBB was, in fact, exactly right, as Miss Pardoe was born in 1806.
12. In *The City of the Sultan; and Domestic Manners of the Turks in 1836* (1837), Miss Pardoe relates how she and her party went to observe the entry of "Mahmoud the Powerful, the Brother of the Sun, and Emperor of the East" into Sultan Achmet's Mosque: "his eyes wandered on all sides, until they fell upon our party, when a bright smile lit up his features ... and [he] looked long and fixedly at us." The Sultan then directed an officer to enquire "who I was and what had brought me to Constantinople" (bk. I, ch. XI).

No. 898 [12 January 1842] 209

13. Miss Pardoe had recently visited Reading while Chorley was also there, this providing her with an opportunity to further her supposed pursuit of him.
14. "Allah the Generous."
15. Edwin Henry Landseer (1802–73) showed his talent for drawing and painting at an early age, exhibiting at the Royal Academy when he was only 15. He was still in his teens when he first met Georgiana (1781–1853), the second wife of the 6th Duke of Bedford, and fell in love with her. He is now acknowledged to have been the father of the last two of her ten children, Alexander George (1821) and Rachel (1826), although at the time they were accepted as the Duke's offspring. The Duke died in 1839, and, after a proper interval, Landseer proposed to the Duchess, who was then in her 59th year, but she declined his offer. Following her refusal, his physical and mental health declined, and in 1840 he went to the Continent to recuperate.

Lord William Russell (b. 1767), younger brother of the 5th and 6th Dukes of Bedford, was murdered on 6 May 1840 by his valet, who was executed for the crime. We have found no corroboration of EBB's story of his portrait being painted posthumously by Landseer.

16. According to legend, Minerva, goddess of war, sprang armed and fully grown from the head of Jove when Vulcan split it open with his axe. EBB presumably means that she hopes the story about Landseer is equally fanciful. He resumed exhibiting at the Royal Academy in 1841, after his sojourn on the continent.
17. EBB's translations of three of Gregory's hymns appeared in *The Athenæum*, 8 January 1842 (no. 741, pp. 39–40).
18. See letter 894, note 3.
19. Underscored three times.
20. *The Last Days of Aurelian; or, the Nazarenes of Rome* (1838) by William Ware (1797–1852), an American Unitarian Minister, author of *Zenobia: or, the Fall of Palmyra* (1837) and editor of *The Christian Examiner* (1839–44). EBB and RB met him in Italy in 1848.

---

898. EBB TO HUGH STUART BOYD

[London]
Wednesday– [12 January 1842][1]

My dear friend,

Thank you, thank you, for your kind suggestion & advice altogether. I had just (when your note arrived) finished two hymns of Synesius, one being the seventh & the other the ninth. Oh! I do remember that you performed upon the latter,[2] & my modesty sh^d have certainly bid me 'avaunt'[3] from it. Nevertheless it is so fine .. so prominent in the first class of Synesius's beauties,—that I took courage & dismissed my scruples, & have produced a version which I have not compared to yours at all hitherto, but which probably is much rougher & *rather* closer!—winning in faith what it loses in elegance! 'Elegance' is'nt a word for me you know, generally speaking. The barbarians herd with me, "by two and three".[4]

I had a letter today from Mr Dilke who agrees to everything—closes with the idea about 'Christian greek poets'—(only begging me to keep away from *theology*—) & suggesting a subsequent review of English poetical literature, from Chaucer down to our times.[5] Well—but the Greek poets. With all your kindness, I have scarcely sufficient materials for a full & minute survey of them. I have won a sight of the *Poætæ Christiani*[6]—but the price is ruinous—*fourteen guineas*—and then the work consists almost entirely of Latin poets—deducting Gregory & Nonnus, and John Damascenus[7] & a cento from Homer by somebody or other– Turning the leaves rapidly I do not see much else—& you know I may get a separate copy of John Dam, & have access to the rest. Try to turn in your head what I sh^d do. Greg. Nyssen did not write poems—did he? Have I a chance of seeing your copy of Mr Clarke's book? It w^d be useful in the matter of chronology.[8]

I humbly beg your pardon & Gregory's, for the insolence of my note. It was as brief as it could be, & did not admit of any extended reference & admiration to his qualities as an orator. But whoever read it to you sh^d have explained that when I wrote "He was an orator," the word ORATOR was marked emphatically, so as to appear printed in capital letters of emphasis.[9] Do not say "you *chose*", "you *chose*". I did'nt & dont choose to be obstinate indeed—but I can't see the sense of that 'heavenly soul.'[10]

Ever your grateful & affec^{te}
EBB

I shall have room for praising Gregory in these papers.

Address: H S Boyd Esqr / Downshire Hill / Hampstead.
Publication: LEBB, I, 96–98.
Manuscript: Wellesley College.

1. The letter is postmarked 13 January 1842, a Thursday.
2. Boyd's translation of the ninth ode was included in his *Select Poems of Synesius and Gregory Nazianzen* (1814). EBB's version appeared in the third of her papers on the Greek Christian Poets (*The Athenæum*, 12 March 1842, no. 750, pp. 229–231), with her acknowledgement that it was "closer if less graceful and polished than Mr. Boyd's".
3. *Macbeth*, III, 4, 92.
4. Cf. Matthew, 18:20.
5. EBB's detailed commentary on *The Book of the Poets* appeared in five numbers of *The Athenæum*, commencing with the issue of 4 June 1842.
6. *Poetæ Græci Christiani, una cum Homericus Centonibus* (1609).
7. Johannes Damascenus, one of the Greek Fathers of the Church, wrote a hymn on the subject of Christ's birth. EBB referred to him in her third paper.
8. See letter 894, note 5.
9. For EBB's comments on Gregory, see letter 894, note 1.
10. *Paradise Lost*, VI, 165.

899. EBB TO MARY RUSSELL MITFORD

[London]
Jany. 12. 1842

I do not take a breath my beloved friend, between finishing your last word & writing my first. I am too anxious to explain what requires explanation—in the first place, first & chiefly, how such an idea as *your hinting* about anything, never entered my head. Oh I speak for the head's credit, I assure you .. to exonerate my own self rather than you—& in my proper defence I must iterate & re-iterate the assurance of it. *You* hint! No indeed. But I was writing out my thoughts just as they came, just as I always do when I turn my face towards you, & so it happened that the idea of the chocolate brought the idea of the ships in its train. Save me, my dearest friend, from the thought of such a thought any more!—& do believe me now, that it was MY pleasure I was dreaming of, in wishing to send you something, & not yours!–

And then again my old obscurity must have muffled the sense of my sentences to admiration, on the subject of Mr. Willis.[1] I pefectly understood that you did not partake Miss Porter's idolatry before that very inadequate idol,[2]—& that your mediation between its defacement & Mrs. Trollope's *iconoclasticism* was limited to his manners & mode of pronunciation. I understood perfectly, however I may have appeared misunderstanding, & so have been misunderstood, my own self, in turn!

But, after all, I wont quite liken him to Moore! I keep a pace behind you, after all! If Moore be not a better poet than Willis, he is surely a better artist. As a versifier to a particular tune, with a fancy singing through it, there never was or will be or can be, I shd. think, an equal to Moore! "Born, with a nightingale singing in his ear"—as somebody said of him![3] *And* quite truly! A tame nightingale, & in the place of Nature's universal harmonies! Still he is excellent in his department—an accomplished artist—the very snuff-box musician of poetry– And such, Mr. Willis is not—or *is he*?

Mr. Kenyon has told me something to the effect of what you have told me as to Trans-Atlanticism. It is surprising that the Americans who hold in their hands the same talisman of literature with ourselves, shd. not be preserved by it from such corruptions of speech. The cultivated man or woman here, however cut off from society & the acquisition through society of colloquial elegance, does not become *provincial* in the loss of it. Why shd. it be otherwise with them? I do not understand.

Still they are a noble people, speak how they may. I love America for its brotherhood with us—& venerate it for its *separated* brotherhood— and look on to the day when, as its chief glory still lies in our literature, our increased glory may be reflected from its own. The day has not dawned yet—but the red light is in the sky–

No. The beloved relative who loved me & whom I loved & love on so tenderly,[4] was *not* the Speaker of the House of Assembly. The Speaker was a cousin of ours, between whom & us there was *no* love[5] . . a man of talent & violence & some malice, who did what he could, at one time, to trample poor papa down . . did trample him at one moment when he felt him under his feet . . but when the moment passed & the Law gave the triumph to other hands, & the Speaker died . . to the astonishment of everybody his will testified, by a particular mention of Papa in which the sentiment only was of importance, . . that he bore to his old victim much esteem & a tendency to friendship. I remember seeing him, when I was a child—& he gave me a subject for a poem about a run away negro which I still have somewhere, in his handwriting.[6] He *was* a handsome man . . after a fashion!—good features & the short upper lip, full, in his case, of expression. Still it was a face, that I, as a child, did not care to look upon. The perpetual scowl spoilt it—and the smile was worse. It was a face, not for a bandit . . oh no—but *perhaps* (altho' I really sh^d not speak so of my cousin, an old enemy too,—& no more!) *perhaps*, . . between us two, . . of an "honest honest Iago"!–[7] But it was good natured of him to write out 'a subject' for me; & I thought so even then!–

My beloved uncle, the only one of my uncles I really loved, & so I may say emphatically, as it w^d be tenderly & gratefully in any case, *my beloved uncle* . . was for many years a member of the English House of Commons, a dear & affectionate friend of Ld Grey's & Ld Durham's,[8] & at one time himself a man of large fortune. He might have lived like a Duke—he *would* live like a Prince—Jamaica failed. Then, he was *talked into* the new South sea bubbles of some years ago—it was his defect to be easily talked over & into. The great failures came—& he found himself responsible for companies to whom he had simply given his name. It was a situation full of perplexity & distress[9] . . & he was not made, like Papa, for battling with adversity. He left it & went to the West—& so ended all!–

Oh to look back & think!– What he might have been! What he was ever! For the talents of general society, I do not know his rival. For playful brilliant *persiflage* . . . . , Mr Kenyon, the most brilliant talker I can think of, was nought to him! And then, that high & delicate sense of honor, agonized by an unpropitious situation till it helped to drive him to the wilderness! A bright, gifted being! His letters worthy of his faculty! His affections—for that memory clings the closest—so tender & strong— passionate yet something wayward. All gone down, like so much else! How awful it is to·love!–

Richard Barrett

Richard Hengist Horne

I have saddened myself now, my beloved friend, for writing any more. I will speak to Papa & secure the Gregory for you[10] .. quite vexed as I am that you sh.d'nt have had it long ago. The bookseller perhaps neglected to send it—for that Papa directed it right, I cannot doubt.

It is arranged between M.r Dilke & me, that I am "to do" the Greek Christian poets, & then pass on to the English.[11] I really am half afraid that it's conceited of me to let myself be lifted up to this "bad eminence"[12] of criticism. Nay—& who knows what evil spirit haunting the place, may render me "seven times worse than before"?[13] At any rate the Athenæum wont be 'cold to poetry',[14] as long as I may burn it with my little finger. Love to D.r Mitford. To y.rself dearest love from

your EBB–

Publication: EBB-MRM, I, 330–333.
Manuscript: Wellesley College.

1. Willis is one of the figures in Miss Mitford's key to *The Blue Belles of England* (see letter 896).
2. Jane Porter secured an invitation for Willis to Sir Charles Throckmorton's seat in Warwickshire while she herself was a guest there (see *Nathaniel Parker Willis*, by Henry A. Beers, 1885, p. 172).
3. We have not traced the author of this particular remark, but on the quality of Moore's singing "the evidence is unanimous. Lockhart, Scott's biographer, said that Moore's was 'the most exquisite warbling' he ever heard. Leigh Hunt compared his voice to a flute ... Sydney Smith declared ... 'what is your singing but beautiful poetry floating in fine music and guided by exquisite feeling?'" (*The Minstrel Boy. A Portrait of Tom Moore*, by L.A.G. Strong, 1937, p. 134.)
4. Her late uncle Sam.
5. Richard Barrett (1789–1839), although of illegitimate birth, was in effect a first cousin of EBB's father. Her antipathy stems from the long and costly litigation he instituted against her father and uncle, regarding ownership of slaves and stock in Jamaica; after more than 25 years, judgement was finally given in his favour, resulting in severe financial reverses for Edward and Samuel Moulton-Barrett. He was thrice elected Speaker of Jamaica's House of Assembly. (See vol. 1, pp. xxix–xxx, and *Richard Barrett's Journal*, 1983, pp. xi–xiii.) Miss Mitford's query arose from reading about him (see SD1165).
6. This is assumed to be the manuscript in Richard Barrett's hand left among EBB's papers at Wimpole Street when she went to Italy; it is now in the Berg Collection. It was published in his *Journal*, pp. 121–123.
7. *Othello*, V, 2, 154.
8. Charles Grey, 2nd Earl Grey (1764–1845), an ardent proponent of parliamentary reform, had been Prime Minister, 1830–34; SD355 is a letter from him to Samuel Moulton-Barrett. John George Lambton, 1st Earl of Durham (1792–1840), Lord Privy Seal in Grey's administration, also strongly supported the reform legislation.
9. Specific details of his difficulties are not known; apart from the burden of the judgement referred to in note 5 above, he was obviously greatly affected by the financial and economic upheaval consequent upon the emancipation of slaves, together with sugar's steadily-declining price.
10. i.e., her translation of three of Gregory's hymns in *The Athenæum* of 8 January (no. 741, pp. 39–40).
11. See letter 898.
12. *Paradise Lost*, II, 6.
13. Cf. Matthew, 12:45.

14. A repetition of her opinion that literature fared less well than music in the magazine's reviews (see letter 829, note 15).

---

900. MARY RUSSELL MITFORD TO EBB

Three Mile Cross,
Jan. 13, 1842.

My beloved friend,

Mr. James, who might do better, has made a complete mistake (a wonder) about hanging in chains.[1] At Mortimer Common, a beautiful tract of wild country, now for the most part planted, near us, there is an inclosure of one hundred or two hundred acres, chiefly covered with heath and gorse, and called "The Gallows Piece;" because a murderer had been hanged in chains there, on a bit of broken ground, the scene of his crime. I remember the relics of the gibbet, and finding a hare just under it, which poor May, after killing, brought to me in her mouth full half a mile, and laid down at my feet. We had an old keeper with us who took the opportunity of telling me the story of the murder and of the execution, at which he had been present (having known both the murderer and his victim), and which he described most graphically. The man was hanged with *a rope* till he was dead, cut down at the expiration of an hour, and then, instead of being placed in a shell, the body was fastened by irons to the gibbet; indeed, some of the rusty "gibbet arms" were still swinging and clanking overhead. My father confirmed this to-night, remembering the circumstance well, and having seen other criminals suspended in the same manner, and often shuddered at the peculiar creaking of the chains. This critique is rather too elaborate for the occasion; but an author like Mr. James ought to take care to be right. Scott did always. It is a part of *truth*, which in art as in everything, is a grace above all graces.

I hope that one day or other you will know Mrs. Niven. She is a very extraordinary person, the client in a very remarkable cause (she was a Miss Vardill) which, at the end of twenty-one years, she has just won; or rather it was decided in the House of Lords, after two or three adjournments, at the end of last session.[2] The story is too long to tell tonight; but shortly, the question was, whether a Scotch marriage could pass an English estate? And such a marriage! So extreme a case! I must tell it. Her uncle—an old debauchee, living on his fine old place in the scenery which Scott copied in Ellangowan[3]—finding that an old relation, a lady of title, was coming to his house to sleep on a journey, ejaculated: "Eh! my leddy's coming and we maun hae a gude wife to receive her! Off wi' ye, loons, to Meg, and Jean, and Katie, and Beenie, and Bakie, and Beckie, and say that she that wins first to the house shall take possession and hae me into the bargain." Off set his myrmidons to all quarters to summon the usual seraglio, and the first that arrived was introduced to the "leddy," to her great horror; and as she happened to have a bare-legged boy of some twelve years old, this coarse frolic passed to that urchin eight thousand a year of Scottish estates, and cost more suits than I can well reckon; for it was litigated in every stage, until it arrived at the House of Peers, and argued there in three different sessions (chiefly on account of the obstinacy of Lord Brougham), in order to secure the English property to the real descendant, no drop of the true blood being in the veins of the boy, who came in so curious a way into the Scottish property; at least the probability is exceedingly against it, the mother being as bad as bad could be.

Heaven bless you! The books shall come back in a day or two, with some flowers.

Ever most faithfully yours,
M.R. Mitford.

Text: L'Estrange (2), III, 133-135.

1. In his latest book, *The King's Highway* (1840).
2. The case hinged on the legitimacy of Mrs. Niven's cousin, John Birtwhistle, the plaintiff, who sued to recover English property to the value of some £1,200 a year. It was claimed that his parents had married in secret in 1795, prior to his birth in 1799, the secrecy being necessitated by his deceased uncle's wife's disapproval of the match and the fear that, if the marriage were known, she would disinherit John's father, Alexander Birtwhistle. After her death, a public marriage was performed in 1805. Under Scottish law, this legitimatized him and gave him a clear title to his father's Scottish estate, regardless of whether there had been an earlier ceremony. Under English law, however, this was not so, and Mrs. Vardill, Alexander Birtwhistle's sister and Mrs. Niven's mother, inherited the English property. The case was brought in 1825, when it was found that the private marriage "was unsupported by any credible evidence." The decision was appealed, and the case progressed by slow degrees to the House of Lords, where, in August 1840, the verdict in Mrs. Vardill's favour was upheld (see *The Times*, 4 April 1825 and 12 August 1840). She had died by this time, but her will had stipulated that the estate should accumulate until Mrs. Niven was 52.
3. In chapter 4 of *Guy Mannering* (1815).

901. EBB TO HUGH STUART BOYD

[London]
Friday evening. [14 January 1842][1]

Thank you, my dear friend, for all your kindness. It is very welcome to me—and indeed, in spite of it, I am in some straight as to how my business is to be completed. I sh.^d not like to be incorrect .. to leave out poets & misplace dates .. when every fault must become prominent, not merely in black & white, but in *printed black*. Would that I c.^d talk to you for one hour.

I return the paper intended for the Athenæum, with a very grateful appreciation of the praise you lavish upon me in it. But dear Mr Boyd, it is too much! You should not have done it. Particularly *that* opposition between *eminent persons, Rollin*² *& me*!! particularly *that*, does strike me & will of course strike others, as so extravagant, that I venture to supplicate you to strike it out. People will think you are "making game" of *me*! Do strike it out, I beg of you—

Well—& then, I fear that the Athenæum, which never will nourish the snake of a controversy in its bosom, may reject your paper altogether.³ Of course you have a perfect right to object to my note,⁴ but the paper you have written might be compressed, shortened .. & thus the chances of its appearance w.^d be increased tenfold. Leave out some of *my compliments*—all about my preface, for instance—& let the "Lover of literary justice" go upon justice, barely & briefly.

If I can find or make room for more translations from Gregory, I will do your bidding faithfully. Depend upon that. But I have just finished the *whole* of that immensely long ode to his soul, asking her what she pleased to do. It is too long for my purpose—I was tempted by the variety of its merits besides the occasional great beauty, & by some touches of satire which you do not find very often out of his prose writings.

God bless you, my dear friend!

Forgive me for suggesting that the Athenæum paper sh.^d be transcribed by somebody who can *spell correctly*.

Your affec.^{te}
EBB.

You shall hear when I have anything in the Athenæum. I shall not, next Saturday. Thank you about Mr Clarke's book.⁵ I wish very much to see that.

Address: H S Boyd Esqr / 21 Downshire Hill / Hampstead.
Publication: EBB-HSB, pp. 243–244.
Manuscript: Wellesley College.

1. This letter was postmarked 15 January 1842, a Saturday.
2. Charles Rollin (1661–1741), author and historian, materially assisted in the revival of interest in the study of Greek while Rector of the University of Paris, 1694–95. His most important work was *Traité des études* (1726–31).
3. EBB was right; his paper was not printed.
4. i.e., the prefatory note to her translation of three of Gregory Nazianzen's hymns in *The Athenæum*. She had anticipated that it would displease Boyd (see letter 894).
5. See letter 894, note 5.

902. EBB TO RICHARD HENGIST HORNE

50 Wimpole Street.
Jany– 18.th 1842

What can you have thought, my dear Mr Horne, of all this loitering with the tragedy?[1] That I was busy pulling apples from your bough myself? & about to add one compliment more to the very flattering & gracious ones of which you tell me, by bringing out a grand new Desert scene at the nearest open theatre I could find? No, indeed! Here it is all safe back for you .. sands & ramparts & all! nothing touched—not even the covetable possessions of the enchantment scene, the old festival table, or the confluence in the desert, of death & victorious music. And thank you, thank you, twice over, for all the–––*pleasure* is the wrong word––– *sensation* is not quite right—the *emotion*, which this fine tragedy has given me.

There are very fine things in it—and I like the great poetic moral of daring in the midst of a stirring & important political crisis, to fix the main interest upon a private grief––of putting away all 'the pomp & circumstance of glorious war'[2] for the contemplation of a private affection, & consenting to hear the heart beat through the trumpets,

"Crowns are dust
But love .. love is not dust, & cannot die!"

Still .. was Emenias quite the person to say those words? You do not give us quite time to forgive him .. so as to suppress our malice & *not* answer "Pray what love are you talking of? what you felt for poor Alsargis, or the new one for that beautiful bold Lady Zenobia who requited you so well, & is now walking at leisure to Aurelian's good music, with as much sand in her shoes as we wish her"? You know there *are such* malicious people in the world!!

Yes—I c.^d find faults in the tragedy after all—rather I c.^d find fault with the tragedy, to speak more with the modesty natural to me!– The first time I read it, Alsargis seemed to me of too soft & gentle a nature to be worked up with so little obvious provocation[3] into a state & attitude of such resolute violence. I still think that she need not have gone mad when her husband w.^d'nt stay to supper––indeed I do still think so. Dejected to the last point of dejection, she might be .. but the phrenzy I venture to protest again. I am afraid too, that there is a little, the least possible, approach to *conjugal teazing*, in some of her early relations to Emenias. You know he really had "a great deal upon his hands", what with the new arrows & the general state of the war, & was often necessarily absent though too often unnecessarily so. It might be womanly in Alsargis to reproach him incessantly as she does (in a soft low voice certainly) but it is not the best woman-way of attaining the purpose of her tenderness. Forgive me for being wrong—or bold. The last, I must be. And yet one word more. Is your Alsargis a true woman in forgetting[4] her children? Such a woman as your Alsargis could not do it, I imagine even in a phrenzy-fit—particularly when they were in a situation of danger. Do consider, if she ought to do it? or could?[5]

And now after all this courage of mine, I shall crown myself with the pleasantness of at least trying to say how very fine all the *movement parts* of the tragedy are & how deeply I appreciate them. The scene with the sorcerer, . . I mean when she goes to him for comfort, is very fine & moving—& the actual sorcery-scene, with that exquisite under-tone of falling dews, is one of the most beautiful things of the kind I can remember anywhere, It is real sorcery. I congratulate you upon it. Then there's the desert scene! the great epitome of the world's destinies, . . beheld under a picturesque aspect—the death & triumph within two paces, & the wide indifferent wilderness sweeping around both. It is very fine. It has a *meaning*, as all your poetry has.

What shall you do with this tragedy?– What is to be its fate? Thank you for letting its light fall upon *me*—but that must not be all. You must not restrain its 'influences'—indeed you must not!–

I have left myself no time to speak of the Magazine– Yet that story whose author's name is equally illegible & unguessable, has much beauty.

Thank you earnestly!

How is your Biography?[6] Do tell me.

Ever & truly yours
Elizabeth B Barrett.

Address: R H Horne Esqr / 30– New Broad Street / City.
Docket, in Horne's hand: 2^d Alsargis. / 1842.
Publication: None traced.
Manuscript: R.H. Taylor Collection.

1. Horne's docket identifies this as "Alsargis"; if finished, it was never published.
2. *Othello*, III, 3, 354.
3. Horne made this annotation: "Miss Barrett was too pure and spiritual to see what the married lady saw. H."
4. Annotation by Horne: "She did not forget them—but regarded them as 'orphans,' and had them cared for. H."
5. Horne wrote, "Yes H."
6. As a rival to the French *Biographie Universelle*, the Society for the Diffusion of Useful Knowledge was sponsoring a *Biographical Dictionary* under the editorship of George Long (1800–79), a classical scholar, one of the founders of the Royal Geographical Society and Professor of Greek at London University, 1828–31. Horne was one of several eminent men invited to contribute articles; he wanted to write on Æschylus, Aristotle and other classical notables, but they had already been allocated to others; he

had completed two biographies when the project was abandoned. Seven volumes were published between 1842 and 1844, covering the letter "A" only. (See *Always Morning*, by Cyril Pearl, 1960, p. 23.)

---

903. EBB TO MARY RUSSELL MITFORD

[London]
Jany. 20.th 1842–

My beloved friend,

I am rejoicing in the honor & glory achieved by our chocolate, with a gladness beyond the honor. Oh that the effect may last!—oh that it may not be the mere change of diet! Whatever it may be, it is happy—so far—and I hope for the happiest!–

But you are overwhelmed with anxieties I see .. , by more than your habitual ones! Do be particular in telling me how the cold is. It is a transient malady my dearest friend .. & God's mercy will give you an adequate patience & consolation. Indeed but it *is* very grievous, very, to our fleshly eyes & fleshly hearts which deal in no better wisdom than their blended love's, that you sh.d be so tried, month by month, year by year, & no possible help from any of us!–

Your romance of the Loves of the Centaur-sylph passes anything of the sort I ever heard of.[1] It is enough for a generation—certainly enough to make anyone laugh à gorge *deployèe*[2] like the lady's affectionateness. That hysteric in the quadrille! .. I conclude is the "en avant"[3] movement .. the whole thing being so remarkably en avant in every sense! No wonder that it was reciprocated by a dos à dos[4] on the gentleman's side! Ah—but it was hard-hearted of *you*, when she went on a pilgrimage to the 'village', all "to make love to you by proxy" as you admit y.rself, to refuse to be made love to! I am afraid you *are* very hardhearted! You might have got up some sort of a sultan for her[5]––a pair of slippers to match the rose-coloured feathers!

Tell me—was she ashamed afterwards? I hope so, for the sake of womanhood.

I have been wishing so to write to you day after day these three or four days; but other letters pressed in .. letters necessary to be written—not that it is'nt necessary my beloved friend, to write to *you*. That is a heart-want. But I c.dnt do it all at once—and then these Greek poets & the Athenæum have been pulling at me, more than I supposed they w.d One is forced to be accurate in print, & absolute accuracy one cant or ought'nt to be content to go to the memory for—& I wanted books out of my reach, & have been beating against my cage till my wings are tired. After all, not a line is written yet.[6]

You are right & wrong too in all the advice you give me & the superfluity of kindness you add to it. I have grown large O my dearest friend, in the mist of your great affectionateness which I prize, believe me, more for the thing it is, than the praise it brings. You overvalue me in all things but in love. Nevertheless you are quite right in telling me not to give up poetry for magazine-writing, or for prose of a higher character. You will be satisfied when you hear me say that I could'nt if I tried. Whatever degree of faculty I have, lies in poetry—still more of my personal happiness lies in it—still more of my love. I cannot remember the time when I did not love it .. with a lying-awake sort of passion at nine years old, & with a more powerful feeling since, which even all my griefs, such as have shaken life, have failed to shake. At this moment I love it more than ever—& am more bent than ever, if possible, to work into light .. not into popularity but into expression .. whatever faculty I have. This is the object of the intellectual part of me—& if I live it shall be done. There will be no bitterness in the process whatever the labour .. because it is not for the sake of popularity, no, nor of a higher kind of fame, but for poetry's own sake—rather, to speak more humbly & accurately, for the sake of my love of it. Love is the safest & most unwearied moving principle in all things—it is an heroic worker.

Perhaps we may differ a little upon what is called religious poetry .. though not at all upon the specimens extant. My fixed opinion is, if I might express it with the deference due to your views of literature, .. my fixed opinion is, that the experiment has scarcely been tried .. & that a nobler 'Genie du Christianisme' than has been contemplated by Chateaubriand,[7] will yet be developped in poetical glory & light. The failure of religious poets turns less upon their being religious, than on their not being poets. Christ's religion is essentially poetry—poetry glorified. And agreeing with you that human interest is necessary to poetical interest, I w^d yet assume that religious interest is necessary to perfect the human—as the great & ever-influencing prospect & crown of universal humanity.

Yes—I shall write poems yet—& perhaps something that may be happy enough to please you, after some imperfect fashion & thro' the perfectness of your affection. I have not quite cast off your Napoleon[8]— nay, I have not even turned my shoulder to him. I must think.

In the meantime, here is the Athenæum. Oh, but for a time, my dearest friend—but for a time. Mr Dilke does not even wish for me for long. And who knows, but what I may break down at the first three paces? Well– Even *I* cant know anything about it, without trying. Only one thing is sure—that I shant be *cold upon poetry*. Another thing, too, is sure, that the Athenæum has been so! You are quite right—I skipped the science & took patience—but I could'nt take it & keep it, when I found them all so deeply interested in American Indians & English travellers, & every sort of savage & steam-engine & musical instrument,[9] .. & all at once, struck cold, indifferent, nay, a little malicious, with a manifest curling of the upper lip (none the better for being M.[r] Darley's who ought to *know* better) when a true poet or tragedian endeavoured to articulate those great thoughts which he inherited of Nature. It was—it is, dispiriting & mortifying. For there *are* true poets, even as literature is now. M.[r] Browning deserved better than that light, half jocose, pitifully jocose, downward accent of critical rallying! [']'Forsooth they are almost tired of him! and yet he has some good stuff—but they have almost lost their sublime critical patience!!"[10] Why what, if he did mouth in his speaking,—was there nothing worth reverence in his speech? worth a critic's reverence— or a world's!– I w.[d] not speak so of M.[r] Browning in a whisper—I w.[d] not dare—even to myself. And then M.[r] Horne! Where is the excuse for the blank silence, or the still worse word![11] The Athenæum provokes me.

Still I like it for much. It has a nobility of its own—it is liberal, & but for poetry, large-hearted. Many pleasant hours of mine are associated with it, & I like this new association, temporary as it is, which is just rising up.

I am so glad you have such a woman as Mrs Niven, for talk's sake & sympathy's—& how kind of both of you ever to speak of me. God bless you dearest

⟨...⟩[12]

Oh I quite forgot D.[r] Chambers! Indeed I dont want him, & .. I promise to see him when I do– I am very tolerably well, which means, very wonderfully so. Oh for the spring & you!– But must it be QUITE the spring?– "Say nay, say nay."[13]

Publication: EBB-MRM, I, 333–336.
Manuscript: Wellesley College.

1. In letter 897, EBB had referred to Miss Pardoe's supposed pursuit of Henry Chorley. She had used a visit to Miss Mitford while Chorley was also there as a means of furthering her aim, and Miss Mitford had apparently made fun of her behaviour and appearance at a dance on 28 December 1841.
2. "To laugh à gorge déployée" is to roar with laughter.
3. "Forward."
4. "Back to back."
5. A reference to Miss Pardoe's being noticed by Sultan Mahmoud during her visit to Turkey (see letter 897, note 12).

6. The first of EBB's four papers on the Greek Christian Poets appeared in *The Athenæum* of 26 February (no. 748, pp. 189–190).

7. François René, Vicomte de Chateaubriand (1768–1848), French statesman and author, had published *Le Génie du Christianisme, ou les Beautés de la Religion Chrétienne* in five volumes in 1802.

8. As a subject for a poem, suggested by Miss Mitford (see letter 873).

9. Volume 1 of *Letters and Notes on the Manners, Customs, and Condition of the North American Indians* (1841) by George Catlin had received lengthy notice in *The Athenæum* of 2 October 1841 (no. 727, pp. 755–759) and 16 October (no. 729, pp. 792–794). Volume 2 received equal treatment in the issues of 12 and 19 February 1842. As EBB's comment suggests, accounts of travels and books on railways and canals, etc. did appear to be given disproportionate attention by the magazine.

10. *The Athenæum* of 11 December 1841 (no. 737, p. 952) had carried a review of *Pippa Passes*, finding RB's "texts nearly as obscure as ever—getting, nevertheless, a glimpse, every now and then, at meanings which it might have been well worth his while to put into English." The reviewer [G. Darley?] commented that "Our faith in him, however, is not yet extinct,—but our patience *is*." (For the full text of the review, see pp. 399–400.)

11. *The Athenæum* had not reviewed his *History of Napoleon*.

12. The remainder of the manuscript is missing, except for the following sentences written in the margins of the first page.

13. Cf. Chaucer, "The Parson's Tale," 590.

---

904. EBB TO MARY RUSSELL MITFORD

[London]
Jany. 20 [–21]. 1842

Oh my dearest friend, how you frightened me with the inscription on the back of your letter "The opium has failed—& now there is no hope"! Thank God it is not as I fancied! But indeed you electrified the handle of your letter . . & I c^d scarcely get it open.

Well—but how did you try this opium. I quite agree in the wisdom & propriety of giving it a fair trial, & I venture to suggest another attempt by way of *morphine*. The muriate of morphine is what I take—what I call my elixir, & I take it in combination with æther & something else. Æther is highly anti-spasmodic. I suggest a mixture of the morphine with the æther—only of course you w^{dnt} think of giving either without a direction as to quantities from your medical adviser. Do speak about it—do try it, if it is not advised against. My elixir has a sort of ubiquitous influence upon all parts of my system—quiets my mind, calms my pulse— warms my feet—spirits away any stray headache—gives me an appetite— relieves my chest—to say nothing of the bestowment of those sudden pleasant feelings belonging by right to better health & extreme youth—to say nothing of causing me to grow all at once, as young at least . . as Miss Pardoe!!^{1} Now I recommend my elixir.– You know I never tried it upon cramp—but I believe in its ubiquitous infallibility, & recommend it. I chalk it up upon your walls, wherever there's a blank one from creepers, at your village of Three Mile Cross!—as *MY ELIXIR*![2]

Ah my beloved friend, how too kind you are—how extravagant in kindness! How you squander it, all gold as it is, among the beggars! Well!. I sh^d certainly be spoilt, ruined, lost for ever, to all intents & purposes of modesty, if I did not feel your love *through your praise*,—but as *I do*, there will always be something that I must care more for than for the last!– May God bless you! You sh^d not speak so, however, indeed!

As to Mrs Niven, gratifying as it must be to me to have the too high appreciation of a woman so singularly accomplished & gifted as you describe her to be . . . she *smells of the rose*, she has been near you; and you have ––– oh no! my dearest friend! That is all too much to believe! My vanity sinks down overpowered, both hands full, & unable to hold any more! Let me love you—and above all things, do not depreciate yourself! Now do consider—! How can praising me & depreciating yourself encourage me, as your kind words mean to do, to any exertion? Do you not see how the depreciation must be a sign of fallacy somewhere? how it turns like a hazel bough in the hand of a diviner?[3]

Ever your grateful
EBB–

Mr. Kenyon, I have not seen since. He was going, as I think I told you, down to Hastings,—& may not have returned.

Do you really think that Æschylus or Chaucer or your Fletcher ever did "adapt their writings to the public taste["]? I doubt—nay, I disbelieve! *Did Milton*? Did Coleridge? Did Wordsworth? Did not the public go to all of them? It seems to me that the poet has to do, has to think of doing, rather with humanity which is grand world-wide & time-wide, than with that limited changeful capricious thing, called a public, & subject to all the base uses of a self made fashion.

All this was written yesterday, laid aside to be sealed & so forgotten. Your letter, this morning, comes in therefore for its share in the answering!

When did you ever "teaze" me? If the solicitude of your affectionateness be *teazing*, do think me worthy of being grateful for such. Dearest kindest friend!

But do not fancy that I am over-worked by the Athenæum. Oh no—I am pretty well supplied with the books I wanted; . . & the actual writing is the least thing—& I think now that I shall not go into chronological & historical detail quite as much as I proposed. It will be best to keep cl⟨ose to⟩[4] the poetry. And really the *body* of the poetry of the first centuries, is not worth a great deal.

My love to dear Dr Mitford. He *is* a little better . . & *I* am so glad!

Papa has just sent up the new Athenæum number by Mr Flush! He ran up stairs, struck his fore paws against my door, sprang dancing with triumph upon the bed, & gave it into my hands with a kiss! He is quite well—& vivid in spirits & affections—but *not* fat like your Flush, the paternal!

Publication: EBB-MRM, I, 336–338.
Manuscript: Wellesley College.

1. EBB's prior comment on Miss Pardoe's age (see letter 897) suggests that Miss Pardoe's pursuit of Chorley was causing her to behave in a more immature manner than one of her years would generally be expected to do. Apparently, she would never admit her age, and, in 1856, strove to be as vivacious as she was at eighteen (*DNB*).
2. EBB used capitals, underscored once.
3. The movement of a forked hazel branch in the hands of a diviner indicated the presence below ground of water.
4. Conjectural reading, due to ink smudge.

905. EBB TO MARY RUSSELL MITFORD

[London]
[?31] Jany. 1842[1]

I hasten to say my dearest friend, how glad I shall be, how proud I shall be .. what is the right word? .. to hear from your M.[rs] Niven both because she is yours & is as you describe her. Do tell her that I c.[d] but feel it as a condescension from any person of that degree of acquirement, of that high cultivation, to take any notice of such an imperfect production as this hard dry unvital translation of mine stands confest to be, in the eyes of its own performer.[2] It is not *scholastically* that I am so ashamed of it .. but poetically. It is correct enough as far as the letter goes—but otherwise I am only surprised that Æschylus does not dog me with his spirit-dog, as he himself might call his soul. But he does'nt think it worthwhile.

I say none of this out of mock-humility—you will do me the justice to believe so. I have heard that Mrs Coleridge said of my translation (Coleridge's daughter!)—"It is a creditable attempt to do what is impossible."[3] I myself w.[d] say far less of it—for I know how much better it c.[d] be done. Even *I* c.[d] do it better now.[4] Coleridge himself, or Shelley had done it well—they w.[d] at least have drawn from the admitted "impossibility," a GRAND POSSIBLE. What M.[rs] Niven w.[d] do me the honor of writing about, is not worth her reading.

My dearest friend—it was my inconsiderateness & not yours which is to blame. You were true to nature (as you always are & w.[d] lose a hundred charms by being less so) in obeying the impulse of a full heart

& writing on the back of the letter. But I, in cold blood, had no business to tell you that the notice had frightened me![5] Forgive it, my beloved friend! And pray—for my sake—dont try to improve those delightful faults of yours in virtue of which you are ours to love & Nature's to claim—"a lady of her own".[6] Why, if you were all smooth angel, how sh^d our hearts hold on to you? Consider us a little—do! I am a *conservative* as concerns *you*—not a reformer! May God bless you my dearest friend!—

I am very sorry about the cough—but I hope for another change before this lovely sun! Does the weather affect the cramp? Oh—may you be more easy at heart very soon!

It seems to me that my Flush likes London very much indeed, from his playful leaping spirits which scarcely become those reverent two years he has almost touched. In the meanwhile, his appetite is perhaps rather better—that is, he signifies a gracious assent to the acceptance of my muffin rather oftener than he used to do. But he is as particular as ever as to what he accepts besides—& objects (even sometimes unto fasting) to taking his dinner alone, when everybody else has done dining. There is also a manifest expansion of soul towards ratafies, spunge cake, barley-sugar & things of that sort—the enunciation of the word '*cakes*' producing an obvious & sudden dilation of the eyes & agitation of the tail. He lies by me night & day as usual .. growing certainly prettier—& certainly *not* fatter—& winning everybody's heart without any loss of personal dignity. As to Papa—why, think of Papa's saying when he is'nt here—"Where's Flush? I miss Flush. I want him to teaze." Now there's a compliment, never paid before to dog!—

Is Mrs Niven eloquent after the manner of Lady Mary Shepherd? declamatory? or conversational? I like that "sweet serenity" when as you say, there is no insipidity—& when, as I say, there is no conventional habitude to enforce it, or no insensibility to secure it. Serene, impassible people who never think or feel *to their outsides*, are an abomination—& the insipid school is more abundant & scarcely less odious. The serenity born of a right *balance* in the intellects & affections, is a beautiful thing & rare.

As for the ancient languages, or any acquirement in the particular department of languages, you cant think how little I care for it. It puts me out of patience to see people glorying, evidently however silently, in the multitudes of grammars, when the glorious rich literature of our own beloved England lies by their side without a look or a sigh that way. And then a dictionary life is the vainest & least exalting of lives. No occupation claims the time which the acquisition of a language does, with an equal non-requital to the *intellect*. I observe *that* .. & have set my face against *linguaism* .. except to certain ends, & with certain means .. for there *are* you know, peculiar aptitudes to languages, which like other talents cry out for cultivation. For my own part, my learning Greek was a child's fancy .. achieved for Homer's sake; & for Homer's sake, .. that is, for poetry's generally, I have never repented one year of my hard working ones. Latin was admitted as a helper—& my little stock of Hebrew, long after, as a distraction in low spirits. But—oh to look round, & measure the high estate of the Greek & Latin man, & then YOURS!![7]

Well—but your Mrs Niven is something better than a mere Greek & Latin woman. I quite fancy from your sketch how delightful she must be: &, that she is able to appreciate *you*, so as to go every year to Reading for the purpose of having your society, though by no means a strange thing, yet helps me to appreciate *her*, beyond all the rest. For oh my dearest Miss Mitford .. you do .. you see .. there is no denying it .. you do so *dilate* your friends .. you do thrust such greatness upon them, whether they be or be not born to greatness![8] Dont, I beseech you, tell her any fairy tales about me! I beseech you, *untell* them, my beloved friend!

Give my love to Dr Mitford!—to Flush too! Dear little Flush. I want to see him very much. I shall in the spring—shall I not. And this is just February. In three weeks, I shall call it Spring.

Your own
EBB–

Did I ever tell you how many of Irving's disciples, are friends of mine—even relatives—cousins?[9] Oh I assure you I have apostles prophets & angels belonging to me!– But they are not strict in the manner you describe. At least I know that one mature angel, above forty &, I mention the age that you should not attribute the act to any heterodox flightiness of youth .. that one real mature angel borrowed Pickwick from this very house, not long ago, "for the purpose of relaxation." Books such as angels read[10] .... sh^d you have said so of Pickwick before you heard my story?

Publication: EBB-MRM, I, 338–341.
Manuscript: Folger Shakespeare Library and Wellesley College.

    1. At the conclusion of the letter, EBB says "this is just February", suggesting that it was commenced on the last day of January.
    2. *Prometheus Bound.*
    3. This was apparently the opinion conveyed to EBB by Kenyon, mentioned in letter 654.
    4. In a letter of 27 February 1845 to RB, EBB said she had completed a new translation, except for a "last polishing."
    5. A reference to Miss Mitford's note regarding the failure of opium (see letter 904).
    6. Cf. Wordsworth, "Three Years She Grew in Sun and Shower" (1800), line 6.
    7. Underscored three times.
    8. Cf. *Twelfth Night*, II, 5, 145–146.
    9. i.e., the Bayfords.
    10. Cf. *Paradise Lost*, I, 620.

906. EBB TO MARY RUSSELL MITFORD

[London]
2 Febr– 1842

Thank you my beloved friend for Mrs Niven's note & all the dearnesses of your own letter. Be sure that I am conscious of the full worth of her good opinion—& not the less so, that I know her only through *you*! The note itself too w.^{d} be ready to help one to a pleasant impression if that were lacking. As it is, I will ask you to let it, the note, stay with me (may it?) as an earnest of an acquaintanceship to come, which you have taught me to lay up on my shelf among agreeable possible futurities!–

Still I cant consent to give away my Prometheus to such "..... uses"[1] as the perfectibility of science—I cant indeed! Do you see how science is taking away all the earth from under our feet, & ploughing up the violets? We shall not have a foot's breadth of ground soon, to stand on & look up from, to the sky. Science has taken more than enough as it is; & I will not hear of her touching this noble Prometheus with her forefinger. He is hung up safe out of her way—& prefers his old vulture to the new patent .... (what grand name shall we find for a perforating engine?),—at his tormented side.[2] Oh no, no, no! Be on my side, my dearest friend, & dont consent to it. Science may triumph gloriously to the freeing of the elements—& let her do it. But what are the elements after all? The symbol is no glory to Prometheus.

Surely he is the sign of this great ruined struggling Humanity, arising through the agony & the ruin to the renovation & the spiritual empire. I cant consent to desecrate him with the badge of a lower symbol. Be on my side. And dont let your accomplished friend think me very bold for all this rebellion.

In the meantime—oh do *you* think me obstinate? Something in your last letter made me half tremble—fancying it. You know, Mr Kenyon used to call me 'perverse'—but *'obstinate'* is a worse word still—& then I dont think I c.^{d} be very obstinate before a wish of yours. My dearest friend, your kindness is dearest to me—your generous praises & encouragement are as dear as ... not *your* love, but love of the common sort. Well then—being sure of that, the inference is plain that I w.^{d} not cast your advice over my shoulder .. even for good luck, as people do or used to do with salt,—& the very reverse of good luck w.^{d} such a foolish action bring *me*! No no– Not obstinate! I plead against the thought of it. I will do *what I can* to satisfy you, & *when* I can do it. I will indeed!

In regard to Psyche, you will admit that I could'nt break with Mr Horne after an agreement & a commencement, .. nay, a *promise* to come to the work when he is free from a certain Biographical dictionary which enchains him now.[3] It w.^{d} not be a kind act—it w.^{d} be something worse,

I think, than simply unkind. I may not do this *duality* of a poem at all even now--that is quite possible. But then *I* must not take a step towards the possibility. And if it is done .. why my dearest friend, I shall not be all my life in doing it .. not intentionally at least. And I will promise you the privilege of losing your place & knowing where to find it. Oh I wish I had shown you the full-length plan—it may not be half as bad as you fancy!

In regard to the *dramatic*, we do not want the thing strictly so called– Mr Horne is *a poet*—is he not? You admit *that*—I know you do.

I am up to the crown of my head in the Athenæum & the Greeks just now—but afterwards there may be a long interregnum between the end of my prose & the beginning of Psyche, & I must think out some subject, perhaps with a Napoleon in it,[4] to dart down upon in that free interval! Oh how kind you are to care so much, to care at all, for my writing at all. God bless you my beloved friend!–

This collection book or selection book sacred to female writers, this *blue* book as people are sure to call it, is another instance. —That you sh^d care for *me*!–

Of course I w^d not refuse any poem I had by me, & I have plenty of short mss half written & half blotted .. but Mr Dion Bourcicault (is *that* right?) has *not asked me* .. which is a necessary preliminary on more occasions than those of quadrilles & marriages. I cant get in amongst you without being asked, can I? & being shut up here, have no possible means of hinting my willingness delicately, by hysterics or otherwise.[5] Seriously, the probability is that he wont apply to me at all. There will be so many crowded names—& if he goes to France for them .. ! By the way, why not embrace, while he was about the plan of the sort, (honi soit qui mal y pense)[6] why not *include* all the female writers of Europe. Germany Spain & Italy w^d fill as many pages as our England—& it w^d give a completeness & interest to the work.

Dear Mr Kenyon has come back & has been to see me. It is very kind of him. I fancied him rather out of spirits. Oh—it might be fancy!

Did I tell you that your Mr Townsend sent me some sheets of a new poem of his to look at, ten days ago? It is on a strange subject!– The departure & farewell sermon of the Bishop of new Zealand, who appears to have been his pastor in England—positively the sermon turned into verse—the identical sermon! Yet there is the sweetness common to Mr Townsend—& more clearness! It is in the course of *publication*.[7] You will like everything but the subject!

The apotheosis of the Charleses in the book you speak of,[8] made me smile—but such things *ought* to make us frown. Yet how shall we marvel,—with that service upon *the* MARTYDOM (!!!) left, in scorn & desecration of every sensible opinion & sacred feeling, within the leaves of what is called the National prayer book?–⁹ Who can wonder at Puseyism? or at any laudation from reverend lips of that "most religious king" Charles the second.¹⁰ His pretty dogs were the best of him. Thank you for my Flush's pedigree!

Your own
EBB

Publication: EBB-MRM, I, 341–344.
Manuscript: Wellesley College.

1. i.e., "base uses" (*Hamlet*, V, 1, 202).
2. Prometheus, as punishment for offending Jupiter, was chained to a rock on Mt. Caucasus for 30,000 years, where a vulture fed upon his liver, which never diminished though continually devoured; he was, however, delivered from his chains after 30 years by Hercules.
3. See letter 902, note 6.
4. Napoleon and Joan of Arc were both mentioned as possible subjects in letters 873 and 874.
5. Dion Boucicault (1820?–90), originally Bourcicault, the Irish actor and dramatist, was apparently planning an anthology of selections from contemporary women writers, and had invited Miss Mitford to contribute; she obviously felt that EBB should be included in such a work. EBB's reference to it as a "*blue* book" anticipates the application of the pejorative "blue-stocking" to its contributors. As far as is known, nothing came of the project. The reference to "hysterics" is an allusion to Miss Pardoe's behaviour while in Reading (see letter 903).
6. "Shame to him who evil thinks," the motto of the Order of the Garter, founded in 1349.
7. The poem was published by Robert Benton Seeley and advertised for sale at 2s.6d., but we have been unable to trace a copy. George Augustus Selwyn (1809–78) had been consecrated Bishop of New Zealand on 17 October 1841, and had sailed to take up that post on 26 December. Townsend may have known him while Selwyn was a curate in Windsor in the 1830's.
8. As EBB speaks of only one book, it seems reasonable to infer that it was *Historical Sketches of Charles the First, Cromwell, Charles the Second and the Principal Personages of that Period* (1828), by William Dorset Fellowes.
9. By Act of Parliament, a special prayer was added to *The Book of Common Prayer* in 1662 for inclusion in the service on 30 January every year, a "day of fasting and humiliation," the anniversary of the martyrdom of Charles I. This prayer, together with three others mandated by Parliament to commemorate important events, remained there until 1859.
10. One of the special prayers mentioned above was required to be delivered on 29 May, which marked both the birthday of Charles II and the date of the Restoration. He personally was renowned for his easy morals, which set the standard for his court, hence the implied sarcasm of EBB's quoting the Prayer Book's description of him.

---

907. EBB TO HUGH STUART BOYD

[London]
Feb. 4. 1842.

My dear friend,

You must be thinking, if you are not a St. Boyd for good-temper, that among the Gregorys and Synesiuses, I have forgotten everything about you. No—indeed it has not been so. I have never *stopped* being grateful to you for your kind notes, & the two last pieces of Gregory, although I did not say an overt "Thank you"—but I have been very very busy besides & thus I answered to myself for your being kind enough to pardon a silence which was compelled rather than voluntary.

Do you ever observe, that as vexations dont come alone, occupations dont—and that if you happen to be engaged upon one particular thing, it is the signal for your being way-laid by bundles of letters desiring immediate answers, & proofsheets or ms works whose writers request your opinion while their "printer waits"?– The old saints are not responsible for all the filling up of my time. I have been *busy upon busy*.

The first part of my story about the Greek poets, went to the Athenæum some days ago, but, altho' graciously received by the editor, it wont appear this week or I sh^d have had a proof sheet (which was promised to me) before now– I must contrive to include all I have to say on the subject in *three parts*. They will admit, they tell me, a fourth *if I please*, but evidently they w^d prefer as much brevity as I could vouchsafe.[1] Only two poets are in the first notice—and *twenty* remain,—& neither of the two is Gregory![2]

Will you let me see that volume of Gregory, which contains the '*Christus patiens*'? Send it by any boy on the heath,[3] & I will remunerate him for the walk & the burden, & thank you besides. Oh dont be afraid! I am not going to charge it upon Gregory but on the younger Apollinaris whose claim is stronger[4]—& I rather wish to refresh my recollection of the height & breadth of that tragic misdemeanor.

It is quite true that I never have suffered much pain—& equally so that I continue most decidedly better notwithstanding the winter. I feel too, I do hope not ungratefully, the blessing granted to me in the possibility of literary occupation . . which is at once occupation & distraction. Carlyle (not the infidel, but the philosopher) calls literature a "fire-proof pleasure"![5] How truly! How deeply I have felt that truth!

May God bless you, dear Mr Boyd! I dont despair of looking in your face one day yet before my last!

Ever your affectionate & obliged
EBB–

Arabel's love.

Address: H S Boyd Esqr / 21 Downshire Hill / Hampstead.
Publication: LEBB, I, 98–99.
Manuscript: Wellesley College.

1. There were four parts in all.
2. The first paper, in *The Athenæum* of 26 February 1842 (no. 748, pp. 189–190), dealt with Ezekiel, author of *The Exodus from Egypt*, and Clemens Alexandrinus. EBB observed that "It has the look of an incongruity, to begin an account of the Greek Christian poets with a Jew".

3. Downshire Hill, where Boyd lived, bordered Hampstead Heath; it was an easy walk from there, across the Heath, to Wimpole Street.

4. In the second part of "Some Account of the Greek Christian Poets" in *The Athenæum* of 5 March (no. 749, pp. 210-212), EBB dealt with Apollinaris the Elder, who taught grammar in Loadicæa, and his son, Apollinaris the Younger, poet, rhetorician and philosopher. EBB ascribes to the latter authorship of *Christus Patiens*.

5. Carlyle, writing in *The Foreign Review* (no. 9, 1830) about the German novelist and philosopher Jean Paul Friedrich Richter (1763-1825), said he "was of exemplary, unwearied diligence in his vocation; and so had, at all times, 'perennial, fire-proof Joys, namely Employments.'"

---

908. EBB TO MARY RUSSELL MITFORD

Wimpole Street.
Febr- 4. 1842

My dearest friend—, do let me see Dryden.[1] Oh yes—I shall certainly like it! I like anything of that sort—anything that brings [us] nearer, or seems to do so, to the *Immortals*. I am capable of all sorts of foolishnesses (which Mr Kenyon thinks so degrading that he does me the honor of not believing a word of them—at least *he says so*) about autographs & such like *niaiseries*.[2] I might, if I were tempted, be caught in the overt act of gathering a thistle because Wordsworth had trodden it down .. of gathering it eagerly like his own ass![3]—and

"the duck
Which Samuel Johnson trod on—"[4]

being left for you, of course! So you dont 'think anything' (as people say) of Samuel Johnson! How Boswell w^d distrust, in his magnanimous 'hero-worship,' your compliment which brushes by Johnson!- And after all, he *was* a fine show giant! a memorable Gargantua![5] He was a 'man'—as Carlyle boasts of him—& a specimen-man![6] and if he does "say things three times over," he says things sometimes which are worth the repetition. Take notice, this is all in the spirit of contradiction, for I have'nt the least bit of real love for this great lumbering bookcase of a man. Oh I quite agree with you in my inner woman. Think how he treated our poets! Even I, who care almost less for Gray than for him, shrink away from the sight of his injustices in the Life of Gray.-[7] Still, there were some fine things about Johnson—& what with them & what with Boswell, one is worked up into an attitude of respect to him from which there is no quite relaxing. I observe that the imitators of his style, are for the most part superficial—they catch his mechanical trick,—but the intellectual atonement for it, the thought which causes us to pardon the re-iterated emphasis, is passed over altogether.

Yes—Wordsworth is wordy sometimes—in his blank verse he is. But he is a Wordsworth—a great poet & true!

As to Dryden .. why perhaps .. nay, certainly, he does'nt lie as near to my heart as yours. And yet how true is every word that you say of him—every word except ... The truth is I never c^d believe him capable of being a true dramatist under any possible combination of favorable circumstances. I do not believe it, simply because I believe that his defect as a poet is, still more than his verbosity, a defect of sensibility & consequent power over the feelings. Dryden always makes me think of Lucan, who was called by the Roman critic, an *orator* rather than a poet.[8] He roars magnificently to be sure! 'Yes'—to the *letter*, my dearest friend! Yes, frankly!

I am impatient to read M^{dme} d'Arblay[9]—I like diaries & letters & all that sort of gossip so much! Have *you* Jephson's *plays*?[10] I never read one of them—& sh^d like to glance thro' them, in à propos to the times! Think of him & Hannah More[11] dividing the stage between them!–

Ever your attached
EBB.

I am so sorry about your new distress! Is it an epileptic affection? How is she now?[12]

As to Flush .. I did hear once of his condescending to stoop his head over the dripping pan—& I will speak to Crow about it. She is gone out to see the show of the Queen & the Prussian king,[13] & not being at home at one o clock, as usual nothing c^d persuade Flushie to go down stairs to his own dinner. He w^{dnt} stir. So the housemaid brought his plate up to my bedside! Pray thank K⎯ for the suggestion about the dripping. But really his extreme particularity makes it difficult to satisfy him. Milk, he likes best—milk & cakes. Hard biscuits unless there is sugar in them, he does'nt like much. Macaroons & ratafies he is very grateful for—but then, one cant exactly feed him upon macaroons & ratafies all day long! He likes pastry too; & buttered muffins—but with no fanatical enthusiasm. The sweet soft kinds of cake are the only things which excite *that*. What do you think Papa said to me a few days ago?– "It is my opinion that you love Flush better than anyone else in the world"!

No—it *is'nt true*. But I DO love Flush & for *two* unanswerable reasons.

Papa has come into the room while I write,—& he desires me to offer you his regards. Mine to dear Dr Mitford! That cramp! How sorry I am!

God bless you both–

Am I to understand from what you say of the Athenæum that you see it regularly? Tell me if I may send it when my papers appear? Because I must *make* you see *them*—you must criticise my criticisms!

I congratulate you on M.ʳ Lucas, O dearest prophetess.[14]

Publication: *EBB-MRM*, I, 344–346.
Manuscript: Wellesley College.

1. Letter 910 makes clear that EBB refers to an autograph letter of his.
2. "Foolishnesses."
3. See "Peter Bell" (1819), lines 1126–30.
4. Johnson, at age five, was supposed to have composed the following epitaph: "Here lies poor duck / That Samuel Johnson trod on; / If it had liv'd it had been good luck, / For it would have been an odd one" (*Anecdotes of the Late Samuel Johnson, LL.D.*, by Hester Lynch Piozzi, 1786, p. 10). However, authorship is ascribed to his father, "foolishly proud of him" (*DNB*).
5. Gargantua, famed for his insatiable appetite, was immortalized by Rabelais in *La Vie Inestimable du Grand Gargantua, Père de Pantagruel* (1535).
6. In his lecture of 19 May 1840, "The Hero as Man of Letters," Carlyle spoke of Johnson as "A strong and noble man ... An original man" (*Heroes, Hero-Worship, and the Heroic in History*, 1841, p. 46).
7. Gray was included in Johnson's *Prefaces Biographical and Critical to the Works of the Most Eminent English Poets* (1779–81), later published separately as *The Lives of the English Poets*. Although owning that "To say that he has no beauties, would be unjust", Johnson's comments are mainly adverse; he considers the odes to be marked "by glittering accumulations of ungraceful ornaments; they strike, rather than please ... the language is laboured into harshness.... there is too little appearance of ease and nature."
8. Lucan, the author of *Pharsalia*, was said by Quintilian to be "fiery and passionate and remarkable for the grandeur of his general reflexions, but, to be frank, I consider that he is more suitable for imitation by the orator than by the poet" (*Institutio Oratio*, X, 1, 90–95, trans. H.E. Butler, 1922).
9. The first volume of *Diary and Letters of Madame d'Arblay. Edited by her Niece* [Charlotte Frances Barrett] had just been reviewed in *The Athenæum* (no. 744, 29 January 1842, pp. 101–104).
10. Robert Jephson (1736–1803), Irish poet and dramatist, wrote *Braganza* (1775), *The Count of Narbonne* (1781) and *Julia, or the Italian Lover* (1787), among others.
11. Hannah More (1745–1833) wrote prose and verse, as well as plays, and was held by Johnson to be the most "powerful versificatrix in the English language" (*DNB*). Her play *Percy* was produced at Covent Garden in 1777 and was revived in 1787 for Mrs. Siddons.
12. Miss Mitford's new maid, Marianne, was subject to fits. EBB, fearing that either Miss Mitford or her father might be physically harmed in the course of one of them, urged Marianne's dismissal (see letter to Miss Mitford, 17 October 1842).
13. Frederick William IV (1795–1861), who had become King of Prussia in 1840, had come to London to act as one of the sponsors at the christening of the Prince of Wales on 25 January 1842. This was the day of his departure, and he and his suite were being escorted in procession to the Woolwich Dockyard by Prince Albert.
14. Miss Mitford had early recognized the talent of Lucas, and was one of his first patrons (see letter 857). He was now painting Prince Albert, the first of four portraits Lucas made of him. Finished in 1842, it is reproduced facing p. 41 of *John Lucas, Portrait Painter, 1828–1874*, by Arthur Lucas (1910).

909. EBB to Thomas Westwood

50, Wimpole Street,
Feb. 5, 1842.

Dear Sir,

I fear to think what inference, unjust to my sense of your kind attention, you may have drawn from my silence. But an invalid with the reading and writing upon her hands, which seem to come to me by nature, may be forgiven perhaps, if she asks it humbly. I assure you I *was* and *am* very thankful to you for the gift of your poems[1] although the gentleman who brought them may have thought hardly of me for neither consenting to see him nor even to trust him with a note. The note I would not write until I was properly qualified to be *fully* grateful by reading the book, and the miserable health, or rather lack of it which, even now that I am beyond expectation better, prevents me from leaving my bed-room—shuts me out from the sight of all faces except those of my immediate friends. I hope, therefore, you will not think worse of me altogether than is absolutely necessary. I mean to try to learn humility of you, and indeed it seems to me that you have a good deal to give away among your fellow poets generally. Your book is graceful and fragrant with that feeling for the beautiful, which is beautiful in itself.

It is invidious, or is it? to praise one poem rather than another, but we all do so, and my pencil has marked my favourites. I like, among others, that song with the pretty wild measure, about the summer, and the song to spring about the "bright-vein'd flowers" (a happy epithet)[2] .... but all this is too long.

With a warm sense of the kindness of what you say of my poetry, which of course is heightened by what I have learnt, through this book, of the value of your opinion.

Believe me, dear sir,
Sincerely yours,
Elizabeth Barrett.

Publication: None traced.
Source: Kenyon Typescript, British Library.

1. Westwood's *Poems* (1840) formed lot 1206 of *Browning Collections* (see *Reconstruction*, A2446).
2. "An Expostulation to Summer on Her Premature Departure" (pp. 77–79) and "A Song of Spring" (pp. 163–168).

910. EBB to Mary Russell Mitford

[London]
Feb. 10.ᵗʰ 1842

Thank you my beloved friend, for the sight of Dryden's interesting letter & for your own of more price. Your letters are angels to me!—messengers of all sorts of good & pleasantness—& by so much better than angels as they come oftener, with no[t] far between visits. How kind, how kind, it is in you to write to me so often! That is my reflection fifty times over, to my expression of it once!–

I had a little note from dear Mʳ Kenyon three days ago,—in which he says that I am not to class him with the butterflies, but that he has been tempted into an expedition to Bath or Bristol for four or five days by his three friends Messʳˢ Landor, Crosse & Eagles. Do you know that Mʳ Eagles is the *Sketcher* of Blackwood?[1]—& that his daughter married my cousin a year since, in the midst of a family tempest? He—the sketcher—is a clever artist besides being able to write so admirably upon art,—a clergyman of the Establishment who was formerly tutor to my cousinship of two young Clarkes of Kinnersley castle.[2] A family living was thereupon given to him to hold until the younger Clarke waxed old enough to take it—and in the meantime a lady Eaglet flew away with the elder one—the 'heir of all'.[3] Oh—it was'nt exactly an elopement!– But an obstinate *engagement* it was, in every sense—the seniors engaging as much in arms, as the young lady ever did or *was* by love!– She is'nt at all pretty they say, & she is older by some years than her adorer is, & looks still older—"forty" says Mʳˢ Clarke .. but in a passion!– My story is quite from ex parte evidence,[4] & even by the light of *that*, I cannot choose but blame the violence of wrath twice as deeply as the violence of love. The senior Clarkes have a vow in Heaven[5] never to see the Helen—never—never! And knowing one of them, I do believe it *will* be never!– Mʳ Eagles has removed since the marriage to Clifton—infinitely to his advantage! For think of the pleasure of living constantly within sight & hearing of one's enemies—nay .. praying with one's enemies on sabbath-days (oh that such things shᵈ be!)[6] & preaching sermons to one's enemies, on the gospel of reconciliation!—the great object in people's minds all the time, being to secure the cut effectual, past each other's pews! I do not say so of Mʳ Eagles. It was not *his* object to perpetuate wrath. But the position altogether was a false & painful one.

Is your Mʳ Bourcicault the 'London assurance' Bourcicault? And being so, is he American?– Tell me the name of your story, my dearest friend—*do!*[7]

I want to know too, if you have any means of knowing, whether Mʳ Merry[8] has joined the Puseyites. It has only come into my head that it may be so—I have no other reason! Puseyism is the consumation of High-Churchism, even as Romanism is of Puseyism—& I did think .. a little .. though with every appreciation of the earnestness & truth of Mr Merry .. that there was .. a tendency to High Churchism visible in him. For my own part, if I held High-Churchism today at noon, I sh^d be a Puseyite by break of day, and if I were a Puseyite in the morning, the twilight w^d find me at confession .. infallibly as any pope!– That is my view of the case! As to the evangelical party, though I honor them for many things & much, & recognize in the belief of my soul, more spiritual & doctrinal truth in them than in other divisions of this so-called national church, they yet do appear to me the most inconsistent body of men, I do not say in that church, but under that sun!– Oh! I can see it, I assure you, between the chimneys!—dont call me presumptuous—and it *is* so hot today! my thermometer trying to get up to seventy!– To go down to the evangelical people, whom *I* am ⟨a⟩ngry with for not going out among the dissenters,[9]—& whom you are angry with for a certain narrowness of view & practice which is equally obvious & to be deprecated .. they are, I do admit (having much respect for the good & truth which are amongst them) the most inconsistent body in Christendom.

Yes—after all there is to regret—you are right! This great movement, as all movements must, will end in good.[10] The more thought & enquiry, the better for Truth. Error is the result of half-thinking: & of half-thinking, altho' more *dangerous* than no thinking at all, the most timid of us can scarcely assert that it is *better*! Half-thinking is half-way to whole-thinking—& everybody may rightly welcome it, as long as nobody is content with it!——

Do tell me my dearest friend, how your new charge is,[11] & how you are. Forgive me for caring most how *you* are—& for being anxious that you sh^d not *continue* to be exposed to a state of things so wearing to body & spirit. Surely you have enough to bear, without stooping your shoulder to another burden. Therefore I think with Mr May—that if the poor girl is not very soon better, you sh^d let her family do their obvious duty & receive her from your hands! I quite quite understand all your reluctant kindness—but you must not sacrifice yourself my beloved friend—you must not, remember, for dear Dr Mitford's sake! The affection being simply hysterical, there is no danger of life—& the injury to *you* as a witness, may in effect, be greater than to her as a sufferer. Change of scene & air may be the best remedy, besides! may it not? Do tell me that you are not wearing yourself out into tatters, in your abundant kindness, my dearest dearest friend!– What distresses do come to you, one after another—& you & your tenderness of heart, to meet all!–

I will be careful not to poison Flushie. He is growing so fine-ladyly delicate, that he expects, I believe, to be nourished upon macaroons &

dews, or some such fairy dieting. For the last few days, he has eaten scarcely any animal food—w^{dnt} touch what used to be his favorite,— beefsteak,—yesterday; but immediately upon Crow's bringing him up from dinner to my room, participated most earnestly in my muffin & the milk which came by its side. As to the dripping—oh no! Crow says, "Flush w^{dnt} condescend to such a thing as *that*'[']—it's quite out of the question! And if we gave him a hard biscuit, he w^d take it & run away & play with it—but as to *eating* it, or anything else which is'nt broken up into very small pieces, Mr Flush w^d eschew the barbarity altogether! His soul is above biscuits—but not more than on a level with sponge cakes. You sh^d see how his eyes flash & dilate, & his ears almost join & cover them, when he catches the sight of a parcel in which cakes MAY be, or hears the mystic word! "Cakes—cakes!" He knows the word well, as is testified by the wagging of his tail,!—which not wagging fast enough for the state of his feelings, he wags his hind legs too!- As to spirits & playfulness even to 'joyaunce',[12] Flush beats himself at them lately! He grows younger rather than older I do believe, as to spirits!——

My dearest friend, I shall *send* you the Athenæum where my papers are, whenever they come out! and ⟨there⟩fore dont, on my account, put out your hand in any other direction. I must make you read my papers— that's a necessary part of my vanity!-

In the meanwhile, not having received a proof sheet, I dont know whether I am to be exposed this week or not—probably not! God bless you. All our love-

Mine to dear Dr Mitford! Try to give me good news of both of you.

Your own attached
EBB

Address: Miss Mitford / Three Mile Cross / Near Reading.
Publication: EBB-MRM, I, 347-350.
Manuscript: Edward R. Moulton-Barrett and Wellesley College.

1. John Eagles (1783-1855) was a contributor, chiefly on art, to *Blackwood's Edinburgh Magazine* from 1831 until shortly before his death. His best contributions comprised a series of papers entitled "The Sketcher," appearing between 1833 and 1835.
2. Eagles had been Curate of Kinnersley, but gave up the living in 1841, perhaps as a consequence of the "family tempest" arising from his daughter's marriage to EBB's cousin (see letter 777).
3. Cf. *Love's Labour's Lost*, I, 1, 7.
4. i.e., from one side only.
5. Cf. *The Merchant of Venice*, IV, 1, 228.
6. Cf. *Macbeth*, III, 4, 109.
7. A reference to Miss Mitford's being invited to contribute to Boucicault's anthology of women writers (see letter 906). His play, *London Assurance*, had been performed in 1841. He was Irish, not American.
8. EBB later (1843-44) corresponded with William Merry, Miss Mitford's neighbour, on religious topics.
9. The Evangelicals were a powerful but unpopular group within the Church of England, their members seldom achieving ecclesiastical preferment. They held no special

doctrines, but emphasized the vital significance of each individual's relationship to God and were convinced of the inherent sinfulness of man and his inability to save himself, ascribing to God alone the sinner's salvation. They were responsible for the formation of the Church Missionary Society in 1799. EBB obviously felt that they ought to have broken away from the Established Church, as had the Methodists and other dissenting bodies.

10. The reforming efforts of the Puseyites became known as the Oxford Movement (see letter 803, note 2).

11. Marianne, Miss Mitford's new maid, who suffered from fits; EBB later urged her dismissal (see letter 908, note 12).

12. A poetical word for delight/enjoyment, coined by Spenser and first used in 1586 (*OED*).

911. EBB TO MARY RUSSELL MITFORD

[London]
Feb. 21ˢᵗ 1842

Flushie's likeness! Is'nt it like? The ears rather too long, the nose rather too short, the eyes rather too round! all the rest very like indeed!— Papa brought it home for me some days ago, as Flushie's *double*. "Thine Infelicia's self"!—¹ What do *you* think of it?

Thank you my beloved friend, for interrupting the question upon my lips with an answer from your own dear ones. Your letters are my sunshines & moonshines & larks & nightingales, & when they dont come, I who shᵈ be ashamed under such a deserved catastrophe—to *complain*, yet begin to fancy all sorts of melancholy reasons, more melancholy if possible than the event. And after all, I am half right—for you have been disturbed, vexed, anxious, unwell! May God bless & strengthen you my beloved friend! I yearn to hear better news. Whenever you write there is something to make me sigh & to balance the rest of the pleasure. Another sick servant! And the first sickness not at an end! And Dʳ Mitford—& you yourself! I turn my head quite quick round for some comfort, but altho' you speak of betterness, I can find nothing for my own use but *hope, hope!*—

The thought of yʳ engagement to Mʳ Bourcicault² gave me to hope last week that the silence might be set to his account—though I received the same misgivingly. And I feared to be in the way by writing to you. My papers are not in the Athenæum yet—seeing that Mʳ Dilke wrote to me to apprize me of his intending, according to "my custom always in the

Athenæum", to wait for the whole series before printing one number.³ If critics & editors ever c^d be wrong, I sh^d call it silly—but as it is, the delay is necessary, I having counted upon the more natural arrangement & dawdled "to suit". He *has* two papers, one of them in printed proof—& my poets crowd round me so, that I shall scarcely have done with them without a fourth paper, which Mr Dilke who only wants three of me, will be sure to smile at, a ghastly smile, in agonized courtesy. How amusing all this must be!– I wanted to explain why you did not receive the Athenæum, & 'all this' *came*!

He—they—that is, M^r & Mrs Dilke, & M^r & Mrs Wentworth Dilke[4] were good enough to leave cards here some days ago. Who are the Wentworth Dilkes? Our cards have gone back, but we are not likely to communicate otherwise from Papa's non-visiting tendencies & my non-visitable necessities.

Mr Kenyon has been seen in London .. but not yet by *me*. He will come when he can. Believe me, *that* was'nt the rumble of a grumble. Henceforward I mean to be more goodhumoured, or goodtempered (not to make a fault in metaphysics) than usual!–

In the meanwhile––what an amusing book these Burneyana *do* make!⁵ There is certainly a *consciousness* which combined with the egoism & the Evelinaism 'in sæcula sæculorum',⁶ suggests no idea of modesty, real modesty—& made me think again & again of the true distinction you held up once for my meditation & advantage, between *modesty*, which is not self-occupied, & *shyness* which *is*. And thus I do not worship the "dear little Burney" as a fair incarnate modesty, though with a grove of rose trees turned into blushes, flourishing upon each cheek. But I do like her book—I do think it full of living pulses & delightfulness, & my heart leaps up at the hum of work-day life issuing thus from the tomb-door of that dead generation. Oh—do read the book—I mean, at once—read it at once. Dr Johnson is softer in it than he is to be seen elsewhere—more as Tetty⁷ beheld him than as Boswell did! And one understands the charm of Mrs *Thrale*⁸ more quickly than by the tradition in other places of her sharp sayings & witty vivacities. It lay, I think, in her quick sympathies of head & heart. After all the book, the Evelina, was wonderfully overpraised⁹—which fact, however certain it may be, gives us leave to praise this book, this diary of Ma^{dme} d'Arblay, .. does'nt it?

Let me say while I remember it—but surely not à propos to either book—that I ventured to send to Three Mile Cross, a day since, a barrel of oysters, & am spoiling myself with fancying that one of you at least may care to receive them.

Did you ever hear of *Arcturus* a New York review? The editors sent me two numbers of it this morning—or rather, they sent it by ⟨the⟩ last packet & I received it this morning—with a benignant criticism in one, & a gracious letter—besides.[10] Flush & I blushed "a Burney, a Burney".[11]

Of course he sends his love with his picture—& mine is with you always.

Your EBB–

I am very well (for me) & *walk to the sofa*.

Thank you, thank you for the praise of George. How like you, how kind of you to tell me! Yes!– He *was* M.[r] Wightman's pupil–[12]

Publication: EBB-MRM, I, 350–352.
Manuscript: Wellesley College.

1. Cf. Dekker, *The Honest Whore*, pt. I (1604), IV, 1, 34. Stationery for this letter was imprinted with the "likeness" (see illustration) which EBB mentions.

2. See letter 906.

3. Despite this, he did not wait; the first paper was printed in the issue of 26 February, the fourth and last in that of 19 March.

4. Charles Wentworth Dilke (1810–69) was the son of the editor of *The Athenæum*, also Charles Wentworth Dilke (1789–1864).

5. Frances ("Fanny") Burney was born in 1752. A backward child, entirely self-educated, she began composing poems and stories when she was 10, but destroyed all her manuscripts on her 15th birthday. She continued to write, and her first work was published anonymously in 1778 as *Evelina, or a Young Lady's Entrance into the World*. Her second novel, *Cecilia, or Memoirs of an Heiress* was published in 1782; both were great successes. She served in the Royal Household from 1786 to 1791 as an assistant to the Keeper of the Robes. In 1793 she married General d'Arblay, who had been Lafayette's comrade, and they spent some time in France. She continued writing novels and plays, but, although financially successful, none quite equalled her early novels. She died in 1840, and the first volume of her *Diary and Letters* had just been published.

6. "Unto the age of ages"; i.e., without end.

7. Samuel Johnson's wife, Elizabeth (1688–1752, *née* Jervis), whom he married in 1735 after the death of her first husband, Henry Porter, in 1734. She was 20 years his senior.

8. Hester Lynch Thrale (1741–1821, *née* Salusbury), later (1784) the wife of Gabriel Piozzi, a talented Italian musician, was the author of *Anecdotes of the Late Samuel Johnson, LL.D.* (1786), whose close friend she had been.

9. *The Critical Review: or, Annals of Literature* said of *Evelina*: "This performance deserves no common praise ... It would have disgraced neither the head nor the heart of Richardson" (vol. 46, 1778, pp. 202–204). Johnson "was so caught by it ... that he has sung its praises ever since,—and he says Richardson would have been proud to have written it" (Mme. d'Arblay, *Diary and Letters*, I, 76).

10. *Arcturus, a Journal of Books and Opinion* had noticed *The Seraphim* in its February 1841 issue (no. III, pp. 171–176). (For the full text, see pp. 388–389.)

11. *Evelina* having been published anonymously, with only a select few knowing the identity of its author, Mme. d'Arblay tells of her embarrassment and fear of disclosure when Mrs. Thrale and Johnson discussed the novel with a friend. Mrs. Thrale told her "you have looked like your namesake in the 'Clandestine Marriage', all this evening, 'of fifty colours, I wow and purtest'." While not accusing Fanny of affectation, Mrs. Thrale felt she was over-delicate: "why should you write a book ... and then sneak in a corner and disown it!" (*Diary and Letters*, I, 74–78.)

12. See letter 672, note 4.

912. RB TO WILLIAM CHARLES MACREADY

[London]
Wednesday M^g [?23 February 1842][1]

My dear Macready,

You have given me "some pleasure" indeed– I shall be happy to dine with you on Sunday as you propose, and to talk over the matter—many thanks, meantime.

Ever yours
R Browning.

Qu: "Sine cretâist"[2]—"he who never '*chalks one*'?"

Publication: None traced.
Manuscript: Armstrong Browning Library.

1. Macready's diary entry for Sunday, 27 February 1842, noted that RB had dined with him that day, the other guests being Forster, Anderson and Bucknill (*Macready*, II, 159). No other Sunday with RB was recorded by Macready; this, together with an 1841 watermark, suggests the conjectural date.
2. "Creta," the Latin for chalk, derived from Crete, where it was found.

---

913. EBB TO HUGH STUART BOYD

[London]
Saturday. [26 February 1842][1]

My dear friend,

I send you the Athenæum,[2] which they have been too long in bringing to me. How will you like it? That is a question I ask myself of you anxiously!– Tell me the exact truth of your impressions.

It w^d have been a great security to my 'remarks' & the translations accompanying them, if you could have seen either previous to publication—but what with the obscurity of my handwriting & the briefness of the time, &, to do myself justice, the consideration I have for your *ease*, I c^d not ask you to do such a thing. The *third* paper is almost going to Mr Dilke—& I believe now that nothing can save him from a fourth–

Arabel sends her love to you. Next thursday she is to take you a visitor,—and on monday she talks of being the visitor to you herself—provided there is fine weather & no obstacle.

Think of my walking to the sofa now! Is'nt that an improvement? God bless you dear Mr Boyd!

Ever your affectionate
& grateful EBB–

Remember! Gregory is in the second paper³—which, by the way, is longer than the first.

Address: H S Boyd Esq! / 21 Downshire Hill / Hampstead.
Publication: EBB-HSB, pp. 244–245.
Manuscript: Wellesley College.

   1. Dated by reference to *The Athenæum*.
   2. *The Athenæum* of 26 February 1842 (no. 748, pp. 189–190) included the first part of EBB's "Some Account of the Greek Christian Poets."
   3. This appeared in the issue of 5 March (no. 749, pp. 210–212).

---

914. EBB TO MARY RUSSELL MITFORD

London–
Feb. 31. [*sic*] 1842.¹

I struggle from under a heap of proof sheets, my dearest friend—just because I must say one word to you before the week closes. If it had not been for writing, writing, .. & such reading of heavy books as makes one[']s arms ache long before one's head, (my head is quite secondary!) you w^d have heard from me some days ago, nay, day by day– So trace up the silence to the source. In the meanwhile, I think of you, dream of you, love you, read your letters three times over & leap up as high as I can when I catch the first ray of them as their orient appears in Crow's hands. Dearest friend—think of my pleasure to hear about the oysters!² Think of my luck turning, or seeming to turn all at once! There seems no end to the new prosperity!– I am proud too, quite proud, of a certain sympathy of destiny between you & me, which I w^d not however, even for pride's sake, extend beyond books, because for all the new flattering in the skies I am not yet near so assured of my present good-luck as of my tender love to *you*—but I *am* proud (to take breath again) of the certain sympathy of destiny as to book-reading between you & me. For I have not very long done with Lewis's memoirs,³—& have actually scarcely laid aside Hayley's Autobiography,⁴ so as to draw two full breaths between concluding it & opening your letter!!

   Therefore you see the inference afar off—you need'nt my dearest kindest friend, send me Hayley—& I need'nt seek for Lewis any more. I agree with you as to the last quite—yet was something less interested than you seem to be, from never having cared much for the man or his works either, or heard him much cared about. Perhaps the biographer is nearly good enough for his subject, bad as he is—yet the man (the subject) seems to have had all the excellent points of character which you mark with a hand so ready to distinguish excellence. His West Indian work I never saw.[5] I rather suspect that when I was a child I used to think Alonzo & the fair Imogen fine poetry[6]—but the opinion past away a very long time before I "put away childish things"[7]—& if it had not been for a hankering 'inexpressive' & highly improper wish of mine to see the Monk, which has led me to hazard my reputation[8] by asking for it at more than one circulating library (& all in vain!) I sh^d have put away "little Mat" altogether from my thoughts at the same moment of antiquity. Still he was better than his books—how much better! Tell me what the West Indian book is like. Not that I shall care to see it—I might you know from the library here if I did care. But I dont think, considering the subject, which is so worn to me, & the author who may be wearing, that I *shall* care.

Well—then! there's the autobiography! I will tell you how it was with *me*! For a long time, I thought Hayley was scarcely put-up-able-with! So powdered & pigtailed! so primly elaborate as to diction—so anointed with fine words & fine phrases—there was no coming between the wind & his nobility!![9] so conscious of his bardship, in the length & breadth of every sentence! so be*bard*ing his readers till they w^d nearly as soon be bombarded! so determined on being very good, & very delicate & very generous & very magnanimous—oh—so magnanimous!—& præter-determined[10] that nobody sh^d miss seeing the full extent & degree of said goodness, delicacy generosity & magnanimity—that I all but threw up the book—or threw it down,—as one for whom the "Halleyan periods" to use his own speech, were full too much!- I all but did it—but I did not actually. I, another "pitiable Eliza,"![11] read on, on the contrary—& by degrees, by slow degrees, & sure I suppose,—the extreme overcoming sense of self-occupation seemed to wear away- I liked the 'poet' better & his phraseology better—at last I almost loved him for his lovingness to his friends—to his son! His tenderness to his son & his grief at that parting won my heart! It is touching & beautiful as love always is.[12]

Yes—the book certainly does grow to be interesting. Tell me if you dont think so. Tell me if you dont think that it *grows* to be interesting, & chiefly through its tenderness. The edition I had from Saunders concluded with the poet's biography of his son, "the young sculptor"[13]—& not impotently, might the feelings speak.

Still the expression of sentiment is occasionally most strange. The funeral sermon he wrote for "his pitiable Eliza" .. a copy of which he sent to his son "to recite" to his friends the Flaxmans in London, while the mournful ceremony was performed at Eartham!![14] The poetical 'recitations' which he prepared on the birthdays of his dying son, wherein his dire estate as a cripple is set forth rather according to the 'bardship' than the fatherhood .. with so little of the shrinking delicacy of love!!![15] It is strange. Tell me 'your thought'. The book is interesting after all!–

I sh^d like to know "the rights & the wrongs" of "his pitiable Eliza"—whether & how, exactly & only, she was blameable.[16] I c^d fancy that "the bard of Sussex'[']"[17] might be a hard person to live with! He did not live in the house even with his dying son. The simple scheme of living together appears unthought of, undesired, amid all the yearnings of their mutual tenderness.

And how little is said of Miss Seward "the Muse"! It disappointed me. Is there a life of *her*?[18] There was certainly a coolness between her & Hayley—you see *that* in her letters[19] .. & I sh^d like to know 'the rights & wrongs' of that too!–

You cant care a great deal more for biography than I do. My thirst for it is not quelled though I sit by a fountain.

If you had not lost the five vols. out of six of Richardson's letters,[20] I sh^d certainly entreat you to let me see them—for I never did,—& w^d give much to do so. But as to Collier's book[21]—no—I thank you my beloved friend for your ready *leaning-forward* kindness; but you shall not send me that!– I do not care much—and it w^d be wrong if I did, to trust a book which c^d not be replaced by the most remorseful desires, on the railroad.

What do you mean by Mr Talfourd's *ratting*? We have heard nothing.[22] What did Mr Milnes say?–

How glad I am, how thankful! that you are all some thing better & easier! God keep you so—or rather increase & complete the happy change.

George goes away on monday. Thank you for your kind words—nay—*thoughts* they are I know–

My beloved friend, your Dilkes stand straight up in the light. I see them perfectly!——[23] I see them *by* you now, & I may, *with* you, some day! God bless you, dearest friend! I love you truly & entirely, & I will let you think such love of some worth, because it is—it must be in this world! You only overvalue the *lover*!

I send the Athenæum, my first Athenæum![24] Try to read it to the end—though I fear it wont be called very readable by the most of those who do try–

Your
EBB–

My love to Dr Mitford– I have not seen Mr Kenyon.—Oh—When & where[?]

Publication: EBB-MRM, I, 352-356 (as 31 [*sic*, for 26] February 1842).
Manuscript: Wellesley College.

1. The editors of *EBB-MRM* believe this to be a misdating for 26 February, based on EBB's sending *The Athenæum* of that date and her remark about writing "before the week closes." There is, however, no indication that EBB was sending the magazine immediately upon its issue, and we do not feel that her remark necessarily shows her to be writing on a Saturday. It seems more probable that she forgot that February had only 28 days; we therefore leave her dating, placing this letter between 913 and 917, without struggling to interpret her error further.
2. Sent on 20 February (see letter 911).
3. Matthew Gregory Lewis (1775-1818), a prolific novelist and playwright, became famous on the publication in 1795 of his first work, *Ambrosio, or the Monk*. It was a popular success despite (or because of?) its indecency, which caused the Attorney-General to seek an injunction against its sale. The prosecution was halted when Lewis undertook to expunge the more objectionable passages from the second edition. *The Life and Correspondence of M.G. Lewis* [by Mrs. Margaret Baron-Wilson] was published in 1839.
4. William Hayley (1745-1820), poet and playwright, is best known for *The Triumphs of Temper* (1781) and for his *Life of Cowper* (1803-04). *Memoirs of the Life and Writings of William Hayley, Esq.... Written by Himself*, ed. John Johnson, appeared in 1823.
5. Lewis, the owner of estates in Jamaica, was known for humane and considerate treatment of his slaves. EBB refers to his *Journal of a West Indian Proprietor*, published posthumously in 1834.
6. "Alonzo the Brave and the Fair Imogine" was a ballad incorporated in *Ambrosio, or the Monk*.
7. I Corinthians, 13:11.
8. Because of its alleged indecency, referred to in note 3 above.
9. Cf. *I Henry IV*, I, 3, 45.
10. "Determined beyond measure."
11. When Hayley broached to his mother the idea of marrying Eliza Ball, the daughter of his guardian, she was concerned that Eliza might take after her mother, who was mentally deranged. He replied that, if such were to transpire, "I should bless my God for having given me courage sufficient to make myself the legal guardian of the most amiable and pitiable woman on earth" (*Memoirs*, I, 87-88). He married Eliza in 1769, but, unfortunately, his mother's fears were realized when Eliza's mind became affected in 1786.
12. Hayley's illegitimate son, Thomas Alphonso Hayley (b. 1780), showed much promise as an artist and sculptor, but in 1798 his health began to deteriorate and, after two years of great suffering, he died in 1800. Hayley wrote in his diary of his hope "for a blissful re-union with my dear filial angel, whose endearing perfections are more and more the wonder and delight of my faithful and affectionate remembrance." John Johnson observed that there could be "very few examples of a father and son in whom the reciprocal affection rose to such a height, and supported itself in so striking a manner" (*Memoirs*, II, 12 and *Memoirs of Thomas Alphonso Hayley*, p. 502).
13. This is the sub-title of *Memoirs of Thomas Alphonso Hayley*, following Hayley's own *Memoirs* in Johnson's edition.
14. In a letter of 16 November 1797, Hayley sent to his son a copy of the "brief occasional discourse" he had composed for Eliza's funeral "that you may ... recite it yourself to our dear Flaxmans, at the very time when it will be delivered to the good people of our village" (*Memoirs of Thomas Alphonso Hayley*, p. 370). For three years (1795-98), Hayley's son was the pupil of John Flaxman (1755-1826), a sculptor of great repute, and had lived with Flaxman and his wife Ann (*née* Denman, 1760?-1820).

15. Hayley had marked some, but not all, of his son's birthdays with verse, starting with the first birthday on 5 October 1781. "Invocation to Patience" was addressed to the "dear Invalid" on his penultimate birthday, 5 October 1798 (*Memoirs of Thomas Alphonso Hayley*, pp. 411–413).

16. i.e., for the separation that took place in 1789.

17. Hayley became known by this appellation following the success of *The Triumphs of Temper*.

18. The only biography available at this time was the memoir by Scott in the 1810 edition of her poems. EBB commented on this in letter 606.

19. In a letter of 9 August 1786, Miss Seward had written that her correspondence with Hayley "is not what it was; but the deficiency . . . proceeds not from me. I honour and love him as well as ever; yet I feel that the silver cord of our amity is loosening at more links than one" (*Letters of Anna Seward Written Between the Years 1784 and 1807* [ed. Archibald Constable], 1811, I, 168).

20. *The Correspondence of Samuel Richardson, Author of Pamela, etc.*, ed. Anna L. Barbauld, 6 vols., 1804.

21. Jeremy Collier (1650–1726) published a number of political pamphlets, including one defending the actions of Charles I, for which he was imprisoned briefly by Cromwell. EBB probably refers to his *Short View of the Immorality and Profaneness of the English Stage* (1698), a courageous and unsparing attack on Dryden, Congreve and other contemporary playwrights.

22. Talfourd acted for the defence when Moxon was brought to trial on a charge of libel arising from his publication of an edition of Shelley's works. The accusation of "ratting" probably reflects Miss Mitford's feeling that Talfourd had compromised his principles in his address to the jury. *The Athenæum* of 13 November 1841 (no. 733, p. 869), commenting on his speech, said that Talfourd "must be fully aware of the facts and their consequence. Why, then, did he pass over them in his argument? The reason is obvious: the sole course which lay open to the learned Serjeant . . . was to flatter the prejudices of the jury . . . His client's escape . . . could only be attained through a side-wind . . . his *amour propre* as a man, and his regard for truth as a logician, were sacrificed to his duty as an advocate."

23. Miss Mitford had obviously responded at some length to EBB's question in letter 911 about the younger Dilke and his wife.

24. The issue of 26 February, containing the first part of "Some Account of the Greek Christian Poets" (no. 748, pp. 189–190).

---

915. EBB TO MARY RUSSELL MITFORD

[London]
[?March 1842][1]

⟨★★★⟩[2] O most encouraging of Mæcænases,[3] by your account of your letter to the Reading poetess![4]

And here am I, one of the race,--'good for nothing'[5] except to be loved a little--if you will continue to be so good to your ever
affectionate EBB–

Publication: EBB-MRM, I, 356.
Manuscript: Wellesley College.

1. We assume that "most encouraging of Mæcænases" refers to Miss Mitford's reaction to the first of EBB's papers on the Greek Christian Poets, in *The Athenæum* of 26 February; hence this conjectural date.
2. The beginning of the letter is missing; this single sheet was numbered "III" by EBB.
3. Gaius Cilnius Mæcenas (70?–8 B.C.), Roman statesman and man of letters, was the patron of Vergil, Horace, Propertius, and others; his name came to signify one who encouraged young writers.
4. Unidentified. The editors of *EBB-MRM* speculate that the reference is to Priscilla Maurice (1810–54), the sister of the theologian Frederick Denison Maurice (1805–72), but we have been unable to verify either that she was a poetess or that she was in Reading at this time.
5. *All's Well That Ends Well*, II, 3, 207.

916. Mary Russell Mitford to EBB

Three Mile Cross,
March—, 1842.

I have only read the first volume of Madame D'Arblay's "Diary." Dr. Johnson appears to the greatest possible advantage—gentle, tender, kind and true; and Mrs. Thrale—oh, that warm heart! that lively sweetness! My old governess[1] knew her as Mrs. Piozzi, in Wales. She was there as a governess—neglected, uncared for, as governesses too often are; and that sweetest person sought her out, brought her forward, talked to her, wrote to her, gave her heart and hope and happiness. There have been few women who have used riches, and the station that riches give, so wisely as Mrs. Piozzi. I used to ask, "Was she happy?" and the answer was, "I hope so; but her animal spirits were so buoyant—she was so entirely one of those who become themselves cheered by the effort to cheer another—that the question is more difficult to answer than if it concerned one of a temper less elastic." As to the little Burney, I don't like her at all, and that's the truth. A girl of the world—a woman of the world, for she was twenty-seven or thereabout—thought clearly and evidently of nothing on this earth but herself and "Evelina."

Ever most faithfully yours,
M.R.M.

Text: L'Estrange (2), III, 143.

1. Miss Rowden, afterward Mrs. St. Quintin.

917. EBB TO HUGH STUART BOYD

[London]
March 2. 1842.

My ever very dear friend,

Do receive the assurance that whether I leave out the right word or put in the wrong one, you never can be other to me than just THAT while I live—& why not after I have ceased to live? And now--what have I done in the meantime, to be called 'Miss Barrett'? "I pause for a reply".[1]

Of course it gives me very great pleasure to hear you speak so kindly of my first paper. Some 'bona avis'[2] as good as a nightingale must have shaken its wings over me as I began it! & if it will but sit on the same spray while I go on towards the end, I shall rejoice exactly fourfold. The third paper went to Mr Dilke today—& I was so fidgetty about getting it away, (& it seemed to cling to my writingcase with both its hands) that I w^d. not do any writing, even as little as this note, until it was quite gone out of sight. You know it is possible that he, the editor, may not please to have the *fourth* paper—but even in that case, it is better for the "Remarks" to remain fragmentary, than be compressed till they are as dry as a *hortus siccus*[3] of poets.

Certainly you do & must praise my number one too much– Number one (that's myself) thinks so– I do really—& the supererogatory virtue of kindness may be acknowledged out of the pale of the Romish Church.

In regard to Gregory & Synesius, you will see presently that I have not wronged them altogether.

As you have ordered the Athenæums, I will not send one tomorrow so as to repeat my illfortune of being too late. But tell me if you would like to have any from me, & how many?

It was very kind in you to pat Flush's head in defiance of danger & from pure regard for me.[4] I kissed his head where you had patted it; which association of approximations I consider as an imitation of shaking hands with you & as the next best thing to it– You understand—dont you? that Flush is my constant companion, my friend, my amuser, lying with his head on one page of my folios while I read the other? (Not *your* folios—I respect *your* books, be sure) Oh! I dare say if the truth were known, Flush understands Greek excellently well.

I hope you are right in thinking that we shall meet again. Once I wished *not* to live—but the faculty of life seems to have sprung up in me again, from under the crushing foot of heavy grief.

Be it all as God wills.

Believe me, your ever affectionate
EBB.

Address: H S Boyd Esq.r / 21 Downshire Hill / Hampstead.
Publication: LEBB, I, 99–100.
Manuscript: Wellesley College.

1. *Julius Caesar*, III, 2, 34.
2. "Lucky bird"; i.e., one that would have furnished good omens to a Roman augurer.
3. "Dry garden."
4. Presumably Arabel took Flush with her when paying the visit forecast in letter 913.

918. EBB TO GEORGE GOODIN MOULTON-BARRETT

[London]
March 2– 1842.

My ever dearest Georgie,
 I said to Papa last night– "We *may* hear from George tomorrow" .. *that* was an ebullition of good opinion of you! But "oh no" .. he said—nothing can be more unlikely. If he writes at all, he wont write tomorrow.
 Thank you my dearest dearest George for the letter which came after all– If you knew how I cared to have it you w.d 'do so again' very soon. You have only to breathe once or twice over the paper & let your hand move at the same time, & the work is done!
 I feel quite triumphant about the six cases, & we are all as pleased as possible. Fortune will come if you wait long enough where the three roads meet[1] & restrain your natural discontent at the dust.
 I am a chronicler with nothing to chronicle, having heard nothing, out of my own heart-beating & head-working, & that not worth repeating, since you went away. M.r Gosset[2] does not dine here today, & Papa was scarcely pleased at his being asked—"Why did George ask him when he was not here to entertain him? Certainly you could'nt have waited dinner for *me*. *I* shall not be back perhaps until half past eight." So spake he yesterday, & Henrietta being abashed never explained how M.r Bell[3] and M.r Somebody else were coming—so there will be a delightful surprise for him at half past eight. Henry met Arabella Gosset yesterday– Of course she enquired after "dearest Ba" but notwithstanding the dearestness leaves town today without coming to Wimpole Street. I had M.r Townsend's poem of 'New Zealand' yesterday too,[4] with a request that I w.d dispose of a few copies, as assistant to Seely in his heavy publishing labors, & in help to the charity. Not knowing nor having access to many buyers of poems (unfortunately for myself) I shall decline the proffered occupation. I shall say "I am still busy with the Seraphim! & have'nt sold it yet by .. how many copies!"

I have no doubt that your Scotchman: your accidental Scotchman, admired you quite as much as he admired me. "Very like a whale"[5] & Carlyle indeed! I suppose Carlyle stands for an author in the far north—& that there's an inversion in those parts of the old phrase—ex Hercule, pedem.[6] M.[r] Boyd approves of my first part but objects to the injustice of including Gregory & Synesius in the canaille of poets, & using one grand swoop of a *they*[7] to all. "My third" inclines to end itself– Sh.[dnt] you like to see the ghastly grin of enforced courtesy, with which M.[r] Dilke will receive the intimation of a fourth's being necessary? I think I must propose *un*paying back—i.e. the taking off of a half guinea for every supernumerary column. Everybody's love. God bless you my own dear Georgie!

Ever your Ba

Do write.

Address: George Goodin M Barrett Esq.[r] / [continued in Henrietta's hand] M.[r] Palmer's / Westgate St / Gloster.
Publication: B-GB, pp. 77–79.
Manuscript: Pierpont Morgan Library.

1. The junction of three roads (*trivium*) had a particular significance for the ancients. The Romans frequently placed there an image of Diana, portrayed with three faces, one looking along each road; in this capacity, she was known as Diana Trivia. It was also at such a meeting of the roads that Œdipus slew his father, fulfilling the first part of the fate foretold by the Delphic Oracle (see Sophocles, *Œdipus Tyrannos*, 707 ff. and 787 ff.).

2. Allen Ralph Gosset, married to EBB's cousin Arabella.

3. The brother of Maria Barrett, the wife of EBB's distant cousin, Samuel Goodin Barrett. In a letter to Henrietta, 7 January 1847, EBB wrote that he "gives up his heiress, then, and is not thinner for it" (*TTUL*, p. 23).

4. See letter 906, note 7.

5. *Hamlet*, III, 2, 382.

6. The usual form is "ex pede, Herculem" ("from the foot, Hercules"). Aulus Gellius (*fl.* ca. 130 A.D.) described in his *Noctes Atticæ* (bk. I, cap. 1) how it was inferred from the size of Hercules' footprint that he was much taller than other men; in a more general sense, the phrase signifies the deduction of the whole from a part. As George's letter is lost to us, so too is the meaning of the reference to Carlyle, but EBB's inversion of Gellius's phrase gives the meaning "from Hercules, the foot."

7. EBB has emphasized her underscoring by printing the word.

919. MARY RUSSELL MITFORD TO EBB

Three Mile Cross,
March 2, 1842.

Since writing to you yesterday, my beloved friend, I have read in H.F. C[horley]'s "Music and Manners" the account of a visit which he made to Madame d'Abrantes, I think in '39. He speaks of the thing among Parisian contrasts. He went to see her, he says, in her two small rooms, humbly furnished; describes her as clumsy of figure, with dim eyes, a hoarse voice, and feverish spirits, and adds that the three last evils were caused by the excess of opiates in which she indulged. He says that the room rung with anecdote and repartee; that she took her full part of the noise; and that, in particular, she cajoled two or three black-bearded men, who wore "Journalist" imprinted in visible letters on every hair of their mustachios. He adds that a few months afterwards she died in a hospital; that almost at the last a party of visitors going through the wards, one of the nurses pointed her out to their notice, on which the dying woman exclaimed, "Are you making a show of me?"[1] Think of the ambassadress, the governess of Paris, the vice-queen of Portugal, labouring as a bookseller's drudge; fancy the wife of Napoleon's first aide-de-camp and friend,[2] the companion of Josephine, of Hortense, of Duroc, of Madame Mère,[3] forced to court such creatures as Balzac has painted in the "Journalists of Paris!"[4]

Is poor King Louis still alive?[5] Hortense is dead, I know. And is the captive of Ham the single or the married brother?[6] One of the two remaining sons of Louis died, I think; but, of these two, one was the husband of a daughter of his uncle Joseph,[7] so that *he* would unite hereafter every right to the Crown that the settlement under the Empire could give. This, I suppose, is Louis Philippe's excuse.

Now, good-night! It has just occurred to me that when a young girl, some eleven years old or less, I went with my father to the pit of one of the theatres—Drury Lane, I believe; yes, Drury Lane—to see a tragedy from "The Monk." Kemble played the hero, and Mrs. Siddons the heroine. *She* had to go into a dungeon where a frail nun had produced an infant, or rather she had to come out of a small door on to the stage, with the supposed baby in her arms. The door was what is technically called "practicable," that is to say, a *real* door, frame and all, made to open in the scene, and to sustain the illusion of a dungeon, as well as in that huge stage such an illusion can be sustained—for, paradoxical as it sounds, so many are the discrepancies in the present ambitious state of scenery, that I am quite convinced that in the days of Shakspeare, when all was trusted to the imagination of the spectator, the fitting state of willing illusion was much more frequently obtained than now—however, to make the scene as dungeon-like as possible, the door was deeply arched, hollow and low; and Mrs. Siddons, miscalculating the width, knocked the head of the huge wax doll she carried so violently against the wooden framework that the unlucky figure broke its neck with the force of the blow, and the waxen head came rolling along the front of the stage. Lear could not have survived such a *contretemps*. The theatre echoed and re-echoed with shouts of laughter, and the tragedy being comfortably full of bombast, not only that act, but the whole piece, finished amidst peals of merriment unrivalled since the production of "Tom Thumb."[8] I remember it as if it were yesterday.

Ever most affectionately yours,
M.R.M.

Text: L'Estrange (2), III, 138–140.

1. Laure Junot (*née* Permon, 1738–1838), Duchess d'Abrantès, was nicknamed "petite peste" by Napoleon. After her husband's death in 1813, she participated in intrigues to restore the Bourbons. Her *Mémoires* (18 vols., 1831–34) were somewhat sarcastic and spiteful, especially with regard to Napoleon. The events mentioned by Miss Mitford were recounted by Chorley in vol. III, pp. 259–261.
2. Jean Andoche Junot (1771–1813), one of Napoleon's generals, was created Duke d'Abrantès in 1807 and made Governor of Portugal. He was defeated at Vimiera by Wellington in 1808 and committed suicide on 29 July 1813 after becoming insane.
3. Joséphine (*née* de La Pagerie, 1763–1814), widow of Vicomte Alexandre de Beauharnais (1760–94), married Napoleon in 1796. Her daughter, Hortense de Beauharnais (1783–1837) married Napoleon's brother Louis and was the mother of Napoleon III. Géraud Christophe Michel Duroc (1772–1813), aide-de-camp to Napoleon, was created Duke de Frioul in 1808. As Grand Marshal of the Tuileries, he was responsible for Napoleon's safety; he was mortally wounded while with Napoleon at the Battle of Bautzen in 1813. Madame Mère was Napoleon's mother, Maria Letizia Bonaparte (*née* Ramolino, 1750–1836).
4. Balzac despised the daily press, revenging himself for adverse criticism of his works by pillorying journalists and their profession in his novels.
5. Louis Bonaparte (1778–1846) was King of Holland from 1806 to 1810.
6. Charles Louis Bonaparte (1808–73), the youngest son of Louis Bonaparte, attempted to overthrow Louis Philippe in 1840. The attempt failed, and he was condemned to life imprisonment in the fortress of Ham, 90 miles N.E. of Paris, but escaped after six years. In 1848 he was elected President of France, and in 1852 proclaimed the Second Empire and himself Napoleon III. At the time of Miss Mitford's enquiry, he was still unmarried.
7. Louis Bonaparte's first son, Napoléon Charles, had died in 1807. The second son, Napoléon Louis (1804–31), had married his cousin, Charlotte Bonaparte (1802–39), daughter of Napoleon's elder brother Joseph (1768–1844), King of Naples (1806–08) and King of Spain (1808–13).
8. The play, based on Lewis's *Ambrosio, or the Monk*, was *Aurelio and Miranda* by James Boaden (1762–1839), the biographer of Kemble, Mrs. Siddons and Mrs. Jordan. It was first performed at Drury Lane on 29 December 1798 (shortly after Miss Mitford's 11th birthday) and was repeated four times in the following week. *The Times* of 31 December 1798, in its review of the first performance, made no mention of the mishap recounted by Miss Mitford, so presumably it occurred in a subsequent performance. The principal roles were played by John Philip Kemble (1757–1823) and his sister, Sarah Siddons (1755–1831).

Tom Thumb, a Tragedy, by Henry Fielding (1707–54), was given its first performance in 1730.

920. EBB TO MARY RUSSELL MITFORD

[London]
March 3.ᵈ 1842¹

My beloved friend too kind always to me, there goes to you today another Athenæum with its burden of Greek poets. I may end by tiring you of them after all . . & yet I almost fancy to myself that you will care something for Gregory's [']'Soul & body" which strikes a sprightly note in the midst of his more solemn minims. In the meantime I embrace as if I were a Brahmin martyr, though in quite a different spirit, your column of prophecy. You the dearest prophetess in the world, & dear M.ʳ Kenyon & I myself shall be nearly sure to walk round it since you say so!² I hail the omen "a good bird" as the old Romans w.ᵈ call it, & singing like a nightingale!

But dear D.ʳ Mitford is not well again—yet better—yet not the more well for being better. Oh that you could take some breath from these anxieties! You are hardly tried indeed. How are his spirits commonly? Do they feel refreshed by this breathing of spring which we can all feel in our faces as she "comes slowly up this way."?³ And that reminds me– Did I thank you—oh no no! I didn't—for that spring-feeling which threaded your violets & kept them fresh on their journey from your garden to my glass, & a day or two afterwards besides! Ungrateful being that I am to have to say 'no' to such a question. Dont *derive* me to be as bad as the premises threaten! I love both violets & you—but you best!–

I have seen M.ʳ Kenyon. I saw him either the day on which my last letter went to you or the day next to it,—& the first word which he, in his evil conscience uttered as he passed the threshold of my door, was . . . *"Dont ask me if I have written to Miss Mitford"*. Well!—then he went on to tell me of his Bath expedition—how immediately upon his arrival there in the midst of his Landors & Crosses & Eagles, a dumb devil took him, in the shape of a cold, & he c.ᵈⁿᵗ speak a word. That was disappointing & vexatious of course to every one of them—& he appears to have scarcely been able to speak again until he went out of hearing, back again on the London road. And thus perhaps he had not much pleasure in being away—at any rate he did not talk of the journey as one talks of pleasures—& between ourselves, dear M.ʳ Kenyon did not seem to be altogether in the satisfied sunny spirits one is used to associate with the name. Not that he did not smile, & laugh even, & talk with gaiety & brilliancy—but the sparks did appear struck accidentally—the buoyancy & abandon were not in their old places. I said to myself "He is out of spirits plainly[']'. My fancy very likely! Dont take much note of it lest it be my fancy. He congratulates himself on his return to his own quiet back room which you may remember, & from which he has shut out the world with his folding doors. That is his illusion! For you know & I know, that the world can slide in at a back door as well as a front, & that our dear friend's solitude is confined to .. perhaps .. half an hour before breakfast. I asked him when he was going away again– "Never!" "So you said the day before you went to Bath". "No, no. I always meant to go in the spring to Bath, if not then—but now I am quite settled". You see we may be sure of him for a fortnight—or even three weeks!—there's no knowing! Dear Mr Kenyon!

Thank you my dearest friend for wishing to lend me Richardson's letters in the five lost volumes—& promising me the one within reach.[4] But since I spoke, I have found them all six at Saunders's library, & they are at this moment waiting to be read at my right hand. I rejoice in my sympathy with you,—(it is more honor!—& a pleasure, oh surely a pleasure, besides!) regarding the love of details, & of all memoirs & letters in which the great Humanity is revealed to us by a thousand little strokes. "Sands make the mountains"[5]—& still lesser grains, this large Human Nature. I quite quite agree with you. It has always been my impression that if Sir Charles Grandison had appeared in three volumes like the novels of our day, he w^d have been *unreadable*.[6] But we come to love the personnages of that work as we do many people in the world, by force of knowing them long, by force of being tired of them, by force of recognizing the neutral tint of our common life in the very tedium of their dulness. I do think just that of Sir Charles Grandison. As to the divine Clarissa she is a book apart, a poem apart—a beatitude in a fiend's mouth! There is no praise fit for her beyond our tears.[7]

Will you give me a handful of sympathy for Flush's misfortunes—not that Clarissa's suggested them,—however "by your smiling you may think to say so."[8] You may have heard of Miss Trepsack, a very dear old family friend of ours, who lived *simply as a friend* in Papa's family, has held him an infant in her arms besides each of *his* infants, & now having lodgings in a street near to us runs in & out (she can still run I assure you) of this house & calls us "her children". Now you understand who our dear *Trippy* is—for we call her impertinently just *that*—& now you have only to learn that dear Trippy who cant bear dogs in general, has dropped down into love before Flushie, & gives him cakes so often that Flushie's first ceremony upon meeting her is to examine both her hands & then push his nose into her bag. Well. Flush went out walking with Trippy & Arabel yesterday, & was taken into a confectioner's shop & presented with a spunge cake for himself. Flush is too great a coward to eat even a cake in a shop, with a strange man staring at him, & far too gentlemanly to eat it out in the street—therefore the gift was wrapt up in paper & given to him to carry home "to Miss Barrett"—all of which he perfectly understood & acted upon. He had carried it with the gravest satisfaction quite up to this door—when on a sudden—behold, there was a vision of the two great dogs, Resolute & Catiline, who also, on their part, were coming in from walking, & met him on the threshold. Now Flush's delight in the society of these great dogs is something quite wonderful—& more especially as they in their tender affection very often almost swallow him up. Even his love of cakes is nought before his love of the dogs! Therefore on he sprang,—into their very mouths—& down in his emotion, fell the precious cake—& up in the same minute was it snatched by his beloved friend Catiline & swallowed with a mouthful. Poor, poor Flush! He did not see the catastrophe—but on the subsiding of his passionate delight he looked about for his cake round & round in vain—smelt into everybody's hands,—went on his hind legs, feeling with his pretty front paws all round my tables, & at last had recourse to most vehement coaxing that somebody might give him his cake. Of course, the end of my story is that I sent out for another one, & that he ate it with many signs of satisfaction. But think—in the meantime—of poor Flushie's anxieties! And that treacherous friend Catiline![9]

God bless you my ever beloved & kindest friend! My love & most affectionate wishes to your invalid. How are the servants.

Your own EBB–

Publication: EBB-MRM, I, 356–359.
Manuscript: Wellesley College.

1. EBB's reference to "another Athenæum" indicates that she was sending the second of her papers on the Greek Christian Poets. This appeared in the issue of 5 March, so it is apparent that EBB received advance copies, or else misdated her letter.
2. Lacking Miss Mitford's letter, we cannot clarify her "column of prophecy." EBB's comment suggests that Miss Mitford had linked EBB's and Kenyon's poetical skills in some manner.
3. Coleridge, *Christabel* (pt. I, 1816), line 22.
4. Miss Mitford referred to having lost five volumes of "Richardson's curious correspondence" in a letter of 4 March 1842 to Miss Anderdon (see Chorley, I, 198).
5. Cf. Edward Young's *Love of Fame, the Universal Passion* (1728), Satire VI, "On Women," line 206.
6. *The History of Sir Charles Grandison. In a Series of Letters Published from the Originals* (6 vols., 1754).
7. Richardson's *Clarissa; or, the History of a Young Lady* (the longest novel in the English language) was published in 1747–48 (8 vols.). The "fiend's mouth" refers to Lovelace, who, in the novel, dupes Clarissa into going to London with him, where he establishes her in what she believes to be respectable lodgings but which, in reality, is a superior brothel.
8. Cf. *Hamlet*, II, 2, 309–310.
9. EBB is comparing Catiline's theft of Flush's cake with the treachery of the Roman Catiline, whose conspiracy to overthrow the Roman government was discovered by Cicero.

921. EBB to Hugh Stuart Boyd

[London]
Saturday night. March 5– 1842.

My very dear friend,

I am quite angry with myself for forgetting your questions when I answered your letter.

Could you really imagine that I have not looked into the Greek tragedians for years, with my true love for Greek poetry? That is asking a question you will say—& not answering it. Well then, I answer by a 'Yes' the one you put to me. I had two volumes of Euripides with me in Devonshire—& have read him as well as Æschylus and Sophocles,—*that* is *from* them––both before & since I went there. You know I have gone through every line of the three tragedians, long ago, in the way of regular, consecutive reading.[1]

You know also that I had at different times read different dialogues of Plato: but when three years ago, & a few months previous to my leaving home, I became possessed of a complete edition of his works edited by Bekker,[2] why then I began with the first volume & went through the whole of his writings, both those I knew & those I did not know, one after another,—& have at this time read, not only all that is properly attributed to Plato, but even those dialogues & epistles which pass falsely under his name,—everything except two books I think, or three, of that treatise "De legibus" which I shall finish in a week or two—as soon as I can take breath from M^r. Dilke.[3]

Now, the questions are answered.

Ever your affectionate & grateful friend
EBB.

Address: H S Boyd Esqr.
Publication: LEBB, I, 101.
Manuscript: Wellesley College.

1. As far back as 1832, EBB had written "I have now read every play of Æschylus Sophocles & Euripides" (*Diary*, p. 229).

2. August Immanuel Bekker (1785–1871), German philologist and critic, Professor of Philosophy at the University of Berlin (1810), was a prolific editor of the classical authors. EBB's copy of his 11-volume, 1826 edition of Plato's works, now at Ohio Wesleyan, sold as lot 989 in *Browning Collections* (see *Reconstruction*, A1861).

3. i.e., her on-going series of papers on the Greek Christian Poets.

922. EBB TO ELEANOR PAGE BORDMAN

[London]
[early March 1842][1]

Dearest Nelly,

You will certainly think that I dont want to see you at all—and yet how untrue!! But I am *forced* to provide a fourth paper and am pressed for time, and you would find me in an agony if you came this week. Put it off to *Wednesday* week—will you, dear? and believe me as ever was truly

your most affectionate,
EBB

Publication: None traced.
Source: Transcript in editors' file.

1. Dated by the preparation of EBB's fourth paper on the Greek Christian Poets, published in *The Athenæum*, 19 March 1842, pp. 249–252.

---

923. EBB TO HUGH STUART BOYD

[London]
Thursday. [10 March 1842][1]

My very dear friend,

I did not know until today whether the paper w^d appear on Saturday or not—but as I have now received the proof sheets, there can be no doubt of it. I have been & *am* hurried & hunted almost into a corner through the pressing for the fourth paper & the difficulty about books– You will forgive a very short note tonight.

I have read of Aristotle, only His poetics, his ethics & his work upon rhetoric[2]—but I mean to take him regularly into both hands when I finish Plato's last page. Aristophanes I took with me into Devonshire—& after all, I do not know much more of *him* than three or four of his plays may stand for.[3] Next week, my very dear friend, I shall be at your commands, & sit in spirit at your footstool, to hear & answer anything you may care to ask me—but oh! what have I done that *you* sh^d talk to *me* about "venturing," or "liberty," or anything of that kind?

From your affectionate & grateful catechumen,

EBB.

Ah—you are not pleased about Gregory! Well but what could I have said? Surely he was *not* a great poet![4] You do not think so yourself!!

Address: H S Boyd Esq.ʳ / 21. Downshire Hill / Hampstead.
Publication: LEBB, I, 101–102.
Manuscript: Wellesley College.

   1. This letter is postmarked 11 March 1842, a Friday.
   2. EBB's 1780 edition of *De Poetica Liber* and 1803 edition of *Ethicorum Nicomacheorum* formed lots 351 and 352 of *Browning Collections* (see *Reconstruction*, A89 and A90). The latter is now at ABL.
   3. In 1838, George had given EBB Brunck's 1814–15 edition of Aristophanes' *Comœdiæ*; it formed lot 343 of *Browning Collections* (see *Reconstruction*, A82).
   4. Although praising Gregory's prose works, EBB had said, in the second part of her essay on the Greek poets, that "monotony of construction without unity of intention is the most wearisome of monotonies, and . . . we find it everywhere in Gregory" (*The Athenæum*, 5 March 1842, p. 211).

924. RB TO ANNA BROWNELL JAMESON

New Cross, Hatcham.
Tuesday [?mid-March 1842][1]

Dear Mrs Jameson,

I shall try hard for the great pleasure of seeing you on Thursday Morning. —I am glad indeed that my play[2] interests you in any degree.

Ever yours faithfully
R Browning.

A thing, by the way, I have longed to ask you– At which of the Colnaghis[3] can one see the Correggio[4] you spoke of one evening at Carlyle's? I am just now hungry for his pictures, and mean whenever I am sore at heart to go and get well before the great cupola at[5]––but why not versify, since that, or something like it, is my trade?–

> Could I, heart-broken, reach his Place of birth
> And stand before his Pictures—could I chuse
> But own at once "the sovereign'st thing on earth
> "Is Parma-city for an inward bruise?"[6]

Publication: N&Q, December 1974, pp. 449–450 (in part).
Manuscript: R.H. Taylor Collection.

   1. This letter could have been written at any time after December 1840, when RB moved to New Cross. The handwriting and form of signature, together with the reference to "my play," provide this conjectural dating.
   2. Assumed to be *King Victor and King Charles*, published 12 March 1842.
   3. London print-sellers and publishers. The firm was founded by Paul Colnaghi (1751–1833) but, at this time, was in the hands of his son Dominic Paul (1790–1879), with premises at 14 Pall Mall East. A separate establishment, at 23 Cockspur Street, was managed by Dominic's son, Martin Henry Colnaghi (1821–1908), hence RB's query.
   4. Antonio Allegri da Correggio (ca. 1489–1534), who developed the illusionist technique pioneered by Mantegna, subsequently used almost always in ceiling paintings.

5. Here RB wrote, and crossed out, the letter "P". Correggio executed two dome paintings in Parma. They were of Christ Ascending (1520) in the church of S. Giovanni Evangelista, and the Assumption of the Virgin (1530) in the cathedral; as RB uses the phrase "great cupola" he is probably referring to the latter. He and EBB visited Parma in May 1851, and EBB subsequently wrote to John Kenyon (8 July 1851): "Correggio ... is sublime at Parma: he is wonderful! besides having the sense to make his little Christs and angels after the very likeness of my baby."
6. Cf. *I Henry IV*, I, 3, 57–58. RB is punning "Parma-city" with Shakespeare's "parmaciti."

---

925. EBB TO MARY RUSSELL MITFORD

[London]
16.th March. 1842

My ever dearest Miss Mitford,

You will laugh at me for my important profession of business!!¹ which c^d possibly stand in the way of the expression of that going out of my heart to you, the reality of which nothing interrupts. Yet for these two, three, four, days past, most particularly for two of them, I really have seemed to myself much like a hare tearing away before the huntsman sweeping over the most fragrant of thyme without the power of pausing to crop the least head of it. Two books were wanting for my last paper—so I waited & waited till Mr Dilke sent for it [']'at my earliest convenience". Whereupon I had to scurry rather than write .. scurry, hand & eyes & pulses—the last, Papa declared was past the hundred, & well it might be—& only finished last evening at seven!² Quite finished though! What a triumph as Lady Mary Shepherd used to say, "to be just in time"—what a triumph to throw one's weight off, not from despondency but completion! What a gladness to get back to one's leisure, & YOU my own beloved friend, .. to one's leisure which may be one's idleness if one pleases,—and to YOU who must be one's happiness besides. I am so glad, the papers are done!—quite *glad*! Writing to the clock is against my nature. Yet Mr Dilke has been very gracious .. & I am not complaining .. & I never was hurried, *chased* at all, until the last paper. Well! you are glad (generously & kindly) that I *was* chased, & you hope now that I have had enough of it & will return to the household gods of my poetry. Yes—very soon! There *is* this 'Book of the poets' still—sent to me to say something about. But I mean to be very leisurely & dawdling & discursive thereupon,³ & make it my last Athenæum task for the present.

Your encouragement—no, not en*courage*ment because you do not approve of the Athenæum-writing at all—but your benignity of affectionateness towards the papers I wrote against your approbation, makes my heart feel *full*! That feeling always marks my sense of your praise—& well it may, because it is in fact *your heart* which praises me, rather than your critical faculty.

My beloved friend, I wish, oh how I wish that I c^d see your face instead of writing to you! I am anxious about you. That you sh^d suffer at last in the body the result of your late anxieties, is only the accomplishment of a painful expectation but when I make up the sorrowful sum of prospective restlessness, of all this house-changing, this bearing your own fatigues & ministering to those of others, together with your present feebleness resultive from past agitations, I quite take a long breath in apprehensive love for you! May God bless & keep you my beloved friend! We come to Him at last, when we can do nothing for each other! Sometimes I wish I were well & able to help you & K⸺ in the shifting of chairs & stools & books—as if under any circumstances, the probability were not that I sh^d be in your way .. just as very "useful people" generally are! But I do yearn from my heart's bottom to do some good beyond these words—& these prayers––and these last, they are not, God be thanked for His pitifulness, as weak as the rest!

Tell me how long the renewing of the old house will take & if there is painting in addition to the white washing. In the latter case, you will not of course hasten to go back. Oh I do wish the whole turmoil at an end! And I wish my Wishes could each turn into a broomstick or a painting-brush or some such useful instrument, after the transformations of the old German story,[4] so as to cast their love-quickness into the accomplishment of the labor!

And here am I writing about wishes & painting brushes, as if I were not to be swallowed up before twelve of the clock on this present Wednesday Night! I sh^d instead be sending you my solemn benediction, & no sort of good wishes except the last! But you see what a tittle tattle Humanity is, even on the edge of an earthquake! Make a little philosophy out of us my dearest friend, I bequeath it to you—and although all your publishing business is over for ever & ever in London,—Bath, or Liverpool may inherit our printing presses with our metropolitanism, & you may bring out somewhere else a new book of the 'Last days of London', with a vein of the melancholy Jaques[5] crossing your own in the marble!–

You know of course,—I am not writing to anyone 'ignorant of the knowledge dearest chuck'[6] .. you know of course how it is with us in the eye of the prophetic & with the cognizance of all almanacks? Of course you know, that London is to be swallowed up bodily to say nothing of a circumference of fifteen miles of country, within these present four & twenty hours .. probably, people say, "in two minutes time", at a gulp!⁷ The sensation excited among the lower classes, in station & education, yes, & the sensation fluctuating & rising up into the bewildered wits of better-informed persons, is more than you w.ᵈ be prepared for. Crowds of the poor Irish have been pressing away out of their holes & corners—householders removing their furniture to Hampstead & Highgate⁸ .. clerks throwing up their offices .. the panic active in absurd gesticulation. M.ʳˢ Orme who was mine & my sisters['] governess for two or three years—quite a woman of the world, agreeable & clever in a certain way, .. said to me seriously the other day—"Are you frightened?"–"No—are *you?*" "Why really it is as likely to happen as not—but I w.ᵈⁿᵗ leave London on any account! All I care for are here, & I prefer sharing their fate"! Quite in earnest really!—in sober wonderful earnest. I have plenty of credulity & superstition myself—but I stand bravely this earth-quake shock—which is far more than might be expected of me.

My dearest friend, I will send you the *Chaucer Modernized*, and two shaddocks besides which you or dear D.ʳ Mitford may grace us by accepting. Will you? I *have* read Marmontel's memoirs⁹ .. & a most amusing book it is—and Ma.ᵈᵐᵉ Roland¹⁰ I was just bestirring myself to see as your question reached me. Those coincidences touch me with a gentle thrill of complacent affectionateness! I do like them so!–

But I am not yet sure whether I shall get Ma.ᵈᵐᵉ Roland. Saunders does not *lighten* his books back quickly on me. There was one you spoke of on the French revolution¹¹ ... your letter has tumbled somewhere out of my reach at the moment .. no, I have not read *that*. I do not know very much about the French memoirs—and until lately, I knew scarcely anything of them—it was from want of opportunity, & I think I once sighed out loud to you about it. Lately, before these Greeks set on me, I breathed a few breaths to try to disperse the ignorance—the more especially undesirable, as these memoirs do in my belief, as formerly in my suspicion, constitute by far the most valuable part of French Literature. Do you not think so?

We must talk more of it, my own dearest friend! I wonder if ever in your secret soul, you say to yourself—"She is over-brave with me—& opiniated altogether." And yet—if you do say so .. I sh.ᵈ not like to know it--unless indeed you ended the saying with such another one as .. "but I love *her* better still than [sic] I know her faults". I could be almost glad at any sharpness I think, closing with such a sweetness!

Your own attached
EBB.

No M.ʳ Kenyon! He does not come—we do not hear a word of him. Perhaps some particular Earthquake is engaged upon him .. aside!–

Will you pray Miss Anderdon to keep the Chaucer as long as she pleases? The shaddocks have come to us unseasonably, "all unaware"![12] The better if you care for them. I only wish they were more numerous.

I remember Miss Harrisson in the Tableaux. The epitaph is beautiful indeed. But no—I never heard of it. I never was in that church to see it![13]

Address: Miss Mitford / Three Mile Cross / near Reading.
Publication: EBB-MRM, I, 359–363.
Manuscript: Wellesley College.

1. EBB emphasized "business" by printing it.
2. The fourth and final part of "Some Account of the Greek Christian Poets" appeared in *The Athenæum* of 19 March (no. 751, pp. 249–252).
3. The first part of EBB's review did not appear until the issue of 4 June.
4. Goethe's "Die Zauberlehrling" ("The Sorcerer's Apprentice," 1797), later set to music by Paul Dukas and now known to millions through Walt Disney's "Fantasia."
5. The lugubrious character in *As You Like It.*
6. *Macbeth,* III, 2, 44–45, slightly misquoted.
7. "For some weeks past a singular impression has been entertained by the lower classes of Irish residing in the metropolis and its environs, that London is to be destroyed by an earthquake, and the day fixed for this event ... is the 16th of March. A great many people have already left the metropolis" (*The Times,* 3 March 1842). This expectation owed its credence to two ancient prophecies dating back to 1203 and 1596; both specified 1842 as the year of the catastrophe, and the latter the specific date of 16 March.
8. On high ground, north of the city.
9. Jean François Marmontel (1723–99), novelist, dramatist and critic, was the author of *Bélisaire* (1766) and *Contes Moraux* (1761–86). EBB's copy of his *Mémoires* (4 vols., 1804) formed lot 904 of *Browning Collections* (see *Reconstruction,* A1545).
10. Marie Jeanne Roland de la Platière (*née* Philipon, 1754–93) knew Voltaire and Rousseau and her salon was frequented by Robespierre and other major personalities of the day. Before being guillotined in 1793, she uttered her memorable cry: "O Liberty! what crimes are committed in thy name!" Her *Mémoires* were published in 1820.
11. *The Athenæum* of 21 August 1841 (no. 721, pp. 639–640) had reviewed *History of the French Revolution till the Death of Robespierre,* by David Wemyss Jobson. This may be the book of which Miss Mitford had spoken.
12. Shelley, *The Revolt of Islam,* III, x, 7.
13. We cannot clarify the reference to this epitaph, also mentioned in SD1171. Henrietta Harrison (?–1879), later Mrs. Acton Tindal, had contributed to the 1838 and 1841 *Findens' Tableaux.*

926. EBB TO MARY RUSSELL MITFORD

[London]
March 17. 1842

Ever dearest friend, here is the book,[1] & here the shaddocks!–

One of the subjects on which I venture to be *two* with you, is just this of Bulwer!– You know it is. He is an unequal artist .. but nearly always, it appears to me, true to the soul of poetic Art, in evolving from each of his books *An* IDEA. In regard to Zanoni, I think with you that there is much in it, one w^د yearn to see cast out of it, in reverence to the unity of the whole.[2] The roaring of the French Revolution grinds horribly through the mystic ideality of the groundwork—we are rent in twain, distracted, as the work is!– Also the supernatural parts are brought certainly as you observe too near the eye . . the Haunter of the threshold being quite a failure to my own instincts![3] At the same time I like that castle scenery—I like the *preparation* . . the hushing of the heart, preparatory to the awakening of the soul. That is all, as it seems to *me*, fine & phil[o]sophical! The struggle too in Zanoni's great nature between the aspiration toward knowledge & the yearning toward love, & the final evolvement of the first in its glory from the last in its devotion—which is the IDEA of the book—all seems to me a noble verity! "Knowledge puffeth up—but Love buildeth up"[4] says God's book! It is a noble verity.

My chief objection to the work, is to the character of Viola. I object to her *sinking* by the influence of Love, rather than *rising!* She sh^d have risen into intellectual sympathy by the mere force of love—she, Viola! She was too high at first or too low afterwards. Am I right, or wrong?

After all, there are beautiful things in the book—beautiful thoughts in eloquent expression. He is a great writer I think in my soul.

Beautiful—exquisite indeed, is the poem—it *is* a poem—of the old musician & his instrument & his daughter![5] So high fantastical[6] yet so true to that lowest simplicity of nature which a child may reach & *feel* true! The man capable of such a conception cannot be, my beloved friend, quite a common man. —You do not think so!

Did you ever read Ernest Maltravers & the Alice which perfects the work.[7] *That* is to my mind, Mr Bulwer's chief work: this Zanoni standing far below ⟨★★★⟩

Publication: EBB-MRM, I, 363–364.
Manuscript: Wellesley College.

1. *Chaucer, Modernized*, for Lucy Anderdon, as promised in the previous letter.
2. Bulwer-Lytton's *Zanoni* (3 vols., 1842) was reviewed in *The Athenæum* of 26 February 1842 (no. 748, pp. 181–183). The writer found it "a strange patchwork of things the most discordant" and feared that readers would find it confused, its purpose "ill-defined." It is interesting to note that the author himself, in a preface to the 1853 edition, held that it "ranks, perhaps, amongst the highest of my prose fictions."
3. In bk. IV.
4. Cf. I Corinthians, 8:1.
5. In bk. I.
6. *Twelfth Night*, I, 1, 15.
7. These two works appeared in 1837 and 1838 respectively. EBB praises the former in letter 596, the latter in letter 621.

927. EBB TO RICHARD HENGIST HORNE

50 Wimpole Street
21. March– 1842.

My dear M! Horne,

I send you my conclusion—with an emphatic self-congratulation in which you will duly sympathize. If I write any more for the Athenæum at present, it will be upon English poetry in the shape of a criticism .. 'save the mark!'[1] *a review* .. on the Book of the Poets.[2] M! Dilke is courteous enough to trust the subject in my hands—rash enough! *for* (among other reasons) I shall certainly be contradictory to the great poet-crasher of that journal, M! Darley, who not satisfied with holding his hopeful doctrine about the absolute extinction of English dramatic literature, takes an opportunity in the last number but one (see the article upon art, having the Darley character on the face of it) to promulgate the same heresy in relation to English poetry generally.[3] It is an old country, forsooth, this England! with a worn-out heart—& the voice of the singing birds can be heard no more, in such a land![4] Qu[er]? *Is it older than the Earth*?

Do not tell of me or of my informant: but I have heard, as well as seen with my eyes in his writings, that this M! Darley's morbidity lieth in his temper![5] He is a shrew of a poet——be witness our Chaucer!–[6] If he sh! be a particular friend of yours besides .. why forgive me for that Chaucer's sake!

By the way, I never heard whether Chaucer accomplished my prophecy, or that of the more sanguine, by selling at all!! But no—I need'nt put such a question—still less, another, .. whether there will ever be a second volume.[7]

But you may tell me one thing, the next time––mind, *the next time* you write– Has the suggestion never occurred to you of publishing a volume of miscellanies—inclusive of your *Fair*, the *odes*, & poems in my remembrance? A few dramatic scenes, w! tell nobly among them,—& the whole w! not be "let die".[8] I do wish you w! think of it—"carve out an hour"[9] or two out of your ebony nights, & think of it!– Do, M! Horne!

Was there some nonsense in the last paper I sent you, about an "*altar* of rose trees". Of course it was a misprint, & sh! be read *attar*.[10]

Ever truly yours
Elizabeth B Barrett.

Publication: None traced.
Manuscript: Wellesley College.

1. *1 Henry IV*, 3, 56.
2. EBB's review of Scott, Webster and Geary's *The Book of the Poets* appeared in five issues of *The Athenæum*: 4 June 1842 (no. 762, pp. 497–499); 11 June (no. 763,

pp. 520–523); 25 June (no. 765, pp. 558–560); 6 August (no. 771, pp. 706–708) and 13 August (no. 772, pp. 728–729).

3. *The Athenæum* of 12 March (no. 750, pp. 219–220) carried a review of the first volume of *A Hand-Book of the History of Painting* by Franz Kugler, ed. Charles Locke Eastlake. In it, the putative writer, Darley, observed that "Literary Germany has not sown her wild oats yet: England has, long since, and is now perhaps come to her chaff.... The days of our Shakspeare and Milton are past; but it is one comfort, we *had* them!"

4. Cf. The Song of Solomon, 2:12.

5. EBB may be recalling a series of letters, addressed to various dramatists and censuring their preference for a "poetic" rather than "rhetorical" style. Written by Darley under the pseudonym John Lacy, they had been published in *The London Magazine* in 1822–23.

6. EBB had spoken in letter 796 of Darley's "tomahawking" of those connected with *Chaucer, Modernized*. She returns to the subject in letter 946, where she castigates Darley as "the Herod of the Chaucer massacre." For the full text of his review in *The Athenæum* of 6 February 1841, see pp. 389–391.

7. EBB's prophecy, in letter 779, was that "the book is sure to be left, for the most part, in the publisher's hands, & that no second volume will be called for."

8. Cf. Zechariah, 11:9.

9. We have not located the source of this quotation.

10. The misprint ("the altar of a thousand rose trees") occurs in her discussion of the works of Synesius, in *The Athenæum* of 12 March (p. 229, col. 1).

---

928. EBB TO MARY RUSSELL MITFORD

[London]
March 21. 1842

Thank you my beloved friend thank you for your abundant goodnesses! I am a mystic fleece—my heart is!—saturated with this dew from high places,—yet falling so softly as love!– When I turn to speak my sense of it, I cannot speak—my only answer must be love again. "Thank you" .. what can *that* say?

But do you know, my dearest dearest friend, that *if you were not so* you w^d undo me by some of your praises. Your critical opinion—your's as Miss Mitford, without relation to friendships & friends—would of course to me Elizabeth Barrett be of great importance, & if favorable of high price! But supposing the impossible supposition that you Miss Mitford did say of me Elizabeth Barrett what you as too tender friend have said of her in this letter by my hand ... why you w^d undo me in the very act of building me up! I sh^d be built up like a pack of cards, & fall by the very breath of my buildor!– For nothing w^d be left to the faculty of my logic, than the miserable inference .. that by some mortal casualty, instability, or imperfection, common to the strongest of the earth-kings & earth-queens, .. Miss Mitford had so far beyond sight over-rated, hyper-exalted, praised above measure said Elizabeth Barrett, that .. (oh what a race of inferences is born from this Œdipus!)[1] .. that .. nobody could be sure whether she Miss Mitford had any cause for thinking any manner of good of said Elizabeth Barrett in any segment of degree! Do you see how you w[d] have undone me,—had you not been my friend? Had *you not!*– Ah! in a way nearer the heart than *that*!

But I am not undone. I am built up—"Love buildeth up"[2]—& I only look to your love—not my prophetess this time, but my beloved friend! caring more for it, wearing it nearer to my inward nature in dearness, than if it had been all your praise, won in open field, .. & *mine* because deserved!

For the rest, I always separate as far as it is possible whatever parts of your opinions can be *true out of love*—I mean apart from it,—& lay them by to muse over or take courage from or counsel from, whenever I want either for my writings. I have been musing these two days, off & on, upon what exactly you meant in relation to "the terms of endearment & appropriation," as applied to the Supreme Being. I my⟨self⟩ have observed & disliked such expressions in a few hymns of Watts[3] & others (motes in my brother's eye!!)[4] but I am blind to them in myself .. with a great beam perhaps lying straight across my eyeballs. Do tell me, where the fault is in myself—.

Perhaps you allude to certain expressions in the Greek translations, such as "O my Jesus," or "my Christ." All such cases are,—I believe without an exception,—literal translations—& you will perhaps reconsider that "my Jesus" is not more than "my Saviour", the word *Jesus* signifying *Saviour*.[5]

Any "familiar expression of endearment" or anything tantamount to such an expression I c[d] not attempt to defend either in others or myself—& I do not think that the Greek christian poets expose themselves, with all their fervency, to a reproach of that particular kind. At the same time you will allow me to suggest in an under-voice .. that there is an opposite fault common to higher poets & better writers than perhaps any of my modern Greeks are, & which consists in spiritualizing away to a dim far Influence, the Divine Glory as beheld in the Saviour's human face. Too much of the Humanity, full & tender & simple as a man-woman-child humanity,—too much of the assured Humanity of Christ Jesus, is put out of sight & out of hearing, when we muse & speak & pray. The result is .. a cold adoration, instead of a worshipping love. The result is that we come to write & to think of the Man-Christ, coldly as Epicurus might of his Possible-gods—at best, solemnly as Plato might, of his God above the æons[6]—& not at all heartfully & with a love upturned, as to Him who is the Love-God,—God in Humanity.

It is this consideration which does seem to me most intensely true, which has acted upon minds of more fervency than delicacy, to the eliciting of the expressions in question. I defend not one of them! & am only anxious to know in which of them I myself have sinned. Tell me—do tell me, my beloved friend—everything which seems to you wrong—everything whether in the poetry or out of it, which you do not like to see in me, yet see!

You like my 'House of Clouds'.[7] Now I will tell you what M.ʳ Boyd said of it to my sister Arabel! He is very much pleased with my Athenæum papers, concluding his praise of them with a climax of this sort—"I am the more pleased, & surprised, because—"--(now listen stedfastly to the 'because'——) "because I had inferred from the "*House of Clouds*" that her illness had weakened her intellect"! There is a subject of congratulation!! Mark it well!–

But *you* liked my House of Clouds—& M.ʳ Kenyon did not take it as a token of idiocy—& I myself like it as well as any trifle of the kind which I have printed. Apart from your kindness, "Cowper's grave'['],[8] has pleased more persons to my knowledge than all the rest put together. Strangers who have written to me, always, almost, have spoken of it—& M.ʳ Powell, a friend of all the poets as I call him, a particular friend of M.ʳ Wordsworth & of M.ʳ Horne, wrote once to me to decide a dispute about a passage in it, held between himself & Leigh Hunt—telling me at the same time that I never wrote up to that poem as a composition. Well—but, I do hope—it is my only excuse for talking so much upon so little .. I do hope to write better hereafter—were it only to give you generous pleasure, my beloved friend! As to justifying your words, I can never do that, otherwise than by my love!–

I am very anxious to hear how you decide about the house-changing, & what will be the first step. No—dont write to me at a period of so much bustle & uneasiness! *No—dont write to me*! It is written, yet I doubt myself! Am I an hypocrite? or so ambitious as to aspire to vanquish you in generosity? And yet, I *am* quite sure that I w.ᵈ not willingly lay a burden upon your burdens—not even of a letter's weight.

I shall take to my dreams the hope that dear D.ʳ Mitford may be better after all. I think he *is* better! And that *you* are so .. what a blessedness *that* is! But the newspapers, the newspapers—& the other reading—& the universal talking .. I can understand it all, without the experience of any of it, & I tremble for the result upon you—for all your strong volitions & endurances of love. I have always been free from such trials—never was forced to read, or to talk much, when & where I did not please—never was called upon for *unnatural attention*. Still I sh.ᵈ always have instinct enough to feel for *you*—even if I had not fancy.

We have all a great anxiety at this moment, our dear Sette ⟨...⟩ being ill with the meazles, and Occy, who never had it, being in full prospect of the same evil. Poor Sette is "going on well" they say, & in that case we need not be quite unhappy—still—but may God preserve him dear fellow & our affections in him.

M[r] Kenyon is here. I must end, & see him—for the post will be fast upon his heels. Dear little poney! how is it now?—[9]

Your own attached
EBB.

Publication: EBB-MRM, I, 364–367.
Manuscript: Folger Shakespeare Library and Wellesley College.

1. The oracle of Delphi had told Œdipus, who was ignorant of his parentage, that he would kill his father and marry his mother; despite his attempts to avoid this fate, the oracular predictions were fulfilled. On finally learning the truth of his birth, and that he had indeed slain his father and committed incest with his mother, he blinded himself. EBB seems to be suggesting that she recoils similarly from Miss Mitford's forecast of coming fame.
2. Cf. I Corinthians, 8:1.
3. Isaac Watts (1674–1748) wrote on philosophical and religious topics, but his continuing fame rests on his prodigious output of hymns. These emphasized a personal relationship with, and affection for, God and Christ in the manner that Miss Mitford is objecting to in EBB's translations.
4. Cf. Matthew, 7:3.
5. These possessives occur in EBB's third paper on the Greek Christian poets (*The Athenæum*, 12 March, pp. 229–231).
6. Epicurus (ca. 340–ca. 270 B.C.) was criticized by contemporaries for representing the gods as being given up to pleasure and unconcerned with the affairs of men. Plato (ca. 427–ca. 348 B.C.) believed that man owed his creation to a divine emanation, and that his soul was immortal, but he did not postulate a loving and concerned Deity.
7. In *The Athenæum* of 21 August 1841 (no. 721, p. 643).
8. One of the poems included in *The Seraphim* (1838).
9. In a letter to Miss Anderdon, 4 March 1842, Miss Mitford had said "my poor pony has been, and still is, very ill of influenza. I believe that I shall lose him" (Chorley, I, 196).

929. EBB TO MARY RUSSELL MITFORD

[London]
March 24 1842.

I write to you my beloved friend in the full gladness of receiving your letter—beyond hope—this morning. Is my beloved friend such a sceptic as one question seems to say? "Do you really care for my gossipping letters"! Care for your letters! what,—*I*? What am I then? (there's the elementary question in philosophy to meet yours!) what am I, that I sh[d] not care for your letters!

If I do not empty my heart out with a great splash on the paper, everytime I have a letter from you, & *speak* my gladness & thankfulness, it is lest I sh^d weary you of thanksgivings! For no other reason, be sure! Your letters have been my palm trees in the desert, my nosegays from the garden, my "sweet south"[1] & singing nightingales, since the first day they came to me. Even Crow's face shines with reflection from my face when she gives them to me—& if Flush is the bearer, as he very often is, it seems to me that he wags his tail & shakes his ears ten times for once under another burden. Your letters—do you know what they are worth, that you should ask me such a question! Why if they were not yours—but that is an impossible hypothesis—why if I did not love you—but that is another—take the letters up in a pair of tongs as an abstraction & hold them in the air, .. what spirit in the world w^d not leap high to catch them? Do you not *know* their price & delightfulness .. as bare letters? Surely you must guess a little at their value! You who care for Hayley's, must devine the higher light. Still—if they were dross, I sh^d care to have them because I love you—and if you were naught to me, I sh^d care to have them because they are so far from dross.

Quæry. Did nobody ever, in all the world except me, my beloved friend, admire your letters loud out to you? I am curious. They on the other hand, are curiously excellent, true to the keynote of your published works but often gifted with a tone both higher & sweeter. The compass of mind is surely greater in the letters—& the expression can scarcely be called less uniformly happy in them. They often make me wonder at the remembrance of what you once told me about the labour you use "in composition". Why this—in this letter of yours .. ,—is "composition" in the sight of our eyes & to the attesting of our intelligences—this, which ran from under your fingers while you wrote it! We want no better composition from you after all—& wherefore sh^d you give greater elaboration? Over this very composition & the rest of its order, editors & booksellers will be quarrelling a hundred years hence,—& readers rejoicing. Miss Mitford's letters will go down to Prince Posterity[2] with her Village & Belford Regis & other of her writings. In the meantime let me beseech of her to believe that a commoner in Wimpole Street cares as much for them now with this living earnest heart, as His Royal Highness of the future ever can!–

We have—that is, Papa has—Miss Seward's Letters[3] (to turn to a very different & lower subject) & you shall have them .. if you will promise to tell me what it is in them that I liked when I ought to have known better. I have read them three, four .. peradventure five times. There is an attraction somewhere, however out of sight may be the loadstone.

Richardson's correspondence has charmed me[4]—"charming" being the right word, since I verily & indeed believed myself wrapt up close in the domestic brocades of the Harlowe family, all the time I spent in reading it. His own letters are letters out of his romances to the very crossing of the t[']s—and they seem capable of eliciting a Miss Howe[5] out of any sprightly correspondent he may be pleased to magnetize with the waving of his pen. Lady Bradleigh [*sic*] is delightful--I dont wonder that he tired himself with pacing up & down Hyde Park in his desire to catch a glimpse of her![6] That he didn't fall in love with her in all gravity, I wonder at more. I read that volume with quite a romance-palpitation. Thank you, thank you for telling me of the book, which I never even *heard* of before .. or at least never with sufficient interest, to remember its entity. It is altogether to *you* that I owe this new pleasure!–

What I grumble at—if I had'nt something to grumble at, this world of ours w^d'nt be *grumbledom*—is that Mrs Barbauld sh^d have thought it necessary to cut down the mss to fit her particular box. Why the materials might have filled twelve volumes instead of six! Oh those sensible editors! what harm they do in the world! If they sh^d treat your letters so!–

And that reminds me of your requirement of Hayley's editor—that he sh^d cut away all the epithets & blow away the Della Crusca!![7] My dearest friend! I start back before such a proposition! I beseech you to whisper it very softly into the ground & plant it up with clay the next time you are tempted to pronounce such a word– In my mind, that race of editors is far too much given to take liberties already! They do not want your encouragement to address their "improvements" to any text open to their attack—while the whole world of books is their oyster, which with their swords they open!–[8] Be the texts of all authors, from Shakespeare to Hayley, sacred from the touch of all editors!– "Aroint ye"—ye, who are *no* witches!–[9]

I have written to Mr Townsend—(owing him an acknowledgement for his pretty azure poem, & having had previously a dumb devil from the Athenæum—) & ventured to take some notice of the expectation he expressed to you. My dearest Miss Mitford, you were quite right as kind, in saying to him what you did. I have no power to touch the Athenæum with my finger, in the behalf of the thing nearest my heart. Neither *do I covet the power*,—— which may be said aside. Therefore indeed he must go to Mr Darley—&—between you & me—if he depends for tender mercies upon Mr Darley, I am very sorry for him.[10] Mr Darley has added to his doctrine lately, his hopeful doctrine of the extinction of Dramatic Genius now & for ever in England,[11] a doctrinal codicil on the exhaustion of the poetical faculty generally. Did you observe what is written in a late article upon Art—a leading article in the Athenæum journal, &

bearing obvious marks of what Hayley w.^{d} call the '*Darleyan* hand'? Did you observe what is set down there on the being-worn-out-edness of this England! That the poets we have had, we have had—& are now superannuated to any poetical purpose whatever!!–[12] Is'nt it too bad that a Literary Journal sh.^{d} freeze up our hearts' blood with such theories? I am very angry indeed.

I like this waste of the public money upon bishops of New Zealand!! & of Jerusalem!![13] as little as you do, & have ventured to be open with Mr Townsend & tell him as much. The utter absurdity (to say nothing at all of money) of forcing out the forms & ceremonies of this Parliament church, out among the savages, I c.^{d} even cry over in utter vexation. Think of the lawn sleeves & the mitre, beautifying a "spiritual lord" under circumstances of such utter incongruity. A bishop of New Zealand!– No—let them send missionaries, simple men with simple words—& I w.^{d} not grudge them the monies from Glasgow or elsewhere. Spiritual wants are crying wants—more touching perhaps to such as know the price of spiritual comfort than any cry of the bare body; & particularly, when we recollect that to such as do *not* know *that*, the physical cry is moving. But let those who are sent, be *missionaries*. The bishops are impotent, have been *found* to be impotent, in all situations of the kind—& as I ventured to tell Mr Townsend, the martyr soul of poor Williams was the true Bishop-Soul for the south seas.[14]

There is great sweetness in his little poem to be sure—a few lines together which one smiles over to oneself as for pleasure. Still—what a subject! I do not mean it theologically—but what a subject for a poet!– He says the sermon ran into rhythm—which was a reason for the preacher of the sermon preaching it rhythmically, but none at all for Mr Townsend's singing the subject-matter of the preaching over again. I must join you in regretting it!–

Ah—but you will not join with *me*. You will make me out to be wrong—& so, no wonder that I sh.^{d} tremble over an ideality of wrongness, such as may be mine! Still—you will let me struggle for an admission (will you not?) that a work without unity is a defective work—& that a work which leaves no sovereign impression, cannot have unity. The reader's impression is the transcript—may it not be called so?—of the author's conception—or rather of the poet's—since the principle refers essentially to works of the imagination. Should there not be a sovereign impression? Should the impression not be a transcript? It appears to me that when the Greeks talked about unity .. they meant something of this sort—& something as far as possible from the French interpretation.[15] And it appears to me—to *me* who dare to babble thus about criticism with your face turned toward me & y.^{r} opinion against me—–that all the chief works of art from Shakespeare's to your M!̣ Haydon's must evolve a *thought* for either reader or spectator. If we looked at nature as the angels do, we might say so of nature too (as indeed we may of particular portions of nature)—but the difference between art & nature is, that we see the whole of art, as the chief angels may, nature—& that each great work of art is a universe suited to the finite embrace of our souls & whose full meaning is evolved in their embrace. Am I mystical past bearing? Have patience with me my beloved friend! And have patience too while I remark in relation to your remark, i.e. that the necessity for an *idea* is as bad as a necessity for a moral,—that I object far more to the base mean stupid kind of morality enforced by the moral-mongers than I can do to their principle. Tell me—has not *Clarissa* a moral? though she perished by tenfold agonies, the moral w^d stand firm! Has not all life, all Nature a moral .. if we c^d discern it always! Has not Shakespeare a truer moral than Miss Edgeworth?[16] I think so.

And oh! have patience with me once more when I dare to whisper that exactly in the *unity of conception* which appears to me the great accomplishment of the artist, Walter Scott appears defective. Forgive me for thinking—& precisely for that reason—lower of him than you do! You know,—you have heard me (with a shudder,—with many a shudder!) speak a whole octave below your enthusiasm on the subject of Scott's genius. Well—behold the reason of it, at last! He is a great writer—but not a poet—a maker—in any high sense! Not at least in my humblest of doxies!-

Can you pardon me? Yes! But you did'nt—nevertheless—answer a question I asked you at the end of one of my last letters—the question .. whether you did'nt sometimes think me opiniative or *ted* .. whether you didn't think I was "too bold" for a cloth of frieze![17] Ah! I feel the needle pricking me through the tender silence!- And so, no more of unities—which have indeed done harm enough in the world without my taking them up in my bravery.

Half way in this letter—dear M!̣ Kenyon came suddenly again!— beyond hope & expectation as I had seen him four & twenty hours before: & his coming prevented the going of all this writing to you. He has dined with Lady Morgan, & seems to be almost under a vow, never to dine with her again. Dont tell anybody. It was whispered to me—& I whisper it back to you—a confidence in both relations:--but he was disgusted, heart-startled at the hardness & worldliness of the talk at dinner. Clever, he said it was—very clever—but of the cleverness which comes by speaking one's soul out "without regard to any social or moral restraint"— the subject, during dinner, the poor people who were to come afterwards— & who, coming, were all welcomed with extended hands, as very dear friends, whom it had been a pleasure to cut up (*not* "into little stars")[18] in their absence. Lady Morgan said to him—"Oh—you have shut your house to us! you wont let us in at all now"—to which he answered that he used to receive ladies at his house but had grown shy & given it up. Before the evening ended the resolution was shut & locked.

It is late—I must shut & lock too. Thank you for letting me see Miss Harrison's graceful & feeling lines.[19] They are just *that*, I think—without showing much power or originality. It is a touching subject taken into the heart! How are you? how is Dr Mitford? And the dear little poney? My Flushie has just had an escape from the jaws of Mr Chichester's great dog[20]—he shrieking & screaming & clinging to Arabel's arms! My poor Flushie!

God bless you! your kindness is too too great! God bless you–
Ever your EBB

Not a word of the *Corn Law* letter.[21] It is very able. What is your mind about the new tax? That Sir Robert Peel! He is "subtlest of the beasts of the field".[22]

Address: Miss Mitford.
Publication: EBB-MRM, I, 367–373.
Manuscript: Wellesley College.

1. See letter 668, note 3.
2. Swift's *A Tale of a Tub* (1704) was dedicated "to His Royal Highness Prince Posterity."
3. *Letters of Anna Seward Written Between the Years 1784 and 1807* [ed. Archibald Constable], 1811.
4. Edited by Anna Letitia Barbauld (*née* Aikin, 1743–1825), the correspondence was published in six volumes in 1804.
5. The Harlowe family's "domestic brocades" are recounted in *Clarissa: or, The History of a Young Lady* (1748); about a third of the work is written in the form of letters. Anna Howe was Clarissa's particular friend.
6. Lady Dorothy Bradshaigh (*née* Bellingham), the wife of Sir Roger Bradshaigh, corresponded with Richardson from 1750 until his death in 1761 and was the model for Charlotte Grandison in *Sir Charles Grandison* (1753). In an early letter, Richardson tells her how "I walked up and down ... the path between the trees and the Mall, my eyes ... looking for a certain gill-o'-th'-wisp ... Yet, she cannot be come, thought I ... And so continued walking, expecting, and sometimes fretting, till the Mall was vacant of ladies" (*Correspondence*, 1804, IV, 372).
7. John Johnson (d. 1833), who edited the correspondence of his cousin William Cowper (1817), also edited Hayley's *Memoirs* (1823). Discussing Hayley's style, he spoke of "that exuberance of feeling, which ... impelled him to invest with endearing epithets, every person and every thing, of which he had occasion to speak—an impulse ... prejudicial to the development of his conceptions as an author" (II, 221). The Accademia della Crusca was founded in Florence in 1582 with the object of sifting impurities from the language ("crusca" means bran); EBB obviously feels that an editor should not blow away the chaff represented by such "endearing epithets."
8. Cf. *The Merry Wives of Windsor*, II, 2, 3–4.
9. "Avaunt, begone." Cf. *King Lear*, III, 4, 124.
10. See letters 906 and 918 for EBB's earlier references to Townsend's poem, "New Zealand." EBB's comments make it apparent that he had hoped for her intercession

with the editor of *The Athenæum* to get it reviewed. Darley, of course, was the magazine's critic who had earned EBB's censure for his reviews of *Ion* and *Chaucer, Modernized*. He did not notice Townsend's poem.

11. The review of *Ion* (*The Athenæum*, 28 May 1836, no. 448, pp. 371–373) included Darley's dismissive comment: "the Drama is *not* dead, for then were there some hope of its resurrection: it is annihilated!"

12. For an extract from Darley's article, see letter 927, note 3.

13. An episcopal council in 1841 had recommended the foundation of a series of colonial sees, of which New Zealand was one of the first. For the consecration of its first bishop, see letter 906, note 7. Palestine, "which in the events of the last 12 months has been brought before Christendom" (*The Times*, 11 October 1841), was another new see. Michael Solomon Alexander (1799–1845), born and raised in the Jewish faith, was baptized in 1825 and ordained in 1827. From 1832 to 1841, he held the Chair of Hebrew and Rabbinical Literature at King's College, London. He was consecrated as the first Bishop of Jerusalem on 7 November 1841, arriving there to take up his duties on 21 January 1842.

14. John Williams (1796–1839), "the most successful missionary of modern times" (*DNB*), spent the years 1817 to 1833 visiting various islands in the Pacific. In 1834 he returned to England, travelling to different parts of the country to address meetings sponsored by the London Missionary Society, one of which EBB attended (see letter 946). Returning to the New Hebrides in 1839, he was killed and eaten by the natives on 20 November 1839.

15. See letter 816, note 2.

16. EBB contrasts Shakespeare's illustrations of the universal human condition with Miss Edgeworth's attention to specific issues (e.g., the relationship of children and servants, mentioned in letter 856).

17. See letter 594, note 3.

18. Cf. *Romeo and Juliet*, III, 2, 22.

19. See SD1171.

20. J.H.R. Chichester, a lawyer, was the Moulton-Barretts' neighbour at 49 Wimpole St.

21. The Corn Laws kept prices unduly high, especially in times of bad harvests (see letter 540, note 3). A letter in *The Times*, 12 March 1842, signed "C.C." and addressed to Sir Robert Peel, the Prime Minister, proposed a sliding scale of duties to alleviate the injustices of the current legislation, import duty to be high when domestic prices were low, but to decrease progressively as the domestic price rose.

22. Cf. Genesis, 3:1.

---

930. MARY RUSSELL MITFORD TO EBB

Three Mile Cross,
March [?27], 1842.[1]

Thanks upon thanks, my beloved friend, for the kindness which humours even my fancies. I am delighted to have the reading of Anna Seward's letters. Perhaps we both of us like those works which show us men and women as they are—faults, frailties, and all. I confess that I do love all that identifies and individualizes character—the warts upon Cromwell's face, which, like a great man as he was, he would not allow the artist to omit when painting his portrait.[2] Therefore I like Hayley, and therefore was I a goose of the first magnitude, when, for a passing moment, just by way of gaining for the poor bard a portion of *your* good graces (for I did not want to gain for him the applause of the public—he had it, and lost it), I wished his editor to have un-Hayley'd him by wiping away some of the affectations—the warts—no—the rouge, upon his face.

My love and my ambition for you often seems to be more like that of a mother for a son, or a father for a daughter (the two fondest of natural emotions), than the common bonds of even a close friendship between two women of different ages and similar pursuits. I sit and think of you, and of the poems that you will write, and of that strange, brief rainbow crown called Fame, until the vision is before me as vividly as ever a mother's heart hailed the eloquence of a patriot son. Do you understand this? and do you pardon it? You must, my precious, for there is no chance that I should unbuild *that* house of clouds;[3] and the position that I long to see you fill is higher, firmer, prouder than ever has been filled by woman. It is a strange feeling, but one of indescribable pleasure. My pride and my hopes seem altogether merged in you. Well, I will not talk more of this; but at my time of life, and with so few to love, and with a tendency to body forth images of gladness and of glory, you cannot think what joy it is to anticipate the time. How kind you are to pardon my gossiping, and to like it.

God bless you, my sweetest, for the dear love which finds something to like in these jottings! It is the instinct of the bee, that sucks honey from the hedge-flower.

I made my father happy in reading what you say of Sir Robert [Peel]: his eyes brightened like diamonds at the sound. For my part, I incline to think with one of Miss Edgeworth's heroines, that "he cannot be so very artful as is said, because everybody does say so." The perfection of cunning is to conceal its own quality. Mortally dull are those debates. I rather have a fancy for Mr. Roebuck,[4] who is as cantankerous and humorous (in the old Shakspearian sense)[5] as Cassius himself. I would know him at any time by half a line—so perfectly in keeping are his speeches—which is more than I can say for any of the rest.

Certainly, in point of wearisome insipidity Sir Robert and Lord John [Russell] are well matched one against the other. Did it ever occur to you to hear the debates read aloud for a whole session? The impression upon me is the exceeding want of power, the flat mediocrity, the total absence of anything like eloquence. I remember a few years ago reading speeches by O'Connell in one of the Irish papers, which, with the faults of Irish oratory, had yet life and power. Now, so far as we have hitherto gone, I really have not met with a single speech that might not have been delivered by any tolerably-taught schoolboy. After all, these men are no such marvels.

Did you ever read Holcroft's Memoirs?[6] If not, I think you would like them. I did *exceedingly*. He was a poor boy, who carried Staffordshire ware about the country; then he exercised the horses at Newmarket. Do read it; I know nothing more graphic or more true. Do you know his comedy, "The Road to Ruin?" The serious scenes of that play, between the father and son, are amongst the most touching in the language.

Dear Mr. Kenyon! How true in him the feeling always is! How few wits are like him—so bright, so playful, and yet so exquisitely kind! Heaven bless you, my beloved!

Ever yours,
M. R. Mitford.

Text: L'Estrange (2), III, 140–142 (as 24 March 1842).

1. L'Estrange's dating of 24 March is obviously a misreading of Miss Mitford's handwriting, for this is clearly a reply to letter 929. As EBB's enquiry in 931 about receipt of Miss Seward's *Letters* shows that she had not received this letter when she finished hers on the 28th, the most probable date for it is 27 March.

2. While sitting for Sir Peter Lely (1618–80), Cromwell is reported to have instructed him to "remark all these roughnesses, pimples, warts, and everything as you see me, otherwise I never will pay a farthing for it" (*Anecdotes of Painting*, by Horace Walpole, ed. Dallaway and Wornum, 1849, p. 444). Hence the expression "warts and all," to denote a truthful depiction including blemishes and defects.

3. A play on the title of EBB's poem.

4. John Arthur Roebuck (1801–79), a friend of John Stuart Mill and an adherent of Jeremy Bentham, had stood for election to Parliament to further his political opinions. He first sat in the reformed House in 1833 as an independent and earned the nickname "Tear 'em" from the vehemence with which he attacked those who differed from him (*DNB*).

5. i.e., having a sanguine, choleric, phlegmatic or melancholic humour, depending on the preponderance in the body of blood, choler, phlegm or bile.

6. *Memoirs of the Late Thomas Holcroft, Written by Himself* (1816), edited by William Hazlitt. Holcroft (1745–1809) was a frequent contributor to various magazines, a translator of numerous French authors, and the writer of many plays, including *The Road to Ruin* (1792).

931. EBB TO MARY RUSSELL MITFORD

[London]
March 28 & 9.th [*sic*, for 27 & 8.th] 1842–[1]

It is Sunday & there is no way of sending a letter to you my beloved friend—but it is a day to speak what is in my heart,[2] & the heart moves your way without thought of the day. And this is what is in my heart!

Are we so far apart my dearest friend? Do we think so differently on a point scarcely unimportant? Ought I to deny my convictions for the love of you? Surely not! you will say so as I say so! That I love & admire & revere you . . *that* you KNOW! But I sh.^{d} be more unworthy of the least of your love than I feel myself to be now, if I c^d sacrifice or *appear* to sacrifice in the cowardice of silence any one opinion or principle which I hold honestly.

In the first place, we do quite differ in regard to our mutual estimation of the mass of persons called "religious", that is,—making high religious professions,—whether in the church or out of it. All these persons—of whom I know more privately & domestically than my beloved friend appears to know—all this mass of persons, except such as are hypocrites, hold strongly by my affection & respect. I believe them to be right & safe—justified before God. I believe that it is right to think earnestly & not to be ashamed of speaking earnestly, our belief in the gospel of Christ & our hope by His death! I believe that Christ's *will* is, that we sh^d speak aloud our love for Him—that it is the natural result of our natural affections that we sh^d speak them all—why not our love which goes upwards? But you will agree with me in your admirable candour my beloved friend, that by the great mass of the world this upward love alone is unspoken! Is it unfelt? Is it a subject of shame? Those inferences remain.

I do believe then that the persons in question, are both in doctrine & in word *right*—& if I do not say 'I am *proud* to be numbered among them' it is because I w^d rather be humble in the same place.

The individual case you mention is exactly twice as revolting (I eagerly agree with you) as connected with a person of the class in question—but I appeal to your justice not to condemn a class for the corruption of an individual! it is as you observe a very large class (I thank God it is) in the church of England & out of it .. almost all the dissenters— *all*, as far as profession goes—with the exception of the ice-bound unitarians; & if in all classes—whether political, philosophical, artistical or philanthropical,—there are hypocrites, why sh^d you expect the religious class to be free from the taint! Even the apostles had their Judas—did you ever mistrust John for Judas?[3] Surely not! Nor shall this infamous man who did you so much harm[4] .. nor SHOULD[5] he .... forgive me my dearest friend .. wrench your opinions & affections into a universal wrong. I could tell you instance upon instance of the actions of noble Christian hearts & hands which might well neutralize the poison of that man's wickedness. There is Mr Groves of Exeter,[6] in the receipt of five thousand a year from his profession, who gave up everything, nay, gave *away* everything, & went into the east without purse or scrip,[7] a missionary on foot, with a noble heroism. The taunt of "Methodism"[8] has drawn tears from many meek eyes I know .. while the heart sate firmly on its throne of a strong purpose. The lives of many have been cast away .. the blood of their life pouring from their dying lips,—through a life-devotion to preaching Christ's truth! And all this to be remembered in

Heaven! Should we forget it here? If God loves it, should we not love it? Let us think twice before we say we do not.

Yes! they are narrow in taste for the most part. They hold strange opinions, strange contractive opinions on the subject of literature & the arts—which I call a contracted spirituality as well as a contracted taste. Because the whole atmosphere of God's creation (man's works being a part of it, even as the bee's geometry is) is a medium of beholding God—& we are not called upon to look away from the creation up to God, but to look *through* the creation up to Him. It thus appears to me that their notions on the subject of literature & the arts are defective *spiritually*—I do think so!

People of very different opinions generally, fall into a similar mistake! M.[r] Dilke for instance, wrote to beg me to avoid as far as possible in my papers the mention of the name of Christ (& I writing upon the Christian poets!!!) because it was painful to people's feelings to see that name mixed up indifferently with the ordinary subjects of the journal. Of course I did not enter upon an argument with M.[r] Dilke—but I thought within myself—"Here is just the mistake of a large religious class. *They* say, Christ's name must not be named in conjunction with ordinary literature—& therefore we who hold by the name of Christ, must shun the ordinary literature." The mistake is identical you see—the inference only being different—religious persons forsaking literature,—& worldly ones avoiding Christ's name! I mean no disrespect to M.[r] Dilke—but I am emphatic upon a mistake which is in my eyes dangerous to the world & melancholy for the religious. I agree with the latter from my heart .. that the place unfit for the naming of the redeemer's name, is unfit for the thoughts of the redeemed. The inference is as right as the premises are wrong!

Still it is not everybody in the class in question who holds the opinion .. & you must not consider it so. The Evangelical part of the establishment, & the methodists are the most narrow—the independents the most liberal.[9] I have heard Shakespeare quoted from the pulpit in dissenting chapels— and M.[r] Hunter a congregational minister, a dear & valued friend of mine, has all sorts of reading even to a partial knowledge of the old dramatists.

For my own part, I holding by the convictions of my soul to these Christian societies in all their chief doctrines & yet so far from being "unco guid"[10] that I am guid in no possible sense, .. you know very well how little I have stayed my thirst in any matter of literature. There are not perhaps many women in England even beyond my age who have tasted of such hundreds of muddy waters as I have—muddy & pestilential as well as the clear & pure—all sorts of abominations in & out of philosophy—as Hume & Hobbes[11] & Voltaire & Bolingbroke,[12] coming down from Lucian in the antique—manifold attacks, atheistical & otherwise on what I reverence as the truth. Reading *everything*, it has been said, does nobody any harm—& yet I sh{.d} scarcely like my sisters to touch all that has strengthened the truth to *me* through an antagonistical iniquity. Still, without referring any more to these philosophies so called, .. my conviction is that general literature sh{.d} be as open to the devoutest soul as the meadows are! I sh{.d} as soon say do not look at the sun—do not listen to the nightingale—as do not read the poets! The opinion is as monstrous in my ears & to my understanding as to yours.

If I could think that my Seraphim were read by the class in question my beloved friend—I should be .. just pleased! I *was* very much pleased to hear once that D{.r} Pye Smith had used it as a "book for Sunday". I have been pleased by hearing of its proving acceptable in a like manner to others: but be sure that the acceptability is far from being general. A baptist minister whom I had known & regarded for years[13] told me with a praiseworthy candour, nay, a thank-worthy candor, that the religion seemed to him made subservient to the poetry, rather than the poetry to the religion—& shook his head over it altogether. Another true & holy christian now dead[14] left a message to me which gave me some pain at the time .. that the book was unworthy of my knowledge of the Scriptures. Well!—should I be irritated at these things? should I respect them less for the contraction expressed in an opinion. Oh surely not! A religious man without literature is nobler in the sight of the angels, than a literary man without religion![15] Surely he must be nobler!

In regard to poetry—whether exclusively religious subjects be or be not the best adapted to poetry—I am sure that we shall agree my dearest friend in the opinion that the tendency of poetry must be upward——that religion should virtually enter into it—that Humanity cannot be considered philosophically without a reference to its relations God-ward & Heaven-ward. One might as well (& better) leave a man's mortality out of his humanity, as his immortality. We shall agree in this—shall we not? *Let us, my dearest friend!*

"We were placed on this earth to love each other"[16]—yes! but we know from the supreme book if we do not from our own experience that the love is warmest, truest, purest, which is the overflow of the love to God—even as we hear your own Coleridge say

'He prayeth best who loveth best'—[17]

love & prayer being reciprocal helps. Therefore it w{.d} not be true in philosophy to insulate in poetry the bare human love! *It has been done* I know! And that it is done too often is exactly what I mean to lament in wishing for "Christ's hand upon our poetry".[18] I wish it for poetry[']s sake & philosophy's as much as I wish it for religion's. I beseech you to consider what I mean before you decide that you will have no sympathy with me in the opinion!–

That your sympathy is very dear to me, that your approval in all things is very precious, I do not disguise to myself for a moment. You will believe it of me always—will you not?—however obstinately & opiniatively I may seem to cling to a particular doxy against (perhaps) your approval. But honesty above all things! honesty *in* all things! it is the best way even for love! Even for us, even in our case, where certainly all the reverence sh!! go from *me* to *you*, . . I believe that an entire openness & honesty on both sides has given more vivacity & stedfastness to the friendship you have honored me by permitting between us, than if I had laid heart & brain beneath your feet. It has been so hitherto—oh may it be so now!

As to the drama, I believe there is a prejudice as well as an opinion— & that your conjecture respecting the revolting influence of the amphitheatre may be connected with it. The theatre I am persuaded *might be* a means of great moral good. That it is not so now however—that it was not so even under James the first, that it was so fearfully the contrary under the second Charles, may justify utterly the absence upon principle of any person.[19] Do not mistake me my beloved friend! I do not blame you or others for attending the theatres—in all liberty of conscience. I sh!! not blame my own brothers & sisters for doing it—if Papa had a less particular objection. But I quite see the sufficiency of the objection as it is seen by him & others. Do you know how M! Macready has been attacked for even trying, even beginning to try to suppress *the saloons*— (the miserable application of which is very well known)—& how it has been declared that no theatre can exist at the present day without a saloon—& how, if it could, the effect w!! be to force vicious persons & their indecencies into full view in the boxes—!![20] Now this appears to me enough to constitute a repulsive objection! & I who have read hard at the old dramatists since I last spoke to you about them,—Beaumont & Fletcher Massinger Ben Jonson all Dodsley's collection,[21]—can yet see that objection in all its repulsiveness! . . & read on!

Dear M! Kenyon came here again yesterday (Sunday) I am writing now on monday—& overwhelmed me with the unexpected supernumerary visit of kindness! M! Browning, the poet, passed saturday & a part of sunday with him, & pleased & interested him very much! He has bad health—swimmings in the head—& a desire (if any loosening of family ties sh!! give him to himself) to go to a Greek island & live & die in the sunshine. M! Kenyon says he is "a little discouraged" by his reception with the public,[22] which I am very sorry to hear . . but "a strong sense of power" which is equally obvious may obviate the effect of the depression. Do you at all doubt that the writer of the Athenæum papers upon the 'Handbook,['] is Mr Darley?[23] Mr Horne—a generous-hearted man he really is—wont believe any harm in the world of Mr Darley—& thinks that all the stings lavished upon the poets' [sic], including Chaucer's modernizers, are the evil work of a certain Dr Taylor.[24] Of "Darley the author of Ethelstane"[25] he wont believe anything but innocense & ill-health! Macready told M.[r] Kenyon on saturday that he was about to read & pass judgment on a new play by Charles Darley, a brother of George's, & which by the glances he had cast upon it already he guessed to be a very extraordinary production.[26] Did you ever hear that there was a brother who was a poet?

Do you know Carlyle's writings? I am an adorer of Carlyle. He has done more to raise poetry to the throne of its rightful inheritance than any writer of the day,—& is a noble-high-thinking man in all ways. He is one of the men to whom it w.[d] be a satisfaction to me to cry 'vivat'[27] somewhere in his hearing. Do you recognize the estate of mind when it waxes impatient of admiration & longs to throw it off at the feet of the admired? I have felt it often!

You have not been well, my dearest dearest friend! Those newspapers—those newspapers![28] Do say particularly how you are! Be sure that I c.[d] not *mistake you*. Try not to mistake *me*—or rather try to love me through what appear to you *my* mistakes—& through what *are*!——

Happy! "you are happy!" You startled me with the sound of the word! I am *content* my beloved friend at least!

George said smiling one day by my bedside a great truth which I smiled at too though sadly. He said "When I hear people say they are content, I always know that they are miserable". It is a great truth with some modification—for certainly I, for one, never felt satisfied, content, I call it—until the illusion of life was utterly gone. When I think of the future *now* . . I think of something to be done, something to be suffered,—not of what is to be enjoyed. It is not when we talk or write lightly that we do not feel heavily—it is not at least so for me. My only individual hopes now are prospective actions & duties. My castle-building is at an end! A great change has passed both upon my inward & outward life within these two years. I scarcely recognize myself sometimes. One stroke ended my youth.[29]

And so be it! even so! It must have ended some time—& it is as well ended suddenly as more gradually. Bearing this vacancy at my side, I may bear the rest patiently.

And I am you see contented—quite calm—fearless even of the future. I am at leisure too & able by God's grace to count the MUCH which remains—to think of the beloved faces near me still—& of such a dear & precious friend as yourself in the same world with me—& permitting me to love her, heart to heart, as at this day!

May God bless & keep you my beloved friend! I never can thank you enough for all the comfort & sympathy I have received from you. I beseech you to bear with, a little longer,

your ever attached
EBB

Yes—I know Mary Wolstonecraft. I was a great admirer at thirteen of the Rights of woman.[30] I know too certain letters published under her name:[31] but Godwin's Life of her I never saw & sh^d like much to do so.[32]

The exquisite letters of Meta Klopstock! *Exquisite* is the only word of them. They have been extracted in different works—& I was familiar with nearly all of those in Richardson's Correspondence before my acquaintance with it.[33]

I have read the 'Cavalier'—but years ago. I must see it again. Nothing in Defoe fastened upon me much, except Robinson Crusoe & The Plague—which last you know of course, & which is still more a romance than the other—[34]

Have you received Miss Seward's letters—with *mine*? I sent them by the railroad on friday I think. I do hope too that you received the last Athenæum—the one containing my last paper?[35] Papa directed it himself to you.

Our dear Sette, is well again, I thank God[36]—breakfasted down stairs this morning—& Occy feels no symptom up to this hour. You need not be afraid of infection through my letters—as he has never entered my room so as to touch a paper in it since he began to be ill!

My love to Dr Mitford—I hope he continues better, & will forbid some of the reading. I think I sh^d dare to whisper that impertinence somewhere in his hearing—if the hearing were attainable to me. What you tell me of Mrs Niven's kind opinions is of course very agreeable to hear. I thank her for her kindness.

I wish you c^d hear how dear Mr Kenyon talks of you! I wish that for two reasons--if not three! Guess them!———[37]

Publication: EBB-MRM, I, 373–381.
Manuscript: Folger Shakespeare Library and Wellesley College.

1. EBB has altered the dating but clearly says in her text that she writes on Sunday and Monday.
2. Easter Sunday.
3. Just as the treachery of Judas Iscariot did not stain the other disciples, so should the corrupt man of whom Miss Mitford had spoken not condemn his peers.
4. We are unable to identify "this infamous man."
5. Underscored three times.

6. Anthony Norris Groves (1795-1853) was one of the founding members of the Plymouth Brethren. In 1829 he and his wife had undertaken missionary work in Bagdad; she died there in 1831 of the plague. In 1833 he went to Bombay, and, except for two brief visits to England, spent the rest of his working life as a missionary in India. EBB had mentioned his second marriage in letters 499 and 504.
7. Cf. Luke, 22:35.
8. The term methodist was first applied to Charles Wesley (1707-88) and a group of his friends at Oxford for their serious application to a particular system of study; it had a slightly pejorative meaning, equivalent to "prig," with no special religious connotation. It was only later, in association with his brother John Wesley (1703-91), that evangelical activities became dominant, and not until after John's death that a separate Methodist Church was established.
9. By "independents" EBB means the Unitarians.
10. "Address to the Unco Guid, or the Rigidly Righteous" (1787), by Robert Burns.
11. Thomas Hobbes (1588-1679), whose philosophical and political views were expressed in *Humane Nature: or, the Fundamental Elements of Policie* and *De Corpore Politico: or, the Elements of Law, Moral and Politick* (1650) and *Leviathan, or the Matter, Forme, and Power of a Common-wealth, Ecclesiasticall and Civill* (1651). EBB's copy of his *Tracts* (1678-81), now at Harvard, formed lot 743 of *Browning Collections* (see *Reconstruction*, A1188).
12. Henry St. John (1678-1751), 1st Viscount Bolingbroke, was a political philosopher whose works included *Letters on the Study and Use of History* and *Reflections Concerning Innate Moral Principles* (1752).
13. The Rev. George Henry Roper-Curzon, who had been appointed Baptist minister in Ledbury in 1828 while the Moulton-Barretts were at Hope End. EBB corresponded with him for some time after leaving there.
14. Probably the Rev. William Marriott Caldecott, described by EBB as "a saint" when she wrote of his death in letter 728.
15. An echo of Burns's "an irreligious poet is a monster," quoted by EBB in letter 534.
16. Cf. I Peter, 1:22.
17. Coleridge, *The Rime of the Ancient Mariner* (1798), line 612, slightly misquoted.
18. In the second of the papers on the Greek Christian poets, EBB had said "We want the touch of Christ's hand upon our literature, as it touched other dead things—we want the sense of the saturation of Christ's blood upon the souls of our poets" (*The Athenæum*, no. 748, 26 February 1842, p. 190).
19. Hence such criticism as Jeremy Collier's *Short View of the Immorality and Profaneness of the English Stage* (1698).
20. Macready was unsuccessful in his efforts to eliminate the sale of alcohol in theatres, but when the Drury Lane Theatre opened under his management in December 1841 the playbill warned that "the room . . . for refreshment attached to the boxes would be strictly protected from all improper intrusion" (*Macready*, II, 151, note 1).
21. Robert Dodsley (1703-64), dramatist and bookseller, issued a *Select Collection of Old Plays* in 1744.
22. The reviews of *Sordello* and *Pippa Passes* were largely negative. The former was criticized for its "pitching, hysterical, and broken sobs of sentences"; a review of the latter found RB's "texts nearly as obscure as ever—getting, nevertheless, a glimpse, every now and then, at meanings which it might have been well worth his while to put into English." (For the full text of the reviews, see vol. 4, pp. 416-417 and 420-424 and this volume, pp. 392-400.)
23. See letter 927, note 3.
24. William Cooke Taylor (1800-49), author, translator and critic, had settled in London in 1829, bcoming a contributor to, and staff member of, *The Athenæum*. He continued to work for the magazine until his death.
25. George Darley's play, *Ethelstan; or, The Battle of Brunanburh*, was published in 1841.
26. Either Kenyon had misunderstood Macready, or EBB had misunderstood Kenyon, because Macready had recorded in his journal on 6 August 1841: "Finished the play of

Plighted Troth—a play written in a quaint style, but possessing the rare qualities of intense passion and happy imagination" (*Macready*, II, 139). The author, Charles F. Darley (1800–61?), was now busy making changes suggested by Macready, prior to the play's going into rehearsal. Despite Macready's initial impression of the script, the play was a failure, and he wrote on 21 April 1842 "I cannot imagine how I could have been so mistaken" (*Macready*, II, 162–165).

27. "May he live."

28. A reference to Miss Mitford's fatiguing chore of reading the papers to her father (see letter 882, note 2).

29. i.e., the trauma of Bro's death.

30. In 1821, EBB's mother had referred to "yours & Mrs. Wolstonecrafts system" (letter 135) and it was about then that EBB wrote her "Fragment of an 'Essay on Woman'" (see *Reconstruction*, D308). Mary Wollstonecraft (1759–97) had published *Vindication of the Rights of Woman* in 1792.

31. *Letters Written During a Short Residence in Sweden, Norway, and Denmark* (1796).

32. *Memoirs of the Author of a Vindication of the Rights of Woman*, written by her husband, William Godwin (1798).

33. Four letters from Margareta ("Meta") Klopstock to Richardson, written in 1757–58, were printed in *Memoirs of Frederick and Margaret Klopstock, Translated from the German, by the Author of "Fragments in Prose and Verse"* [Elizabeth Smith], (1808), where EBB probably first read them. They were also printed in Richardson's *Correspondence*. The *Memoirs* also contained eight "Letters from the Dead to the Living," letters to her family containing thoughts on her own death. EBB had spoken of Meta Klopstock in letter 488.

34. *Memoirs of a Cavalier* (1724) by Daniel Defoe (*né* Foe, 1661?–1731). *Robinson Crusoe*, one of his best-known works, was published in 1719, and *A Journal of the Plague Year* in 1722.

35. The issue of 19 March 1842.

36. As letter 928 indicates, he had had measles.

37. The three reasons are enumerated in letter 938.

932. EBB TO HUGH STUART BOYD

[London]
March 29.th 1842.

My very dear friend,

I received your long letter & receive your short one, & thank you for the pleasure of both. Of course I am very *very* glad of your approval in the matter of the papers[1]—& your kindness could not have *wished* to give me more satisfaction than it gave actually– Mr Kenyon tells me that Mr Burgess has been reading & commending the papers—& has brought me from him a newly discovered scene of the *Bacchæ* of Euripides, edited by Mr Burgess himself for the Gentlemen's magazine, & of which he considers that the *Planctus Mariæ*, at least the passage I extracted from it, is an imitation.[2] Should you care to see it? Say 'yes'—& I will send it to you.

Do you think it was wrong to make *eternity* feminine? I knew that the Greek word was not feminine; but imagined that the English personification should be so.[3] Am I wrong in this? Will you consider the subject again?

Ah, yes! That *was* a mistake of mine about putting Constantine for Constantius. I wrote from memory—& the memory betrayed me–[4] But say nothing about it. Nobody will find it out. I send you Silentiarius & some poems of Pisida in the same volume–[5] Even if you had not asked for them, I sh^d have asked you to look at some passages which are fine in both. It appears to me that Silentiarius writes difficult Greek—overlaying his description with a multitude of architectural & other far fetched words! Pisida is hard too occasionally from other causes—particularly in the *Hexaëmeron* which is not in the book I send you but in another very gigantic one[6] (as *tall* as the Irish giant!)[7] which you may see if you please. I will send a coach & six with it if you please.

John Mauropus of the three towns,[8] I owe the knowledge of to *you*. *You* lent me the book with his poems, you know. He is a great favorite of mine in all ways– I very much admire his poetry–

      Believe me ever
        your affectionate & grateful
         Elizabeth B Barrett–

Pray tell me what you think. I am sorry to observe that the book I send you, is marked very irregularly—that is, marked in some places, unmarked in others, just as I happened to be near or far from my pencil & inkstand. Otherwise I sh^d have liked to compare judgments with you.

Keep the book as long as you please—it is my own.

Address: H S Boyd Esqr. / Downshire Hill.
Publication: LEBB, I, 102–103.
Manuscript: Wellesley College.

1. i.e., her papers on the Greek Christian Poets.
2. George Burges (1786?–1864), classical author, editor and translator, contributed to *The Classical Journal* and *The Gentleman's Magazine*; the scene from the *Bacchæ* was printed in the latter in the issues of September and December 1832 (pp. 195–199 and 522–524). EBB, in the fourth of her papers (*The Athenæum*, no. 751, 19 March 1842, pp. 249–252) had quoted a passage from "Planctus Mariæ" ("Mary's Lament") by Simeon Metaphrastes (*fl.* 950–1000 A.D.).
3. In the third paper (*The Athenæum*, no. 750, 12 March, pp. 229–231), EBB, in her translation of the ninth ode of Synesius, had ascribed the feminine gender to Eternity.
4. In the second paper (*The Athenæum*, no. 749, 5 March, pp. 210–212), EBB had quoted a remark of Gregory Nazianzen, saying it was spoken of Constantine. Julius Constantius was Constantine's brother.
5. In the third paper, EBB had discussed the works of Paul Silentiarius (*fl.* 550 A.D.) and George Pisida (*fl.* 630 A.D.). The volume EBB refers to is *Corpus Scriptorum Historiæ Byzantinæ*, ed. August Immanuel Bekker, 1837. EBB's copy formed lot 593 of *Browning Collections* and is now in the Brighton Area Library (see *Reconstruction*, A711).

6. The *Hexaëmeron*, Pisida's chief work, is discussed by EBB in the third paper, on p. 230. The "very gigantic" book was probably the 1777 folio edition of his *Opera*.

7. We assume this to be a reference to Murphy, the celebrated Irish giant of the late 18th century, who was 8 ft. 10 in. tall.

8. "John Mauropus, of Euchaita, Euchania, Theodoropolis" was discussed in the fourth paper.

933. EBB TO MARY RUSSELL MITFORD

[London]
March 30. 1842

I should like to be near you my beloved friend, to kiss both the dear hands twenty times which wrote & touched the paper of this most tender letter![1] I smiled half for pleasure & half for wonder as I read some of it, & ended all with such a heavy sigh that Crow turned round quickly to see what was the matter with me. What—do you not know—can you not guess, dearest kindest most indulgent friend, that all these words of yours must have the effect of humbling me to the ground? at your feet? At your feet! That sounds better! & I can be content with any humility which brings me nearer to *you*!–

I need not however say any more, or describe to you picturesquely the mountains of faults which are all mine! While I read your letter, my last one was effectually disenchanting you. And now—perhaps!– Ah! what are you thinking of me now? I am afraid to think myself.

Do not in any case cease to love me I beseech you. Do not punish me now or at any time for your own mistake—seeing that my love for *you* is true, actual, & has never been exaggerated even by your love to *me*. That you sh^d have so overprized everything else about me is the result of no cunning or intentional fraud of mine, but of the creativeness of your own faculty, & of the remissness of your own Imagination who takes, without a second thought, the shining of your own face in the glass for the loveableness of another's. You who are so acute in all other things, are in no degree aware how blind you are & *testa lunga*[2] (as was said of me) how headlongly blind, to the true characteristics of the persons you love. Forgive me! but indeed you are! You are blind as any cupid with wings. Your love of truth remains unimpaired through your love of persons—but you do not see what truth is—the moon is in a haze. And then, when .. all at once & much against your will, it shines full upon you .. then—ah then! what will become of *me* for one! Yet love me I beseech you, still, & in all cases. I cannot "do" now without your love!

How unwell you are! I am beginning to be quite restless about you, lest it end in an illness—for I see plainly that you are sacrificing yourself in spirits & health. What can be done? I say *that* restlessly to myself again & again & have no answer. If you sh^d be really ill you know, you *could' nt* read—& then dear Dr Mitford w^d reproach himself for permitting this labor which he does not think of now. If I were by, I sh^d certainly ask him to think of it.

Oh if there were anybody who would read & spare you! & if somebody w^d read even the newspapers, it w^d spare you a little! You are killing yourself with these newspapers–

Indeed I never did read or even make believe to listen to all the debates of a session—& if I seemed to listen, be sure that it w^d be '*make believe*'. I like Lord John Russel[3] for a certain nobleness & simplicity of purpose, which one does not see in that narrow paltry slippery artful (without *art* as you say) statesman Sir Robert Peel.[4] I have the sort of dislike to that man which some people have for cats or spiders—a half-fear & half-contempt. There is more nobleness of instinct in a "schoolboy's" oratory than you find in his,—which gives no breathing-room much less a breathing-out, for a generous sentiment. The man's ideality is in his father's mills[5] .. going towards manufacture—& indeed his whole mind rather revolves like a mill-wheel than advances or aspires. In regard to *power*, there is not a redundancy of it on either side, I readily grant to you. The country is sinking on one side like a willow tree, for the lack of power—for the want of a supporting soul. We have hands enough, & tongues rather more than enough, but of souls there is a deficit. So it appears to *me*. I could have wept when the whigs went out, with a very little fluttery of the eyeballs—but I go as far beyond them in my sublime ignorance as you in your knowledge, & peradventure something farther! I aspire to the republicanism of the Fortunate islands,[6] & to the distinguishing of my citizens by their heads & hearts rather than their pedigrees & landed estates. Besides—I do not believe in aristocracies, as my dearest friend does, in a manner!

What irritates me, pricks me as with a spur[7] or 'by'r Lady'[8] with a pin—is this sly way of flagellating the Country with a rod of office loaded on one side, so that the heaviness of the striking falls altogether upon the operative & commercial classes. I am the more angry, from having been beguiled at my first glance of the measure & by Sir Robert's august peroration rather to like this Income tax!!–[9] If anybody is wicked enough to take us in ...... why how very very wicked he must be!

You will thank me for this letter—it being almost as good as a newspaper—& quite redolent of one. If I am in luck, & you fall a little asleep instead of *all*, it may pass for a fragment of Col. Sipthorpe's last speech.[10]

You make me glad with the thought of that precious drawerful of letters! I for my part, have a precious box-full[11]—which if Sir Robert Peel had an inkling of, he w^d certainly tax.

But the drawerful will be published first .. & the prospect of your being at leisure to unfold its treasures to us in the spring, is a new spring-joy in hope to me! The public will leap at the collection, as I leap at every several letter. The post goes—I must be done—though with so much more to say. I expected Mr Kenyon today—but he did'nt come.

Your own
EBB—

Publication: EBB-MRM, I, 381–383.
Manuscript: Wellesley College.

1. Miss Mitford's letter (930) voicing her expectations for EBB's future fame.
2. "Headlong"; said of EBB by her Italian master (see letter 705).
3. Lord John Russell (1792–1878), later (1861) 1st Earl Russell, was the third son of the 6th Duke of Bedford. He first entered Parliament in 1813, representing the family borough of Tavistock. He had been an ardent proponent of electoral reform, and was Home Secretary and then Colonial Secretary in Melbourne's 1835–41 Whig administration, but with the advent of Peel's Tory administration in August 1841 became Leader of the Opposition.
4. Sir Robert Peel (1788–1850) had been Prime Minister in 1834–35, but gave way to Melbourne after being defeated on votes in the Commons six times in six weeks. He had now been returned to power after carrying a vote of "no confidence" in Melbourne's ministry.
5. Peel's grandfather had founded the family fortune by establishing in 1764 a calico-printing works, the business being continued by Peel's father.
6. The Fortunate Islands, otherwise the Islands of the Blest, were imaginary islands where good souls lived in eternal bliss. The name was also applied to the Canary Islands.
7. Cf. *Macbeth*, I, 7, 25–26.
8. *Richard III*, II, 3, 4.
9. *The Times* of 12 March 1842 carried a report of a long speech made by Peel the previous day, when he had announced to the House of Commons an anticipated budget deficit of £4.7 million for the two years ending May 1843. After reviewing several possible solutions, he recommended the imposition, for a limited period, of an income tax of not more than 7d in the pound, levied on incomes of over £150, and a tax on leaseholds at 50% of that rate. In his "august peroration," Peel spoke of the "increased prosperity and wealth" of the upper classes, and exhorted the Commons to put an end to "the public evil of financial embarrassment," saying that failure to do so would engender "a reflective and retrospective condemnation."
10. *The Times* of 25 February, reporting the previous day's parliamentary business, summarized a speech of some length by Col. Charles Sibthorp (1783–1855), the Member for Lincoln, on the Controllership of the Exchequer. An ultra-Tory, his "delivery was rambling and uncouth ... His speeches ... too often personal and violent" (*DNB*).
11. EBB refers, first, to the letters to Sir William Elford which Miss Mitford had been encouraged to publish (see letter 737, note 1), and, secondly, to her own growing collection of letters from Miss Mitford.

934. EBB to George Goodin Moulton-Barrett

[London]
March 30.th 1842.

My ever dearest George,

I marvel at myself for not having answered your letter with the first breath I drew after receiving it—but I knew that you had letters if not mine—& the last paper tired me so utterly & I had such a heap of letters to answer after the accomplishment of the Athenæum business, & you yourself besides offered me such a pattern of intersectory spaces between writing & writing—, that I being tempted, sinned in my silentness. Forgive it—write directly: I beseech you, George, write!

You have heard of the measles & our dear Set together. This morning he has gone to the baths for purification,—& therefore you may be well assured there is nothing more to be uncomfortable about. I have not seen him yet—because--I dont know why!! for he has been down stairs to breakfast & dinner & might with equal impunity come into my room. Occy complains of nothing up to this now. I hope he may escape it after all.

My dearest George I w.^{d} give a whole penny piece to amuse you for one half hour—not knowing however where the amusement is to come from. You have heard, I suppose, all the vibratory movements here upon mirrors, & pictures, & a house in Harley Street (contemplated for purchase!!!) & how "the income tax will prevent many persons from keeping their carriages, who had thought of doing it"—& of the proposal & election by persons unknown of Papa to the Reform Club![1] The vibratory movements of the house are not much more than such! For the rest there is dining as usual—& breakfasting with the Fortescues[2]—& drinking tea with Trippy. There is nought to tell you that is either 'curious or improving'.

Uncle James heard you speak—& Bummy gives me the echo of his commendation of the speaking. *I* will hear you speak too, George, some day,—if I ever have life long enough & strong enough to suit the purpose. In the meantime or otherwise, I fancy the speaking to myself—& clap you with the (wings?) hands of my imagination!

Papa is pleased I think—indeed I am sure—with his election to the Reform Club—inclusive of the privilege of paying forty five guineas entrance fee,—ten annually. He wishes that it had been always so with him since his settlement in London—but the rein upon his neck was a most transcendental fear of being blackballed! Therefore he w.^{dnt} be proposed! and was startled by the notice of his election one morning at breakfast, from the propriety of the eating of muffins, into an honor uncourted, unsought, unexpected. *I* am quite glad too!

Miss Mitford writes to me every two days just as she used– I am not sure that I c^d do without it now—not without the missing as of a morning star in any case. I love her better & better certainly—& she does not seem to love me much less—which is more wonderful. Her father seems to have lost both health & hope—the natural result of a strong man *in the body only*, losing the strength of the body!—, mere animals spirits departing with the animal health, & the soul bending like a reed. Nothing keeps him up, she says, but reading one newspaper after another all through—& she, poor thing, just reversing his condition, she, strengthening her feebler frame by her strong heart, is reading, reading from morning to night—reading her very breath away! It is most lamentable to think of––thinking too what *she* is! Some of her friends cry aloud, Mr Kenyon tells me, "I wish he was dead!"—but that is a want of faith in the love which is in her! She w^d droop lower beneath that stroke than beneath any burden!

Mr Kenyon has multiplied kindnesses lately in coming to see me— three times last week—& promised for today or tomorrow– He brought me the last time my series of papers as marked & remarked upon by Burgess the Grecian & Browning the poet—& Mr Burgess sent me, *gave* me, a lost scene of the *Bacchæ* of Euripides, restored by himself & imitated long ago (according to his view) by my Simeon Metaphrastes.[3] He is going to send me moreover a concatenation of his remarks on the *Christus Patiens*—& rather wished to bring me himself, until that was explained to be out of the question. Mr Kenyon proposed also to introduce to my sofa-side . . Mr Browning the poet . . who was so honor-giving as to wish something of the sort! I was pleased at the thought of his wishing it—for the rest, *no*! You are aware how I estimate . . admire (what is the sufficient word?) that true poet—however he may prophecy darkly. Mr Kenyon says that he is a little discouraged by his reception with the public—the populace, he sh^d have said. "Poor Browning," said Mr Kenyon. "And why poor Browning?"—"Because nobody reads him," —"Rather then, poor readers!" Mr Carlyle is his friend—a good substitute for a crowd's shouting!

I have been reading Emerson–[4] He does away with individuality & personality in a most extraordinary manner—teaching that what Cæsar did, we did—(*we-everyman*), & (which is scarcely so "pretty to observe") what Cæsar's bondslave did, we did—& that every man's being is a kind of Portico to the God Over-soul—with Deity for background– This malformation of philosophy does not, you may be sure, admit other than a malformation of theology in this side—there are heresies thick as blackberries.[5] Still the occasional beauty of thought & expression, & the noble erectness of the thinking faculty gave me "wherewithal to glory".[6]

M.' Kenyon brought me the book of M.' Crabbe Robinson's lending–'Holla'—quoth Robinson the next morning! [']'*You* have lent *Emerson* to Miss Barrett!! You have done very wrong indeed!" To which M.' Kenyon responded that Miss Barrett read "an infinite deal of *everything* & had a healthy digestion". "A healthy digestion perhaps—but you sh.^{d} not on that account overtry it, to the extent of distension &–––"

It was a pretty simile but not over delicate—& so I will stop there. M.' Kenyon on the other hand without stopping at all set off to me, hoping that he had committed no offensive solecism—in lending me a book which he had'nt read!—that "the book in question was in fact "too strong" for Crabbe Robinson himself who leant towards heresy, & might haply prove so to *me*!" Upon which I begged to keep it one day longer than I sh.^{d} have done otherwise. And there is a story & a moral for you, both together! I hope they may be profitable.

Dear M.' Hunter was here yesterday for an hour or two—& although it is not certain that he is now on his road to Brighton, it is left to us as a probability. He speaks at once sadly & bitterly of his position at Brighton—& altogether appeared to be in spirits most oppressed & oppressive. He wants abstracting by the exertion of an outward-working energy. The very owl leaves its ruin sometimes or would hoot out its own knell—& a self-conscious heart is a ruin, if old enough. Mary is quite well, I am glad to say besides. He evidently does not like my papers—"they are written, not gravely enough, & with an obvious effort which is fatiguing to the reader". Otherwise—I mean by other people, they seem favorably received.

Arabel has just come in, having dined with the Bazalgettes–[7] She was at the Suffolk street exhibition, with Occy, two days ago, & very much pleased.[8] In association with which subject—M.' Haydon has stabbed his foot with a javelin.[9]

My dearest George, what shall you do about Frocester. If Miss Hayward[10] or any other person there continues to have the typhus fever, *I entreat you not to go*! That is my entreating & beseeching to you. Otherwise you will do right to refresh yourself with a little ease, to the uttermost. The weather is delightful & my fire extinguished. I am very tolerably well—& also (tolerably I hope)

your ever & ever attached
Ba

Address: G. Goodin M Barrett Esq.' / Barrister at Law / Oxford Circuit.
Publication: B-GB, pp. 79–84.
Manuscript: Pierpont Morgan Library.

1. The Reform Club was founded in 1836 to promote "the social intercourse of the Reformers of the United Kingdom," with Edward Ellice (1781–1863), brother-in-law of Earl Grey, the former Whig Prime Minister, as its first chairman. Members included

Thackeray, who joined in 1840, and it was from the Reform Club that Phileas Fogg set forth in Jules Verne's *Around the World in Eighty Days* (1873).

2. Acquaintances made by EBB and her sisters during their stay in Torquay (see letter 695).

3. See letter 932, note 2.

4. Ralph Waldo Emerson (1803–82), philosopher and poet, had published *Nature* (1836) and *The American Scholar* (1837). EBB was probably reading his *Essays: First Series* (1841), as her comments are similar to those in the mainly-negative review of *Essays* in *The Athenæum* of 23 October 1841 (no. 730, pp. 803–804), which said "Denying the relative and the contingent, [Emerson] is forced to deny man's individuality; to save humanity, he absorbs it into one 'universal mind'."

5. Cf. *I Henry IV*, II, 4, 239.

6. Cf. Romans, 4:2.

7. Acquaintances first mentioned in 1838 (see letter 666).

8. The annual exhibition of the Society of British Artists at the Suffolk St. Gallery had opened to the public on 28 March.

9. Haydon's diary entry for 22 March read: "Painted 2 hours, finished musket & Bayonet. The musket fell down. I did not see it, & ran my foot against it, & the bayonet right (½ an inch) into my left foot. It bled copiously." The next day's entry read "Laid up all day—with my bayonet wound" (Pope, V, 138). He later became one of EBB's principal correspondents; for details of their friendship, see the biographical sketch, pp. 370–373.

10. Unidentified.

935. EBB TO FANNY DOWGLASS[1]

50. Wimpole Street.
March 31. 1842.

My dearest Fanny,

The sight of your letter pricks my heart through! What have you thought of me? What can you have thought of my unkindness, before your kindness, growing too strong for it & yourself, induced you to write to me? I am ashamed—quite cast down before you. And now it is too late to try to prove to you that if you had delayed writing two days, you would have heard from me at last! Every assurance of the kind must look suspicious & of a disreputable aspect!

Nevertheless do believe as far as you can that not without thought, not without love, if without word or sign, this long interval has passed. I love you dearest Fanny & your dear mother affectionately as I ever did: & all that you have told me in your tender forbearing way of your illness & the result it leads to & of your wish to see me—& *not* to reproach me!—has touched me very nearly. You are ill & going away! May God's will be accomplished in the fulness of His love- "Yet not alone"[2]—yet not afar! These words will always be true for you in blessing & blessedness while God is truth.

But I had thought, had *hoped*, you were so well & so much strengthened! I had hoped that your constitution had cast off its bands & freed you into a comparative health which might endure. And now comes this disappointment even as others have done! But dearest Fanny, I must not moan over you who belonging to the family of the *Great hearts*[3] never moan for yourself—there being indeed far more good cause for the cheerfulness than for the moaning with my dear hopeful friend—& I shall now turn my head backwards & tell you the story you are kindly desirous of hearing about my own tongue-tied self.

In the first place—last summer I was better. The unspeakable agonies of the year before passed as agonies will[4]—it was not the divine will that I sh^d die *so*– The latter part of the winter, passed in weakness & depression, yet passed too, & with a certain dreary staleness: & then in the summer, to my own surprise I rallied & was better in health, & caught eagerly at the first possibility of leaving that dread⟨ful⟩ place. My medical friends & indeed all my other friends w^d scarcely admit it to be a possibility,—& I was argued with & persuaded against & talked to in every manner of eloquence to no use. Certainly I may judge now that it scarcely looked like a possibility! I had only just attained to being lifted from the bed to the sofa for an hour in the day without dead fainting fits which were once apprehended to be dangerous: & it did seem like a sort of mania to insist upon travelling two hundred miles for the sake of spending a winter in London, in the state I was in then! ["]Nevertheless,["] said the medical man, ["]you must take her, if she insists." You know (in other words) working oneself into a fever through obstinacy, is an evil of evils.

And so, Fanny, if I had died on the road,—dear Dr Scully w^d have dedicated to my memory in his secret soul, an epitaph exalting my obstinacies above all obstinacies, even female, he ever had the privilege of knowing.

On the other hand, I was self-justified (applaud my self-righteousness) in the resolve I came to . . not instant thought, as well as through suffering. Apart from the weight which lay day & night upon my body & soul in that miserable place, so that every sound beneath my window was as "the waters going over my soul",[5] & every separate breath a separate pang— apart from every personal consideration-–& yet what a life it was, shut up face to face with the greatest grief of one's life . . & yet what a life it was, never for a whole year to bear to look even at the sky—& I could not bear it in that place!—but apart from every personal consideration, there was poor Papa, obliged to be in London & his hearth made desolate to him for *me* & by my means. He had not one daughter with him—to pass the rest which I cannot speak of more even to *you*—he was dreary for my sake & through *me*! I felt it all miserably! The change was blessing & blest to me—& I thank the Blessed Giver who when His hand was heaviest, moved it softly in this last Paternal caress!

Moreover the improvement in my health which began last summer has gradually increased rather than diminished– I have grown fatter, stronger .. do not look at all as I did! My voice has come back to me which had fainted to a whisper,—I have not had one attack this winter: & I walk every day from the bed to the sofa where I pass two hours. My impression is, my belief is, notwithstanding the uncertainty of the complaint, that I am essentially better—that I may, if it so please God, praise Him in my *life*. Ten times a day the thought has touched the very quick of my heart, that if I died, the dearest in the world to me w^d be the happier for it, in some manner—able at last to live together. To make an effort therefore to get away & get home was imperative upon me—& whatever the consequences had been to myself personally I never sh^d have had one regret for what was called my self-willedness. You will understand everything my dearest Fanny, just as it happened.

Well! Papa sent a patent carriage down for me & went himself to Exeter as he was afraid (poor dearest Papa!) to see me set off, but he met me at Exeter & travelled the rest of the way with us. Ten days we spent upon the road. I suffered in the manner that was apprehended by renewed & increased spitting of blood, but not to the extent—& altho' exhausted day after day to fainting & speechlessness I came into London perfectly alive & inclined to remain so. Indeed I am a marvel to myself for this winter past. The restoration to my family flushed my spirits back to what they never thought to be again—it was the opening of the dungeon to the captive! I looked at the chimney pots & at the smoke-issuing of this London .. all I c^d see from my bed .. with the sort of exaltation & half-incredulity with which you have looked at the Alps! I could believe again in a smile!

You are very very kind to care to come & see me. Dearest Fanny—I see nobody– I tell you, heart to heart, that I love you & shrink to see you—the more, not the less, because I love you! Ah—you will understand that.

Angela Owen was in the house not many days ago & she asked earnestly to see me & she is my cousin .. & I loved her much once & love her still at this moment, but I *could not* see her.

Still .. will it be possible *not* to see *you* my dearest dearest Fanny! I think I cannot let you be so near a whole month—or you going away! & not see you! I think I shall not find it possible. Tell me when you come to St Johns Wood, & let us write a little more one to another– Will you answer this letter soon? Will you let my silence be as if it had not been?

For indeed I cannot justify it. At Torquay I thought .. [']'if ever I get to London I will write to her"—and when I was in London & the fatigue had worn away, other reasons arose for "putting off, putting off" .. as is always the way with unkind idle silent people! So I will not apologize! I deliver myself up to you rather, bound hand & foot, to be dealt with according to the measure of your ... mercy! 'Not *justice*', dearest Fanny I beseech you.

What makes me most of all ashamed is that you sh^d have heard I have been writing. Writing .. and not to *you*!! But as to my writing, it has only been some papers in the Athenæum on literary matters, a slovenly sort of survey of the Greek Christian poets, which I was asked to write .. *because* perhaps, the Athenæum rejoices in its cruel soul over the confusion of all poets, christian or profane—

You asked me once—& this reminds me of it,—to send you some of my MS poems—but your letter was never read until four or five months after it was written, & when read, the poems, such as they were, lay in a chaos of illegibility & I who only c^d read, had no strength to transcribe them. Otherwise believe me I never c^d neglect a request of yours—still less one which I c^d not receive without an emotion of thankfulness for the affectionate interest it expressed. I will look out .. even now .. for one or two things—if you care ⟨...⟩ to such a late hour, to have them—[6]

Dearest Fanny, tell me a little more particularly of yourself! Have you pain? Is the cough bad? the expectoration returned? Do you sleep at nights? And my dear dear Mrs Dowglass! I recognized her handwriting at once & felt glad through all my shame. Ask her to try to go on loving me. I say "go on" in my vanity, because I thought once in the same, that she did love me a little! Dearest Fanny, may the great God-Love in the Filial Love be with you perceptibly as He must be indeed!—making known to you as the end of suffering, the enjoyment of Him, even as the beginning of wisdom is His fear.

We were concerned for poor Mr Drummond,—in hearing of his loss, which has been generally accounted more sudden than you represent it.

May I ask if it is true that he has united himself to the Puseyite party (as it is called) in the church of England.[7] I lie here separated in the body from all the visible churches—as if almost my gravestone were between me & them—

Ever your as ever
affectionate E B Barrett
commonly called
Ba–

We are all together here—all on earth– I returned early in September last.

Address: Miss Dowglass. / Dr Thompson's / Albury / Guilford.
Publication: None traced.
Manuscript: University of Texas.

    1. This friend was, like EBB, troubled with health problems, and she spent considerable time in Italy for that reason. The two corresponded in the 1840's and '50's, but none of Fanny's letters has thus far surfaced. Miss Dowglass is mentioned only indirectly in the voluminous correspondence which EBB conducted with Mary Russell Mitford during that time. From the tone of this and other letters from EBB to Miss Dowglass, one surmises a long and fairly close friendship, probably based on ties between their families, but specific details are lacking.
    2. Cf. Numbers, 11:17.
    3. In the second part of Bunyan's *The Pilgrim's Progress* (1684), Mr. Great-heart was the guide of Christiana and her children to the Celestial City.
    4. i.e., those following the deaths of Sam and Bro.
    5. Cf. Psalms, 69:1.
    6. Any verses EBB may have sent with this letter are not now preserved with it.
    7. Malcolm Henry Drummond had died on 25 March, aged 21. He was the eldest surviving son of Henry Drummond, M.P. (1786–1860), of Albury Park, and his wife, Lady Henrietta Drummond (*née* Hay, 1783?–1854). Drummond was an enthusiastic adherent of Edward Irving and a co-founder of the Irvingite Church, in which he was ranked as apostle, evangelist and prophet. As he paid for the erection of an Irvingite church in Albury, and remained an active member of the movement almost to the end of his life, his purported union with the Puseyites was obviously just rumour.

936. EBB TO JOHN KENYON

50 Wimpole Street
Thursday Night. [31 March 1842][1]

I send you the Prometheus, my dear Mr Kenyon & have written to Duncan to desire that an Essay on Mind may be sent to you.[2] *As you please to have it*, I have done so,—& you are of course at liberty to do with it what you please—only I hope that thro' consideration for me you will save it generously from any risk of general circulation .. I mean of circulation anywhere, at home or abroad, where the extenuating circumstances of its production cannot be known– Now you will be sure to laugh at this!—as if 'general circulation' were an evil plenty as blackberries,[3] now a days! But a bad conscience you know, always was a great coward!

My note of thanks to Mr Lowell, I enclose to you—& two Prometheus's instead of one (in case you may care to have two) with the House of Clouds written in one, *past reading*, by my hand.

                                      Ever affectionately yours
                                      Elizabeth B Barrett.

Dont forget the gypsies .. & the gods.

Friday night– Dear M:͟ Kenyon, you will see my willingness to do your bidding quickly by the date of the last page. But after I had transcribed a stanza of the House of Clouds into the book last night, I found that my m·s. wanted certain variations which were only to be found in the printed copy, while not an Athenæum containing *that* c.^{d} be found in the house. I waited in vain—& it was only tonight that I set about rifling my memory & brains generally & discovered the thing missing. In the meantime you come!– Well!—since you have a Prometheus, I will send you only one instead of the two I intended—& you will find in it both the Cloud House & the "Confiteor tibi"[4] which you desired to have & which expresses my disturbance of conscience much as I feel it. You will receive also an Essay on Mind from Duncan, to whom I wrote yesterday directing a copy of that melancholy 'lusus naturæ'[5] to be sent to you. All that it is worth to *me* consists in some verses towards the end, of no work as poetry, but precious to me from their association . . & as witnesses of happy emotions & satisfied affections which never more can move me or bless me on this side the grave!

Dear M:͟ Kenyon, how kind & like yourself (*because* kind) is your proposal to take Henrietta with you to Strawberry Hill. She is very much pleased.

Affectionately yours again
EBB

Address: John Kenyon Esq:͟ / 4. Harley Place.
Publication: None traced.
Manuscript: Dartmouth College.

1. Dated by the enclosed note to Lowell (letter 937).
2. EBB's father had previously given Kenyon a copy of *An Essay on Mind* in November 1840; Kenyon subsequently (1845) gave it to RB (see *Reconstruction*, A327). Kenyon sent this second copy to George Ticknor, the American scholar and historian, together with *Prometheus Bound*. Both books, together with this letter, are now in the Ticknor Library of Dartmouth College, Ticknor's *alma mater* (see *Reconstruction*, D345, M41 and M67).
3. Cf. *I Henry IV*, II, 4, 239.
4. "I confess to thee," the opening words of the liturgical General Confession; cf. Psalms 32:5. The copy of *Prometheus Bound*, given to Kenyon and subsequently to Ticknor, contained 10 of the 13 stanzas of "The House of Clouds." "Confiteor tibi" apparently refers to the following apologia, written facing the title-page: "For this version, which is cold stiff & meagre, unfaithful to the genius if servile to the letter of the great poet, too hastily executed & altogether immature, the translator's only apology is — — *her remorse*. EBB."
5. "Freak of nature."

937. EBB TO JAMES RUSSELL LOWELL[1]

50 Wimpole Street– (London).
March 31.st 1842.

Sir,

I beg you at last to receive my very earnest thanks for the volume of graceful poetry which I received from you some months ago[2] through the hands of our mutual friend Mr Kenyon. I felt obliged to you & gratified by such a mark of your attention both as a poet & an American—& if I did not say so directly, circumstances have had more to do with that negligence than any degree of insensibility could. Will you try to believe this? There is a natural bloom upon the poems, a one-heartedness with nature, which it is very pleasant to me to recognize. I hope—if you will not scorn the *hoping* of the stranger whom you first honored .. I hope that you will write on, & not suffer your " year's life" to be only *one* year's life.

And I remain, Sir,
your obliged
Elizabeth B Barrett–

Address: James Russell Lowell Esqr / Boston.
Publication: None traced.
Manuscript: Harvard University.

1. For details of EBB's friendship with Lowell, see the biographical sketch, pp. 373–374.
2. *A Year's Life* (1841).

938. EBB TO MARY RUSSELL MITFORD

[London]
April 1.st 1842.
Is'nt it *spring*?

Your dearest & too touching letter O my beloved friend, is among the things for which I cannot thank you adequately when my heart & eyes are fullest!– May God bless you—*love you*!

For my own part you have mistaken my figures—my 3's you have read into 8's, my 0[']s into 10's—"the full sum of me"[1] must of course be wrong. And, some time hence, when the sun shines upon the slate & the dimness passes from your eyes & you *find it out* to be wrong,--will you promise me *now*, my dearest friend, to struggle *then* with the new wisdom & try in spite of it to love me further & longer than you c.^{d} overvalue me? Will you try to do it? Perhaps you will, for the sake of this love which goes out to you truly & clearly & cannot be exaggerated like the rest.

Do you remember what the old poet said of love[:] "It is the toothache or like pain—"?[2] Well! *your* toothache or face ache seemed to act like that poetical aching. It acted like love! "Embittered your letter"! No indeed! I felt no bitterness, I tasted none—& my lips were close enough to the paper to do so if any bitterness had been there.

My question was—wasn't it?—"Can you guess the three reasons why I wished you to hear M^r. Kenyon talking of you?"–[3] You guess only one of them—& here are all three. 1st Because it w^d. have pleased you. 2^d. Because it w^d. have pleased me to see you pleased. 3^d. *Because you w^d. have been here*. There's my climax of a reason! Guess why I sighed in writing *that*. 1st Because of my selfishness! 2^d *Because you were* NOT *here*! And there's another climax. How improveable the world is, to begin with *me*!

Well! but he was here again yesterday, & we had more talking of you—& he told me how a certain society in which he had been the day before, was talking incense about you .. & how M^r. Harness extolled the magnificent positions in your Otto—& how the novel was marvelled at, that it had been cast down[4]—& how delightful it w^d. be for you to come to London & light up the smoke of it with the shining of you. Then M^r. Kenyon & I talked of the novel, & I denied the casting down of it in what some of M^r. Kenyon's friends call my "insolent" way, & felt sure of its being up on its pedestal ready for all worshippers before very long. He told me that you had developed something of the story to him & that it promised everything. Was'nt the name "Mary Gray" thought of for it? I think you told me so once—long ago—& that was the second day we met.

Often & often do I look back, leap back in spirit over the great gulph of darkness between my *now* & my *then*, & think of the moment when the door was first opened to me of the permission to love you. Did I ever tell you just how it was? M^r. Kenyon had been asking me, asking me,—like a king beseeching a beggar to take a dukedom—pressing me on all sides with kindness to pass an evening at his house & see Wordsworth. Now I w^d. have gone on a pilgrimage to see Wordsworth ever since I was eight years old—& if the indispensable condition had been pebbles within side of the pilgrim shoon,[5] I w^d. have gone even so. But at the end of a pilgrimage, I sh^d. have seen Wordsworth alone in his niche,—kissed his feet & come away .. & he peradventure w^{d}nt have seen *me*! It was altogether different going into M^r. Kenyon's den of lions & lionesses—& I was frightened into absolute shame at the sort of roaring implied by my imaginativeness. I know M^r. Kenyon was half angry, thro' all his kindness, at my long drawn perversity—& I was near crying in the conflict between what I wished & feared, & what dear M.ʳ Kenyon tried to press beyond the fear. Who can judge aright for another who has lived a peculiar life, in no sort of society except of books, & shy at the best, as to manners—? "I loathed that I did love"!–⁶ Well—at last the temptation took the form of a softer devil. He, not the devil but our dear friend, asked me to think no more of the great party but to consent to come to a very small one, where Wordsworth w.ᵈ be again—& *Miss Mitford* . . & then he told me of your gentleness & dearness. So then I said "Yes"—half ashamed & half afraid still!—and then again in the morning came a note from him to propose my going with himself & *you* . . & *you*! to the Zoological gardens. Oh how I remember the words? I am sure he measured them so as to encourage me into some estate of common sense—"you will become acquainted" (thus they ran) "with an amiable person whom you will be certain to like, & who is prepared to like you". Prepared to like *me*! I resolved at once to go, & set my teeth as for the desperate purpose of it—couldn't do anything during all the interval at books or writing . . dawdled about . . walked up & down stairs, looked out at the window—said to myself so as to keep myself firmly buckled up in resolve, "I shall be glad *after it is over*! I shall be glad I have seen her, all my life afterwards (O unconscious prophetess!) & in the meanwhile it will only be a few hours pain". Think of me as you please, but I do assure you that when the carriage was heard to be at the door, my knees trembled so that it was a hard thing for me to get down stairs to it. And then, . . the first sound from your lips which reached my ears . . embleming all the rest . . was said in reply to something M.ʳ Kenyon said & I c.ᵈ scarcely hear in my confusion, something to the effect that I "sh.ᵈ have a protectress now"—"*I hope, a friend*". Those were the first words I ever heard from your lips—& there was a tone, a significance of kindness in them which went beyond the words & made me love you in [a] moment. I loved you before as all the world does & for much the same reasons—but the heart-to-heart love began just then! You were Cæsar to me in a moment!–⁷ Dearest friend . . bear with me as you have done. It is for *you* to bear with *me*!

Your eyes are growing older you say & you cant see the violets so well this year as on others. Now do not anticipate the growing older. When your eyes grow older,—I mean when age begins to affect them,—you will see more clearly than you do now. You are short-sighted—are you not?—like me & M.ʳ Kenyon & Papa. Well—that species of defective sight *improves* with age—because it arises from the too great convexity of the pupil, which it is the effect of age to flatten. So YOU SEE you have made a mistake & are growing younger instead of older. I am so glad!–

Poor M.ʳ Browning! Was that extreme irritability of nerve supposed to be occasioned by the disappointment, or the exercise of an overwrought faculty?[8] After all I cannot wish with you that he be turned to occupations of less excitement. In the first place, C^D he so turn? In the second, dare we ask silence from such a poet? It w^d be like asking a prophet to forbear his prophecy—he has a word to speak from Nature & God, & he must speak it!–

Certainly Mr Browning does speak in parables—& more darkly than .. even .... some other of your friends. But he is a true poet. I estimate him very highly—& so do you—& so must all who know what poetry is & turn their faces towards its presence willingly.

The 'Rhymed Plea'[9] is admirable "after its kind"[10]—but with all my true & admiring regard for its author & his writings I could not be content to receive it as sole comforter for the absence of higher inspirations.

My prose style like Carlyle!– To remind anyone in the world of Carlyle were praise enough & too much! Miss James's[11] praise made me feel glad for a moment .. as if it c^d be true.

And yet you are quite right. He does not write pure English .. no, nor quite pure German—nor pure Greek, by any means. But he *writes thoughts*. He reminds me of Leibnitz's plan for an algebraic language,[12]— altho' *his* plan is not algebraic—but he *writes thoughts*. There is something wonderful in this struggling forth into sound of a contemplation bred high above dictionaries & talkers—in some silent Heavenly place for the mystic & true. The sounds do come—strangely indeed & in unwrought masses, but still with a certain confused music & violent eloquence, which prove the power of *thought* over *sound*. Carlyle seems to me a great prose poet. At any rate he is a man for the love & reverence of all poets, seeing that he, almost sole among the present world's critics, recognizes the greatness & the hopefulness of their art.

I, presume to offer my admiration to Mr Carlyle, my dearest friend! No—you have not spoiled me quite up to that point or pinnacle yet.

Thanks upon thanks for the lovely violets. They deserve to lie enfolded in your letters– I wish I deserved to receive them, as well!

May God bless you ever. They always drive me away from you with this post hour. Say how the face-ache is! & go on to love

your own grateful
EBB–

I read the Beggar girl, when I was very young—'Vicissitudes' I must try to get.[13] Always I remember too late so much I forget to write to you of—my remorseful memories beginning with the sealing up.

Poor Mr Haydon! Indeed it was an accident suggestive of less martial ideas than seem to have occurred to him.[14] You amuse me so with your description of Mr Darley and Mr Darley's handwriting—"turned the wrong way". Have you any philosophy on the subject of handwritings? Mr Dilke's is a very strange one—sufficiently *retorted* too!–

Dear Set is quite well, & nobody else ill.

Address: Miss Mitford / Three Mile Cross / Near Reading.
Publication: EBB-MRM, I, 383–387.
Manuscript: Edward R. Moulton-Barrett and Wellesley College.

1. *The Merchant of Venice*, III, 2, 157.
2. Sir Walter Raleigh, "The Shepherd's Description of Love," line 15.
3. EBB's question was contained in the postscript to letter 931.
4. These references are to Miss Mitford's play, *Otto of Wittelsbach*, and *Atherton*, the novel not published until 1854. Harness had pronounced *Otto* to be "quite excellent" but feared that "If Bunn and Kean were to write to you to-morrow and promise that the play should be acted ... my opinion of them is, that they would make no scruple of flinging you and the play over on the most frivolous pretence ... So *don't depend too much* upon them, and go on with the *sure* game of the Novel" (*Miss Mitford and Mr Harness: Records of a Friendship*, Caroline M. Duncan-Jones, 1955, p. 51).
5. Cf. *Hamlet*, IV, 5, 26.
6. Thomas Vaux (1510–56), "The Aged Lover Renounceth Love," line 1, in *The Paradyse of Daynty Devises*.
7. EBB first met Miss Mitford in May 1836 (see letter 527, note 3). The reference to Cæsar, of course, is as conqueror.
8. Miss Mitford had obviously added her own comments on RB's health, following EBB's speaking of his "swimmings in the head" in letter 931.
9. Kenyon's *Rhymed Plea for Tolerance* was first published in 1833. EBB's copy of the second edition (1839) formed part of *Browning Collections* (see *Reconstruction*, A1362).
10. Genesis, 1:11, 12.
11. Miss Mitford's Richmond friend, who stayed frequently at Bertram House prior to the Mitfords' moving to Three Mile Cross. Miss Mitford tells how, on being driven into Wokingham by her, Miss James was unruffled by Miss Mitford's erratic driving, saying "she was not at all afraid, being so assured of my being reserved to be hanged, that she would not mind going with me even in a balloon" (Vera Watson, *Mary Russell Mitford*, [1949], p. 119).
12. Gottfried Wilhelm Leibnitz (1646–1716), philosopher and mathematician, had invented a calculating machine in 1673 and in 1676 formulated the differential and integral calculus, independently of Isaac Newton.
13. Agnes Maria Bennett (d. 1808) had published *The Beggar Girl and Her Benefactors* in seven volumes in 1797 and *Vicissitudes Abroad; or, The Ghost of My Father* in six volumes in 1806.
14. For details of Haydon's accident, see letter 934, note 9.

---

939. EBB TO HUGH STUART BOYD

50 Wimpole Street
April 2. 1842–

My very dear friend,

I am sorry I should have omitted to notice any part of your letter—but I did not neglect it really. M[r] Hunter spent an hour or two with us the other day, having come to London upon business, & I did not neglect making the enquiry of him you desired. The enquiry was vain—he did not know of any young person likely to suit you. Arabel will speak about it either to M[r] Stratten or his wife—& take courage, for we shall succeed at last. There must be many young persons who would be delighted to make themselves useful to you. The difficulty is to take knowledge of them.

Arabel is much obliged to you for wishing to see her still oftener—& would I am sure go oftener to you if the distance were not so great & herself engaged much in different ways. She talks of paying you a visit next week.

Is this better writing? I try to make it clear.

In regard to Mr Burgess I mean to repeat what you have said to me to Mr Kenyon, that, the mistake being cleared away, you may have your visitor again.[1]

As to your kind desire to hear whatever in the way of favorable remark I have gathered for fruit of my papers,[2] I put on a veil & tell you that Mr Kenyon thought it well done altho' "labor thrown away from the unpopularity of the subject"—that Miss Mitford was very much pleased, with the warmheartedness common to her,—that Mrs Jamieson read them "with great pleasure" unconsciously of the author,—& that Mr Horne the poet & Mr Browning the poet were not behind in approbation! Mr Browning is said to be learned in Greek, especially in the dramatists—& of Mr Horne I sh.^{d} suspect something similar. Miss Mitford & Mrs Jamieson altho' very gifted & highly cultivated women are not Græcians & therefore judge the papers simply as English compositions–

The single unfavorable opinion is Mr Hunter's who thinks that the criticisms are not given with either sufficient seriousness or diffidence, & that there is a painful sense of effort through the whole. Many more persons may say so whose voices I do not hear. I am glad that your's, my dear indulgent friend, is not one of them.

Believe me
Your ever affectionate
Elizabeth B Barrett.

Address: H S Boyd Esqr / 21. Downshire Hill / Hampstead.
Publication: EBB-HSB, pp. 245–246.
Manuscript: Wellesley College.

1. George Burges (1786?–1864), classical scholar and editor, had called on Boyd, but was rebuffed by what he felt was an unfriendly reception, so had not repeated the visit. Boyd lamented his "unhappy manner" and told EBB that he had been very glad to see Burges; EBB related this to Kenyon (see letter 962) in the hope that he would pass it on to Burges.
2. i.e., the series on the Greek Christian Poets.

940. MARY RUSSELL MITFORD TO EBB

Three Mile Cross
April 4, 1842.

I am an inconsistent politician, I confess it, with my aristocratic prejudices and my radical opinions. By-and-by, perhaps, when education is more diffused, these prejudices may lose their ground; at present there is certainly a great difference between the well-born, well-bred, simple, frank, and gentle people who had grandfathers, and the fine, fussy pretenders who have never known such progenitors. All the Whigs seem to me, in all their measures, afraid of the people—afraid to make any popular concession. Moore said once, in my hearing, that he "liked the Whigs when they were out of power." And certainly they are better then. But even then they seem as if always guarding against whole measures— devoted to bit-by-bit legislation. If they had flung themselves upon the people heartily and honestly, they might have set the Tories at defiance. Free trade—that seems to me the one great want now; and I cannot but believe that we shall live to see the principles advocated by Grote and Warburton (neither of them now in Parliament),[1] in the ascendant. O'Connell is versatile in his words and ways, and the Repeal seems to me incomprehensible;[2] nevertheless, *as an Irishman* (for doubtless he looks upon us as the English enemy), I cannot but think him a great patriot. And if you had but to read all those dull speeches you would feel the relief of coming across his eloquence.

Ever your own,
M.R.M.

Text: L'Estrange (2), III, 143–144.

1. George Grote (1794–1871) agreed to stand for Parliament in 1831 to work for parliamentary reform, of which he was an early proponent. He remained a Member until 1841, when he declined to stand for re-election in order to devote himself to the completion of his 12-volume *History of Greece*, begun in 1822 and published in stages between 1846 and 1856. Henry Warburton (1784?–1858), philosopher and economist, was first returned to Parliament as a radical in 1826 but resigned his seat in 1841 when there was a suggestion that his agent might be implicated in charges of bribery. He was re-elected in 1843, but retired from political life in 1847, when all the reforms he had advocated had been effected.

2. In 1840, feeling that Parliament was not seriously addressing Ireland's many problems, O'Connell had founded the Repeal Association with the object of working for the repeal of the Act of Union of 1801, which created the United Kingdom of Great Britain and Ireland; this was an issue he and his followers were still strenuously advocating.

941. EBB TO MARY RUSSELL MITFORD

[London]
April 6. 1842.

My beloved friend,–
Your delightful letter reconciles me to myself, for the pleasure I used to take in Anna Seward. That *you* can be attracted by her now, is my absolution.

Her filial sentiment & your's have often occurred to me together[1]— but otherwise you are easts & wests—the expression of her warmest friendships being attended to my mind with a certain self-conscious folding of the robes which is altogether opposed to your *abandon* & heart-impulsiveness .. & the characteristics of mind & style & outward developments in every manner being opposite as pole to pole. As to the obstinacy,—my beloved friend .. do you really set up for being obstinate? I have seen no type or symbol of it in anything I have seen in you—& really .. if it is lawful to disappoint you so far .. I am afraid that you cannot be qualified. Obstinacy of the forehead as marked to your observation in Miss Seward's, you certainly have not—& the inward quality you must pardon me for putting no sort of trust in, until "proven".

A moment ago & Crow brought me a little parcel from Mr Haydon containing a gift of his late Lecture on Fresco. And now I am in a doubt! "With Mr Haydon's respects to Miss Barrett"– "Miss Barrett" quite plain. But is it really for *me*? Perhaps for one of my sisters, both of whom he knows while of me he is innocent. Perhaps for Arabel, because she paints & he means to be good-natured. That he sh^d mean to be goodnatured to *me* is more unlikely perhaps, & I dont know what to do with my thanks, & I am afraid of standing out in the foreground with both hands open when all the time my rightful place may be to be *blacked* out of sight in the far background. Tell me—is the Lecture for *me* do you suppose, or not? Because if it is for ME I must write & thank him for it—while if for my sister, *she* must.[2] There is the difference. Very kind of him, either way!–

I know very little of many of Miss Seward's gods & goddesses—& nothing at all of the "domestic epic—"[3] but that same Whalley is shown I think in Ma^{dme} d'Ar⟨blay's⟩ Bath picture-gallery under a languishing aspect.[4] Even Helen Williams I have not caught a glimpse of out of those letters[5]—altho' trying once or twice or thrice. No—& I dont know the Lives of Milton & Romney—nor the Pleader's Guide nor the Siege of Gibralter (but *shall*) nor any of Jephson's play[s],[6] but w^d gladly if you have any to lend—mo⟨st⟩ gladly if you have any to *bring*. There's a list of alibis. I am almost ashamed of them. I always liked Hayley's Life of

Cowper altho' he did not understand the *man*.⁷ Of Cowper as a religious man he was intensely ignorant—& the sort of confusion which he made between the sentiment & the insanity is obvious & unphilosophical everywhere. There is a Life of Cowper written by a biographer of his own opinions whose name has quite escaped me, but insufficient in a literary point of view—in one volume & nearly as one-sided as Hayley's, only of a different side. I met with it & lost sight of it at Sidmouth.⁸ The best & fullest biography in all ways appears to me to be poor Southey's— the life published together with the works a few years ago.⁹ Do try to get it from Reading. It extends over four or five volumes I think or more, including the letters & every detail known on the subject of the insanity. You will see the conclusion clear . . without room for a vapor of scepticism . . that poor Cowper was mad, not in consequence of his theological views but altogether apartly from them—so apartly, that before he entertained them or was the subject of any strong devotional impressions of whatever character, he was *mad enough to attempt his own life*.¹⁰ It is very important that the truth sh^d be rightly apprehended on all accounts—& you will admit unhesitatingly from the testimony of these volumes that no modification of religious belief can be charged with the madness. Southey does indeed say that he was treated injudiciously by his religious friends—but really *he* could scarcely believe so from *his evidence* as it strikes my perceptions. I read the book some years ago—Mr Kenyon lent it to me—& that is my impression now. Mr Southey is far too steeple-high & stiff as a theologian for me, & there are traces of the church*yard* in the biography.¹¹ Still, his love of truth was stronger than his hatred of Calvinism¹²—& there are traces of *that* superiority in the biography too. What is called the doctrine of reprobation is a very evil one certainly, & pestiferous with the fruit of its cruelty—but the doctrine is rather *imputed* to the highest Calvinists than believed by them; & I, having known many high calvinists, many who *call* themselves high calvinists & are so,—have yet never stood face to face with any human being who confessed to a belief in that reprobative doctrine¹³ except once—& then its believer was a woman. It was however held obviously by Luther himself.

But Cowper did not hold the doctrine of reprobation in the Lutheran, Calvinistical, or any other ordinary sense—& is wrongly represented in the common opinion as a victim to it. His belief was, his madness was, that he alone of all the universe stood without hope—never to be accepted into the bosom of God's mercy,—though clinging to it in his despair!— never to be cleansed by the dropping of the Sacrificial blood, though waiting in its fall, with the whole patience of his desolation. His belief was a madness in its obvious nature.

I do not know why I sh^d ask you to read that book of Southey's—except that you were speaking to me of Cowper—for when I had done I felt sorry myself that I had read it. I never had doubted at all about the madness & the physical causes of it—& really that book lay upon my heart like a weight of lead for days & days. It is the dreariest, most melancholy, most pathetic story I ever read, & drew tears enough from me to serve the sorrows of six romances. Do not read it when your spirits are not strong. The only consolation is the certainty of *his* consolation now—& the only bearable manner of realizing to one's own soul the sunless moonless darkness of his, is to regard it as a sign of the inward cross of martyrdom, conferred rather than inflicted, in preparation for its perpetual crown. Otherwise there is no hope—no comfort! no view beyond! The curtains of his desolation are drawn close.

How singular in its mournful coincidence is the fact that this biography should be almost the last work from his hands—the very last being (was it not) a final collection of his works. Yet even the head of our poor Laureate is not bent as low as Cowper's was.[14]

You will love Cowper very much in that book. I never loved him so much, setting no high enthusiasm upon his poems, as when I closed it. Moreover it is very beautiful, written with the full Southey charm.

I agree with you altogether about Mason.[15] He is a Mason to me & I am a stone to him- As to Gray—do you not know my heresy about Gray? Was I always afraid to tell you of it? Yet Mr Horne told me once that I was right in it—yet YOU *wont*—yet you must hear the truth, if only for conscience's sake. Suppose me then to be a stone to Gray too—quite cold, quite impenetrable—not a breath quickened, or pulse stirred! It is true! I am a stone to Gray. He seems to me to be elaborate rather than inspired, worked up & made up—artificial .. yet too far from Nature to admit of true Art. There seems to me in his poetry what Horace Walpole complained of in his manhood .. a fine cold pride .. an *hauteur* which is by no means *height*.[16] Oh—I know it is heresy. But I cannot help it. The fault may be in me—but the misfortune is on me surely—he does not *act* on me.

Speaking of Horace Walpole, Mr Kenyon in his great kindness took both my sisters with him yesterday .. with him & *Mrs Jameson*—to Strawberry hill[17]—& they came home in the full glow of all the pleasure he had given them. I asked a good deal about Mrs Jameson .. & have her now in her whole anatomy. No!—the externities have nothing very striking or graceful—but the countenance has its intelligence & the voice its agreeableness .. & the bearing is unassuming & not unpleasing. I asked if there was eloquence—or anything else brilliant in the conversation—"No,"—they said—"they did'nt observe anything peculiar in any way"—they w.^{d} not have guessed if they had not known!-

What do you want to puff me up into doing? About Carlyle .. I mean![18] Oh no, no, no!

And now tell me— There is a mystic phrase in your letter[19]—something to the effect that you w^d not have had me praise another, who ...!
Do tell me if you have a meaning in particular! I catch at a sort of meaning I see a glimpse of. Do tell me the whole of it—& believe me my beloved friend, that you could not vex me by speaking out to the uttermost word.

Mrs Jameson was praising yesterday her dear friends the Kembles,[20] but said that 'Adelaide was the cleverest of the sisters.' Did you ever hear it? She was speaking of their comic powers in conversation—drawing a general inference which the premises I heard of, seemed to disclaim.

My dearest dearest friend!—you say little of yourself—& I am anxious about you. Can I ever cease to love you? Do you think it possible? Did anyone ever cease to love you? They have done so to me oftener than once!—but *you*!–

No sooner do you think a thought than the thought lightens upon me thro' a quicker electricity than the post's– Blake! Mr Kenyon had just lent me those curious "Songs of innocense"[21] &c with their wild glances of the poetical faculty thro' the chasms of the singer's shattered intellect— & also his life by Cunningham.[22] The particular book you mention I have not seen.

Oh the post, the post!– I must go! Papa came while I was writing & told me to mention his name to you!–

May God bless you! I love you more & more.

Your own EBB–

Do you know Ma^{dme} de Genlis in her *Memoires*?[23] They are very amusingly characteristic—amusing indeed in all ways!

Dear ⟨Occ⟩y has the meazles now, but is pretty well. How you amused me about Mrs Dupuy's mistake in my *antiquities*! You see how it is possible to be mistaken in me in all sorts of ways– How *is* Mrs Dupuy? You spoke of her being out of health. Tell me of Mr Haydon.

Address: Miss Mitford / Three Mile Cross / near Reading.
Publication: EBB-MRM, I, 388–393.
Manuscript: Wellesley College.

1. Like Miss Mitford, Anna Seward was a devoted attendant during her father's declining years. Thomas Seward (1708–90), a friend of Dr. Johnson, was Canon of Lichfield and of Salisbury and had collaborated—not very successfully—on an edition of the works of Beaumont and Fletcher. After his death, she wrote to Cary that she had lost "the helpless object of those sweet, though anxious cares, that were their own reward" and other letters abound in lamentations (see *The Singing Swan: An Account of Anna Seward*, by Margaret Ashmun, 1931, pp. 187–188).

2. EBB was persuaded that the gift was indeed meant for her, and she acknowledged it with letter 945.

3. The phrase "gods and goddesses" refers to the eminent persons who were known to the Sewards; apart from Dr. Johnson, they included Boswell, Darwin and Hayley. The "domestic epic" is Anna Seward's 1784 poetical novel, *Louisa*.

4. Thomas Sedgwick Whalley (1746-1828), author and Rector of Hagworthingham, was described by Mme. d'Arblay as "a young man who has a house on the Crescent ... He is immensely tall, thin, and handsome, but affected, delicate, and sentimentally pathetic" (*Diary and Letters*, I, 306).

5. Helen Maria Williams (1762-1827) was a friend of Miss Seward. She passed much of her adult life in France, espousing revolutionary ideals and spending some time in prison. She published three separate collections of letters written from France, describing her impressions and experiences.

6. EBB's references are to *The Poetical Works of John Milton. With a Life of the Author* (1794-97) and *The Life of George Romney* (1809), by William Hayley; *The Pleader's Guide: a Didactic Poem* (1796), by John Surrebutter, Esq. (i.e., John Anstey); *The Siege of Gibraltar, a Poem* (1795), by Joseph Budworth; and the plays of Robert Jephson (1736-1803), which included *Braganza* (1775), *The Count of Narbonne* (1781) and *Conspiracy* (1796).

7. *The Life and Posthumous Writings of W. Cowper*, 3 vols., 1803-04.

8. One-volume accounts of Cowper's life were written by John Corry (1803), Samuel Greatheed (1803, revised 1814), and Thomas Taylor (1833); we cannot deduce which one EBB had read.

9. *The Works of William Cowper, Esq., ... With a Life of the Author*, by Robert Southey (15 vols., 1835-37).

10. In November 1763, Cowper had attempted to hang himself; his life was saved only because the strap he was using for the purpose broke and he fell to the floor, unconscious. Following this, "symptoms of a violent attack of madness rapidly developed themselves.... He was convinced that he was damned" (*DNB*); in December, he was confined in a private asylum, where he remained for more than a year. After this episode, Cowper, previously caring little for religion, became intensely devout. Late in 1772, his madness returned, together with a recurrence of suicidal tendencies, and he was again confined until 1774. Yet another attack, and a further attempt at hanging himself, occurred in 1787, and thereafter he was subject to frequent strange fancies and delusions.

11. Southey's religious views were contained in *The Book of the Church* (3 vols., 1824). By the play on church*yard*, EBB is probably suggesting that his 15-volume work on Cowper suffered from the prolixity of which Thomas Churchyard (1520?-1604) was accused. In the second part of her review of *The Book of the Poets* in *The Athenæum* (no. 763, 11 June 1842, pp. 520-523), she said that Churchyard was one of the poets "who had their hand upon the ore if they did not clasp it!"

12. The principal tenet of the Calvinists was that the Bible was the only authority in matters of belief. (See letter 499, note 1.)

13. i.e., rejected by God and thus condemned to eternal misery, as in Cowper's belief (note 10 above) that he was damned.

14. Southey also suffered from mental ill-health, the last year of his life being "one of insensibility to external things" (*DNB*). An edition of his works, "collected by himself," had appeared in 1838.

15. William Mason (1724-97), a friend and disciple of Thomas Gray, published *The Life and Letters of Gray* in 1774. He was a prolific poet, his writings including *Elfrida*, a poem in classical style (1752), *Caractacus* (1759), and collections of poems in 1762 and 1764.

16. In a letter of 3 September 1748, Walpole said of Gray: "he is the worst company in the world—from a melancholy turn, from living reclusively, and from a little too much dignity, he never converses easily—all his words are measured, and chosen, and formed into sentences; his writings are admirable; he himself is not agreeable" (*Horace Walpole's Correspondence with George Montagu*, ed. W.S. Lewis and R.S. Brown, Jr., 1941, I, 76).

17. The Twickenham estate of Horace Walpole, the house resembling a miniature Gothic castle.

18. Whether or not Miss Mitford encouraged EBB, she did write some thoughts on Carlyle in 1843, used by Horne for *A New Spirit of the Age* (1844); see *Reconstruction*, D1282 and the 1900 Porter and Clarke edition of EBB's *Complete Works* (VI, 312-321).

19. Letter 944 makes clear that the "mystic phrase" referred to Queen Victoria.
20. Charles Kemble (1775–1854), his daughters Frances Anne ("Fanny") Butler (1809–93) and Adelaide (1814?–79, later Mrs. Sartoris), and his son John Mitchell Kemble (1807–57). In 1826, Kemble had created the title role in Miss Mitford's *Foscari*.
21. *Songs of Innocence and Experience* (1789, 1794), by William Blake.
22. Blake is one of the subjects of the second volume (pp. 143–188) of *The Lives of the Most Eminent British Painters, Sculptors, and Architects* (6 vols., 1829–33), by Allan Cunningham (1784–1842).
23. The *Mémoires Inédits* of Stéphanie Félicité, Comtesse de Genlis (1746–1830) were published in 8 vols. in 1825–26, together with an English edition produced by Colburn.

---

942. MARY RUSSELL MITFORD TO EBB

Three Mile Cross,
April 9, 1842.

It will help you to understand how impossible it is for me to earn money as I ought to do, when I tell you that this very day I received your dear letter, and sixteen others; that then my dear father brought into my room the newspaper to hear the ten or twelve columns of news from India;[1] then I dined and breakfasted in one, then I got up. By that time there were three parties of people in the garden; eight others arrived soon after—some friends, some acquaintances, and some strangers; the two first classes went away, and I was forced to leave two sets of the last, being engaged to call upon Lady Madalina Palmer, who has an old friend of both on a visit at her house.[2] She took me some six miles (on foot) in Mr. Palmer's beautiful plantations in search of that exquisite wild flower the buck-bean (do you know it—most beautiful of flowers? wild, or as K―― puts it, "tame?"). After long search we found the *plant*, not yet in bloom. Then I hurried home, threw my own cocoa down my throat, and read to my father Mrs. Cowley's comedy, "Which is the Man?"[3] and here I am (after answering, as briefly as I can, many very kind letters), talking to you.

My father sees me greatly fatigued—much worn—losing my voice even in common conversation; and he lays it all to the last drive or walk—the only thing that keeps me alive—and tells everybody he sees that I am killing myself by walking or driving; and he hopes that I shall at last take some little care of myself and not stir beyond the garden. Is not this the perfection of self-deception? And yet I would not awaken him from this dream—no, not for all the world—so strong a hold sometimes does a light word take of his memory and his heart—he broods over it—cries over it! No, my beloved friend, we must for the present submit. There may be some happy change. He may himself wish me to go to town, and then—. In the meanwhile my heart is with you.

Ever yours,
M.R.M.

Text: L'Estrange (2), III, 144-145.

1. Details had just reached England of the massacre in January of a force of British and Indian troops, support personnel, and camp followers, during its withdrawal from the Afghan city of Kabul. According to the first reports, of more than 13,000 men, women and children, only one English doctor and three Indians reached the safety of the English fort at Jalalabad.

2. Lady Madalina Palmer (née Gordon, 1772?-1847) was the daughter of the 4th Duke of Gordon and sister of the 5th Duke. In 1805 she married, as her second husband, Charles Fyshe Palmer (d. 1843) who, until 1841, represented Reading in Parliament. In a letter of 12 March 1842 to Miss Harrison, Miss Mitford speaks of Lady Madalina's house as East Court [4 miles from Wokingham], and identifies Mr. Palmer as being related to Elizabeth Fyshe Gisborne (née Palmer), the wife of Thomas Gisborne, the politician (Chorley, I, 288).

3. Hannah Cowley (née Parkhouse, 1743-1809) was the author of several volumes of poetry and numerous plays, the best of which were "sprightly and vivacious" (*DNB*). Her comedy, *Which is the Man?*, was first performed at Covent Garden in 1782.

943. EBB TO JOHN KENYON

50. Wimpole Street–
April 13– 1842.

My dear Mr Kenyon,

I send you back the *two* books with a great many thanks.

The Tragedy will be considered probably "naught" as a whole, but of considerable entity of beauty in detached parts. It appears to *me* that there are even fine dramatic touches in it although it is not a fine tragedy— & I would assuredly far rather be the poet of it than of half or three quarters or *more*, of those "fine tragedies" which pass & are acted as such– There are also very noble passages which are not dramatic—for instance that noblest of the noble which the poet employed before—long ago—as a motto—& which seemed then to belong to the great 'didactic poem' in the treasure-house .... "Action is transitory .. a step, a blow".[1] Altogether we surely ought to be grateful for it .. call it tragedy .. poem—discrepancy .. what you please. And I for one, *am* grateful.

For the rest—there is much which is beautiful & powerful—only you have *to dig for it*– Do read the sonnets to the painter .. & the next *palinodia* sonnet—& the one beginning "A Poet"—& that composed on

May morning 1838 & that immediately following & commencing "Life with the lambs",—& think if they may not take rank with the crowned sonnets, the very most royal, of even Wordsworth himself. The 'Windermere widow' too– O yes! & much besides! & I like the 'Norman boy'— only there is something wanting to the *wholeness* of the impression.[2]

There is one poem affecting in its subject, & treatment too I think— too affecting to me personally to read to an end.[3]

The Shakspeare society appears to labour under an antiquarian delusion to the effect that this book—which I return thanking you, .. involves much valuable novelty.[4] To be honest I cannot say that it has interested *me* .. beyond a few scattered notices with almost a quarter of the volume between each pair.

Dear Mr Kenyon's "perverse",
affectionate cousin
EBB–

I heard from dear Miss Mitford yesterday. A very sad account of her father!–

Publication: None traced.
Manuscript: Wellesley College.

1. "The Borderers," line 1539.
2. The subject of these paragraphs is Wordsworth's latest publication, *Poems, Chiefly of Early and Late Years; Including The Borderers, a Tragedy* (1842). The title-page of "The Borderers" dates its composition to 1795–96. EBB was later asked to write a review of the volume for *The Athenæum*; it appeared in the issue of 27 August 1842 (no. 774, pp. 757–759).
3. EBB may be referring to "Composed by the Sea-Shore" (pp. 180–181). As it deals with the dangers faced by those who sail the sea, it is probable that it would evoke painful memories of Bro's death.
4. The Shakespeare Society of London sponsored various publications, dealing in the main with the theatre, but not exclusively with Shakespeare. EBB's reference may be to *Memoirs of Edward Alleyn ... Including Some New Particulars Respecting Shakespeare, Ben Jonson, Massinger, Marston, Dekker, etc.* by John Payne Collier (1841).

---

944. EBB to Mary Russell Mitford

[London]
April 13. 1842

My beloved friend you grieve me by what you describe as your situation. It is most touching in description—it must be most painful in endurance— & oh—be sure of my sympathy. But the spring, the spring!– I look forward beyond these east winds which are depressive to the spirits of ill health & debility to an extent unguessed by those not personally sufferers,—to the hopeful & cheerful influence of sunshine & green leaves.

He will be better then *I think*– I hope & pray that he may. In the meantime try to hold fast the conviction that the despondency is "all desease"[1] at all times—& that if the desease were more of a fatal character the patient would probably be *less* apprehensive & cast down than you see him now.

As for myself—wistfully as I have looked & dreamed for the spring *in two senses* (with the metaphysical sense turned uppermost) much & earnestly as I longed to look at your dearest face at the time your goodness fixed for its *orient*—still—do not think of me—still help me not to think of *me* my beloved friend—& be very sure that I c^d not wish you *even to be here* if you were uneasy either before or after or at the time of such an arrangement. I quite see now that you cannot come now– We must wait.

When the sunshine is settled, & the spirits follow the example of the sun & *shine* .. why then we may begin to talk again of it—or at least you will begin to talk of what becomes a possible subject to you. And I will not teaze you in the meanwhile more than appertaineth to mortality.

Dear Mr Kenyon lent me Wordsworth's new volume two days ago[2]— & I have read the last line & end gratefully to the poet. The tragedy *fails*, to my apprehension—fails utterly *as a whole*, yet has more dramatic feature occasionally than I had expected to find. There are also fine things in it here & there which are *not* dramatic but which we have not force (overborne by the beauty) to wish away. The old man left to starve, reminds me of a position in Schiller, but falls short.[3] It is NOT[4] a fine tragedy—altho' having hear⟨d⟩ no single opinion except this of my own, .. I ought not to thunder it so emphatically. But to my mind it is NOT[4]—even while that same mind vibrates sensitively to the much beauty contained in it.

Among the other poems there are some four or five sonnets which are supremely excellent—most noble & beautiful—most instinct with Wordsworth in his full, great, divine life—& the poems on the Clouds, on the Widow of Windermere are fine also. And there is a ballad on a "Norman boy" which I like—& other things. The clay however lies thickly & heavily around the brightness of the diamonds—and we have to work hard to get at them. Those sonnets in favor of the punishment of death, which appeared first by grace of the Quarterly & Mr Taylor, grind harshly on my idea of the office of the poet & the tender-heartedness of *this* poet.[5] And I do not like *very* much better (altho' *much*) the Puseyite note towards the close of all.[6]

You relieved me my beloved & kindest friend by what you said . . . . of the queen! I had inferred after my illogical fashion, from the previous saying, that some idol of mine with a crowned head like Wordsworth rather than Victoria, had scorned me from the heights of his regality.[7] Now .. if it is only Victoria .. why I peradventure can be regal too. My dearest friend, I never had a thought until you put it into me that she w^d look at verses of mine, or that looking I sh^d ever be aware that she did.[8] Many probabilities were against the former,—all etiquettes against the latter!. & after all your pleadings on the other side, I by no means feel aggrieved, to the breadth of this line _____ which my bad pen (by the way) has made broader than my bad temper desired to do—by the quodlibets[9] of queenhood.

But if I had learnt from you that someone near the sphere of Wordsworth (not Wordsworth himself because I have heard otherwise of his kind thoughts but some one near his sphere) had been punishing me with "hard thoughts"[10] .. why then perhaps after I had thanked you for your candor my beloved friend .. perhaps, nay, *certainly*, I sh^d have sighed very heavily the next minute & felt very very sorry.

Your remarks on Anna Seward's Letters water them to my recollection—& they are all up & green & fresh, just like mustard & cress. Your remarks run like water from a fountain—which is properly called 'living water[']'[11]—& I hear your own living personal voice in them all. No! not a bit like! You like Miss Seward! No! not a bit– We will except the filial devotion, the perversity of over-estimating *friends*, the love of truth, the fervidness in all things—make those exceptions & there is not a bit of likeness remaining. And even in those exceptions you must except much—for you are after all a daughter, a friend, an enthusiast, in a different way from the sentimentalist of Lichfield—without the self-consciousness & without the ornateness of phraseology. Your's my beloved friend is a *free* as well as a noble nature—& it is not necessary for you to elaborate your attitudes to attain your gracefulness—nay, it is not possible to you, *through* your gracefulness, to elaborate your attitudes—for that is the right manner of putting it. She was certainly in love with Mr Saville. She was perhaps *ornately* mournful in her lamentation for "my Honora".[12] There now! You have done it! I am quite ashamed of myself for my maliciousness—but it is all your fault. And you will finish by forcing me to dislike this Anna Seward whom I have had a liking for all my life, & only by saying that she is like *you*! Like *you*! Is'nt it enough to make anyone who knows *you*, stone her with stones out of their own hearts, in utter jealousy & malice?

You sent me Miss Anderdon's letter with your writing crossing its ends—& so I hope you dont mean me to send it back to you. I shall keep it safe for the dear autograph's sake, unless you say "No, you shant".

I have written you a short dull exchange for your delightful letter—but my hand has begun aching before its time .. I am physically tired—not otherwise, *you know*! It is the east wind—I think it must be.

My dearest friend, I maintain that your eyes are not growing weaker *through age*—that is my position; but is natural enough that they sh^d bear their part in the agitation & weariness to which your whole frame has been lately subjected.

You shall have the account of Williams the missionary—tomorrow if possible . . & I save the opportunity by venturing to send you "mine oysters"[13] again.

My love to your poor invalid. God bless you ever & ever.

Your own EBB.

You who are fond of likenesses—can you make out a likeness between Mrs Thrale & *you*? Not a perfect similitude, I grant you, but I stand on my ground for more points of approximation than exist between yourself & the ephemeral muse of 'Lichfield town'. The *abandon* is very like—taken apart from the *lightness*. Altogether I c^d make a better case of my suggestion than you c^d of your's–

Have you heard how the queen subsides before the tories[14]—whether she subsides at all—how she treats them—how she bears up under the circumstances—whether she cares enough for certain opinions to *bear up* in the strict sense, in any manner? Do tell me if you hear.

Send me too (pity the sorrows of a blind idle person!)[15] Mr Harrison's direction.[16] I know it is safe in one of your letters, but I search & re-search again vainly. I am ashamed of the pamphlet's remaining still 'to be sent'.[17]

Publication: EBB-MRM, I, 393–396.
Manuscript: Folger Shakespeare Library and Wellesley College.

1. Cf. Deuteronomy, 28:60.
2. See note 1 to the previous letter.
3. EBB apparently sees parallels between Old Herbert in "The Borderers" and Old Moor in *Die Räuber*.
4. Underscored three times.
5. "Sonnets Upon the Punishment of Death," advocating capital punishment, appeared on pp. 166–179 of Wordsworth's *Poems*. They had been printed previously in an article on his sonnets in *The Quarterly Review* of December 1841 (pp. 1–51). However, EBB is mistaken in associating their publication with Taylor, who was on the staff of *The Athenæum*. The editor of *The Quarterly Review* at this time was Lockhart.
6. In a note to "Musings Near Aquapendente" on p. 402 of *Poems*, Wordsworth speaks of "the religious movement that, since the composition of these verses in 1837, has made itself felt . . . throughout the English Church;—a movement that takes, for its first principle, a devout deference to the voice of Christian antiquity." He speaks of his own "repugnance to the spirit and system of Romanism" and says he draws "cheerful auguries for the English Church from this movement."
7. Miss Mitford had apparently clarified an earlier reference, deemed by EBB "a mystic phrase" in letter 941.
8. EBB refers, in letter 735, to a proposal by Miss Mitford to use the offices of her friend Marianne Skerrett to bring "The Crowned and Wedded Queen" to Victoria's attention.
9. "What pleases, or is agreeable to."

10. *As You Like It*, I, 2, 183-184.
11. John, 4:10.
12. Anna Seward spoke of John Saville, eight years her senior, as her "almost next-door neighbor" and admitted that, since making his acquaintance in her twelfth year, her "esteem and friendship for him have never known abatement." A most devoted regard for Saville, her "soul's chosen friend," is expressed in her letters, even though he had a wife (from whom he was separated) and daughter. Honora Sneyd, after the death of her mother, had lived in the Seward household for 14 years, and Miss Seward "had trained up the little girl with devoted care ... had made her a constant and intimate companion ... That she should have felt the pangs of separation upon the marriage of the younger girl is not unnatural. But her poems and letters reveal a degree of grief and misery which is accounted for only by a sense of total estrangement and loss." (See *The Singing Swan: An Account of Anna Seward and Her Acquaintance* ..., by Margaret Ashmun, 1931, pp. 58-63 and 178-187.)
13. Cf. *The Merry Wives of Windsor*, II, 2, 3. For "the account of Williams the missionary" see letter 946.
14. At the time of Victoria's accession, a Whig ministry was in power under Melbourne, who tactfully tutored the young Queen on her duties. A mutual affection and regard developed between them, and Victoria deplored the necessary withdrawal of his solicitude and advice when a Tory administration, under Peel, supplanted Melbourne's in 1841.
15. Cf. "The Beggar's Petition," line 1 (*Poems on Several Occasions*, 1769), by Thomas Moss (d. 1808).
16. The Rev. John Harrison, the father of Miss Mitford's correspondent Henrietta Harrison, later Mrs. Acton Tindal.
17. Presumably the pamphlet borrowed by Miss Mitford from Miss Harrison (see SD1171).

---

945. EBB to Benjamin Robert Haydon

50 Wimpole Street.
[mid-] April 1842.[1]

Permit me Sir, to thank you for your kind attention in sending me your interesting & animated treatise on the subject of fresco painting[2]—an attention of which I am abundantly sensible,—though ignorant of practical art & shut out from all especial revelations of *the angel Uriel*.[3] But I can understand the advantage the glorious advantage of a new (old) grand dialect for the use of the Imaginative faculty .. & how, the most imaginative artists being naturally most earnest in aspiration toward such sufficient expression, M[r] Haydon finds himself in heart & voice first in the pursuit. May he find besides success & victory—for the sake of the Houses of Parliament—for the sake of British art, & for the sake of his own fame in its connection.

I count it among my deprivations that I was not able to see him when he did us the kindness of calling here some time ago—but my health unhappily for me, was & is weaker than my will.

It is not possible to close this note without saying that I heard from our dear mutual friend Miss Mitford, my very precious friend Miss

Mitford, a few days since,—& that she speaks with something more [of] hope of the infirm state of her father than her anxieties have suffered her to do for a long while past—

I remain Sir
Your obliged & faithful serv.![
Elizabeth B Barrett.

Publication: EBB-BRH, pp. 1–2.
Manuscript: Wellesley College.

1. This letter falls between 941, in which EBB mentions having just received Haydon's gift, and 947, in which she tells Miss Mitford that she has written to him.
2. Haydon's diary entry for 4 March 1842 recorded that he "Lectured at the Royal Institution on Fresco & made a great hit" (Pope, V, 134). The lecture was published with the title *Thoughts on the Relative Value of Fresco and Oil Painting as Applied to the Architectural Decorations of the Houses of Parliament.*
 (In this note, and some others relating to the series of letters to Haydon, we have drawn on material researched by Dr. Willard Bissell Pope for his *Invisible Friends: The Correspondence of Elizabeth Barrett Barrett and Benjamin Robert Haydon, 1842–1845.* We here record our debt to his scholarship.)
3. A reference to Haydon's first attempt at fresco, on the wall of one of his rooms, seen by Arabel and Septimus Moulton-Barrett, and also by Miss Mitford, in October 1841. (For their reaction to it, see letter 861.)

---

946. EBB TO MARY RUSSELL MITFORD

[London]
[mid-] April– [1842][1]

No, my beloved friend I am not ill—only dull & lower than usual through this simoom of the west, this east wind! It lights up a fire within me & blows, blows at it continually—so that I lose my hold of old occupations & feel flagged & fagged & wearied & wearisome. I did not write on that account. I shall not write much today—for my hand burns till the very pen grows warm & my heart stops unduly & I am *out of sorts* (there's an expressive phrase for me!) altogether.

You will wonder at me for sending you that great stout history of Williams[2]—& in fact whether the quality keeps any measure with the undeniable quantity, I am in absolute ignorance. The book went to you from the library & I never read a page of it, altho' Papa likes it—but it is [*sic*] does not contain the last details of his life .. ending I believe with his last visit to England from whence he went again for ever. He came to England principally for the sake of inducing other missionaries to accompany him out & partake his labor—and at one of those religious meetings which I like better than you do, & was present at myself, .. four or five years ago at Sidmouth,—I saw him & heard his south sea story from his own lips. He was rather a large man belonging in appearance

& manner to the middle classes of society . . rather coarse than otherwise in his *externities*—with a countenance of a certain intelligence & an exceeding benevolence & a smile that made it shine all over. He rather talked than disserted—& his voice was agreeable & his language characteristic & picturesque. Of eloquence or of any high toned enthusiasm there was not a spark or breath: his abundant matter flowing away through the smile on his lips without effort or emotion. I was much interested & could have listened for an hour longer. I remember particularly the description of his farew⟨ell⟩ to the natives—how they followed him down to the shore & stood & hung in groups on the rocks crying in their clear soft musical voices "Come back to us—come back to us—& bring more friends". "This" he said . . turning to the people . . "this was their message to you . . they told me to bring them more friends". And this is what in truth they want—*friends* & not bishops.

His friendship to them he made-manifest[3] more variously than in his religious teaching. He had a remarkable aptitude for mechanics—& he taught them to build houses & ships & to acquire habits of civilization & aspire to its comforts. In return they loved him with a reverence & faithfulness most touching & true—& listening in child-hearted submission to the sound of his religious teaching, "saw his face as the face of an angel"[4] & blessed him to it, as a very messenger of God. It was testified to by others than himself. For himself he spoke of his influence humbly & simply—yet tenderly—as a father might of a child's love. I liked to hear him speak of it, very much. Of course you saw in the papers what the end of all was! how nearly immediately upon his return, passing, as was his custom, from island to island, he touched a strange shore & landed with one or two of his friends while the others remained in the boat. The savages scarcely received his salutation ere they struck the blow. It was all seen from the boat but help was impossible—& they passed away with the story of death. Of death & life at once! God received upwards His own witness to *see* what he had testified!

As to the book which I sent you, I cant answer for the readableness of it—but you may care to read it "with your fingers"[5] or peradventure *thumbs*. Is your story for the Lady-Book,[6] of the South Seas? Do tell me.

How kind of dear Dr Mitford—& what *precious* kindness! And if I in my infinite grumbleness ever sigh in thinking of the long way to the geraniums, why then I think again of the meazles & 'take note'[7] how impossible it w^d be to wish to have you here until all the different forms of infection had been spirited away. Occy has been well some days—& now Alfred is unwell! Alfred!—altho' he had the meazles years ago! But—headache, . . watering of the eyes,—even to an appearance of eruption, are all obvious symptoms, & we cannot resist their evidence.

He is not *ill*—& indeed all the attacks have been as mild as possible—Still I w^d not have you here for the world.

Oh yes—he will be better dearest friend (*your* invalid)—be sure he will .. when this wind has departed. May God bless & revive you my dearest friend!

Miss Anderdon not only left her card with the books but a very kind note for which I must ask you to thank her in my place. Mr Kenyon has not been here very lately—but meeting Papa a few days ago he told him to tell me that Mr Wordsworth was either coming or come. Oh you sh^d be here *now*!

I will write again—perhaps tomorrow—perhaps the next day. An incubus sitteth on my wits today. This wind—which blows *nobody* any good!—[8]

I heard from Mr Horne two days since, & he seems neither windbound nor otherwise limited in spirits—& wont believe either for you or for me that Mr Darley was the Herod of the Chaucer massacre.[9] It was he says, Dr Taylor.

For my own part I have left hold of my obstinacy .. ever since I heard of a writer in the Westminster review insisting to George, upon circuit, that Mr Darley wrote my articles on the Greeks .. being as certain of it from the internal evidence "as that *that* dish is a dish".!![10]

There's poetical justice done upon my opinionativeness! But is there really any feature of likeness in the styles?

Mr Horne begged to be remembered to you, whenever I wrote.

Can you read what I write?

Adieu .. How is the witlow?

        Ever your attached EBB–

Publication: EBB-MRM, I, 396–399.
Manuscript: Wellesley College.

 1. This letter falls between 944, in which EBB promised to send "the account of Williams the missionary," and 949, in which Miss Mitford replies to EBB's query about her story for "the Lady-Book."

 2. Williams had just been memorialized in John Campbell's *The Martyr of Erromanga* (1842), but, as EBB says that the book she is sending does not deal with "the last details of his life," it is probable that she is speaking of Campbell's *The Missionary's Farewell* (1838). For an earlier reference to Williams, see letter 929.

 3. Cf. I Corinthians, 3:13.

 4. Cf. Acts, 6:15.

 5. We take this to be a reference to the reading system developed in 1826 by Louis Braille (1809–52), who was blinded in a childhood accident.

 6. We have not found a story by Miss Mitford published at this time. EBB's description, "Lady-Book," fits a number of publications, of which *The Ladies' Cabinet of Fashion, Music and Romance* or *The Ladies' Magazine and Museum of the Belles Lettres* would seem the most probable recipients.

 7. *Othello*, III, 3, 377.

 8. Cf. the proverbial "It's an ill wind that blows nobody any good."

9. For EBB's earlier remarks regarding "tomahawking" by *The Athenæum*'s critic, see letter 796; for her belief that Darley was responsible, see letter 799. Matthew, 2:16 tells of Herod's massacre of the children.

10. Assumed to be George Stovin Venables (1810–88), a barrister on the Oxford Circuit, where George Moulton-Barrett also was, and a frequent contributor to various journals. EBB makes several references to him in her letters to George, one of them (13 March 1845) querying Venables's authorship of an article in *The Westminster Review*.

947. EBB to Mary Russell Mitford

[London]
April 25. 1842

My beloved friend,

How hot it is & how cold! the east wind threading the sunshine through with its black mournful thread. It is scarcely kind to you, beginning to write to you while my heart beats & stops, beats & stops as it does .. uncertain every other minute whether it shall not stop 'for good & all' as people say, & have done with me. But I feel farther away from you than usual—I have not heard from you—which is the whitlow's fault I know & I have not written to you beyond a letter which went staggering on its road to you stupidly & blindly as this one is likely to do—& I must creep a little nearer again for comfort's sake & love's too. I am not ill, my beloved friend—dont expect a tragedy from such a prologue! only uncomfortable as in duty bound to an east wind of determined volition.

Did you see a notice of M:̲ Darley's 'Plighted Troth'—the new tragedy? I was writing à propos of tragedies—in the Morning Chronicle?[1] It was by M:̲ Fox I understand, & confessed the genius displayed in that drama--a confession which c^{dnt} be wrung from friendship & the Athenæum.[2] *Mr. Darley's* tragedy, the 'Troth' is considered—but then I remember how his brother had one in Macready's hands & conjecture it may be his.[3] If you know do tell me whenever I am happy enough to hear again from you.

And that is'nt to say "Write soon if you suffer from writing or not",—because believe me if you c^d hear my heart speak in a whispering gallery you w^d never hear such a sound! No—do *not* write, until the thumb is quite well!—and may it, oh may it be well soon for both our sakes.

I saw M:̲ Kenyon for a short time the day before yesterday—& M:̲ Wordsworth does not come to London quite as soon as was in his first intention. M:̲ Kenyon told me a story which I must tell you though he told me to tell nobody—because you who live so close to whole groves of roses must be sacred to Harpocrates[4] all over– I rely on your secrecy.

It is what M.[r] Wordsworth says of his daughter's marriage—she having married last year M.[r] Quillinan, *your* M.[r] Quillinan, *my* M.[r] Quillinan the author of the 'Conspirators'. He says "I am satisfied with the marriage, but I really dont see why I should. For my son in law is a Roman catholic—and an Irishman—and a widower—and the father of a family & a beggar".!![5]

M.[r] Kenyon was telling the story one day without names .. as an anonymous gentleman's reasons for satisfaction with an anonymous son-in-law—when somebody cried out to his consternation, "Why that description can only apply to M.[r] Quillinan". Our friend had the presence of mind .. he was "base enough" as he says of himself .. to turn the current of enquiry by asking quietly "Is M.[r] Quillinan an Irishman? I was not aware & ..." Quitte pour la *bassesse*.[6]

Papa & Set & Occy are gone to Strawberry Hill—& they have a lovely looking day for it indeed, & may forget (having harder hearts than I have) the east wind in the golden sunshine. I am fancying too that dear D.[r] Mitford may perhaps get out into the garden today—so that .. with such thoughts .. I am not so badly off after all.

Of course you know Ma[demoiselle] de Monpensier's Memoires.[7] They are most characteristically delightful—yet I am only just now reading them—& the Duc de St Simon's also.[8] I have a sort of Memoir brain fever at the present season– Dont you think so?

Hard thoughts you have of poor Victoria![9] And not unreasonably, seeing the evidence, I do admit—while hoping that there may still be some of another character & beyond our access. She gave two hundred pounds to Leigh Hunt I believe, unsolicited. That was well.

Tell me if you can that D.[r] Mitford's spirits are better, & that you have heard some soothing account of the family of your poor friend.[10]

I think over & feel over all your sorrows & joys my beloved friend as you permit me to look at them!–

God bless you ever & ever . [.] as long .... oh *longer*! God forbid that the divine sh.[d] depend upon the human .. as long I was going to say as I love you—& that may be as long as the other.

Your EBB–

I have written to M.[r] Haydon–

Publication: EBB-MRM, I, 399–401.
Manuscript: Wellesley College.

1. *The Morning Chronicle* of 21 April reviewed the previous evening's performance of *Plighted Troth*, seeing in it "unquestionable marks of power and genius, intermixed with defects of construction and development, that show the hand of an unpractised writer.... We concur, with the audience of last night, in withholding from this drama the meed of unmingled approbation." *The Times* of the same date was less generous, saying that the play "was fairly demolished, and, we must add, most deservedly.... There is no doubt that this piece should never have been produced."

2. *The Athenæum* of 23 April, in a notice much shorter than that in the newspapers, spoke of "the condemnatory opinion unequivocally expressed at the conclusion" and hoped the play would not be performed again, "for the attempt would be unsuccessful, and only provoke hostility."
3. The author was Charles Darley, brother of *The Athenæum*'s contributor. Macready had entertained high hopes for the play, and was surprised by its failure (see letter 931, note 26).
4. In Egyptian and Greek mythology Harpocrates was the god of silence and secrecy. EBB had once before associated him with roses (see letter 692).
5. Edward Quillinan (1791–1851), the author of *The Conspirators* (1841), a widower with two daughters, had taken Dora Wordsworth as his second wife on 11 May 1841.
6. "Escaped through baseness."
7. The *Mémoires* of Anne Marie Louise d'Orléans, Duchess de Montpensier (1627–93) were published in 6 vols. in 1728. She supported unsuccessful efforts to curb the power of Cardinal Mazarin over Louis XIV and consequently spent some years away from court in disgrace.
8. The ideas of Louis de Rouvroy, Duke of Saint-Simon (1675–1755) were surprising for a man of his time and background: greater social equality, availability of education for all, and the abolition of hereditary privileges. His *Mémoires* were published in 7 vols. in 1788–89.
9. Apparently a reference to a change in the supervision of the royal nursery. Early in 1841, on the recommendation of the Archbishop of Canterbury, the Queen had appointed a Mrs. Southey to superintend the four nursery staff, but quickly became dissatisfied with Mrs. Southey's attitude and her inability to control her staff's squabbles. The appointment was offered to one of the Ladies of the Bedchamber, Sarah, Lady Lyttelton, widow of the 3rd Baron Lyttelton; she accepted on 18 April 1842, and Mrs. Southey was discharged. Miss Mitford would, one assumes, have been made aware of these developments through her friendship with Marianne Skerrett, the Queen's Dresser.
10. Doubtless Lady Sidmouth, who died the day after this was written.

---

948. RB TO WILLIAM CHARLES MACREADY

Forster's Rooms. [London]
Tuesday M[g] [26 April 1842][1]

My dear Macready,
I have forborne troubling you about my Play[2] from a conviction that you would do the very best possible for us both in that matter: but as the Season is drawing (I suppose) to an end, and no piece is at present announced in the Bills, it has struck me that in all likelihood the failure of "*Plighted Troth*"[3] may render it inexpedient in your opinion to venture on a fresh Trial this Campaign;[4] and I stand, if I remember rightly, next in succession on your List. I need not say that I would not for the world be the cause of any considerable anxiety to you .. much less of loss in any shape—and that I shall therefore most entirely acquiesce in whatever you consider expedient to be done or left undone. —But, here is my case .. that quiet, generally-intelligible, and (for me!) popular sort of thing, was to have been my *second Number* of Plays[5]—on your being gracious

to it, I delayed issuing any farther attempts for nearly a year—and now have published a very indifferent substitute, whose success will be problematical enough.[6] I have nothing by me at all fit to be substituted for the work in your hands. Will you have the kindness to say if I am mistaken in my conjecture as to your intentions?—and if you will at all object to my withdrawing it, in that case, and printing it at once—the booksellers' season being now in the prime?[7] I write this in haste, and without much consideration, but you will interpret for the best.

Ever yours faithfully,
R Browning.

Publication: NL, pp. 25-26.
Manuscript: Yale University.

1. Dated by RB's reference to the failure of *Plighted Troth*, which had its one and only performance on 20 April; the 26th was the first Tuesday after this.
2. RB had left the manuscript of *A Blot in the 'Scutcheon* with Macready in September 1841; Macready, however, feeling the need for another opinion, had asked Dickens to read it and was still waiting for his comments (see letter 850, note 2).
3. Macready had thought that Darley's play had "rare qualities of intense passion and happy imagination"; when it failed, he wrote in his diary: "I cannot imagine how I could have been so mistaken" (*Macready*, II, 139, 162-165). See letter 947, notes 1 and 2, for excerpts from the reviews.
4. Macready brought the season at Drury Lane to a close on 23 May; a month earlier than intended, RB told Domett in letter 964.
5. After *Pippa Passes*, published in April 1841.
6. Lacking Macready's assessment of *A Blot in the 'Scutcheon*, RB had made *King Victor and King Charles* the second number of *Bells and Pomegranates* (see letter 883, note 6).
7. Perhaps RB hoped this proposal might spur Macready to action, but the text of the play was not published until 11 February 1843, the day of its première at Drury Lane.

---

949. MARY RUSSELL MITFORD TO EBB

Three Mile Cross,
April 27, 1842.

No! my dear love, I am not now about to write on the subject of the South Seas. The first volume of any size that I printed was on the story—which came to me from a friend of the American captain who visited them—of Christian's Colony on Pitcairn's Island. A large edition was sold. Then I published a second edition of a volume of miscellaneous poems; then another volume of narrative poems called "Blanch and the Rival Sisters."[1] All sold well, and might have been reprinted; but I had (of this proof of tolerable taste I am rather proud) the sense to see that they were good for nothing, so that I left off writing for twelve or fifteen years, and should never have committed any more pen-and-ink sins, had not our circumstances become such as to render the very humblest exertions right. My dear mother's health was then almost what my father's is now; only then we were three, so that, except by staying at home, I was not so absolutely chained as I am now.

Well, perhaps if I could be all the time I covet, among the sweet flowers and the fresh grass, I should not enjoy as I do the brief intervals into which I do contrive to concentrate so much childish felicity. Who is it that talks of "the cowslip vales of England?"[2] is it you, my beloved? The words are most true and most dear. Oh! how I love those meadows, yellow with cowslips and primroses; those winding brooks, or rather *that* winding brook, golden with the water ranunculus; those Silchester coppices, clothed with wood-sorrel, wood-anemone, wild hyacinth, and primroses in clusters as large as the table at which I write! I do not love musk—almost the only odour called sweet that I do not love; yet coming this evening on the night-scented odora with its beautiful green cups, I almost loved the scent for the form on which it grew. But the cowslips, the wild hyacinths, the primroses, the violet—oh, what scent may match with theirs? I try to like the garden, but my heart is in the fields and woods. I have been in the meadows to-night—I ran away, leaving my father asleep—I could not help it. And oh! what a three hours of enjoyment we had, Flush, and the puppies, and I! I myself, I verily believe, the youngest-hearted of all. Then I have been to Silchester too. My father went there; and I got out and ran round the walls and coppices one way, as he drove the other.[3] How grateful I am to that great gracious Providence who makes the most intense enjoyment the cheapest and the commonest! I do love the woods and fields! Oh! surely all the stars under the sun, even if they were brighter than those earthly stars ever seem to me, could not compare with the green grass and the sweet flowers of this delicious season!

I mistrust the feeling of poetry of all those who consent to pass the spring amongst brick walls, when they might come and saunter amongst lanes and coppices. To live in the country is, in my mind, to bring the poetry of Nature home to the eyes and the heart. And how can those who do love the country talk of autumn as rivalling the beauty of spring? Only look at the texture of the young leaves; see the sap mounting into the transparent twigs as you stand under an oak; feel the delicious buds; inhale the fragrance of bough and herb, of leaf and flower; listen to the birds and the happy insects; feel the fresh balmy air. This is a rhapsody; but I have no one to whom to talk, for if I mention it to my father, he talks of "my killing myself," as if that which is balm and renovation were poison and suicide.

Heaven bless you, my most precious! My father's love.
Ever most faithfully your own,
M. R. Mitford.

Text: L'Estrange (2), III, 146-148.

1. Miss Mitford's first publication was *Poems* (1810), with a second edition in 1811, in which year she also published *Christina, the Maid of the South Seas.* The next work she mentions is not listed in the catalogue of the British Library or in *The English Catalogue of Books*; *DNB* gives its title as *Blanch of Castile* (1812).
2. We have not located the source of this quotation.
3. Silchester, about 6 miles S.W. of Three Mile Cross, was the site of the Roman town of Calleva Atrebatum; the walls, over a mile in circumference, still stand.

---

950. ALFRED DOMETT TO RB

[London]
Saturday [*Docket:* 30 April 1842]

Dear Browning-

I return your books with many thanks- I need not assure you of my love nor that my wishes for all good for you will be as lasting as life. God bless you for ever- *Write* (to *the world*)—& to me at New Zealand.[1] Say goodbye for me to your family- I have no time to call-

Yrs ever
Alfred Domett

Docket, in RB's hand: (April 30, 1842).
Publication: None traced.
Manuscript: Alexander H. Turnbull Library.

1. Domett was emigrating to New Zealand, where he had bought land and where his friend and kinsman, William Curling Young, was already established. E.A. Horsman, in his introduction to *The Diary of Alfred Domett* (1953), states that Domett set sail on 30 April aboard the S.S. *Sir Charles Forbes.*

---

951. MARY RUSSELL MITFORD TO EBB

Three Mile Cross,
April [?30], [1842][1]

How startling coincidences are! Sometimes how painful! Just as I had sent to you the little jar of honey from Hymettus,[2] brought from thence by Sir Robert Inglis,[3] and sent to me by a dear old friend, Lady Sidmouth, two letters arrived from her at the same time, of which, that which bore the latest date, anticipated with delightful cheerfulness our speedy meeting; and, not five minutes after dispatching that trifling token of honor to the muse, I found, in reading the paper to my father, that poor Lady Sidmouth was dead![4] Imagine the shock! She was, you know, daughter of Lord Stowell,[5] niece of Lord Eldon,[6] and wife of Lord Sidmouth, all remarkable men in themselves, and connected with the most memorable personages of the last half-century. And fully worthy was she of such association.

I have seldom known any one more thoroughly awake and alive to all that was best worth knowing. She had an enlightened curiosity, a love of natural history, of antiquities, of literature, of art; was herself full of talent, intelligence, and gayety, and had a quick and peculiar humor; the more surprising as her physical sufferings were great and constant. For many years she had suffered under a spine complaint—suffered to such an extent that, for very many years, instead of being (as she used to be) dragged between two strong supporters round my garden, she had been carried in the arms of an old servant into the greenhouse, and there deposited until her visit was over. In the fine season she used to pass many hours of every day in her carriage or in a garden chair; but frequently her sufferings were so severe that the perspiration would pour down her face from pain, and for days and weeks together she remained unable to see her favorite friends. She had submitted to that tremendous operation, the actual cutting down either side of the spinal column (I forget the technical phrase), but without any benefit; and had tried Dr. Jephson's system[7] equally without success. Still, such was her sweetness, that Lord Sidmouth told me that some sculptor (I think Behnes)[8] earnestly wished to be allowed to model her face for the expression, which, as he said, was more full of lively sweetness than any he ever saw. She was twenty-seven years younger than the husband who now has to mourn her loss.

The first thing she did when coming into her father's large fortune was to portion her two step-daughters, each of whom had been for many years engaged to a man too poor to marry a poor lord's daughter.[9] All her dealings about money were munificent in themselves and most graceful in the manner. She gave to the Berkshire Hospital six acres of land (valued at a thousand pounds an acre for building leases), standing on the finest situation of the outskirts of Reading, and told every body that it was Lord Sidmouth's gift! And in the same way she built a new market cross in his name in the town of Devizes, of which he is high steward.

I have lost a most kind and affectionate friend, one of the very many of whom the last two or three years have deprived me. Lord Sidmouth retains his unmarried daughter, who officiated as his private secretary when he was prime minister, and is a very cultivated and excellent person;

but not to me what Lady S. was. We, indeed, had many mutual ties. Her father, like mine, was of Northumberland; and we had connections and friends near Newcastle—her cousins married to cousins of mine. The most amiable of these—a young and lovely girl of remarkable talent—died last autumn.[10]

Every body that loves me does die! Oh! take care of yourself, my very dearest! Did I tell you that her father, Lord Stowell (the Sir William Scott of Dr. Johnson's time), died at a very advanced age in a state worse than idiotcy? The old servants have told me that his expressions were awful. That must have been a great grief. Her only brother, too, killed himself by drinking.[11] At the same time that Lord Stowell was wearing out the dregs of life so painfully four miles on one side of us, Sir Henry Russell, the only other survivor of the "Literary Club," was lingering in equal imbecility four miles on the other; a remarkable and humbling fact to the pride of intellect.[12]

At Stowell (poor Lady Sidmouth's estate)[13] is a hazel coppice of such extent that all the fairs of the south of England are supplied from it with cob-nuts—the favorite present of a country lad to his sweetheart. Gypsies and other wanderers pitch their tents around it in the nutting season; and for three weeks the coppice is as populous as a vineyard or a hop-garden in their gathering-time. Poor dear Lady Sidmouth! how fond she was of distributing little bags of her own nuts, purchased from the licensed plunderers! You would have liked Lady Sidmouth.⟨★★★⟩

Text: L'Estrange (2), III, 113–116 (as 20 April 1841).

1. This letter is dated by the reference to Lady Sidmouth's death, announced in *The Times* of 28 April 1842. L'Estrange's dating of 20 April 1841 obviously resulted from a misreading of Miss Mitford's handwriting.

2. A mountain, about two miles from Athens, famous for its bees and excellent honey.

3. Robert Harry Inglis (1786–1855), one-time private secretary to Lord Sidmouth, M.P. for Oxford University from 1829 until his retirement from political life in 1854, was an opponent of parliamentary reform and of all attempts to ease the religious and civil disabilities still suffered by Roman Catholics and Jews.

4. Marianne, Lady Sidmouth had died at Richmond on 26 April; as stated above, the notice of her death was in *The Times* of 28 April. She had married Thomas Townsend in 1809 and, after his death, in 1823 became the second wife of Henry Addington, 1st Viscount Sidmouth (1757–1844), whose first wife, Ursula Mary (*née* Hammond) had died in 1811. He had been Prime Minister (1801–04) and Home Secretary (1812–22).

5. William Scott, 1st Baron Stowell (1745–1836), an intimate friend of Dr. Johnson, had been a lecturer in ancient history at Oxford, but, after inheriting his father's estate, resigned his tutorship in 1777 and took up law, becoming in 1782 Advocate-General for the Office of Lord High Admiral. He entered Parliament in 1790, and, like his friend Inglis, was a steady opponent of reform and the relaxation of restrictions on Catholics. At his death, his daughter, Lady Sidmouth, inherited property producing £12,000 per annum, as well as considerable personal effects.

6. John Scott, 1st Earl of Eldon (1751–1838), was the younger brother of Lord Stowell. He had been successively Solicitor-General, Attorney-General, Lord Chief Justice of the Court of Common Pleas and Lord Chancellor.

7. Henry Jephson (1798–1878) practised medicine in Leamington Spa; we have not been able to establish the nature of his system.
8. William Behnes (d. 1864) achieved high repute as an artist and sculptor, making a bust of Macready, among others.
9. Her step-daughters, Charlotte and Henrietta Addington, were both thus enabled to marry in 1838, one to a clergyman, the other to an army officer.
10. Not identified.
11. William Scott had died in November 1835, his death leaving Lady Sidmouth as inheritrix. Because of Lord Stowell's mental deterioration, he was never aware of his son's death.
12. Henry Russell (1751–1836), of Swallowfield Park, near Three Mile Cross, had been Chief Justice of the Bengal Supreme Court. He died ten days before Lord Stowell. The Literary Club, founded in 1764 by Dr. Johnson and Sir Joshua Reynolds, met regularly for conversation; other members included Edmund Burke, Edward Gibbon and Oliver Goldsmith.
13. Stowell Park, in Gloucestershire, had been purchased from Lord Chedworth, although Lord Stowell lived principally at Earley Court, near Reading, and, as noted above, Lady Sidmouth died in Richmond.

---

952. RB TO EUPHRASIA FANNY HAWORTH

New Cross, Hatcham, Surrey
Sat^y M^g_e [May 1842][1]

Now, was *ever* such a strong-head such a wrong head? My dear friend, as I am to be believed, I read your note twice before I found out its drift—having clean forgotten all about the reading-proceeding, and supposing you had misunderstood some part of the Moxon-disquisition. All I meant, as I thought I had said, was that my recitation of my own verses is too bad for any deliberate purpose, & that, if you were expecting even a little, you would be sadly disappointed: what I meant to try, would have done tolerably well "next morning"—do you see? Do you see? *And* do you NOT see, that if you seriously so please, I will run over now, then, howsoever, whensoever, and give you enough & over that! Do you but get a pretty girl (mind!)—and a low reading table—but the girl's prettiness matters most.

When I wrote, (it is but just to say) I was in real sorrow of heart,—for my dear friend Alfred Domett, God bless him, left that night (was it not Saturday?)—for New Zealand– Now, he, to my knowledge, presented himself to Moxon with the poem I send you,—and not even his earnest handsome face (the proffered Amount-in-full-of Expenses, I knew would not avail—but—) not his sincere voice & gentlemanly bearing, could tempt Moxon to look at a line of it. So, he printed it where you see[2] .. they would print Montgomery's execrabilities.[3] And the poem fell dead from the press—that poor creature Wilson, who had paralleled Domett with Milton in his customary bleating-speech, and praised away at a mad rate so long as his poems were contributions to Blackwood[4]—never said a little sneaking Scotch word about *this*! —I told D. how Moxon would act—and as simple telling succeeded so indifferently with him, I wanted really to spare you, (by telling it you a little more explicitly, a mortification—as there is no doubt it would be. I shall now tell you (*au secret*) that the MOST bepraised Poetess of that Time, met with the same rebuff just after—thro' a real friend's mediation) too!

Write and say your favour rests again on

Yours ever,
RB.

The copy is a proof sheet—pray keep it safely.

Publication: NL, pp. 26–27.
Manuscript: Yale University.

1. Dated by the reference to Domett's recent departure (see letter 950, note 1).
2. Domett's poem, *Venice*, was published by Saunders & Otley in 1839 (see *Reconstruction*, A810 and 811).
3. Robert Montgomery (1807–55), author and preacher, who combined "an unfortunate facility in florid versification" with "no genuinely poetic gift"; Macaulay had described him as a writer of "detestable verses on religious subjects" (*DNB*). It was Saunders & Otley who had printed *Pauline*, at the expense of RB's aunt; the implication is that they would print whatever the author would pay for.
4. An unsigned article entitled "Our Two Vases," in *Blackwood's Edinburgh Magazine* (April 1837, pp. 429–448), included two poems by Domett, introduced by this comment: "Sit close, and we shall sing thee a song—by—by ALFRED DOMETT—a new name to our old ears—but he has the prime virtue of a song-writer—a *heart*." Domett later made several contributions to *Blackwood's* (see, for example, the issues of May 1837 and March 1839).

---

953. WILLIAM CHARLES MACREADY, JR.[1] TO RB

[London]
[May 1842][2]

My dear M.[r] Browning

I was very much obliged to you, for your kind letter. I liked exceedingly the Cardinal and the dog.[3] I have tried to illustrate the poem, and I hope that you will like my attempt.[4] I cannot go to school because my cough is so bad.

I remain your affectionate friend

W. C. Macready.

Publication: BN, No. 3 (Fall, 1969), p. 34 (in facsimile).
Manuscript: Armstrong Browning Library.

1. "Willie" (1832–71) was the Macreadys' eldest son.
2. Based on RB's own statement (see below) this letter preceded no. 961.
3. This letter and no. 961 were preserved together in a single envelope, which also included the following note, made by Sarianna Browning after RB's death: "In May, 1842, Macready's eldest little boy was confined to the house by a cough. To amuse him, Robert wrote two poems which the child was to illustrate—'Crescentius, the pope's Legate' and the 'Pied Piper'– At first, there was no thought of publishing them, but I copied the Pied Piper and showed it to Alfred Domett who was so much pleased with it that he persuaded Robert to include it in the forthcoming number of Bells and Pomegranates– 'Crescentius', he did not publish till the last, in Asolando– These are the boy's illustrations." Both Mrs. Orr (p. 122) and DeVane (pp. 127 and 534) give this date for composition.

RB himself, in a letter to Furnivall on 1 October 1881, also states that both poems were specifically written for Willie, "The Cardinal and the Dog" being first. However, that cannot be true, as his draft of this poem, in the margins of p. 611 of his copy of Nathaniel Wanley's *The Wonders of the Little World* (now in the editors' possession) is dated 27 February 1841, well before the illness which is supposed to have prompted composition; RB's statement—or lapse of memory—is all the more surprising as he offers to send Furnivall a copy of the poem "when I can transcribe it from the page of the old book it remains upon." "The Cardinal and the Dog" was not published until 1889, when it was included in *Asolando*; the text then contained significant changes from an undated facsimile reproduction, in RB, Sr.'s hand, printed in *The Bookman*, May 1912, pp. 68–69, which itself differed slightly from RB's original draft (see *Reconstruction*, E45 and J68).

4. Willie's three drawings are now at ABL (see *Reconstruction*, H89). They are reproduced facing page 331.

954. EBB TO MARY RUSSELL MITFORD

[London]
May 2—1842.

Your honey reached my hands late yesterday evening my beloved friend, yet too early for my will. It was so kind of you to think of making that transfer yet so wrong altogether, that my 'no' was ready to fly to you when the haste of your goodness intercepted the interception. What shall I say now? Nothing but an impotent 'thank you'? 'Sweets *from* the sweet'[1] reverse equally the quotation & the proprieties by sending away Hymettus honey from YOU to another![2] How kind—how wrong! How obliged I am, .. how ashamed! Do you not know how Ælian[3] writeth that the flies do not dare for their unworthiness to taste the honey from Hymettus? And your ..

"Little fly,
Drink with me & drink as I'['][4]

would rally (Raleigh)[5] me out of the modest traditions of his 'Natural history.' Must it be so really?——

I was sorry that K's sister had the trouble of bringing the precious deposit here just at the time when Crow was out at chapel. It was sunday

My dear Mr Browning
　　I was very much obliged to you, for your kind letter. I liked exceedingly the Cardinal and the dog. I have tried to illustrate the poem, and I hope that you will like my attempt. I cannot go to school because my cough is so bad. —
　　　I remain your affectionate friend
　　　　W. C. Macready.

When rising to refresh himself / He saw a monstrous sight

His servants in the anteroom / Commanded every one

To drive away the dog / That leaped on his bedside

"The Cardinal and the Dog." Pencil sketches by Willie Macready.

evening:—and the housemaid who gave me the parcel could not persuade the messenger to go to the housekeeper's room.! I am sure Crow would have been glad to make the acquaintance of a sister of your K–

I waited & would not write on saturday because I expected Mr Kenyon in the afternoon & he did'nt come until Sunday .. & after all you will hear more satisfactorily of him from himself (he is talking of writing to you immediately) than you can do from me. On friday he sent me & lent me Mr Reade's new poem 'A Record of the Pyramids',[6] & was so considerate as to stand between the author & myself & save me from the present of a copy which he did me the honor of meditating, & the very serious *consequences* either to my veracity or his vanity. The *vanity* by the way w^d have suffered—if it had not taken shelter under the innocuousness generally of such a thing as an opinion of mine—since I hold fast my single point of supremacy over Walter Scott, & am resolute to speak what seems to me the truth with whatever painfulness in the utterance.[7] As to the 'Record' I am glorying you see in the security won for me. *You* will be sure to have the new poem—the new Prometheus!! a Prometheus taken out of his cloud,[8]—out of the sphere of his poetry & exhibited in a Parliamentary sort of coat & waiscoat, as a type of Sir Robert Peel!! to whom the work is dedicated. Do explain to Mrs Niven this satisfactory solution of the great riddle. And then, the preface, the preface!! He takes high ground for Poetry abstractedly, which of course is to be applauded, but when he ends all by saying 'Here is my throne' it spoils all too![9] Mr Kenyon describes his personal sensitiveness & selfassurance as something wonderful—as, in fact, they appear in his books. *Can* he be safe in unconsciousness of the plagiarisms wherewith he has girded up his loins?–[10] It is a phenomenon in my eyes.

His friends are said to say that he has spent fifteen hundred pounds in printing & advertizing poems .. which are to be read by Prince Posterity![11]

He *loves* poetry too. It is hard that he sh^d not be praised for *loving* poetry—& if he would .. if he could .. but throw off this consciousness of other poets & determine to be something else than their shadow on the wall, he might write .. not greatly I think .. but worthily. In the meantime this new Prometheus is very much past bearing. It is a desecration—a blasphemy!–[12]

Mr Kenyon talks of going in June to Torquay for a fortnight, & then to Scotland—provided he does not go to Vienna instead of either. In the latter case it will be for 'a run'—to be accomplished at comet-pace, in eight weeks.

He was telling me of Mr Tennyson—that he is tall, pale, with black hair—looking 'a mild brigand'—for the rest, uncomfortably shy .. quite without assumption & pleasing in many ways. A new book of poems—true poems be sure—we are to have from him soon.[13]

Think where George dined on saturday! At M[r] Serje[t] Talfourd's. It was a law dinner . . & no lions!

Alfred . . who had the meazles last, was pursued to the death almost, with agony in the face, & is only just emancipated from bed & bedroom— while my poor Arabel has suffered too from the common plague of swelled faces & rheumatic pains in the shoulders. She goes out today the first time for a week. My heart waxes better & worse as the wind blows,—& forced me to take wine last night, in the night, as an alternative to fainting, altho' it beat more regularly for some previous days . . and altho' M[r] Kenyon praised the improvement he heard in my voice only yesterday. Today, he might praise me again.

Thank you . . how can I enough? for your delightful letter—the 'sweet south'[14] blowing *from* a bank of violets, being less fragrant! And you wished me with you, did you my dearest kindest friend in that walk?[15] But I walked it all over again in your footsteps, by the spell you sent me. Your delightful letter smelt of the fields—the stream ran in it—& the garden-wind blew!– For me, I leapt & walked—as if indeed I were walking with you.

Tell me, are you out in the garden room yet? Is dear D[r] Mitford there? I must write more another day.

Ever your EBB–

What a scribble! My hand does shake so!–

Publication: EBB-MRM, I, 401–404.
Manuscript: Folger Shakespeare Library and Wellesley College.

1. Cf. *Hamlet*, V, 1, 243.
2. Miss Mitford mentioned sending the honey in letter 951.
3. Claudius Ælianus (ca. 170–235), known as Meliglossus ("honey-tongued"), was the author of *De natura animalium*, a collection of anecdotes of animal life.
4. William Oldys (1696–1761), "On a Fly Drinking Out of a Cup of Ale" (first published anonymously in *The Scarborough Miscellany*, 1732). EBB misquotes the first two lines of the poem.
5. Oldys edited the 1736 edition of Raleigh's *History of the World*, prefacing it with a 282-page "Life of the Author"; hence EBB's pun.
6. *A Record of the Pyramids: A Drama, in Ten Scenes*, by John Edmund Reade (1842).
7. A reference to Scott's volte-face regarding Miss Seward's poetry (see letter 606, note 6).
8. Reade's preface commences by referring to his "idea of abstracting the character of Prometheus from the grand ideal in which he lived . . . and bringing him within the pale of humanity . . . labouring for the welfare of his fellow-men . . . sharing their common sympathies and oppressions."
9. Reade devotes a number of paragraphs of his preface to an expression of his view of the duties of a poet, charging him to "fulfil the impulses impregnated in him from the Ineffable Being. His, above all others, is a holy mission . . . to teach to each man

... that he is 'a little lower than the Angels;' ... He is the Priest of Nature, as of Humanity."

10. I Kings, 18:46. Reade's persistent plagiarism was the subject of comment by EBB in letters 643 and 687.

11. EBB is perhaps making an oblique reference to Peel, to whom Reade had addressed the fulsome dedication of his book; Prince Posterity was the mythical recipient of Swift's dedication of *A Tale of a Tub* (1704).

12. EBB's view is shared by the author of a savage review in *Blackwood's Edinburgh Magazine* (July 1842, pp. 113–119), who dismissed the work as "eight or nine thousand verses strung like empty birds' eggs" and again made reference to Reade's plagiarism. EBB later identified the author as Landor (see letter of 14 September 1842 to Miss Mitford).

13. A two-volume edition of Tennyson's poems was published later in the month and was immediately sent to EBB by Kenyon (see letter 958).

14. See letter 668, note 3.

15. i.e., the visit to Silchester, described in letter 949.

955. MARY RUSSELL MITFORD TO EBB

Three Mile Cross,
May 4, 1842.

Charlotte Smith's works, with all their faults, have yet a love of external nature, and a power of describing it, which I never take a spring walk without feeling.[1] Only yesterday I strolled round the park-like paddock of an old place in our neighbourhood—an old neglected ride, overgrown with moss, and grass, and primroses, and wild strawberries—overshadowed by horse-chestnuts, and lilacs, and huge firs, and roses, and sweet-briar, shot up to the height of forest trees. Exquisitely beautiful was that wild, rude walk, terminating in a decayed carthouse, covered with ivy; and, oh! so like some of her descriptions of scenery! My mother knew her when her husband[2] was sheriff of Hampshire; and she lived in a place (about four miles from the little town of Alresford, where I was born) where the scenery and the story of the "Old Manor House"[3] may still be traced. There was a true feeling of nature about Charlotte Smith.

Of the three—Wordsworth, Southey, Coleridge—how very much the greater poet Coleridge seems to me! Poor Cowper![4] I never doubted his insanity, knowing as I did his kinswoman, whose melancholy tale I must have told you (Mrs. Frances Hill, sister to the Eve Hill of the letters, and his first cousin) whose madness was always said to be hereditary. There could be no question of the taint in the blood. That the hands into which he fell were not likely to administer the best remedies, even with the best and purest motives, there can be as little doubt. So you have actually seen and known one who believed in that melancholy tenet![5]

I always held the imputation to be untrue: it seemed to be so impossible that any one mind could at once believe *that* and the mediation.

Yours ever,
M.R.M.

Text: L'Estrange (2), III, 148–149.

   1. Charlotte Smith (*née* Turner, 1749–1806) was a popular and prolific poetess and novelist. Her earliest publication was *Elegiac Sonnets and Other Essays* (1784), followed in 1785 by a translation of *Manon Lescaut.* Her first novel, *Emmeline, or the Orphan of the Castle*, appeared in 1788 and met with great success.
   2. In 1765, she had entered into an arranged marriage with Benjamin Smith (d. 1806), the son of a director of the East India Company. His extravagance and enthusiasm for impractical schemes caused the couple to fall into debt, for which both were imprisoned for seven months in 1782.
   3. *The Old Manor House*, held by Scott to be Mrs. Smith's best work, was published in four volumes in 1793.
   4. Miss Mitford is responding to EBB's comments about Cowper in letter 941.
   5. i.e., the reprobative doctrine mentioned by EBB in letter 941.

---

956. Mary Russell Mitford to EBB

Three Mile Cross,
May 5, 1842.

Mr. Kenyon's kind letter, my beloved love, arrived just soon enough to be answered—that is to say, to have a very long postscript appended to a very brief letter. Some friends of his have come to Silchester, and I shall go to see them to-morrow or next day. Oh, that you could be of the party! Well, in spite of the manner in which the winds have affected *that dear heart*,[1] I will hope that the hour may come when we shall see that lovely scene together. The poem on Silchester[2] first made Mr. Kenyon and me friends, and that friendship was the remote cause of one to me still more precious—there is one reason for loving Silchester. But the scene is itself so beautiful! Fancy a hundred acres of the highest land in the south of England, the crown of a ridge of hills, mostly covered with the richest woodland, enclosed by a wall some twenty feet high, and nearly twenty feet thick,[3] surmounted by huge pollards, high timber-trees, hedgerow shrubs (such, for instance, as fine old thorns, maple-bushes, &c.), with enormous masses of ivy, and wild service trees, and long, pendent shoots of the briar-rose hanging down the old grey, cliff-like walls. Everywhere the ground at the foot of these walls sinks down into a narrow fosse at the depth of some hundred feet, rising again on the opposite side—some part of this outer ditch being rich meadow-land— other portions in the most beautiful coppice—joining again to the other copses—on the most beautiful ascents and declivities. Nothing was ever so exquisitely mantled about. Just at one of the gates of the old city, a huge crag clothed with ivy and crowned with magnificent timber-trees, stands the pretty country church; adjoining to that an old rustic farm-house; and at a little distance, in a magnificent grove of oak-trees, the amphitheatre, with its five rows of seats still to be traced—huge elms growing on the top and sides, and the large oval space in the bottom perfectly clear, a fine level arena of smooth and verdant turf. On one side of the amphitheatre is a piece of water, dark as a mirror; another deep pool reflects the hoary walls and some noble oak-trees; and on the opposite side of the city the parsonage, a beautiful house, very large for a pastoral mansion, with its pretty grounds, sweeps away into the woodland scenery of the south side of the walls. A short avenue leads to the fine, open, breezy common, golden with furze and broom, and from that commodious upland you look down upon the hundreds, ay, thousands, of acres of the most wild and exquisite sylvan scenery. Pamber Forest is spread beneath your feet; on one side the dark fir-plantations of Mortimer Common rise over a clear little lake with its decoy and its millions of wildfowl—on the other, High Clere; the Beacon hills stretch away over the wild district of North Hampshire, where Mr. Chute's curious old place The Vine (*vide* Horace Walpole),[4] and the still more remarkable moated grange of Bear[5] carry back the eye and the fancy to the days of Clarissa, and of manners and scenery more primitive still. Oh, how I should love to stand with you upon Silchester Common! Its floral beauty I have endeavoured to describe to you in my scrawl of last night—but the purity of the air, the fragrance of the budding woods, the enormous fir-plantations, the wide expanse of richly-scented, blossomed gorse, the acres of wild hyacinth and of lilies of the valley, defy all description. It must be felt. Oh, that we were there together! I so love Silchester—always loved it. Always a drive to Silchester, or ramble through the woods, was to me joy and delight, health, freedom, and happiness; and since I have learnt to think of it as a link in the chain of our friendship, I have loved it more and more. Surely a wish so ardent will one day realise itself. We shall stand together in that lily coppice, where terrace hangs over terrace crossed with its thousand trees, carpeted with its myriad flowers, vocal with the blackbird and the nightingale. Surely, surely, we shall some day go together to Silchester. You will think, my dearest, that I rave. But so well do all here know my passion for the place, that, when very ill, my poor father years ago has often said, 'We will go to-morrow to Silchester,' and that was a never-failing specific. Even now *he* goes there. It is a strange feeling that—for he himself has not my enthusiasm for the spots, and *now* thinks, persuades himself that it tires me, but it is a sort of imitation. He recollects my love for it, my persuasion of the good that it did always effect upon me (the benefit resulting partly from the delicious purity of the air, partly from the love), and now without the love, he, from pure imitation, persuades himself that what used to be good for me will be good for him, so (although too far, as I fairly tell him) he goes.

You are far too good, my most dearest, in what you say of my poor letters. They come from my heart, and therefore go to yours—but that is all their merit—merit to us only—to the lover and the loved. Was there enough of the honey to taste? It seemed so light that it might be all but empty. From two other 'tastes' of the same 'honouring gift' (and who should have it, if not you?) it seemed to me strongly myrtle-flavoured—tasting exactly like the scent of a bruised myrtle leaf. The most delicious honey that I ever met with came from the orange groves of Sicily, and had the exact flavour of that delicious perfume. Would the myrtle taste keep away the flies, or was it an exaggeration?[6]

Upon reading over my wretched scrawl I see that, with my usual curious infelicity,[7] I have contrived to make it appear that the one hundred acres within the walls of Silchester are partly woodland—whereas *they* are clear, open fields. It is the hills and declivities around that seem hewn out of some vast forest. One sweet village close by (Mortimer West End) goes straggling down one steep hill and up another—partly coppice, partly meadow, partly field—a clear bubbling brook crossing the road at the bottom, and the road itself winding and twisting, so as to give it at every step a fresh landscape. Oh, the beautiful cottages of that West End! In many of them piles of long, straight poles, and neatly arranged staves are leaning against the ends of the dwellings, giving token of the sylvan trade of the inhabitants! But for the distance from Mr. May, I should long since have coaxed my father into migrating as far towards Silchester as Mortimer End West. Only how K―― would dispense with the streets and shops of Reading I can't tell. She is most thankful for your kind and condescending notice of her sister, who lives as lady's maid with the Misses Pepys—Sir William Pepys' sisters—in Bryanston Square.[8] I have a good opinion of their sense, for I find that they leave their town house in May (not letting it, but shutting it up), and resort to their country seat to stay the fine season in the pretty scenery of Kent.[9]

Did you find the leaf of the *humea elegans* between two leaves of Sir William's book?[10] Did you like the scent? It is the fashion, and the plant came to me from Strathfieldsaye; the gardener there and I having a traffic in flowers. In days of yore I used to get books from the Strathfieldsaye library—Lord Rivers[11] and my father being great friends and fellow coursers. He was a man of taste, and from him I borrowed more volumes than I can recollect of French memoirs. They are delightfully amusing. I must go over them again when I have time, not from Strathfieldsaye, I doubt if the great Duke's library be half as well furnished as was that of his predecessor, who had a noble collection of the best books—but from Sir Henry Russell, whose wife, a Frenchwoman,[12] has caused her accomplished husband to add the literature of her native country to his own.

Heaven bless you! I am tired to death, and I presume that my sleepy letter bears sufficient marks of my condition—thrice happy if it may come in aid of opium, and bring sleep to your eyelids.

. . . .

Once again heaven bless you, my most dearest! My father sends his kindest love.

Your faithful,
M. R. Mitford.

P.S.—How is your Flushie? Mine becomes every day more and more beautiful, and more and more endearing. His little daughter Rose is the very moral of him, and another daughter (a puppy of four months old, your Flushie's half-sister) is so much admired in Reading that she has already been stolen four times—a tribute to her merit which might be dispensed with—and her master, having upon every occasion offered ten pounds reward, it seems likely enough that she will be stolen four times more. They are a beautiful race, and that is the truth of it.

Text: L'Estrange (1), II, 66-72.

1. The italicized words were "inserted conjecturally" by L'Estrange.
2. Not traced.
3. The wall of the Roman city of Calleva Atrebatum (see letter 949, note 3).
4. In March 1793, Walpole sent a description of The Vyne to John Cowslade, tracing its history from Lord Sandys, Lord Chancellor to Henry VIII, to its acquisition by Chaloner Chute, Speaker of the House of Commons in Cromwell's Parliament, and its descent to Walpole's friend William John Chute (see *Horace Walpole's Correspondence*, ed. W.S. Lewis, 1973, 35, 641-642). The house is now owned by the National Trust.
5. Not identified; no "moated grange of Bear" is listed in *Moated Houses of England*, by R. Thurston Hopkins (1935), or in the several guides to Hampshire architecture we consulted.
6. See the first paragraph of letter 954.
7. A reversal of Petronius Arbiter's "curiosa felicitas" (*Satyricon*, 118, 10).
8. Sir William Weller Pepys (1778-1845), brother of the 1st Earl of Cottenham, lived with his unmarried sisters Maria Elizabeth (d. 1850) and Anne Louisa (d. 1876) at 36 Bryanston Square.
9. *Robson's Royal Court Guide for 1840* lists Sir William's country seat as Tanbridge Court, Godstone; this is in Surrey, not Kent.
10. Presumably a book belonging to Sir William, as we have found no evidence that he himself was an author.
11. George Pitt, 2nd Baron Rivers (1751-1828) had inherited Strathfieldsaye; in 1817, the estate was purchased by Parliament for £263,000 and presented to Wellington.
12. In 1816, Sir Henry Russell (1783-1852), of Swallowfield, had taken as his second wife Marie Clotilde (d. 1872), the daughter of the Seigneur de la Motte et de la Fontaine.

957. EBB TO MARY RUSSELL MITFORD

[London]
Saturday– [7 May 1842][1]

Thank you my beloved friend for the two bunches of pleasure .. nosegays of delight .. your two letters. I get your letters in time for breakfast, & have a fashion (*doing* all my eatings & drinkings by myself) of reading & taking coffee .. that is, now sipping of the coffee & now of the nectar.

You frighten me by suggesting the possibility of Flushes being lost.[2] And my Flushie never contemplating such a thing, is very naughtily fond of running away from his two-footed companions, sometimes to the end of a street & back again, just for the pleasure I do believe, of achieving something very naughty. Flushie has that natural taste in him. He is, as Crow says, "just like a spoilt child", & rejoices in his own way. Tell him to go to the chair—& altho' he likes the chair in question very well under other circumstances, .. he w^d rather,—being commanded,—lie down on the floor ten times over– Let him fancy that he is wished to be out of the way, .. instantly he siezes upon the opportunity to squeeze himself close to you with his head upon your shoulder. Ask him to eat his dinner & he wont touch it! or offer him bread & butter & buttered muffin or anything of the sort, & he recoils, shuts his mouth quite close, & looks another way. Pretend to submit to the coquetterie, .. in two minutes, the little paw will be patting on your arm, the first of a series of coaxings—"he will be glad to have the muffin now, if you .. *dont* please"–

So you see Flushie is pretty well altho' I dont say,—have not said lately,—much about him. He is lying in his eternal place on my bed, close beside me now,—& when the time comes (which it will in half an hour) for me to go to the sofa, he will leap up full of vivacity to superintend my toilette, to kiss both my feet before I put on my shoes, & to sieze the moment of my reaching the sofa for kissing face & hands too with an obvious eagerness of congratulation, & instantly afterwards to throw himself quite *into* my arms as a settlement until one of us is tired .... I dont say which.– I mean every respect to Flushie, & in fact if I did'nt, he understands the readiest manner of enforcing it. But it is strange & dear of him—is it not?—that he sh^d without beck or word, move from the bed to the sofa the moment I move, & back again with the same exactness. Even when he was ill,[3] & unwilling to stir otherwise, he performed that migration of his own accord. I love him—dear little Flushie—as far as dog-love can go—& that is farther than I supposed possible before I had knowledge of him.

For the rest, .. he keeps to his resolve of never leaving this room upon any person's invitation *except Crow's*, unless the inviting person have a hat upon her or his head. He never will, even to dinner. And yesterday it happened as usual that Crow having spent the day out, with her family, it was found necessary to bring M? Flush's beefsteak up stairs to him, to my bedside—an attention which evidently by his manner was no more than he expected to be paid. & you wont think me hardhearted—but I am certainly amused sometimes at Crow's mode of counteracting my spoiling system by her system of discipline. Flush is very fond of her, & also very afraid of offending her—& it is impossible to help smiling through one's pity sometimes, to hear her scolding him, & his crying responses. He cries most piteously in response—& then comes to me to kiss me almost to death that I may persuade Crow to be friends with him!

And do you observe it of your Flush, that in respect to language, he understands words but not grammar. Nobody can say of my Flush as was said of Bentley to his great discontent,—that he is 'magnus grammaticus.'[4] His vocabulary is very much enlarged—but the 'Ladie Grammere' is no lady of his.[5] For instance—the word 'cakes' in his ear, is like Bruce in a Scotchman's[6]—but if you say 'You shant have any cakes' or 'I have not any cakes for you' he leaps up in as much expectation as if you said 'I will give you some cakes'! In the same way, it is with the phrase 'go out'—'kiss me'—& sundry verbs. The negative 'no', he understands perfectly—but 'not' in a sentence goes quite for nothing.

Behold! I submit all this learned observation to the subtlety of your philosophy.

Henrietta & George & Alfred were at M? Kenyon's yesterday evening—& heard him speak his joy & satisfaction in your 'graceful & gratifying note'. M? Forster was there—whom he calls 'a tribune of the people'--(ah! that's a high name—& I something doubt the application!) & M? Fellowes from Lycia,[7] & heaps of other celebrities, inclusive of the poet M? Reade. The latter spoke in such a kind tone of interest of me, that I have been in sackcloth & ashes of selfreproach ever since I heard what he said. But after all, is it my fault to be afflicted with that particular impression? Is'nt the feeling of admiration far pleasanter than any of the critical faculty can be? Even *you* think as I do!- And if he w.^d but give to his heart, his soul, the active pre-eminence which he bestows upon his memory—if he would but feel & think *outwards* in his poetry, it might be poetry still. For sentiment there is nothing to find fault with. The moral intonation of what he utters is always excellent & elevated—& the thoughts are those of the cultivated, the too well cultivated, & the rightminded. I hear that he is remarkably gentlemanly—the most strikingly so, say the dear people who belong to me,—of any in the room last night saving M? Kenyon himself.

Yes—the business with Fraser was terrible.⁸ Even *I*, who do not understand the heartbreakingness of an illnatured criticism, quite shrank within myself at the thought of what that mortification must have been. Two notes if not three, one upon another, presupposing the lost estate at the postoffice of its predecessor, & all crying out for mercy—& all with the author's name & dated from his private residence at Bath! And then, Fraser's commentary upon these humble petitions! His inference that M.ʳ Reade who never w.ᵈ be read (such was the joke!) had used the same process of eloquent coercion upon every periodical editor with a heart to be worked upon,—& how Fraser having only brains, responded to them . . . thus! If it had'nt been for the anticipated glories of another age, surely M.ʳ Reade in his morbid sensitiveness might have cut his melodious throat on the provocation of it. I was really really sorry for him. But Fraser is twice a savage. The wonder is, how the victim could in the first instance, through his very sensitiveness, debase himself to such an application!—& to 'such a Roman'!!⁹

Dearest dearest Miss Mitford, believe me I have felt deeply the shock which poor Lady Sidmouth's death must have been to you¹⁰—altho' trusting that from the circumstance of her long painful illness, you may be more quickly reconciled to grief involving that valued friend's release from a hopeless degree of suffering. You are tried many ways my beloved friend—but not one of them can be more than enough—& while my eyes are fullest of tears for you, the conviction is strong with me. May the comfort be present always & as near as the pain! May God bless you twice for every trial—I pray that for you, my dearest dearest friend!–

Thank you for letting me see the characteristic letters!¹¹ I understand what you observe in Miss Niven—& both understand & agree with your reasoning upon the phenomenon. Few things in ordinary life are more provoking to me than that impassiveness—that dull insensateness—which some people call quietness, & others want of animal spirits, & I, want of sensibility. Do you remember Burns–

> Chords that vibrate sweetest pleasure
> Thrill the deepest notes of woe.¹²

And yet—it is possible, I have been thinking—*is* it possible?—that she may be a *little afraid of you*? You who forget yourself, forget also that other people remember you.

By the way—M.ʳ Kenyon's friends, he told me, have taken to Silchester both Belford & the Village, in order to saturate themselves with Miss Mitford! Happy people! By the time the saturation is accomplished, I shall be ready to love them—& then . . *dear* people!–

Your story of Silchester,¹³ being saturated with you of course, I love very much. Shall I—shall I indeed, ever be there with you? Ah! but I say so, as if I looked up to the stars & fancied ... [']'shall I ever be *there* with you?"

My heart has been better for two days—altho, tremulous as a candle low in the socket, even now. Still I shall avoid—if you will let me, the catastrophe of Dr Chambers: & as to enquiring about the liberties of the summer prophetically, I know like an Irish sybil that I WILL do what I *can*. Certainly if it proves possible in any way, I shall be in the drawing room if it were only to please Papa! & I am very wonderfully well, all but the heart—& *that* is better—"upon my honor," as the peers say with their right hand to their left side![14]

I was stupid about the leaf—never doubting that it came by an accident. Yet I remember the odor—I did not particularly like it, I do believe! Was it wrong of me? Do tell me, whether the fashion is to talk of it & Arabia together?[15] What do you think of it?

My dearest friend, I am distressed at my folly about the Tableaux. Long & long ago, one of my brothers heard at some bookseller's, that Finden—(no—*that* is not right!)[16] that Finden was about to reissue the Tableaux, engravings & all, in monthly numbers. I heard it giddily, taking for granted that he had a right to do it, & never thought one word more of it either in writing to you or in meditation with myself. I am distressed & ashamed of my dulness! It never struck the obtusity of me, that you c.^{d} be ignorant of the disposal of your mss[17]—& this was long ago! Do tell me how you dis-arrange it all--& good bye—or I shall be late for the post. Take in change for all your abundant kindness, the grateful
                                            affection of your EBB——

Oh yes—you introduced me to the strange letters in Fraser—including Miss Edgeworth's![18] So unlike her book Miss Edgeworth!

Publication: EBB-MRM, I, 404–409.
Manuscript: Folger Shakespeare Library and Wellesley College.

1. Internal references show that this is a reply to letter 956.
2. In a postscript to the previous letter, Miss Mitford had told of one of her Flush's offspring being stolen four times.
3. EBB had mentioned Flush's illness in letters 886 and 893.
4. "A great philologist." Richard Bentley (1662–1742), Master of Trinity, Fellow of the Royal Society, and Keeper of the Royal Libraries, established his reputation as a scholar by addressing a long letter, in Latin, to Dr. John Mill, who was editing *The Chronicle of Malelas*, correcting many of the references in the Greek text. When the *Chronicle* was published in 1691, Bentley's letter was included as a 98-page appendix. In 1697–99, Bentley engaged in a celebrated feud with Charles Boyle regarding the authenticity of *The Letters of Phalaris*.
5. An allegorical figure in *The Passetyme of Pleasure* (1506) by Stephen Hawes (d. 1523?).
6. Robert de Bruce (1274–1329), the national hero of Scotland, took up arms against Edward I in an effort to gain Scottish independence. Crowned Robert I of Scotland in 1296, he suffered defeat and excommunication before finally winning Scotland's freedom from Edward III in 1327.

7. Charles Fellows (1799–1860), traveller and archæologist, had discovered the ruins of Xanthus, the ancient capital of Lycia in Asia Minor. He published his findings in *An Account of Discoveries in Lycia* (1841).
   8. EBB refers to some scathing remarks about Reade in *Fraser's Magazine* (see letter 732, note 8).
   9. *Julius Caesar*, IV, 3, 28.
  10. See letter 951.
  11. Subsequent letters show that these were from Darley, Chorley and Miss Anderdon.
  12. "Sensibility How Charming" (1792), lines 15–16.
  13. Miss Mitford had described a visit to Silchester in letter 956.
  14. A reference to a peer's oath on taking his seat in the House of Lords.
  15. EBB refers to the leaf of *humea elegans* sent with the previous letter, and Miss Mitford's enquiry regarding its scent; not herself liking its odour, in asking whether it is "the fashion," she apparently had in mind Shakespeare's "all the perfumes of Arabia" (*Macbeth*, V, 1, 50–51).
  16. After "Finden" EBB had written and deleted "as having sold the last c[opy]."
  17. The Finden brothers were infringing what Miss Mitford believed to be her copyright by reprinting material from *Findens' Tableaux*. This problem is dealt with in more detail in the following letter, and crops up in the correspondence periodically for some months.
  18. The "strange letters" were "A Letther from Mr. Barney Brallaghan, Piper at the Paddy's Goose Public-House, Ratcliffe Highway, to Oliver Yorke, Exquire" and "A Sickund Letther ..." in *Fraser's Magazine* (January 1842, pp. 65–80 and February 1842, pp. 160–179). Two letters from Miss Edgeworth appeared in the issue of November 1833 (pp. 633–634).

---

958. EBB TO MARY RUSSELL MITFORD

[London]
May 14. 1842

Dearest dearest Miss Mitford,

You are welcome as more than daylight at all hours of the day .. & I c.^{d} not restrain my exclamation—acclamation it was rather .. of 'Oh how delightful!' when I felt by the thickness of the substance between my fingers & thumb what a long letter I had before me for coffee time at six oclock, instead of at nine in the morning. Two sheetfulls in your own handwriting!! Flushie jumped up in a sympathy of rapture, & wanted very much to hold it all in his mouth—but no! Flushie!—you may eat my muffin if you please but nothing at all, .. not the least bit in the world, .. out of my letter!– There, you & I have our divided interests!–

Which reminds me that I c^{dnt} help reading to Crow your beautiful story of your Flush,—& that mine immediately took up the gesture of listening intently gathering his ears over his great eyes as if he saw a hare, or rather a crow in a field (his more familiar wonder & a very favorite subject of observation out of the carriage window in the days of his travelling—)^1 & patting about his little paws everytime the word

'Flush' 'Flush' occurred. Be sure he thought I was reading about *him*! I know he thought so!– It was very natural that he sh^d., you know!

And I must say one thing more in reference to Flush's tastes. He likes walking out of course—particularly on the grass: he likes walking out with the great dogs most particularly—that is an especial pleasure; but his distinct taste is to go out in a carriage!– Think of his jumping into a lady's carriage the other day—& she quite a stranger to him .. & refusing, positively refusing to come out again. There was nothing for it but to carry him out by main force! We ought to have a carriage I say—if it were only for Flushie!– But I think it a strange taste. An open carriage as in the taste of your Flush is less to be wondered at—but these flies & shut-up vehicles .. except for the glory of the thing .. one w^d scarcely imagine covetable by an unconventional will whether of man or dog.

Is his sister found at Reading?[2] Yes! I take courage from Ben's argument– I had thought of it before. If anybody stoops to hazard a salutation upon Flushie's head—a most awful growl together with a shrinking gesture are the consequences. Supposing that his cowardice may preserve him from any possible danger, I certainly need not be uneasy. Still, there are peculiar risks here, in London. Dogstealing is carried on as a profession—& only the other day, while Henry & Major Nugent .. a blind neighbour of ours were walking together, a little spaniel belonging to the latter was snatched up, thrown headlong into a sack, & run off with. The poor little thing was recovered .. but after several days anxiety—& what w^d my Flush do & what sh^d I do under such circumstances? Flushie w^d cry piteously—& I sh^{dnt} be very much wiser I dare say. He always cries, directly anything goes wrong––if you go on reading for instance without paying him proper attention! nay, just now .. just as I was writing of this morbid sensibility,—up came a little plaintive note of complaint as much as to say 'Oh how dull it is!'!—but I have patted him well & he has kissed me in turn & now he has re-disposed himself into a ball close beside me with very sufficient resignation.

Oh! your Flush is a genius! he is worthy of hero-worship in M^r. Carlyle's sense[3] & all others. Do you not suppose that the peculiar & close intercourse with Humanity which dogs in the position of yours & mine too have, influences or develops their intelligence in a manner not observable generally in their race? What philosophy can we bring to bear on it?

While I write, M^r. Kenyon's ready kindness has sent me Tennyson's new volumes, which I see include the old—or at least some of the old[4]— with a little note to explain his more kindness of having wished to get to me & of having been 'circumvented'! I had not sent him your message because I expected to see him day after day—but now I shall use no delay & write to him what your wishes are about his going to you. I *cant* doubt that he will go if he can—and I *dont* doubt that he can!

All this writing & nothing of yourself! & you not well again, my beloved friend! I am afraid—I am much afraid that that guilty Finden has made you ill besides making you unhappy.[5] My dearest, dearest friend—take courage about it, at least until the evil be proved complete. M[r] Dawson[6] being at work for you, gives me strong hope & expectation too, that the business may yet be happily arranged. Surely Finden had no right, & cannot *make* a right to a copyright under such circumstances. Surely it is not possible. The Tableaux was a periodical work . . just as The New Monthly Magazine is! Now conceive the publisher of the New Monthly proposing to republish the papers of the contributors, editor & contributors, against or without their permission!– The inference is obvious! And this suggests to me that if it c[d] be supposed to do the least shade of good, I w[d] send George directly to protest on my own account (without a word about *you*) against the republication of my Ballads. They have no right whatever to re-publish my ballads . . & I w[d] far rather that they did no such thing . . seeing that of any volume I might hereafter hazard, those ballads w[d] naturally form a part; & I know M[r] Finden does not think of excepting them from the universal compliment of re-publication, because it was of them in particular which I heard in the time of my obtuseness. Believing you to be interested in the business very differently from the manner in which you were actually, I never thought, of course, of even *thinking* an objection. Now I am ready, quite ready to *utter* twenty. Shall I send George with a protestation from myself? Shall I tell M[r] Kenyon to do anything? Rights are rights—and altho' my ballads will neither win nor lose me "money in my purse",[7] still it is quite worth making as malign a stir as possible about the thing, were it only out of revenge for your wrongs. I feel like Shylock already. Let me send George. Write & tell me if I may, without doing any harm. The ballads were given to *you*, & by no means to Mess[rs] Finden, & it is impossible that they can legally touch a line of them!–

Thank you for the interesting & characteristic letters which your kindness let me look at. There is something *apart* in M[r] Darley's which I like—a tone above the commonplace. M[r] Chorley's is lower.[8] I quite see what you mean—and oh! I am so glad you answered as you did! At the same time I feel sorry for M[r] Chorley too . . the want of literary sympathy being a bad want—and I feel more than you seem to do my beloved friend, the actuality of emotion connected not with the mere 'love of fame'[9] which is "base common & popular",[10] but with the working out of the faculties in the perfecting of a worthy work. There are strong motives of which in your case, the affections have taken the place, crowding around you so closely as to prevent your perceiving their strength & naturalness in the case of others,—& motives imply emotion. Perhaps even *you*, in another position, might have been .. not insensible to some of them. I myself am in no sort insensible—oh you must not indeed lift me up so, above the infirmities of the 'pen & ink people'.[11] There are anxieties of the intellect as well as of the heart—not *afflictions*[—]we will unite in not endowing them with so grave a name—but anxieties there are, & perhaps ought to be—nay, certainly ought to be—because otherwise it w^d be for the grand interests of humanity that authors & authoresses & all qualified by nature to become such, be kept poor by Act of parliament.

In much of this, you will perhaps, upon thinking it all over, agree with me. The point on which we rather differ is connected with the question whether a pen & ink person must necessarily become selfish in becoming sensitive. I say 'No' to it, in the very loudest voice I have the power of attesting with. Those who yearn most for sympathy are according to my impression, the very people who sh^d be readiest with sympathy— and if they are backward instead of ready, why my doxy is, not that it arises from their being of the Pariah race pen-&[-]ink people, but radically & independently of all 'inkhornisms' as Hall the satirist says,[12] .... *selfish* people. Agree with me my beloved friend as far as you can—and for the rest forgive me the differing–

Nobody in the world can have more sympathy "on her sleeve for daws to peck at"[13] than *you*—it is your virtue most in sight .. & for which you are—w^d be without a thing else .. at sight too, so most loveable. No wonder that you sh^d be struck by the want of it, or the comparative want of it in many! I think we may venture to count on the excellence of your Otto above the three unnamed Acts of the Uncompanioned![14] I think we may! At the same time I do quite appreciate his pleasant & lively, & sometimes elegant writings—yes, & do it so heartily as to feel more sorry than the strangership justifies perhaps, that he sh^d be entangled *with the theatres*. Well! I am ignorant enough of it all .. but from my own impressions, & from what you have said of your experience, it seems of all literary positions in the world the one least calculated for a young author whose object & ambition it is to pass out of the periodical low atmosphere of literature into the high serene of a success which will not in its turn, pass. It sounds impertinently—but is'nt it true that Mr Chorley tries all sorts of literature—as if he were bent rather on trying his faculties than using them?[15]

I send the letters back, thanking you once more. It pleased me very much to read all three of them—& not least of course Miss Anderdon's gracious words—which . . 'smell of the rose'![16] But you sh^d not teach people the illusions which belong to the love you cannot teach! altho' I hope to see *her* some day under the sun yet, & so, disenchanting her at leisure, prevent any serious mischief.

Ah poor Arabel! Her face was well, . . & we were hoping to get rid of all the moveable invalidships—when two days ago, she became less absolutely unwell than attacked by symptoms resembling *meazles*! I am afraid it is certainly meazles—and there, she is, dear thing, shut up again in a room to herself . . not feeling much more the matter with her than a headache but suffering the inconvenience of the eruption.

After all, with all my regrets, I couldn't dare to have you in the house even if you c^d come—& you c^{dnt} come, I suppose, if I c^d have you! O miserable consolation!—— as Job might say.[17]

Still there is hope in the stars! Henrietta went today with a party to the Cheswick [*sic*] flower-show—& your geraniums must be at theirs very soon. When is it? I hope—& hold fast dear Dr Mitford's dear promise– Tell him so, will you—with my love?–

And tell *me* how you are. I am anxious about you through all this nonsense. For my own part, I am better—yet have been "bad at heart"[18] since I wrote last. Oh yes! I have two prophets for good—you & Dr Mitford—& I believe you both as in duty & hopefulness bound–

Your own EBB.

Alas!—my ingratitude! Thank you (at last) thank you for the most lovely & welcome gift of lilies of the valley! You will make a wrong inference from my benighted thankfulness—& yet indeed they were delightful to me to look upon & hold in my hands! Worth a hundred of the fashionable Humea . . what is its aristocratic title?–[19]

Publication: EBB-MRM, I, 409–414.
Manuscript: Wellesley College.

1. Flush, of course, made the slow journey from Torquay to London with EBB in September 1841.
2. In letter 956, Miss Mitford had told how a half-sister of EBB's Flush had been stolen four times.
3. A reference to Carlyle's series of lectures in May 1840, subsequently published as *Heroes, Hero-Worship, and the Heroic in History* (1841).
4. A two-volume edition of Tennyson's poems had just been published; the first volume contained reprints of earlier works, with revisions, while the poems in the second volume were new.
5. In a letter of 1 June 1842 to Miss Harrison (Chorley, I, 294–295), Miss Mitford explains how Charles Tilt, having agreed that copyright of the contributions to *Findens' Tableaux* should remain hers, had, in contravention of that understanding, arranged to republish the *Tableaux*. On the basis of Tilt's original statement, Miss Mitford had

contracted with Henry Colburn for a three-volume edition of stories, two volumes to be reprints of material from the *Tableaux,* and she was concerned that Tilt's action would damage her financially. She tells Miss Harrison that she has sought legal advice— and this contretemps continues to concern her well into 1843.
 6. Apparently, Miss Mitford had enlisted the help of her neighbour, G.B. Dawson, in contesting the copyright infringement.
 7. Cf. *Othello,* I, 3, 339–340.
 8. As Darley and Chorley had contributed to *Findens' Tableaux,* both would have been affected by the copyright issue, and we infer that Miss Mitford had communicated the problem to them, and had sent their replies to EBB.
 9. Marlowe, *Tamburlaine the Great,* pt. I (1590), V, 2, 117–118.
 10. *Henry V,* IV, 1, 38.
 11. See letter 737, note 16.
 12. Joseph Hall (1574–1656), Bishop of Norwich, wrote "In mightiest Ink-hornismes he can thither wrest" (*Virgidemiarum,* 1598, Satires, bk. I, viii, 12). It connotes a learned or bookish usage (*OED*).
 13. *Othello,* I, 1, 64–65.
 14. The remainder of this paragraph indicates that "the Uncompanioned" refers to Chorley, a confirmed bachelor. EBB may be suggesting that Miss Mitford's *Otto of Wittelsbach* is more deserving of a stage presentation than the three plays by Chorley that did receive performances, with limited success. Alternatively, "the three unnamed Acts" may be a reference to his unstaged drama, "Fontibel," written in 1837. Its "conceptions of character offer no original features, and its language no beauties of thought or fancy" (Hewlett's *Autobiography* of Chorley, 1873, I, 132).
 15. "As an author ... his career was a succession of failures. With adroit talent, serious purpose, and indomitable perseverance, he essayed a succession of novels and dramas which one and all fell dead upon the public ear" (*DNB*).
 16. Cf. *II Henry VI,* I, 1, 254–255.
 17. Cf. Job, 16:2.
 18. Cf. *Hamlet,* I, 1, 8. EBB had mentioned this indisposition in letters 954 and 957.
 19. A further reference to the leaf of *humea elegans* sent by Miss Mitford (see letters 956 and 957). The editors of *EBB-MRM* state that the plant, of Australian origin, was named for Lady Hume of Warmleybury.

---

959. EBB TO JOHN KENYON

50. Wimpole Street.
Sunday night– [15 May 1842][1]

My dear Mr Kenyon,

Having missed my pleasure today by a coincidence worse for me than for you, I must, .. tired as I am tonight, .. tell you, .. ready for tomorrow's return of the books, .. what I have waited three whole days hoping to tell you by word of mouth. But mind, before I begin, .. I dont do so out of despair ever to see you again .. because I trust stedfastly to your kindness to *come* again when *you* are not 'languid' & I am alone as usual—only that I dare not keep back from you any longer the following message of Miss Mitford. She says .. "Wont he take us in his way to

Torquay? or from Torquay? Beg him to do so—& of all love, to tell us *when*."² Afterwards, again—"I think my father is better. Tell Mʳ Kenyon what I say, & stand my friend with him & beg him to come."

Which I do in the most effectual way, in her own words–

She is much pleased by means of your introduction. "Tell dear Mʳ Kenyon how very very much I like Mʳˢ Leslie.³ She seems all that is good & kind—& to add great intelligence & agreeableness to those prime qualities".

Now I have done with being a messenger of the gods—& verily my caduceus is trembling in my hand–⁴

O Mʳ Kenyon! what have you done? You will know the interpretation of the reproach, your Conscience holding the key of the cypher!

In the meantime I ought to be thanking you for your great kindness about this divine Tennyson.⁵ Beautiful, beautiful! After all it is a noble thing to be a poet!

But notwithstanding the poetry of the novelties—& you will observe that his two preceding volumes (only one of which I had seen before . . having enquired for the other vainly) are included in these two,—nothing appears to me quite equal to *Œnone*,⁶ & perhaps a few besides of my ancient favorites. That is not said in disparagement of the last, but in admiration of the first. There is in fact more thought, more bare brave working of the intellect in the later poems, even if we miss something of the high ideality, & the music that goes with it, of the older ones. Only I am always inclined to believe that philosophic thinking, like music, is involved however occultly in high ideality of any kind.

You have not a key to the cypher of this at least—& I am so tired that one word seems tumbling over another all the way.

Ever affectionately yours
Elizabeth B. Barrett.

You will let me keep your beautiful ballad & the gods a little longer–⁷

Address: John Kenyon Esqʳ / 4 Harley Place.
Publication: LEBB, I, 108–109 (as September 1842).
Manuscript: Wellesley College.

1. This letter falls between no. 958, in which EBB promises to pass on Miss Mitford's message to Kenyon, and no. 963, telling her that it has been delivered. The only Sunday between these two letters was the 15th.

2. EBB told Miss Mitford of Kenyon's intention of visiting Torquay in letter 954; by the time of letter 963, however, he had altered his plans.

3. Kenyon's friend has not been further identified. In a letter to Miss Mitford (31 October 1842), Mrs. Leslie is said to be critical of Kenyon, whom EBB defends.

4. i.e., Mercury, whose wand was usually represented as entwined with two snakes.

5. Kenyon had sent EBB Tennyson's just-published *Poems* (see previous letter).

6. "Œnone," originally published in 1832, was included in volume 1 of the 1842 edition.

7. Kenyon had apparently sent EBB the manuscript of his poem "The Gods of Greece," paraphrased from Schiller. Published in *The Keepsake for 1843* (pp. 77–80), it inspired EBB's "The Dead Pan" (Taplin, p. 113).

960. EBB TO HUGH STUART BOYD

[London]
May 17. 1842–

My very dear friend,

Have you thought all unkindness out of my silence? Yet the inference is not a true one, however it may look in logic.

You do not like Silentiarius *very much* (that is *my* inference:) since you have kept him so short a time. And I quite agree with you that he is not a poet of the same interest as Gregory Nazianzen, however he may appear to me of more lofty cadence in his versification. My own impression is that John [Mauropus] of Euchaita is worth two of each of them as a poet– His poems strike me as standing in the very first class of the productions of the christian centuries. Synesius & John of Euchaita! I shall always think of those two together—not by their similarity but their dignity.[1]

I return you the books you lent me with true thanks—and also those which M.[rs] Smith, I believe, left in your hands for me.[2] I thank *you* for them—& *you* must be good enough to thank *her*. They were of use—although of a rather sublime indifference for poets generally.

Arabel will take this packet to your door—but she will not go in to see you because she is only just convalescent from the meazles, making the fourth victim within the last few weeks in this house. They are well now,—I thank God! But I have not seen Arabel for nearly a week,—& therefore I leave you to judge whether it w[d] be right to expose *you* to a hazard from which her carefulness has preserved *me*. She had had the meazles *before* this attack; & so had Alfred–

I shall send you soon the series of the Greek papers you asked for—& also perhaps, the first paper of a Survey of the English poets, under the pretence of a review of "The Book of the Poets" a bookseller-selection published lately. I begin from Langland of Piers Plowman & the Malvern Hills. The first paper went to the editor last week, & I have heard nothing as to whether it will appear on saturday or not[3]—& perhaps if it does, you wont care to have it sent to you. Tell me if you do or dont. I have suffered unpleasantly in the heart lately from this tyrannous dynasty of east winds, but have been well otherwise, & am better in *that*. Flushie means to bark the next time he sees you in revenge for what you say of him.

Good bye dear M.ʳ Boyd. Think of me as
your ever affectionate
EBB

Address: H S Boyd Esq.ʳ
Publication: EBB-HSB, pp. 246–247.
Manuscript: Wellesley College.

1. EBB commented on all the writers named in this paragraph in "Some Account of the Greek Christian Poets."
2. EBB had borrowed *A Concise View . . . of Sacred Literature*, commenced by Mrs. Smith's father and completed by her brother, and a copy of Synesius (see letter 894).
3. The first instalment of EBB's review did not appear until the issue of 4 June.

961. WILLIAM CHARLES MACREADY, JR. TO RB

[London]
May 18.ᵗʰ 1842

My dear M.ʳ Browning

I have finished the rest of the illustration of the Pied Piper, which I hope you will like as well as the others but I am sorry to say I do not think them so good as the Council chamber, or the other one that I did.[1] Hoping that they will be as great a success as the others

I remain your affec.ᵗ friend

William C. Macready Jun.ʳ

Address: R. Browning Esq.ʳ
Publication: The Times Literary Supplement, 15 September 1921, p. 596.
Manuscript: Armstrong Browning Library.

1. This letter and no. 953 were preserved in a single envelope bearing the following note, made by Sarianna Browning after RB's death: "In May, 1842, Macready's eldest little boy was confined to the house by a cough. To amuse him, Robert wrote two poems which the child was to illustrate—'Crescentius, the pope's Legate' and the 'Pied Piper'– At first, there was no thought of publishing them, but I copied the Pied Piper and showed it to Alfred Domett who was so much pleased with it that he persuaded Robert to include it in the forthcoming number of Bells and Pomegranates– 'Crescentius', he did not publish till the last, in Asolando– These are the boy's illustrations." The drawings for "The Pied Piper" are now at ABL (see *Reconstruction*, H88). They are reproduced facing pages 350 and 351.

Sarianna's statement that "The Pied Piper" was shown to Domett is suspect, as all the evidence points to his having sailed for New Zealand before Willie's illness prompted composition. RB himself, in a letter to Furnivall on 1 October 1881, states that the "more picturesque subject" was only attempted after Willie made his "clever drawings" for "The Cardinal and the Dog"; if RB's memory of these events is correct, it would not have been possible for Domett to have seen the poem before leaving England.

"The Pied Piper" was published in November 1842 in *Dramatic Lyrics*, the third in the *Bells and Pomegranates* series, with the sub-title "A Child's Story. (Written for, and inscribed to, W.M. the Younger.)"

Only a scraping of shoes on the mat

And step by step they followed dancing

"The Pied Piper of Hamelin." Pencil sketches by Willie Macready.

And to Koppelberg Hill his steps addressed

Its dull in our town since our playmates left

"The Pied Piper of Hamelin." Pencil sketches by Willie Macready.

962. EBB TO JOHN KENYON

[London]
Friday– May 20– 1842.

My dear Mr Kenyon,

I hope you will express to Mr Burges my sense of his kind attention in allowing me to witness the experiment upon Demosthenes;[1] & that— .. should it appear to you necessary to give any account of my thoughts of it .., my honesty may be received as simply a part of my gratitude.

Really & sincerely, the translation seems to me inadequate .. a Demosthenes without his Demosthenisms– The vehemence & fire .. the harmony in abruptness—the *characteristics*, in fact .., are not there. And if it were not impertinent to compare a failure of mine, with the supposed one of so learned a critic, I sh.^d opine that he had fallen almost as low from the heaven of a high purpose, as I did myself when I thought to copy Prometheus & went a-stealing of fire .. with liberal allowance of three days & nights to me & Vulcan, for falling down withal!–

The translation is too close to be faithful—& I complain on the other hand of its not being too close to exclude such .... *not Atticisms* .. as "fore gad"!– They are not for Demosthenes; nor for Peel!

Dear Mr Kenyon—mind you do not say any of this to Mr Burges unless it is pressed for– My own private opinion being that Demosthenes is untranslateable by any possible process .. & more beyond our ken & apprehension *even in Greek* than even Æschylus .. (because Æschylus was a poet—& high ideality is a *common* country—) I was the less malleable to the translation in question.

It all reminds me that I sh.^d be glad if you w.^d explain to Mr Burges Mr Boyd's yearnings towards him of which he has told me more than twice– Mr Burges called upon him once, *but never again* .. & a mutual friend explained the reason to be that "*Mr Boyd did not seem glad to see him*". —"What an unhappy manner I must have!", ejaculated poor Mr Boyd to me—"because I really *was* VERY glad to see him!!"–[2]

Would it be wrong to tell Mr Burges this? and if it w.^{dnt} be wrong, will you do it? sometime you know—when there is an opportunity!

Mr Boyd cares so much for Greek company, & has so little, that I am sure he has worn out one suit of sackcloth already in expiation of an unintentional sin which did such mischief of deprivation.

Ever affectionately yours
Elizabeth B Barrett.

Publication: None traced.
Manuscript: Wellesley College.

1. George Burges had contributed a long and very detailed review of Lord Brougham's translation of Demosthenes' *De Corona* to *The Times*. Totalling some 20 columns, the

review (unsigned) appeared in eight issues of the paper, between 21 March 1840 and 4 April 1840; it was subsequently published as *A Review of Lord Brougham's Translation of the Oration of Demosthenes on the Crown* [1840].

2. See letter 939.

963. EBB TO MARY RUSSELL MITFORD

[London]
May 21. 1842–

I am longing to hear from you my dearest friend,—longing & wondering why I dont! You spoil me for all common delays—you spoiled me—I am spoilt! That's done! and the next thing is that you must go on with kindness upon kindness as fast almost as breath follows breath, or I shall be "*low* fantastical'['],¹ & getting up all sorts of distresses for suppositious causes! It certainly does seem to *me* a long time since I heard from you! Certainly *I* wrote last! Is'nt it? Did'nt I? Certainly I am half uneasy at your silence! That's a certain 'certainly'.

Mͬ Kenyon knows all the kindness you invite him to—but he is *not* going into Devonshire, he is *not* going to Scotland, and he *is* going to the continent! There's a change of plan! He remains in London until August, & then he sets off with Mͬ Bezzi, .. sees his brother at Vienna, helps his companion to four days' vision of his family at Florence, & returns home at the close of eight or nine weeks. No! I am not very sorry! He was bent on going somewhere—and eight or nine weeks spent in Scotland & Devonshire might as well be over the Alps—and then, besides,—*August is further off than June is*. I shall be sure to miss him very much whenever he goes, he has been so kind in coming to see me. I see him most weeks, once at least! That is very kind—considering what a milky way of habitable stars he revolves in day & night without stopping.

My dear Arabel is down stairs again & pretty well, except some weakness from the meazles, & a tendency to a swelled & painful face—and I am beginning to hope that we may see no more victims marked for seclusion.

Mͬ Kenyon & I were longing so for you, two days ago when he was sitting in this room. "Oh!" he said "how I do wish she were here—*living* in London! We might all pet her & do all the honor we could to her, & enjoy her delightfulness! Instead of that, she must, in some degree at least, be thrown away upon the society round about Three Mile Cross! in a degree she must!" Of course I said yes & yes & yes to it—and so that's the way in which we modest people wish you to belong to *us* as the only relative position in the world not altogether unworthy of you.

Oh you wont thank us for such wishes! You w^d rather be in the Silchester woods,—with that proper gratitude for our orizons, for which I give you credit.

In the meanwhile these meazles came just when they should not. I dare not even wish for you in this house .. as a sleeper in the rooms up stairs .. with this possible probable almost necessary infection in the air of them. I cudgel my brains[2] for a hope apart from a risk to *you*, & do not dare to take one up. What can be done? How is Dr Mitford? How are the geraniums? How do you think of it all?

Dont let me forget to tell you that Tennyson's new volumes rapt me in Elysium.[3] *New*, they are not altogether—the first of them containing every poem of those formerly published which the poet intends to [let] live. Of the new poem[s] we may say, there is less of the quaint peculiarity, more individuality, more *power* in the sense of nervous utterance, more thought under the obvious ordinary forms, & *less* of that high ideality which distinguished the old Tennyson lyrics, & includes always however occultly a higher degree of philosophic thought than the critical world wotteth of. That is my doxy about the poems—the poet being divine as I always felt him to be .. by his step—as the Greeks detected the godship of their gods–[4] Well! but what I wanted to tell you was that one of his idyll's .. perhaps the most beautiful of all—nay, certainly the most beautiful of all, was by the author's confession in a note, "suggested .. by a pastoral of Miss Mitford's"—or "by one of Miss Mitford's pastorals".[5] It made my heart leap up to see your name—as 'at a rainbow in the sky'![6] I think it will please you a little. I think within myself that fancying myself *you*, it w^d please *me* a good deal—I think such a godship of Tennyson!!–

The story is your beautiful one of the son marrying against his father's consent—and of the manner in which his child after his death, is adopted & embraced, after a Ruth-scene in the corn-fields.[7]

Mr Wordsworth goes out of town on friday; but it is only for a week or two to Harrow, & his intention is to return. He has been holding his court royally in London—breakfasting five or six times every morning, & taking evening refreshments as polyglottically. His wife bent over his chair, as Mr Kenyon stood by some evenings ago, & said, stroking his "sublime gray hairs"[8] gently .. "Ah William—you are tiring yourself"!– Do you not like to hear it?

To pass to a lower personnage altho' still a royal one, I was glad to be told two days since by one of my brothers who had it as a true tradition from somebody called "a silver stick in waiting" a Colonel Read,[9] that the only gentleman with whom the queen shook hands at her last drawing room was Ld Melbourne. And her eagerness of joy was obvious both in the act & the manner! Poor queen! there may be good in her yet: and it is a merit (*for a queen*) to be cordial to a friend in adversity—! To do another thing attributed to her by silver stick .. i.e. hating Sir Robert .. is a merit in anybody.[10]

I had proofsheets of my Book of the Poets' review sent to me last week, with a command to send it back next wednesday. If the Athenæum sh^d have it on saturday, I shall certainly intrude my insolence upon you as in the case of my Greeks—because it is more than a review & accomplishes Mr Dilke's desire to me of attempting a survey of the English poets.[11]

Dearest dearest friend, how I do trample on your forbearance with wooden shoes[12] & on every possible occasion. Bear with me still—love me so as to make it possible. Do write to me. The longer I think of the silence the blacker it looks. Surely you received my last long letter?

God bless you ever & ever! I am sure I am yours *so*

EBB.

Publication: EBB-MRM, I, 414–417.
Manuscript: Wellesley College.

1. A reversal of Shakespeare's phrase (*Twelfth Night*, I, 1, 15).
2. Cf. *Hamlet*, V, 1, 56.
3. In ancient mythology, Elysium was a place of bliss in the infernal regions, where the souls of the virtuous found themselves after death. EBB's enthusiasm for Tennyson was reflected in an essay she wrote and sent to Horne in December 1843 as the basis for a chapter in *A New Spirit of the Age*. He cut up her autograph and pasted it in place in his own manuscript; it is now at the University of Virginia (see *Reconstruction*, D1374). The essay was included in the 1900 Porter and Clarke edition of EBB's works (VI, 322–325).
4. *Æneid*, I, 405.
5. A note at the end of the volume states that "The Idyl of 'Dora' was partly suggested by one of Miss Mitford's pastorals" ["Dora Creswell" in *Our Village*].
6. Wordsworth, "My heart leaps up when I behold" (1807), line 2.
7. See Ruth, 2:2–23.
8. We have not located the source of this quotation.
9. *The Times* of 20 May 1842, reporting a reception held the previous day to mark the Queen's birthday, listed Col. Reid of the 2nd Life Guards, Silver-Stick-in-Waiting, as one of the gentlemen present.
10. As noted previously (letter 944, n. 14), Victoria had been distressed when her close and affectionate relationship with Melbourne had, of necessity, been interrupted when his administration was ousted by Peel's.
11. The first part of EBB's essay on *The Book of the Poets* appeared in *The Athenæum* of 4 June 1842 (no. 762, pp. 497–499). It was continued in the issues of 11 June (pp. 520–523), 25 June (pp. 558–560), 6 August (pp. 706–708) and 13 August (pp. 728–729).
12. EBB may have had in mind Goldsmith's "I hate the French, because they are all slaves and wear wooden shoes" ("The Distresses of a Common Soldier," *Essays*, 1765, XXIV).

964. RB TO ALFRED DOMETT

New Cross, Hatcham, Surrey,
May 22. 1842.

My dear Domett,

This is the third piece of paper I have taken up to put my first-words to you on—*this* must do, for time is urgent. I cannot well say *nothing* of my constant thoughts about you, most pleasant remembrances of you, earnest desires for you—yet I will stop short with this . . as near "nothing" as may be. I have a sort of notion you will come back some bright morning a dozen years hence and find me just *gone*—to Heaven, or Timbuctoo, and I give way a little to this fancy while I write, because it lets me *write* freely what, I dare say, I *said* niggardly enough—my real love for you—better love than I had supposed I was fit for: but, you see, when I was not even a boy, I had fancy in plenty and no kind of judgment—so I said, and wrote, and professed away, and was the poorest of creatures: *that*, I think, is out of me, now! but the habit of watching & warding continues and—here is a case where I do myself wrong. However I am so *sure*, now, of my feelings, when I *do* feel—trust to them so much, and am deceived about them so little—(I mean, that I so rarely believe I like where I loathe, and the reverse, as the people round me do)—that I can speak about myself and my sentiments with full confidence. There! And now, let that lie, till we meet again . . God send it!

I shall never read over what I send you,—reflect on it, care about it, or fear that you will *not* burn it when I ask you. So do with me. And tell me all about yourself, straight, without courteously speculating about my being, "doings & drivings"—(unless there is some special point you want to know)—and by my taking the same course,—(sure you care for all that touches me—) we shall get more done in a letter than when half is wasted. Begin at the beginning—tell me how you are, where you are, what you do and mean to do—and to do in *our* way: for live properly *you cannot* without writing—and to *write* a book now, will take one at least the ten or a dozen years you portion out for your stay abroad. I don't expect to do any real thing till then: the little I, or anybody, can do as it is, comes of them *going to New Zealand*—partial retirement and stopping the ears against the noise outside—but all is next to useless—for there is a creeping magnetic assimilating influence nothing can block out. When I block it out, I shall do something. Don't you feel already older (in the wise sense of the word—) farther off—as one "having a purchase" against us? What I meant to say was—that only in your present condition of life, so far as I see, is there any chance of your being able to find out . . what is wanted, and how to supply the want when you precisely find it. I have read your poems—you can do anything—and (I do not see why I should not think—) *will* do much. I will, if I live. At present, I don't know if I stand on head or heels—what men require, I don't know—and of what they are in possession, know nearly as little.

Of me: a couple of days after you left, I got a note from Macready[1]—the disastrous issue of the Play you saw of Darley's brother, had frightened him into shutting the house a month earlier than he had meant. Nothing new this season, therefore—but *next*, &c. &c. &c. So runs this idle life away!. while *you* are working! —I shall go to the end of this year, as I now go on—shall print the Eastern play you may remember hearing about[2]—finish a wise metaphysical play (about a great mind and soul turning to ill)[3]—and print a few songs and small poems—which Moxon adv⟨ised m⟩e to do for popularity's sake–[4] These things done (and my play out) I shall have tried an experiment to the end, and be pretty well contented either way.

The 7th of May last was my birthday (your's is the 20th, tho' you did not say so at our parting dinner, when I spoke about May and birthdays![)]—and on that day I dined with dear Chr. Dowson and your sister[5]—we were alone and talked of you and little else. I got your books, and slip of note—⟨which⟩ is under the paper I write on! With this, I send you your Sordello–[6] I suppose (am sure, indeed) that the translation from Dante in the fly-leaf is your own: I had been fool enough (I told you, I believe) to purpose giving you my whole wondrous works in a stiff binding—good against rats– But I thought twice! The true best of me is to come and you shall have it—and I shall certainly never be quite wanting in affection for essays that have got me your love—as you say, and I believe– But, I don't know that I shall ever read them again. Along with *Sordello**, take & keep for my sake and its own, Notre Dame,[7]—you would *not* read here, and *shall* read there– I mean to send you more of Hugo's books when I can get them. Meanwhile, begin with this.

Give my kindest regards to Young[8]—the books‡ I promised *him*, he must have, I suppose! The press-blunders, too, sicken me. I look for a letter from him, and will answer it. As for this to you, I mean it to be short—for I shall let no ship I hear of, sail without a few lines—and I want to avoid the feeling of having a deal to do on every such occasion.

Tell me if I can do anything for you– My Father, Mother, & Sister are urgent that I should send their very kindest regards to you. I saw your Father[9] (from a distance) this morning at Chapel—very well apparently. It seems, even yet, as if you would "run over" some fine morning; but you are better away. See what good one gets from one's friend *staying* .. I have not seen Arno⟨uld⟩[10] since the last night—just because I may if I will. I shall not wait (nor ever wait) "for an answer," friend-like, but write by next opportunity.

Ever yours,
R. Browning.

‡I do not send him, say, (nor send you) a "Strafford," because I have made up my mind to correct it in most ways and publish it in "Bells &c."[11]

*I send your copy to Young along with his books.

Address: Alfred Domett Esq, / Port Nelson, / New Zealand.
Publication: RB-AD, pp. 33–39.
Manuscript: British Library.

1. A reply to RB's enquiry about staging his play (letter 948).
2. *The Return of the Druses*, published in January 1843 as the fourth number of the *Bells and Pomegranates* series.
3. *A Soul's Tragedy*. Despite RB's comment, it was not published until April 1846, as the last part of *Bells and Pomegranates*.
4. *Dramatic Lyrics*, published in November 1842 as the third *Bells and Pomegranates* pamphlet.
5. Dowson had married Domett's sister Mary in 1836.
6. RB had originally given *Sordello* to Domett in March 1840 (see letter 739), but had later borrowed it to study Domett's annotations; when he returned the book, he had added his own comments, responding to Domett's (G & M, p. 301). The book is now in the British Library (see *Reconstruction*, C562 and E446).
7. RB had previously spoken of Hugo's *Notre-Dame de Paris* (1831) in a letter (no. 492) to Ripert-Monclar.
8. Domett's kinsman, William Curling Young (1815–42), was a member of the set that included RB and Domett (Maynard, p. 99). He had emigrated and established himself at Nelson in 1841, but met his death by drowning while Domett was still in transit to New Zealand.
9. Nathaniel Domett (1764–1849), who had had a career in the Royal Navy and the merchant marine prior to his marriage.
10. Joseph Arnould (1814–86) was also a member of RB's set, sharing chambers for a time with Domett after both were called to the Bar in November 1841. E.A. Horsman states that Domett borrowed £70 from Arnould to finance the purchase of land in New Zealand (*The Diary of Alfred Domett*, 1953, p. 14).
11. RB changed his mind; not only was the play not included in the *Bells and Pomegranates* series, but it was excluded from the 1849 edition of RB's works, and was not reprinted until the 1863 collected edition.

---

965. EBB TO MARY RUSSELL MITFORD

[London]
28.th May. 1842

My dearest friend, I beg your pardon & my own too, for teazing each of us so far more than the occasion required—for really I had made up my mind that something very bad was the better [*sic*, for matter] either with yourself or with dear D.ʳ Mitford——whereas it was only with my imagination. Your letter was *'twice* blessed'[1] in consequence of it however, —& now I beseech you to forget, to throw out of the window into the midst of the flowers so as to be buried evermore, the remembrance of the dunning, .. & not to write a bit oftener to me than comes by the inspiration of your kindness, instead of by the exhortation of my never-to-be-satisfied-ibleness!–

No to be sure!– May is not the time for doing anything but standing out in the new grass under the new sun, with the running of a stream threading all the mixed sounds of jubilee, as clear in sound as its own water though so soft!– It is a beautiful, beautiful month! the prophecy,— the hope of the year—with an earnest of performance besides! I wish you my beloved friend, all the May wishes in the world—ah benedicite! as old Chaucer says at the first thought of May.[2]

But then, there is this terrible work about the Findens. Are you aware that the publication has actually begun? I had understood that it was only a prospectus which had been seen—and now George tells me that he saw long ago a first number at the Temple, containing my 'Child's dream'[3] among other things, & which was sent to him at his chambers in the way that those cheap periodicals have the fashion of passing round. Still, on the ground of remuneration, & also of *arresting* the further publication, you must be safe. George says there can be no question about it—particularly as your retention of right of copyright was mentioned in your agreement. Do not be too vexed I beseech you—& do not be uneasy at all—if the thing be possible. You will see that everything will work right again. And as to this partial publication——why it must really be partial in every sense. Not an advertisement have I seen of it, by 'any kind of light'[4]—& I am a surveyor general of advertisements of books, always looking to them as my "leading article'['] in a newspaper. So I do encourage myself into hoping strenuously that after all the engagement with Colburn may stand good & profitable.[5] Tell me, my dearest friend,— I beg of you to tell me, the whole event of it.

You must make allowances for the weakness (in reason & philosophy) of such people who living themselves in London would fain transplant you out of the woods to have & to hold & to water gently in a flowerpot of their own. We know very well that you laugh us to scorn all the time—and yet I stand by M.ʳ Kenyon, & M.ʳ Kenyon stands by me & we both wish you lived close to us!–

And that throws me into party-spiriting, & makes me take M.ʳ Kenyon's part again in the affair of the travelling. You would'nt care to see Italy by the light of that sun? nor the "great sublime"[6] of nature in the Alpine passes? nor the Hartz mountains of Germany?– You w.ᵈⁿᵗ *fly*, if you could? Now I would! Nay—in the exaggeration of my malignancy, I would have YOU with me & fly *so*!–

Are you afraid of me my beloved friend—of the consummating strength of my wishes, .. which is in your creed I know? Yet do not be afraid. The thing is too impossible—taking the full sum[7] of my weakness & your unwillingness—to be wished very hard!—and—(which I sigh for most of all!) my evil eye[8] might be twice as evil as it is, without achieving any evil to you, seeing that it cannot see you!–

&[9] all this illnature comes of yours to the generation of poor poets. You talk with a Bilboa blade[10] for a tongue, when you talk of *them*—that is certain! Tell me how far is a young lady who trembles when she is asked to sing, less morally morbid & naughty than the worst of the poor poets, scolded so for being sensitive? Tell me again. Is not the very extremity of the sensitiveness in question compatible with a sensitive *sympathy*? Tell me again– You who were ennobled out of these "base uses"[11] by the holiest of affections, are you not also lifted away from the comprehension of them by another circumstance .. to whit [*sic*], your own literary *success from the beginning*? Suppose it had ever occurred to you to feel yourself depreciated .. your right price denied .. your place in literature given to the unworthy before you! Such things *have* been,[12] as we all know—& Wordsworth was not the last victim we all fear.[13] Can you not conceive the bitterness—yes, the bitterness embittering in its turn? the injustice, can you not shrink at the very imagination of *that* .. you who speak so expressively in this very last letter of the deep inward feeling which a sense of injustice, even pecuniary, involves?– Do, do forgive me for my surpassing impertinence. I quite wonder at myself for my impertinence I assure you—& so you may well open your eyes!— VERY well, as long as you dont at the same moment, knit the broad Coleridgian department above them![14] To be sure you are by no means a hero-worshipper—& I *am*, by all manner of means!–

I am so glad you have had Martha with you. What she said ... I was glad to hear it! because it was a reflection in the glass, of the face of your kindness!

It is very very hot indeed! and we want a little wind (not east if you please) but a little more wind of the sweet south-west than we have, first to dilute the strong sunshine & secondly to play on an Æolian harp[15] which Papa has just bought for the drawing room. They ("the boys") brought it up to my room this morning & held it out of the window ... "Blow, Blow"[16] &c—but very few breaths w.^{d} come, & all our bravos w.^{d} not incite King Æolus to "favor us"!– Think of my being so innocent as never in my whole life to have heard an Æolian harp before! I *did* just hear it this morning, in a whisper, tho' "marvellous sweet."[17]

I do not send you the Athenæum, having no part in this week's.

And now goodbye— God bless you, my dearest dearest friend!— Oh! but I must tell you!— Flushie was thought to be *lost* today! quite lost! *I* did not think so, or know anything of the suppositious danger. Henrietta walking with two strangers (to Flushie) took him out & missed him in Bond Street. Oh! Flush was'nt to be seen—was'nt to be heard of. She came home in despair, & found him *here*—M!̣ Flush evidently not liking his company, & coming back all that way by himself half an hour before she came! She wont have Papa told of the adventure—because he prophecied & said just as she left the house "You will lose Flush! and if you do, *you had better not* come *back at all.*"!—

You may suppose what high favor Flushie is in with Papa! Perhaps it was a little for love of me—still, love of Flushie was much!

God bless you ever. My love to dear D!̣ Mitford. Arabel is well again, & she & *I too*, thank you again & again for your kindest sympathy. Dearest friend,

Always your own
EBB

No more meazles! You w^d not have me give up my vision?[18] Oh— surely surely not!—

Publication: EBB-MRM, I, 417–420.
Manuscript: Folger Shakespeare Library and Wellesley College.

1. *The Merchant of Venice*, IV, 1, 186.
2. *The Cuckoo and the Nightingale*, line 1. In all editions of Chaucer published in EBB's lifetime, this poem was ascribed to him; since 1878, its author is believed to have been either John Clanvowe (d. 1391) or his son Thomas (d. 1410).
3. "The Dream" was one of EBB's contributions to the 1840 *Findens' Tableaux*. The subject of this paragraph is the alleged infringement of copyright in the material published in *Findens'*, mentioned in letter 957 and subsequently.
4. Cf. *King John*, IV, 3, 61.
5. Miss Mitford was concerned that the problem over copyright would diminish her recompense from Colburn, discussed in more detail in a letter from EBB to R.H. Horne ([ca. June 1842]).
6. Pope, "Essay on Criticism" (1711), 680.
7. *The Merchant of Venice*, III, 2, 157.
8. An ancient belief held that certain individuals had the power to harm or even kill with a glance. Vergil speaks of lambs being so harmed (*Eclogues*, III, 103).
9. EBB has altered this paragraph by inserting an ampersand.
10. The Spanish city of Bilbao was famous for its finely-tempered sword blades.
11. *Hamlet*, V, 1, 202.
12. Cf. *Macbeth*, III, 4, 109.
13. Taken to be a reference to Wordsworth's having been passed over in favour of Southey for the Laureateship in 1813.
14. EBB had compared Miss Mitford's forehead to that of Coleridge in letter 828, and Chorley tells how Hablot Knight Browne spoke of "that wonderful wall of forehead" (Chorley, I, 15).
15. An Æolian harp, named after Æolus, ruler of the winds, produced sounds by the passage of air over its strings.

16. *As You Like It*, II, 7, 174.
17. *The Tempest*, III, 3, 19.
18. Probably the wish of EBB and Kenyon that Miss Mitford move to London, mentioned in letter 963.

966. EBB TO JOHN KENYON

50 Wimpole Street.
30.th May. 1842–

My dear Cousin,

I thank you much for the sight of Mr Ticknor's letter[1]––& altho' "very well *for* . . anything—or *for* . . anybody" never seems to me praise worth anything to anybody,—yet of course what he writes is quite enough, more than enough, to make me generally thankful—& without a recoil at the stab to the transcendentalism–

With the letter I return you the old black book, which is better than a *red* book—& rich in that building up of heavy & high sentences, the architectural music of our fathers, out of which their sons are disinherited.

Yes—thank you! I am much better for the departure of the east wind. And Papa has just given me (in his too great kindness) an Æolian harp, a double one of new construction, which turns all the surviving winds into music—so that we are on the best terms possible. Flushie is jealous of it!—he thinks it alive & does'nt like to hear me call anything "beautiful" except his ears–

And so, you will come to hear it some day—will you not?–

With double thanks, affectely—yours

EBB—

Publication: None traced.
Manuscript: Wellesley College.

1. Presumably Ticknor's acknowledgement of *An Essay on Mind* and *Prometheus Bound* sent him by Kenyon (see letter 936, note 2). They are now in the Ticknor Library at Dartmouth (see *Reconstruction*, M41 and M67).

Appendices

APPENDIX I
Biographical Sketches of Principal Correspondents and Persons Frequently Mentioned

THOMAS CARLYLE (1795–1881)

This famous British writer was a long-time friend of RB, and an early object of EBB's admiration. Born at Ecclefechan, Scotland, on 4 December 1795, he was eldest of the nine children of James and Janet (*née* Aitken) Carlyle. His father was a mason and small farmer, providing for his family an adequate but frugal living. As a child, Carlyle showed great promise, devouring knowledge from all the books that came his way, and it was decided to send him to Edinburgh University. He enrolled in 1809, walking 100 miles to do so, and there acquired a substantial knowledge of mathematics, though his eventual goal—not given up until some years later—was the ministry. He spent a number of years as a schoolmaster and tutor, during which time he formed a close friendship with Edward Irving. The latter was to become a prominent London preacher, whose name cropped up frequently in EBB's letters. While in his twenties, Carlyle came strongly under the influence of German literature, undertook some writing of his own, and went through a spiritual crisis later reflected in his *Sartor Resartus* (1833–34). On 17 October 1826, Carlyle married Jane Baillie Welsh (1801–66), daughter of a Scottish physician. The temperamental natures of both parties made the marriage a stormy one, but it endured until Mrs. Carlyle's death in 1866. In 1834 the couple moved from Scotland to London, settling at 5 Cheyne Row, Chelsea, where Carlyle resided for the rest of his life. There he wrote his great historical work, *The French Revolution* (1837). Another memorable production, *On Heroes, Hero-Worship, and the Heroic in History* (1841), was based on a lecture course he had presented in the previous year. Carlyle became an outspoken writer and commentator on British political and economic issues, taking first a liberal and later a conservative viewpoint. In his writing he combined richness and complexity into a style that came to be known as "Carlylese." He was under much financial stress during the early part of his life, and—despite later fame and honours—never received the benefits of a government pension, as did certain other literary figures. When finally offered one late in life by the Prime Minister, Benjamin Disraeli, a long-time foe, he rejected it (along with a proposed knighthood). Increasingly gloomy in his outlook during old age, he died on 5 February 1881. Despite the offer of a final resting place in Westminster Abbey, he was buried—in accordance with his own wishes—at his Scottish birthplace, Ecclefechan.

On 18 March 1881, shortly after Carlyle's death, RB discussed him in a letter to Madame Bessie Rayner Belloc. "He confessed once to me," RB wrote, "that, on the first occasion of my visiting him, he was anything but favourably impressed by my 'smart green coat'—I being in riding-costume: and if then and there had begun and ended our acquaintanceship, very likely I might have figured in some corner of a page as a poor scribbling-man with proclivities for the turf and scamphood." Carlyle, whose opinion eventually changed, was among the numerous literary acquaintances whom RB acquired shortly after the appearance of *Paracelsus* (1835), and he is known to have visited RB in Hatcham (G & M, p. 49), where the latter lived with his parents from 1840 until the time of his marriage. Carlyle's first extant letter to RB (no. 822) carried criticism and encouragement based on *Sordello* (1840) and *Pippa Passes* (1841). It is noteworthy for the advice (not followed) that "your next work" should be "written in prose!" At the end of the same year, in letter 883, RB wrote to Euphrasia Fanny Haworth of having "dined with dear Carlyle and his wife ... yesterday." When Carlyle was preparing *Oliver Cromwell's Letters and Speeches: with Elucidations* (1845), RB lent him a copy of *Killing, no Murder* (1659), (see *Reconstruction*, A48). A copy of the second edition of Carlyle's *Cromwell* was inscribed to RB by the author on 20 June 1846 (*Reconstruction*, A731). In 1849 Carlyle told the Irish politician Gavan Duffy—as reported much later in Duffy's *Conversations with Carlyle* (1892)—that he, Carlyle, regarded RB as one of the few current English writers from whom it was "possible to expect something" (G & M, p. 135).

As for EBB, she wrote in March 1842 (letter 931) to Mary Russell Mitford: "I am an adorer of Carlyle. He has done more to raise poetry to the throne of its rightful inheritance than any writer of the day,—& is a noble-high-thinking man in all ways. He is one of the men to whom it wd. be a satisfaction to me to cry 'vivat' somewhere in his hearing." In a letter to her brother George on 30 March 1842 (no. 934), EBB noted a remark by John Kenyon that "nobody" was reading RB's poetry. Her own comment to George was: "Mr. Carlyle is his friend—a good substitute for a crowd's shouting!" Carlyle was among the literary figures discussed in R.H. Horne's *A New Spirit of the Age* (1844), and the author drew heavily on material supplied by EBB for the sections on Carlyle (*Reconstruction*, D1282) and various others. Engravings for five of the eight full-page portraits appearing in *A New Spirit* were hung on the walls of EBB's room at 50 Wimpole Street—those of Carlyle, RB (reproduced in vol. 3, facing p. 164), Harriet Martineau, Alfred Tennyson, and William Wordsworth. EBB sent Carlyle a copy of her *Poems* (1844), telling Miss Mitford on 14 August of that year: "I have taken a great gasp of courage, & sent a copy to Carlyle, .. as 'a tribute of admiration & respect.' I pray all the heroes that he may not devote the entrails of my votive sacrifice to make curlpapers for Mrs. Carlyle,—but can scarcely aspire to a higher destiny." On 1 September 1844 she told Miss Mitford of receiving "kind letters from Carlyle." However, just as he had suggested prose-writing to RB, he had written "that a person of my [EBB's] 'insight & veracity' ought to use 'speech' rather than 'song' in these days of crisis." The letters that passed between RB and EBB in 1845-46 were sprinkled with references to Carlyle. On 17 February 1845, for instance, EBB referred to herself as "a devout sitter at his feet," and RB on 26 February 1845 said: "I know Carlyle and love him." On the following day EBB called him "the great teacher of the age." RB frequently mentioned visiting the Carlyle home. Carlyle's comment on the RB-EBB marriage came quite late but was worth waiting for; on 23 June 1847 he wrote to RB: "No marriage has taken place, within my circle, these many years, in which I could so heartily rejoice: You I had known, and judged of; her too, conclusively enough, if less directly; and certainly if ever there was a union indicated by the finger of Heaven itself, and sanctioned and prescribed by the Eternal Laws under which poor transitory Sons of Adam live, it seemed to me, from all I could hear or know of it, to be this!" At this time, EBB had never met Carlyle, but the deficiency was remedied when the Brownings visited London in 1851 and when, upon their departure, he accompanied them to Paris. On 22 October 1851 EBB wrote to Miss Mitford: "Carlyle ... I liked infinitely more in his personality than I expected to like him, and I saw a great deal of him for he travelled with us to Paris & spent several evenings with us, we three together. He is one of the most interesting men I could imagine even—deeply interesting to me: and you come to understand perfectly, when you know him, that his bitterness is only melancholy, & his scorn, sensibility. Highly picturesque too he is in conversation. The talk of writing men is very seldom as good." The Brownings were with Carlyle again during their 1855 London visit. Indications are that EBB and Carlyle's wife could have become, under different circumstances, close friends and correspondents. Their relationship was stunted, however, by the mutual dislike between Mrs. Carlyle and RB. There was frequent contact between Carlyle and RB after the latter returned to London following EBB's death. On 4 March 1869, shortly after completion of RB's *The Ring and the Book*, several notables, including RB and Carlyle, were presented to Queen Victoria. In her journal, the Queen referred to RB as "a very agreeable man" and to Carlyle as "a strange-looking eccentric old Scotchman, who holds forth, in a drawling melancholy voice, with a broad Scotch accent, upon Scotland and upon the utter degeneration of everything." Apparently referring to the group as a whole she wrote: "It was, at first, very shy work speaking to them." These comments are printed in *The Letters of Queen Victoria, Second Series*, ed. George Earle Buckle, (1926, I, 586-587). In 1877, RB published *The Agamemnon of Æschylus*. Both in the book's preface and in a letter to Carlyle dated 17 October 1877, RB mentioned that Carlyle had desired (or, as the preface says, "commanded") him to undertake the work. Although the copy of RB's *Agamemnon* which presumably accompanied his 17 October letter has not been traced, RB presented and inscribed to Carlyle various other books which are listed in *Reconstruction: Sordello* (1840), C560; *Bells and Pomegranates* (1841-46), C225; and *La Saisiaz* and *The Two Poets of Croisic* (1878), C375. Letters from Carlyle to RB were among the many papers which the latter destroyed in his old age. An account is given in *LRB* (p. xii) of an 1884 visit to RB's London home by T.J. Wise and F.J. Furnivall, during which Wise "saw letters of Carlyle go into the fire." A few years after Carlyle's death in 1881, RB reminisced extensively about him during conversations in Venice with the American painter Daniel Sargent Curtis. An account of the reminiscences appears in *More Than Friend*, ed. Michael Meredith (1985), pp. 168–169. (See also *Reconstruction*, L84.) In the conversations as reported by Curtis, RB spoke very unfavourably of Mrs. Carlyle, commented on Carlyle's "contempt for all which he did not know or think," and expressed admiration for his "power of description." According to Curtis, RB "saw Carlyle a week before his death . . . lying comatose" and taking "no notice of anything."

CHARLES DICKENS (1812–70)

Born on 7 February 1812, three months ahead of RB, this Browning acquaintance and correspondent was the most popular English writer of his time, possibly because of childhood experiences that helped him to identify closely with the common people. His parents were John and Elizabeth (*née* Barrow) Dickens, and his birthplace was Portsea, near Portsmouth, where the father was a Navy clerk. Before long John Dickens's job took the family to London and to Chatham. Amiable and improvident, the father is recognized as Charles Dickens's model for Mr. Micawber in *David Copperfield*. He was finally imprisoned for debt; and Charles, at an early age, learned first-hand about child labour in a factory warehouse. With little formal schooling, he went to work as an office boy at age 15, then became a reporter by about 20. As a sideline, he wrote fictional magazine sketches, which were collected and published as *Sketches by Boz* in 1836; hence EBB's occasional reference to Dickens as "Boz" in her letters. Serialization of the famous *Pickwick Papers* began in 1836, and they appeared as a collected edition in the following year. The success of these sketches, first appearing piece by piece, encouraged RB and his publisher Edward Moxon to use a similar procedure for *Bells and Pomegranates*, which appeared in eight parts from 1841 to 1846. The works of Dickens are remarkable for their social commentary and their creation of unforgettable characters. He was a writer who showed a "sense of identity with the human lot everywhere" (Maynard, p. 130). Despite an enthusiastic reception in the United States and Canada during an 1842 visit, for various reasons he became soured, and subsequently his *American Notes for General Circulation* (1842) and *Martin Chuzzlewit* (1843–44) depicted his erstwhile hosts in an unfavourable light and gave great offence. An 1867–68 visit went more smoothly. His marriage to Catherine Hogarth, which occurred in 1836, ended in separation in 1858. Dickens worked hard until the time of his death, which came on 9 June 1870 after a sudden collapse the previous day. Burial was in Westminster Abbey. Charles Dickens is mentioned at least twice in Queen Victoria's journal. Of a conversation with him on 9 March 1870 she wrote: "He is very agreeable, with a pleasant voice and manner. He talked of his latest works, of America, the strangeness of the people there, of the division of classes in England, which he hoped would get better in time. He felt sure that it would come gradually." On 11 June of the same year, two days after Dickens's death, she wrote: "He is a very great loss. He had a large, loving mind and the strongest sympathy with the poorer classes. He felt sure that a better feeling, and much greater union of classes would take place in time. And I pray earnestly it may." These passages are printed in *The Letters of Queen Victoria, Second Series*, ed. George Earle Buckle, (1926, II, 9 and 21).

Personal association between Dickens and RB began in the 1830's. G & M (p. 112) pictures the latter in 1838 as "day after day" attending play rehearsals with Dickens and others. RB's first known letter to the novelist (no. 859) was written on 7 October 1841 while Dickens was ill, and offered a "get well" gift of apples, presumably from the Browning family's garden at Hatcham. Dickens had a peculiar involvement with RB's not-very-successful *A Blot in the 'Scutcheon* (1843). Before the publication and production of this play, RB's acquaintance John Forster showed it to Dickens, who on 25 November 1842 responded: "Browning's play ... is full of genius, natural and great thoughts, profound and yet simple and beautiful in its vigour.... And if you tell Browning that I have seen it, tell him that I believe from my soul there is no man living (and not many dead) who could produce such a work." Forster did *not* tell RB of Dickens's involvement, but he quoted the letter in his *The Life of Charles Dickens* (1873), II, 25. There RB eventually saw it, more than 30 years after the writing. He made a copy on Athenaeum Club stationery and noted: "I was never 'told' a word of the above, and read it for the first time thirty years after the telling would have been useful to me" (*Reconstruction*, E579). However, whether RB knew of it or not, Dickens's high regard for *A Blot* was publicly mentioned long before 1873. An article by Gertrude Reese Hudson in *Modern Language Notes*, 63 (April 1948), 237–240, cites references to his favourable opinion, published in 1848 and 1849. (*Graham's Magazine*, reviewing an American edition of RB's poems in December 1849, said Dickens regarded *A Blot* as the finest poem of the century.) Dr. Hudson observes that RB was "somewhat isolated in Italy" at the time, and thus may not have learned of these published comments.

EBB lacked early personal contacts with Dickens, but she got an interesting glimpse of him in a letter written from London by her brother Sam to Henrietta in Torquay on 14 June 1839 (SD1009): "Tell Ba I met 'Dickens' alias [']Sam Weller'—& a number of other Lions & Lionesses at Mr. Kenyons ["a feeder of lions"; see vol. 3, p. 316] the other night ... Dickens is my height *exact*, rather darker, about my age & wears his hair '*à la Brosy*' [their brother Edward], very animated but I should not have given him credit for so much real fun & talent." Four years after this, in a letter to Mary Russell Mitford dated 30 June 1843, EBB declared herself not to be a great "enthusiast" about Dickens, then went on to say: "But he makes me feel his power again & again & again—he has the heart of a man & it beats audibly, & I must confess that I hear the vibration of it." In a letter to Miss Mitford dated 30 December 1844 she wrote of "Boz": "I never sent to ask him for his hair. I do not enter into the madness of his idolaters in any degree: & my secret opinion has always been that he is of that class of writers who arrive during their own lives at the highest point of their popularity. ... But to deny his genius ... No—I could not, & would not." EBB deplored Dickens's treatment of Americans in *Martin Chuzzlewit*. She wrote to Miss Mitford on 4 September 1843: "To think of a man .. a man with a heart .. going to a great nation to *be crowned* ... & then to come home & hiss at them with all the venom in his body! ... I am as angry as if I were an American." She was willing to give credit where credit was due, however, in writing to Miss Mitford on 27 December 1843 concerning *A Christmas Carol*: "The exquisite scenes about the clerk & little Tiny [Tim]; I thank the writer in my heart of hearts for them."

Much earlier, on 1 January 1838 (letter 605), she had admitted to Miss Mitford that her young brothers Septimus and Octavius were avid fans of Dickens's Mr. Pickwick—"great Pickwickians," as she put it. RB referred to Dickens occasionally in his 1845–46 letters to EBB. On 24 September 1845 he mentioned attending an amateur theatrical performance given by Dickens, John Forster, and others. On 11 January 1846 he mentioned meeting "Dickens and his set" the previous night. On 21 May 1846 he wrote of Dickens's *Pictures from Italy* (1846): "He seems to have expended his powers on the least interesting places,—and then gone on hurriedly, seeing or describing less and less, till at last the mere names of places do duty for pictures of them." RB and EBB visited Paris at the same time as did Dickens in 1856; and EBB, writing a letter to her sister Henrietta on 10 and 11 April of that year, mentioned RB's having been "at Dickens's." On 22 April 1864, after EBB's death, RB wrote from London to his son, Pen: "I dine with Dickens, Wilkie Collins, and Forster at Greenwich." Dickens is known to have owned copies of EBB's *Aurora Leigh* and *Casa Guidi Windows* (*Reconstruction*, M15, 30). A substantial number of Dickens's works were given and inscribed by RB to Pen on the latter's fifteenth birthday, 9 March 1864 (*Reconstruction*, A786–789, 792–798). Some years after Dickens's death, RB reminisced about him in a conversation with American painter Daniel Sargent Curtis, whose report appears in *More Than Friend*, ed. Michael Meredith (1985), p. 172. (See also *Reconstruction*, L84.) RB recalled Dickens's father ("Micawber was easily recognizable") and the novelist's account of his grandmother as "housekeeper to Lord Crewe." Curtis quoted RB as saying that Dickens "in dress and manners was rather like a shop-keeper."

Benjamin Robert Haydon (1786–1846)

Possessing undeniable talent as an artist and writer, but characterized by EBB's biographer Gardner B. Taplin as "vain, self-assertive, impetuous, quarrelsome, touchy, and embittered," this EBB correspondent might well have become the subject for a tragedy by one of the Brownings. However, they made no such use of his real and imagined woes. Haydon was born in Plymouth on 26 January 1786, the only son of a prosperous and respected bookseller. He was encouraged by his parents in artistic and literary pursuits, and in 1804 went to London to study art at the Royal Academy. His first exhibit of a painting there ("The Road to Egypt") was in 1807, when he was only 21 years old. A lifelong quarrel with the Academy began in 1809 over the placing of another of his pictures, "Dentatus." More difficulty came in the following year, with the stoppage of an annual £200 allowance from his father. In 1814 Haydon travelled to France, where he studied briefly at the Louvre. He became interested in the famous pieces of Greek sculpture known as the Elgin Marbles and was instrumental in persuading the British government to purchase them in 1816. In 1821 Haydon married a beautiful young widow, Mary Hyman. The marriage proved to be a reasonably happy one—despite Haydon's various difficulties, his frequent attention to other women, and the deaths of several children in infancy. Haydon's pictures were well received by critics and by viewers in general, but they did not provide enough income to cover his extravagances, and he was four times imprisoned for debt—first in 1823. During one period of incarceration he produced a picture entitled "The

Mock Election," which was purchased for £525 by King George IV. Starting in the mid-1830's, Haydon built a substantial reputation as a speaker on fine arts, travelling widely and eventually publishing two volumes of his lectures. Also he wrote a lengthy entry on "Painting" for the seventh edition of the *Encyclopædia Britannica*. As a painter of their portraits Haydon became acquainted with a number of contemporary national leaders such as Lord Grey, Lord Melbourne, and the Duke of Wellington. In 1843 there was a competition in which artists were to offer designs, or "cartoons," for frescoes in the new Houses of Parliament. Haydon laboured hard over some entries and became deeply resentful when they were not selected. According to *RB-EBB* (p. 810), he then "set out to 'educate' the British public and his presumption and uncritical self-esteem became a regular butt of laughter in *Punch* and elsewhere." A great humiliation came in the spring of 1846, when Haydon mounted an exhibition at the Egyptian Hall in London. Unfortunately for him, the American midget Charles Sherwood Stratton, better known as General Tom Thumb, was appearing at the same time in a nearby chamber of the Hall under the sponsorship of showman P.T. Barnum. Tom Thumb attracted great crowds, while Haydon's exhibition was a failure. That was the last straw: the distressed and despondent Haydon committed suicide on 22 June 1846. A group of friends, including Thomas Noon Talfourd and Sir Robert Peel, came to the financial rescue of Mrs. Haydon and her daughter, Mary.

EBB's friend Mary Russell Mitford knew Haydon as early as 1817, and it was through Miss Mitford that EBB herself became acquainted with the eccentric and tormented artist. Some of Haydon's letters to Miss Mitford were sent on to EBB in 1841, who acknowledged them on 21 September (letter 853): "Mr. Haydon's letters . . . interested me much. . . . They spring up like a fountain among the world's conventionalities . . . He is said, you know, to be a vain man, & it may be true for aught the letters say." On 6 April 1842, Haydon sent a gift directly to EBB—one of his lectures. Her first letter to him, no. 945, dated "April 1842," was written in acknowledgement. From its context we learn that Haydon was already preparing for the 1843 Houses of Parliament competition. EBB never met Haydon, but her sisters did. When they visited him in the autumn of 1842, they saw an unfinished portrait of Wordsworth and mentioned how much EBB would enjoy viewing it. He immediately sent it to Wimpole Street for her inspection. She responded with a letter dated 17 October, and a sonnet (*Reconstruction*, D615–620). In the next two years there was extensive correspondence between EBB and Haydon. Most of the extant letters are from him. On 6 December 1842 EBB commented to Miss Mitford: "Mr. Haydon & I have been & are corresponding by little notes on great subjects." On at least two subjects there was disagreement. First, concerning the leaders who had been antagonists at the Battle of Waterloo: EBB felt a degree of sympathy toward Napoleon, while Haydon was an acquaintance and admirer of the Duke of Wellington. Second, on mesmerism: EBB was intrigued—though somewhat fearful—about the practice, while Haydon was scornful. On 30 December 1842 Haydon gave EBB a 60-line fragment of John Keats's "I Stood Tip-Toe Upon a Little Hill" in the poet's own handwriting (*Reconstruction*, L127). In early January 1843 Haydon sent EBB "what no human eye but my own has seen," the first portion of his autobiography. He called for her "opinion of it," and asked that it be kept "sacredly confidential." So began an episode which was later to cause EBB a great deal of trouble and worry. The main problem in 1843, however, was Haydon's failure in the competition to design frescoes for the Houses of Parliament. In late June he reported to EBB: "*My Cartoons have no reward.*" Then, fearing that creditors would close in on him, he began depositing some of his private papers and other valuables with her. He complained bitterly about the results of the competition, and of being victimized by his "enemies"; but EBB on 19 July wrote: "Now try to forgive me for not being sure of the existence of this conspiracy against you.... Your late disappointment ... is not worse than other men of genius have sustained, & risen higher in consequence of." Haydon, however, did not respond to the challenge in any such positive way. Correspondence with EBB had ceased by the time of the 1846 episode when Haydon's art exhibition failed while "Tom Thumb" attracted great crowds. Haydon's subsequent suicide on 22 June was, of course, felt deeply by EBB. By coincidence, she had visited a private art collection and viewed one of his pictures on the very day of his death. On 23 June she wrote to RB: "*I cannot help thinking—Could anyone .. could my own hand even—have averted what has happened?* ... for a year & a half or more perhaps, I scarcely have written or heard from him—until last week when he wrote to ask for a shelter for his boxes & pictures." In writing to Miss Mitford on 30 June about the same situation, she said: "Once before, he had asked me to give shelter to things belonging to him, which, when the storm had blown over, he took back again. I did not suppose that, in this storm, he was to *sink—* poor, noble soul!–" Beyond her understandable shock and grief, EBB faced a problem of a more practical nature. On 10 July 1846 she wrote to her brother George: "It appears that poor Mr. Haydon has left a paper declaratory of his last wishes, now in the hands of Mr. Serjeant Talfourd, in which to my infinite astonishment, he makes a bequest of his memoirs & other papers to *me* desiring that I should edit & place them for publication in Longman's hands." She felt unequipped for the task, and soon was rescued by Talfourd, who advised her through RB that the materials were the property of Haydon's creditors and that she should have nothing further to do with them. Eventually, in 1853, they were published with the title *The Life of Benjamin Robert Haydon* under the editorship of journalist and dramatist Tom Taylor. (Taylor is linked historically with another violent death, that of Abraham Lincoln. He wrote *Our American Cousin* (1858), the play which President Lincoln was viewing at the time of his assassination.) EBB read the Haydon-Taylor book, and on 19 March 1854 wrote about it to Miss Mitford: "Oh—I have been reading poor Haydon's biography– There is tragedy! The pain of it one can hardly shake off. Surely, surely, wrong was done somewhere, when the worst is admitted of Haydon. For himself, .. looking forward beyond the grave, .. I seem to understand that all things when most bitter, worked ultimate good to him—for that sublime arrogance of his would have been fatal perhaps to the moral nature, if developed further by success. But for the nation, we had our duties—& we should not suffer our teachers & originators to sink thus–" In at least two letters written by EBB in 1854 she mentioned Haydon's surviving daughter, Mary, whose mother had recently died. To Mrs. David Ogilvy, in Scotland, EBB wrote on 28 August 1854: "Do you happen to know any lady who wants a companion & would be kind & gentle to her? Poor Haydon's daughter writes to me in a desolate state. She has fifty six pounds a year of her own, but it is not enough to keep her in any comfort of course, & she wants protection. She wd. like to go abroad she says. Under thirty she must be: father & mother gone! Will you tell me if you hear of anything?" A little while later, on 4

September 1854, EBB wrote to Miss Mitford that Mary Haydon had enquired about coming to Florence. But, she said, "I fear to recommend her to come so far."

JAMES RUSSELL LOWELL (1819-91)

This writer and diplomat, whose poem *The Vision of Sir Launfal* (1848) became known to generations of American schoolchildren, corresponded with EBB as early as 1842 and with RB as late as 1885. He was born in Cambridge, Massachusetts, into one of New England's most prominent families, on 22 February 1819, son of the Rev. Charles Lowell and Harriet (*née* Spence) Lowell. He attended Harvard, was a mediocre student despite his affinity for literature, and graduated in 1838 notwithstanding a misconduct suspension in his final year. After pondering various careers, he entered Harvard Law School, but by the time he had completed his work there and gained admission to the bar, he had already begun contributing prose and verse to various magazines. He became engaged to the intellectually-gifted Maria White in 1840 (they did not marry until 1844), and she exerted much influence upon his life and work until her death in 1853. Lowell's first book, *A Year's Life and Other Poems*, appeared in 1841. Two years later he and a friend, Robert Carter, launched a literary magazine known as *The Pioneer*, but it survived for only three monthly issues. In the mid-1840's he published a volume entitled *Poems* and another book, *Conversations on Some of the Old Poets*. At about this time he became involved in the anti-slavery movement, especially as a writer for the *Pennsylvania Freeman* and the *National Anti-Slavery Standard*. The year 1848 was a highly productive one, in which Lowell published *A Fable for Critics*, the previously-mentioned *Vision of Sir Launfal*, and a second series of *Poems*. Appearing in book form were his *Biglow Papers*, previously serialized in the Boston *Courier*. These consisted of nine "letters" in Yankee dialect criticizing U.S. policy in connection with the annexation of Texas and the war against Mexico. Lowell's wife, Maria, died in 1853, leaving him with a daughter, Mabel. Four years later he married his daughter's governess, Frances Dunlap. Lowell became editor of the newly-established *Atlantic Monthly* in 1857, and of the *North American Review* in 1863. Both magazines served as vehicles for presentation of his views during the Civil War era. Meanwhile Lowell was a professor of modern languages at Harvard, working in this capacity for 20 years beginning in 1856. He continued publishing poetical works and essays, then embarked on a diplomatic career, becoming Minister to Spain in 1877 and to Britain in 1880. His second wife died in 1885, and he retired from the diplomatic service later in the same year. Having become highly popular in England, Lowell now treated that country as a second home; but he died in Cambridge, Massachusetts, in the same house where he was born, on 12 August 1891.

A copy of Lowell's first book, *A Year's Life and Other Poems* (1841), reached EBB via John Kenyon shortly after publication. She thanked the author in her letter of 31 March 1842 (no. 937), mentioning "our mutual friend Mr. Kenyon." On 13 December of the same year Lowell sent a belated acknowledgment, told of his plan to establish a magazine (*The Pioneer*) in Boston, and asked: "Might I hope to print a poem of yours every now & then? I cannot afford to pay for it now, for I am poor." EBB sent some poems (*Reconstruction*, D394,

506, and 932), but there was time for only one of them—"The Maiden's Death"—to be published in the short-lived *Pioneer*. At about this time, an apparently jealous Cornelius Mathews, EBB's other young American correspondent, offered a discordant comment about Lowell. In a letter of 30 March 1843, saying that he meant to keep EBB "advised on all these American points," Mathews called Lowell "the most amusing specimen of mature & rampant conceit I ever happened to encounter . . . overtly treacherous—not a little selfish withal, so that one should have a caution in their dealings." In her reply, on 28 April, EBB wrote: "You surprise & disappoint me in your sketch of the Boston poet,—for the letter he wrote to me struck me as frank & honest." The extent to which Mathews' outburst influenced EBB is not really known. Her next contact with Lowell was when he sent her an inscribed copy of his *Poems* (1844), (*Reconstruction*, A1490), and she returned "an expression of cordial thanks" in July of that year. In February 1845 Lowell inscribed to EBB a copy of his *Conversations on Some of the Old Poets*, a work which EBB and RB criticized between themselves later that year. RB, on 19 December 1845, commented that Lowell "would propound his doctrine to the class always to be found, of spirits instructed up to a certain height and there resting." On the following day EBB responded: "How right you are about Mr. Lowell!– He has a refined fancy & is graceful for an American critic, but the truth is, otherwise, that he knows nothing of English poetry—or the next thing to nothing," and she called Lowell's effort "a curious proof of the state of literature in America." She admitted that Lowell had shown kindness toward her, and that she had shown some ingratitude toward him, but then concluded: "When one's conscience grows too heavy, there is nothing for it but to throw it away!——" A year later, on 23 December 1846, while the new Mrs. Browning was in Pisa, Italy, she sent Lowell a manuscript of her "Runaway Slave at Pilgrim's Point" (*Reconstruction* D805). This poem then appeared in the 1848 issue of *The Liberty Bell*, a Boston anti-slavery annual with which Lowell was connected. Also in 1848 (April) Lowell wrote generously of RB in the *North American Review*, saying that "he appears to have a wider range and greater freedom of movement than any other of the younger English poets." The Brownings met the Lowells when both couples were in London in 1852. Some months afterward, on 20 May 1853, EBB wrote favourably of Lowell in a letter to Mary Russell Mitford. After referring to him and Ralph Waldo Emerson as "the best poets in America," she went on to say of Lowell: "I think highly of him—& I liked him personally & his interesting wife [Maria], when we met in London."

 Years later, RB had numerous contacts with Lowell and his second wife in London, Lowell then having been made U.S. Minister to Great Britain. Also, Lowell was acquainted with RB's American expatriate friend Mrs. Katharine Bronson and was a frequent guest at her home in Venice while visiting that city in 1881. Correspondence between RB and Lowell dealt with matters such as international copyright arrangements and, of course, poetry. A note from Lowell dated 5 November 1882 relates to a third party's query or comment about RB's "How They Brought the Good News" (1845). Not surprisingly, Lowell acquired and owned a number of volumes of RB's works. Those listed in *Reconstruction* (Section M) range chronologically from *Paracelsus* (1835) to *Pacchiarotto* (1876).

Thomas Westwood (1814–88)

Described in *DNB* as a "minor poet and bibliographer of angling," Thomas Westwood carried on a substantial correspondence with EBB, especially in the 1840's prior to her marriage. His father, likewise named Thomas, had worked as a haberdasher but was retired and living in Enfield at the time of the son's birth on 26 November 1814. The Westwoods were on friendly terms with Charles Lamb, who called the father "Gaffer" Westwood and who encouraged the son in his literary interests. These interests bore fruit, and over the years the younger Westwood produced a number of poetical works, at least three of which found their way into the Brownings' library: *Poems* (1840), *Beads from a Rosary* (1843), and *The Sword of Kingship* (1866), (see *Reconstruction*, A2445–47). The 1840 volume prompted an *Athenæum* critic to credit Westwood with "a poetical eye, a poetical heart, and a musical ear." Despite this, Westwood was not fully devoted to a poetical career, and on 10 December 1846 he wrote to EBB of having taken up a "mercantile" vocation. According to *DNB* he eventually became director of a railroad in Belgium and "spent most of his later life" in that country. However, EBB wrote to him at a London address as late as 2 October 1849. Meanwhile, through a lifelong interest in angling, he developed into a leading authority and bibliographer on that subject. He published *A New Bibliotheca Piscatoria* in 1861 and *The Chronicle of the Compleat Angler* in 1864. In 1883, with help from Thomas Satchell, he greatly expanded the 1861 volume into a work of more than 5,000 entries. Westwood died on 13 March 1888, in Belgium.

The earliest extant letter in the correspondence between Westwood and EBB is no. 895, which she wrote to him on 7 January 1842. From the context it is evident that he had requested a copy of her *Essay on Mind* (1826), which she was sending (*Reconstruction*, C34). Her next letter, no. 909, dated 5 February 1842, acknowledges a copy of his *Poems* (1840), (*Reconstruction*, A2446). In a letter to Mary Russell Mitford on 5 November 1842, EBB described Westwood as "the author of a volume of poems with poetical feeling in them & grace—not much power or originality." She wrote to him on a wide variety of subjects, but seems never to have developed as much enthusiasm toward him as she did toward certain other intellectuals, for instance B.R. Haydon and R.H. Horne, with whom she corresponded. As was the case with Haydon, and with Horne until 1851, EBB and Westwood did not actually meet. After she began seeing RB, EBB's correspondence with Westwood tapered off. The last known letter to him before her marriage was sent on 6 September 1845. It told of her plan, which never materialized, of going to Pisa for the winter of 1845–46. Over a year later, on 24 November 1846, after she finally *did* reach Pisa as the wife of RB, she wrote again to Westwood, acknowledging his "kind word of remembrance" which had been forwarded by her sister. On 10 December of the same year he sent a long letter saying "I honour the new name," discussing his own current activities, and commenting on contemporary writers. In 1850, after the death of Poet Laureate William Wordsworth, the *Athenæum* at least twice recommended EBB as his successor. Then on 23 November, after Alfred Tennyson had been selected, the magazine argued—without actually mentioning EBB's name—that she would have been a better choice. Westwood sent her a copy of the 23 November article, and on 12–13 December she wrote to him from Florence: "If you had not sent me the Athenæum article I never should have seen it probably, for my husband only saw it in the reading room, where women dont penetrate, (because in Italy we cant read, you see) & where the periodicals are kept so strictly . . . that none can be stolen away even for half an hour." On 13 December she mentioned Westwood's thoughtfulness in a letter to Miss Mitford and went on to describe him as "interesting & amiable—an old correspondent of mine & kind to me always." The last extant letter between EBB and Westwood was written by her in February 1856. She mentioned "Mrs. Westwood" and went on to say: "Oh—it is all I ever wished for you, dear Mr. Westwood,—a happy marriage!" RB may have had some correspondence with Westwood after EBB's death. A letter in RB's handwriting dated 27 March 1880, and quite likely intended for Westwood, was found in the latter's copy of RB's *Men and Women* (*Reconstruction*, M163). Westwood knew the Brownings' son, Pen, in Belgium in the 1870's. A letter printed in Florence Compton's *A Literary Friendship: Letters . . . from Thomas Westwood* (1914), p. 195, describes the young artist as "a droll little figure . . . very popular."

APPENDIX II
Checklist of Supporting Documents

IN EDITING THIS volume of the Brownings' collected correspondence, we have studied all known original items of Browningiana during the period it covers. Besides primary sources (listed in *The Browning Collections: A Reconstruction*) there exists an extensive body of significant secondary source material, most of it relating to the Barrett and Moulton-Barrett families.

These supporting documents have been invaluable in editing the correspondence which appears in this volume. In numerous cases they helped us assign dates; and, even more, they have helped with notes to enhance the meaning of the letters. We have decided, therefore, to provide a listing of such items—thus sharing them with others contemplating in-depth Browning studies.

Listed below is the supporting material for the period covered by this volume. Subsequent volumes will carry similar appendices of material parallel to their primary-correspondence contents.

Relevant extracts are given where the material includes comments directly pertaining to EBB or RB, or comments impinging on events covered in the primary correspondence.

Following the practice established for our *Checklist*, in all cases where the writer, recipient, or any part of the date is conjectured, we give the first phrase, for positive identification. This is also done in cases where there are two letters of the same date to the same recipient. Location of the document is given, as a cue title or abbreviation, in square brackets at the right-hand margin.

SD1145] 1 January 1841. A.L.s. Samuel Goodin Barrett to George Goodin Barrett (1792–1854). [ERM-B]

SD1146] 25 February 1841. A.L.s. W.W. Anderson to Edward Moulton-Barrett (father). [ERM-B]

SD1147] [27 February 1841]. A.L.s. Lord Sandys to John Ellis. *Our friend Seymour* ... [MM-B & RAM-B]

SD1148] [March 1841]. Draft of Letter. Edward Moulton-Barrett (father) to W.W. Anderson. *Thank you for your very kind letter* ... [ERM-B]

SD1149] 4 March 1841. A.L.s. Anderson & Kemble to Edward Moulton-Barrett (father), enclosing account from January 1839 to September 1840, with memorandum by Edward Moulton-Barrett (father) on 20 October 1841. [ERM-B]

SD1150] 4 March 1841. A.L.s. Edward Moulton-Barrett (father) to Henrietta Moulton-Barrett. ... *By the bye talking of great Men, I heard an anecdote of the Prince Albert which speaks much for his good sense as well as of his natural feeling– After he had finished his lesson with Mr. Selwyn who teaches him the constitutional law of England, he said, perhaps Mr. Selwyn you would like to see the Princess Royal, of course the reply was that he should wish to have the honor; upon which the Child was sent for & the Prince took her in his arms & holding her out to Selwyn, observed I dare say you see nothing more in this Child than in any other,* BUT I DO THOUGH. *Is it not faculty. Dont you think our Ba will like the sentiment contained in it—and cannot I in presenting* her *to any one, who is discriminate, say more than the Prince felt himself warranted, namely, not only I see a difference between her & others, but they also must acknowledge it– Dear Puss, I meant to have written to her, after I had finished this, but I have such a pain in my eyes that I must postpone doing so until to-morrow, when I will write before I go out if possible, in order that she may hear from me on the 6th. ... My eye is so bad that I cannot write to my precious one to-day, but tomorrow I will; it is some thing of the influenza so prevalent here–*
[Altham]

SD1151] 13 March 1841. A.L.s. J.S. Buckingham to Edward Moulton-Barrett (father). [MM-B & RAM-B]

SD1152] [ca. April 1841]. A.L.s. Eliza Flower to Catherine Bromley. ... *I send you* Bells and Pomegranates, *not because you will like the thing any more than I do, but because you won't like it less than I do. It is just like* his *way. This time he has got an exquisite subject, most exquisite, and it seemed so easy for a poet to handle. Yet here comes one of those fatal ifs, the egoism of the man, and the pity of it. He cannot metempsychose with his creatures, they are so many Robert Brownings. Still there are superb parts, the very last is quite lovely. But* puppets, *what a false word to use, as if God worked by puppets as well as Robert Browning!* ... Garnett, p. 194. [   ]

SD1153] [April 1841]. Cover Sheet. Addressed in Unidentified hand to John A. Graham-Clarke. [PG-C]

SD1154] 17 May 1841. A.L.s. Adam Cliff to Edward Moulton-Barrett (father). [ERM-B]

SD1155] 22 May 1841. File Copy of Letter. Edward Moulton-Barrett (father) to Adam Cliff. [ERM-B]

SD1156] 21 July 1841. File Copy of Letter. Edward Moulton-Barrett (father) to W.W. Anderson. [ERM-B]

SD1157] 25 August 1841. A.L.s. William Symons to Edward Moulton-Barrett (father). [ERM-B]

SD1158] [3 October 1841]. Mary Russell Mitford to Lucy Olivia Anderdon. ... *Yes! I do hope that you & my beloved Miss Barrett will still know each other* *personally! She travelled at the rate of 25 miles a day—her bed being drawn out of the carriage like a drawer out of a table, & deposited (with a shawl over her face) in a bedroom at the different Inns. But she certainly seems to have suffered less from the journey than I had feared—& has enjoyed her return home with no more partings to fear or meetings sometimes worse than partings as entirely as I expected from her affectionate spirit. She writes to me now almost every day, & I cannot resist the Temptation of going by train to see her—returning the same evening....* [Yale]

SD1159] November 1841. A.L.s. Mary Russell Mitford to Lucy Olivia Anderdon. ... *Besides that sweetest and highest of women, our precious Miss Barrett, you will like the rest of the family. They have some fine pictures, and there is a miniature of Miss Barrett when a child, with wings, upon a snuff-box, which really seems a foreshowing of her character, it is so spiritual and lovely. See how I go back to that beloved one! But you will pardon the fondness that prompts the repetition; and some day or other you will join in the feeling as thoroughly as myself....* Chorley, I, 190–191. [   ]

SD1160] [14 November 1841]. Envelope. Addressed in unidentified hand to Mary Russell Mitford. [ERM-B]

SD1161] 15 November 1841. File Copy of Letter. Edward Moulton-Barrett (father) to William Symons. [ERM-B]

SD1162] 30 November 1841. A.L.s. Mary Russell Mitford to Henrietta Harrison. ... *My beloved Miss Barrett writes more and more exquisitely. "The House of Clouds," printed a few months back in the "Athenæum," seems to me one of the most beautiful poems in the language. I told you, I believe, of the death of her favourite brother, who, giving up every other object to reside with her at Torquay, went out in a sailing boat which sank in sight of the house, the body not being recovered. Of course this terrible catastrophe not merely threw her back in point of health—for some months she was on the very verge of the grave—but gave her a horror of the place, so that reviving a little this summer she insisted upon returning home to Wimpole Street, and accomplished the journey by stages of twenty-five miles a-day in one of the* invalide *carriages, where the bed is drawn out like a drawer from a table;—one of her reasons for wishing to get to town being the desire to be within reach of me. I left my father for two nights, and took the railroad, not having spent even an evening from him since last November. I found her better than I had dared to hope....* Chorley, I, 281–283. [   ]

SD1163] [ca. December 1841]. A.L.s. Mary Russell Mitford to Henrietta Harrison. ... *for finish, and melody of versification, there is nothing approaching to Miss Barrett in this day, or in any other—also for diction. her words paint....* Chorley, I, 283–285. [   ]

SD1164] [5 December 1841]. Mary Russell Mitford to Lucy Olivia Anderdon. ... *Perhaps before the Spring is over I may revisit Wimpole Street & then I shall try [to see] if I cannot express my favorite wish by bringing you & my precious Invalide together! She is as you may guess difficult to reach—however much she respects & admires the person & however ready she may be to write to her– Never leaving her bedroom—only at uncertain times & hours her own—I doubt if she has admitted a single soul since her return to Town besides her own family Miss Bordman & myself– However I am a good deal privileged in that I* *see her, & knowing her feelings towards you I think that I might venture upon the measure of taking you to her bedside—certain that the after pleasure would amply compensate for a nervous half hour. Even before her illness she was very retired & shy– Mrs. Dupuy who saw her the year after I was in Town told me that she said she had not been out of an evening since the one when she met Mr. Wordsworth & myself at Mr. Kenyons—& you can imagine how much this feeling grows on any one by sickness– Even the indulgence of such a habit as she has it—but when such illness is added to the habit of seclusion the result is inevitable. I doubt if any of the family except the young lawyer (the second son who goes the Oxford Circuit) visit much—& yet Mr. Barrett is an exceedingly clever agreeable man with very easy highbred manners, & the daughters (I mean the two younger ones) remarkably elegant & pleasing– The way of living of the whole family is exactly what Mr. Anderdon would like, full of quiet respectability—fine pictures—rich plate—all the marks of affluence without the slightest show or finery—& a gathering together round their father's table—& looking up to him—& a conduct & satisfaction in their own happy & elegant home which is one of the truest pledges of a careful & successful education.– My beloved friend suffered much during the short early frost—but is now much better again– I hear from her two or three times a week—& such letters!– Put Madame de Sévigné & Cowper together & you can fancy them—I doubt though if ever the French woman wrote so frequently or so diffusely.– She & I have been much puzzled by the impression which Miss Garrow's poetry has made upon certain very competent & usually very fastidious critics—Mr. Kenyon, Walter Savage Landor, &c, &c . . .*

[Yale]

SD1165] [12 January 1842]. A.L.s. Mary Russell Mitford to Lucy Olivia Anderdon. *No, my sweet love, that charming drawing from Carlo Dolce is not, nor ever can have been, at all like our exquisite friend. Its beauty, great as it is, is the result of harmony; hers proceeded from contrasts—a slight, girlish figure, very delicate, with exquisite hands and feet, a round face, with a most noble forehead, a large mouth, beautifully formed, and full of expression, lips like parted coral, teeth large, regular, and glittering with healthy whiteness, large dark eyes, with such eyelashes, resting on the cheek when cast down; when turned upward, touching the flexible and expressive eyebrow; a dark complexion, with cheeks literally as bright as the dark China rose, a profusion of silky, dark curls, and a look of youth and of modesty hardly to be expressed. This, added to the very simple but graceful and costly dress by which all the family are distinguished, is an exact portrait of her some years ago. Now she has totally lost the rich, bright colouring, which certainly made the greater part of her beauty. She is dark and pallid; the hair is almost entirely hidden; the look of youth gone (I think she now looks as much beyond her actual age as, formerly, she looked behind it); nothing remaining but the noble forehead, the matchless eyes, and the fine form of the mouth and teeth—even now their whiteness is healthy. Your dear mama, so well versed in the appearances of sickness, will understand what I mean, and read in it a symptom favourable to our beloved friend's restoration. The expression, too, is completely changed; the sweetness remains, but it is accompanied with more shrewdness, more gaiety, the look not merely of the woman of genius—that she always had—but of the superlatively clever woman. An odd effect of absence from general society, that the talent for* *conversation should have ripened, and the shyness have disappeared—but so it is. When I first saw her, her talk, delightful as it was, had something too much of the lamp—she spoke too well—and her letters were rather too much like the very best books. Now all that is gone; the fine thoughts come gushing and sparkling like water from a spring, but flow as naturally as water down a hillside, clear, bright, and sparkling in the sunshine. All this, besides its great delightfulness, looks like life, does it not? Even in this weather—very trying to her—she has been translating some hymns of Gregory Nazianzen, which I send you together with "The House of Clouds" (you can return them when quite done with), and is talking of a series of articles for the "Athenæum," comprising critiques on the Greek poets of the early Christian centuries, with poetical translations. I had rather she wrote more "Cloud Houses," and have told her so;—and, above all, I had rather see a great narrative poem, of an interest purely human (for one can't trust her with the mystical), doing justice to that great man, Napoleon, to whom no justice has yet been done in any English work, from Lord Byron's "Ode," to Scott's "History." ... Dear Miss Barrett knows you, and your dear mama, through me, as well as you know her, and mentioned you only yesterday, with high regard, as my "sweet young friend." Did I ever tell you that I have another young friend, Henrietta Harrison, whom I should so like to make known to you? ... Surely, some day I shall be able to make you known to each other; but Miss Barrett first. If my dear father be well enough, I must come to town for a day or two in May or June; and then, if it please God to continue her present amended health, I will take you to her bedside. I would go to town on purpose, so sure am I that the acquaintance—the friendship, for such it will prove—will conduce to the happiness of both, living as you do so comfortably within reach of each other, caring for the same things, and with parents who would, on either side, be so ready to promote the intercourse. You will meet exactly on the table-land of that best class in the whole world, I do verily believe—the affluent and cultivated gentry of England; and they seem as domestic, as free from mere fashionable dissipation, as yourselves. In reading "Tom Cringle's Log" to my father, the other day, I find that Mr. Scott, the author, speaks of the Speaker of the House of Assembly in Jamaica as the handsomest and most agreeable man in the island. Now, he must have been Miss Barrett's uncle, who held that station for very many years before his death, which occurred two or three years ago, without children, so that his property came to our friends; and I can well believe that such a description would apply to Mr. Barrett's brother. Most unexpectedly, this dear friend has done my health much good. She (with a kindness like your own, my dear and kind friends) sends frequently to my father whatever she thinks likely to suit him, and forwarded, since I saw you, some of the rare West India chocolate, entirely free from oil, which cannot be bought in England. He dislikes the flavour, and did not taste it; but I, having heard that Dr. Jephson recommended it to the most difficult amongst his dyspeptic patients, tried a small quantity, and have found astonishing relief from the use of it with a dry crust of brown bread. This was a real blessing; for, in consequence, I believe, of anxiety and watching (my poor father's cramp requiring me to be with him often all night), I had been falling back exceedingly. This may not last, but even the remission is a blessing for which I cannot be sufficiently thankful. A charm seems to hover over such kindnesses as hers ... Chorley, I, 180–185.* [ ]

SD1166] 23 January 1842. A.L.s. Mary Russell Mitford to Lucy Olivia Anderdon. ... *Keep the books and the leaves of the "Athenæum" as long as you like, my dearest. Mrs. G―― says of the Gregorian translations, that they are "Englished in words which in their point and richness are almost Greek;" and yet I had rather see more "Cloud Houses," and still rather a long, clear, unmystical narrative poem, full of picturesque description, of dramatic dialogue, and of human interest. Let her (Miss Barrett) once give the world such a work as that, and she will not only sit on the very throne of poetry, but give an impulse to public taste at once elevating and purifying.* ... Chorley, I, 194–195.
[   ]
SD1167] [ca. February 1842]. A.L.s. Mary Russell Mitford to Henrietta Harrison. *Dear Miss Barrett is, I hope, rather better; still, however, confined to her bed. Her last poetical effort was on "Chaucer Modernised," in conjunction with Mr. Wordsworth, Leigh Hunt, &c. It is a charming volume, and the introduction by Mr. Horne is, I think, the best essay upon English metre in the language. Every poet ought to read it, and you would agree with every word.* ... Chorley, I, 285–286. [   ]
SD1168] 23 February 1842. A.L.s. Mary Russell Mitford to Lucy Olivia Anderdon. ... *Miss Barrett is busy with Madame D'Arblay. She says that Mrs. Thrale's charm seems to have been her quick sympathy both of heart and intellect. I knew that before; my old governess, Mrs. St. Quentin, having known her in Wales, and described that as her peculiar characteristic. Miss Barrett says that she is quite well (for her), and walks to the sofa—words of great hope for the summer. Oh, how kind it was of you to get Hayley! How can I enough thank you, my precious young friend? I shall tell Miss Barrett of it, and her love will help to pay you—will be gold added to my silver.* ... Chorley, I, 195. [   ]
SD1169] 3 March 1842. A.L.s. Mary Russell Mitford to Henrietta Harrison. ... *my dear Miss Barrett is, I bless God, stronger and better than for the last three years. She is now printing in the "Athenæum," accounts, with translations, of the "Early Christian Poets," better known as orators and theologians under the name of the Fathers. Do look at these fine papers, if the "Athenæum" is within your reach, as it is probably taken in at the nearest circulating library; she has as yet only published two numbers, one of which was in the last "Athenæum," the other in one some weeks back. I do wish that you and this sweet creature knew each other, and I hope some day or other my wish may be realised. I owe my knowledge of her to my kind friend, Mr. Kenyon, to whom she is distantly related, and for some years back her health has been such as almost to confine her to her bed; but she has borne this winter in Wimpole Street better than the two preceding, and that, I think, affords some grounds of hope that her life may be spared, and even that a comparative recovery may be anticipated; she now walks from the bed to the sofa, which she had not done for years before, and the brilliant and graceful prose of her last papers is in itself an omen of life.* ... Chorley, I, 286–288. [   ]
SD1170] 4 March 1842. A.L.s. Mary Russell Mitford to Lucy Olivia Anderdon. ... *Do you see the "Athenæum?" I should suppose that any circulating library would lend it to subscribers. My reason for asking is, that dear Miss Barrett has published in the last number another article on the early Greek*

Christian poets, and will publish two more, which I should like you to see. The prose is quite as extraordinary as her poetry—so rich, and powerful, and brilliant. There is about it, too, the same vitality, the same allusion to out-door things—things of the day (Trafalgar Square and the Column to be therein erected), which, as your dear mama observed, with the fine sense of the relation of things for which her observations are so frequently distinguished, holds forth a welcome hope of her own comparative recovery, at least of her prolonged life. She has gained strength, too, during this wretched winter, for she now walks to the sofa; and altogether I am hopeful as to her health. Is it not a remarkable instance of sympathy that she had just finished Lewis and Hayley, the memoirs of both? She enquires for a book which has often excited my curiosity, but which I never saw—the six volumes of Anna Seward's "Letters" ... If you cannot procure the "Athenæum," I'll contrive to send you the numbers. The poetry in the last paper is quite worthless. It is our dear friend who turns all she touches into gold.... Chorley, I, 196–199. [   ]

SD1171] 12 March 1842. A.L.s. Mary Russell Mitford to Henrietta Harrison. ... *I shall take the admirable letter, which I have read over twice to-night to my father, to East Court, and leave it with Lady Madalina for a day or two, in case she should not have seen it, and if she have, I shall send it to Miss Barrett, who will enclose it back to you.... It is really a privilege to read such a production, more like "Junius" in point, and sarcasm, and triumphant reasoning than any pamphlet that I have read this many a day. I thank you heartily for your kindness in trusting me with it, and shall double the gratification by enclosing it to my sick friend. I am sure that you may depend upon her for returning the treasure.... How very beautiful the epitaph in question is? May I ask for a copy of the lines which it suggested? I confess that my motive, one of my motives, is to send it to dear Miss Barrett, who already knows you by name and character, and would be so sure to love yourself. She has stood this winter in London bravely, gaining rather than losing strength, so that we begin to hope for improved health, for a change of room at least (she already walks from the bed to the sofa), and, perhaps, for even more....* Chorley, I, 288–290. [   ]

SD1172] 19 March 1842. A.L.s. Mary Russell Mitford to Lucy Olivia Anderdon. ... *I have written to ask dear Miss Barrett the exact title of the volume of Chaucer, edited by Mr. Horne. I have no doubt that the modernized Chaucer, with the editor's verse, would be sufficient; still, as my beloved friend has the book, she will, I am sure, send me the exact words of the title-page....* Chorley, I, 199–202. [   ]

SD1173] 25 March 1842. A.L.s. (in French). William Shergold Browning to André Victor Amédée de Ripert-Monclar. *Je viens de recevoir de Robert un exemplaire de sa novelle tragedie, pour vous ...* [Yale]

SD1174] 10 April 1842. A.L.s. Mary Russell Mitford to Lucy Olivia Anderdon. ... *The same post that brought your dear letter brought one from Miss Barrett, whose two sisters accompanied Mr. Kenyon and Mrs. Jameson to see the place* [Strawberry Hill], *on Friday or Thursday ... I send the passage about dear Miss Barrett, by to-night's post, to herself, so that she will comprehend your visit exactly. I earnestly wish she were well enough to admit the hope of her seeing you. At present she remains exactly as before.... I have been reading*

also Miss Seward's "Letters," which dear Miss Barrett happened to possess, and, I confess, with strong interest, so does she.... Chorley, I, 202–205.
[   ]
SD1175] 22–23 April 1842. A.L.s. Henry Crabb Robinson to William Wordsworth. *... I called on Kenyon this morning. He read me a charming letter from Miss Barrett full of discriminating adoration....* [Williams's Library]
SD1176] 4 May 1842. A.L.s. Mary Russell Mitford to Lucy Olivia Anderdon. *I have had a great shock lately, in the death of poor Lady Sidmouth. I received from her two letters at once, on the Tuesday, accompanying a small portion of honey from Hymettus, which I sent, in right of Museship, to Miss Barrett; and on Friday I read her death in the newspaper. This honey from Hymettus is a fashionable gift of honour.... Have I, all this time, fulfilled Miss Barrett's commission of thanking you for your charming note? She prayed me to do so. I had hoped she would have done it herself.... Chorley, I, 205–206.*
[   ]

SUPPORTING DOCUMENTS: INDEX OF CORRESPONDENTS

(References are to SD number, not page number.)

Anderdon, Lucy Olivia, 1158, 1159, 1164–1166, 1168, 1170, 1172, 1174, 1176
Anderson, W.W., 1146, 1148, 1156
Anderson & Kemble, Messrs., 1149
Barrett, Edward Moulton- (father), 1146, 1148–1151, 1154–1157, 1161
Barrett, George Goodin, 1145
Barrett, Henrietta Moulton-, 1150
Barrett, Samuel Goodin, 1145
Bromley, Catherine, 1152
Browning, William Shergold, 1173
Buckingham, J.S., 1151
Clarke, John A. Graham-, 1153

Cliff, Adam, 1154, 1155
Ellis, John, 1147
Flower, Eliza, 1152
Harrison, Henrietta, 1162, 1163, 1167, 1169, 1171
Mitford, Mary Russell, 1158–1160, 1162–1172, 1174, 1176
Monclar, André Victor Amédée de Ripert-, 1173
Robinson, Henry Crabb, 1175
Sandys, Lord, 1147
Symons, William, 1157, 1161
Wordsworth, William, 1175

APPENDIX III

Contemporary Reviews of The Brownings' Works

RB AND EBB, understandably, showed much interest in the reviews—favourable and otherwise—which their works received. Frequently mentioned in their correspondence, the criticisms unquestionably influenced their subsequent writings. Because it is difficult to convey the full impact of the reviews through brief quotes, and since many of them would be hard for readers to locate, we here reproduce—in chronological order for each poet—all reviews whose publication we have traced for the period covered by this volume.

We have, however, excluded reviews of *The Poems of Geoffrey Chaucer, Modernized* in *The Court, Lady's Magazine, Monthly Critic, and Museum* (January 1841); *The New Monthly Magazine* (January 1841); and *The Church of England Quarterly Review* (April 1841) because no mention is made of EBB's contributions. Also excluded is a review of *The Seraphim*—under the general title "Modern English Poetesses"—in *The Museum of Foreign Literature, Science, and Art* (February 1841), as this is reprinted from the September 1840 issue of *The Quarterly Review*.

WORKS BY EBB

THE POEMS OF GEOFFREY CHAUCER, MODERNIZED. *The English Journal: A Miscellany of Literature, Science, and the Fine Arts*, 2 January 1841, pp. 7–9.

IF THIS WORK succeed, as it ought, and as we see every reason to think it must, it will most probably bring about a new era of poetry. We shall find that the immense advantages we have latterly derived from science and the steam engine have not been purchased by the sacrifice of our ideal life and all its finest enjoyments. Should such an era supervene, it is sure to be one of health and strength, and kind feelings and genuine impulses; all of which are found, even to overflowing, at the fountain head of English poetry—the primitive verses of DAN CHAUCER.

The design of this publication, originating with Mr. WORDSWORTH, and carried into operation by Mr. R.H. HORNE, with the able assistance of Mr. LEIGH HUNT, RICHARD MONCKTON MILNES, ROBERT BELL, THOMAS POWELL, Miss E.B. BARRETT, BARRY CORNWALL, &c., is of an entirely novel kind. If it has not been generally felt by the many, it has certainly been

[385]

long known to the few, as a *desideratum* in English literature. To confess the truth, we know very little of CHAUCER in this country, though his own. Whatever we may believe of the richness of his soul—his sweetness at heart—his obsolete dialect has always been felt as a wild crab apple, and one taste of its pungent roughness has usually proved sufficient to settle all further desires. Mr. HORNE, in his Introduction, following and developing the argument of the old commentator, SPEGHT, would have us believe that all the fault rests with us, and that CHAUCER is in reality, and when properly understood, as easy and harmonious to be read as we are fastidious and indolent. It may be so. But all these black-letter gentlemen and poets should remember that it is not every one who can devote the requisite time to the study, even if it had great charms for them, and suited their taste. It is not a fair ground of complaint against us, which Mr. HORNE makes, with sundry indirect but trenchant reproaches, that we have studied glossaries in order to read BURNS and the Scotch novels, while we have refused to do as much for so great a poet as CHAUCER. The cases are not parallel. There was a whole country ready at once to understand the former, and assist other countries. Again, CHAUCER is more difficult at all times than the most difficult passages which are here and there found in BURNS and SCOTT: besides this, we have continually observed, that both the latter, and SCOTT in particular, "so contrive it" that when they use words not at all known to the general readers of the English public, you may still know pretty well, from the context, what the meaning of them is most likely to be. You find nothing of this kind in CHAUCER'S "hard words." In fine, the class that reads CHAUCER in the original is for the most part identical with the readers of Anglo-Saxon, the Norman romances, and old French fabliaux. It may be easily seen how small in numbers this class must be, from the obsolete character of the languages, and from the scarcity of the books; for even the Canterbury Tales are at this time nearly out of print, while to obtain a good black-letter copy of all CHAUCER'S known works is a matter of no small difficulty. Mr. HORNE thus opens his Introduction:—

"The present publication does not result from an antiquarian feeling about CHAUCER as the Father of English Poetry, highly interesting as he must always be in that character alone; but from the extraordinary fact, to which there is no parallel in the history of the literature of nations, that although he is one of the great poets for all time, his works are comparatively unknown to the world. Even in his own country, only a very small class of his countrymen ever read his poems. Had CHAUCER'S poems been written in Greek or Hebrew they would have been a thousand times better known;—they would have been translated. Hitherto they have had almost everything done for them that a nation could desire, in so far as the most careful collation of texts, the most elaborate essays, the most ample and erudite notes and glossaries, the most elaborate and classical (as well as the most trite and vulgar) paraphrases, the most eloquent and sincere admiration and comments of genuine poets, fine prose writers, and scholars—everything, in short, has been done, except to make them intelligible to the general reader."

Objecting only to the assertion, that "almost everything has been done" for CHAUCER'S poems, in the way of "the most careful collation of texts," (for this can only apply to TYRWHITT'S edition of the Canterbury Tales,) we think the above passage is full of very striking truth, and not the less forcible from its being stated for the first time. To put an end to this national reproach, the above-named gentlemen, acting, we believe, under the patriarchal guidance of Mr. WORDSWORTH, have united in the very praiseworthy attempt, not of paraphrasing CHAUCER'S poems, but of translating or rendering them into modern English, retaining as much as possible of the original. Nor has Mr. WORDSWORTH only given his sympathy and advice in the undertaking. He has laboured in the vineyard with his own hands—weeding, clearing, and transplanting, but very rarely pruning away any of the antique luxuriance. Fruit, flower, and leaf, and boughs and "tendrils fine," all are left by his careful and reverent hand—well knowing what is due to a great author who has been subject to the neglect of ages.

The following verses are taken from Mr. WORDSWORTH'S modernisation of CHAUCER'S beautiful poem of "The Cuckoo and the Nightingale:"—

The God of Love—*ah, benedicite!*
How mighty and how great a lord is he!
For he of low hearts can make high; of high
He can make low, and unto death bring nigh;
And hard hearts he can make them kind and free.

Within a little time, as hath been found,
He can make sick folk whole, and fresh, and sound;
Them who are whole in body and in mind,
He can make sick; bind can he, and unbind,
All that he will have bound, or have unbound.

To tell his might my wit may not suffice;
Foolish men he can make them out of wise;—
For he may do all that he will devise;
Loose livers he can make abate their vice,
And proud hearts can make tremble in a trice.

In brief, the whole of what he will, he may;
Against him dare not any wight say nay;
To humble or afflict whome'er he will,
To gladden or to grieve, he hath like skill;
But most his might he sheds on the eve of May.

For every true heart, gentle heart and free,
That with him is, or thinketh so to be,
Now against May shall have some stirring—whether
To joy, or be it to some mourning; never
At other time, methinks, in like degree.

For now when they may hear the small birds' song,
And see the budding leaves the branches throng,
This unto their rememberance doth bring
All kinds of pleasure mixed with sorrowing,
And longing of sweet thoughts that ever long.

And of that longing, heaviness doth come,
Whence oft great sickness grows of heart and home;
Sick are they all for lack of their desire;
And thus in May their hearts are set on fire,
So that they burn forth in great martyrdom.

In sooth, I speak from feeling: what though now
Old am I, and to genial pleasure slow,
Yet have I felt of sickness through the May
Both hot and cold, and heart-aches every day,—
How hard, alas! to bear, I only know.

Such shaking doth the fever in me keep
Through all this May, that I have little sleep;
And also 'tis not likely unto me,

That any living heart should sleepy be,
In which Love's dart its fiery point doth steep.

But tossing lately on a sleepless bed,
I of a token thought which Lovers heed;
How among them it was a common tale,
That it was good to hear the Nightingale
Ere the vile Cuckoo's note be uttered.

The whole poem is rendered with the same poetical faithfulness to the original. Of a similar kind of excellence are Mr. WORDSWORTH'S extract from "Troilus and Cressida," Miss E. B. BARRETT'S version of the pathetic poem of "Queen Annelida and False Arcite," and the "Squire's Tale" by LEIGH HUNT. Mr. R. H. HORNE'S version of the "Franklin's Tale" is close to CHAUCER. Mr. BELL'S "Mars and Venus," so far as we have at present examined it, is very faithful to the original, and reads flowingly. The "Flower and the Leaf," by THOMAS POWELL, is highly commendable on the former grounds: it is one of CHAUCER'S most picturesque and beautiful poems, and great credit is due to the care with which it has been rendered by Mr. POWELL. "The Manciple's Tale," rendered by LEIGH HUNT, is excellent for its vivid and graceful execution. We have not, however, compared it with the original throughout, but were we to venture any criticisms on so admirable and accomplished an author as LEIGH HUNT, they could only be offered as the result of more time than we can at present devote to the examination. With the closeness of the following passage, however, we have been almost as much attracted, as by its excellence in poetry, quaint humour, and homely philosophy:—

Take any bird, and put it in a cage,
And do thy best and utmost to engage
The bird to love it; give it meat and drink,
And every dainty housewives can bethink,
And keep the cage as cleanly as you may,
And let it be with gilt never so gay,—
Yet had this bird, by twenty-thousand fold,
Rather be in a forest wild and cold,
And feed on worms and such like wretchedness;
Yea, ever will he tax his whole address
To get out of the cage, when that he may:—
His liberty the bird desireth aye.

So, take a cat, and foster her with milk,
And tender meat, and make her bed of silk,
Yet let her see a mouse go by the wall,
The devil may take, for her, silk, milk, and all,
And every dainty that is in the house;
Such appetite hath she to eat the mouse.

Lo, here hath Nature plainly domination,
And appetite renounceth education!

Of the graphic powers of CHAUCER in painting character, the following, as rendered by Mr. R. H. HORNE, is a rich specimen:—

A Monk there was, of skill and mastery proved,
A bold hand at a leap, who hunting loved:
A manly man, to be an abbot able.
Full many a dainty horse had he in stable;
And when he rode, men might his bridle hear,
Jingling in a whistling wind as clear,
And eke as loud, as doth the chapel bell
Where reigned he lord o'er many a holy cell.

The rules of Saint Maure and Saint Benedict,
Because that they were old and something strict,
This sturdy monk let old things backward pace,
And of the new world followed close the trace.
He rated not the text at a plucked hen,
Which saith that hunting fits not holy men,
Or that a monk beyond his bricks and mortar
Is like a fish without a drop of water—
That is to say, a monk out of his cloister:—
Now this same text he held not worth an oyster!
And I say his opinion was not bad:
Why should he study and make himself half mad,
Upon a book in cloister ever to pore,
Or labour with his hands, and dig and bore
As Austin bids? How shall the world be served?
Let the world's work for Austin be reserved.
Therefore our monk spurred on, a jolly wight.
Greyhounds he kept, as swift as bird of flight:
In riding hard and hunting for the hare,
Was all his joy; for no cost would he spare.

I saw his large sleeves trimmed above the hand
With fur, and that the finest of the land;
And for to keep his hood beneath his chin,
He had of beaten gold a curious pin,—
A love-knot at the greater end there was:
His head was bald, and shone like any glass;
And eke his face, as it had been anoint:
He was a lord full fat, and in good point.
His eyes were deep and rolling in his head,
Which steamed as doth a furnace melting lead.
His boots were supple, his hose right proud to see;
Now certainly a prelate fair was he;
He was not pale as a poor pining ghost
A fat swan loved he best of any roast.
His palfrey was as brown as is a berry.

That the two foregoing extracts will bear comparing line for line with the original, may be cheerfully conceded; but as Mr. HORNE seems almost to challenge this comparison throughout his translations, we shall perhaps avail ourselves of a future opportuniy, and endeavour to point out several instances in which we think, if he has not misunderstood, he cannot be said to have accurately rendered his author. Of Mr. HORNE'S Introduction we have not left ourselves sufficient room to speak. It is, however, a bold undertaking in several respects, and not unlikely to prove a well-armed pioneer in various new marches which seem about to be made through the present weak condition of the realms of English poetry. The "Life of CHAUCER" is evidently written with great care, and is well condensed. On the whole, however, and speaking generally, all these versions are faithful copies as well as transcriptions from the original. Nothing like them in fidelity and poetry has ever before appeared in a collective form. They are a boon which we shall be much deceived if the public do not accept with gratitude, and even avidity. They are all creditable to the authors, and some of them bespeak the possession of the highest faculty for producing and appreciating the finest and loftiest poetry. There is not one of *these* modernisers that old DAN CHAUCER would not heartily shake by the hand, could he rise again in his "gipon of dark velvet."

THE SERAPHIM. Arcturus, February 1841, pp. 171–176.

IN SPITE of the various machinery which is kept in agitation by authors and publishers, to invent and circulate literary reputation, it still not unfrequently happens that some very admirable authors are a long time in finding their way to the public. A good book, like a modest man of worth, is often overlooked for awhile in the crowd. Criticism cannot either always aid public justice; it cannot forestall the practised judgment or cultivated taste, which must exist in the mass of readers before the author can be appreciated. Originality, the element of true success, is at first an obstacle to favor, though novelty, (generally a very different claimant,) often gains the day. Excellence of the highest order cannot indeed be hid from the world, but it not seldom happens that talent is overlooked and neglected till by some influence or other it suddenly becomes fashionable. The literary tastes of each age involve something of fashion even among critics. Reputation, with writers of a limited degree of merit, is often a matter of accident, depending upon a particular connection with some reigning author, a favorable review, a temporary interest by which the subject is of importance, the support of a clique, or the notoriety of excellence in some other department. Various are the tenures by which the middle classes among authors hold their rank. A few great names rule the world, while the rest are subject to caprice and fortune, illustrations of the vanity of fame, and the folly of authorship.

By what accident the poems of Miss Barrett have been so long neglected by American readers, we do not stop to inquire. It is not the fashion now with booksellers to republish poetry, though the taste for it, if we may judge from some recent illustrations, appears to be on the increase. A cause of popular neglect in the present instance may lie nearer home, and be attributable to the fair authoress herself. The first impression on opening the volume at the long poem of the Seraphim, is a sense of mysticism and obscurity in a dim philosophizing, which an experienced reader is apt to distrust. We are not at home in speculating on the minds of angels; but as we proceed in the book the eye lights upon passages of earthly description, and sentiments of earthly actors, which claim for themselves a place in our hearts. No cultivated reader can lay down the volume without a consciousness of love and holy thought, the parting gifts always borne away from the company of true poets.

One of the chief poems in the collection is entitled The Poet's Vow. It is written to teach the need of sympathy to the human heart, without which it 'languishes, grows dim, and dies;'* that though

> Thou mayest not smile like other men,
> Yet like them thou must weep.

It is picturesque in its style, and has stanzas which partake a fine legendary spirit, and would do no discredit to the best days of the ballad. The Poet's Vow is to Solitude, to the retirement of his high vocation in the enjoyment of an ideal philosophical revery, which he mistakes for happiness, and the true means of his calling. The introduction of the poet has the fastidiousness and inventive grace of Keats, and seems written to illustrate some antique painting of monk or scholar. After an artist-like opening of the poem at even, with its silent call to the sympathies with those we love, the glare of noonday makes us often forget we are called away to the poet.

> A poet sate that eventide
> Within his hall alone,
> As silent as its ancient lords
> In their coffined place of stone;
> When the bat hath shrunk from the praying monk—
> And the praying monk is gone.

In his thoughts of man and life he would not be included in the common curse; he would not barter or sell or vex the soul with gain, or the countenances of bad men, so he foreswore all human society, to rest unpolluted, undisturbed in his own proud heart. But mark the falsehood of his self-taught philosophy,—the first step to his fancied innocence of living is over the graves of two human hearts; he must first trample upon friend and lover. The touching address of Rosalind, whom he had caused to love, moves him not, nor the manly expostulation of his friend. While the latter thought to win him back to sound sense and feeling, by talking of the humanity of the Saviour on earth, he listened not, but all the while, (how false is the human heart!) he thought of celestial rivers and 'white cold palms' of immortals of his own device. How lived the poet in his solitude? Let the poetess tell, for her knowledge is sound, and her imagination vivid enough to tell us the truth—

> He dwelt alone, and sun and moon,
> Perpetual witness made
> Of his repented humanness—
> Until they seemed to fade.
> His face did so; for he did grow
> Of his own soul afraid.

For years he bore that solitude, 'the pressure of the infinite upon his finite soul;' but years could not dry up the fount of sympathy in the heart, and he looked out upon the world a sorrowful man—

> The poet at his lattice sate,
> Three Christians passed by to prayers,
> With mute ones in their ee.
> Each turned above a face of love,
> And called him to the far chapelle
> With voice more tuneful than its bell—
> But still they wended three!

> There passed by a bridal pomp,
> A bridegroom and his dame—
> She speaketh low for happiness,
> She blusheth red for shame—
> But never a tone of benison
> From out the lattice came!

> A little child with inward song,
> No louder noise to dare,
> Stood near the wall to see at play
> The lizards green and rare—
> Unblessed the while for his childish smile
> Which cometh unaware!

But where was Rosalind all the while? Where could she be to the true unselfish sight of poetry but sad, grieved, heartbroken in *her* solitude. The worldly man may have looked for her elsewhere in reckless gaiety, surrounded

---
*Wordsworth.

by new lovers, but it is not the manners of the world the poet is tracing, but the history of the heart, and most naturally do we find Rosalind heartbroken.

> The loving nurse leant over her,
>   As white she lay beneath—
> The old eyes searching—dim with life—
>   The young ones dim with death,—
> To read their look, if sound forsook
>   The trying, trembling breath.
>
> When all this feeble breath is done,
>   And I on bier am laid,
> My tresses smoothed for never a feast,
>   My body in shroud arrayed—
> Uplift each palm in a saintly calm,
>   As if that still I prayed.

By the last wish of Rosalind she was gently carried on her bier by the side of the kirk-yard, the brook, the hill, and forest, to the door of the poet's ruined hall. At night came the Revenge—need we tell the rest?

> For when they came at dawn of day
>   To lift the lady's corpse away,
>   Her bier was holding twain.

We have dwelt long upon this poem, not only for the sake of the choice poetry, but for the sound philosophical lesson it inculcates. Nature will be revenged on the man who deserts his fellows. The world is harsh to the desires of the youth who has built up for himself, as youth ought, a world of his own, but let him not shun the manly strife of the real world. If the desertion be done in pride, pride will sting the soul by its sharp goadings to despair; if the world be abandoned to avoid its cares in a spirit of selfishness, life without motive will be without honor. It is too much the fashion with a new sect of writers to overestimate the benefit of solitude, retirement, and silence. Verily, there is little chance of the quiet sentences of wisdom dropping like the eloquent words of Nestor upon the ear softer than snowflakes in the babble of the exchange, or the noisy political meeting. These are the extremes. Yet in the midst of action, in the pauses of business, out of the excitement of passion, the very heart of conflict comes the language of truth and eloquence. Thinking, by itself, if we can imagine any such process, would be but 'an idle waste of thought.' Resting on the 'motions of the incessant soul,'* we would soon pause in the charmed circle, not of philosophy, but of madness. Wisdom has marked out the proportion of thought and action in appointing six days of labor and one sabbath of rest.

If the reader desire to hear more of the true poetry of our authoress, let him read the poems entitled Sounds, Earth and her Praises, the Sleep, the Student, Cowper's Grave. The following is of surpassing beauty, from the poem of The Seaside Walk.

> We walked by the sea,
> After a day which perished silently
> Of its own glory—like the Princess weird,
> Who, combating the Genius, scorched and seared,
> Uttered with burning breath, 'Ho! victory!'
> And sank adown, an heap of ashes pale.
>   So runs the Arab tale!
>
> The sky above us showed
> An universal and unmoving cloud,
> Athwart the which, yon cliffs did let us see
> Only the outline of their majesty;
> As master-minds, when gazed at by the crowd!
> And, shining with a gloominess, the water
>   Swang as the moon had taught her.
>
> Nor moon, nor stars were out.
> They did not dare to tread so soon about,
> Though trembling, in the footsteps of the sun.
> The light was neither night's nor day's, but one
> Which, life-like, had a beauty in its doubt;
> And silence's impassioned breathings round
>   Seemed wandering into sound!

These stanzas are the very breath of poetry, the unconscious whisperings of the Muse.

> I MAY sing; but minstrel's singing
> Ever ceaseth with his playing.
> I may smile; but time is bringing
> Thoughts for smiles to wear away in.
> I may view thee, mutely loving;
> But *shall* view thee so in dying!
> I may sigh; but life's removing,
> And with breathing endeth sighing!
>   Be it so!
>
> When no song of mine comes near thee,
> Will its memory fail to soften?
> When no smile of mine can cheer thee,
> Will thy smile be used as often?
> When my looks the darkness boundeth,
> Will thine own be lighted after?
> When my sigh no longer soundeth,
> Wilt thou list another's laughter?
>   Be it so!

---

*Emerson.

THE POEMS OF GEOFFREY CHAUCER, MODERNIZED. The Athenæum, 6 February 1841, p. 107.

CHAUCER IS THE morning star of our verse:—
  His light those clouds and mists dissolv'd
  Which our dark nation long involv'd.
But Chaucer dead, there was no revivification of his spirit till Spenser wrote, who more than once insinuates (and here are genealogies in song as well as in heraldry) that the soul of Chaucer was transferred into his body. The father of our verse had all the qualities of a great poet; imagination, fancy, pathos, humour peculiarly English, and descriptive power. The English language which, to use Addison's expressive phrase, *sunk under Milton*, rose with Chaucer; his works, indeed, are essential to a perfect understanding of the history of our language: though not one jot more so than to a history of the manners and morals of the nation—to the history of our civilization. Chaucer made our language a written and a poetical one;—

>   And as much as then
> The English language could express to men,
> He made it do.

There were rhymers, it is true, before him, but the line of the English poets begins with Chaucer; nor is this unfelt, for he has had the homage of genius in every age, with but two exceptions, Cowley and Byron.

In "the file of our heroic poets" Chaucer was the first in time, nor is he much behind in rank; in popularity he is low, from the too-much talked of antiquity of his language, and the bugbear difficulty of his rhythm. But the heavy "Gothic cloud of night" that hangs over the learning of his age and obscures the lesser lights, is a fog or mist that time and language have thrown over his thought, to haze rather than eclipse his genius, for "the lost glories of his numbers," that Waller laments, exist more in fancy than in truth. A taste for Chaucer is thought an antiquarian relish; and the multitude are frightened at the rough shell that incloses the sweet kernel.

To extend a taste for this great poet has been the task of the several writers who have united to produce the work before us, which we venture to predict, without much pretension to prophecy, will do no more to make Chaucer read, than Ogle, or Lipscombe, Pope, Dryden, or Wordsworth, have done already. To our thinking, the greatest help ever given to Chaucer has been in the cheap reprint of his 'Canterbury Tales,' in Dove's Classics and Bell's Poets; the low price of the volumes induced purchasers; and if men will only attempt to read, they will soon relish and appreciate, for Chaucer is as much a poet for the many as Shakspeare himself. He is the most enlivened of our tale-tellers, the most dramatic by far of all our undramatic poets, the most vivid of our painters in words, and the most characteristic and discriminatory, now humorous, now pathetic, and now both.

If a mob of gentlemen, etchers and engravers, anxious to make Vandyke or Velasquez popular, were to trick out their glorious pictures in the costume of to-day, the attempt would not be more idle than this to give Chaucer a modern dress, and make him write as these gentlemen believe he would have written, had he lived, not in the time of the Plantagenets and Edwards, but of the Guelphs. To hold consistently to their argument, Occleve's drawing of Chaucer should have stood before the writer, not in the gipon or garb he wore, but after the fashion of Stultz or Nugee. Chaucer, in this modern version, is as much like old Geoffrey as Sprat and Flatman are like Pindar. The father of our poetry stands like a time-worn tower, overgrown with ivy, which these Malone-like modernizers have stripped fearlessly off, that they may cover it with a coat of whitewash. If you cannot restore the tower to its pristine splendour, it is a sort of sacrilege to rob it of those beauties which nature, to atone for the injuries of time, has bestowed upon it. It is impossible to change the spelling of Chaucer without injustice to his metre, and yet the spelling is but a small impediment. Despoil him of his words, and you strip him of that beauty, that Doric dialect which lends, as Ben Jonson said, "a kind of majesty to style," for words in writing are what colours are in painting. You rob him too of the characteristic peculiarities that reflect his age. You rob him of those touches which, like the lisp in Lord Douglas's speech that Barbour speaks of, is a beauty that becomes him "wonder well;" that, in his own words—

—make his Englishe swete upon his tonge.

To modernize an author is, in other words, to translate him: and what is translation but an endeavour to make an author write as he would have written in our time and in our language? What Dryden and Pope attempted was to work in the spirit rather than the letter of their author, and they wrote pretty poems of their own, which are as much like Chaucer as the 'Iliad' of the one, and the 'Æneid' of the other, are like Homer and Virgil. They interpolated largely, forgetting a rule of one of their own favourites:—

Excursions are inexpiably bad,
And 'tis much safer to leave out than add.

They mis-metred Chaucer, and mis-wrote lines, the very things he prayed to escape from. Their ornaments, too, are as incongruous as the modern monuments in Westminster Abbey with the surrounding architecture—as Sir Cloudesley Shovel's full-bottomed wig with his Roman sandals and naked body. They made him write after the fashion of their day, syllabically, not as he really wrote, as Gascoigne assures us, rhythmically, that is, upon the same principle on which Coleridge composed his 'Christabel,' a kind of versification to which the public ear is not yet attuned, but, thanks to Coleridge, Shelley, Wordsworth, and others, it must and will learn, and, when it has acquired the taste,—

Then, such as *Dryden* is shall *Chaucer* be; his rhythm will be mastered, and the public will know more than the clock-work note of the heroic couplet, which in a long poem lulls to mellifluous drowsiness. He will then no longer be thought "to fayle in a syllable,' to be lame "for want of half a foot," but will have a music of his own, as every true poet has.

Shakspeare is supposed to have met his commentators in another world, and was found to have no previous acquaintance with them or they with him. When these "mere moderns" meet Chaucer, a recognition there will be, a friendly shake of the hands, perhaps, for intentional kindness, but nothing to infer intimacy or to encourage it. Kindred spirits live together, and where Chaucer is his modernizers cannot be. Do they know more of Chaucer, let us ask, than they know of Wordsworth? We hope they do; for Wordsworth never supplied them with the motto to their volume, which is the work of *on* Michael Drayton, who addressed a delightful epistle, in verse, 'To his dearly loved Friend, Henry Reynolds Esq., of Poets and Poesy,' where the very lines occur which these modernizers attribute to Wordsworth. This blunder at the threshold, and print their ignorance on the title-page of their work.

"Everything has been done for Chaucer's poems," say Mr. Horne, in his Introduction, "but to make them intelligible to the general reader,"—that is, to dilute them down to the level of cockney comprehensions. This therefore, is the object of the present volume; and accordingly the nerve, vigour, and manliness of *Father Chauce* is reduced to sickly weakness and effeminacy, and he sons (but are they of his *sealed tribe?*) have gone, to us Sir Philip Sydney's phrase, "but stumblingly after him. Chaucer's native manners-painting verse would defy even a kindred genius to modernize it; and the same ma be said of the freshness of his descriptive scenes, for description in Chaucer is something for both ear and eye Heighten his nature you cannot, or enliven his humou or deepen his pathos. He is as graphic as description ha ever been, or as words will allow. "I see the pilgrims in the Canterbury Tales," says Dryden, "their humour their features, and their very dress, as distinctly as if had supped with them at the Tabard in Southwark." The are, indeed, all but visible; their characters are distin and individual as human nature itself; their wit, the humour, their wisdom, their manners, even when the are only varieties of the same class, are all obvious distinct: he brings the scene and the actors before us in life; we laugh, talk, eat, drink, sport with them; the can no more pass into the dark backward and abysm time than nature herself; they yet live glowing from t hand of their creator, as fresh to the understanding eye, though five hundred years old, as if the work of yesterday. Words with Chaucer, too, are things—they are pure gold, with the mint stamp sharp and clear on them, not counters of arbitrary value, to be changed at pleasure; they are never vague, characterless, inappropriate, like our modern language; in their use there is often manifest the refined delicacy of genius, which must be lost by the slightest change. They are essential, too, to the melody of his verse, of which no poet in our language has left finer examples. Chaucer was master of all and every variety of linked sweetness. Can this be preserved in a modern paraphrase? To us, indeed, it is strange how men could be found to embark in so hopeless and thankless a task, for if they succeed in directing but one poetic spirit to Chaucer, he will despise the copy, in proportion as he prizes the original. After all, one half the difficulties are local, for the people north of the Humber and south of the Tay, would understand Chaucer without much labour, for they speak a language still rich in Saxon words, and they use to this day many of his expressions, for the meaning of which a cockney turns to a glossary.

But it was idle to waste more words on the subject. Let us give a specimen or two. Here is the first half-dozen lines of the true poet, and for the convenience of readers not familiar with Chaucer we have here and there marked the accent:—

Whanne that April with his shourés sote,
The droughte of March hath percéd to the rote,
And bathed every veine in swiche licoúr,
Of whiche vertue engendred is the flour;
When Zephirus eke with his soté brethe
Enspiréd hath in every holt and hethe
The tendre croppés, and the yongé sonne
Hath, &c.

Here is the counterfeit presentment:—

When that sweet April showers with downward shoot
The drought of March have pierc'd unto the root,
And bathéd every vein with liquid power,
Whose virtue rare engendereth the flower;
When Zephyrus also with his fragrant breath
Inspiréd hath in every grove and heath
The tender shoots of green, and the young sun
Hath, &c.

Now, the *downward shoot*, and *liquid power*, and *virtue rare* of the April showers, the reader will observe are so many gratuitous flourishes of the modern versifier. This is a pretty dilatation and dilution of four lines and one idea. Then again, in the second line, there are wanton changes, which affect both the sense and rhythm; and where is the exquisite melody of the last, in the lame and disjointed modern verse,—"The tender shoots of green, and the young sun"? But it is needless to proceed further, although, on turning over the first half-dozen pages, more obvious objections present themselves—for example, in the graphic description of the Prioresse, we are told—

At mete was she wel ytaughte withalle,
She lette no morsel from hire lippes falle,
Ne wette hire fingres in hire sauce depe;
Wel coude she carie a morsel and wel kepe,
That no drope ne fell upon hire brest:
In curtesie was sette ful moche hire lest:
Hire over lippe wiped she so clene

The *in hire cuppe was no ferthing sene*
Of grese whan she dronken hadde hire draught.

Now it is very probable that if the reader be not familiar with our old writers, he may not understand the passage in italics,—is it more intelligible in Mr. Horne's version?—

—in her cup there *was no farthing seen*
Of grease!

If the reader does not understand the old poet, how is he to understand the modern? In the one case the exact meaning of the words is obscure, but the sense is obvious; a ferthing must mean something very small, a flake, a scale, a crumb, as we should say, if speaking of bread instead of meat: but in the other, the words *a farthing of grease* are intelligible, and their meaning and their application absurd. Again, Chaucer tells us of the Clerk of Oxenforde—

As lene was his hors as is a rake,
And he was not right fat I undertake,
But loked holwe, and thereto soberly.
Ful threadbare was his overest courtepy.

This, we admit, is not very intelligible, and accordingly Tyrwhitt adds a note, to explain that "overest courtepy" signifies "his uppermost short cloak;" and Mr. Horne, by way of making the reader acquainted with the *Poet*, puts the prose commentator into verse, and the line is thus rendered:—

His uppermost short cloak was a bare thread!

But in every page, almost every line, Mr. Horne stumbles, and often from mere wanton tampering with the original. The *hosiers* shops, for example, must have made the reader familiar with the word *hosen*, and yet, where Chaucer tells us of the Wife of Bath,—

Hire hosen weren of fine scarlet rede,

Mr. Horne must needs alter it to—

Her stockings fine were of a scarlet red.

Mr. Horne has surely mistaken the Wife of Bath for the Prioresse: Madam Eglantine, it is true, was too modest to allow her hosen to be seen, or Chaucer might have described them as Mr. Horne has characterized those of the Wife of Bath—as hosen fine,—but Chaucer knew better the tastes of the Wife of Bath—he does not say that her hosen "were fine," but of a fine flaming scarlet red, and she was very proud of them.

To keep up the dramatic interest so remarkable in the Canterbury Tales, and which the Prologue awakens, it is followed in this modern version by—The Cuckoo and the Nightingale, The Legend of Ariadne, and other poems, which have no relation or connexion whatever with the Pilgrims and the Prologue. Mr. Wordsworth, like a worshipper of genius and a true poet, selected the purely imaginative poems to try his skill on. Mr. Powell, Miss Barrett, and Mr. Bell are entitled to like praise. Mr. Leigh Hunt, Mr. Horne, and Z.A.Z. venture boldly on the tales. Of Mr. Horne we have spoken—Z.A.Z. keeps somewhat closely to his text, and where he finds a difficulty he leaves it as he found it. There is a natural, easy, and colloquial air about Mr. Hunt's versification that is in keeping with his author: he is the best refashioner of Chaucer, and seems to have a just and appreciating relish for the old poet; but when he tells us that *love* will warrant liberties, he should not have forgotten that *Love* commands respect, *Age* reverence, and *Genius* something on this side of idolatry.

Appendix III

WORKS BY RB

PIPPA PASSES. *The Spectator*, 17 April 1841, p. 379.

THIS IS A publication intended to comprise a series of "dramatical pieces" by the author of *Paracelsus*, and to appear at intervals; the object of the writer being to procure by such means their introduction to the stage. Allowance is to be made for every first number; especially when it exhibits only part of a play, and that part of necessity the least stirring in its action and the least interesting from its passion. But, judging with this qualification, the scheme of Mr. BROWNING is not likely to conduct to the wished-for end, unless he greatly change his mode of execution. In *Pippa Passes*, (which title apparently means that Pippa, the heroine, only *passes* over the stage, talking to herself, and stimulating the conduct of others by her appearance,) though there is nearly enough letterpress for a short tragedy, we are merely introduced to the actors, and apparently not to all. So far as we have yet the means of judging, *Pippa Passes* is not a drama, but scenes in dialogue, without coherence or action; not devoid of good thoughts poetically expressed, but perfectly ineffective from being in a wrong place. Nor does the moral tone appear to be of the kind likely to be tolerated on the stage, or approved of anywhere. In one scene, a young wife and her paramour discuss their loves and the murder of the "old husband,' needlessly, openly, wantonly, tediously, and without a touch of compunction, sentiment, or true passion. In another scene, common courtezans of the poorest class are introduced; one gloating, naturally enough perhaps over what such people in England call a "blow-out," to which an admirer had lately treated her, and giving the recipe by which she wheedles her dupes. The story itself as we gather from the last pages, will probably turn upon the endeavours of an uncle to get his niece, brought up as a peasant, (*novel* incident!) inveigled to Rome as a prostitute, in order that he may get possession of her property—*novelty* again!

PIPPA PASSES. *The Monthly Review*, May 1841, pp. 95–99.

[The review deals with three other titles; we give here only those comments relating to *Pippa Passes*.]

"Bells and Pomegranates" marks an epoch, as the French say, in the history of literary publication in England. In no previous instance, we believe, has a poet put forth his first edition in that cheap form, in which so many interesting reprints have been given to the public by Messrs. Moxon, Smith, Whittaker and others. The author tells us that the number before us is meant for the first of a series of Dramatical Pieces, to come out at intervals, and "I amuse myself," he says, "in fancying that the cheap mode in which they appear will for once help me to a sort of pit-audience again." We heartily wish success to his experiment, for surely *he* has large claims on our sympathies, who, with high poetic endowments, and a fervent desire to influence through his art the thoughts, feelings and characters of his fellow men, yet finds his lot cast on these gloomy days for poetry, in which so few are they who will pause to listen to the voice of the charmer. The plan of the poem is singular. The opening scene introduces us at daybreak to the sorry chamber of Peppa, [*sic*] one of those pale maids of Asolo in the Trevesan, whose

"Twelvemonth toil,
Is wearisome silkwinding, coil on coil,"

at the moment when she is debating with herself how she shall spend the opening New Year's Day, her one sole annual holiday. She will wander wherever the changing hours may lead, through meadow and wood, and by the habitations of men, indulge her human sympathies as she watches, but judge not their doings, and for once delight her fancy by imagining herself each one of all those beings of her little world who think so little of the poor girl from the silk-mills, nor dream that her slighted existence can have any bearing on their own destiny. The proud voluptuous Ottima and her paramour, the enthusiastic artist and his fair Greek bride, the fond mother and her son, high in soul but weak and visionary in intellect, and the pious bishop who comes that night to bless the house, and pray for the soul's repose of his dead brother; all these she will look on, and be in fancy each of them in turn. Then follow four scenes, morning, noon, evening, and night, in which these individuals are set before us, scenes which would be altogether detached from each other were they not connected by the agency of the silk-girl, whose snatches of song, heard from without, fall like oracles upon the ears of the already passion-wrought listeners, give to their wavering feeling a decisive bias, and produce the climax of each scene. Thus Peppa's *passings*, apparently of such trivial moment, are really seen to be the moving causes of effect incalculable, and the moral of her New Year's hymn wrought out:—

All service ranks the same with God:
If now, as formerly he trod
Paradise, God's presence fills
Our earth, and each but as God wills
Can work—God's puppets, best and worst,
Are we; there is no last nor first.

Say not a small event! Why small?
Costs it more pain this thing ye call
A great event should come to pass
Than that? Untwine me, from the mass
Of deeds that make up life, one deed
Power shall fall short in or exceed!"

The poem, as will readily be surmised from the analysis of it, is fragmentary, and perhaps the consciousness of this has insensibly acted on the author's mind and caused that obscurity that offends us in some parts of the poem, particularly in the scene between the artist and his young bride. The very language seems in places fragmentary and enigmatical, not merely from the abstruseness of the thoughts it embodies, but from a own mechanical imperfection. In the lyric parts the ear is often pained by the involved and difficult construction of the words, the awkward breaks, and misplaced pauses. Something of this will have been noticed in the first of the stanzas quoted above. That this defect, however, is but the result of want of care, witness the strange music of this mythic strain. It is sung by Peppa, and over-heard by Luigi, the enthusiast, and his mother, at the moment when the anxious parent has almost won upon her misguided son to forego his desperate design upon the life of the Austrian despot.

> *Peppa (without)*. A king lived long ago,
> In the morning of the world,
> When earth was nigher heaven than now:
> And the king's locks curled
> Disparting o'er a forehead full
> As the milk white space 'twixt horn and horn
> Of some sacrificial bull—
> Only calm as a babe new born:
> For he was got to a sleepy mood,
> So safe from all decrepitude,
> Age with its bane so sure gone by,
> (The Gods so loved him while he dreamed)
> That, having lived thus long, there seemed
> No need the king should ever die.
> *Luigi*. No need that sort of king should ever die!
> *(Without)*. Among the rocks his city was:
> Before his palace, in the sun,
> He sate to see his people pass,
> And judge them every one
> From its threshold of smooth stone.
> They hailed him many a valley thief
> Caught in the sheep-pens—robber chief,
> Swarthy and shameless—beggar-cheat—
> Spy-prowler—or some pirate found
> On the sea sand left aground;
> Sometimes there clung about his feet
> With bleeding lip and burning cheek,
> A woman, bitterest wrong to speak
> Of one with sullen, thick-set brows:
> Sometimes from out the prison house
> The angry priests a pale wretch brought,
> Who through some chink had pushed and pressed,
> Knees and elbows, belly and breast,
> Worm like into the temple,—caught
> He was by the very God,
> Who ever in the darkness strode
> Backward and forward, keeping watch
> O'er his brazen bowls, such rogues to catch:
> These, all and every one
> The king judged, sitting in the sun.
> *Luigi*. That king should still judge sitting in the sun.
> *(Without)*. His councillors on left and right
> Looked anxious up, but no surprize
> Disturbed the king's old smiling eyes,
> Where the very blue had turned to white.
> A python passed one day

> The silent streets—until he came,
> With forky tongue and eyes on flame,
> When the old king judged alway;
> But when he saw the sleepy hair,
> Girt with a crown of berries rare,
> The God will hardly give to wear,
> To the maiden who singeth dancing bare
> In the altar smoke by the pine torch lights,
> At his wondrous forest rites,—
> But which the God's self granted him
> For setting fire each felon limb
> Because of earthly murder done,
> Faded till other hope was none;—
> Seeing this, he did not dare,
> Approach that threshold in the sun,
> Assault the old smiling king there.
> [*Peppa passes*.
> *Luigi*. Farewell, farewell—how could I stay? Farewell!

The scene between Ottima (an Italian Lady Macbeth, whom lust has steeled, as ambition did the other,) and her German paramour, Sebald, is too long to extract, and must not be garbled. The following vigorous passage will, however, bear to be detached from the context:—

> *Otti*. Then our crowning night—
> *Seb*. The July night?
> *Otti*. The day of it too, Sebald!
> When heaven's pillars seem o'erbowed with heat,
> Its black blue canopy seemed to descend
> Close on us both, to weigh down each let each,
> And smother up all life except our life.
> So lay we till the storm came.
> *Seb*. How it came!
> *Otti*. Buried in woods we lay, you recollect;
> Swift ran the searching tempest overhead;
> And ever and anon some bright white shaft
> Burnt through the pine-tree roof—here burnt and there,
> As if God's messenger thro' the close wood screen
> Plunged and replunged his weapon at a venture,
> Feeling for guilty thee and me—then broke
> The thunder like a whole sea overhead.—

That universal philanthropy and sentimentality, with "tears of compassion trembling on its eyelids," are often the disguise of a cold hard heart, has frequently been said, but seldom with more point than in the following passage:—

> If patriotism were not
> The earnest virtue for a selfish man
> To acquire! he loves himself—and then, the world—
> If he must love beyond, but nought between:
> As a short-sighted man sees nought midway
> His body and the sun above.

And now we must bid farewell to Mr. Browning, thanking him for what he has done, and looking forward to his doing still better; and when he next makes his bow to an audience, assuredly we shall be in the pit.

PIPPA PASSES. *The Atlas*, 1 May 1841, p. 287.

HAVING ACQUIRED some reputation as a poet by the publication of *Paracelsus*, and some applause as a dramatist by the performance of a strange tragedy called *Strafford*, Mr. BROWNING has devised a plan by which he endeavours to sustain his reputation in both ways at the same time. The publication, of which the first number, with the above incomprehensible title, is now before us, is dramatic in form, and poetical in treatment; and the author says, very explicitly, in his introduction, that a pit-full of good-natured people having applauded his play, he amuses himself by fancying that the cheap mode in which the present work is issued may help him to a sort of pit-audience of readers. The cheapness may possibly produce an audience—but will they give him their hands when they come? We are afraid they are more likely to get sulky and hiss.

In the first place, the whole affair, from beginning to end, as far as this first part proceeds, is a chaos of speeches, dialogues, and figures, in which we can discover neither coherency nor positive meaning. As to *Pippa*—a young lady who *passes* across the stage from time to time for some sinister purpose that we suppose will be revealed by-and-by—we are in total ignorance of her mission, her position, or her destiny. We have a group of students talking like mad, but nobody can tell what it is all about; and we have also a wife and her paramour who talk very leisurely about the murder of the husband, but to what end, Mr. BROWNING alone knows. In fact the work is so deficient in unity, action, and human character, that, unless it develop some very unexpected interest in the ensuing parts, it will not be difficult to anticipate the issue of the experiment. We have not the most remote suspicion of the enigma concealed under the title of *Bells and Pomegranates*.

Yet in this maze of crudities there are some highly poetical passages—some, indeed, that are not quite as intelligible as we could desire, but others replete with that wild and fanciful beauty which Mr. BROWNING pours out so richly into his productions. The following is the best entire specimen we can find. It is from the scene between *Ottima*, the guilty wife or widow, and her paramour *Sebald*:—

    Seb.   Hark you, Ottima,
One thing's to guard against. We'll not make much
One of the other—that is, not make more
Parade of warmth, childish officious coil,
Then yesterday—as if, sweet, I supposed
Proof upon proof was needed now, now first,
To show I love you—still love you—love you
In spite of Luca and what's come to him.
—Sure sign we had him ever in our thoughts,
White sneering old reproachful face and all—
We'll even quarrel, love, at times, as if
We still could lose each other—were not tied
By this—conceive you?
    Otti.   Love—
    Seb.   Not tied so sure.
Because tho' I was wrought upon—have struck
His insolence back into him—am I
So surely yours?—therefore, forever yours?
    Otti. Love, to be wise, (one counsel pays another)
Should we have—months ago—when first we
    loved,
For instance that May morning we two stole
Under the green ascent of sycamores—
If we had come upon a thing like that
Suddenly—
    Seb.   "A thing" .. there again—"a thing!"
    Otti. Then, Venus' body, had we come upon
My husband Luca Gaddi's murdered corpse
Within there, at his couch-foot, covered close—
Would you have pored upon it? Why persist
In poring now upon it? For 'tis here—
As much as there in the deserted house—

You cannot rid your eyes of it: for me,
Now he is dead I hate him worse—I hate—
Dare you stay here? I would go back and hold
His two dead hands, and say, I hate you worse
Luca, than—
    Seb.   Off, off; take your hands off mine!
'Tis the hot evening—off! oh, morning, is it?
    Otti. There's one thing must be done—you know
    what thing.
Come in and help to carry. We may sleep
Anywhere in the whole wide house to-night.
    Seb. What would come, think you, if we let him lie
Just as he is? Let him lie there until
The angels take him: he is turned by this
Off from his face, beside, as you will see.
    Otti. This dusty pane might serve for looking-
    glass.
Three, four—four grey hairs! is it so you said
A plait of hair should wave across my neck?
No—this way!
    Seb.   Ottima, I would give your neck,
Each splendid shoulder, both those breasts of yours,
This were undone! Killing?—Let the world die
So Luca lives again!—Ay, lives to sputter
His fulsome dotage on you—yes, and feign
Surprise that I returned at eve to sup,
When all the morning I was loitering here—
Bid me dispatch my business and begone.
I would—
    Otti.   See!
    Seb.   No, I'll finish. Do you think
I fear to speak the bare truth once for all?
All we have talked of is at bottom fine
To suffer—there's a recompense in that:
One must be venturous and fortunate—
What is one young for else? In age we'll sigh
O'er the wild, reckless, wicked days flown over:
But to have eaten Luca's bread—have worn
His clothes, have felt his money swell my purse—
Why, I was starving when I used to call
And teach you music—starving while you pluck'
Me flowers to smell!
    Otti.   My poor lost friend!
    Seb.   He gave m
Life—nothing less: what if he did reproach
My perfidy, and threaten, and do more—
Had he no right? What was to wonder at?
Why must you lean across till our cheeks touch'd
Could he do less than make pretence to strike me
'Tis not the crime's sake—I'd commit ten crimes
Greater, to have this crime wiped out—undone!
And you—O, how feel you? feel you for me?
    Otti. Well, then—I love you better now than
    ever—
And best (look at me while I speak to you)—
Best for the crime—nor do I grieve in truth
This mask, this simulated ignorance,
This affectation of simplicity
Falls off our crime; this naked crime of ours
May not be looked over—look it down, then!
Great? let it be great—but the joys it brought
Pay they or no its price? Come—they or it!
Speak not! The past, would you give up the past
Such as it is, pleasure and crime together?
Give up that noon I owned my love for you—
The garden's silence—even the single bee
Persisting in his toil, suddenly stopt

And where he hid you only could surmise
By some campanula's chalice set a-swing
As he clung there—"Yes, I love you."
   Seb.   And I drew
Back: put far back your face with both my hands
Lest you should grow too full of me—your face
So seemed athirst for my whole soul and body!

There is power in this, and vivid dramatic truth, in spite of the radiant obscurity of its diction.

Here is another specimen of a different kind—a lyrical snatch, which we extricate from the dialogue:—

A king lived long ago,
In the morning of the world,
When earth was nigher heaven than now:
And the king's locks curled
Disparting o'er a forehead full
As the milk-white space 'twixt horn and horn
Of some sacrificial bull—
Only calm as a babe new-born:
For he was got to a sleepy mood,
So safe from all decrepitude,
Age with its bane so sure gone by,
(The gods so loved him while he dreamed,)
That, having lived thus long, there seemed
No need the king should ever die.

Among the rocks his city was:
Before his palace, in the sun,
He sate to see his people pass,
And judge them every one
From its threshold of smooth stone.
They haled him many a valley-thief
Caught in the sheep-pens—robber-chief,
Swarthy and shameless—begger-cheat—
Spy-prowler—or some pirate found
On the sea-sand left aground;
Sometimes there clung about his feet
With bleeding lip and burning cheek
A woman, bitterest wrong to speak
Of one with sullen, thickset brows:
Sometimes from out the prison-house
The angry priests a pale wretch brought,
Who through some chink had pushed and pressed,
Knees and elbows, belly and breast,
Worm-like into the temple,—caught
He was by the very God,
Who ever in the darkness strode
Backward and forward, keeping watch
O'er his brazen bowls, such rogues to catch:
These, all and every one,
The king judged, sitting in the sun.

His councillors, on left and right,
Looked anxious up,—but no surprise
Disturbed the king's old smiling eyes,
Where the very blue had turned to white.
A python passed one day
The silent streets—until he came,
With forky tongue and eyes on flame,
Where the old king judged alway;
But when he saw the sweepy hair,
Girt with a crown of berries rare
The God will hardly give to wear
To the maiden who singeth, dancing bare
In the altar-smoke by the pine-torch lights,
At his wondrous forest rites,—
But which the God's self granted him
For setting free each felon limb
Because of earthly murder done
Faded till other hope was none;—
Seeing this, he did not dare,
Approach that threshold in the sun,
Assault the old king smiling there.

These passages may not be thoroughly appreciated without a knowledge of the scenes in which they are studded; but the reader may still discern a ripe spirit of poetry in them.

Pippa Passes. *The Morning Herald*, 10 July 1841, p. 6.

UNDER THIS piquant and poetic designation a publication, which promises to be one of the most remarkable of the day, has just made its appearance. Mr. Browning, its author, already so favourably known to the public by his "Paracelsus" and tragedy of *Strafford*, thus announces, in a brief and modest preface, its purport:—"Two or three years ago I wrote a play, about which the chief matter I care much to recollect, at present, is that a pit-full of good people applauded it. Ever since, I have been desirous of doing something in the same way that would better reward their attention. What follows, I mean for the first of a series of Dramatic Pieces, to come out at intervals; and I amuse myself by fancying that the cheap mode in which they appear will, for once, help me to a pit audience again." Thus have we introduced us, and with a winning courtesy, the first sample of Bells and Pomegranates," "Pippa Passes," or more correctly "Pippa *passes*," for in truth Pippa is a delicate little thing, half maiden of earthly mould and half spirit—a "wandering Una," who seems intended to bring into something of unity four different actions with different *dramatis personæ*, which, in this libretto, are thrown into juxta-position. Pippa, an innocent girl of the silk mills at Asolo in the Trevisan, wanders forth at sunrise on the holiday of New Year's-day, full of pleasant fantasies, and as she "passes" along throughout "the livelong day," at morning, noon, evening, and night approaches the scenes of the four actions alluded to, and her voice is heard by those engaged in them, carolling some strain of song, which happily in its seemingly unwitting effusion, comes home with a touching significance to their feelings. The scenes thus set forth are highly dramatic, glowing with strong and original conception, and combining the darker and more gentle passions in vigorous contrast. They are marked through out with a certain waywardness of tone, which occasionally tends to obscurity, but contain, also, abundant compensating contributions of genuine poetry. Could we conveniently afford the necessary space in our columns, we should be glad to give our readers one of these scenes to answer for its own and the merits of its context; that, however, not being the case, we shall but offer the following short extract from the lyric outpourings of Pippa, as a particle of evidence of the music of our poet's Bells—of the fragrance and flavour of his Pomegranates:—

A King lived long ago,
In the morning of the world,

When earth was nigher heaven than now—
And the King's locks curled,
Disporting o'er a forehead full
As the milk white space 'twixt horn and horn
Of some sacrificial bull—
Only calm as a babe new-born:
For he was got to a sleepy mood,
So safe from all decrepitude,
Age with its bane so sure gone by,
(The gods so loved him while he dream'd)
That having lived thus long, there seemed
No need the King should ever die.
Among the rocks his city was:
Before his palace, in the sun,
He sate to see his people pass,
And judge them every one,
From its threshold of smooth stone.
They haled him many a valley-thief,
Caught in the sheep-pens—robber chief,
Swarthy and shameless—beggar, cheat,
Spy—prowler—or, some pirate found
On the sea-sand left aground.

Sometimes there clung about his feet,
With bleeding lip and burning cheek,
A woman bitterest wrong to speak,
Of one with sullen thickset brows;
Sometimes, from out the prison-house
The angry priests a pale wretch brought,
Who through some chink had pushed and pressed
Knees and elbows, belly and breast,
Wormlike into the temple—caught
He was by the very god
Who ever in the darkness strode,
Backward and forward, keeping watch
O'er his brazen bowls, such rogues to catch.
These, all and every one
The King judged sitting in the sun.

When it is stated that this masterly and singular dramati
composition is presented to the public at the price o
sixpence, Mr. Browning's expression in his preface, c
a hope that the cheap mode in which his sketches appea
will help him to a sort of pit-audience again, may b
understood.

PIPPA PASSES. *The Examiner*, 2 October 1841, pp. 628–629.

PARACELSUS announced a new and original poet—one of the rarest things met with in these days, much cried out for, much sought after, and, when found, much objected to. We dare say that *Paracelsus* did not succeed: we never heard of a second edition: but we find it an agreeable circumstance to remember, that from this journal it had its first and heartiest acknowledgment.

Mr Browning has published since then: in our opinion, not so well. But yet not so, as to falsify any anticipation formed of the character of his genius. To write a bad poem is one thing: to write a poem on a bad system is another, and very different. When a greater curiosity about the writer shall hereafter disentomb *Sordello*, it will not be admired for its faults, but, in spite of them, its power and its beauty will be perceived. It had a magnificent aim, and a great many passages in which justice was done to that, and to the genius of the designer. The temptations which too easily beset a man's pride in his own originality; the enticing and most dangerous depths of metaphysics, which are, to the young and genuine thinker, as the large black eyes of Charlotte were to Werter, *a sea, a precipice;* into these the poet fell. But to rise again. The misfortunes which are apt to occur in this literal world of ours, the seas and precipices that receive one here, the bogs and pitfalls, are seldom recoverable: but he that

has been led astray
Through the HEAVEN'S wide pathless way

finds, soon or late, the guide that brings his footsteps home.

This *Pippa Passes* is worthy of the writer of *Paracelsus*. We call it, without doubt, a piece of right inspiration. It is in a dramatic form, and has fine dramatic transitions, but its highest beauty is lyrical. It gushes forth, an irrepressible song. Its rich variety of verse, embodying the nicest shades of poetical and musical rhythm, flows in a full tide of harmony with each lightest change of sentiment. We want no better assurance of entire sincerity, for the Idea presented in the poem. No one ever yet managed to get utterances of this kind, out of what M Carlyle calls the region of *Sham*.

The story of the poem is, simply, one day's adventure of a little, black-eyed, pretty singing girl, of Asolo the Trevisan: a poor, ragged little thing, employed in th silk mills of the place: what we should call a factor child, of some fourteen years of age, and with but on single holiday all the year round, yet inspired, by th healthy Italian sky and air, with songs and cheerfulnes New Year's Day has arrived; that single holiday of her and with the first line of the poem she has sprung out her little bed in her "large, mean, airy chamber," full anticipations of a day of unalterable gladness, in whic she shall be free to go singing and enjoying herself she pleases, all around the little old town of ASOLO.

DAY!
Faster and more fast
O'er night's brim day boils at last;
Boils, pure gold, o'er the cloud-cup's brim
Where spurting and supprest it lay—
For not a froth-flake touched the rim
Of yonder gap in the solid gray
Of eastern cloud, an hour away—
But forth one wavelet then another curled,
Till the whole sunrise, not to be supprest,
Rose-reddened, and its seething breast
Flickered in bounds, grew gold, then overflowed t
  world.
Day, if I waste a wavelet of thee,
Aught of my twelve-hours' treasure—
One of thy gazes, one of thy glances,
(Grants thou art bound to, gifts above measure)
One of thy choices, one of thy chances,
(Tasks God imposed thee, freaks at thy pleasure,
Day, if I waste such labour or leisure,
Shame betide Asolo, mischief to me!

But then, in turn, the light-hearted singer asks of th long waited for, great joy bringing Day, not to be sul to her, or spoil mirth with frowns or storms:

For let thy morning scowl on that superb
Great haughty Ottima—can scowl disturb
Her Sebald's homage? And if noon shed gloom
O'er Jules and Phene—what care bride and groom
Save for their dear selves? Then, obscure thy eve
With mist—will Luigi and Madonna grieve
—The mother and the child—unmatched, forsooth,
She in her age as Luigi in his youth,
For true content? And once again, outbreak
In storm at night on Monsignor they make
Such stir to-day about, who foregoes Rome
To visit Asolo, his brother's home,
And say their masses proper to release
The soul from pain—what storm dares hurt that peace?
But Pippa—just one such mischance would spoil,
Bethink thee, utterly next twelvemonth's toil
At wearisome silk-winding, coil on coil!

So come into the little silk-winder's head, people she has heard great talk about, in "the little town below." The first is the handsome ill-tempered wife of the miserly old owner of the neighbouring silk mills, with whom spiteful gossip has of late connected a foreign lover, the German Sebald: the second is a pair that hang more pleasantly about her thoughts, a young sculptor and his young bride that have just come to Asolo, and of whom she herself had caught a glimpse the night before:

So strict was she the veil
Should cover close her pale
Pure cheeks—a bride to look at and scarce touch,
Remember Jules!—for are not such
Used to be tended, flower-like, every feature,
As if one's breath would fray the lily of a creature?
Oh, save that brow its virgin dimness,
Keep that foot its lady primness,
Let those ancles never swerve
From their exquisite reserve,
Yet have to trip along the streets like me
All but naked to the knee!

The third are a mother and son who live in an adjoining turret, and whose love for each other, and supposed quiet happiness, have made a deep impression upon her: the fourth is a great Monsignor, the youngest of three brothers, who have a large family estate in Asolo, and who, the second and childless brother having now followed the eldest to the grave, has left his priestly duties at Rome to say mass for the dead, and possess himself of the inheritance.

Morning, noon, eve, night—little *Pippa*, still at her humble toilet, delightedly dwells upon all the treasures of that holiday, difficult to be exhausted by her, and still those four sets of human figures come back upon her, as filling up, somehow, the morning, the noon, the evening, the night. They are for all the year far from her, but then for that day she is free, she has a holiday, and may go near to them. Why, she even thinks, she could love, be happy, feel content, say masses, just like them. Why should she not, for all that long day at the least, *be* as they? Well .. she will pass by them, look at them at all events, and who knows if she may not even move them somehow, be almost important to them, ragged little silk girl as she is? For the new year's hymn of Asolo has come into her head, with what it says about all service ranking the same with God, and about His presence filling each corner of the earth, and about every one working only as He wills, and being, best or worst, His puppets only: "no last, no first." And so she ends her talk to herself and trips off into the street.

I am just as great, no doubt,
As they!
A pretty thing to care about
So mightily—this single holiday!
Why repine?
With thee to lead me, Day of mine,
Down the grass path gray with dew,
'Neath the pine-wood, blind with boughs,
Where the swallow never flew
As yet, nor cicale dared carouse:
No, dared carouse! [*She enters the street.*

The division of the poem into four scenes is now begun, and the first is the house of Ottima at this early morning. We find that the previous night had witnessed a dark action: the murder of old Luca by the wife and paramour. It is told in a scene between the guilty pair, written with an intensity and, if we may so call it, a sensual extravagance, which issue rightly from such a drunken deed of passion and of blood. In the mind of the paramour, however, the sense of guilt gradually weighs down every other, till scarcely the stronger and more sustained will of Ottima can drag him from the now palpable and not to be evaded horror which threatens, out of his repentance and remorse, to discover and overwhelm them both. But at the last her will prevails; Sebald yields; guilt triumphs; and he is crowning Ottima his spirits' arbitress again, "magnificent in sin,"—when a girl's voice, singing cheerfully without, arrests him. It is a song about the spring of the year and the morning of the day, about the lark on the wing and the snail on the thorn, about God in His heaven, and all being right with the world. The conscience of Sebald is more fatally struck; the scales that fenced and hardened it, melt and drop off; Sin fascinates no longer; the little peasant's voice has righted all again.

And this, carried with the light, unconscious steps of *Pippa*, from morning to noon, from noon to evening, from evening to night, is the purpose and Idea of the poem. It is to inculcate the faith in higher than mere actual things: it is to encourage the hope that all who do rightly and cheerfully what duty they are called to, however humble, may aspire to their share of influence on the whole great scheme of the world: it is to express the truth that, at once encircling the meanest and the greatest, there is a fulness of divine life which acts upon our own existence, to be made suddenly visible or sensible by the lightest thing; and that all, even when the greatest contraries appear to be at work, is yet, to the mind of thoughtful insight, interdependent and harmonious.

Pippa's Noon song restores the artist to more real views of his art, and to that true bride from which the disease of his mind would else have parted him: *Pippa's* Evening song falls upon a troubled scene in the turret of Luigi, and, restoring him to that patriotic resolve from which his mother's fears were fast dissuading him, averts the levelled bayonets of Austria: *Pippa's* Night song penetrates the palace of Monsignor, and disperses a design by which the over-tempted priest would have worked her own destruction. And then, unconscious of it all, she returns to her little bed, in her large, mean, airy chamber.

Full of wise and *naïve* thoughts is she, of what she has passed and seen: the sanctity of those people about Monsignor, for example, who had been driving her and other poor girls from the palace gate:

> The pious man, the man devoid of blame,
> The ... ah, but—ah, but, all the same;
> *No mere mortal has a right*
> *To carry that exalted air;*
> *Best people are not angels quite—*
> *While—not worst people's doings scare*
> *The devils; so there's that regard to spare!*

And full of tired happiness she is, at having really been, in fancy, all she had designed to be at her morning's toilet:

> And now what am I? .. tired of fooling!
> Day for folly, night for schooling ..
> *New year's day is over—over!*
> Even my lily's asleep, I vow;
> Wake up—here's a friend I pluckt you.
> See—call this a heartsease now!

But as she is placing them together, the red sun drops into a black cloud; there falls a drear, dark close to her poor holiday; and thus the poem closes.

> [*After she has begun to undress herself.*
> Now one thing I should like to really know;
> How near I ever might approach all these
> I only fancied being this long day—
> ... Approach, I mean, so as to touch them—
> so
> As to .. in some way .. move them—if you please,
> Do good or evil to them some slight way.
> For instance, if I wind
> Silk to-morrow, silk may bind
> [*Sitting on the bedside.*
> And broider Ottima's cloak's hem—
> Ah, me and my important passing them
> This morning's hymn half promised when I rose!
> True in some sense or other, I suppose.
> [*As she lies down.*
> God bless me tho' I cannot pray to-night.
> No doubt, some way or other, hymns say right.
> *All service is the same with God—*
> Whose puppets, best and worst,
> Are we..... [*She sleeps.*

We are told no more, but can guess what the morning brings. This good *Pippa* is no longer the ragged little silk-winding girl; but *Felippa*, the rich and wealthy niece of Monsignor, the daughter of his elder brother, whom the wicked second brother had removed for seizure of her inheritance.

The defect in the execution of the work—the whole conception seems to us to have extraordinary beauty—lies in the scene with the young sculptor and his bride. Here, with some few exquisite exceptions, the language is so fitful and obscure, the thoughts themselves so wild and whirling, the whole air of the scene so shadowy and remote, that, with its great blots of gorgeous colour too, we are reminded of nothing so much as of one of Turner's canvasses—pictures *of* Nothing, as some one has called them, and remarkably like. But the very reverse of this, is the general style of the poem: suited to what it has to express; now crisply cutting out the thought, now softly refining or enlarging it; swelling or subsiding at the poet's will; and never at any time failing of originality.

Our sketch has omitted mention of two incidental scenes. The first is of some German students: the second of the poor girls at the gate of Monsignor. From the first, which is written in clear and manly prose, we shall take an admirable glimpse of character:

1 Stu. Schramm (*take the pipe out of his mouth, somebody*), will Jules lose the bloom of his youth?

Schramm. *Nothing worth keeping is ever lost in this world;* look at a blossom—it drops presently and fruits succeed; as well affirm that your eye is no longer in your body because its earliest favourite is dead and done with, as that any affection is lost to the soul when its first object is superseded in due course. *Has a man done wondering at women? There follow men, dead and alive, to wonder at. Has he done wondering at men? There's God to wonder at;* and the faculty of wonder may be at the same time grey enough with respect to its last object, and yet green sufficiently so far as concerns its novel one; thus ...

1 Stu. *Put Schramm's pipe into his mouth again*

The dramatic truth, the local colouring, is invariably well kept. Our extract from the other scene is a song of touching sweetness:

> You'll love me yet!—and I can tarry
> Your love's protracted growing:
> June reared that bunch of flowers you carry
> From seeds of April's sowing.
>
> I plant a heartfull now—some seed
> At least is sure to strike
> And yield—what you'll not care, indeed,
> To pluck, but, may-be, like
>
> To look upon .. my whole remains,
> A grave's one violet:
> Your look?—that pays a thousand pains.
> What's death?—You'll love me yet!

A few lines more, and we have done. They shall be from the scene of mother and son in the turret of Asolo, and brief as they are beautiful.

When the mother seeks to calm the son's ardent Italian indignation against Austria, by suggesting the impossibility of escape from her bloodhounds, the young man answers:

> *Luigi.* Escape—to wish that even would spoil all!
> The dying is best part of it—I have
> Enjoyed these fifteen years of mine too much
> To leave myself excuse for longer life—
> Was not life pressed down, running o'er with joy,
> That I might finish with it ere my fellows,
> *Who, sparelier feasted, make a longer stay?*
> I was put at the board head, helped to all
> At first: I rise up happy and content.

He is afterwards reminded that patriotism is sometimes an easy virtue for a selfish man:

> he loves himself—and then, the world,
> If he must love beyond,—but nought between:
> As a short-sighted man sees nought midway
> His body and the sun above ..

—and, more persuasive still, he is reminded of his loved Chiara

> .. with her blue eyes upturned
> As if life were one long and sweet surprise.

And *Luigi* must then have perished, but that *Pippa Passes*, and saves him.

Let us conclude with a hope that she may get the welcome she deserves. Whomever she passes, she cannot but do good to—opening generous hopes, suggesting cheerful thoughts, awakening virtuous impulses.

[John Forster]

PIPPA PASSES. The Athenæum, 11 December 1841, p. 952.

MR. BROWNING is one of those authors, whom, for the sake of an air of originality, and an apparent disposition to *think*, as a motive for writing,—we have taken more than common pains to understand, or than it may perhaps turn out that he is worth. Our faith in him, however, is not yet extinct,—but our patience *is*. More familiarized as we are, now, with his manner—having conquered that rudiment to the right reading of his productions—we yet find his texts nearly as obscure as ever—getting, nevertheless, a glimpse, every now and then, at meanings which it might have been well worth his while to put into English. We have already warned Mr. Browning, that no amount of genius can fling any lights from under the bushel of his affectations. Shakspere himself would, in all probability, have been lost to the world, if he had written in the dead languages. On the present occasion, Mr. Browning's conundrums begin with his very title-page. "Bells and Pomegranates" is the general title given (it is reasonable to suppose Mr. Browning knows why, but certainly we have not yet found out—indeed we "give it up") to an intended "Series of Dramatical Pieces," of which this is the first; and 'Pippa Passes' is a very pretty exercise of the reader's ingenuity, which we believe, however, on reading the poem, we may venture to say we have succeeded in solving. A curious part of the matter is, that these "Dramatical Pieces" are produced in a cheap form (neatly printed in double columns, price sixpence,) to meet and help the large demand—the "sort of pit-audience"—which Mr. Browning anticipates for them! How many men does Mr. Browning think there are in the world who have time to read this little poem of his? and of these, what proportion does he suppose will waste it, in searching after treasures that he thus unnecessarily and deliberately conceals: "Of course," he says, "such a work as this must go on no longer than it is liked;"—and, therefore, we are speaking of it, now, with that reverence and forbearance which one is accustomed to exercise towards the dead. Still-born, itself, it is also, no doubt, the last of its race—that is, if their being maintained by the public is a positive condition of their being begotten. Yet it has its limbs and lineaments of beauty, and exhibits the traces of an immortal spirit.

The idea of this little drama is, in itself, we think, remarkably beautiful, and well worth working out in language suited to its own simple and healthy moral. One of the daughters of labour, Pippa, a young girl employed in the silk-mills of Asolo, in the Trevisan, rises from her bed, on new-year's morning,—her single holiday of all the year: and, as she pursues the long, but willing, labours of her toilet, the map of its boundless enjoyments unfolds before her imagination. Then, among the light-hearted girl's thoughts, come those which *must* intrude upon the speculations of the poor—the contrasts with her own lowly lot presented by the more fortunate forms of life which she sees everywhere around her. Her neighbours of the little town of Asolo pass in review before her, with their several circumstances of what, to the outward eye, is advantage; and a touch of the envy and ill will, from which even the humble cannot be wholly exempt, mingles with her purer fancies, and dims the brightness of her holiday morning. But, in the breast of this joyous-hearted girl, these feelings soon take a healthier tone,—resolving themselves into reliance upon providence, contentment with her lot, which has in it this *one* chartered day—now only beginning—and a sense that she is a child of God as well as all the others, and has a certain value in the sum of creation, like the rest:—and so, she breaks away out into the sunshine, merry as a May-day queen,—

Down the grass-path grey with dew,
Neath the pine-wood blind with boughs,
Where the swallow never flew
As yet, nor cicale dared carouse,—

with a song expressing such sentiments, and her own joy:—

The year's at the spring,
And day's at the morn:
Morning's at seven;
The hill-side's dew pearled:
The lark's on the wing,
The snail's on the thorn;
God's in his heaven—
All's right with the world!

And then, the poem, which has no unity of action,—is held together by the single unity of its moral, and is dramatic only because it is written in dialogue-form—introduces us, by a series of changes, into the interiors of certain of those dwellings which the envious thoughts of Pippa had failed to pierce: and we are present at scenes of passion or intrigue, which the trappings, that had dazzled her eye, serve to hide. One of these, between the wife of a rich miser and her paramour,—on the night which conceals the murder of the husband, by the guilty pair, but just as the day is about to dawn upon it—is written with such power of passion and of painting (with a voluptuousness of colour and incident, however, which Mr. Browning may find it convenient to subdue, for an English public) as marks a master-hand,—and makes it really a matter of lamentation, that he should persist in thinking it necessary for a poet to adopt the tricks of a conjuror, or fancy that among the true spells of the former are the mock ones of the latter's mystical words. Into this scene of guilt and passion,—as into all the others to which we are introduced,—breaks the clear voice of a girl, singing in the young sunshine. By each and all of them, "Pippa passes,"—carolling away her one untiring burthen of gladness,—carrying everywhere her moral that "God's in his heaven," and the world beneath his eye—scattering sophisms and startling crime. Before this one natural and important truth, taught to a cheerful and lowly heart, the artificialities of life severally dissolve, and its criminals grow pale. Surely, there is something very fine in this! Not only have we the trite, but valuable, moral that happiness is more evenly distributed than it seems, enforced in a new form,—but also that other and less popularly understood one, which it were well the poor should learn,—and still better that the rich should ponder,—that the meanest of them all has his appointed value in God's scheme,—and a higher part may be cast to him who has to play it in rags, than to the puppet of the drama who enacts king, and walks the stage in purple. This despised little silk-weaver, like a messenger from God, knocks at the hearts of all these persons who seem to her so privileged,—and the proudest of them all opens to her. Again, we say, this is very fine;—and Mr. Browning is unjust both to himself and others, when he subjects it to the almost certainty of being lost. Why should an author, who can think such living thoughts as these, persist in making mummies of them?—and why should we, ere we could disengage this high and beautiful truth, have had to go through the tedious and di[s]agreeable process of unwrapping?

We could not give our readers any specimen of the author's beauties, exceeding a few lines in length, without stumbling upon some of his obscurities: and will content ourselves, therefore, with a short example or two of his manner, when it is most natural and unencumbered:—

> I have
> Enjoyed these fifteen years of mine too much
> To leave myself excuse for longer life—
> Was not life pressed down, running o'er with joy,
> That I might finish with it ere my fellows,
> Who, sparelier feasted, make a longer stay?
> I was put at the board-head, helped to all

> At first: I rise up happy and content.
> God must be glad one loves his world so much—
> I can give news of earth to all the dead
> Who ask me:—last year's sunsets and great stars,
> That had a right to come first, and see ebb
> The crimson wave that drifts the sun away—
> Those cresent moons, with notched and burning rims
> That strengthened into sharp fire, and there stood,
> Impatient of the azure—and that day,
> In March, a double rainbow stopped the storm—
> May's warm, slow, yellow, moonlit summer nights—
> Gone are they—but I have them in my soul!

And the following song:

> You love me yet!—and I can tarry
> Your love's protracted growing:
> June reared that bunch of flowers you carry,
> From seeds of April's sowing.
>
> I plant a heartful now—some seed
> At least is sure to strike,
> And yield—what you'll not care, indeed,
> To pluck, but, may be, like
>
> To look upon .. my whole remains,
> A grave's one violet
> Your look?—that pays a thousand pains.
> What's death?—You love me yet!

[G. Darley?]

KING VICTOR AND KING CHARLES. *The Spectator*, 5 March 1842, pp. 233–234.

VICTOR AMADEUS, the first King of Sardinia, determined at the age of sixty-four to resign his crown to his son, and to marry the widow of the Count ST. SEBASTIAN, who was then about fifty, but to whom he had been long attached. Being rather a pompous personage, and probably verging towards dotage, VICTOR had every thing connected with the abdication arranged in exact imitation of that of CHARLES the Fifth: and for a little time after his resignation, he was satisfied with his condition; but as the novelty wore off, and the attention which was at first paid by his son and his ministers in taking his opinion on affairs was discontinued, he grew dissatisfied, and expressed a wish to recall his abdication. Some unsuccessful attempts on the fidelity of his son's officers failing, he was forcibly arrested in bed, and was confined, first in one castle or mansion and then in another, pretty much as he wished. His death occurred in about a twelvemonth after his arrest, previous to which he seems to have fallen into a sort of fatuity.

The interest of this story is historical: and very interesting it is in many of its details,—as the surprise and agitation of Victor's own grenadiers when they saw him led down under arrest, and the promptness by which the threatened mutiny was quelled by the Count de la Perouse—or the old King's agitation at the sight of the regiment of dragoons that had formerly distinguished itself under his own eye, and his attempt to address them, drowned by beat of drum. These and several other points of a kindred nature are omitted by Mr. BROWNING; partly, it would seem, because they are not even adapted to what is called dramatic poetry; partly because he has a theory of his own upon the historical part of the case,—which is, that Victor having got himself into difficulties, with his subjects by his tyranny and with his allies by his tricks, resigned in order to let his son overcome these obstacles, after which he intended to reclaim the crown: but as the poet could not bend the *facts* of history to these refinements, he constrains his characters to his purposes. Charles, the son, is intended to exhibit "extreme and painful sensibility, prolonged immaturity of powers, earnest good purpose, and vacillating will": his sensibility, however, savours of mawkishness, and he holds the crown with a tenacious gripe enough when he gets hold of it, though he proposes to resign it at the last, when his father is dying within a speech or two. D'Ormea, one of the ministers of the true story, but the only one of the poem, is designed as a compound of "ill-considered rascality and subsequent better-advised rectitude": but his conduct is a tissue of incomprehensibleness. Victor Amadeus is intended to be drawn as of a "fiery and audacious temper, unscrupulous selfishness, profound dissimulation, and singular fertility in resources": but in the execution, it is difficult to say whether he is an old gentleman in his dotage or an over-cunning politician with a scheme too fine for use. To the character of a drama *King Victor and King Charles* has no pretension, scarcely to that of a modern dramatic poem. It is a Dialogue of the Dead in blank verse, where the interlocutors are made to express the author's theory of their character and purposes, but without that regard to consistency which nature requires; for no attorney or confidential clerk was ever systematically abused and insulted by a patron as King Victor and King Charles both insul D'Ormea. As the exposition of an historical theory, the poem has this defect—that, presenting results without the reasons on which they are founded, and very often in an allusive and mystical way, it will not convince those who are acquainted with the period and will be unintelligible to all others. Considered merely as a poem, it has some passages of a quaint and peculiar beauty or power; but the whole inspires regret that Mr. BROWNING should persist in marring the ability he possesses, by affectation and singularity; or that Nature should have fixed these qualities so deeply in him that he cannot favourably develop his own powers. We suspect, however, that Nature ought not to bear all the blame; for, though Mr. BROWNING may have excelled *Paracelsus* in particular passages, as a whole that first work was his best. Mr. BROWNING appears a man who rather cultivates his weeds than his flowers.

KING VICTOR AND KING CHARLES. The *Examiner*, 2 April 1842, pp. 211-212.

THIS IS A PIECE of modern history of a startling kind, thrown into dramatic form.

The King Victor is that notable person whose energy secured for the Dukes of the House of Savoy, some century and a quarter since, the place among Sovereigns of Europe which they hold to this day, with the title of Kings of Sardinia. He has also some special claims upon the interest of Englishmen, from having married a niece of Charles the Second: an alliance which might have dropped the English Crown into his family, but for the settlement of '88. All the incidents and associations of his life, however—even to the memory of that indomitable spirit which, having sustained a petty dukedom against all that even the Fourteenth Louis could bring against it, ultimately regalised its race—have been absorbed in his sad and surprising death. And over this sufficient mystery still hangs, to make it the more appropriate subject for a tragic poet.

After reigning in his Dukedom thirty years, and seventeen years in his kingdom, Victor, in a hale and vigorous old age, abdicated in favour of his son. His motives are doubtful. Mr Browning finds them in a restless passion for intrigue; and makes the abdication a mere expedient by which the wily politician, still resolved to die a king, would have slipped his pliant and docile son for a time into the danger-woven mesh of his sovereignty, which, when youth and innocence had disentangled, craft and old age should again enjoy. And the manner in which this tribute to the simplest kind of honesty is wrung from the hardened veteran in subtle policy, is no doubt the conception of a true poet. But we suspect that Victor's reasons lay much more upon the surface. In all probability the case was the precise counterpart of what we have witnessed in a neighbouring kingdom within the last three years: a king abdicating in his son's favour, that he might as a private man indulge a passion unquestioned, from which decency would have interdicted royalty.

Be this as it may—and whether *to return* was a part of the original design, as Mr Browning would make it; or, as we think more likely, a part of the original weakness of the old man's subjection to an infamous woman, for whom he had resigned his crown, and impelled by whom he came to ask for it again—Victor, within a year of his abdication, *did return*. But he found his son less docile and pliant than he had left him. And here equal doubts as with the motives of the father, occur respecting the conduct adopted by the son. It seems questionable whether there were needless cruelty and harshness in what he did, or whether he was urged and sustained through it all by a noble sense of duty. Mr Browning uses the poetic privilege admirably, in reconciling the external facts on which these questions arise; and the decisive measures which are said to have broken the heart of Victor, are with great beauty and masterly skill made quite compatible with the generous character which history gives to Charles. But the mere facts as they stand on record in relation to Victor's return, we take to be these. At first, his son would not believe that his father seriously entertained the intention attributed to him; but on receiving serious proofs to that effect, took council with his nobles, and had him at once arrested. Victor then passed twelve wretched months in solitary detention at Rivoli, and miserably died. The old man's heart was broken, but his passionate temper stayed to the last. It is even said, in some of the more private details of this unhappy time, that from his death bed he drove away the priests of the church, to which he had theretofore never failed in duty, appalled by the nature of his denunciations against King Charles. "Bring no consolation to me," he said, when they reminded him of the Great Sacrifice for the remission of suffering and of sin: "He of whom you speak, had a son to die for him: *I die for my son.*"

The characters in Mr Browning's tragedy are four: Victor and Charles; Polyxena, the wife of Charles; and D'Ormea, the minister of both kings. Of these, we like Victor the most; and, notwithstanding some exquisite management in relation to him, Charles the least. Until near the close indeed, he is in such a continual and most painful fret and worry that we long for all our sakes to have him any way out of it. The secret of Mr Browning's error in this, we suspect to be one very common with the best young poets: the love of a too decisive contrast. But it needed no such artifice to recommend the more strikingly, the calm and quiet figure by Charles's side. Polyxena is a charming conception, adequately sustained: a delightful picture of the high-toned Love in woman, which without other aid gives brightness to the intellect and irresistible moral strength to the soul. We like D'Ormea too: the rascally, conscience-scared old minister, who suddenly finds himself infected with the disease as with an influenza, and is very nigh falling a martyr to it.

The general fault of the tragedy, as a poem, is in its defects of versification; and, as a dramatic work, in its substitution of the metaphysics of character and passion for their broad and practical results. These mistakes, which have a wilful and deliberate air, are easily pointed out, and much effective abuse vented upon them without much trouble. But it is worth more trouble to be able to discover, even in these, the wayward perverseness of a man of true genius. Such is Mr Browning. We ought not to extenuate what we hold to be a grave error; but we think it not difficult to see that, by the very passion for his art, such a man may be so betrayed. Time is the great correcter: as Time is the disinterested, the immortal witness on Poetry's behalf, that her ways are very old and very settled ways, not admitting, like those of steam and other wonderful inventions, of many novel or useful improvements. She has now been current in the world for some thousands of years, and it is generally admitted, we believe, that the first effort she made—the first at any rate of which there is written record—*continues to be the best.*

We cannot subjoin all we could have wished, from the tragedy itself: but the reader who is wise enough to take our word, and act on it, will find his reward in many beautiful, powerful, and pathetic passages. Meanwhile, what little we can quote may go in illustration of old Victor: the master-piece of the composition, as he ought to be. The constant reaction upon his habits of craft and mere politic purposes, of the nobler part of his nature and the grand recollections of his life, is at once an instructive and affecting piece of truth.

> Oh, Victor—Victor—
> But thus it is: the age of crafty men
> Is loathsome—youth contrives to carry off
> Dissimulation—we may intersperse
> Extenuating passages of strength,
> Ardour, vivacity, and wit—may turn
> E'en guile into a voluntary grace,—
> But one's old age, when graces drop away
> And leave guile the pure staple of our lives—
> Ah, loathsome!

So is the pleading of the poor outwitted old man, when the change of character in his son dawns terribly upon him.

> ... he forgot his promise, found his strength
> Fail him, had thought at savage Chamberri
> Too much of brilliant Turin, Rivoli here,
> And Susa, and Veneria, and Superga—
> Pined for the pleasant places he had built
> When he was fortunate and young.

Again:

> ... he could not die
> Deprived of baubles he had put aside
> He deemed for ever—of the Crown that binds
> Your brain up, whole, sound, and impregnable,
> Creating kingliness—the Sceptre, too,
> Whose mere wind, should you wave it, back would beat
> Invaders—and the golden Ball which throbs
> As if you grasped the palpitating heart
> Indeed o' the realm, to mould as choose you may.

In the closing speech of the tragedy, there is great art, beauty, and effect. The best and worst of Victor are here for the last time brought together, side by side with the lesson they teach. It is very striking, that grand kind of vanity in the old man—already sufficiently far from life to behold himself a figure in history.

> *Vic.* Past help, past reach!
> 'Tis in the heart—you cannot reach the heart:
> This broke mine, that I did believe you, Charles,
> Would have denied and so disgraced me.
> *Pol.* Charles
> Has never ceased to be your subject, sire—
> He reigned at first through setting up yourself
> As pattern: if he e'er seemed harsh to you,
> 'Twas from a too intense appreciation
> Of your own character: he acted you—
> Ne'er for an instant did I think it real,
> Or look for any other than this end.
> *I hold him worlds the worse on that account;*
> *But so it was.*
> *Cha.* I love you now, indeed!
> (*To Victor.*) You never knew me!

> *Vic.* Hardly till this moment,
> When I seem learning many other things,
> Because the time for using them is past.
> If 'twere to do again! That's idly wished.
> *Truthfulness might prove policy as good*
> *As guile.* Is this my daughter's forehead? Yes—
> I've made it fitter now to be a Queen's
> Than formerly—*I've ploughed the deep lines there*
> *That keep too well a Crown from slipping off!*
> No matter. Guile has made me King again.
> Louis—'twas in King Victor's time—long since,
> *When Louis reign'd—and, also, Victor reign'd—*
> *How the world talks already of us two!*
> God of eclipse and each discoloured star,
> Why do I linger then?
> Ha! Where lurks he?
> D'Ormea! Come nearer to your King! Now stand!
> [*Collecting his strength as D'Ormea approaches.*
> But you lied, D'Ormea! I do not repent. [*Dies.*

This should be our last extract, but that we wish to show the writer's dramatic faculty, in passages of ordinary dialogue. If we had space, we should have given the whole scene which closes the first part, beginning with the entrance of the crowned Charles: as it is, we content ourselves with what follows.

> *Cha.* First for the levies.
> What forces can I muster presently?
> [*D'Ormea delivers papers which Charles inspects.*
> *Cha.* Good—very good. Montorio .. how is this?
> —Equips me double the old complement
> Of soldiers?
> *D'O.* Since his land has been relieved
> From double impost this he manages:
> But under the late monarch ..
> *Cha.* Peace. I know.
> Count Spava has omitted mentioning
> What proxy is to head these troops of his.
> *D'O.* Count Spava means to head his troops himself.
> Something's to fight for now; "whereas," says he,
> "Under the Sovereign's father" ..
> *Cha.* It would seem
> That all my people love me.
> *D'O.* Yes. [*To Polyxena, while Charles continues to inspect the papers.*
> A temper
> Like Victor's may avail to keep a state—
> He terrifies men and they fall not off—
> Good to restrain; best, if restraint were all:
> But with the silent circle round him ends
> Such sway. Our King's begins precisely there.
> For to suggest, impel, and set at work,
> Is quite another function. Men may slight
> In time of peace the King who brings them peace:
> In war,—his voice, his eyes, help more than fear.
> They love you, sire!

Sooner or later—unless he defers it till too late!—Mr Browning will write an entirely worthy, manly, and well matured dramatic work. It is *in* him, and ought to be *out*.

KING VICTOR AND KING CHARLES. *The Athenæum*, 30 April 1842, pp. 376–378.

THIS IS THE SECOND of a series of poems which, under the whimsical title of 'Bells and Pomegranates,' Mr. Browning promises to the world. We have before predicted that Mr. Browning's audience would be limited, and, inasmuch as he has doubled the price of admission, we are led to conclude that our prediction has been fulfilled. If such be the case, even in the teeth of our infallibility, we regret it, for we have faith in Mr. Browning, and trust to see him realize a higher destiny than that of the thousand and one claimants to the laurel crown.

The "plot" of 'King Victor and King Charles' is taken from an episode in the history of Sardinia, peculiarly adapted for dramatic treatment. Victor Amadeus, second Duke of Savoy of that name, has involved himself, by tortuous policy, in the danger of a war, both with Austria and Spain; and in order to put off the fatal day, he conceives the project of resigning his crown to his son Charles. Charles Emmanuel bears a striking resemblance to Schiller's Don Carlos; and his wife Polyxena, his counsellor, is not unlike a female *Posa*. By her advice, Charles accepts the proffered crown, and the unswerving rectitude of his conduct restores Sardinia to tranquillity and happiness. Meanwhile the ambition of the abdicated King returns—the crown and sceptre, with all their associated excitements, are an ever-craving want to his restless mind, and he resolves to regain them, even by force, should persuasion fail. Charles, who has long turned a deaf ear to the information conveyed to him by a crafty Prime Minister of his father's "conspiracy," at last authorizes his arrest. Victor is brought before him, claims the crown, which his son restores, and the old man, after a minute's enjoyment of his accustomed dignities, expires!

This plot, it will be seen at a glance, is highly dramatic; and Mr. Browning has worked it out with skill. His characters are drawn with breadth and great distinctness of colouring. The sensibility, the true-heart, the vacillating will of Charles at the commencement of the drama, his subsequent energy and developed talents, when the crown is placed on his head, and the noble aim of a nation's welfare, which gives concentration to his powers, are finely conceived. The restless ambition and selfishness of Victor, the bold dishonesty and sarcastic deceit of D'Ormea (the Prime Minister), and the calm, lofty, pure-mindedness of Polyxena, are pictured with unity and vigour. But in giving an extract, or two, we must once again, and emphatically, express our regret, at the extent to which Mr. Browning allows his manner to interpose between his own fine conceptions and the public. Full of thought, full of learning, full of fancy as his poems would have them to be, they also exhibit him as cumbered, rather than strengthened by the number of his possessions, and neither few nor far between are the portions where this inability to do justice to his own meanings, takes forms, which might be confounded by the superficial observer with commonplace.

This protest recorded, we will give some extracts from the scene in which Polyxena first learns of the resignation of the crown by Victor to his son. She sees the crown and exclaims,—

    Polyxena.   So, now my work
Begins—to save him from regret. Save Charles
Regret?—the noble nature! He's not made
Like the Italians: 'tis a German soul.
          CHARLES *enters crowned.*
Oh, where's the King's heir? Gone:—The Crown-
    prince?
Gone—
Where's Savoy? Gone:—Sardinia? Gone!—But
    Charles
Is left! And when my Rhine-land bowers arrive,
If he looked almost handsome yester-twilight
As his grey eyes seemed widening into black
Because I praised him, then how will he look?
Farewell, you stripped and whited mulberry-trees
Bound each to each by lazy ropes of vine!

Now I'll teach you my language—I'm not forced
To speak Italian now, Charles?
[*She sees the crown.*]   What is this?
Answer me—who has done this? Answer!
    Cha.   He:
I am King now.
    Pol.   Oh worst, worst, worst of all!
Tell me—what, Victor? He has made you King?
What's he then? What's to follow this? You, King?
    Cha. Have I done wrong? Yes—for you were not
    by!
    Pol. Tell me from first to last.
    Cha.   Hush—a new world
Brightens before me; he is moved away
—The dark form that eclipsed it, he subsides
Into a shape supporting me like yours,
And I alone tend upward, more and more
Tend upward: I am grown Sardinia's King.
    Pol. Now stop: was not this Victor Duke of Savoy
At ten years old?
    Cha.   He was.
    Pol.   And the Duke spent
Since then just four-and-fifty years in toil
To be—what?
    Cha.   King.
    Pol.   Then why unking himself?
         *   *   *   *
                Ah, it opens then
Before you—all you dreaded formerly?
You are rejoiced to be a king, my Charles?
    Cha. So much to dare? The better;—much to
    dread?
The better. I'll adventure tho' alone.
Triumph or die, there's Victor still to witness
Who dies or triumphs—either way, alone.

Victor enters, and strives to instil into his son the leading maxims of his own policy. Charles finely asserts his higher views:—

    Vic. You are now the King: you'll comprehend
Much you may oft have wondered at—the shifts,
Dissimulation, wiliness I showed.
For what's our post? Here's Savoy and here's
    Piedmont,
Here's Montferrat—a breadth here, a space there—
To o'er-sweep all these what's one weapon worth?
I often think of how they fought in Greece
(Or Rome, which was it? You're the scholar,
    Charles)
You made a front-thrust? But if your shield, too,
Were not adroitly planted—some shrewd knave
Reached you behind; and, him foiled, straight if
    thong
And handle of that shield were not cast loose
And you enabled to outstrip the wind,
Fresh foes assailed you either side; 'scape these
And reach your place of refuge—e'en then, odds
If the gate opened unless breath enough
Was left in you to make its Lord a speech.
Oh, you will see!
    Cha.   No: straight on shall I go,
Truth helping; win with it or die with it.
    Vic. Faith, Charles, you're not made Europe's
    fighting-man.
Its barrier-guarder, if you please. You hold,
Not take—consolidate, with envious French
This side and Austrians that, these territories
I held—ay, and will hold . . . which you shall hold
Despite the couple!   *   *

About the People! I took certain measures
Some short time since . . . Oh, I'm aware you know.
But little of my measures—these affect
The nobles—we've resumed some grants, imposed
A tax or two; prepare yourself, in short,
For clamours on that score: mark me: you yield
No jot of what's entrusted you!
    Pol.   No jot
You yield!
    Cha.   My father, when I took the oath,
Although my eye might stray in search of yours,
I heard it, understood it, promised God
What you require. Till from this eminence
He moves me, here I keep, nor shall concede
The meanest of my rights.
    Vic. [*aside.*]   The boy's a fool.
—Or rather, I'm a fool: for, what's wrong here?
To-day the sweets of reigning—let to-morrow
Be ready with its bitters.

We will now endeavour to exhibit the three principal *dramatis personæ*, in passages which shall do their creator credit. The first is a portion of King Victor's soliloquy on his unexpected return—in which we cannot but think, that the struggles of unscrupulous ambition and remorseless shame, are happily conceived.

Why come I hither! All's in rough—let all
Remain rough; there's full time to draw back—nay,
There's naught to draw back from as yet; whereas
If reason should be to arrest a course
Of error—reason good to interpose
And save, as I have saved so many times,
My House—admonish my son's giddy youth—
Relieve him of a weight that proves too much—
Now is the time,—or now or never. 'Faith,
This kind of step is pitiful—not due
To Charles, this stealing back—hither because
He's from the Capital! Oh, Victor—Victor—
But thus it is: the age of crafty men
Is loathsome—youth contrives to carry off
Dissimulation—we may intersperse
Extenuating passages of strength,
Ardour, vivacity, and wit—may turn
E'en guile into a voluntary grace,—
But one's old age, when graces drop away
And leave guile the pure staple of our lives—
Ah, loathsome!
        *   *   *   *
                Here am I arrived—the rest
Must be done for me. Would I could sit here
And let things right themselves—the masque
    unmasque
Of the King, Crownless, grey hairs and hot blood,—
The young King, crowned, but calm before his time,
They say,—the eager woman with her taunts,—
And the sad earnest wife who beckons me
Away—ay, there she knelt to me! E'en yet
I can return and sleep at Chamberri
A dream out. Rather shake it off at Turin,
King Victor! Is't to Turin—yes or no?
'Tis this relentless noon-day-lighted chamber
That disconcerts me. Some one flung doors wide
(Those two great doors that scrutinize me now)
And out I went mid crowds of men—men talking,
Men watching if my lip fell or brow changed;
Men saw me safe forth—put me on my road;
That makes the misery of this return!
Oh, had a battle done it!

The next passage shall display the aroused Charles, determining on the arrest of his father. Here, again, (and it is no mean exercise of the dramatist's power) the contention between obedience and duty—between the Son, the King, and the Master of the treacherous Minister, is indicated with a clearness, which would justify us in yet a stronger desire, that one who can conceive so forcibly, should write as he conceives.

    Cha.   There!
About the warrants! You've my signature.
What turns you pale? I do my duty by you
In acting boldly thus on your advice.
    D'O. [*reading them separately.*] Arrest the
    people I suspected merely?
    Cha. Did you suspect them?
    D'O.   Doubtless: but—but—sire,
This Forquieri's governor of Turin;
And Rivarol and he have influence over
Half of the capital.—Rabella, too!
Why, sire—
    Cha.   Oh, leave the fear to me.
    D'O. [*still reading.*]   You bid me
Incarcerate the people on this list?
Sire—
    Cha. Why you never bade arrest those men,
So close related to my father too,
On trifling grounds?
    D'O.   Oh, as for that, St. George,
President of Chamberri's senators,
Is hatching treason—but—
[*Still more troubled.*] Sire, Count Cumaine
Is brother to your father's wife! What's here?
Arrest the wife herself?
    Cha.   You seem to think
It venial crime to plot against me. Well?
    D'O. [*who has read the last paper.*] Wherefore
    am I thus ruined? Why not take
My life at once? This poor formality
Is, let me say, unworthy me! Prevent it,
You, madam! I have served you—am prepared
For all disgraces—only, let disgrace
Be plain, be proper—proper for the world
To pass its judgment on 'twixt you and me!
Take back your warrant—I will none of it.
    Cha. Here is a man to talk of fickleness!
He stakes his life upon my father's falsehood,
I bid him—
    D'O. Not you! Were he trebly false,
You do not bid me—
    Cha. Is't not written there?
I thought so: give—I'll set it right.
    D'O.   Is it there?
Oh, yes—and plain—arrest him—now—drag here
Your father! And were all six times as plain,
Do you suppose I'd trust it?
    Cha.   Just one word!
You bring him taken in the act of flight,
Or else your life is forfeit.
    D'O.   Ay, to Turin
I bring him; And to-morrow!
    Cha.   Here and now!
The whole thing is a lie—a hateful life—
As I believed and as my father said.
I knew it from the first, but was compelled
To circumvent you; and the crafty D'Ormea,
That baffled Alberoni and tricked Coscia,
The miserable sower of the discord

'Twixt sire and son, is in the toils at last;
Oh, I see—you arrive—this plan of yours,
Weak as it is, torments sufficiently
A sick, old, peevish man—wrings hasty speech
And ill-considered threats from him; that's noted;
Then out you ferret papers, his amusement
In lonely hours of lassitude—examine
The day-by-day report of your paid creatures—
And back you come—all was not ripe, you find,
And as you hope may keep from ripening yet—
But you were in bare time! Only, 'twere best
I never saw my father—these old men
Are potent in excuses.
   * * * *
Charles [*pacing the room.*]   And why
Does Victor come! To undo all that's done!
Restore the past—prevent the future! Seat
Sebastian in your seat and place in mine
... Oh, my own people, whom will you find there
To ask of, to consult with, to care for,
To hold up with your hands? Whom? One that's
 false—
False—from the head's crown to the foot's sole,
 false!
The best is that I knew it in my heart
From the beginning, and expected this,
And hated you, Polyxena, because
You saw thro' him, though I too saw thro' him,
Saw that he meant this while he crowned me, while
He prayed for me,—nay, while he kissed my brow,
I saw—
 Polyxena. But if your measures take effect,
And D'Ormea's true to you?
 Cha.   Then worst of all!
I shall have loosed that callous wretch on him!
Well may the woman taunt him with his child—
I, eating here his bread, clothed in his clothes,
Seated upon his seat, give D'Ormea leave
To outrage him! We talk—perchance they tear
My father from his bed—the old hands feel
For one who is not, but who should be there—
And he finds D'Ormea! D'Ormea, too, finds him!
—The crowded chamber when the lights go out—
Closed doors—the horrid scuffle in the dark—
Th' accursed promptings of the minute! My guards!
To horse—and after, with me—and prevent!
 Pol. [*seizing his hand.*] King Charles! Pause you
  upon this strip of time
Allotted you out of eternity!
Crowns are from God—in his name you hold yours.
Your life's no least thing, were it fit your life
Should be abjured along with rule; but now,
Keep both! Your duty is to live and rule—
You, who would vulgarly look fine enough
In the world's eye deserting your soul's charge—
Aye, you would have men's tongues—this Rivoli
Would be illumined—while, as 'tis, no doubt,
Something of stain will ever rest on you—
No one will rightly know why you refused
To abdicate—they'll talk of deeds you could
Have done, no doubt,—Nor do I much expect
Future achievements will blot out the past,
Envelop it in haze—nor shall we two
Be happy any more; 'twill be, I feel,
Only in moments that the duty's seen
As palpably as now—the months, the years
Of painful indistinctness are to come—
While daily must we tread the palace rooms
Pregnant with memories of the past—your eye
May turn to mine and find no comfort there
Through fancies that beset me as yourself—
Of other courses with far other issues
We might have taken this great night—such bear
As I will bear! What matters happiness?
Duty! There's man's one moment—this is yours!
 [*Putting the crown on his head, and the sceptre
  in his hand, she places him on his seat.*

Of a like quality is the closing scene of the chronicle. It may give our author little popularity among the many: but it must confirm the few in their anxiety to see him take "the one step more" out of the labyrinth in which he lingers too fondly.

List of Collections

(References are to letter number, not page number.)

Armstrong Browning Library, Baylor University, Waco, Texas, 791, 871, 878, 884, 885, 890, 912, 953, 961

Barrett, Edward R. Moulton-, Platt, England, 792, 832, 840, 852, 879, 882, 893, 910, 938

Barrett, Myrtle Moulton-, Ringwood, England, 817

Barrett, Ronald A. Moulton-, Aberdeenshire, Scotland, 817

Berg Collection, The Henry W. & Albert A., The New York Public Library, Astor, Lenox and Tilden Foundations, 822

British Library, Department of Manuscripts, London, 883, 909, 964

Brown University Library, Providence, Rhode Island, 889

Dartmouth College, Hanover, New Hampshire, 936

Fitzwilliam Museum, Cambridge, England, 811, 862, 875, 880

Folger Shakespeare Library, Washington, D.C., 829, 832, 865, 893, 905, 928, 931, 944, 954, 957, 965

Harvard University, Cambridge, Massachusetts, 795, 802, 813, 818, 937

Huntington Library, The Henry E., San Marino, California, 859

Iowa, University of, Iowa City, Iowa, 800, 810

Jones, Mrs. E.E. Duncan-, Cambridge, England, 896

Morgan Library, The Pierpont, New York, 784, 788, 789, 793, 794, 796, 798, 799, 803, 805, 812, 814, 815, 821, 824, 830, 831, 833, 838, 842, 864, 868, 918, 934

Scripps College, Browning Collection, The Ella Strong Denison Library, Claremont, California, 850

Taylor Collection, R.H., Princeton University, Princeton, New Jersey, 785, 876, 902, 924

Texas, University of, The Harry Ransom Humanities Research Center, Austin, Texas, 786, 935

Texas Christian University, Fort Worth, Texas, 831

Turnbull Library, Alexander H., Wellington, New Zealand, 950

Wellesley College Library, The English Poetry Collection, Wellesley, Massachusetts, 787, 792, 797, 801, 804, 806, 816, 819, 823, 826–829, 832, 834, 835, 837, 839–841, 843–849, 851, 853–856, 858, 860–863, 865–867, 869, 870, 872–875, 879–882, 886–888, 893–895, 897–899, 901, 903–908, 910, 911, 913–915, 917, 920, 921, 923, 925–929, 931–933, 938, 939, 941, 943–947, 954, 957–960, 962, 963, 965, 966

Yale University, The Beinecke Rare Book and Manuscript Library, New Haven, Connecticut, 808, 809, 836, 948, 952

List of Correspondents

(References are to letter number, not page number.)

Anster, John, 808
Barrett, George Goodin Moulton-, 798, 803, 805, 815, 821, 824, 830, 833, 864, 918, 934
Barrett, Septimus Moulton-, 817
Blanchard, Samuel Laman, 810
Bordman, Eleanor Page, 922
Boyd, Hugh Stuart, 813, 846, 849, 858, 878, 887, 894, 898, 901, 907, 913, 917, 921, 923, 932, 939, 960
Carlyle, Jane Welsh, 890
Carlyle, Thomas, 822, 836, 876, 892
Dickens, Charles, 859
Domett, Alfred, 884, 950, 964
Dowglass, Fanny, 935
Flower, Eliza, 784
Haworth, Euphrasia Fanny, 883, 952
Haydon, Benjamin Robert, 945
Horne, Richard Hengist, 788, 789, 791, 793, 794, 796, 799, 802, 812, 814, 818, 831, 838, 842, 868, 902, 927
Jameson, Anna Brownell, 785, 924
Kenyon, John, 871, 881, 888, 936, 943, 959, 962, 966

Lowell, James Russell, 937
Macready, Catherine Frances, 885
Macready, William Charles, 807, 850, 912, 948
Macready, William Charles, Jr., 953, 961
Martin, Julia, 804
Mitford, Mary Russell, 787, 790, 792, 797, 801, 806, 811, 816, 819, 820, 823, 825–829, 832, 834, 835, 837, 839–841, 843–845, 847, 848, 851–857, 860–863, 865–867, 869, 870, 872–875, 877, 879, 880, 882, 886, 893, 896, 897, 899, 900, 903–906, 908, 910, 911, 914–916, 919, 920, 925, 926, 928–931, 933, 938, 940–942, 944, 946, 947, 949, 951, 954–958, 963, 965
Monclar, André Victor Amédée de Ripert-, 809
Montagu, Anna Dorothea, 786
Moxon, Edward, 795
Powell, Thomas, 800
Talfourd, Rachel, 891
Westwood, Thomas, 895, 909

Index

Index

(For frequently-mentioned persons not covered by the biographical sketches in Appendix I, or for places or topics frequently named, the principal identifying note, if in this volume, is italicized. If the principal identifying note occurs in a prior volume, its page reference is given in square brackets at the beginning of the entry.)

Aberleigh, 109
Ackermann, Rudolph, 145
Addington, Charlotte, 326
Addington, Henrietta, 326
Ælianus Meliglossus, Claudius, 330
Æneid, 354n
Æolus, 359
    Æolian harp, 157, 359, 361
Æschylus, 26, 223, 224, 256, 351
    Agamemnon, 367
    Prometheus
        EBB's translation of, 226n, 351
        quotation from, 44
        see also *Prometheus Bound*
Agamemnon, 367
Albert, Prince, 136, 145, 378
Alexander the Great, 4n, 152
Alford, Henry, [vol. 4: 16]
    Poets of Ancient Greece, 200
Alice, or the Mysteries, 19, 263
"Alonzo the Brave and the Fair Imogine," 243
Alps, Recollections of ..., 196
Alps, The, 196, 294, 352, 358
Alresford, 333
"Alsargis," 217–218
Ambrosio, or the Monk, 243, 251–252
Amelia, Princess, 198
America, 86, 87, 203, 211, 368
America, A Diary in, 153
American Stories for Children, 157
Anderdon, Lucy Olivia Hobart, 207, 262
    letters from, 314, 319, 342n, 346
    letters to, 201n, 255n, 268n
Annan, 99
Annie, *see* Hayes, Ann Henrietta

Anster, John,
    letter from, 38
    letter to, 38
Apollinaris the Younger, 230
Apuleius, Lucius, 1
Arabia, 341
Arcturus, 239–240
Argo, 29
Arianism, 186
Ariel, 199
Aristophanes, 257
Aristotle (The Stagirite), 51n, 257
Arnould, Joseph, 356
Asolando, 330n, 350n
Athenæum, The, 11n, 13n, 17, 20, 24, 42n, 57n, 73n, 74, 76n, 77, 78, 79n, 83, 95, 150, 156n, 169, 206n, 213, 216, 221, 224, 233, 239, 246n, 248, 263n, 264, 265n, 268n, 270, 281, 283n, 292n, 320, 360
    EBB's contributions to, 117, 146, 151, 159, 195n, 201, 207, 210n, 213, 216, 219, 220–221, 223, 228, 230, 233, 237, 238–239, 241–242, 244, 248, 253, 256n, 257, 258n, 259–260, 262n, 264, 267, 282, 284–285, 289, 295, 297, 309n, 312n, 349, 354, 379, 382–383
    Miss Mitford's contribution to, 109
Atherton, 11n, 299
Atlantic, The, 87
Aurelian, 217
Aurelian, The Last Days of, 208
Aurelio and Miranda, 251
Aurora Leigh, 370
Austen, Jane, 72

[411]

Avernus, 115

Babbage, Charles, [vol. 2: 293], 31
Bacchæ, 284, 290
Baillie, Joanna, [vol. 3: 269n], 31, 116, 141, 203
Baldwin, Miss, 54
Balzac, Honoré de, 251
Barbauld, Anna Letitia (*née* Aikin), 270
Barrett, Alfred Price Barrett Moulton- ("Daisy"), (brother), [vol. 1: 293–294], 153, 280, 339
 health, 318–319, 332, 349
Barrett, Arabella Barrett Moulton- (sister), [vol. 1: 291], 10, 11, 20, 22, 31, 33, 36, 41, 43, 44, 47, 52, 53, 55, 59, 78, 85, 93, 106, 117, 118, 119, 127, 128, 129, 135, 136, 138, 139, 142, 143, 145, 150n, 155, 163, 168, 174, 194, 230, 241, 249n, 254, 261, 267, 273, 279, 280, 291, 302, 303, 305, 307, 317n, 349, 380
 health, 22, 53, 54, 143, 332, 346, 349, 352, 360
 letter from, 152
 letter to, 138
Barrett, Charles John Barrett Moulton- ("Storm"), (brother), [vol. 1: 292], 4, 21, 33, 41, 44, 59, 70, 93, 128, 132, 134, 152, 280
 health, 22, 53, 54
 letter to, 21
 shyness, 31, 47, 93
Barrett, Edward Barrett Moulton- ("Bro"), (brother), [vol. 1: 289–290], 69
 death, 18, 43, 57–58, 82–83, 92n, 126, 140n, 166, 169, 281, 293, 312n, 379
Barrett, Edward Barrett Moulton- (father), [vol. 1: 286–288], 21, 22, 23, 25, 31, 34, 35, 36, 41, 46, 47, 50, 52, 54, 55, 56, 57, 58, 59, 60, 63, 66, 68, 69, 70, 82, 84, 87, 88, 92, 101, 102, 103, 109, 110, 115, 117, 120, 123, 125, 127, 128, 134, 137, 141, 142, 144, 148, 151, 153, 155, 160, 164, 166, 169, 175, 185, 198, 200, 207, 212, 213, 225, 232, 238, 239, 249, 254, 259, 269, 280, 282, 289, 293, 294, 297n, 300, 308, 317, 319, 321, 341, 359, 360, 361, 380
 health, 378
 letters from, 21, 66, 85, 92
 letters to, 46, 63
 likeness of, 35

Barrett, Elizabeth Barrett Moulton- ("Ba"), [vol. 1: xxvi–xxxiv]
 dreams, 20, 160
 first meeting with Miss Mitford, 299–300
 health, 4, 7, 12, 13, 18, 20–21, 23, 26, 27, 31, 32–33, 44, 45, 47, 48, 49, 54, 55, 92, 115, 117, 131, 138–139, 148, 153, 158, 160, 162, 172, 174, 175–176, 185, 186, 208, 221, 230, 234, 240, 241, 267, 291, 293, 294, 316, 317, 320, 332, 341, 346, 349, 361, 379–380, 381, 382, 383
 hæmorrhages, 47, 48, 125, 138, 294
 medical consultants, *see* Chambers, William Frederick, and Scully, William
 use of opiates, 6, 23, 222
 languages, 225
  Greek, 226
  Hebrew, 226
  Latin, 226
 literary opinions, 11, 15, 16, 17, 19, 24, 60, 72, 74–75, 77, 78–79, 81, 82, 83, 89–90, 93, 94–95, 96–97, 101–102, 103, 107, 120, 122, 129–130, 138, 145, 148–149, 157–158, 162, 169, 172–173, 175, 176, 182, 184–185, 186, 192, 193, 194, 199, 200, 207, 209, 211, 217–218, 220, 223, 228, 231–232, 234, 239, 242–244, 254, 262–263, 269–270, 271–272, 281, 282, 285, 290, 298, 301, 306–307, 308, 311–312, 313, 314, 321, 331, 339, 348, 349, 351, 353, 366, 369, 372, 374, 375, 376
 love of poetry, 220
 opinion of the theatre, 5, 7, 14–15, 280
 pets, 152
  see also Flush
 political opinions, 95, 287
 portraits of, 34–35, 36, 41, 50, 56, 59, 379
 reading, 101, 291
  biographies/letters, 72, 74, 96–97, 148–149, 153, 172–173, 200, 239, 242–243, 261, 269, 270, 306–307, 308, 321
  Greek, 256, 257
  novels, 19, 72, 184, 193, 262–263, 282, 301
  philosophy, 172, 278–279, 290
  plays, 15, 24, 130, 175, 185, 280
  poetry, 25–26, 29, 138, 186

religious works, 182, 186
religious opinions, 181–182, 186, 220, 236, 266, 271, 277–279, 306
return to London, 55–56, 63, 67–68, 115, 117, 120, 123, 124–125, 127–128, 293, 294, 379
works, 172n, 173, 228, 295, 309n, 314, 344
"A Day from Eden," 146
"A Drama of Exile," 147n
"A Madrigal of Flowers," 167–168
An Essay on Mind, 202, 296, 297, 361n, 375
Aurora Leigh, 370
Casa Guidi Windows, 370
"Cowper's Grave," 267
"Essay on Woman," 284n
"Lessons from the Gorse," 159
Poems (1844), 147n, 170n, 366
Prometheus Bound, 26, 44n, 224, 227, 296, 297, 351, 361n
"The Cry of the Children," 32n
"The Dead Pan," 349n
"The Dream," 358
"The House of Clouds," 117, 146, 151, 159, 267, 275, 296, 297, 379, 381, 382
"The Maiden's Death," 374
"The Poet's Record," 102
"The Romaunt of the Page," 86n, 135, 162
"The Runaway Slave at Pilgrim's Point," 374
The Seraphim, 175, 249, 268n, 279
review of, 240n, 388–389
translations, 194, 201, 207, 209, 213, 216, 226n, 285n, 381, 382
see also *Chaucer, Modernized*; "Greek Christian Poets"; *New Spirit of the Age, A*; *Poets, The Book of the*; "Psyche Apocalypté"
Barrett, George Goodin Barrett Moulton- (brother), [vol. 1: 292–293], 54, 128, 132, 163, 193, 198, 240, 244, 280, 281, 319, 332, 339, 344, 358, 380
letters from, 21, 30, 34, 46, 84, 109, 152, 249, 289
letters to, 21, 30, 34, 46, 63, 67, 84, 92, 152, 249, 289, 366, 372
Barrett, Henrietta Barrett Moulton- (sister), [vol. 1: 290], 10, 11, 20, 22, 31, 33, 35, 41, 44, 46, 47, 55, 59, 85, 93, 118, 119, 131, 142, 153, 155, 164, 249, 261, 279, 280, 297, 305, 307, 339, 346, 360, 380
letters to, 195, 369, 370

Barrett, Henry Barrett Moulton- (brother), [vol. 1: 293], 128, 132, 134, 152, 249, 280, 343
letter from, 31
Barrett, Octavius Butler Barrett Moulton- ("Ocky"/"Joc"), (brother), [vol. 1: 295–296], 4, 31, 33, 41, 44, 47, 54, 59, 63, 67, 147n, 280, 291, 321
health, 22, 53, 268, 282, 289, 308, 318
Barrett, Richard (cousin), 212, 381
Barrett, Samuel Barrett Moulton- (brother), [vol. 1: 290–291]
death, 170, 293
letter from, 369
Barrett, Samuel Barrett Moulton- (uncle), [vol. 1: 288–289], 184, 212
letters from, 212
Barrett, Septimus James Barrett Moulton- ("Sette"), (brother), [vol. 1: 294–295]; 34, 127, 128, 132, 145, 147n, 153, 164, 280, 317n, 321
at London University, 153
health, 268, 282, 289, 302
letters from, 31, 34, 52
letter to, 52
Bastille, The, 42
Bath, 235, 253, 254, 260, 305, 340
Bayfords, The, 226
Bayley, Sarah, 116, 141, 164
Bazalgettes, The, 291
Beacon Hills, 335
Bear Grange, 335
Beattie, James
quotation from, 112
Beaumont, Francis, [vol. 3: 209n], 5, 280, 308n
Bedford, Duchess of, 207
Bedford, Duke of, 95
Beelzebub, 199
Beethoven, Ludwig van, 157
Beggar Girl, The, 301
Behnes, William, 326
Bekker, August Immanuel, 256, 285n
Belford Regis, 269, 340
Bell, Mr., 249
Bell, Robert, 82, 101n
Bells and Pomegranates, 75, 323n, 330n, 350n, 357, 367, 368, 378
see also component titles
Ben, see Kirby, Ben
Bennett, Agnes Maria, 302n
Bentivoglio, Guido, 49
Bentley, Richard, [vol. 2: 57], 339
Beresford, Jane, 203
Berkeley Castle, 156

Berkshire Hospital, 326
Bermuda, 199
Bezzi, Giovanni Aubrey, [vol. 4: 100], 4, 10, 98, 116, 119, 120, 130–131, 164, 169, 352
Bible, The, 88, 134, 138, 140, 181, 279
  quotations from, 10, 15, 17, 20, 22, 25, 43, 48, 71, 75, 77, 81, 99, 110, 112, 114, 125, 130, 133, 138, 140, 141, 168, 170, 173, 185, 199, 202, 209, 213, 243, 263, 264, 266, 273, 279, 290, 292, 293, 301, 313, 314, 318, 331, 346
Bilbao, 359
Biographical Dictionary, 218, 227
Bird, Robert Montgomery, 19
Birmingham, 203
Birtwhistle, Alexander, 214–215
Birtwhistle, John, 215
Bishop, Henry Rowley
  quotation from, 143
Black Mountains, The, 34, 35
Blackwood's Edinburgh Magazine, 91n, 103n, 235, 329, 333n
  Domett's contributions to, 329n
  EBB's contribution to, 32n
Blake, William
  "Life of," 308
  quotation from, 117
  Songs of Innocence, 308
"*Blanch and the Rival Sisters*," 323
Blanchard, Samuel Laman
  letter to, 40
  Life of L.E.L., 61, 62, 72, 93, 96–97
  Lyric Offerings, 40
Blessington, Marguerite, Countess of, 120, 141, 172
  see also *Keepsake, The*
Blomfield, Charles James (Bishop of London), [vol. 3: 91n], 87
Blot in the 'Scutcheon, A, 124, 322–323, 369
Blowsabella, 14
Blue Beard, 206
Bolingbroke, Lady, 47, 153
Bolingbroke, Viscount, 278
Bonaparte, Charles Louis (Napoleon III), 251
Bonaparte, Charlotte, 251
Bonaparte, Hortense (*née* de Beauharnais), 251
Bonaparte, Joseph, 251
Bonaparte, Louis, 251
Bonaparte, Maria Letizia (*née* Ramolino), ("Madame Mère"), 251
Bonaparte, Napoléon, 87, 110, 171, 206n, 220, 228, 251, 381

Tyas's Illustrated History of, 88, 222n
Bonaparte, Napoléon Charles, 251
Bonaparte, Napoléon Louis, 251
Bond Street, 40, 360
Book of Beauty, The, 120
Book of Common Prayer, The, 228–229
"Borderers, The," 311, 313
Bordman, Eleanor Page, [vol. 3: 177n], 123, 139, 149–150, 165, 167, 168, 171
  letter from, 171
  letter to, 257
Boswell, James, 87, 231, 239, 308n
Boucicault, Dion, 228, 235, 238
Boyd, Hugh Stuart, [vol. 2: 339–341], 250, 351
  comments on EBB's poetry, etc., 267
  letters from, 117, 123, 138, 209, 230, 256, 284, 302
  letters to, 43, 117, 123, 138, 181, 194, 201, 209, 215, 229, 241, 248, 256, 257, 284, 302, 349
Boz, see Dickens, Charles
Bradleigh, Lady, 270
Bradley, Mr., 203, 206, 207
Bradshaigh, Lady (*née* Bellingham), 270
Bride-cake, 95, 114, 121–122, 174
Brighton, 69, 291
Bristol, 69, 235
British Artists, Society of, 291
British Association, The, 151
British Institution, The, 189
Broadstairs, 56, 60
Brougham and Vaux, Lord, [vol. 3: 142n], 215
  translation of Demosthenes, 351
Browne, Mary Ann, 157
Browning, Robert, [vol. 1: xxiv–xxvi], 75, 83n, 280, 290, 297n, 300–301
  EBB's comments on his poetry, 75, 78–79, 221, 301
  health, 40, 280, 300
  languages
    Greek, 303
  literary opinions, 40
  wishes to meet EBB, 290
  works, 258, 328
    A Blot in the 'Scutcheon, 124, 322–323, 369
    A Soul's Tragedy, 356
    Agamemnon, 367
    Asolando, 330n, 350n
    Bells and Pomegranates, 75, 323n, 330n, 350n, 357, 367, 368, 378
    Dramatic Lyrics, 190n, 350n, 356
    "In a Gondola," 189
    King Victor and King Charles, 37,

189, 258n, 323
  reviews of, 190n, 400–405
 La Saisiaz, 367
 Men and Women, 376
 Pacchiarotto, 374
 Paracelsus, 366, 374
   EBB's comments on, 75, 79
 Pippa Passes, 16, 37, 38, 39, 40, 64, 78, 115, 129, 323n, 366
   EBB's comments on, 75, 78–79
   reviews of, 38n, 222n, 283n, 392–400
 Sordello, 37n, 38, 64, 79n, 283n, 356, 366, 367
 Strafford, 357
 "The Cardinal and the Dog," 329, 350
 "The Pied Piper of Hamelin," 350
 The Return of the Druses, 37, 356
 The Ring and the Book, 367
 The Two Poets of Croisic, 367
Browning, Robert, Sr. (father), [vol. 3: 307–309], 189, 330n, 356
Browning, Sarah Anna (*née* Wiedemann), (mother), [vol. 3: 309–310], 356
Browning, Sarianna, [vol. 3: 310–311], 330n, 350n, 356
Browning Collections, 9n, 35n, 61n, 91n, 94n, 118n, 157n, 197n, 234n, 256n, 258n, 262n, 283n, 285n, 302n
Bruce, Robert de, 339
Brutus, Marcus Junius, 157
Bryanston Square, 336
Buckingham, Duke of, 28
Buckinghamshire, 178
Bulwer-Lytton, *see* Lytton, Bulwer-
Bunn, Alfred, 5, 302n
Burges, George, 284, 290, 303, 351
Burlington, Lady, 110n, 145, 149
  Miss Mitford's verses on, 42n, 109, 147n
Burney, Fanny, *see* D'Arblay, Mme.
Burns, Major, 189
Burns, Robert, 189
  quotations from, 85, 87, 279, 340
Butler, Charlotte Mary ("Arlette"), (EBB's cousin), [vol. 1: 222n], 152
Butler, Cissy (EBB's cousin), [vol. 3: 221n], 152
Butler, Isabella Horatia (EBB's cousin), 198
Butler, Thomas (EBB's uncle), 195n
Byron, Lord, 74, 98, 156
  Hunt's memoir of, 156
  Parisina, 89
  quotations from, 20, 192

Cæsar, Julius, 97, 290, 300

Caldecott, William Marriott, 279
Caliban, 199
Calvinism/Calvinists, 306
Camberwell, 16, 40
Campbell, Thomas, 77
  quotation from, 106
Canada, 147n, 199
"Cardinal and the Dog, The," 329, 350
Carlyle, Jane Baillie (*née* Welsh), 99, 177, 189
  dislike of RB, 367, 368
  letter to, 196
Carlyle, Thomas, 82, 189, 191, 196, 231, 250, 258, 281, 290, 301, 307, 343
  biographical sketch, 365–368
  EBB's essay on, 309n
  letters from, 64, 99, 177, 197, 367
  letters to, 99, 367
  Oliver Cromwell's Letters and Speeches, 197n, 366
  opinion of RB's work, 64–65
  quotation from, 230
Carter, Matilda, 35, 56, 59
  see also EBB, portraits of
Casa Guidi Windows, 370
Cassius (Gaius Cassius Longinus), 275
Castle of Otranto, The, 185
Castruccio Castracani, 97
Catherine, Empress, 117
Catholics/Catholicism, Roman, 181, 236, 321
  see also Rome, Church of
Catiline (dog), 134, 152, 255
Cavalier, Memoir of a, 282
Cecilia, St., 110
Céleste, Mme., 160
Cerberus, 54
Chambers, William Frederick, [vol. 3: 299n], 66, 175, 176, 221, 341
Channing, William Ellery, 186
"Chapeau de Paille, Le," 136
Chapel Street, 155
Charles I, King, 228, 246n
Charles II, King, 228, 229, 280
Charon, 2
Chateaubriand, François René de, 220
Chaucer, Geoffrey, 17, 25–26, 210, 223, 358
  quotations from, 206, 221, 358
Chaucer, Modernized, 3, 4, 10, 13, 14, 33, 82, 83n, 261, 262, 382, 383
  reviews of, 15n, 17, 20, 24, 25, 264, 281, 319, 385–387, 389–391
Chelsea, 99
Cheyne Row, 99
Chichester, J.H.R., 273
Chiswick, 58, 346

Chorley, Henry Fothergill, [vol. 3: 185n], 20, 62, 76, 78, 80, 82, 84n, 207, 345
 "Fontibel," 347n
 health, 76
 letter from, 342n, 344
 Music and Manners in France and Germany, 72, 76, 251
Christ, Jesus, 44, 58, 112, 170, 182, 186, 220, 266, 277, 278, 279
Christian, Fletcher, 323
Christianisme, Le Génie du, 220
Christina, The Maid of the South Seas, 323
Christus Patiens, 230, 290
Chryses, 138
Chudleigh, 68, 69
Churchyard, Thomas, 309n
Chute, William John, 335
Cinderella, 87
Civil Wars, A Chronicle of the, 197
Clarissa, 254, 272, 273n, 335
Clarke, Adam, [vol. 2: 162], 140n, 202, 210, 216, 350n
Clarke, Arabella Sarah Graham- ("Bummy"), (EBB's aunt), [vol. 1: 297–298], 114, 152, 183, 185, 198, 289
Clarke, Emma Jane Graham- (*née* Eagles), 235
Clarke, James Graham- (EBB's uncle), [vol. 1: 299], 185, 289
Clarke, John
 quotation from, 69
Clarke, John Altham Graham- (EBB's cousin), 158, 235
Clarke, John Altham Graham- (EBB's uncle), 235
Clarke, Joseph Butterworth Bulmer, 202, 350n
Clarke, Leonard Edmund Graham- (EBB's cousin) 158, 235
Clarke, Mary Graham- (*née* Parkinson), (EBB's aunt), 235
Classical Journal, The, 285n
Clifton, 52, 55, 57, 63, 66, 68, 69, 235
Cockney School, The, 98, 159n
Codrington, Christopher, 122
Colburn, Henry, [vol. 1: 160n], 347n, 358
Coleridge, Samuel Taylor, 78, 149, 223, 224, 333, 359
 quotations from, 253, 279
Coleridge, Sara, [vol. 4: 64n], 31, 224
Collier, Jeremy, 244, 283n
Collier, John Payne, 312n
Colnaghi, Messrs., 258
Congregationalists, 186, 278
Congreve, William, 246n
Conspirators, The, 19, 321
Constantine the Great, 285

Constantinople, 207
Constantius, Julius, 285
Contrarius, 203, 206
Cook, Eliza, 157
Cooper, James Fenimore, 203–204, 206
Corn Laws, 273
Correggio, Antonio Allegri da, 258
Cosmo de' Medici, 4, 5, 10, 15, 30, 107, 115, 162
Covenanters, 181
Cowley, Hannah (*née* Parkhouse), 310
Cowper, William, 273n, 333
 Life of, 305–307
"Cowper's Grave," 267
Cox, Mrs., 193
Critical Review, The, 240n
Cromwell, Oliver, 197, 229n, 246n, 274
 Letters and Speeches of, 197n, 366
Crosse, Andrew, [vol. 3: 243n], 235, 253
Crow, Miss (maid), [vol. 4: 80n], 10–11, 20, 30, 53, 68, 84, 93, 104, 105, 106, 109, 112, 127, 128, 146, 161, 164, 176, 185, 200, 232, 237, 242, 269, 286, 305, 330–331, 338, 339, 342
Crusca, Accademia della, 270
"Cry of the Children, The," 32n
Cunningham, Allan, 308
Cupid, 1, 2, 286
Curzon, George Henry Roper-, [vol. 2: 189n], 279
Cymon, 176

D'Abrantès, Duchess (*née* Permon), 251
D'Abrantès, Duke, 251
Dacre, Lady (*née* Ogle), [vol. 3: 245n], 158
 Translations from the Italian, 204
Damascenus, Johannes, 210
Daniel, 161, 194
Dante, Alighieri, 91n, 356
Danton, George Jacques, 163
D'Arblay, Mme. (Fanny Burney), 240, 247, 305, 382
 Diary, 232, 239, 247
 Evelina, 239
Darley, Charles F., 281
 Plighted Troth, 281, 320, 322, 356
Darley, George, [vol. 4: 264n], 17, 18, 21n, 24, 221, 222n, 264, 270–271, 281, 301, 319
 Ethelstan, 24, 281
 letter from, 342n, 344
 Thomas à Becket, 24
Davidson, Lucretia Maria, 148–149, 157, 174
Davidson, Margaret Miller, 149, 174
Dawson, G.B., 344

De Legibus, 256
"De Virginitate," 138
Deans, Douce Davie, 203
Death penalty, 313
Defoe, Daniel, 282
Dekker, Thomas, 312n
 quotation from, 238
Demosthenes, 351
Denmark, 87
Devizes, 326
Devonport, 100
Devonshire, 75, 119, 122, 168, 256, 257, 352
Devonshire, Duke of, 148
Devonshire cream, 4, 10, 41, 61, 75, 87, 115, 116, 122, 167
Diary of an Ennuyée, The, 192
Dickens, Charles ("Boz"), 124n, 193, 204
 biographical sketch, 368–370
 letter to, 140
Dilke, Charles Wentworth, [vol. 3: 189], 17, 83, 146, 213, 220, 230, 239, 241, 248, 250, 256, 259, 264, 278, 301, 349, 354
 letters from, 201, 208, 209, 238, 278
Dilke, Charles Wentworth, Jr., 239, 244
Dino, Dorothea, Duchess de, 136
D'Israeli, Isaac, 101, 102
Dissenters (Non-Conformists), 181, 236, 277, 278
Dodsley, Robert, 280
Dog stealers, 337, 343
Dogs, Isle of, 112
Domett, Alfred, [vol. 4: 315–317], 328–329, 330n, 350n
 letter from, 325
 letters to, 190, 355
 Venice, 328
Domett, Nathaniel, 356
Donne, John
 quotations from, 154, 161, 193
"Dora Creswell," 353
Dort, Lady, 193, 203, 204, 206
Dowglass, Mrs., 292, 295
Dowglass, Fanny
 letter from, 292
 letter to, 292
Dowson, Christopher, Jr., [vol. 3: 124n], 356
Dowson, Mary (*née* Domett), 356
"Drama of Exile, A," 147n
Dramatic Lyrics, 190n, 350n, 356
Dramatic unities, 51n, 271, 272
"Dream, The," 358
Dresden, 195
Drummond, Henry, 295
Drummond, Malcolm Henry, 295

Drury Lane Theatre, 191, 251, 283n, 323n
 EBB's shares in, 7
Druses, The Return of the, 37, 356
Dryden, John, 91n, 232, 246n
 letter from, 231, 232, 235
 quotation from, 146
Dublin, 38
Dugdale, William, 197
Duncan, James, [vol. 1: 226n], 297
 letter to, 296
Dupuy, Sophia, [vol. 3: 182n], 308
Durham, Lord, 212
Duroc, Géraud Christophe Michel, 251

Eagles, John, 235, 253
Earine, 12, 16
Eartham, 243
Echo, 30, 131
Eden, 47
"Eden, A Day From," 146
Edgeworth, Maria, [vol. 1: 33n], 134, 272, 275, 341
 "Manœuvring," 204
Egeria, 89
Eldon, Lord, 326
Elford, William, 107n, 288n
Elizabeth I, Queen, 163
Ellangowan, 214
Elysium, 353
Emenias, 217
Emerson, Ralph Waldo, 290–291
England, 60, 87, 115, 168, 225, 228, 264, 270, 271, 278, 317, 324, 327, 334
 Church of, 182, 277, 295, 315n
England, The Blue Belles of, 193, 203–204, 206, 207
English Journal, The, 4n, 11n, 13
Epicurus, 112, 266
Ernest Maltravers, 19, 263
Essay on Mind, An, 202, 296, 297, 361n, 375
"Essay on Woman," 284n
Estmere, King, 15
Ethelstan, 24, 281
Etty, William, 2n, 188
Euripides, 256
 Bacchæ, 284, 290
Europe, 203, 228
Eustace, John Chetwode, 127
Evangelicals, 236, 278
Eve Effingham, 203, 204, 206
Evelina, 239, 247
Examiner, The, 40n, 73n, 76n, 90, 132n, 163n
Exeter, 277, 294
Exposition of the False Medium, 80, 88, 101–102, 115, 129–130

Fame, 275
Fates, The, 167
Faust, 7, 49
"Feats on the Fiords," 90
Fellows, Charles, 339
"Fetches, The," 25
Finden, Edward Francis & William, 341, 344, 358
Findens' Tableaux, 25, 59, 262, 341, 344, 360n
Fisher, Harriet, 119
Fitzgerald, Mrs., 204
FitzHardinge, Lord, 156
Flagellum, 197
Flaxman, Ann (*née* Denman), 243
Flaxman, John, 243
Fletcher, John, [vol. 3: 209n], 5, 74, 223, 280, 308n
Flora, 127
Florence, 352
Flower, Eliza, [vol. 3: 311–312]
  letter to, 1
Flower and the Leaf, The, 167
"Flower in a Letter, A," 170n
Flush (EBB's dog), 3, 4, 10, 20, 23, 28, 30, 36, 42, 44, 51, 53–54, 76, 77, 91, 93, 98, 104–107, 112–113, 116, 127–128, 131, 132, 134, 151–152, 154, 160, 164, 167, 188, 224, 225, 229, 236, 238, 240, 248, 254–255, 269, 273, 337, 338–339, 342–343, 349, 360, 361
  cowardice, 28, 53, 105–106, 115, 254, 343
  eating habits, 10, 23, 28, 105, 109, 112, 151, 154, 225, 232, 236–237, 338
  health, 193, 200, 338
  intelligence, 20, 53, 91, 93, 104, 339, 343
  misdeeds, 30, 360
Flush (Miss Mitford's dog), 11n, 20, 28, 30, 36, 53, 76, 90, 98, 112, 113, 116, 134, 135, 151, 224, 226, 324, 337, 339, 342, 343
Forster, Charles, 12
Forster, John, [vol. 3: 169n], 62n, 73n, 124n, 140, 189, 193, 241n, 339
Fortescues, The, 289
Fortunate Islands, The, 287
Fortune, 103
Foscari, 310n
Fox, William Johnson, [vol. 3: 313–314], 1, 37, 81, 320
  Hymns and Anthems, 1n
France, 228
France, Music and Manners in, 72, 76, 251
Francis the First, 102

Franklin, Benjamin, 87
Fraser's Magazine, 88, 340, 341
Frederick William IV, King, 232
Free trade, 304
French language & literature, 51n, 261, 271
French Revolution, The, 261, 263
Fresco, Thoughts on ..., 305, 316
Frocester, [vol. 3: 55], 152, 291
Furnivall, Frederick James
  letter to, 330n, 350n

Gallow's Piece, The, 214
Gardiner, Mrs. Stewart, 193
Gargantua, 231
Garrow, Joseph, 121n, 183
Garrow, Theodosia, [vol. 4: 105n], 119–120, 176
  lines on Miss Landon's death, 169
  "The Doom of Cheynholme," 120, 169
Garrow, Theodosia (*née* Abrams), 121
Garrow, William, 183
Garrows, The, 169
Garth, Samuel, 122
Gaston de Blondeville, 184–185
Genlis, Comtesse de, 308
Gentleman's Magazine, The, 187n, 284
George III, King, 179
Georgina, Lady, 204
Germany, 192, 228, 358
Germany, Conversations on the State of Art and Literature in, 192
Germany, Music and Manners in, 72, 76, 251
Germany, Social Life in, 200n
Gibraltar, The Siege of, 305
Glasgow, 271
God, 7, 9, 10, 11, 20, 22, 23, 28, 31, 32, 33, 35, 42, 43–44, 46, 47, 49, 50, 54, 58, 61, 62, 64, 65, 66, 70, 76, 85, 86, 90, 91, 94, 99, 102, 107, 108, 111, 112, 113, 117, 118, 120, 121, 122, 123, 125, 128, 130, 134, 138, 143, 146, 149, 150, 153, 156, 158, 160, 161, 164, 165, 166, 167, 169, 170, 171, 174, 176, 181, 182, 183, 184, 185, 186, 188, 193, 200, 208, 216, 219, 221, 222, 223, 225, 228, 230, 232, 237, 238, 241, 244, 248, 250, 255, 260, 266, 268, 273, 275, 277, 278, 279, 281, 282, 290, 292, 294, 295, 298, 301, 306, 308, 315, 318, 319, 321, 325, 328, 340, 349, 354, 355, 360
Godwin, William (1756–1836), 282
Goethe, Johann Wolfgang von, 60
  "Die Zauberlehrling," 260
  Hermann and Dorothea, 173
Goldsmith, Oliver, 328n
  quotation from, 146

Gosset, Allen Ralph, [vol. 3: 207n], 249
Gosset, Arabella Sarah (*née* Butler), (EBB's cousin), [vol. 1: 21n], 249
Graham-Clarke, *see* Clarke, Graham-
Gray, Thomas, 307
 Johnson's "Life of," 231
Great-heart, Mr., 293
Greece, 23–24, 280
"Greece, The Gods of," 348
Greece, The Poets of Ancient, 200
"Greek Christian Poets, Some Account of the," 201–202, 208, 209–210, 213, 216, 219–220, 223, 228, 230, 238–239, 241–242, 244, 248, 253, 256n, 257, 258n, 259–260, 261, 262n, 264, 266, 267, 278, 282, 284–285, 289, 290, 291, 295, 303, 319, 349, 354, 381, 382–383
 RB's comments on, 290, 303
Greeks, The, 271
Gregory, *see* Nazianzen, St. Gregory
Gregory VII, 4
Gregory VII, 15, 30, 107, 115, 162
Grey, Lord, [vol. 2: 331n], 212, 291n
Grimaldi, Signor, 205
Grote, George, 304
Groves, Anthony Norris, [vol. 3: 130n], 277
Guido, 87

Hall, Joseph (Bishop of Norwich), 345
Ham, 251
Hamlet, 180
Hammersmith, 149, 150
Hampshire, 333, 335
Hampstead, 43, 117, 128, 261
Hand-Book of the History of Painting, A, 265n, 281
Handel, George Frederick, 157
 Hallelujah Chorus, 179
Hanford, Mr., 33
Hanford, Mrs. C., [vol. 2: 79n]; 32–33
Hanford, Fanny, 33
Harley Street, 289
Harlowe family, The, 270
Harman, Mr., 63, 69
Harness, William James, [vol. 3: 215], 299
 letter to, 188n
Harpocrates, 320
Harrison, Henrietta, 262, 273
 letters to, 311n, 346n
Harrison, John, 315
Harrow, 353
Hartley, Mrs., 204
Harz Mountains, 358
Hastings, 174, 208, 223
Haworth, Euphrasia Fanny, [vol. 3: 314–315]
 letter from, 328
 letters to, 188, 328
Haydon, Benjamin Robert, 135, 143n, 145, 156, 159, 185, 272, 308
 biographical sketch, 370–373
 health, 291, 301
 lecture on fresco, 305, 316
 letters from, 127, 129, 132, 163, 164, 371, 372
 letters to, 135, 316, 321, 371, 372
 "Uriel Disturbed by Satan," 129, 145, 163–164, 316
 visits Wimpole Street, 174
Haydon, Frederick Wordsworth, 131n
Hayes, Ann Henrietta (*née* Boyd), 117, 123, 139
 letter from, 43
Hayley, Eliza (*née* Ball), 243, 244
Hayley, Thomas Alphonso, 243–244
Hayley, William, 242–245, 269, 271, 274, 308n
 Life of Cowper, 305–306
 Life of Milton, 305
 Life of Romney, 305
 Memoirs, 242, 243, 270, 275
Haymarket Theatre, 160
Hayward, Miss, 291
Hazlitt, William, 6–7, 276n
Heath, James, 197
Heckfield Heath, 135
Hedley, Frances ("Little Fanny"), (EBB's cousin), 54
Hedley, Jane (*née* Graham-Clarke), (EBB's aunt), [vol. 1: 299–300], 114
Hell, 1
Hemans, Felicia Dorothea (*née* Browne), 62, 75
Hemel Hempstead, 69
Heraud, John Abraham, 56
 The Roman Brother, 175
Hercules, 250
Herefordshire, 46, 101, 102, 122, 164
Hermann, Johann Gottfried Jacob, 12
Hermann and Dorothea, 173
Herod, King, 18n, 25, 319
Hessey, Lady, 203
Hexaëmeron, 285
High Clere, 335
Highgate, 261
Hill, Eve, 333
Hill, Frances, 333
Hingson, Edwin, 106
History of a Flirt, The, 72
History of Imbanking ... divers Fenns, 197
Hobbes, Thomas, 278
Holcroft, Thomas, 276
 The Road to Ruin, 276

Holders, The, 46
Holme Park, 180
Homer, 5, 138, 210, 226
Honiton, 122
Hood, Thomas
  quotation from, 106
Hopkins, Mrs., 139
Horne, Richard Hengist, [vol. 4: 317–320], 22, 41, 42, 49, 50, 58, 59, 60, 76n, 79n, 80–82, 83, 115, 130, 142–143, 146, 158, 161, 221, 227, 228, 267, 281, 307
  A New Spirit of the Age, 83n, 309n, 354n, 366
  "Alsargis," 217–218
  comments on EBB's poetry, etc., 161, 303
  contributions to *Biographical Dictionary*, 218, 227
  Cosmo de' Medici, 4, 5, 10, 15, 30, 107, 115, 162
  Exposition of the False Medium, 80, 88, 101–102, 115, 129–130
  Gregory VII, 15, 30, 107, 115, 162
  health, 45, 55, 60, 86, 100–101, 110
  History of Napoleon, 88, 222n
  introduction to Schlegel's *Lectures*, 89
  letters from, 6, 12, 15, 24, 31, 45, 60, 80, 86, 128, 130, 146, 160, 162, 319
  letters to, 4, 6, 9, 12, 14, 16, 23, 29, 42, 45, 55, 86, 100, 110, 162, 217, 264, 360n
  member of Royal Commission, 31, 51
  "Orpheus," 29
  petition to Parliament, 4–5, 7, 8, 116n
  "The Fetches," 25
Hosier, Francis, 140
Hour and the Man, The, 11
"House of Clouds, The," 117, 146, 151, 159, 267, 275, 296, 297, 379, 381, 382
Howe, Anna, 270
Hughes, John, [vol. 4: 76n], 178
Hugo, Victor, 356
Hume, David, [vol. 2: 58n]; 103, 278
Hungary, 207
Hunt, James Henry Leigh, 14, 26, 81, 89, 90, 267, 321
  Lord Byron, 156
  The Story of Rimini, 89
Hunt, John, 90
Hunt, Thornton Leigh, 90
Hunter, George Barrett, [vol. 3: 315–316], 278, 291, 302, 303
Hunter, Joseph, 199, 200

Hunter, Mary, [vol. 3: 87n], 22, 31, 157, 291
Hyde Park, 270
Hymettus, Mt., 325, 330

Iago, 212
"In a Gondola," 189
Income tax, 287, 289
India, 310
Indicator, The, 90
Inglis, Robert Harry, 325
Innocence, Songs of, 308
Innocents, The Holy, 17, 25
Ion, 274n
Ireland, 304
Irving, Edward, [vol. 2: 31n], 226, 296n
Iscariot, Judas, 277
Italy, 204, 228, 358

"Jack and the Beanstalk," 71
Jacob, 71
Jago, Francis Robert, 123, 138, 149, 150
Jamaica, 198, 212
James, Miss, 301
James, George Payne Rainsford, [vol. 4: 190n], 214
James I, King, 280
Jameson, Anna Brownell (*née* Murphy), [vol. 4: 320–323], 192–193, 198–199, 303, 307, 308
  Conversations, 192
  letters to, 1, 258
  marriage, 192
  Social Life in Germany, 200n
  The Diary of an Ennuyée, 192
Jameson, Robert, 192, 198, 199
Jaques, 260
Jephson, Henry, 198, 326, 381
Jephson, Robert, 232, 305
Jerdan, William, 63n, 72, 157
Jerusalem, Bishop of, 271
Joan of Arc, 171, 172, 173, 185
Joan of Arc, 171, 173, 185
Job, 346
Joc, *see* Barrett, Octavius Butler Barrett Moulton-
John, St., 277
John Bull, 88
Johnson, Elizabeth (*née* Jervis), ("Tetty"), 239
Johnson, John, 270, 275
Johnson, Samuel, 231, 239, 247, 308n, 327
  Anecdotes of, 233n, 240n
Jones, Inigo, 144, 146

Jonson, Ben, 280, 312n
  The Sad Shepherd, 12, 16
Josephine, Empress, 251
Jove, 49, 116, 157
Judgement, The Last, 153
Juliet, 72
Jungfrau (mountain), 85

K., *see* Kerenhappuch
Kean, Charles John, 20, 302n
Keats, John, 29, 157–158
Keepsake, The (1842), 120, 171, 172, 174
  Kenyon's contribution to, 167, 169, 174, 176
  Milnes's contribution to, 173, 176, 182
  Miss Garrow's contribution, 120, 169
  review of, 170n
Keepsake, The (1843), 349n
Kemble, Adelaide, 308
Kemble, Frances Anne ("Fanny"), 102
Kemble, John Philip, 251
Kembles, The, 308
Kent, 167, 336
Kenyon, Edward, [vol. 3: 229n], 352
Kenyon, John, [vol. 3: 316–318], 3, 31, 34n, 58, 76n, 78, 80, 81, 86, 87, 95, 98, 102, 107, 108, 109, 113, 116, 118–119, 120, 121–122, 132, 133, 141, 144, 152, 164, 165, 168, 174, 182, 183, 185, 188, 192, 193, 198, 199, 200, 205, 208, 211, 212, 223, 226n, 228, 231, 239, 244, 253–254, 261, 267, 268, 272, 276, 280, 281, 282, 284, 288, 290, 291, 298, 299, 300, 303, 306, 307, 308, 313, 319, 320, 321, 331, 332, 334, 339, 340, 343–344, 352, 353, 358
  health, 164, 165, 253
  letters from, 195, 235, 300, 334, 343
  letters to, 166, 168, 186, 195, 259n, 296, 311, 344, 347, 351, 361
  Rhymed Plea for Tolerance, 301
  "The Gods of Greece," 348
  "Upper Austria," 167, 169, 174, 176
Kerenhappuch ("K."), (Miss Mitford's maid), 61, *62n*, 66, 112, 115, 134, 144, 148, 161, 178–179, 182, 232, 260, 310, 330, 331, 336
King Victor and King Charles, 37, 189, 258n, 323
  reviews of, 190n, 400–405
Kinnersley Castle, [vol. 1: 9], 152, 158, 235
Kirby, Ben, 20, *21n*, 28, 42, 70, 91, 105, 112, 134, 135, 192, 200, 343
Klopstock, Margareta (*née* Moller,

("Meta"), [vol. 3: 102n], 282
Knyvett, Charles, 179, 180

La Fontaine, Jean de, 174
La Harpe, Jean François de, 182
La Saisiaz, 367
Laila, 102
Lake Poets, The, 20, 98
Lamartine de Prat, Alphonse Marie Louis, 30
Lampedusa, 199
Landon, Letitia Elizabeth, [vol. 3: 183n], 74, 75
  Castruccio Castracani, 97
  Life and Literary Remains of, 61, 62, 72, 93, 96–97
  lines on Miss Landon's death, 169
Landor, Walter Savage, [vol. 3: 182n], 78, 82, 119, 120, 191, 235, 253, 333n
Landseer, Edwin Henry, 203, 207
Langland, William, 349
Lawrence, Thomas, 136
Leamington Spa, 198
Lear, King, 252
Leibnitz, Gottfried Wilhelm, 301
Lenient, 203
Leslie, Mrs., 348
"Lessons from the Gorse," 159
Letters from Abroad, 74, 77, 85–86, 87, 94, 205
Lewis, Matthew Gregory, 242
Lichfield, 314, 315
Lieven, Dorothea Christopherovna, Princess de, 136
Literary Club, The, 327
Literary Gazette, The, 79, 94, 157
"Little David," 4n, 11
Liverpool, 203, 260
Lockhart, John Gibson, 82, 205n
  Ancient Spanish Ballads, 187n
Loddon (river), 168
London, 5, 18, 25, 27, 30–31, 33, 34, 35, 42, 44, 45, 46, 47, 48, 49, 52, 56, 63, 66, 68, 80, 85, 87, 99, 100, 101, 103, 109, 113, 115, 116, 127, 128, 131, 144, 164, 171, 179, 193, 198, 204, 225, 239, 243, 253, 260, 289, 295, 299, 302, 320, 343, 352, 353, 358
  EBB's return to, 55–56, 63, 67–68, 115, 117, 120, 123, 124–125, 127–128, 293, 294, 379
  Miss Mitford visits, 142, 144, 148, 154–155, 157, 160
  predicted earthquake, 260–261
  see also specific places and streets

London, Bishop of, *see* Blomfield, Charles James
London Assurance, 235
London Journal, The, 3
London Magazine, The, 265n
London University, 153
Longfellow, Henry Wadsworth
 quotation from, 118
Longinus, Dionysius Cassius, 127
Louis Philippe, King, 251
Love and War, 51
Lovelace, Richard
 quotation from, 114
Lowell, James Russell
 A Year's Life, 298, 373
 biographical sketch, 373–374
 letter to, 296, 298
Lucan (Marcus Annæus Lucanus), 232
Lucas, John, [vol. 3: 195n], 109n, 118, 129, 135–137, 143n, 145–146, 149, 233
Lucas, Mrs. John (*née* Morgan), 137
Lucas, Mrs. William (*née* Calcott), 136
Lucian, 279
Luther, Martin, 306
Lutherans, 181, 306
Lycia, 339
Lyric Offerings, 40
Lyttleton, Lord, 192
Lytton, Edward George Bulwer-, [vol. 3: 54n], 83n, 101n, 154n, 262–263
 Alice, or the Mysteries, 19, 263
 Ernest Maltravers, 19, 263
 Night and Morning, 19
 Zanoni, 262–263
Lytton, Rosina Bulwer- (*née* Wheeler), 193

Maclean, George, 62, 97
Maclise, Daniel, 189
Macready, Catherine Frances (*née* Atkins), [vol. 3: 183], 37
 letter to, 191
Macready, Letitia Margaret, 37
Macready, William Charles, [vol. 3: 318–319], 140n, 189, 191, 280, 281, 320, 328n
 letter from, 356
 letters to, 37, 124, 241, 322
Macready, William Charles, Jr.
 letters from, 329, 350
 letter to, 329
Madagascar, 99
"Madrigal of Flowers, A," 167–168
Mæcenas, Gaius Cilnius, 246

Maginn, William, 62n, 73n
Magyar, The City of the, 207
Mahmoud, Sultan, 50, 207, 221n
Mahometanism Unveiled, 12
"Maiden's Death, The," 374
Malvern, 164
Malvern Hills, 349
Manchester, 203
Manfred, 49
"Manœuvring," 204
Mansoor the Hierophant, see *Druses, The Return of the*
Marchmont, Mr., 193
Marianne (maid), 232, 236
Marlowe, Christopher
 quotations from, 21, 344
Marmontel, Jean François, 261
Marryat, Frederick, 153
Martha (maid), 62n, 359
Martin, James, [vol. 2: 342–343], 32, 33
Martin, John, 153
Martin, Julia (*née* Vignoles), [vol. 2: 342–343]
 letter from, 32
 letter to, 32
Martineau, Harriet, 90
 "Feats on the Fiords," 90
 The Hour and the Man, 11
Martinuzzi, 116n, 125, 130, 142, 143, 162
Marylebone, 85
"Mary's Lament," 284
Mason, William, 307
Massinger, Philip, 280, 312n
Mathias, Thomas James, 204, 206
Mauropus, John, 285, 349
May (dog), 214
May, Mrs. Edward, 118
May, George, [vol. 4: 112n], 8, 9, 58, 62, 108, 111, 114, 222, 236, 336
Medea, 55
Melbourne, Lord, 54n, 56, 90, 288n, 316n, 353–354
Men and Women, 376
Mercury, 348
Merry, William, 235–236
Metaphrastes, Simeon, 285n, 290
Methodism/Methodists, 277, 278
Mexico, 89
Michaelchurch, 46, 47, 69
Miller, Lockhart, 203
Milman, Henry Hart, 205n
Milman, Lockhart, 203
Milnes, Richard Monckton, [vol. 4: 29n], 31, 82, 176, 244
 "On the Death of the Princess Bor-

ghese," 173, 176, 182
One Tract More, 182
Milton, Henry, 136
Milton, John, 14, 130, 223, 265n, 329
  Life of, 305
  quotations from, 10, 16, 20, 22, 58, 72, 97, 127, 210, 213, 226
Minny, *see* Robinson, Mary
Mitford, George, [vol. 3: 177n], 3, 21, 29, 41, 50, 58–59, 61, 62, 72, 76, 94, 95, 107, 111, 113, 116, 121, 125, 128, 131, 133, 135, 137, 142, 143, 144, 145, 146, 148, 158, 160, 164, 169, 174, 185, 187–188, 198, 206, 213, 214, 223, 226, 232, 236, 237, 244, 261, 273, 287, 310, 311, 312, 318, 321, 324, 325, 326, 327, 332, 335, 336, 337, 346, 353, 358, 360
  health, 8–9, 10, 19, 144, 148, 149, 161, 169, 172, 180, 185, 187, 188n, 219, 222, 223, 225, 232, 238, 244, 253, 255, 267, 282, 290, 312–313, 315, 317, 319, 324, 335, 348
  portrait of, 136
Mitford, Mary (*née* Russell), 324, 333
Mitford, Mary Russell, [vol. 3: 319–321], 13, 24, 44, 52, 85, 87, 162, 166, 290, 303, 317n, 347
  accidents, 61–62, 65–66, 70, 71, 90, 107, 111, 113, 115
  copyright dispute, 342n, 344, 358
  description of, 96n, 149
  health, 27–28, 50, 58–59, 61, 62, 66, 70, 71, 108, 111–112, 115, 149, 176, 187, 188, 236, 238, 244, 260, 267, 281, 287, 301, 310, 315, 319, 320, 344
  letters from, 8, 17–18, 19, 21n, 27, 28, 29n, 42n, 57, 61, 66, 67n, 70, 74, 77, 78, 85, 86, 90, 92n, 108, 111, 114, 115, 118, 124, 133, 135, 136, 141, 159, 164, 170, 178, 182, 187, 188n, 191, 203, 207, 211, 214, 223, 225, 227, 235, 238, 242, 247, 251, 255n, 265, 268, 269, 274, 286, 288, 290, 298, 299, 304, 305, 308, 310, 311n, 312, 314, 315, 316, 323, 325, 332, 333, 334, 338, 339, 342, 346, 359
    plan to publish, 288
  letters to, 3, 10, 19, 27, 36, 41, 48, 57, 65, 71, 73, 77, 80, 88, 94, 96, 100, 101, 104, 108, 111, 113, 114, 118, 121, 124, 125, 126, 129, 132, 133, 141, 143, 148, 151, 154, 157, 159, 163, 165, 167, 170, 172, 175, 181, 184, 187, 191, 198, 206, 211, 219, 222, 224, 227, 231, 235, 238, 242, 246, 253, 259, 262, 265, 268, 276, 286, 298, 305, 310, 312, 317, 320, 325, 330, 338, 342, 352, 357, 366, 367, 369, 370, 371, 372, 373, 374, 375
  likeness of, 59, 136, 145–146, 149
  literary opinions, 62, 162, 171, 176, 182, 185, 203, 204, 242–243, 262–263, 272, 274–275, 276, 314, 333, 336
    comments on EBB's writings, 135, 265–266, 379, 382, 383
  moving house, 260, 267
  political opinions, 304
  reading
    biographies, 62, 156, 247, 274
  visits London, 142, 144, 148, 154–155, 157, 160
  works, 20, 27, 29, 41, 42, 48, 49, 59, 145, 157, 269, 318, 323
    American Stories, 157
    Atherton, 11n, 299
    Belford Regis, 269, 340
    Blanch and the Rival Sisters, 323
    "Dora Creswell," 353
    Foscari, 310n
    "Little David," 4n, 11
    "On the Portrait of the Countess of Burlington," 42n, 109, 147n
    Otto of Wittelsbach, 8, 20, 115, 160, 164, 183, 299, 345, 347n
    Our Village, 109, 269, 340
Monclar, André Victor Amédée de Ripert-, [vol. 3: 321–322]
  letter to, 39
Monclar, Joseph Anne Amédée François de Ripert-, 39
Monclar, Mary Clementina de Ripert- (*née* Jerningham), 39
Monk, The, 243, 251–252
Monmouth, 30
Montagu, Anna Dorothea (*née* Benson)
  letter to, 3
Montagu, Basil, 3n
Montgomery, Robert, 328
Monthly Chronicle, The, 5, 15, 26n, 82, 101, 111, 170n
Monthly Critic, The, 14
Monthly Magazine, The, 40n, 56
Monthly Review, The, 38n

Montpensier, Mme. de, 321
Moore, Thomas, 81, 89, 103, 211, 304
More, Hannah, 232
Morgan, Lady (Sydney Owenson), 203, 272–273
Morning Chronicle, The, 91n, 320
Mortimer, Henry, 193, 203
Mortimer Common, 214, 335
Mortimer West End, 336
Moses, 168
Moss, Thomas
  quotation from, 315
Moxon, Edward, [vol. 4: 328–330], 85, 86, 246n, 328, 329, 356
  letter to, 16
Mudge's Farm, 54
Murphy, Denis Brownell, 192
Murray, John, Sr., 14
Music and Manners in France and Germany, 72, 76, 251
Myrtle (dog), 23

Naples, 204
Napoleon, *see* Bonaparte, Napoléon
Napoleonis Reliquiæ, 171
National Gallery, The, 137n, 146
"Nature's Voice," 26
Nazianzen, St. Gregory, [vol. 2: 39n], 117, 123, 138, 210, 229, 230, 242, 248, 250, 257, 285n, 349
  "Address to His Soul," 216
  "De Virginitate," 138
  EBB's translation of, 194, 201, 207, 213, 216, 381, 382
  Poemata Dogmatica, 139n
  "Soul and Body," 253
Necker, Jacques, 74
New Cross, 16, 39, 40
New Monthly Magazine, The, 344
New Spirit of the Age, A, 83n
  EBB's collaboration on, 309n, 354n, 366
New York, 203, 239
New Zealand, 325, 328, 355
  Bishop of, 228, 271
  Townsend's poem on, 228, 249, 270, 271
Newcastle-upon-Tyne, 327
Newmarket, 276
Newton Abbot, 93
Niagara, 94
Nick of the Woods, 19
Night and Morning, 19
Niven, Miss, 340
Niven, Mrs. (*née* Vardill), 174, *175n*, 176, 185, 221, 223, 224, 225, 226, 282, 331

  letter from, 227
  litigation over inheritance, 214–215
Niven, Agnes, [vol. 4: 225n], 174
Nonnus Panopolitanus, 210
Normanby, Lord, 203
North, Christopher, *see* Wilson, John
Northampton, Lord, 82
Northumberland, 327
Notting Hill, 192, 198
Nova Zembla, 8
Nugent, Major, 343
Nyssen, St. Gregory, 210

Ockwells Manor, 71
Ocky, *see* Barrett, Octavius Butler Barrett Moulton-
O'Connell, Daniel, [vol. 3: 221n], 275, 304
Œdipus, 250n, 266
"Œnone," 348
Old Manor House, The, 333
Oldys, William
  quotation from, 330
Olympus, Mt., 1
"On the Death of the Princess Borghese," 173, 176, 182
One Tract More, 182
Orme, Mrs. C., [vol. 1: 115n], 81, 101, 142, 152, 163, 261
Orpheus, 130
"Orpheus," 29
"Osier's Ghost," 140
Otto of Wittelsbach, 8, 20, 115, 160, 164, 183, 299, 345, 347n
Our Village, 109, 269, 340
Overreach, Sir Giles, 20
Owen, Angela (*née* Bayford), (EBB's cousin), 294
Oxford, 186
Oxford Movement, The, 32n, 183n, 236

Pacchiarotto, 374
Palmer, Charles Fyshe, 310
Palmer, Lady Madalina, 147n, 310
Pamber Forest, 335
"Pan, The Dead," 349n
Paper Buildings, 22, 34
Paracelsus, 366, 374
  EBB's comments on, 75, 79
Pardoe, Julia, 207, 219, 222
Paris, 196, 203, 251
Paris, Notre-Dame de, 356
Parisina, 89
Parliament, 87, 229n, 271, 316, 327n, 331, 337n, 345
  debates, 188n, 275, 281, 287, 304
  Horne's petition to, 4–5, 7, 8, 116n

House of Commons, 212, 288n, 304, 311n
  elections, 54, 72, 76, 87, 156n, 194n, 276n
House of Lords, 214, 215, 342n
Parma, 258
Peel, Robert, [vol. 3: 113n], 54n, 194n, 273, 275, 287, 288, 316n, 331, 351, 354
"Pen and ink" people, 345
Pepe, Guglielmo, 204
Pepoli, Countess (née Fergus), 196
Pepys, The Misses, 336
Pepys, Samuel, 153
Pepys, William Weller, 336
Petrarch (Francesco Petrarca), 204
Philip van Artevelde, 203
Pickwick Club, The Posthumous Papers of the, 226
"Pied Piper of Hamelin, The," 350
Piers Plowman, 349
Piozzi, Mrs., *see* Thrale, Hester Lynch
Pippa Passes, 16, 37, 38, 39, 40, 64, 78, 115, 129, 323n, 366
  EBB's comments on, 75, 78–79
  reviews of, 38n, 222n, 283n, 392–400
Pisida, George, 285
Pitcairn Island, 323
Plague Year, A Journal of the, 282
"Planctus Mariæ," 284
Plato, 146, 256, 257, 266
  De Legibus, 256
Pleader's Guide, The, 305
Plighted Troth, 281, 320, 322, 356
Plotinus, 195
Pneumatology, Theory of, 172, 173, 176, 183n
Poems (1844), (EBB), 147n, 170n, 366
Poetæ Græci Christiani, 210
Poets, The Book of the, 210, 213, 259, 264, 309n, 349, 354
"Poet's Record, The," 102
Polidoro da Caravaggio, 188
Poole, John, 188
Pope, Alexander
  quotations from, 56, 89, 168, 192, 358
Porter, Jane, 206, 207, 211
Portland Place, 203
Portugal, 251
Posterity, Prince, 269, 331
Powell, Thomas, [vol. 4: 330–331], 81–82, 267
  letters from, 82, 267
  letter to, 25
  "Nature's Voice," 26
Powell, Mrs. Thomas, 26
Princess Royal, The, 12, 90, 378
Procter, Anne (née Skepper), 3n

Prometheus, 227, 331
Prometheus Bound, 26, 44n, 224, 227, 296, 297, 351, 361n
Proserpine, 1, 2
Prospero, 199
Prussia, King of, 232
Psyche, 1–2, 14, 25, 49, 50, 59–60
"Psyche Apocalypté," 4, 6, 7, 9n, 12–13, 14, 15, 16, 18, 22, 23–24, 31, 41, 42, 45, 49–50, 56, 59–60, 72, 88–89, 110, 135, 146, 153, 160, 162, 163, 227, 228
Puritans, 181
Pursuits of Literature, The, 204
Pusey, Edward Bouverie, 32n, 183n
Puseyism/Puseyites, 31, *32n*, 182, 186, 229, 235–236, 295, 313
Pyramids, A Record of the, 331

Quarterly Review, The, 82, 84n, 158, 313
Quillinan, Dora (née Wordsworth), 51, 321
Quillinan, Edward, 19, 51, 321
  Love and War, 51
  The Conspirators, 19, 321
Quintilian (Marcus Fabius Quintilianus), 232

Radcliffe, Ann (née Ward), 184–185
Raleigh, Walter, 330
  quotation from, 299
Raphael (Raffaello Sanzio), 145
Reade, John Edmund, [vol. 4: 45n], 339–340
  A Record of the Pyramids, 331
Reading, 8, 69, 85, 103, 109, 122, 174, 179, 226, 246, 306, 326, 336, 337, 343
Reform Club, The, 289
Reid, Colonel, 353
Reni, Guido da, 163
Resolute (dog), 134, 152, 255
Reynolds, Samuel William 135–136
Rhine (river), 196
Richardson, Samuel, 240n
  Clarissa, 254, 272, 273n, 335
  Correspondence of, 244, 254, 270, 282
  Sir Charles Grandison, 254, 273n
Rimini, The Story of, 89
Ring and the Book, The, 367
Ripert-Monclar, *see* Monclar, Ripert-
Rivers, Lord, 336
Road to Ruin, The, 276
Roberts, Emma, 72
Robinson, Lady, 203
Robinson, Henry Crabb, 291
Robinson, Mary ("Minny"), [vol. 1: 47n], 23
Robinson Crusoe, 282

Roebuck, John Arthur, 275
Rogers, Samuel, 81, 203
Roland de la Platière, Marie Jeanne (née Phlipon), 261
Rolfe, Mr., 204, 206
Rollin, Charles, 216
Roman Brother, The, 175
"Romaunt of the Page, The," 86n, 135, 162
Rome, 182, 186
  Church of, 248, 315n
  see also Catholics, Roman
Romney, George, 305
Roper-Curzon, see Curzon, Roper-
Roscoe, Thomas, 206
Rose (dog), 337
Rousseau, Jean-Jacques, 262n
Rowden, Miss, 247
"Runaway Slave at Pilgrim's Point, The," 374
Russell, Lady, 337
Russell, Henry, 327, 337
Russell, John, 275, 287
Russell, William, 207
Ruth, 36, 353

Sadler's Wells Theatre, 204
St. John's Wood, 294
Saint-Simon, Duke de, 321
Salisbury Plain, 63
Sappho, 120
Saunders & Otley, Messrs., [vol. 3: 74n], 171, 208, 329n
Saunders' Library, 243, 254, 261
Saville, John, 314
Scheherazade, 104
Schiller, Friedrich von, 60, 313
  Kenyon's paraphrase, 349n
  The Maid of Orleans, 171
Schlegel, August Wilhelm von, 89
Schloss's English Bijou Almanac, 61n
Scotland, 331, 341n, 352
Scott, Walter, 62, 97–98, 169, 214, 272, 331, 334n
  quotation from, 164
Scott, William, 327
Scully, William, [vol. 4: 203], 18, 31, 33, 34, 36, 44, 46, 49, 52, 53, 55, 63, 66, 67–68, 69, 70, 92, 93, 95, 100, 103, 115, 117, 120, 123, 293
Sedgwick, Catharine Maria, 74, 77, 85–86, 87, 94–95, 122, 174, 205
Seeley, Robert Benton, 229n, 249
Self Culture, 186
Self-formation, 184
Selwyn, George Augustus (Bishop of New Zealand), 228, 378
Seraphim, The, 175, 249, 268n, 279
  review of, 240n, 388–389
Serle, Thomas J.
  Joan of Arc, 171, 173, 185
Set/Sette, see Barrett, Septimus Barrett Moulton-
Seven Sleepers, The, 7
Seward, Anna, [vol. 4: 4n], 98, 244, 305, 314, 332n
  Letters of, 269, 274, 282, 314
  Louisa, 305
Seward, Thomas, 308n
Shakespeare, William, 5, 14, 74, 77, 199, 206, 251, 265n, 270, 272, 275
  quotations from, 5, 6, 7, 11, 14, 21, 24, 26, 28, 37, 40, 48, 49, 53, 56, 74, 75, 80, 82, 84, 87, 97, 101, 102, 103, 112, 116, 119, 130, 133, 153, 155, 156, 160, 161, 162, 163, 172, 174, 185, 199, 209, 212, 217, 226, 227, 235, 243, 246, 248, 250, 254, 258, 260, 263, 273, 278, 287, 290, 296, 298, 299, 314, 315, 318, 330, 332, 340, 344, 345, 346, 352, 353, 358, 359
Shakespeare Society, The, 312
Shelley, Percy Bysshe, 60, 130, 224, 246n
  quotations from, 24, 164, 262
Shepherd, Lady Mary (née Primrose), [vol. 2: 156n], 225, 259
Shepherd, The Sad, 12, 16
Sherbourne, Mrs., 193
Shylock, 344
Sibthorp, Charles, 288
Sicily, 336
Siddons, Sarah (née Kemble), 233n, 251–252
Sidmouth, 119, 306, 317
Sidmouth, Viscount, 326
Sidmouth, Marianne, Lady, 322n, 325–327, 340
Sigourney, Lydia Howard (née Huntley)
  letter from, 51
Silchester, 324, 333n, 334–335, 336, 340, 353
Silentiarius, Paul, 285, 349
Sir Charles Grandison, 254, 273n
Sismondi, Jean Charles Léonard Simonde de, 203
Skerrett, Marianne, [vol. 3: 292n], 90, 204, 315n, 322n
Skinner, Mrs., 203, 204–205
Smith, Benjamin, 333
Smith, Charlotte, 333
Smith, John Pye, [vol. 3: 149n], 279

Smith, Mary Ann (*née* Clarke), 139, 349
Smith, Sydney, 203
Smith, Thomas Southwood, 82
Sneyd, Honora, 314
Socinians, 186
Socrates, 162
Solway Firth, 99
Sonning, 179
Sophocles, 256
Sordello, 37n, 38, 64, 79n, 283n, 356, 366, 367
"Soul and Body," 253
Soul's Tragedy, A, 356
South Seas, 212, 271, 317, 318, 323
Southey, Caroline Anne (*née* Bowles), 132
Southey, Robert, [vol. 1: 28n], 102, 132, 307, 333, 360n
  Joan of Arc, 171
  Life of Cowper, 306–307
Spain, 228
Spectator, The, 38n, 91n, 190n
Spohr, Louis, 153
Spowers, G., 43
"Staffa," 26
Staffordshire, 276
Statira (ship), 93
Stephens, Lady, 203, 206
Stephens, George, 130, 143
  Martinuzzi, 116n, 125, 130, 142, 143, 162
Sterne, Laurence
  quotation from, 167
Stilling, Johann Heinrich Jung-, 172–173, 176, 180, 181, 182, 193
Stone, Tom, 142
Storm/Stormie, *see* Barrett, Charles John Barrett Moulton-
Stowell, Lord, 326, 327
Stowell Park, 327
Strafford, 357
Strathfieldsaye, 135, 336
Stratford-upon-Avon, 207
Stratten, James, [vol. 3: 211n], 302
Stratten, Mrs. James (*née* Wilson), 302
Strawberry Hill, 297, 307, 321
Styx (river), 192
Suffolk St. Gallery, 291
Sunbeam, The, 175
Sussex, 244
Synesius (Bishop of Ptolemaïs), 202, 229, 248, 250, 265n, 349
  EBB's translation of, 209, 285n

Talfourd, Rachel (*née* Rutt), [vol. 3: 161n]
  letter to, 196
Talfourd, Thomas Noon, [vol. 3: 323–324], 72, 145, 196, 244, 332

Ion, 274n
Recollections of . . . the Alps, 196
Taylor, Henry, 203
Taylor, William Cooke, 281, 313, 319
Tempest, The, 199
Temple, The, 358
Tennyson, Alfred, 331–332
  EBB's essay on, 354n
  Poems (1842), 332, 343, 348, 353
Tetty, *see* Johnson, Elizabeth
Thomas à Becket, 24
Thrale, Hester Lynch (*née* Salusbury), 239, 247, 315, 382
  Anecdotes of the Late Samuel Johnson, 233n, 240n
Three Mile Cross, 20, 141, 223, 239, 352
Ticknor, George, 297n
  letter from, 361
Tilt, Charles, [vol. 3: 253], 346n
Timbuctoo, 355
Times, The, 132n, 252n, 262n, 274n, 288n, 321n, 327n, 351n, 354n
Tolerance, Rhymed Plea for, 301
Tom Thumb, 252
Tophet, 25
Torquay, 10, 63, 67, 68, 100, 109, 126, 131, 145, 164, 165, 168–169, 174, 182, 185, 293, 295, 331, 348
  EBB leaves, 123, 125
Toussaint L'Ouverture, Pierre Dominique, 11
Townsend, Richard Edwin Austin, 102, 271
  letter from, 100
  letter to, 270
  "New Zealand," 228, 249, 270, 271
Trant, Mary (*née* Barrett), 47
Treppy, *see* Trepsack, Mary
Trepsack, Mary ("Trip"/"Treppy"), [vol. 1: 301–302], 23, 152, 254, 289
Trinitarians, 186
Trollope, Frances (*née* Milton), [vol. 3: 68n], 10, 136, 193, 203, 204, 211
  The Blue Belles of England, 193, 203–204, 206, 207
  Vienna and the Austrians, 10
Troy, 193
Tunbridge Wells, 69
Twickenham, 52, 69, 85
Two Poets of Croisic, The, 367
Tyas, Robert, 88

Ulfried, 27
Unitarianism/Unitarians, 187n, 200, 277, 278
"Upper Austria," 167, 169, 174, 176

Upton, 53, 85
Uriel, 129, 145, 316

Varley, John, 111
Vaux, Thomas
 quotation from, 300
Venables, George Stovin, 320n
Venice, 189
Venice, 328
Venus, 1, 2
Vergil (Publius Vergilius Maro), 360n
 Æneid, 354n
 quotation from, 115
Vicissitudes Abroad, 301
Victoria, Queen, 54, 56, 90, 105, 145, 193, 232, 310n, 313–314, 315, 321, 353–354, 367, 368
Vienna, 10, 331, 352
Vigor, Mrs., 32
Voltaire (François Marie Arouet), 262n, 278
 quotation from, 174
Vulcan, 351
Vyne, The, 335

Wales, 109, 247
 Prince of, 233n
Walpole, Horace, 307, 335
Walthamstow, 69
Warburton, Henry, 304
Watts, Isaac, 266
Wellington, Duke of, 136, 336
Wesley, John
 quotation from, 89
West Indian Proprietor, Journal of a, 243
West Indies, 4, 93, 110, 212
 chocolate from, 198, 199, 206, 211, 219, 381
Westminster Review, The, 319
Westwood, Thomas
 biographical sketch, 375–376
 letter from, 203
 letters to, 202, 234
 Poems, 234, 375
Whalley, Thomas Sedgwick, 305

Which is the Man?, 310
Whitbread, Mrs., 153
Wightman, William, 240
Williams, Helen Maria, 305
Williams, John, 271, 315, 317–318
Willis, Nathaniel Parker, 204, 206–207, 211
Willoughby, Lord, 203
Willoughby, Solomon, 69
Wilson, John (Christopher North), [vol. 4: 70n], 103n, 328–329
Wimpole Street, 31, 41, 46, 47, 55, 59, 60, 68, 85, 92, 110, 123, 142, 249, 269
Windsor, 52, 85, 90
Wollstonecraft, Mary, 282
Wolverhampton, 31, 51
Woman, Vindication of the Rights of, 282
Woolsack, The, 22
Wordsworth, Dorothy ("Dora"), *see* Quillinan, Dora
Wordsworth, Mary (*née* Hutchinson), 353
Wordsworth, William, 17, 20, 51, 82, 83n, 120, 223, 231, 232, 267, 299, 300, 313, 314, 319, 320, 321, 333, 353, 359
 Poems (1842), 311–312, 313
 quotations from, 49, 78, 148, 225, 353
 religious views, 315n
Wortley, Emmeline Charlotte Elizabeth Stuart- (*née* Manners), 204
Wraxall, Nathaniel William, 27

Xeniola, 38

Year's Life, A, 298, 373
Young, Edward
 quotation from, 254
Young, William Curling, 325n, 356, 357

Zanoni, 262–263
"Zauberlehrling, Die," 260
Zenobia, 217
Zion, 22
Zoological Gardens, 300

This book is a work of fiction. Names, characters, places, and incidents either are products of the author's imagination or are used fictitiously. Any resemblance to actual events or locales or persons, living or dead, is entirely coincidental.

Copyright © 2019 by S. Blake Thews

All rights reserved. This book may not be reproduced or stored in whole or in part by any means without the written permission of the author except for brief quotations for the purpose of review.

ISBN: 978-1-7338973-6-5

Thews. S. Blake
The Rightful King

Edited by: Elizabeth Russell

Warren publishing

Published by Warren Publishing
Charlotte, NC
www.warrenpublishing.net
Printed in the United States